To Jen Arribau,
Fine Artist,
with Best Wishes
for Success in the
Things which
Really Count.
Craig McConnell
11-5-06

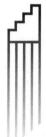

Cafe Whyoming

Diving into the Sky

by Craig McConnell

BIG LAKE
NIMAN

Author's Note

Cafe Whyoming is a work of fiction. Characters originated and portrayed, and names ascribed to those characters, are entirely imaginary. At the same time, however, many of the settings, some events, and a few actual persons, groups, and companies, while genuine, are used fictitiously for the sole purpose of creating realistic context; and any resemblance to actual events, locales, or persons, living or dead, is entirely coincidental.

Credits

Front cover painting, "Jingle Belles" (excerpt of the original triptych), Copyright © 2002 by Sandra Okuma. Used by permission.

All other cover images Copyright © 2002 by Craig V. McConnell.

Edition

This 2003 Big Lake-Niman Books printing is a limited first edition. Copies 1 through 100 are individually numbered and signed by the author.

ISBN 0-9726171-0-8
Manufactured in the United States of America

Trademarks

Publishing and Distribution

Big Lake-Niman Books
P.O. Box 12645
Prescott, AZ 86304

Visit our website at: www.biglake-nimanbooks.com

To the presence of natives, and women of gentle spirit.
A sappy Cowgirls and Indians love story it may be,
but a love story nonetheless.
That's got to count for something.

Preface

In those days I took more than I gave. Much more. Even when it was detachment, silence. I still struggle with that. Wrapped up in myself, dwelling in streams of consciousness, on tour, on thousand mile drives, making notes, keeping journals, recording rambling commentaries. Later, I needed the linkages, because of what happened in the Mojave. To remember who I was; to build a foundation for new travels in geography, contemplation, music, and love; beyond that, to learn who I am.

Let it be said I was a great romantic who never got started, despite the promise and beauty which is spring. Wait a minute, you say, you're Craig Maxwell—I've heard the songs, read the accounts, seen the pictures. But I'm sticking to my statement. Surely, the truth is in the clouds silently watching long rides on Navajo horses, warrior paint from black seeping springs, the blessing and honor of new creation.

I was born in a dawn of coincidence and had no childhood, none that I recall. A still-startling revelation. My consciousness seems to have been switched on when I was 14; before that remain only the vaguest transitional shadows from blankness, void. I think I played baseball, seemingly after an unknowable version of, "and then there was light." Games on a field far from sandstone cliffs or portages of the Voyageurs. Years ago, when I asked my parents the perpetually profound question, "where did I come from?" why did they answer, "you don't want to go there"? I don't look like them, and often see the world from a much different perspective. They point to a tree, an object; I'm learning, perhaps recalling, its spiritual significance, a presence connected to all living things.

Of course, none of it may be true. I've also learned that valid conclusions do not necessarily follow indisputable facts. If we are our memories, I could be anyone, or no one—a mystery to the few who know me, even more so to myself. With that threshold uncertainty, I'm back to California, where the tour began six months ago, really started five years before that. I couldn't wait to get home and head north. Off the bus. By myself, deciding when to appear, deploy illusion, play it straight, or simply blend in. That's how all great romances must start.

You might wonder about the tenses and persons. Sometimes present, first person; at other times, past tense, third person; subjunctive in a language which doesn't permit it. Ragged writing. Maybe it's finished, my work. Maybe not, someone else's struggle to melt the ends of ravelling dreams, seal, circumscribe and finally render inert the openendedness of my litany of neoprecognitive misnomers.

In a life where experiences are counted down as flights on a skydiver's discount punchcard, I've figured out that when malfunction is revealed, or overlooked exercise of the parachute option realized, during the final glissando the facts are indisputable, theoretical and applied models of inelastic behavior applicable, and the freefall conclusion inevitable. *Ni´ nikinítłizh*. He fell to earth. And memories, all which we may have in the end, are as the finest of the earth's dust on our fingertips.

1

You will be driving a Healey, in Nevada

I knew a girl who bent her knee that way. Her own, unique way. Swaying gently to the music I played, she would open her eyes, look deeply into mine. As deeply as you can when 17. Certainly more innocently, perhaps more clearly than we ever will again.

And I would look back, play a love song. For that girl. For myself. Unknowingly, we were weaving from our essence a pattern of our everything. Like the Navajo do on levels conscious and unconscious, rugs of profound, textured content. Hung on a wall, intact, now a collected specimen; underfoot, worn, fraying. Regardless, over the years cherished as indistinguishable fragments of our lives; exhibits to unending arguments, witnesses to the debates, contradictions, beauty we were meant to be, sometimes are.

In our shared summer, truly the love song was no less heartfelt, no less valuable than any before or after. Played over and over to the quiet of an empty house, pianissimo in the understanding seclusion of a summer afternoon, Germantown eye-dazzler print looking on from the bright, whitewashed wall. The emotion was there, forthright, honest. Yet, we did not know that it was for us.

Ten years have passed, we're both long gone. The soundtrack is an anachronistic compilation, then unwritten cuts in the future indefinite tense, "Helplessly Hoping", "Wooden Ships", now presented in modified space-time as a post-modern, revisionist account of my youth. The version I sometimes prefer to remember, to live—inauthentic, with smoother corners, more exciting, entertaining content; but occasionally, in the darkness, revealed to have sharp, troubling angles. Instead of Natalie at 17, warped into a *Lilith* retrospective. Film and music, reality and opulent fantasy which, like that love, slipped away with no forwarding address. I gave up looking for her, but not for that love, albeit in ways now with harder curves, many more complications. Ultimately, a dramatic romance of my own invention.

"I never thought of women that way." Great line to start a short story. Saying it, I think of Cindy. A short one, alright.

What brought her to mind? It's been a long time, although nothing happened between us, whatever that means. Almost a third of my life. Yeah, I can see Cindy as Jean Seberg, but in a different film. Reading a book with her round, tortoise shell glasses while in the background, continuing the CS&N ambience, "Guinnevere" floats on the cool air of my minimalist vignette.

Cindy and Natalie. On the long grass, sweet grass, lodge grass; above Blue Mountain, whether Cumberland County or Jamaica. At least they're real, or once were, neither of them *Lilith*. In the morning, when the thin strands of that web of creeping monochrome madness still bearing droplets of dew are revealed to be just that, their memory is an encouraging start to a better, noncinematic day. One to touch. Breathe.

The part about not having a past is, of course, not entirely true. Let me restate that. The part is relatively untrue. It's just another speculative fiction, occasionally launched on the unwary as a playful cuffing. They're not unwary for long. I explored it in considerable detail once in an essay for Philosophy 45 entitled, "Attributes and Attitudes of the Wary and Unwary." It was a master-work of transparent though exceedingly accretive exchanges, dangerous as ice buildup on the rigging of the classic schooner I wanted to believe was my imagination:

> "You're not Craig Maxwell, are´ you?" A question abandoned to diacritical disinterest.
>
> "Got me."
>
> "Doubt it." Tacit. Implied.

Though the professor knew enough of the unfathomable Sartrean French in which it was written to realize that even beginning to read was to embark on a joyriding intellectual crime spree, nevertheless, the paper copped an Ace, eliciting subsequent dialogue:

> "I must say, impressive delusions. Where did you study?"
>
> "*Je suis dans vôtre classe.*" I'm in your class.
>
> "Really, how extraordinary. *Eh bien*, next time translate it *en Anglais*, Jean-Paul."

Threateningly illustrated in the future-conditional, an egregious Ralph Steadmanesque splotch of fountain pen ink looking to be between tight-lipped, furrowed grimace and full mouthed scream. Every day a stage play—$25,000 a year for this?

Something brought me here. To Laramie. These last five years of living felt like twenty. Dog years. I was swimming in a land of junk, an Account Manager for Deep End Specialists: "Survive the Plunge!" Cork-bobbing in another litany,

The Interim Realities, little more than a grinning coyote dead on the fence around the Lake of Cumulative Impact. Expert tinfoil collector. Eventually, I knew that my life would be all about complications, vulnerability, damage, with energy no longer as freely available.

Though I am here, that doesn't explain why. Zen non-here? A yin-yang exercise, attempted awakening in a California way? What the print trade calls, "a uniquely California way?" The trade does indeed trade in the unique. The look, the ambiance, and in my trade, the sound. Rinzai! Bonzai! Deadeye! Uniqueye! A zzzz-zen Sundays-only casual subscriber to denouement, unprotected and susceptible, pistol-whipped and then pearlharbored in an unprecedented gong pounding. In that moment, All Woe! All Emptiness! All Fullness! All Sonny! All Cher! As empty as an unplugged, UL listed lamp cord, inspected, approved, attested to by Cyrenely Unsmiling Zen Roshi No. 32, "You can call me Walt." Still unplugged before the supersharp but metallurgically brittle intellectual plywood blade, menace of 80 teeth per inch hidden in attractive spin, softly aesthetic blur, waiting for the fun of an unpulled nail. What "rip" is all about.

This insulated lifestyle of mobility, both blessing and curse. Constantly moving, too few pauses, I rationalize but do not admit, to build strong relationships. Motion—too many layers of motion, like electrons orbiting a nucleus, only a probability of being in a particular region at a particular time, but the position never a certainty. Caught in a stairwell, flock of steps, moving elbows visible over the rail, going up or coming down? Read the last row without squinting and tell me again. Watch it. Until you and the hollow ground carbon steel are one in Blade Union.

Between the highs, mundane structure: my schedule after breakfast, tomorrow, what's next, while suppressing the fact that my life's essentially a monologue. It's true with my family, my work, my friends, the women I've known. Guilty of a lack of dialogue, sentenced to a travelogue, a monologue. A constant tug of war between clutter and simplicity, confusion and coherence. Moving to get away and arrive, forget and remember; seek new experiences, splice them into the fabric of my life, or push them out, to the margins of rock and sky beyond. Just one pitch away from the starting rotation, on a 3-2 count, now in my career, as never before:

I NEED A JUMP START

Four years after entering the University of Pennsylvania in 1967 for an institutionally-installed baseline upgrade, the Faculty, Board, and Trustees awarded a civil engineering degree, one I would not, could not use. Another data point along the Obscure Spectrum—thankfully not frontline 'Nam, but the stateside, urban Philly reaction to it. Meanwhile, I endeavored to reconcile the discipline of engineering with the artistic expression of music. The nominal reconciliation was in structure—the physical structures of engineering, compositional structures of music. The music *I* like, that is.

I would do it on my own. Sort of. With the help of widescreen color, movies downtown on Chestnut Street and Rittenhouse Square. Charlie Chan and the Crass Brothers monkey in non-o-chrome. *Partitas* at the practice keyboard in the warmly incandescent, silky hours after midnight.

The discipline demanded of engineering similarly fostered development of a concise, intensely personal musical style, and productive use of very limited time. I had taken classical lessons for ten years, starting at six, according to those indisputable facts, stool at the grand piano cranked up so high I couldn't reach the pedals. Soul music seasoning and gigs were added at 15, extending through high school. Years of noise under the silent presence of that eye-dazzler print on the wall, very bright for a 1960's CPA (Central Pennsylvania) ruled by Cold War low pile and rusty shag, drapes drawn to mourn the nescient everyday off-price specials on gloom.

My mind was awash in music—eras, styles, modes, progressions. Scratching for time, I practiced classical drills, each cascading scale reinforcing my resolve to never design culverts for subdivisions, determine the length of traffic queueing at an intersection, or calculate the stresses in manufactured concrete shapes. My father had done those, made and overpaid the Maxwell family's contribution to the rigid-engineered environment, all while observing an exceedingly conservative factor of safety, with no chance of a refund.

If only integral calculus or tensor analysis could explain life in my little ego niche, provide an heuristic bridge to the girl with the long brown hair in what was a memorable case study of interpersonal dynamics and virtual work trial solutions, I would have had it knocked. No luck there. I was left with King Richard and Gulf, Big Power and Big Oil, Nix 'n Nox. Along with the rest of America, insured, and waiting to be healed.

Evenings brought refinery exhaust, walking to dinner with a dime's worth of three-star edition *Philadelphia Bulletin* in hand, eager for the sports and entertainment sections, averting my eyes from the front page global corruption update so as not to, as The Four Tops warned, "Turn to Stone". I didn't want to read another word about The World. *Leges sine moribus vanae.* "Laws without morals are invalid," the University's motto pronounced. Since when? *Mottoius sine veritas emptius.* Mottos without truth are empty. The World ran on fabrications, representations, hype, mottos, slogans. Conceived and dispensed in the name of commerce. Rifled barrels and calculations, too. Was it any wonder that on one "commonwealth's" version of the license plate was to be found, "The Polynomial State"? Solve it and send a man to the moon.

Ronnie's Sandwich Shop, once at 37th and Spruce before they knocked down the building across from The Quad and moved it to 40th Street, was both refuge and testimony. Shovels turned to dismal identity erosion paraded as redevelopmental renaissance in another variation upon the classic work, *The Wrecking Ball Cantata*.

So boil it down to something approaching meaningful, essential sludge. Here goes. Though fundamentally a mathematical abstraction, I've discovered extraneous roots and learned how they pervade all areas of life, analytical and nonanalytical. These roots are nothing less than the throwaway pretenders of solution sets, and the possibilities for encountering them are limited only by imagination. Beware the self-created, homegrown paradox, however: in certain contexts, extraneous roots may be real. Examine tightly packed digressions, broken seal spaceouts, and all wild cards equally meticulously, keeping in mind there is no such thing as a convincing argument.

Back to 40th and Spruce. The call came at the end of the last semester, in 1971, while I was eating a Supreme Roast Beef Hoagie from The New Ronnie's with The Works leaking through The Improved Wrapper, listening to Mahler's *Symphony No. 3* while pretending to study for The Important Final. It was a time when continuation of the cultural-political weirdness of the late 60's/opening of the 70's was taken for granted, to wit, The Osmonds, Three Dog Night, and Grand Funk Railroad; *Women in Love* and *Patton*; Native Americans' Alcatraz occupation; the Paris Peace Talks' fourth year; and les coups de grace, *All in the Family* and *Well-Meaning Blonde Airheads at a Famous Medical School* on the Meathead Channel, cracking markets where relevant.

Among the bizarre concepts like "crimes against property", and its corollary sticker, found only on bumpers with Vermont plates, QUESTION YOUR PROPERTY, I had to keep things in a clear, nonchemical focus. "Synthetic" had a lot of meanings. Instead of mescaline, I steered toward a mix of preppie "high cotton" easy-care fabrics at Dean's, occasionally the cableknit elite of J. Press and Brooks Brothers if I happened to be in New York, and alternatively, the wave-particle duality of hip urban denim and leather. Huxley, once read, was left behind in the spiralling fall of a feather through the vacuum of his own creation. Licit or illicit? Who cares. Give me *licht*.

Late in the day, before the *Bulletin* promenade, window open for fresh air, WFLN countered the racket of buses noisily accelerating, swooshing along Spruce Street with crystalline Vaughan Williams. As time went on, during frequent digressions of increasing amplitude, I detected many of those extraneous roots, doodling crescendi before predictably lapsing yet once more into the Stones' "You Can't Always Get What You Want" on WMMR, or inadvertently tuning to the ethnic folk music of WXPN, noise without a beat sounded on instruments lost in caves for centuries, found and restored in error. Soul deficient, negligent compared to the really good stuff on Philly jazz stations, Carmen McRae, Nina Simone.

Now dusk, windshift paying homage to the refineries, my book lit by a yellow metal gooseneck desklamp, within the fourth floor numbered space defined more by walls than the bamboo matchstick-blinded windows, I heard, will always hear Simon & Garfunkel sing, "...down from Berkeley to Carmel...," thinking, that's where *I* want to be, banging on the glass:

ELAINE !!!

And if Simon & Garfunkel contributed simple chords and smooth harmonies to the vignette, so did Sviatoslav Richter. More than I knew, playing Handel's *Keyboard Suite No. 5 in E major*, for a ballerina's perfect dance, while the rain came down on an empty stage.

All a montage styled as cinematic, illusory detachment, before I understood the real alienation of *Winter in the Blood*, sought one sweet nepenthe after another, attempting to calibrate other myths. Because I still wanted Natalie.

I missed graduation, oh too bad, but earned the degree. The diploma sent to me in the stiff, "Do Not Bend" mailer said, "Bachelor of Science in Civil Engineering, Magna Cum Laude." Perfect groundwork for a future Earth Depletion Award. No surprise there. Dylan's "Blowin' in the Wind" had succumbed to the doldrums. After freighting the four years, Mom and Dad, the deduction-claiming benefactor-pair, didn't get to do the graduation weekend thing, primarily staged for future "Alumni and Parent Annual Giving" anyhow. In search of the considerable bequeath. Can't make everybody happy.

Listen to another song which has held up much better, "Like a Rolling Stone". Get the message, it's not "Like a Robot". Even before the offer came, I was looking for career alternatives. Alternatives to a career, not alternative careers. I completed the University degree for several obvious reasons: because it was a challenge, to roll at least one snowball to which my parents could ever relate, and not excited about anything in the world of conventional jobs, I simply wanted to put off the day of reckoning.

I had never considered being a music major. Ultimately, I didn't have confidence the classical talent was there. Let's face it, you have to know by college that you're not the 16 year old Korean Liszt prodigy you've always wanted to be. If I couldn't be the best, it would be a demoralizing waste of effort. Suffice it to say, the offer from ESO was timely. I didn't have to be Beethoven. It was an opportunity for rehabilitation from a not entirely imaginary war in the streets of academia; invitation to extruded life, indented fame. Tasty, Crunchy Life. The Peerless Waffled Cone.

So with a measure of musical talent trending toward the *de minimus* end of the spectrum, according to my aesthetitometer, whether I could do anything with it was uncertain. More variables than equations, an abundance of those quirky extraneous roots. I wouldn't be getting closer to mental stability with pipe hydraulics or organic esters. Were my synergistic amalgams, variations on themes by YES, Allman Brothers, and Eric Clapton healthier, marketable? Had I been finer-tuned, more conscious, the drift and confusion evident in Mary Wells' music might have caused some concern: "My Guy" to "Sometimes I Wonder" to "Stop Takin' Me for Granted" to "Two Lovers" and finally, "Bye Bye Baby". From Natalie to free, but broke.

Back to '67, The Summer of Natalie. The scene was changing rapidly, already leaving Stax and Motown behind, headed to grass and pills, highs and bummers, impossibly compounded predicates. In blew the more challenging progressive rock I wrote and played. Intricate changes, metal lathe-turned power grooves disrupted by searing solos, expressionistic sketches, keyed transitions, helical shreds of shiny biting alloy, doubly vulcanized ear paint. Though expressive and perhaps eventually lucrative, nevertheless, Portfolio Non-Handel.

What saved me during that political, musical, and social tumult was a combination of the oft-cited discipline; an elasticity to be able to rebound from intermittent abuses to sufficiently clean living; artistic curiosity, not only musical, but visual and intellectual; and, baring all, a well disguised, though narrow, stratum of conservatism, exercised in the form of restraint. There, I've said it. One is, of course, only able to articulate such things later, attributions not the least of which are more of an appreciation of Natalie, formatively, symbolically and tangibly; and a dread of flashbacks, some inevitably, undeniably chemical. Respect the enemy: synthetics. All synthetics.

There was family conflict with the music career, not to the point of overt alienation or disinheritance, but rather terse interrogations ("for your own good") filled with economic admonishments, and finally, silence. Like donuts on wire shelves, even when turnover is rapid, the sugar and grease of the issue remain: howlongwilltheincome lastandthenwhat? Nobody in a campus industrial, tilt-up engineering sweatshop would want to put a 30 year ex-rocker with platform heels to work during a recession after the thrill was gone. But then the entertainment economy was booming, appearing to be downturn proof. I mined a mindset: "As outrageous as this reality is, we must stand together as a society of consumers. We simply will not stand for this recession." Somebody actually said that. A person with a hairstyle as high as the interest rates, paisley tie wide as the economic gulf. Medallioned aftershave swinger with a seriously chafed, turtlenecked weekend disco habit.

So above the dust of a life gon' bad appeared the smoking disclaimer, one nevertheless extended in an abundance of good faith: "All flaws are revealed in due time, to their most dramatic effect; we are not and cannot be responsible in any manner whatsoever." Sign or make your mark here.

My invitation to the anti-recession campaign came from LA. We had opened for (the earlier version of) ESO at the Power Factory in Philadelphia, three nights in late winter of my senior year. It was a time when a band, singer, player could just explode onto the scene, before even being allowed to get near the scene became a closely held business decision. Although we stayed in the city during summer vacations to gig, during the academic year our band was a weekend special, primarily playing dates at area colleges. I was writing originals, fighting those *Concrete Structures* at Penn, wearing a fitted black leather jacket, riding a motorcycle, and throwing an intentionally angular urban musicscape out to the crowds. Progressive, arguably Möbiusianally Regressive, Rock. Bouncing it off the walls, darker and more subversive than a light show. That was, after all, only *licht*.

Right place at the right time, like a bottle of Heineken Dark at that new bar just up from 34th and Walnut, a Bryn Mawr 8th round knockout with me, in town for the evening, strictly casual. How did I do it? An ESO personnel change, a call from LA, just a nonstop away, and I've got a high draft number to boot. Needed: one technical specialist. The garage bands were staying in their garages, while the Cars pulled out. The new music required polymodal machineheads comfortable with microprocessor controlled gear. It didn't hurt that this walk-on had an engineering degree, pondered realism at the Museum of Art, read Zen for entertainment, and played the musical equivalent of Richard Wagner meets Thelonious Monk at the Brecker Brothers' for Hai Tai Chi, processed through an Eventide Harmonizer. Music for No-Mind Artful Combat. Slant light disquiet.

This was after the purely intellectual encounter with Sonya, Frank's friend, strictly talk, no sport driving the curves which dominated the viewshed marked with European driving plates: *Pelligro!* Her close Afro was as a sumac tassel in the twilight obscure of the hofbrau, refracted a purple-black, melanzane hue, unbelievable and fantastic. Seeing the look she gave me through wire rims while Stokely Carmichael ran through her psyche, I wondered, does she have an arsenal of M-16's? How would that be translated in Cuba? Should I buy her a beer, the Bryn Mawr gamer notwithstanding? What would I order? Workers' Plight? People's Uprising?

As a man of suspicious origin, one who played music, I guess I was tolerable to a point, whatever or wherever that point was. I knew it didn't include my bottle of Bourgeoismeister Bier on the thick table of this booth, already carved with graffiti, the British pop laureate, Rod Stewart, or his classic, rhetorically dogmatic observation long since chiseled with accompanying punctuation above the entrance of one of the new "urban concrete box commons" at Penn, aka a dormitory:

"Every Picture Tells A Story, Don't It?"

Maybe all this is just pondered neorealism, internally inconsistent, empty of chronological or chromatographical accuracy. Purely vapid chimery. I know I can't remember what we were talking about, or more accurately, the titles of our lectures to one another. I was sidetracked by the melanzane parmagiana, *belle, dangereuse,* thinking, "beautiful woman, Soul Sister, are you ever going to get a life?" Meaning, as usual, one I can understand. But then I looked into the fabfauxpubantique Guinness mirror on the wall of the booth and wondered the same thing about myself. I wasn't exactly kicking field goals from 50 out or starring as Wally Kahuna in my next film.

Forget the philosophy, radical politics, and *pas de deux* with the 'Sister sure to be packing unseen hardware, firmware, software. The synch wouldn't handshake with the Sheila in the next booth either, high draft pick of an Australian professional rugby squad that she was. Headed West, to join ESO, chart competitor of YES and ELO with a tour starting in a month and a half. I had the chopped and channeled Hammond B-3 rig, Fender-Rhodes electric piano, triamped death ray monitor with neutron "rumor", new MOOG and ARP synthesizers. Management wired money for travel and shipping the gear. Rapid-fire weapons and money, so right for the times. I'd be driving my Austin-Healey 3000—you've enjoyed it enough, now wreck it—day and night, no TWA for me. Not using drugs, now or yet, that is. A straight, licit, first transcontinental road trip. Another round. Yeah.

Nobody believed it could be true, that the garnets of Wissahickon schist were to be replaced with Angeles Crest gneiss, the serpentine and jade of Big Sur, banded agate, jasper, vesicular basalt and secondary common opal of Last Chance Canyon. After reading of gravitational lensing, I wondered myself about the change, as intriguing and potentially deceptive as the multiple images of galactic presence recently intercepted, thought to be maneuvering into a bay at the coin-operated Phantom Nebula Dharma Wash. The ever-unknown motives of on-the-edge physics at play. Star collapse or only a multidimensional high pressure hosing? The future, once wet brown mud on the grate, now only a one-way trip away. I even had the extra quarters for WAX, GLEAM.

The last miles down steep and curving Cajon Pass on a rainy Sunday night, four lanes of 80 mph California freeway terror, were a prelude to midnight, surreally lighted, I-10 overpasses crumbled by the February earthquake. All blamed on the cryptic "Richter 6.6" code hidden within so many newspaper articles, widely believed to be the secret signal for Alien Reserve activation. Shadows of eucalyptus and oleander lined the freeway, gauntlet for traffic returning from Vegas or, as I learned, dune running/dirt biking in the high desert. To the Pacific, waves crashing as I hit the Santa Monica hotel, unable to sleep for hours from exhaustion and anticipation. Little did I know that those aliens had specifically chosen to settle here because it reminded them of their home planet in the deci-eons immediately preceding the ultimate depletion of plasmodic energy. Seamlessly Welded Masters at Concealment become Mentors with Suspicious Intentions, Motors without Bearings, Mothers of Invention.

The initial weeks were intense, learning the tunes all morning, rehearsals from 4 until midnight, trying to get some sleep in the new place, repeating it day after day. Getting used to stucco. Preparing for Big Time Romance.

Cut to fast forward. I made $200,000 the first year. All legit, no herbal importing or exporting from remote airstrips, no bundles of goods carried across the Tijuana border by nuns of the Church of the Blessed Unspoken Economy. A tour, record royalties, bonus, high interest rates, tax shelters, all those things that real businessmen use. Unmarked bills, motel rooms. Forced compromise. Pharmaceuticals. Surveillance.

The beach, much bigger than the Beach Boys

One weekend getaway was pivotal, to unwind in Santa Barbara, stopping in Ventura for a look at beach property whispered to be in play for a marina. The coast will always be golden. Every spare dime went into it. As fragrant as the flowers were on upper State in Santa Barbara, the return on the beach property was even sweeter. Five years later, with SEVERAL MILLION to celebrate the bicentennial, check it out, all caps, there was no need to worry about money. Like the time I drove a Larry Gill fastball up the power alley in left on a perfect day. Connecting with power, striking with authority, driving metaphorically regardless of the run. Getting good wood.

Neither had the drive come down yet, nor had I rounded the bases. There was no fence on that field and sooner or later, there would be a throw. It was the same now. I was still running, mindful any headroom that remained before clipping and burnout was disappearing fast. If there was to be hope beyond the tour bus, other interests would be needed—classical music, literature, photography; perhaps even people.

Looking back, well beneath the magazine-hyped superficialities, in more lucid stretches my life could be seen as a quest to recognize, find, and dwell within the Defining Sea of Importance. Not self importance, but the importance of self worth. The attributive Sea of the Past, Present and Future; its galaxy of island pairs—active/passive, good/bad, giving/taking, vital/numb, full/empty, to name only a few. It had to be out there. Somewhere, something more fundamentally valuable than simply having a talent or two and living for myself. Beyond the Hip Quip.

I became a creative co-leader in the band, and with that, predictably, an artistic rival. As with many leaders, there was enough unpredictability to keep things on edge. The dynamics of the rivalry produced some great work, but even more tension. Malibu, Laurel or Coldwater Canyon were destinations for the others, not me. I hadn't found a city where I wanted to live, but rather had the sense that I didn't want to live in a "city" at all. Where could I really settle in, achieve some kind of balance between self-interest and sharing a life with another? Had I ever walked on the beach of that Sea?

As often as I thought I was "ready", getting to the next level with that one, special woman continued to be elusive. Face it. I didn't have any idea what it even meant to be ready. "Ready", what a dumb word, useless as saying, "well yes, mankind did come to an END, but I got it all down and we were relatively unaffected anyway." Five years in too few episodic pages, edited for content and to play in the allotted time. It wouldn't be hard to stop here. Give up, forever stymied by the implications of a line I heard crawling into a remote, dust choked, low desert dive where you didn't want to look too carefully into the dark corners: "The World just doesn't turn like it used to."

A note of disclosure at the outset; whether important or not, it'll be your call. My life *is* besieged by all the fame stuff—shows, noise, pictures, clubs, capers, autographs, calls, interviews, benefit appearances, industry dates. I've filtered out most of it. This is what's left, my reality, what's going on in my head. If you want the tours, debauches, fights in private jets, closed door frenzies "leaked to the press", all the stuff rock stars think they have to do, wait outside the door or read the magazines. Behind these eyes, beneath the music, within a space filled by the pungent smudge of sweet grass, forever changing and the same, I'm in *here*. This is *my* life.

Or so I thought.

2

Really, but not literally, in the Banana Belt

Don't give up. Eventually I'll engage someone in conversation other than myself.

I don't know much about Laramie, but then, this is America, The Union. Performances daily at the Grate Maul of the Mined, where living on the ore dumps, we need know little of anything. Surely not The Great Books to take the test for a Brotherhood of Minimal Thinkers card. Where truth is too often parked in hidden garages, leaving us to live not according to the Ten Commandments, rather, the Three C's: Complexity, Confusion, and Chaos. We've hunted out the buffalo and felled old growth forests; harvested the Grand Banks and dammed rivers; dug the copper and extracted groundwater; pumped the oil and built smokestacks; penned up the Indians, taken the land, sold it on credit; defined and institutionalized "business cycles", made boom, bust, and recovery into the unquestioned national mantra. All verbs in the past tense. Get the picture?

America. You're entitled to any and all expectations and exploitations, limited only by imagination. As the historians term it, "exceptionalism"; and business schools, "commerce." We're different, unprecedented. Translated: delusional; mindless over matter. Is this sandwich one a thinking person would order?

Among all the perfect places to test Life-as-Hypothesis, The Spur Bar is equally perfect, away from the University and its elaborately derived trivialities, yet close enough to process the raw data. Stochastically speaking, events of varying probabilities linked within set theory only by commonality of the old railroad end of downtown. A zone of working and relaxing but never recovering, hours wasted fouling line, tangling reels with no trout stream to be found. South of the District of Assorted Motels, a strip of wielding, yielding, winding and unwinding. In short and no particular order, a land of neon signs, package goods, two-steps, smoke, dirty darkness, flimsy romances, and train wrecks, where the motto is "Don't Ask," and the sign in the broken window says "No Data Today." Leave that baseline behind.

The U. UWY. UWHY. There's a music program, although I wonder about the mix of musical cowpokes, locally 'Pokes, who would actually come here to study. What kind of kerchiefs would they wear? Chaps? Consider the downstate melodic rumination found blown up against a range fence:

(to the music of *Que Sera, Sera*)

… Would they be wooly, would they be white?
Here's what they said to me …

Musical Montana heading south for A Near Denver Experience or Banana Belt weather? Some banana belt in Laramie when the wind's blowing in January, and the radiator, like most things in the vicinity, is Not Near Enough. There's also an engineering school, but I'm not planning on running a road crew in Meeteese, trying in futility to push back winter when the gray flakes start, fighting the snow with giant plows, salt and cinders, losing out until spring when in a good year, an early rain washes away old grime. A hypothetical, hypo-thermial question: when did you first think of going back to school in Laramie? When I realized that aside from all the important things in life, I'm theoretically a smart guy and could do the program, get good grades, overachieve.

Though one with a few tragic hangups, like holding out for a mezzo-soprano. I wonder, would Frederica von Stade accept my collect call? "Hi, Talk Radio, this is Craig in Wyoming with a question about the *rondo reclusivo* in the third act of *La Schtalla*. Some have called it a *rondo mañana*. Viewed as a lazy-eyed metaphor for life in a moderate climate, *rondo sempre rondo*, how would you voice it, Frederica? *Tremuloso, Sturm und Drang, acequia madre, chile verde*?

Hearing the crunching skid on those cinders, fishtailing to an argued stop, "Let me out!" Or waves growing larger, breaking over the gunwales, in panic, "Turn into the wind, turn into the wind!!" Make for shore, if you can get there, along a coast though rugged and menacingly dramatic, safely overlooking the crashing, howling danger spit from the Roaring 40's. To an exhale in appreciation of Near Placid Water Days, more subtle tides of art and nature. The opportunity for sin on less wildly shifting decks.

With respect to the band, the clinical evidence pointed to a zenith—five years of albums, sold out stadium dates, helicopters; guided fear-calming, stress reduction, and personal training; catering, staff handling everything. There was even a cover in the Sunday paper magazine section—"ESO's Five Years of American Hits." The show was now performance drama, not music, an increasingly competitive, world weary effort with walls of Marshall amps, ten Leslie speakers, stacks of keyboards, trick effects. A battalion of trucks hauling tour gear, like ZZ Top's 75 tons of fun including a Texas-shaped stage and live buffalo. Critter Rock. Although to the market we appeared to be constantly capturing, defining, and communicating fresh material, too much of it these days was within a creatively unhealthy, earsplitting milieu. "It's no worse than … you know what they always want … they have no idea of … ." The universe of *it*, we and they, us and them. *We*'ll work on the most recent trend back in LA. *It* definitely has possibilities. For *us* to sell to *them*.

After a gold album or two and heavy duty touring, if you scored over 1200 on the college boards, found a 50% off coupon, or maybe just took them, you couldn't escape the fact that The LA Life was only a transparent media creation, clear noodles in broth bland without the hot ginger, a carnival in an empty box. And plenty of the cast just weren't too bright. In fact, the longer you were there, the dimmer you became. Without exception. I know, 'cause I heard it through the crepevine. Hardly revelations.

I'd hear fragments of *Tour Conversations, The Movie*, a Françoise Dorleac lookalike unloading on Slam, "So, I'm just a piece of meat, is that it?" Unfortunately, yes. Groupies yelling at roadies, in a final gasp sometimes at a headliner; headliners yelling at management. A business in which appearing to be logical was as bad as being honest, and there was always the last quarter point of the deal to be chased. Supergroup-produced background music for programming cultural games. Go to the *Setup Menu* and toggle away—Accomplice: *Blonde Babe*; Motto: *Eat Death*; Weapons of Choice: *Drugs and M-60 Machine Guns*.

As time went on, it became tougher to break the hold. Put on shades and walk out the front door of the hotel, fight off the diehards lurking there, and all you were left with were concrete and downtown traffic. Not surprising that drinking and other much more expensive, quicker-acting destructive activities began early, at subsidized group rates. A TV was always on, morning-noon-and-night, cooking shows with audible crowd gasps as the dessert creation was unveiled; vital observations such as, "the black pepper was the problem"; KC Ford's Jumbo Jungle, the Elephant of Marketing Disbelief, "we'll beat any peanut-brained deal"; and, of course, the strange clay jerky animated dachshund knockoffs found hidden like Easter eggs within the snowbanks of UHF.

Every tour was a crunching rush, much more tension than creative opportunity. The outrageous, ludicrous was amplified, pursued with a vengeance, anything to relieve the compression of travel, numbness of standing up night after night, mouthing words wornout long ago. We don't all want to live an endlessly looping Rock Star Minute. Some would much rather play than perform. Windsurf burning prairie waves in Asia.

In the studio, instead of creative overlay, it was so easy to default to production repoussé, musical decoration formed from the reverse side—pressure of "the business" to recycle marketable riffs into airtime and "unit sales". Meanwhile, the real talent was winnowed, rode away on the winds, leaving only a residue of promotion, production, and marketing sharks: "Get out of my face. The record's a loser. Don't you have to go to New York for new material, or something?"

I didn't want to dwell in that space in any way. The David Essex movie was sobering—a chemically induced alternative ending to one's own little world weariness. Upon the circumstantial evidence, it might be reasonably concluded that regardless of the alternative, the outcome was simply a predictable fulfillment of a tale of increasingly woeful self indulgence, syncopated by the inescapable, "The Beat Goes On". Lives, once green and thriving, become sterile gray silt, useless to plow, blown away in choking clouds. I'd try to escape it, or in the end if nothing else, either change the beat or fire a torch and play with charcoal lighter fluid. Straight from the can.

Looking around here at the Spur on this September late afternoon, lifting on a mug of Bent Wheat Lager, as they say up here, "A Hailstorm of a Beer Without the Chaff," I realized it could have been the Oarhouse, with the slightest channel change, in what had been Santa Monica in another time (meaning anytime prior to last week). Instead of *The Who? Play Falstaff*, substitute *Kris Sings Merle*. How much is there in the Well of Originality to go around?

Headed back into the studio upon return, I'll have to get into the right frame of mind. Will I be able to even recognize the inspirational path toward artistic tension, like that heard in the music of Jack DeJohnette, a master of playing off the beat, much less take it to creative resolution? And in that resolution, find soothing tranquility, expressed so well in a Zen verse I came across how many rebirths ago?

> You will have lived,
> memories become dreams,
> when the light of a clear heart
> lifts the mist of time,
> forever.

Does the verse offer faith, reflect it, or simply provide a perspective? Is going to church by itself a religious experience? If God's real name was *CLEM*, would *HE* be revered outside South Carolina? Is God a wooden cross? Is God in a wooden cross, in a set of car keys? In a specially marked box of Tide? Could what we heard be true, that the holy man rents shoes at a bowling alley in the town nobody else can see?

What is ballet? Does anyone really live in the City of Industry? Is it true freighters of bananas were stockpiled in a hollowed out mountain near Cheyenne in foreknowledge of The Great Kong? How have they kept them fresh? Will I need a nephelometer? Was John Shaft a real person?

Flashing back on the trip here, over the Sierra, making a square knot to secure all that was good on that day. Road ramblings like water wrung from a wet towel, a rush of cultural icons. I fit right in. I'm a cultural icon now, too. With considerable nod to Jacky the K, in that earlier time colored, enriched by exaggeration and editing, let's call this *Under the Road*.

… It *was* a sweet morning, even by local standards. Donner and its trees were left behind as I motored through the dryness of Reno, pointed toward the basin and range desolation to the east. Escape from Urban California, its economic engine simmering in a foreboding flash of speculation, one which would find only an empty tank when the day of the next reckoning approached—next year, decade, or century, certain nevertheless.

Hall of fame country and western commercials on the box, the absolute worst, pitching feed stores and AMURIK'N VALYOOZ, distracting me from litter become mental, the rubbish, detritus of a post-universal society which has lost touch, but from what? Where are the clues? How do I start looking for them— drink whatever I can find to break up the monotony, work myself into a frenzy, hallucinate until I reach "truth"? Shop for a survivable collision, look for another station? Am I on the road to find truth, "where the rubber meets the road," or is all this just more skid marks?

Where do they get tires that big? Mines again, secret ones in Nevada. Full dress, black outlaw pickyups driven by denizens of this Age of Mechanics in the Land of Real Draft, custom front plates: NOCODE, RSTLESS, BADATUD, HOSTILE, TRYME, HOSTAGE, SAYWHAT, FSTDRAW, WRSTDRM, BAKNBAD, BUTNO, BUTTNO, TERMNAL. Or in da northern part of California, possibly Orinda, BIGBUKS, NEWMONY, VIEWLOT. Kustom Kams and manually locking hubs, Camels in soft packs on the tuck and roll Nauga. Allure of the West. Heavy Awakened Iron. We're talking serious desert dirtwear.

In that dirt of the future, everything will be property. Tangible, intellec- tual, iconic, verbal. Life as copyrighted performance art. Atlantic®, the official ocean of The America's Cup®. Copyright yourself, or someone else surely will.

Another beer. My unborn children appear through memories, of other families, even my own brothers as we grew up, in the station wagons at this market, seeing them put bats and gloves into the back while I drive through small towns I do not know, on yet another summer night, headed east. Where is the mother of our children, my kids, brought from the future to make a present? Who is she? They cut their lawns here, and at least at midnight, all is quiet, at peace.

That money, DOLLRS in Orinda. Taken for granted, now. Yes, it's still there, the means of mobility, escape, insulation. But if I had a handle on the bigger picture, I wouldn't be out here roaming the range, driving all night to sunup in Laramie. I'd be sitting on the front porch, looking at the stars pulsating in darkness, that which is Zencalled void and, fundamentally, both is and is not. Or would I be out here anyway, needing to be on the move, filling the void and nonvoid with motion, looking for emotion unemotionally? Wondering where to find the porch?

What's insight, what's gibberish? Mostly the latter, road talk and sensory data, uninterpreted seismographs, thermographs, you pick a graph. You mean we actually have to work through this stuff? I keep buying books on consciousness and communication, visual creativity, but never open the covers, thinking that what needs to be dealt with is really much more basic. The roll is taken, and for all practical purposes, I'm unaccounted for, missing from the case. This isn't who I am. This is what I've become. Leaving the City of Industry, entering the City of Commerce. Carrots gone wrong. Reverse polarity. Tapering to the top. The very matter of carrot greens awry.

It's a warm September day, 1976, but fall is never far, bite on the clear air of Gallup always with me from another time, when I headed north on U.S. 666 to the science fiction set of Shiprock under a cobalt sky toward dusty red haze on the horizon. Legacy of everburning coal at Four Corners. The sad, angry streets of Gallup, tragic Saturday nights. In Panguitch there was no Saturday night. Their teenagers dreamed "anywhere but here," of California, the Gulf of Mexico, within a reality where Bryce just continued to pinnacly erode. While I was on another trip guided by familiar chords, finding new ones, synthesized "voices" speaking in harmonic complexity. Sagebrush rustling from my wake, grains of sand rearranged. Then I'm gone. But the chords remain, often familiar, occasionally new, sometimes ungraspable, foreign.

Is that what I want to do—become an underground classic, or just go underground classically? Ego ascending, simply disappear into one of those Shiprock basaltic crevices? Or with hope, flourish from a new beginning? Like chiles, wild or mild? Umbra or penumbra? Select your gray scale, graph, or intensity in this land of memories and memorymaking.

Maybe try a multiple choice to pass the miles:

57. Select the personaton with which you most closely identify
    ☐ paragon
    ☐ amazon
    ☐ automaton
    ☐ megaton
    ☐ wonton
    ☐ polygon
    ☐ longgon

Before I left, I mentioned that I was searching for a place without modules—this must be it, no isomodulars detected out here. No filter-tracking mods, triangle waves, or bipoles; compression, limiters, or aural exciters; time machines or synchs to tape. Just prickly pears, jumpin' chollas, rigs hauling green hay, mysteries of the Continental Divide. Behind dusty glass.

I got a haircut for the trip, shaved my beard but kept the moustache. Usual undercover roadtrip. Road performance art. On the road, in disguise, I can be who I want, within an accelerating vortex of new places and ideas. I'll grow it all back when I return. With the Healey, I look like a preppie, perhaps a little darkly complected, overbaked. Scotch-Irish in name, though with a taste for porter, n'er the ruddy cheeks.

Always keep at least one set of wheels registered in Nevada. California plates tend to get you the wrong kind of attention. Packed away was a Flying Burrito Brothers shirt, should it be warranted by an occasion I can't imagine. The beaded Plains Indian jacket, trademark, was back in the closet in Santa Monica. Special events only, rarely worn on the street. I was wearing the matched Hopi overlay bracelets, however, one on each wrist. More about those later. When the show's over, smoke clears.

Maybe not so undercover. Out here, they know I'm from another world. Mysterious, if I work at it, exotic, an undefined variable, wild card. That's why we sell out the stadiums, coliseums, field houses, and record bins. *New West Press* propagates the myth, fans the questioning fires become rebellion, protest, counterculture, while marketing camouflaged material status quo. It's scary, all the youth wanting to join a tribe they don't know or understand; many already so emotionally burned out they've been permanently released on their own recognizance. Nobody else will ever recognize them. Casual affiliations of nonthinkers mobilized to do that which is right, organic, obvious. But how about righteous? That word seems like it should be reserved for something deeper, the dope crazed exclamation notwithstanding. There's a whole rack of books on it at Cody's, in Berkeley. Closely watched for new titles, surreptitiously. Attractive new theories to believe, embrace, sleep with.

Laramie. Six weeks at hand. Enough time to pick a place on the map and point the Healey. The Ferrari 330GT back in LA would be a bit much for Wyoming and Montana; the Ford van with chrome rims and custom paint likewise, no doubt an invitation to a succession of moving violations. Living the luxury of time. Disappear for weeks, then return, to Santa Monica, a house in suspended animation, sealed, preserved and maintained. Time and money are only two terms of the equation, of course, quality a third. Starting with a piece of local peach pie along the Pecos, and extending far beyond. Remember the pie thing. It's suspicious, may be an extraneous root.

While we're living the "Me Generation" of the self-involved, self indulgent 70's, as Tom Wolfe put it, there are serious things going on in this world, in places near and far, known and unknown. In my heart of hearts, I feel ignorant, disinterested, detached, guilty. Running a bumper car, pushing a shopping cart. Maybe that'll change if I invest in a few exploitative ventures in the national interest—join the company of most others, stockholders all. Can anyone really know what's going on, figure it out through the ceaseless barrage of hype, slogans, simplifications, polarizations, smokescreens, agendas? It's not just the *Bulletin*. For sure, little information resembling truth could be found in either the six o'clock news I saw in a Berkeley hotel room a few days ago, or reliance upon the facades put up by the world, even when as tangible as the Walnut Street hofbrau melanzaniness years ago.

The program after the news was an eye opener. Nibbling Critter Fritters, I'm watching *60 Minutes* and there's Sonya, a fed with blown cover; Frank, her attorney, in a total role reversal, looking street angry, like he's the one packing now. No Bryn Mawr 8th round knockout in sight. Thinking back, I thought I felt Sonya's leg brush me a time or two under the table, but couldn't reconcile it with what I understood to be the ex-hofbrauten encaptionally manifestoed, hotlead-dispensing, chainwhippingly ensloganned Simba! Black Power! intellectual taking up arms. A salt withan in tent to ... Sonya just took the deal and went undercover earlier than the rest of us!

So what's the lesson in all of this? I don't like it, but I haven't yet acquired total immunity to reality. That I should just be out there consuming, recycling all the money from ticket sales and record royalties, the fruits of popularity, because it's all nothing more than shoddy sequences of images which can be overturned without even a moment's notice? Well, come to think of it, I would like to step up architecturally to custom handrails for the balcony, art glass, dramatic foliage lighting. That's not so selfish, is it? The same pronominally italicized *it* Tom Wolfe was talking about? Buy into *it*, then buy every*thing. I* become *them.*

Alien in a Healey, on a low budget Route 66 simulation, no matter how much centerline stretches in the rearview, there's always an unlimited supply ahead. Looking at the map and dirt roads which disappear into places like Smoke Creek Desert, Black Rock Sink, Alkali Flats ... and I know intuitively that this dysorganized, overdeveloped, panprogressive, post-industrial thick-crusted pizza of a society in which we live is only one zone, an O-zone in the much larger context. These generations who consider smug, all knowing hipness their manifest destiny. Or postulating, for discussion, that there is no such thing, it's only a fabrication, and without the benefit of any spiritual grounding, shop for philosophies, foreign gods, and other escapes; fight with the previous generation; and consume at the expense of the future genera-tions. Like I said, there will be days of reckoning. Until then, there will always be another motel with space available, The Eons of Comfort, Explorer Class View Rooms looking out on the New Forest of NonSense, the Transitional Rivers of Netherworld Numbbb.

On my way to where? Here, Laramie, but dimly. A university, yes, but one of the high plains, red gravel roads, those cowboy bars down by the tracks, an actual alternative to the UCLA/Westwood version, purporting to be so tuned-in and radikal, but in reality intellectually nominal, fully tenured with parking privileges, nauseating, out of it. Don't get me wrong, I'm not calling for a preemptive strike, rather a sense of creative life balance. What we're all looking for, if we ever bother to ask the first useful question. After just the right number of eons have elapsed in motelled comfort. We'll know when the movie hits the theaters. When we get the credit card receipt. The summons or black-mailable photos strictly for negotiation. "We don't want to make them public."

Lots of those movies in Westwood.

I dreamed she put on a beret, a bandana, tried to fit in, blend, be sufficiently pale for the season; walked on the late Saturday afternoon streets there, feeling invisible to the post football game en-Bruined throngs. Hurting, because she knew why.

"Look at me!" Saw only herself, freeze-framed, stuck to Westwood backgrounds, where else?

After tripping gracefully on a sidewalk crack, now proudly smiling, shaking her hair loose. Resentment gone, clothed in pure buckskin, falling from stutter steps into an old dance, surrounded by her people. A dance about real bruins. Power. Became one she had nearly forgotten as faceless traffic passed, others stood aside amazed, seeing but not finding, in silent indifference to, denial of, their own lost generations.

Revealed, a fragment of what had been before *they* invented wilderness. Revealed, in this modern wilderness *they* had not intended to invent, didn't care enough about to lament. Advancing, closer. I took her hand.

None of which and all of which were only more marketable sneers, new movies opening in Westwood. Possibly more blackmail.

Relax. This isn't Westwood, it's Laramie, a different dream of creative avoidance. And we're the ones with the posable thumb, though itchy trigger finger.

What is the draw of Laramie? Less chance of being recognized (when I don't want to be), interviewed, questioned, fingerprinted, requested, commended, congratulated, invited, booked, or prosecuted. In short, more anonymous, despite the Healey with California plates. A life of explanations and excuses, just clean cut and vacationing. Laramie—a quick draw, twitch. Bang.

Bad, so bad. Frederica, you elegant songbird, pick up on line two. Now we're getting to the *calzone* crux! About singing the heart, *l'amour*. About Native women in buckskin, become real. And only to me. Intellectual property. Protected not by law but tradition, heart and truth.

Towing icebergs, with a serious case of screen flicker

I was towing a lot of icebergs, in many ways, needing fresh water in a land of salt and bitterness. Unmet expectations in relationships. Expecting what and why? All the diagonal arguments and semantic paradoxes you plow again and again, alone in a bar.

I'm hearing a once private conversation a couple of tables over, wandering away, unleashed by alcohol:

"Are you happily married, Ed?"

"Huh?"

"Are you still happily married? Yes or no?"

"You don't understand. If you did, you wouldn't be asking a question like that."

Well, there's your answer. Possible diagnosis: antiphoniously tensile cognophobia, the fear of knowledge while under the influence of alternating, opposed noise generators. Like the reversing carrots, a rondo gone bad.

Since I'm in Wyoming, I can divulge a few secrets of my own. For some reason, I have never really synched with women from California. So far. I admit it. I've had to work way too much, even when backing off on the expectations. My feelings about the whole thing, anyway. Perhaps it's cultural and I don't have the map to navigate the waters. Maybe I was too circumspect at the start, and never really fit in. ESO has been primarily employment with little genuine socializing—just the way it is. After five years, that's not going to change much, particularly when I'm tiring of the whole thing. So maybe I just don't speak the language, can't see the trail markings.

In a daydream, She had come close, asking whether this was my "life in terms of the movies" phase. Unfortunately, the answer, had I rendered it, would have been uncomfortably close to "yes." Instead of the question, though, I got a command: "quit stalling; make a decision." Inquisition by the woman I know so well, but have never met. The woman starring in, defining another of my dream categories: Miss Heavy Accountability 1976. There are others, some more alluring, others much more heroic. In no case extravagantly muscled or earring over-hooped; never wearing a big watch.

When I'm on the road by myself, it's a different story. Where I want to be, doing what I want to do, meeting women who are interesting to me has never been difficult. So if meeting Her is a plausible future, chances are, it'll be outside LA.

Most of the pressure, on or off-tour, is attributable to THE SHOW, anxiety over tracks that won't come together, mix down to coherence. A curve which has unexplainably lost its snap. I know, I've just been over this, but I'm still trying to think it through. And even when the tracks seem to work, doubts linger whether the product will sell. Frayed extension cords connected in series, heating up for too long, trying to keep the power on to this electric cowboy, phosphorescent bison with a serious case of screen flicker. On the other side of the hill must be prairie grass, safety, until you reach the top and see the buffalo jump for what it is. A shortcut with only one possible outcome. You bought it for real. Even in a dream. Mountains on radar that weren't there before final approach. For many of us, as real as it gets.

I got started running at Penn. Now I need it, can't stop. Without the exercise and escape, surely I would have been history long ago. Just this side of striking confusion, I watch what I eat and workout six days a week, without exception. Keeps bad habits away a little while longer. I've seen a few in this business of music, rife with "creative", unreliable misfits pulling down the big bucks, working a dulling edge, ending up either the authentic dead, or soon to be, gripping the wheels of runaway lives, rushing toward unavoidable, incompressible objects specifically placed there for the crash. Useless material excess, those uncharted mountains again, without a stunt double.

That's another clue, "why Laramie?" To escape the handlers, middlemen, spin doctors, ministers of speculation, managers of zodiac depository accounts, custom upholsterers, and grovelling gurus of higher places, usually in first class and well below 35,000 feet. But let me get off this and resip that sweet Nevada morning through a fresh beer.

It was as if I was living impossibly dense prose, monumental as One Peak set upon the earth by an ancient, alien civilization. Folded as metamorphic rock origami, bearing hidden inscriptions, indecipherable meanings. And now, the more I write, the deeper I go, the less I know what's pure fact, if there is such a thing, what's interpretation, what's fabrication.

In that movie, seeping between the pages of this road rant like the hot sauce at Ronnie's, there's an arrow in the bull's eye, piercing a target lost within an immense forest. Or was it on a freshly mown green? I can't remember. Doesn't really matter, there's a fence around it, the place where they all speak so calmly, too calmly. Within the high rent postgraduate institution of the unbalanced, from which there is no extrachemical release or return. Synthetic High. School of Learning Low.

To myself: "Stop talking about me. I'm no more than an abstraction, a device. A reality jig holding no material. A unit black hole, standard issue. Attracting, pulling, consuming, obliterating. Thankfully, running."

Past a fire on a dry lake in the desert, temperature dropping to zero. Gathering driftwood, where there is no forest, river, or ocean. Unanchored. As I am in my Drift Healey, buoyant on the land, caught by an undertow. In the shadow of a boulder, wanting to come out into the light, warm by the fire, walk on the coals. Flames which we appreciate, but do not really understand. As I am, lost in the fires of antiquity, art of the Mimbres, Anasazi; the beauty of women.

A new trip, love letter to another woman who doesn't exist. Yet. It has to be yet, or truly, there would be no hope.

How about if I take a different tack? "Hey, baby, I'm going to rescue your lips from that cigarette." Maybe a problem here. Real Cowgirls don't smoke, do they?

"Rescue your lips from that longneck." Easily convince you that the value of an empty beer bottle is much less than a full one minus the beer. The diminution of value cannot be explained mathematically, only poetically. You need to understand this postcard to myself, Cowgirl. Having a great time, wish you were here. I want to hold your ... body language.

"Rescue your lips," period. Incomparably embouchured, unrestrainably, bioelectrically beckoning. Confrontational, unable to be withstood. Drawing me closer and closer.

Forget the third beer, enough rambling in this mental matinee which is starting to resemble the cover of *Workers' Playtime*. I'll have a tabletop of empties and be fresh out of elocution and equitation by six. Before I fall off my horse, let's just say Bent Wheat is not Anchor Steam, leave it at that. Get back on the road in the morning after an oil change, trade the admittedly vague promise of Laramie for a road southwest to Grand Junction, Moab, Indian Country, Route 66. Places of myths I haven't fully explored, appropriated for their emptiness. I'm in a hurry, to get back home. To get back home, to be alone.

Dirt®, when clean just won't do. Covered with the dust of memories and plain dirt, incognito, there are no introductions or arrangements. You just do it on your own. Freelance®. My exciting new designer *Travel Solo* line.

3

That Palomino ringer from Sheridan

Was I getting anywhere, or simply restuffing the sofa cushions of conjecture? Sawing pieces from a state of mind that comes off the shelf in 4×8 sheets? Taking out an uncollateralized loan on life, bringing to the table only closing costs, nothing down? The victim of my own story, with no tragedy to be found?

Sorry, just hungry.

Physically out of the zone of road shear hazard and reverted to a Type A Swedish perssønality in my intermittence, I dropped into an Italian-Chinese place across from UWY on Grand wondering, "okay, what can be made of this?" The kungfu-trattøria hybrid could only have made its reputation on the basis of, well, being close to the campus. The working-student-waitress was evidently more highbred Palomino than Sino-Caesar, considering her sleek, anythingbutsisal mane. I know, a horse analogy, no matter how noble or poetically drawn, brings only the wrong kind of salt. Delayed anguish as final as a dry watering hole a hundred miles out, ringed by alkali, relied upon in a prior moment of foolish miscalculation. But this was a private association, a musing aside to the poignant lyricism of "Monkey Time" as I snowshoed along the anxiety scale from frenetic to no longer clinically dangerous. Aside, not downside.

The chow mein noodles looked to have been left over from the last century, possibly the first noodles in Wyoming. For those hungry for the past, a real find. Then there was the ashtray—you can count on finding amazing stuff in those. Check that later—she's coming over.

My opener, I recall, was, "and how is the Pollo Larghetto this evening, *molto bene?*"

I wasn't prepared for the reply: "as slow as a wrangler in love getting around to saying what's really on his mind." Was it mere coincidence, rote, or the stunning imprint of an extratropospheric IQ, a real story too unbelievable for "Lives of Laramie", the Friday feature in the TV section? A syzygy forcefully Jupiterian? More delicately Venutian? Were we barrel racing? Who was wearing the saddle?

"I'll accept that challenge. Assuming that you're a college student who's taken more sociology and philosophy than you'll ever need, what would you say to, 'life, more than demography'?" Gouda and Edam, more than red wax rind? Engaged in offshore deependmanship, or a single stroked into right, Purely Yaz?

She began to respond, another coy keepaway coming with a side of creamy ranch, but stopped as if hung up in mid-dipthong, pondering the phonetics, thinking better of it.

"Let's start over. May I take your order, sir? A preference for Italian or Chinese this evening?" Professionally, sincerely, beautifully voiced.

Not barrel racing now, Lippizan dancers on old brick, a balcony above the piazza, silk gown, long white gloves. She could play that part. Easily. It wouldn't be acting.

Scanning the menu, I seriously considered the Pollo Non Sequitur, but instead launched into other, uncharted nonverbal malapropismic headwaters, looking for coarses I could imagine, but not quite stear. Eventually I gave up, and in the absence of a grease pencil to mark my selections on the plastic covered menu, just pointed to a few items, nodding in the order while coincidentally wondering, did Palooka originate as a verb? In a forest abundant with game, he made camp and built a fire; despite pressing hunger, looked into the flames for a purifying vision. Surrounded by darkness, in the crackling embers, the ancient, infinitive wisdom would not be denied: that to palooka is all.

Glancing at the next table, I wondered if I should intervene on the patrons' behalf, insist that they take back the joint of *vitello* and make the cheese sauce yellower.

"Italian," now getting my cheeses straight, realizing thick yellow was not on that country's wheyscape, mindful too that mozzarella can be tricky when heated.

Now with the *formaggio* well in hand, business quiet and boss mostly back in the kitchen, we talked in panels, narrated dream frescoes sequenced with what proved to be a very provincial Wyoming-Italian production: primo, Angelo's Famous Tortellini (it wasn't); and secondo, Scalloppini a la Casper, as oily and apparational as its nemeses, presented in a moderately Louisiana Purchase-sized portion. To nominally validate Angelo's concept, while wondering whether there actually was such a person, I did accept a fortune cookie. As is the case with all fortune cookies, the message was vague; and biscuit, shell, or whatever you call it, hardly dessert.

Cathy was "down from Sheridan," a senior who didn't want to return to ranch forever, did want to be an editor, maybe even a writer someday. I listened intently, framing glamour shots in my viewfinder while she dragged out a hitch with strong arms, work gloves, unmistakably gouging the conversational ground we had otherwise smoothly established, then dropping the hood, welded it on her future in a shower of hot metal, disclosure, and notice, that I might get the whole picture blindingly and concisely:

I've got my mind made up.

The erratically scissored message from the cookie, just out of a bulk pack from the San Francisco distributor, still crisp, was equally unusual:

Tread water or sink.

I rode over that one and while armwrestling with her to see *how* strong, encountered both the muscles and resolve of twisted wire on fence posts, that hard day's ride beyond the draw. You knew she meant it. Accept my decision or I'll send around the boys. A couple of war parties. Northern Cheyenne. Painted with bad news.

There was some tension in her family, to which I could relate, regarding the future she sought although, I gathered, the concern was mild. While one part of it was more about letting a daughter go than a break in the ranching lineage—her brother was already working the spread—the other was much deeper, about leaving the land. Out here regardless of whether romance or misfortune, in the end it's the land, always the land.

She got off work at nine, and I was there to meet her. *Ex parte.* In a street scene made up of all the slot machine bells, bars, numbers, and fruit in Vegas. PULL.

Walking later on Ivinson, in the old downtown by the railroad tracks, we ended up back at the Spur. Regardless of the prospects, voluble or tongue-tied, rain or shine, I was only one beer away from my daily limit. Period. It would be an early evening. Really. I promise.

We sat at the bar for awhile and talked while nursing a couple of Old Candors, Old Downtowns, Old Deceptions, some kind of brew. I wasn't paying too much attention to the brand of suds now, but liked the fact that Cathy was comfortable with a beer and didn't have to try ordering an absinthe because she'd read about it, or the gimlet of a Lauren Bacall movie. While I mentioned LA and the "music production business," she spoke of authors, Wyoming, and the future unfolding after graduation next spring. When somebody put a quarter in the jukebox, I asked her to dance three slow numbers, one after another. Neither of us made a move to waste the music.

Cathy was by all appearances a strong, fine woman, on the threshold of being spectacular. In my arms, dancing, she felt wonderful. Three Sevens. Rush of silver.

"Not bad for somebody from LA with no prior experience," she commented, with a hint of much deeper interest, body language in passing. Attractive in what seemed to me an honorable way. What, if not that, was slow dancing about, anyhow? Arrows.

"Pleased to know that those boxcars in the yard brought a few spirited palominos to this wind whipped, once and always territorial end of the trail cowtown."

"You sound like you're from Denver, not LA. They just scoff at us, pump out the oil, and take back all the money." The beef too, and everything about it.

That was also pretty close to summing up LA. A greasy box of fries to go, delivered a few short and with contempt. When all was said and done, "Where's the beef?"

After the beer, for me it was time to shut it down. "Gotta go, make an early start tomorrow." Shoving off early, unilaterally, is always impressive. Shows you've got your own life. A good move.

"You leave a generous if not imposing tip, awaken my sleeping heart by dancing close, show uncommonly good manners and intelligence for this wind whipped cowtown, as you put it, then are gonna just slip out of Dodge at dawn, pardner?"

Slip got my attention. Slip, falling, aching. Draw and shoot me. Already have.

"Let me amplify that. I like to get up early, go running in the dark. Maybe take a ride to see how far the plains extend in each direction."

"Oh, one of those. White training suit and yogurt. Attitudes toward space. California."

"Somewhat, though not entirely, guilty. I do occasionally draw a line. Don't ask me where, though."

We walked to her place, a cottage on Bradley, and after a few more minutes of small talk, said goodnight. A couple of rodeo hands appreciating the quiet moon after a tough job penning the rough stock. If there was a soundtrack, the selection would be "Variation No. 9" from Elgar's *The Enigma Variations*, "Nimrod". Great grandson of Noah, The Hunter.

I wasn't on tour, and didn't have to be in a hurry. Cathy was the type of woman to whom I'm invariably drawn. We'd just see what might happen. I definitely owed the guy who put the quarter in the juke.

⊹ ══════ ⊹

The next day stretched into more than two weeks. We saw each other often, after class or work—talking, drinking coffee, even a Saturday trip to the Medicine Bow Range. I suppose I was a rarity in Laramie—someone who was not a rancher, tireshop employee, student, or professional academic. A head case who didn't act out his personal scenery in the usual ways?

Rare and interesting enough for Cathy to want to "keep you away from my girlfriends," she said. What had to be a brief relationship for me, at least for now, eventually became intimate. Grew to intimacy? Slipped into intimacy? Took on a measure of intimacy? As eventual and intimate as two weeks can be. Cathy showed me, maybe began to give a part of, her warm, sincere heart. I had mixed feelings about that but said nothing. After all, weren't we both giving and taking?

To occupy time by myself, I checked out The U, crashed a couple of classes to get the feel of the place, and found a piano in a soundproof studio at Frank's Music where I could practice daily. While they did a decent business, mostly oriented to beginner County & Western guitar, I did Hanon and Bach exercises, played at composing, developing and polishing new riffs. I was realistic about my capabilities, closer to Roy Orbison than Chopin. Let me see, did I have the diamond horseshoe pinky ring then? If so, I must have left it under the pillow. At Cathy's.

Speaking of her place, it was small and bright, with a senior's knicknacks, by now winnowed U. Cowboy memorabilia, cookbooks, picture books, and interesting reading material. Somewhat predictable was *Angle of Repose*, Stegner's portrait of several generations on the American frontier. James Welch's *Winter in the Blood* was less so, being about the Blackfeet, though the family/search for truth theme was consistent.

Two other books, well thumbed, were unknown to me: *The Optimist's Daughter* by Eudora Welty, and Annie Dillard's *Pilgrim at Tinker Creek*. Hardly typical reference material for a cowgirl, the former being about a young woman dealing with the death of her father in the South; the latter about nature, observation, and learning. Families, seeking meaning, our place—what most books are about, I suppose.

I was reading quite a bit, not because I necessarily wanted to, rather, the time was there to fill. My preference was to go, see, breathe (gasp), touch, regret. I could relate to Nicholas Payne pursuing Ann Fitzgerald in McGuane's *The Bushwacked Piano*; and *Zen and the Art of Motorcycle Maintenance*, the message of which to me was to forget the convoluted deadends of philosophy, just ride the trip. More Meaning might be around the next bend. In a tree, a cloud, a river. Delivered poetically in a town, a crash, eye contact. Pursuit.

Cathy was going to classes, and neither knew of the time at the music store, nor of the specifics of my career. I was used to keeping it quiet. She remarked, in passing, that music production must pay well, if I could just take off a few weeks, and drive a mint Healey around Wyoming.

We talked about where I lived, a two story house in Santa Monica, but not in much detail. Being an engineer by training, she could tell I was organized, and probably very orderly, the kind of guy who keeps up to date on interferometer technology, carries a roentgen gauge. It was an understatement, supersaturated with irony. An ordered world, but one which often seemed to be so in all the wrong ways. It wasn't ordered in my head, that's for sure. Occasionally flashing back on major inhales ... "I'm sooo wrecked!!" ... before laughing bedlam. Entire lives lived within, indexed under, While in the State of Being Wrecked. Which state plate would that be?

Despite enjoyable getaways like this one, I saw myself as effectively insulated by lifestyle back in LA, being restrained, in the end, among art and paper, music and walls. What had happened to the days when girls wore perfume that smelled like Play Doh, and I liked it? Before they were carrying stash or packing that calibered hardware? After the creativity and peaks of ESO, unable to relate to the "reality" of the NOW, was a slow fade coming, symptomatic of an ending marked first by creative attrition, followed by loss of heart? *My* heart.

"Maybe I'll come out there after graduation, make my fortune in the publishing business," she said, "but then maybe Cheyenne will just have to do." Strong willed.

The difference in our ages, recently 21 and nearly 27, never really came up, but *I* felt it, knew it was there.

The same *I* had to constantly fight for awareness of the need to loosen up, get away from overdisciplined methodicalities—cowboy it. While Cathy was busy, to supplement my time at Frank's, I took pictures with the Nikon or Leica, day hiked. Looking out over Laramie from a nearby hill, I wondered whether she was the one in the famous story, *Here's How We Met*. How many chances do you really get in a lifetime? More than I deserve, but there always seemed to be another forthcoming, with the level of interest empirically observed to be directly proportional to the distance from LA. That could be self-fulfilling. I was thinking about it way too much.

Oh, yeah. Before I leave, I'll have to tell her about the fame thing. With each day, I'm closer to being out of time. Slow it down, like the Chambers Brothers, "Time!"

Sorry, I'm not done thinking about it. Now and again, and particularly during moments like this, alone on the road in the great wasteland (of the unenlightened), numbed by the roar of the Healey (a classic), the implications of "peace", "quiet", and where they might lead, are unsettling (theoretically). For each clause, a parenthetical qualification. In each picture, a bridge on the horizon. Always on the horizon, never closer. Obvious much?

How can I get closer, bring it closer? Will the explanation, if non-answer, be only existential acceptance and emulation of the "no-mind" Zen warrior, or an ultimately incessant, passive intellectual "all-mind" boredom expanded to occupy all the available time? Maybe something else quite different?

Contemporary musician that I am—resident of yet another counterculture, my generation, possibly a selfishly ego-unique epoch of human-time submerged in noise, some of it actually aural-recognizable, compounded by incessant distraction, too often self deceptive—where is the value to be found? Take away the noise, and what's left—peace, or a disturbing withdrawal from the empty addiction of, when you really get down to it, just killing time? Are you in, or out? When you're out, you're left behind. The technology advances, but since you no longer need to have "the edge", there is less and less motivation to learn how to apply it. That's not necessarily bad for those of the mechanistic school, simply the natural order of *things*.

Driving toward Medicine Creek this afternoon. These heavy thoughts, trying to relate Cathy to my context, determine where to place her on the set. My context? Huh?

I know that although this mindstream is inevitable and necessary, most of the attitudes, approaches, and theories arising from it will be dead ends. Behind the noise, my sense is that there is a message to be heard, like the one which has stuck with me, sometimes in my throat, for the last two years. The message that keyboard wizards, intellectuals, street sweepers, machine collectors, one generation or the other, will have pointless lives if they do not make their number one priority a search for True Worth, not the hardware brand or kind measured in dollars; seek answers that may or may not be found; and in the process gain some small measure of understanding, aware "synthesis" is literally that, an action which leads to synthetic results.

I could take comfort in a temporary excuse: at the time he was officially self-classified as a "device", and therefore, not responsible for any and all actions and/or inactions whatsoever. May it please the court, the classic noncognitive "device defense".

Talking of pointlessness, the stranger on the plane, who may as well have thrown me out the door, was right when he mused that you won't find True Worth in the chimery of Buddhism, the mind-game maze of existentialism or other "philosophies", or communicating with unmapped, weird cosmic energies emanating from mysterious objects usually orbiting just beyond the limits of detection but summonable with the flick of a switch, truly a random cosmic surprise when turning on the blender. "You Win!" Indeed, something more is at work. There was no stranger. There was no plane. But Cathy does exist. The faultless arguments assembled in a vacuum *meaning* what?

That the switch on the blender is wornout, the stranger did throw me out the door. I didn't mind it at all. And in falling through space much bigger than my imagination, triumphing over myself in an inspiration of acumen more impressive and ordered than epoxied-copper coils, I realized that the secret began to be understood if one never neglected to regularly check line voltages, tire pressures, and thermostats. Vital stats of The Comfort Zone.

With an inexhaustible power supply and frictionless surfaces, I could take the mechanics of life for granted. That rig next to me filled with sorry, bawling cattle on the way to market, roaring by to pass, was somebody else's problem. Combustion, movement, angular momentum, torque, transfer, motion. All those vehicular travel-vectors headed down the road, with magnitude and direction, at least in the physical sense. Merging trajectories with seeming, self-imposed urgencies to speed toward, disappear at, the vanishing point. But do they really reach it, or not? It doesn't matter. Like I said, I can take the mechanics for granted. I don't have to derive them for this test. I keep telling myself.

There's always another nightfall and awakening the next morning, in Grand Junction or Rock Springs, Laramie. On second thought, are they vanishing points? Is any place not a vanishing point? For the cattle? For me? For the Duke of Earl?

Okay, so I admit I'm still turning this over in my mind … we all do. Who is that on the decal, smoking a cigar and eating nails—early Woodie, an angry, bad-boy SluggoBird, way beyond the Saturday morning cartoons? Voted Most Dangerous Woodpecker of the 60's, marking a time which had to end decisively, or we'd be in "analysis" forever. The clothes and incense were too much, the undeclared war too heavy for the nation to deal with. I was able to steer around the road junk: television force feeding, the cause; primetime war in your living room, whether Flint, Tupelo, or Wax 'n Wenatchee, the logical effect. Then again, maybe it didn't end decisively, and I'm one of those blankeyed casualties, a battle unit which didn't escape after all, who/which even when standing before the shrines can't remember anything, but need a cigarette.

Shuffling, counting cards. Jotting thought fragments in my notebook, black & white world views on film. Laramie, cowboy town, within a day's drive of the Medicine Bows, Bighorns, one restrained by university antibodies. When the Country & Western gets too loud, recover at a classical recital, without having to check the Colt at the door. Now there's a pipedream for you.

I happened to look at what had appeared on the napkin, my pen still smoking:

refraction	by the prism of reality
resolution	through the stories of truth
reflection	on the dust of dreams
retreat	in surrender only to timelessness

And so the musings and doodlings went on in the days of rambling, before that intervening event, when things became increasingly tangled, the most favorable outcome, "go to your room." More modal, then tangible. And on. And on. In a surrender. Of sorts.

During a moment of solitude within this Big West Trail Drive, I thought again about the different directions we were headed. They didn't have to be opposite. Tremendous insight at work, fog lamps working overtime; even in the clouds of confusion, hot enough to seal the real. What could be clearer? Cathy would finish her degree, start a career. Just suppose that we could meet at that all important point of coincident inflection, and hence departure, where multiple futures are possible. Would that point be five years from now? Where? In a rearview mirror? Hole in the sky, diffracted edge effect?

Last timeout of the first half, sitting on the bench, towel over my head. Wakeup, Craig Maxwell. Why does any of this matter? Because in that rearview, turned to her side, Cathy is applying a hint of lipstick. Imagine that pardner-scape, Cowgirl in Wyoming. In my Healey. Lipstick and everything that goes with it. Scent, texture. Smile.

Back in town, on the way to an early dinner out, we stopped at Frank's Music. Dan asked how it was going; time to introduce the lady. Cathy. Goes to the U. I just want to play a few things for her in the studio.

"I've heard that before ... who did it? That's really good!" We left and went to Square Two, the record shop down the street, where I showed her an album cover.

"Look closely at the picture and liner notes."

"Why didn't you tell me? You're that guy, huh?" Aka Captain Eddie Stocks and the Market Gyrations.

Tripped while skating in on the goaltender in a short seller's market. My advice, take the penalty shot, Cathy. Always take the shot.

It was a quiet dinner. The kind that when you think about it, you don't know why you choose to live under all of it. In my case, the absolute mass of the universe. I guess you could call it concealment. I may be guilty. I'm not who I said I was, even though I never said who I was. Extenuating circumstances—I don't know who I am to say who I was.

"I've got to get back to LA. We're going into the studio to do another album, which will take a few months. I don't want what's between us to fade away to nothing. Let's just see what happens." Knowing that it would be uphill all the way, but interested enough to hope that it would be otherwise. I liked this woman.

"It's a dream from which I haven't awakened," Cathy said, really meaning, "I don't know if you're starring in it or not."

You guess the inflection. I have my own opinion. I'm sure it will come to me, if I think about it enough. But I'm not going to now. I would just feel bad about the way she's so strong, yet holding on in unseen ways, like all of us are.

It was a dream, a play, story of lozenge-lives set at the PHhosphoric Loounge, your place of choice for time stretching, controlling the hack, where the freeways meet in Downey. Meeting the vague headon, with energetic ambivalence, my character an expert in selfstarting, openended arguments.

Remembering days when it was beyond food, all about control: "eat that dessert or else!" And resistance. "Make me."

I've gotten very good at the things which don't count or matter. This time, I wanted to believe more than the truth, I wanted to know that I could make up my own mind about dessert, that finally I was a free agent on location:

Deep in Paradise.

4

The Cigar Museum—showcase
with a shelf life

Driving to Wyoming, chances are you'll drive back from Wyoming. It's something I just realized and wanted to pass along, what some would term the natural order of things. And while you're out here, rip favorite clothing on barbed wire; learn firsthand about mine spoil, the Weird Code of the West, what the few women, unattached or otherwise, share with snow fences; and always and inevitably, EATDIRT.

Populating the empty, geographical disconnect, where all maps are at best approximate and more often contrivances, are Golconda, a town denoted but actually in Chile; Owyhee, with nothing but wishful thinking in common with the Luau State; and all five Jacks dealt from the bottom of the deck: Jackpot, Jackrabbit, Jackpine, Jackson, and Jack's Place. The extra Jack calls for a shot on the house, '45, and it ain't malt liquor. In The Orebusters Lounge this week, the only available choice is between programming produced locally in your own head, or the ambient trigger-happy sounds of Slade Palladin and the Last Draw. One never really knows what DSTRESS will be playing in this BeeHiveNevadaWyoming MultiScream Regional Complex until the shots actually ring out, gunsmoke settles.

This lounge Jack built or not, it's the perfect place for mindmeanderings among the basin and range, silhouetted desolate peaks, parhelic visions. Musical siege replaced by the expanse of skyrock and evenmoreunendingsky, city leash left behind, hooked to the MotelKafka as I peeled out of the pack n' park 'em lot, signs flashing, "Vacant" and "To Write is All". It would be leashed again. DUSTRUS. Was it love or just the damp fruit of overaggressive lips? Now hiding out as if my life depended upon it, and it did. Writing and listening to the land. Ignoring the tourist brochures for "Maelstrom Rides—The Last Thing You'll Remember." Babbling into the recorder, reflecting on taking off heavy, long airtrips ending in Parisian cafes, walks along the river, pensive napkin notes. Reflecting on Cathy. Writing my Suite for World Domination, planning a personal assault of Thelos Tworld, without reservations or Sherpas, accessible only by crashlanding.

The interviewer asked the question and I had answered it, realizing that I was among those of the pre-Galileo model. No sense talking about orbits, eccentric or otherwise, planetary escape velocities. It was definitely flat and linear, nothing but. I kept my temper, thought again about needing to crash-land in that Los Tworld, why the consonants were migrating. If I survive, I'll really survive.

Using the word "realize" more these days, but the doors, while closed, are still on the ground floor. I "realize" I'm only in a box held up by somebody else's cable, reading a certificate signed by someone I don't know, over and over. "Realizing" as the fog burned off, the layers were peeled away, these last were of my "it's much worse than I expected" phase. "Realizing" now more choices for new mottos with underutilized capacity: "No Excuses! Just Bungle It!" Even the largest of wires could be overloaded, or in the locally responsive alternative, EATMYTAX.

Stopping again, with the tape playing, I stepped into another Dirt Reality and so rapidly as to be virtually undetectable, deployed my favorite "Freestyle Potato Signature Model" boomerang from that factory deep in the woods on an unknown road in Pennsylvania cranking out clear-finish sleds, yoyo's, snow-shoes for export, everything hardwood subcontracted to Santa's toy line. Rockin' to the beat: "Boomerang Luv, jus' when-u think-u on da roll, it come back an' hitch-u …"

Making a career of restating the obvious, with an E minor bridge. But it was as revelation to those, many as they were, whose depth of thought was drier than the lakes and salt flats, yea chemical rings, of Canaan, New Canaan, Death Valley, Sevier, El Mirage, whatever the next one ahead is Canaamed. Years in places where, in large part, disbelief had been suspended. Obvious downsides, hazards, exposures just ignored until the impending event, another Echoplexed tired dialogue on "the issues". Which in my lostworld were always about guarantees and percentages of the gate, sexdrugs, rock 'n roll. The FastLife as FastFood paradigm. Is that sorry, or what?

Americans demand a sustained supply of noble savages, catalog-orderable rugged remnants with which to identify on multiple levels, starting at the top floor, of course. Acquirable traces of the expropriated, acculturated, extermi-nated, with accompanying genuine certificate of authenticity. Once tribal mountaineers, now 2 ounce titanium-cookstoved, exoticpacked, covert Inner/Outer Mongolian fieldtooltested operators, above the final wave of happy discount campers extending into grubbiness, contour-mapped depths fueled by Old Milwaukee. Ballantine, ROLLIN ROK, Black Ribbon. Overnourished on empty food, become big, thick, overstuffed with brickstyle uncheddar from a waxed box. Where am I going here? Back to the remote, cushions.

Speaking of oblique references, consider the case of Sherry, Sheri, Cheri, or whatever the name was, in the California manner a person from somewhere else redefining herself as a physical constant of the universe. An Avogadro with Avocado served at the Capitol short stack along the 101 Freeway in Hollywood.

Mu and Wu. But then, that could be said of any of us, cosmic textbooks that we want to be, sometimes actually are, singular and unique interchangeable menacing plaintiffs in a militant class action for group identity. Occasionally with better pictures, rhetoric, more printings, yet in the end all trivial first and only editions, one hit wonders, breathtakingly, ". . . sooo wrecked!!"

Good judgment—not valid in 50 states

How did I get here (again)? They say it started with lumber. Abducted and pushed out of a moving car, blindfolded … plate said "SNOOK." Get this (after Art Blakey, Trane, Bud): all movies are not good movies. Confirming the truth of "… ashes to ashes, dust to dust … ." Elko, Deeth, Silver Zone Pass, Oasis (a liberal interpretation). Then the flats, millslaglands, glut and spume of Salt Lake, the city, Deseret of a place, water you can't drink, theological marketing, calendar captions like "Ladder Day" making no sense. A place where the sunups quickly become years, the children grow, more dry waves break on salty flats; where the plea is cultural separation, alienation, if not disorientation; noise is rationed, and duplicate thoughts inexhaustible in supply. Motion denied, class action pleading unsuccessful. Final tally, Desert Stars 8 DenimedNondenizen 0. Posted on a new, modern scoreboard yet to be shipped.

The car narrowed, I drove down a sidewalk, any sidewalk, while dreaming paramorphically of the San Francisco Peaks, Sawtooth, Tetons, pines above the cinders, sky somehow still blue.

Continuing to plead on appeal, the by now familiar dual defense of ignorance and omniscience, explaining how rational it really is, the point being that only others are responsible for their transgressions, not me. And they received the word summing it up, descriptive and imaginative: BAMBOOZLED. Received it favorably and went home, to prepare for new adventures in marginal lawlessness, manipulation, professional, ethical, moral fraud, to reap more resources to buy cars with more accessories, identity-sucking isolation booths of the shortest distance and fastest time, between the same two points where one always is stopped by nonfreemarket forces, awaiting those further adventures in stress and anxiety, edging perceptibly forward for advantage in gridlock. And it was received. And it is here. And it is now. And in LA, it is I.

Take Park City, stroll down Main Street, sip an All Tastes the Same Brut outside on the boardwalk. The old mining town was experiencing *enboutiquement*, the state of being boutiqued, now an unsettled mix of stores pushing hunting licenses and outdoor lore, next to pointless decorator emporia with names ending in i's (heidi's, micki's, charli's). The subdivisions of Deer Valley were pushing out the rustdented Jeeps, leaving a residue of plushed "Suburbans", ski racks and 2-door couples with Colorado plates, $100 felt hats with feathers and Indian silver bands, deerskin jackets and fringe. For Moms shopping at ReBozo, the playful challenge of being re-enclowned. For the remainder, not evenly divisible, lipstick on crystal champagne brut-flute, a life of metaphors charged to your card, perhaps now beautiful, but predictably colored within the preprinted lines, little original content.

Some lived for haiku painted with doodads below the pegs on gift shop coat racks, even with a German slant:

> Shoppink für ßeaver
> Zat lustrous felt springëntime
> Mäde un würthwhile

It met the definition, but was nothing I would consider celebrating. I remember the rapid cabin decompression, then the oxygen masks falling. Had I stumbled into the set of *Giant*? Steers around camp looking on in disbelief as the cowboys, liquored up, thinking of *A Streetcar*, raised their bottles and erroneously chanted "Liz Taylor's Slip" before falling into the fire.

There was still a bite on the early morning air which made the coffee more enjoyable, but not so much that I wanted to spend serious time here. Particularly after painting an attempted haiku rebuttal of my own on the side of a building, and obviousness that the history of this town had been paralogismically reinvented, leased at market competitive rates. The truth soldout to imagination, imaginatively packaged. National ice cream chains were coming in the name of hand-packed consistency and convenience with imaginative flavors. Imagine It!™ Once. Then register it.

Threatening parking restrictions, too—hard, fast, and tight. POSITIVELY NO PARKING. PARKED VEHICLES OWNERS AND DOGS WILL BE TOWED. $10,000 MINIMUM FINE FOR PARKING. DON'T EVEN THINK OF PARKING. PARKED VEHICLES WILL BE CONFISCATED AND OFFENDERS PROSECUTED TO MAXIMUM PENALTY. Brushed back from the plate, I got the message. It would be more comfortable to ponder dinosaur fossils back in Green River, gateway to scenic Rock Springs. Of course, with a nod to the nice flat map in the atlas, the right machine, attitude, and resources, that might mean an 800 mile shortcut through Boise. Or according to the Weird Code of the West, start a new personal open pit mine—POPM, in the parlance.

The sign in front of the Healey said, "MECHANICAL REMOVAL WARNING." I didn't like the sound of that.

Susan/Suzanne/Susanna(h) slipped back into my consciousness. By now nearly fictional, left behind on First Street in Long Beach, where the lawn wasn't grass, rather some kind of *dichondra* which looked like clover; the islands weren't islands but oil derricks; the Plow Boys didn't plow, and "surplus" was frequently applied, but never to Susan/Suzanne/Susanna(h).

When dawn had to do with the sunrise, not a dishwashing detergent; and on the right side of the equation were exotic dark beers on tap from Dresden and München. When Crosby and Nash spun harmonies, and it always seemed there was an open channel.

On the left side was the incomparable S/S/S(h), roughly parallel to Pynchon's *V*, although 20 degrees south and westerly, relative to parallels and meridians. Yes, that's it. Navigating a torn piece of *V*, the wordmap. Would it have sold if the title was *Stencil and the Mysterious Disappearance*? S/S/S(h) had very nice meridia. Wahine quality. *Ne plus ultra*. I miss everything about her. Everything.

"Move on!" the Parking Cop snarled, tapping his club for emphasis, reawakening me to the hegira my life was resembling these days; reinforcing MECHANICAL REMOVAL.

I could handle a romance with Cathy, and a SkilSaw, too. Pound nails, frame walls, put up a hip roof. It would come in handy sometime. Maybe build my own place in Wyoming, if Laramie is a solid lead, the right stop. Downplay the OwyheeDonHoLuau influence, go for shakes and timber, decks overlooking roaring cascades, plunging rapids, thermal spring trout dancing in a quiet pool. They would be right, that it started with the lumber, was all about carefully selecting your hammer, nails. That of course, you'd need a river, too.

Always "headed out," in this case, "out past" the Cigar Museum, showcase with a shelf life, studying the fascinating bands, finding a Dead Cola in a vending shrine filled with unrecognizable dispensables. A caffeine-laced foaming drink like hot hydraulic fluid. Mr. Seenitall Knownitall navigating the Realm of the Census in yet another film noir, *Smell of the Precincts, Roar of the Crowd*, perusing an import Penguin paperßack shipped in error, found in the Literature Section of a drugstore in an abandoned town, empty streets hiding their hashed and hushed secrets, the work of a would be fight/flee, flog/fog master not yet resigned to the fading orbit above a red giant, measurably falling to extinction.

Among all the cults and come-ons, shopping both sides of the street for mental clarity, stillness, peace … it just took a lot of cash to be listened to, and then, in the end, you were only talking to yourself, barking at Sirius. Same words rattling around the same can, not an empty hangar to be found filled with white light left behind by the alien civilization. But then, of those "Going Mobile", who really needed to deal with any of it? Why not move on, rent space in a new place, avoid the face to face with a different face? Setup shop again, as usual, *tertium quid* to reality.

Now a mirage, those serious beach shots the last time through, liquid night air, better ice cream melting in the darkness, corroded roadside rebar stains, tile roofs, looming bushes, grass overgrown, forever. An offday escape to classic woodie tailgate picnic country, contrast to the screaming mobs the nights before and after. Even so, noise negligible compared to that afternoon's black thunderstorm wall and lightning strikes which cleared the beach, whipped up the waves, knocked down trees, started inland fires. All that after so calm and beautiful a morning. At least I can still get my eyes open, input, and interpret … it's not all completely dulled. The shells and breakers, sea oats and sand spurs are 2000 miles away, the flight delayed. Because of the studio. Would Cathy wait until the spell was broken? Would either of us wait at all? Wait for what again? Neogenetic intervention? Ness? Which Ness?

I don't want to go back to LA. At least not yet. If only I can scratch out a day or two more. Because what I'm really looking for is just around the next bend, behind the building in the alley, hidden by the rise of the highway ahead. The me in search of the real me. I can take the long way back through Monument Valley, stay at Gouldings. I'm sure to find it there.

Provo, Price, then Moab, where the land gets really interesting. Green ribbon of cottonwoods and willows in reassuring contrast to the hard, rocky canyonsides of the Colorado, red and purple. Concentrated uranium spoil piles with "unusually high" background radiation. Some surprise. Continuing south, mostly flat, a land of buttes until you finally drop down into Bluff, Mormon bottom land beneath the Twin Rocks, across the iron icon bridge at Mexican Hat, and up the other side into "Navajoland."

Not LA. Please, not yet.

Before leaving on this trip, I visited a more conventional museum. The dehumidor kind where smoking's prohibited inside, and not a Coke machine to be found. Up the Pasadena Freeway, the old Arroyo Seco Parkway— formerly Route 66, then simply, "The 11." Past Academy Road and (Dodger) Stadium Way to the tight 5 MPH killer ramps at Avenue 43. The Pasadena started the LA freeway building craze, back in 1940, before cars had fins and roadrage was a gleam in the eye of *Future Shock*.

The Southwest Museum. There's a little amphitheater above the parking lot, hard-stuccoed and raspberry-tinted, the sand rough, angular, hard. Below, the freeway hummed like AC line juice, traffic headed upstream, at best seeking a source; more likely, making an escape. Swinging a counterclockwise arc, northerly to Pasadena, the San Gabriels were invisible, lost in smog.

Southern California is about keeping the pipelines full and flowing with water, oil, media myths and Spam-O-Velveeta programming, "innovative new products and services." Days of smog, asthma attacks, congested dreams. At the very least. On that particular day an overlook not of beauty, but exhaustion. Telling me to get off the road which is LA, away from the crammed flatroofs and Sunset palms like tired old, toothless lions. To follow the grass somewhere still green in summer canyons, under a blue sky. Not there.

Inside the Museum, the artifacts, Hopi rabbit sticks and wands looking like the end of a hoe, carried by dancers depicting clouds, rain and lightning. Tablitas, vertical headdresses worn by the women during their butterfly dance. Zuni prayer for growth of the corn which I jotted down to bring with me:

> All different kinds of corn in our earth mother
> We shall lay to rest.
> With our earth mother's living waters
> Into their father's daylight
> They will come out standing.
> To all directions they will stretch out their hands
> Calling for rain.

All cleansing preparation for my escape here. To help center me over the miles, this sunny afternoon in Monument Valley. Even so, I can't help think about the Museum, their fact sheet noting over 250,000 items in the collections, including 11,000 baskets, 1,200 Navajo textiles, and 8,000 pottery vessels. There was exhibition space for a minute fraction of those. The rest were locked up, out of sight. If you had the right Ph.D., credentials, maybe research privileges. Otherwise, you were out of luck. Same thing with the Peabody at Harvard, Smithsonian, School of American Research in Santa Fe, others across the nation. What were they saving it all for, dissertations? To trade to aliens? The end of the world?

I guess a good reason I'm out here is because it's a more accessible museum of ancient rock, sky, dunes, unconcreted arroyos, and visible traces of different cultures. One living, interactive.

A dust devil had formed to the southeast, rolling up a dirt road leading to the "Mittens".

"Whirlwind," I said to the man outside the trading post, a recess conversation on the Playground of *Diné* Creation Stories.

"Yes, *nááts´ó ´ooɬdísii* we call it." Can you spell that for me? Conversation over. Talkative today.

No two views, no two moments here the same, constantly changing landscapes of spires and shadows, clouds, rippled dunes, wind, dust and quiet. The "Sanctus" of Mozart's *Requiem* in my mind, so incongruous yet right for one of those unsame moments in this cedarland of wool. Looking over at the seat beside me, occupied only by the clutter of road stuff, I wanted someone to be there. A special passenger, once an intriguing fiction of falsifying, mystifying, become a true story of caring, purifying. As deep as the loose sand along the road, just outside the window.

The quiet dignity of the Navajo behind the bullpen counter at the remote Oljeto Trading Post counterbalanced the fiction, a woman found in a house with a history. And me, Presumed Yuppie Invader in a Healey, way off the road. Caution Loose Sand. Up to my axles—that's what it meant. Exactly.

I went up in a plane for an hour, from the airstrip at Gouldings, visual entertainment by Ed Mell and the Anvils. Above mesas and buttes, without the climbing work. But I wasn't really on top, only looking at it. Shopping for vistas. A sheepherder below tended their flock, the inverse of geese flying south. From above how would they see us, in our cities? Herds milling around. Larger, more pointless, if there are degrees of pointlessness.

So different from where I grew up. I've come to love this land, as someday I hope to love a woman. Not just one feature—a mesa, mountain, or desert— but the whole picture, the open land itself. As a woman.

I lived in a town, where life seemed to be mostly about the town, not the people who made it that. Hardly ever thought of the land except, perhaps, when the seasons changed, couldn't be ignored. A town in a state where rivers were made to run straight, because that's what they wanted. In this country it's all about land and sky, vast regions where there are no towns, only landandsky, and the San Juan runs anything but straight. Like the look from the woman next to me in the empty seat.

Reading about the inhabitants, I found a variety of names, spellings: Navajo, Navaho; *Diné, tsé táá 'áanii*, the Rock-Extends-Into-Water people, other clans. We have only last name, first name, middle initial. Saying nothing about where we live, who we are. Names too often without connection. An occupant identified, house number affixed. Submitted, acknowledged for informational purposes only, filed.

Night fell, illustrated by the powerful view of the Mittens beyond the windows. A quiet dinner, little overheard from the few tourists in the dining room. Later, the rustle of wind outside the screen of my open window. Desert smells, magic as the moon rose and drums gave way to the *Requiem*'s "Communio". Wanting to hear it in the Latin. Wondering, what do other people hear when they're alone out here, with the radio off?

The next day, on the recommendation of the trader at Gouldings, I turned north of U.S. 160, halfway between Kayenta and Tuba City, a brief detour to Shonto. For accessible history go to Hubbell; for dramatic setting, Gouldings; for a return to the authentic Navajo trading post past, Shonto, the "place of sunlight water." Shonto, an enclave of the longhairs, traditionalists who escaped the "Long Walk" to Bosque Redondo, and have been battling cultural erosion ever since. "Holdouts, pockets of resistance," the soldiers would have said. Now a golden cottonwood grove set against pink cliffs, a gem under the bluest of skies.

Sitting outside enjoying a bottle of Welch's from the cooler, I saw Navajos come and go, a surprising number for such an "empty" place. Some walking, others on horseback, in pickups. What do we have that they don't?

Purple lips from the grape juice.

Some would say too many *things* to list, but they could not be right. Material relics, intrinsically, are not culture at all. A better question would be, what can we learn from them? What of value can we give to our brothers?

Savoring Shonto, I drove to Tuba City, made a left on U.S. 89 and passed Cameron, once again postponing an encounter with Vishnu Schist at The Canyon, "a half billion years of unexplained erosion experience." Heading south to Flag, nearly Seven Grand In The Air.

Having found a coffee joint on Beaver Street, I ordered and sat down to partially decompress on the trip. More road notes, collected fragments. "I'm *not* … who I didn't say I was." Write that down this time.

What jumped to mind was *not* of this trip at all, this planet, this mind. Rather, another elegy on returning to California—LA, San Francisco, anywhere. Evidence that my thoughts, personality, entire being seemed to be changing like Archimedes' spiral.

Under intense acceleration. Purple lips mathematically flattened by the calculus.

Metro Cinema on Union Street, gone deco golden peacock, red walls, lights like blue plastic squirt guns, faded falling leaf tapestries, footlights. Greasy hands grabbing popcorn, much too yellow. Stumble outside, caught in a cloud of old carbon, more smoke than I remember. Rains washed away all the paper and gutter junk, into the Bay. Mudflat harvest sculptures, dirty foam, anything that floats. Grapefruit, jersey, Vacuumville Football. Rust brown deathsky, the only sunrise a peeling billboard. Pack of Camels, done Marin, Mendocino, second set, crumpled, Semi-Live. In the rains, yes, heavens are OPEN (neon). NUDE. Don't go there. Gravity as negative lift, why argue.

Chin resting on right palm, open, one of my Camels between fingers, looking askance, making her point. 15-Love. Zero. "This affair," she asked, french onion soup at the trendy place off Lake, cold, "one of your students?" I only saw, stared at memory, soft blonde hair catching the light, shining in the silence. Scares me, sipping wine and popping reds, chain smoking, face half in shadow, freefall depths in her eyes. Stranger, always passing just beyond my grasp. At the night hotel, boarded up but still receiving mail, dim streetlamp glow on a jacked '57. Smoking automatic weapons. Goin' down hard. Prop wash.

"Hey!" Waving her hand in my face. "Come back; tell me, is this a real conversation?"

"There's a smile hiding ... ," another said pushing hard against a serious lack of rapport. Definitely way down. Grim change of subject. Coaxed out on the way back. Halfway across the Bay Bridge. Way down. Way back. All in a moment so new, hadn't even been reviewed. Not smiles, grudges. Against everyone and everything. "What do you take pictures of?" Nothing. Meant it.

Snowing sunlight on water below.

What's *IN*, suzie wong slits, stumbling around drugged. Smile offered, unanswered by sunglassed princess, toppled regime exile. Beauty erased, click by hammer click, cylinder spin. Empty rage. California, by choice, mistake.

Noticed the mirror, talking on the phone, shrugged. That who I am? Shrugged again, Main Street night outside the window.

Driving back. The snapshots, textbook I'm writing about Charms and Sugar Babies in waxed packages, *Wax Life USA!* Near-cultural artifacts under lock and key at any southwest museum, hoarded and boarded in the names of irreproachable ethnoscience and preservation. Superimposed, maybe inherently-residing, force field of American Indians, Native Americans, or whatever the official terminology is these days.

Another force field of a woman recently 21. Not the name of a club.

Kingman, west on I-40. Might as well drive through to LA. Cross the Mojave at night. By the time I hit Barstow it won't matter, anyway. Well before being blinded by Shonto, the "place of sunlight water," years before the purple lips, I had misplaced the Mittens.

All driving back. Into and out of dreams. Only of the past.

5

Albuquerque and Ft. Collins;
more fire at Tomasita's

The 32-track recorder ground on, studio takes nearing completion. In my view it was our best work yet, although the others didn't agree, wanting to change arrangements, chords, and lyrics, roll more tape, argue about details. I knew I was right. Listen to the alternate cuts sometime.

By now it was December, with several months of mixdowns, post production, and rehearsals ahead to finish the album and prepare for the spring tour. Always the tour—another six month warp of major markets, repetitive checks: hotel checkins and checkouts, soundchecks, checking off dates, tiring logistics of tourists passing through with a couple of tractor-trailers full of gear, all checked and double checked daily.

A month ago, Jimmy Carter, "friend of the Allman Brothers," had been elected President with the help of Charlie Daniels and Lynyrd Skynyrd passing the hat for Southern money. Maybe his outsider administration could reverse the sorry state of the country in some way, although I couldn't come up with any specifics. How creative can an administration ever be? California rock stars, always complaining.

Talking on the phone in November, I told Cathy I was considering flying up to San Francisco for The Band's *Last Waltz* at Winterland over Thanksgiving. Bob Dylan, Robbie Robertson, Joni Mitchell, and many other Names were locked, and the gig was going to be filmed by Scorsese. It would be an identifiable change point in the archiving of music and careers ascending, descending, ending. I was thinking in those terms myself.

She was interested in things San Francisco but since the Rousseaus did Thanksgiving at home, and Cathy felt it important to be there the last time before graduation, she wouldn't be able to go with me. Someday we might meet in the City. Until then, we decided on a weekend before her semester finals and the Christmas holidays, closer to the Rockies. I booked a trip to Denver, from which I would drive up to Ft. Collins. A stop in Albuquerque would make it that much better. A week and a half after returning to LA, I planned to go home to Pennsylvania for Christmas, the first one since the move to California five and a half years ago.

At the gate before leaving LAX, a well dressed, professional-looking woman with an Airport Authority ID badge capably forced me aside at pencilpoint to do a tourism survey. Knew I should have stayed in the SkyLounge.

Final destination? Denver. Why did you select LAX? Did I have a choice? Business or pleasure? Are they mutually exclusive? Ha ha. Business or pleasure, sir? Business? Type of business? Invasion of privacy. Ha ha. Type of business, sir? Engineering. Purpose? Out gathering material. Purpose? A colloquium on shallow foundation dynamics in cohesive soils. That's a new one. Passenger's name? Could it be different than mine? Ha ha. Maxwell.

"You're Craig Maxwell." Falling over The Rim.

"Yes I am. Business or pleasure?" Ha ha.

"I had a feeling this morning I'd interview someone interesting. It must be fate." Or fateful. And while we're at it, define "interesting", or I'll do it for you.

Want to quit your job and come to Albuquerque with me this morning? Thought so. While we're waiting, please tell me the unique story of your high school years in Marina del Rave. Possibly San Bernardino or Pacoima? No, definitely Marina del Raze.

"Long Beach City College. Grew up in Long Beach, live in Marina del Rey now. Saw you play a couple of years ago at the Forum." The land before time, before Igneous Coliseum Rock.

"The music sure has changed since my college days." You could say that about a lot of things. Maybe everything.

"How might I contact you if you can't come to Albuquerque with me today?"

"Not that I wouldn't want Craig Maxwell to, but you wouldn't really call me."

"You never know. Sometimes surprises are indeed surprising." Rich in intrigue.

You figure out how this one actually unfolded. A faded leaf pressed in the pages of a book? Her telephone number like the key to a secret Swiss account? Rodomontade? According to Steve Miller, "just a passing fancy in a midnight dream"? I already knew while it was still folded, her pencil still had a point. And I'm not telling.

Renting a car at the Albuquerque Airport, one of few tolerable places to fly into because of its Pueblo Revival architecture and unhurried quiet, I drove north on *El Camino Real de Tierra Adentro*. The King's Road of the Interior, by now with 400 years of history or so, stretching from Mexico City to Santa Fe.

Fresh, cold air overcame the acrid jet exhaust, while under the intensely blue sky, passing Santo Domingo Pueblo, I recalled feast dances a couple of years back. Lines of brilliantly costumed dancers stepped to the drums, bells and shaking olive shell tinklers. It had been what I needed, a thousand years of culture in an afternoon, watched from the rooftop of an adobe. Dust from a stray gust on that cloudless day blanketed the Pueblo, dancers—applying another increment of the sands of time. There is comfort when one does not have to worry about how deep the sands will become.

Climbing the escarpment, *La Bajada*, I passed the wagon wheel on the stone pillar at the top. Santa Fe was near. I was staying at La Fonda, the inn at the end of the Santa Fe Trail. Like much of the city, which was being intensely hyped in the magazines as another "last best place," La Fonda was neither as old nor original as the promoters would have you believe. But then built in the early 1900's, within the inventory of our increasingly disposable architectural masterpieces, it was already officially designated as "historically relevant." It didn't really matter to me. After Hollywood and Santa Monica, the ambiance, sights and smells were invigorating, exotic.

There is a cafe off the lobby where I could get a cappuccino and pastry, a convenient and very strategically placed niche on the leading edge of the java and fine wine wave of yuppiedom breaking over the City Different. Across the street was Packards and the Wheelwright, up near St. John's College, had an exhibition of exquisite Anasazi pottery. Fine arts of the savages, or savagely fine art—your stereotypical choice. The fire in the lobby crackled as I sat in an old leather chair, pleasantly lost in the road trip, Cathy, music, memory of the pueblo dancers. The upcoming tour, album, my place in the galaxy were more problematic.

Was I a meteor or comet? A pound of intergalactic slag making a big deal out of trying to enter the atmosphere, only to be incinerated, or Iceman with shimmering tail, bound to return? The children, as yet unconceived, unborn, were a key hidden deep within a profound story still unwritten. One of so many. I didn't know how to find the right lock to unlock. I did know comet tails always point away from the sun. Could that be important?

For every stage, there's a backstage. And a backstage door leading to an alley, private entrance, secure delivery avenue, limo or helo waiting. Not today. I walked these streets, shooting black and whites with my Nikon F, seeking to interpret them in texture, composition, focus; ultimately, chasing shades of gray. Pictures relating me to the land, to this city, to reality, but only as I see and define it. Though the music is crucial, it's not, cannot be, everything.

Those mountains burned into the afternoon's landscape behind me will see more snow. Roads will ice, trucks chainup; lakes freeze, geese migrate. Then the tracks in the snow will be mine, here now, gone in the spring. As the comet. As this device for reflection on all kinds of things, old friend and side-kick, the rental rearview.

The skylights in the dining room of La Fonda flashbacked Santa Barbara. Trigonometry lectures. Slender dark-haired women. A black dress. Starched white apron tied, untied, abandoned. Vineyards, orchards and oak packing-house barrels, flagons.

Sitting by the railing, menu chalked on green board, clams and fish, risotto. Looking up, that light shaft painted blue, stretching to blinding day-white, flying lobsters and whales swimming in the skylight planes, somehow third dimension-restrained so as not to fall on the patrons below. Perrier and frothy cappuccino that day, while an old black man vamped it out at the upright. Ordering an arpeggio, for the thirties, forties, maybe one for my friend here, sleeping in the corner booth. Cat walked in, hair swept back in the dark, looked like Stone Mountain, Georgia, in progress.

Sunshower was as many dimensions as there were, more. You'd follow a trail, navigating by barrel light from the glowing sax, be lost in an Eicherian maze, rooms wallpapered with fish and exclamation points, moving … infinite magnetic mind plasma. Pulse of expanding rays, needles, the venturi, vorticular gasp of a world draining. As the truth I seek, that which can never be packaged.

They came down from the hills, put their amps up on milk crates, taped cables to the floor. Blew a set so hot it hurt. I couldn't stand it. Was there a purer tone anywhere, more perfect synch with all positive and natural? She smiled, folding the apron. Kept smiling.

So build on that smile, define yourself! Get goggles, a bike, rule a thousand cubes. Combustion Containment! *Your Hot, Finned Alloy Specialists!* Deep, five o'clock spring sky, tall eucalyptus, peeling. Straight road following poles into the dropping sun.

Cymbal crash, running backward. Wild bullfight posters, table debris, brown bottles of Secret Ale, glasses and smokes, dark corners lined with inhaled riffs, night vibrations. What key was that? 1963 in B flat. Around a corner with an old silver sign. Night blooming jasmine, Santa Barbara bayberry, apricot. And it's closed, mostly. Except for lower State, half pints, late hours, and a place named Baudelaire's. Is that the new moon, or a slice of pipe?

An unseen hand pulled down the voltage-controlled filter on this scene, set it to a drone spiral plunging hard to the street. We're into the experimental, improvisational here. Yeah. Emotionless. They barricaded the hole in the pavement, unexplained cause of damage, maybe a utility break, meteorite, assault by music we don't understand.

Somewhere, there are charts, the whole complexity reduced to lines, notepoints. A hidden well of harmony, off the local map. Space abandoned, overrun by a multiplicity of would be dominants. In the end chaos, freeform *maché* defying meter, a dissonant string, adynamic drone ride. So right for the times.

Crash! A porcelain cup, member of the team of objects moving locally under the influence of planetary gravitational fields, fell to the floor, jarred me awake. La Fonda, City Different, New Mexico, USA. Remember? It better be.

The word, "visionary," what I've been called by some critics. Why? Seeing what? Visions of art, expression, boom and bust, maturity, angst? A painting of a dharma bum, trudging through Chama on a train day stilled by winter, needing no special film to capture the overwhelming, cold grayness?

Vision? A sinistral alternate take? *Passe-partout*? Mostly I felt only the fanning of the Deck of Life.

"Are you ever going to deal?"

I got to your choice of juked visions by the uniquely human, cross-pollinated genetics of Motown, Hanon, Bach, ApproximatedChopin, and the 1970's. Sprinkled with science fiction, spliced with the polished chrome of the Seeburg at the City Line Diner, gritty dirtsnow of Steelton, the seething, thick energy of lush summer nights, lights of the Susquehanna viewed from the bluffs. Only a speck of the Creator's grand, cosmic scale. Set to backbeat rimshots of "Nowhere to Run". Women, how I love that song.

There's another word, "scale"—the perspective so important for me to keep. Mozart I am not, and don't know how I could even scratch that surface, but maybe it's only an acquired limitation of imagination. Nevertheless, my style is as distinctive as anybody's, and these days delivered at much higher voltage and amplitude than most. A frenzy of the smoking, ultra-fortissimo lightning bolts, flaming music demanded by "event management" which I am more than equipped to supply. What persona will it be today? Who was that redundant stutterer, that UomoPersonaforte?

The flames continued to flicker as I thought about my family. Even after these years, my parents didn't seem to have moved beyond the decision I had made to go on the road. All that college work, those job applications, inter-views, strings pulled for naught. At 21, about the only decision of importance bearing on MY future was whether or not to get out of bed to take the call. And so, insulated by ambition and ignorance, I took it, signed up for the gig, packed up the B-3, sharpened my chops, and pointed the car out the driveway. Headed for The World, I hadn't even consummated a relationship with a 1040, and couldn't tell you my home precinct. What do those have to do with power chords, anyway? Why am I still thinking about this? I've been over the ground. Over and over. Leave it. Lose it.

Within the chords, those changes, some serious searching was going on, is still going on; maybe just starting, now that I think of it. That could be the mark of true searching—it's always just starting. I'm looking for a sense of future, seeking alternatives to things major, mega, massive, explosive—all the incendiaries, pyrotechnics, and ritual obliquity. Alternatives to the popular, market-driven music product which must constantly be updated using new tools and "vision". I'm searching for a different vision. A healing of sorts, more than buying tips and "anger management".

This would be an easy point of departure. A man with his youth intact, and not enough bad habits to constrain or doom the proverbial quest for meaning before it really got started. And the destination is … ? What intact?

The soothsayer on the payroll again interrupting, telling me, "you will be driving a mint, classic Healey in Nevada … ." Without a cowboy hat. Those won't work in a Healey. Without a map. That would have.

I walked under the porticos of W. San Francisco Street, sat on a cast iron bench in the Plaza, looking at the Official Obelisk, designated end of the Santa Fe Trail. This city is about driving in long, waking up to surprisingly brisk, brilliant mornings. About sugilite, coral and turquoise, bracelets and beads, sunscreen. Enigmatic notes written on cream stock from Marcy Street Card Shop. Snakeskin boots and chrome belts, dusty sandals of impossibly complicated construction, Andean, Hindu Kush, worn even in winter with thick ragg socks. Sitting in a deep chair, considering the perspective from closer to the floor, carrying on a conversation with a dog. World class and world crass. Agua Fria dirt drive dreadlocked casitas. Chocolate-dipped biscotti, morning people sipping warmth. Healing, dealing, and careening. Lilacs on Don Gaspar when the season's right. Woolen shawls, shearling, and red cheeks against the wind. Dancing too many dances, dragging too many smokes in life-ending contemplation of losses vague and specific at Club West. All at a Pueblo crease.

Suppose Natalie had walked in. Alone. Would I have been in the cafe waiting all these years later? How about if it was at Club West and she was with some guy, bending her knee that way for him? Could I picture it? Could I?

About as much as "Don't Mess With Bill" covered by a Zydeco band not used to the high altitude sun, recovering from a winter burn.

An old truck went by, handpainted reversion, travelling an open seam frayed ten years back in the Heart of the Sixties. "It Runs, Therefore It Is." With a broken windshield, of course—it *is* New Mexico.

With evening approaching, I overheard flamenco at the Ore House when the door opened, reminiscent of La Boheme in Berkeley, fingers tapping the beat, counterpoint on the Spanish guitar. It could have been La Salamandra, I thought, slipping on the curb outside Ortega's, dirty ice, clouds of red dust as cars passed. There was the smell of corn tortillas, posole, chile, sage, piñon smoke; the architecture of vigas, corbels, latigas, portales; wooden gates on Camino del Monte Sol. Hilltops from which Doug West hand pulled art views seen nowhere else, Limited Edition. Hearing castanets, staccato heels, seeing her long, jet black hair again. Run down by a memory.

And then I blacked out.

Seeking one more cup of Santa Fe before dinner, I went into another cafe to recover, looking at the menu hung above the register, considering a mocha instead of the usual capp. A girl in a dull green shawl sweater walked by, headed for the back. I noticed as she tried to open the Ladies door, which was locked, kicked it, sighed and went into the Men's instead. Assertive, the gender-sensitive observer might say.

I don't know how gender-sensitive I am, since I can't always figure out whether to use "woman", "young woman", or "girl". I've never really paid much attention to it. I suppose one my age or younger can be, maybe always will be, a girl. Woman sounds older than me. If I'm careful to avoid "babe" or "chick", I'll probably be okay most of the time. Complicated subject, not worth the thought. Just say the wrong thing and it'll fit snugly. Those of us who were destined to laugh will indeed laugh. The glaring others with statement hair don't count.

Mid-20's, a guess, does sound kind of old for a "girl", though.

Musing about the restroom scene, I theorized that it was a one way street. A woman could use the Men's, but a man was inviting trouble by going into the Women's. The most important question seemed to be whether there was a lock on the door. Affirmative in this cafe. Affirmative Action. Affirmative Reaction.

When she returned, I had nearly exhausted the nominal gender musings, but made little progress in ordering. Despite the scenery, the expertly restored pine floor, intensely fragrant ground coffee, the java jump had become a molasses moment.

"I can't make up my mind, don't have a clue," I confessed. Comfortable in the stupor of indecision, I yielded my place to Green Sweater Girl. "Go ahead." Don Quixote, ascending.

She laughed and said, "I don't either." I liked that. Anything other than, "huh?" usually works. Interest generation through humorous self-deprecation. A queen and jack of clubs. Now we're moving.

Prescription for the Santa Barbara flashback, chaser for the crashing cup. Gimme a bar chord with Bigsby while I trip again, wwwaaahh...aaaa.

Eventually, both of us managed to order, got our drinks and went to sit down. Green Sweater Girl sat at a table in front of the window, got out a book, and made motions of starting to read. Clothbound, with no title I could see. Maybe empty, a blank journal, only a prop. After reading feverishly, one eyebrow raised, she set it down, took a sip of coffee, turned around, looked at me, and smiled. Sharing secrets.

Okay, back turned, I couldn't see her eyebrows. You're paying more attention than I would.

Cafe Whyoming

As she resumed "reading", I admired her Dorothy Hamill hairstyle, graceful neck. I've got to sketch that, I thought, opening my own journal. Since reading *Drawing on the Right Side of the Brain*, I could do decent feet and ankles, and was looking forward to moving right along, up and at 'em. At least the sketch of her hair was somewhat accurate; before it would have looked like a crude, surreal version of a porcupine. Was Picasso really that good? I mean, his people were rolled flat.

When turning again, she unmistakably mouthed the words, "you're Craig Maxwell," and pointed at me. I waved off the maneuver and mouthed back, "no, I'm not." The expressive motions brought to bear on the statement remained fresh, provoking.

She laughed, reddened the tiniest bit, then turned back to sip more coffee. I liked her laugh, her lips, everything I could see, everything I could imagine.

Santa Fe, scintillation sold by the cup.

I finished my coffee and rehearsed a line while walking over to her table.

"Relax, Jennifer, you may be assured that I won't try anything crude or ineffective," I mumbled silently to myself, deciding it was a little too passive and opting to try something more direct, add an irresistible emphasis drawn from tales of macho and mestizo, *mole* sauce, sprigs of herbal this and that.

"Thank you for the opportunity to drink my mocha in peace, admiring a woman, in a very comfortable place." Mr. Moka riding off into E. Martin Hennings' sage and chamisa.

The macho part didn't quite make it in. Not exactly what was running through my mind, but sufficient for a "so long" as I strolled out. This trip was about Cathy, not to expand my address book with a new crop of eyewatering *senoritas chiles de Santa Fe*. I think I walked out; can't seem to remember now. Why does Jennifer sound so familiar?

Green Sweater Girl was superb, the cult of her memory remained strong. I've got the sketch to prove it. Every cafe should have a girl in a green sweater. If I had a cafe, it would include that girl in my overdub; she'd be a notorious soprano exquisitely singing the "Credo" of Haydn's *Missa Sanctae Caeciliae* in a perfect performance, melodious and dramatic, by invitation only:

> *Et resurrexit tertie die*
> *secundum Scripturas …*

Amen. I don't know what it means, but I like the music, and wrote down the words in my notebook. Right now, whatever the meaning, it's being eclipsed by GSG. The Latin will have to wait. This is about business. Get her under an exclusive contract.

More fire at Tomasita's, down by the railroad station, from the combo plate: enchiladas, tamales, and chile relleno ("in the badlands of chiles relleno, our batter's badder"). Smokin' salsa to commemorate GSG. I'll bet she's from Texas. The obvious choice. Like California Girls, I don't understand Texas Women either. For every öberbuilten Stella from Dallas, there's a Green Sweater Girl who's more Boston than Austin. And your point is? Hook 'em horns?

Walking after dinner, my beard grown back and longer hair kept away the night cold. The Plaza was still, nearly silent now under a huge sky black with brilliant stars, shadowed by the massive adobe buildings. A wind came up, blew through the barren trees, over ice from a previous storm. Far from LA, Pennsylvania, anywhere else, in so many ways.

Tomorrow I would drive up to Taos by the High Road. The wooly tribes had arrived in Taos, but the battle with the NeoHispanish and DecoPueblo forces had not yet been decided. Predictably, El Victor would be none of these factions, not even Victor Higgins, but rather the developers and retailers over-running, packaging, and marketing a complex mix of cultures in which they had no real interest, of which a nonpanorama of understanding. An empty in which/of which sandwhich. The Money Men pulling a Park City, Kingsmen pulling a "Louie, Louie", paving over, building on top of, obliterating in the name of restoring, redefining, reinventing. All simply a matter of return on investment. "A Louie, Loueye, oh, no; we gotta go." Penned in the dismissive tense, a real challenge to deploy in all but the vulgate form.

Little change was evident along the High Road. Decades after classic monochromes of the 30's, 40's, and 50's, the church at Truchas was indifferent; Picuris adobe continued to melt in the rain like the badlands of Chimayo. On any given day, the sky was the same, depending upon the season, waterholes full or empty, the shadows and scarves of the old ones still hid their secrets. In a wall, a door was open, but learning what was on the other side was not as easy as just going through.

In this arid hardship, *albondigas* and triple decker lunch special stuffed with cultural deli cuts, the wagon wheel broke, the Taos Artists set up shop, and the rest is history. A history of marketable images, legends, and superstars. Served up daily. All it takes to embark upon a unique pueblo experience is a couple of bucks to park. Until you have the courage to really look into their eyes, and realize before, you saw nothing; now, you know nothing. A start.

And then tomorrow was today. Where did it go?

To the cafe on Camino del Pueblo Norte, a few doors north of Kit Carson Road.

"*Comment dites-on 'blueberry muffin' en française,*" I asked, hearing French music, eyeing a muffin.

"Ze muffin ees not French, ees Eenglish, I theenk …," she said as I lost the rest of the statement in the smoothness of her arm. T-shirt and jeans in December, brown skinned, must ski, I thought, eat well and burn a lot of calories. A little North African mixed in there?

"*Comment vous appellez-vous?*"

"Françoise." No *et vous*?

I got the muffin and a double cappuccino to go. Sitting in the car, it came to me: *un petit gâteau aux bleuets*. Blueberry muffin, although it applied to Françoise equally. Seeing her in ways I won't go into, I shook my head to break the spell, wondering how long it would take me to spill the coffee and after that, whether I should end the day by plunging off the road into a canyon. There's a deep one nearby. Real deep. Convenient.

But actually thinking, are *you* holding out for all-consuming love, Françoise, trusting that you'll know when it happens? Is that the shadow of waiting in your eyes? Are you footnoted, "after O'Keefe," or in economic exile? Can I be of help in any way?

"*Merci bien, monsieur,*" Françoise had said as I left. *C'est tout.*

The questions remained unanswered, finally pushed out of my consciousness by growing anticipation of tonight's rendezvous with Ze Cathy.

Leaving Taos, I dropped off the plateau, following the Rio Grande. Thickets of willows along the river between steep walls, no peach pie overlooking the whitewater in Pilar this time through, on to Velarde and Espanola without stopping.

In Santa Fe again on the way back to Albuquerque to catch the plane for Denver, I bought a squash blossom necklace for Cathy, fine old turquoise, exquisite silver work. Traditional and elegant. The shop also had several excellent bracelets, Hopi, Navajo, and Zuni. In an exuberant, "I've got to have everything" crescendo, I bought them all. Buying is the easy part; sorting out emotions and motivations much more difficult.

The flight was only about an hour, mostly dark north of Santa Fe and Taos, until Colorado Springs. The woman in the seat next to me immediately started a conversation, describing a morning fire suppression exercise. Not something you hear about every day, casually, on a flight. I imagined the floods of water now frozen into terraces and pools, like Mammoth Hot Springs. Ice sculpture in some fireman's dream tonight.

A house was to be removed for freeway construction, so the City Fire Department burned it down, for training. Apparently it had made an impression on her, some excitement was still evident. Did she ever make it clear what her role or association was to the exercise? No matter, it was entertainment for the short flight. In an interlude of conscience, I decided not to ask her name.

She was energetic, early thirties, I guessed, with orthodontic bands occasionally making a word difficult to enunciate, and glasses. Dressed in navy blue, sweater, skirt, and nylons, she looked like one of the stewardesses on the plane. I tried to picture her ten years later, but didn't come up with much different. Her nails were a good sign. In my view, shorter is better, usually evidence of work; a pearl clearcoat just fine. I wondered if she was *firmly* energetic, strictly academically at first, but then concentrating on her lips as she struggled to carefully enunciate the story, I got caught up in other things. The fireman can have his icedream, let's you and I play paper dolls, change the blouse and sweater first, try a different skirt, play with the length. A dramatic yawn. Time for ... you know.

When she asked me what I did, I started to say, I'm a visualist, most recently reductive, but caught myself with a variation of the recently rehearsed, "an engineer living in LA ... taking a few days off to visit a friend from Wyoming." In an instant, somehow she took the conversation in a totally different direction: had I accepted Christ?" The way she asked it was not uncomfortable in any way. It was simply another question. Not really sure what she meant, I could only answer, casually, that like many things, even those navy blue, I had thought about it from time to time.

Well okay, where are we going with this? Was this a pickoff attempt by a proselytizer? I wonder, had I really said, "even those navy blue?" *Bleuet*? That you, Françoise?

No throw over.

A minute later Ms. Unidentified and I were talking about something else, maybe the darkness outside the window. That subject wouldn't sustain much of a conversation beyond Newton's Laws. Now I remember, she got to light the fire.

I had moved on to different fires. Any woman could tell you by now what was on my mind. The only thing on my mind. Green Sweater Girl. For one.

Proper name, capitals and all, GSG monogram. "You're looking crisp tonight," I complimented her in my best Southern drawl, a brief line in a little air travel fantasy, seated at tray tables in the nonupright position, chomping on ice cubes in plastic cups next to empty, miniature bottles of hooch, at the Five Miles High Dinner Theater.

Goodbye, Ms. Unidentified Navy Blue. You too, Green Sweater Girl. Enjoy Santa Fe before you go back to Austin. You see, I got her name and telephone number after all. It wasn't a guess. It was fascination. An unfilled prescription. GSG wasn't Jennifer, and I'm no fool.

Cafe Whyoming

6

Open season on the open range

"I don't know that there's anything about me to understand, but I guess you understand me best."

The extent of a conversation in the kind of place where you walk in, "Voodoo Chile" is playing, and she unquestionably looks the part. Outside, no refuge, the shadows of trees clenching fingers of darkness. Side effect recollections in a unidirectional question and answer with myself, inescapable as the so-called rental car counter VIP line at an airport mobbed with travellers looking for any delay they can hold with a major credit card. A half hour later, commencing a new history, in the Stapleton lot, looking for the car while snow fell on a cold night. I-25 North was open, but getting worse. I left town quickly, having already received the sacrament of departure in the name of Single-Minded Travel Experience. Trespassing in the world.

When we played Denver, I wanted to leave quickly then, too. Lakewood, Colorado or California, they're all the same. Tract homes like strings of fish in a vacation snapshot—smilingly exaggerated, overabundant—the sport of life become a pathetic, value-subtracted Robert Frank-Gary Winogrand desolation-scape of twisting green wood, sheetrock, rusty mesh, broken doorbells, cracked lights. Pickups in spec driveways, Chief Likes-Your-Rollbar, Rez-ervations of a much different kind. No one on the street, only bumper stickers to welcome you to the veneer—Hockey Moms Against TV Violence! Live for Bingo! Surf Naked Colorado! M'am, let me sponsor your wave.

My life may not be over after all. If I can just hang around here on earth awhile longer, find a contest with better odds, I know I can win. Luck's changin', can't you feel it? Bum a Camel?

So it goes in a fishscape where all life's essentials are props. The monotony of rooftops interrupted only by TV antennas, disappearing like the open land, in the hidden wiring of cable, the uniformity of commerce and content it brings. Standard floorplans, shells on the production line. In reality, shells of a different kind, chambered for rising suburban conflict born of past, present, and impending neglect, lack of interests and identities, evidenced by domestic strife, juvenile crime, drugged dysescape. What other future could there be in The Budget Motel of 100,000 Rooms? Affordable, but unendurable. Two hands, two barrels. Damage, yet irrevolverable.

Scream! Lidda bit louda now. Just my opinion.

I arrived first, pulling into a hotel parking lot with several inches of snow on the ground and a lot less rooms left, to await my rendezvous with Laramie's best looking Real Cowgirl. Cathy got there at about 10:00 pm after a controlled slide down U.S. 287.

"You look different with a beard. I do see a striking resemblance to the guy on the album cover, what was his name?"

"Your resembling date, now reassembled, as from 'Up on Cripple Creek'."

"It's a long way from California for a date. What's the draw?"

"Functional design. I can think of only one song which even begins to relate the mind-blowing entirety of the young and dynamic shape, I mean original artwork before me—Mose Allison's 'Your Molecular Structure'." Torsion, flexion, free energy.

"Not exactly at the top of charts the last time I checked."

"Oh yes you are." Height 5-6, weight 116. Heavy duty alternator. Custom skirts and pinstriping. All the options.

"Take a deep breath, exhale, and say 'aaaahhhhhh'."

Yeah, I can do that. There're these funny little things she does ... but I'm not telling.

We needed to get out and break the ice, avoid plastic cups. Friday night in Laramie meant The Spur. Our immediate challenge was to find the Ft. Collins equivalent, eventually successfully located—The Range. Depending upon your perspective, maybe lack thereof, The Blur ... Blerrr ... With a brew *en glass*, we were getting warmed up for the C&W band's second set when a girl walked up and asked me for my autograph.

"I know you're Craig," she said, pointing at my Hopi bracelets and handing me a felt tip pen, "I'm Leslie, from Denver." So I wrote, "To Leslie and Great Times at The Range! Craig/ESO 12/10/76." Cathy just looked on kind of blankly, and then it was over. The band started to play, and while we got up to dance, I marvelled about all the stuff girls have on them. I mean, like pens in their purses.

Cathy didn't say anything until we were back at our table, after a slow number danced cheek to cheek, very close. I liked that she was lithe and strong, no doubt a bale thrower on the ranch from way back. Just the right size and shape. Smart and young. Pretty with her cowgirl Stetson. Beautiful in fact.

"Being with you all the time would take some getting used to. When people come up and just start talking, asking for your autograph, saying the first thing that comes into their mind, I'm not sure I like it." Particularly, pretty girls with big ... eyes.

She didn't like it at all when the parade started—within a minute, we were surrounded, and they were all talking to me. Country was edging toward mainstream. Though a C&W joint, it was college too. They know everything about music. How else are you going to remain lucid while enduring four years of prepackaged, predosed educational institutional feedlot drivel?

"Craig Maxwell, from ESO, here at The Range, unbelievable. So, man, what's it like to live in LA and be a star?" I signed everything in sight, declined many offers of free drinks, and after 10 minutes of questions, perfunctory answers and wisecracks, suggested to Cathy that we get out of there. So much for dancing.

Slipping into the night, we got a pizza and went back to the hotel. As the late movie came on, we looked at each other in unspoken communication, turned off the TV, and moved on to our version of that old ballad, "Body and Soul". From very close to even closer. Circuits Maximus—become almost human, I thought.

Later, in the darkened room, I went over to the window and opened the curtains to look at the falling snow. Cathy lay sleeping, hair now tied back, oblivious to the peaceful, resting beauty of her nakedness revealed by the dim light from the parking lot outside. Turning back to the window, so mindful of what could only be a divide in my life, I heard the churning introduction to Beethoven's *Missa Solemnis*, before it explodes into the dramatic, emotional "Kyrie".

I felt as deeply for her at that moment as I have for any woman, thankful for her presence, the trust she silently, gently communicated. "Have mercy on us," continued the "Kyrie". The weighty forces in that work were echoing in my life. At the time he began writing it, Beethoven was uncertain about the direction his music was to take, and the previous years had been difficult. To listen to the work, one was necessarily drawn into dealing with the contrast of Divine glory and the pathos of man. It would not be resolved within me in the darkness of this night, despite the loveliness of the sleeping woman. Is it ever fully resolved in life, or only in death?

With our tenderness there was some tension, most immediately from the experience at The Range, but underlying it, currents of each thinking ahead. For Cathy, increasingly of graduation, the first job, finding her place, making her mark. For me, returning to LA, touring, recording again, replaying the last five years for who knows how many more. Enough reasons to get hung up, make it easier to rationalize turns onto different roads instead of staying on the one taken tonight in beauty, togetherness.

In the late morning, as the snow continued, it was obvious that if Cathy was going to get back to start studying, she would have to leave now, while the snowplows still had the roads open. I wanted to stay here all weekend with her, let room service take care of us. As we talked about it, a hand placed on her upper arm grew to a tight embrace as she pressed against me, crying. In that moment, without speaking, Cathy told me she loved me. What should have been a joyous admission was overshadowed by silent despair: "if only you were with me." If only headed in the same direction. If only so many things.

A little while later, we had coffee in the dining room, talking more about the future, what was coming up, what we had to do. "Love her back, now, with all your heart," I thought, but then counterargued, "get real, she's 21 and hasn't even graduated from college. Remember where you were at that time in your life?" On the outermost point of the edge of control, plunging down Cajon Pass toward the Ocean of the Future.

I gave her the necklace from Santa Fe, while she unknowingly acted the lead in a draft of my private play, one she had never been given the opportunity to read. A continuing performance piece about a musician held from the fullness of life, perhaps now more than ever, by his own choices.

She drove north, I went south, listening to Dexter Gordon blow "Where are You", a melancholy 1962 cut. Reflecting on our parting, I realized what arguing both sides of the issue really meant—I wasn't making any commitment.

"Where are You?" On the road back to Denver, the way back to LA. Hopefully, not "In a Snowdrift Off the Road in the Rockies".

And They built it, and They themed it, and They came

While driving to the airport, I thought about the Pan Am brochure on the seat, "Around the World!" Instead of going south, should it be east or west, geographically, spiritually? Only a thought. I wouldn't want to stay away from New Mexico too long. Jung and Suzuki haven't lead me to any answers. Neither the emptiness of a 50 foot Buddha carved in a Chinese cave would do it, pondering Zen koans that gave me no ride to anywhere, nor trying to navigate the briar patch of psychoanalysis "with help." I need to throw things out, simplify as much as I can, without becoming void in the unhealthy sense, devoid, celluvoid.

Headphones plugged into the cassette player, whether the highway patrol liked it or not, I chased Dexter's "GO" with a song about whales. Four-fifths of the earth's surface is water, yet unable to withstand man's harvesting, exploitation. The song was rightly concerned. *Our* "nature" has always been about material gain, greed, power. Maybe there will be a day when the shark bionics move ashore on bulldozer tracks, join their evolutionary relatives to prey on Fords and Chevies, blasting their way into, through, and over our shallow consciousness. The terrestrial branch is already here, waiting … 396 Stingray, Hemi Barracuda, Mako … got a chassis in the pattern with a desert package, lights, bar … moving to intercept, acquire, terminate, dismantle, salvage. Life: nothing more than a food chain.

Cafe Whyoming

Man, it's cold. Winters here Out West can be so brutal. Twenty below in Elko, the land frozen solid, while the casinos burn megawatts to pull travelers off a desolate road, radiating heat into space. Did I make a wrong turn in the snow? Is this Kansas, Oz, only a road dream at another Holiday Inn? An alternate reality in which I didn't get the major gig, couldn't bear to work a conventional job, was overcome by "personal problems", but had a "solid" handshake deal to do three sets nightly in a money losing swizzle-stick lounge for an army of salesmen on the prowl for the few local women they met in the hospitality suite? Regulars conscripted by a lack of imagination, initiative. My happenin' band, *Spectators in Love, featuring Uneek*. There's the poster, the picture outside the lounge, glue where the glitter fell off. Soluble experience. Hourly workers in Piece 'O Pie, the land of contracted ambition.

What happened to the eloquence of the "Kyrie"? This is the atonal version. Have murky. Have mercury.

Mind wandering again, beyond the lounge, the giant slalom outside the car window. I-10 from Tucson through New Mexico. THE THING? Continental divide, lines of Santa Fe and Rio Grande rail cars along the tracks. The wide open hot sky of summer, scrublands, maybe tougher but somehow better to me than these overgrazed, faded, graywhite opportunityfields just waiting to be subdivided into Colorado Hobby Shop-A-Long Ranchitos. And that RENO RODEO sign. When did I get that close, dose of The Dodge Boys among the hip-deficient, nonmaintained Sculpted Hair Gambling Ice Cold Air Cadddy Creatures sightseeing at the slots inside the barbed wire museum?

Either I punch out of the increasingly techno-musical event horizon, or I'll become THE THING? There is enough money on hand, even with double digit inflation. My years deserve to be filled with more than the emptiness of these miles rolling by, actually slipsliding today. As if "years" were animate, interdependent, samples establishing my identity, could deserve anything.

More and more, what I read or think about seems to be fragmented, incomplete, explained away. Even my relationship with Cathy, as lovely as she is. A succession of telephone books, each missing the one yellow page I'm looking for, in the M's, ripped out by some force always a step ahead. Anticipating my every move, instead of the kernel of insight and understanding I need, leaving only an empty husk. Unidentified smoke. "Meaning" is gone, but there are eighty-seven listings under "Money".

The soothsayer continued, "... and They built it, and themed it, and They came to the Land of Spin, and gave up Their prospects, became Prisoners to Investment; and it was Reno, Jackpot, Lakewood, Vegas." It was *The Dead Zone*, *Killing Fields*, *Mean Season*, and *Never a Great Notion* all thin-sliced and wrapped into a terrifying hoagie. It was the THING?

7

Guns blazed, but only in my imagination

In my business, you meet exotic women with consistently exotic names. Romy, Char, Monique, Briquette, Marisa (nondomestic). Too many exotic women, met too briefly in glistening, dimensionless encounters. I have been trained my entire life to pay a lot of attention to dimensions and details—length, rate, time, intensity—but am realizing that the essence of my existence, maybe all human existence, burgers aside, is more about intangible, nonphysical dimensions. It's not as easy as picking up a box of Einstein's Relativity Flakes or Unified Field Nuggets. They won't fit into the bowl. There's always a missing piece in the physics of women.

Nearly ten years have passed on earth since I graduated from high school on Earth and was launched into space. Coming in now near the speed of light on my long loop solar foray, I'm only five years older. It could be the other way around, or may not be at all. Regardless, asynchronous similitude demands that one define a unique scenario for the calculation. Any way you slice the pie, then, that one piece is missing. It's the gap between each of us and the rest of the world. The five mile an hour, more accurately five year, bumper. The absence of pie. It's an unnatural law, and comes in optional, unavailable finishes. Fitting introduction to a sordid interlude.

Exotics superabundantly continental. Presentations *au courant*, lives *beau monde*, attitudes *carte blanche*. The French or German first born, accents acute, characters I don't recognize, written or otherwise. In contrast, those who discarded theirs for, or accepted nicknames telling way too much about, themselves. Da, Do, Duh and Dough.

My comfort zone seems to be somewhere in between—Catherine, Susan, Samantha. Just once, I want to meet Susanna The Authentic, with or without the (h), triumph in what has become a deepseated, unresolved compulsive movie from youth, mysterious in origin, never entirely grasped, never forgotten. One of imagination and dreams overcome by growing realities and boundaries, dimensions. One offfff ... a stuck key.

I had done time with the Hollywood Hills and Canyons crowd, a few actresses and singers with reasonable names. Even had been approximately one question away from being engaged: "Okay, so we're hip. Now what?" Not exactly the question, but close.

Erica "Gita" Schneider, to all appearances "normal", but fractured way down deep.

A woman who drove what could only be described as a drug dealer's car with deadened windows, menacing lines, and V-8 mill. Who read Kierkegaard before going to sleep, occasionally a strapless red velvet dress shopping. A woman who worked out and didn't want to hear a man sing. Ever.

Once, she described having cried for four years, but never mentioned the reason. Seeing little evidence, at first I had taken it to be an exaggeration. "Don't leave me, don't you leave me," she pleaded-threatened, waving the pointed finger-thumb, internationally recognizable, semi-automatic, small caliber manic-dee gesture, continuing to "sort of" cry. "I won't, I won't." That sort of grabs you—you realize you're being taken prisoner in one manner or another, makes you want to help. You have to try to help. Sort of.

Then she dismissed me, with a perfectly understandable explanation. "You don't live like you're famous, do things rock stars and movie stars do. I want to live like that, enjoy it. I'm well on my way to becoming an actress. Can you accept that? Can you?" Yes. Completely. Utterly. "I thought we were totally together on you buying the jacuzzi, installing the deck and screening, solar water heater and thermal blanket, lighted mailbox with kinetic geese, glassed sunroom; the new car just like my old car you promised to celebrate the part in my upcoming, first film … ." Extreme shopping, acquired or genetic? Count the "you's" throughout what she said; then *you* make the call.

In the kitchen, taking a hard look at an "accident" to end the washed out, grainy French New Wave melodrama it had become. Not to be happily resolved, beyond my capability to ever fix. No dependents or beneficiaries to worry about.

We've been brought up to never use a toaster when taking a bath, and outside California it's been good advice. How about toaster fishing, though? They didn't mention that. Do I have to fill up the kitchen, or just the sink to locate the short circuits by immersive methods? To find fin. The big *FIN*. The End. Without caterer, best boy, gaffers, or grip revealed. Obviously, I was the one utterly looking.

Instead squinting, inescapable commentary rolled as screen credits, while I remembered that the safety precaution was about portable electric heaters, not toasters:

> She'll not always want to be alone with me.
> Nor is that what I will ever ask.
> She'll think, you'll never be enough.
> I'll know that. No one ever is.
> You'll never be enough, I'll want to be with others.

Don't you understand?
They'll never be enough, either.
That'll be your problem. You'll just never get it.

Who would use such a heater to warm a bath anyhow? How dumb do they think we are?

Change the tense from future to present, then past dismissive. Because it's long gone over. As a formative experience, I guess that's what "romantically linked" means.

Now let's look at more evidence on point. Nary a *prima facie* clue found outside the gourmet kitchen of this ritually unkempt eightthousandsquare-foot bungabunga low, warehouse of implements, land of specialized cake pans, wonderland of corkscrews and cordon bleu spatulas.

Mark Green Sweater Girl and a few other favorites Exhibit A. Inadmissible. Actresses, doyennes supremes of raved-up ilk, Exhibit B—shielded by the witless projection program, entered into evidence but sealed, accessible only by press release. Categorical imperatives defined by the two strange home movies found taped underneath a motel table, running side by side, split screen, too rapidly to absorb. One a progression of Romy and her kindred, strangers about whom I knew little—where they came from, who they were. The other screen, just me, thinking furniture, a consumer with unlimited choices. The upholstery I want so difficult to find as to be nearly impossible, the universe being perpetually obscured by Big Tweed.

Reverse the reels. On the edge, a workingman's store in a nameless industrial town. Women in whose faces I see family pictures at 11, last call lounge regulars in high school yearbooks, future Food Court and/or Family Court queens in newspaper listings announcing their engagements too late. Weary faces in old articles that were never news, in pictures to ever-remain unretouched by a happier marriage, great job. What went wrong, Dough? Where did your smile go? Why did you buy that honey-tone swivel unit? That tweedinal davenport? How much of it is your husband's fault? Is total cultural breakdown to blame? Can you estimate the percentage for our baseline data?

All exaggeration, of course. The truth is much worse.

"Wouldn't a real parrot be better," she had asked, "more decorative?" As if you just opened the box, swagged the cord, and plugged it in.

"These horrible trees," guilty for simply existing. Bad trees. Bad.

"I just love Elvis' imagery," like he wrote the songs and we're all able to define the terms. She read it somewhere.

"I'm tired of the rims on your car. (Angrily) Get new rims!"

Gita was a real person, we were "romantically linked", but the rest of the story, all of it, is once again untrue. Do I look like a man who would date a

"Gita" anyhow? After all, I went to "drink a highball at nightfall" Penn. Survived Skimmer's fearsome, oarsomely swizzled and debauched, "Hurrah, Hurrah Pennsylvania," four years running.

Actually, it began with the toaster. I was leaving her place, going to buy a new one. It's easier than cleaning out the crumbs, although with the models always changing, you can never again buy what you've got that works. That and I've always chafed at the thought I was born to shop for housewares and small appliances. Frustrating. While I was out, she wanted me to pick up a leopard skin watch band. "A what?" I asked. That sparked the reaction.

She said something, I said something louder, then she said loudest of all: "I'm … not who … you … want me … to be … and … never will. Get … out … goodbye." Like talking to a 3-year old, very long pauses so even I could get the message.

"I didn't mean most of what I said, that's enough of an apology, isn't it?" I tried. No sale.

I got the message, blew off the toaster and watch band, drove to San Diego instead, and never spoke with her again.

Thinking on the way down, would I pick her out of a crowd? Would she point at me in a lineup? Why bother thinking about it? Who knows how these things work? "Overheating and Fire is a Normal Occurrence." That's what the decal in an inaccessible place under the steering column said as I chanted *Carpe Obversis*, seize the obverse (of the day, insideout sweatshirt, dime).

Pointed toward gutter climbs and curb grinds of the skateboarders at Balboa Park, I had a latte in the Ken District over *The Reader*, what was left of an afternoon varnished by phonies in shades, yet all offering more than anything LA had in stock. The Erica "Gita" thing is true—I can play you the tape: "you are so cool in your cryptic-poetic RayBans." Meaning, in our lack of knowledge, abundance of willful disorientation, we oppptttt for confusion, and in the end, accepppttt symbolism as meaning. So there. The finale of my *Rhapsody for Dead Shorts and Multiple Gunshots*. Erica "Gita" Schneider? Never heard of her.

Mr. Potato Head—finally, a man we can trust

That's some of what I was thinking, while catching TWA out of LA, fleeing a land where people had names like Tommy 8. The itinerary was to Chicago and then Harrisburg, winter night flight, what would ordinarily be quiet time for building reasonable holiday expectations. Watching the smoke curl in the cabin over the newspaper two rows ahead, though, I wondered whether I had it all wrong, was only hotriveting the seams of dysexpectational contrivances for episodic, interludenal coping. Spaced out instead of outspaced or inter-laced. Expecting it all to be brought to fruition, but simply being enfruited in the analytical semantics, whines of possessive individualism. Wondering how to apply the "tips" of the in-flight magazine article to my life, striking words highlighted in a box on the top of the next page:

Favorite book:	Profiles in Golf Courage
Music:	Pompadour Cowgirls Swingfest
Movie:	Diary of a Mad Housewife
Hot gift this year:	Handheld Swede-O-Norge Sauna

A silent opera flight with no libretto. *Othello* without the IQ. *Madame Butterfly—The Bold Country & Western Version*. He developed a thinking habit, smoking habit, drinking habit at age 27. Something just snacked. But I would be different, an island of consciousness within a stream of income.

Just kidding. I don't always do air travel well. I took two of these pills. California people do that. To handle it. Don't mmined me. Waaah … oooh.

Heavily populated coats moved along the concrete curves in the ORD terminal, flights were cancelled due to weather, children were crying or asleep on seats. There were Muzak carols, boot privates in poorly tailored uniforms back from Missouri basic ordering drinks wrong for the rocks, cheese and cracker crumb crops on the carpeted beachhead of gated mobility, burning hot coffee in styrofoam Host cups.

I sat down for a moment, closed my eyes to clear the scene. The gun pointed at me could have been intimidating if not for her reassuring, "look at it this way, you're going to a better place." Darn. The bottle said to "take four tablets twice every fifteen minutes for anxiety," not two. Ah, that's better nnnooowww.

It was indeed beginning to look a lot like terminally poinsettia'd, candle'd, elf'd, holly'd, ribbon'd and ornament'd *Christmas, The Material Frenzy*.

Let's play *Celebrity Watch!* Let's not. Or *Celebrity Watch Band!* either.

I had procured an excellent pair of widewale cords to go with a yellow crewneck sweater and sport jacket—protective coloration for the field work upon which I was embarking. To all appearances, prep school junior faculty. My best friend from the old days, Marco, aka The Meteor, drove us to O'Reilly's, a would-be pub featuring little more than darts, blank looks, and a permanent cast dispatching Rolling Rocks, while the juke poured out heavy metal over electric shuffleboard clang. Big Tweed had seized this market and would not be dislodged. Was this an illegal chokehold, way outside the Zen ring, beyond the referee's view? Caught by a Sleeper in the land of *Il Dormiglione*? Coiffed with a mullet?

Well, yes, what else could it be? If only I could figure out how to loosen the grasp, up against the cigarette machine with its chromed, explosion-proof lock. It didn't do any good to wonder why I had come here at all. The minute we walked in the door, I recognized the controlled burn gone bad, billowing dense toxic smoke of this refamiliar pseudo-opiated den of local under-achievement. Same story, the high school marrieds' lament: "I never got to live my life, and I blame *you*."

Tonight, I was a contract bit player, only one scene, among a legion of extras awaiting the big fade passively, mixed drink by sweet mixed drink, jailed in a bar without bars.

> OK, you bozos, come in and get me!
> Guns blazed.
> But only in my imagination.

Marco pointed her out, sitting on a stool, nudged me from fixation on previously antique metal signs for Atlas Batteries, Burma Shave, Chevrolet. I nodded and took another sip of brandy that reminded me of lighter fluid, went along with him on a right turn, through a drama darker than they remembered, into a replay from way more than five years back. Earth time, that is.

While he had survived massive changes in a still unfolding expansion of interests and intellect, attributable in no small measure to embracing a curious mix of IBM Big Blue culture and soldier of fortune physical training, a regimen hardened and pointed as a missile silo, his onetime cat toy, b. brooks, no capitals pleaze, was frozen at sixteen (there's a tabloid headline for you), truly a manne-quin unchangé. Why is it that she would not ever know about the little adobe in Santa Fe, or cottage outside Camp Hill for that matter, never be willingly lost in ice crystallizing on the widow above steaming cups of coffee as fall became winter in a single afternoon? Was she to blame for that? Was it Catholic school? Who are we, calculative elitists? *Agents provocateur*?

And how could two so completely different women be hanging out together? In polar contrast, her friend, Elaine, was blond, naturally attractive but obviously in the tears and coping State of Hurt, estranged with a young child pending divorce, driving a winter-aspirated Olds convertible, silver with tattered black ragtop, kid-seat in the back, reverb, the works. Caught in a time machine looping only flashbacks, leaving for a destination, but never arriving anywhere new.

The four of us departed, ended up on the other shore, in yet another 'burg down the river, recap slagtown pizza place. It was a shooting gallery for Marco and I, who had neither the biceps nor optional millhand assault rider in our benefits wrap. Too late to bind now.

I drank orange juice, killing time before we could escape from this cast iron exile. Incongruous college types among the steelshovers, unable to secure the hot zone, on threatening turf with local honeys, the enemy clothed in camouflage, occasional deer tag still pinned to an OD shooting sweater with leather shoulder pad. Cleverly flipping oblique asides, we carefully watched for rogue mammoths in the frozen swampland of unmapped Steeltown wilderness, while making plans for tomorrow. It wouldn't matter that I lived in LA, in fact, that would make it worse. I could see the headline:

Star in Metal Town Melt Down

After a subtle diversion, "call for you from the Police Chief," we escaped into the cold, drove back to the West Shore, then returned the next night, but not to Dangerous Pizza. Picking up b. brooks, Marco and I motored out to Elaine's semi-milltown-all-no-view-sort-of-duplex, for home boiled Russian and lots of talk about people we didn't know. It wasn't on a cul de sac along whispering waters.

She brought down her child for a minute in a gesture of both pride and serving notice, a strong boy, sleepy and yawning to be returned to bed. The soon to be ex, jobless, was still living at home until the situation was legally resolved. I wondered whether he might walk in at any moment and open fire. Elaine was, after all, a desirable woman, emotional object now hardwired to a blasting cap, hot load of TNT.

It was a scenario right out of the old days, visiting basements of unsettled homes. The signs were always there. Pillows and sleeping bag in the living room by the TV, nearly empty quart bottle of vodka on the kitchen counter. Still in use, soon to be depleted. Two day shelflife. Even more bottles in the bushes, wheelruts in the flower beds. Sharp-edged Mr. Peanut key 'n ribbon cans full of cigarette butts, burns on the Formica countertop. Too many packs of gum, airfreshener. Foreign cologne. A getaway car cached under branches in the back yard. Evra thing but da mondo jumbo of evra day life. In short, more trouble coming. Fast.

Guns blazed again.
But there was little left to imagine.

Trouble was indeed brewing, though likely nonfatal. Bad vibes between The Meteor and brooks. There appeared to be more to it than just incompatible chemistry. Maybe the affair had ended very badly, the long quiet after seeming final shots now reopened in random border violence. Whatever, it hacksawed their Saturday night.

Despite the friction, rocking in a comfortable chair, listening to Elaine was enjoyable. As she spoke, I looked into her eyes, as deeply as I could, until inevitably, the first resistance was encountered. It might be a fence with gate, but there was little chance I'd find out. Leaving the next day, I had no reason to think I'd ever see her again.

Elaine realized who I was from the start. Years ago, in high school, she saw our band play at the Highspire firehall, a feudal outpost in the Land of the Steamrollers. I would have liked to have known her then; hoped that it would all work out now, fear and desolation would not claim her.

We didn't talk much about Craig Max-swell. Elaine wasn't looking to be thrilled, for easy escape, only to make a life with her son. It made her beautiful, worthy, placed her way beyond those at the cheesy corners of Laverne & Shirley in Hollywood, Romy & Suzette in Beverly Hills. As quietly worthy as she was, as romantic as the fantasies in my mind might be spun, if I let them, the woman was living in a minefield of pain, fatigue, and necessary healing to which I couldn't relate in any meaningful way. *Prohibito toccare.* She was unapproachable.

Luna Tunes, Tuna Loons, Tuna Looms, Looming Tuna

The coast dragged me back, renewed its hold with the tough stewardess' complicity: "… choice of *Capon Marseille* or *Steak Champignons.*" You MUST choose, choose NOW, ONLY from the available choices. NO substitutions. They have ways of dealing with you, red wine spills, beverage cart on toes 'n elbows. Even in first class.

Thousands of feet below, salt flats stretched across a wasteland, Monday work for a mapmaker's hangover, featureless nonumental valley that it is west of the snow covered Wasatch. The trip last fall had been a slipstreamed ground retreat from the overthrust into Wyoming, a rhapsody de Healey set to the pulsating roar of flaming combustions ignited at top dead center, exhaust perfectly tuned.

Valuable intel garnered through a plainclothes investigation. The woman in Laramie located, "we've got pictures. Definitely on the up and up." Cathy.

It all sounded so good then—"Desolation Angles, Dissolution Angles", something catchy, vaguely familiar like "Luna Tunes, Tuna Loons, Tuna Looms, or Looming Tuna". I had overcome the broken handheld recorder, gone to documenting that slipstream of consciousness by cryptic, approximate methods. The same woman I saw a couple of weeks ago in Ft. Collins. I wanted it to be a smooth continuum, elegant calculus, change point, proof to a new life. Instead, I was blindly throwing out emotions, tossed in the air, shooting them again as skeet. "Pull!"

Les McCann breathed, "… my soul runs deep … ," remembered from intermission music at the Keystone Korner in San Francisco. We're as wild as we want to be, can get away with—too wild for our own good, our survival. But underneath it all hums (thumbs) the fundamental question, day in, day out, not much different than the refrigerator or Pasadena Freeway. The question not whether it's original, but rather personal, true, valuable … nonmaterial. The crates of iced fish are in North Beach today, will be there tomorrow morning, too. Even as jazz night edges, planes, and shadows fade.

I knew it must be close to over when I was preoccupied by expense accounts, scheming how to translate the tiger in the tank into a business deduction. Ten bucks for Tony, three bucks for me. Am I an unknowing lead for the next remake of *A Star is Born*? There has to be a different, better ending. For every bloomin' bottlebrush, oleander, or jacaranda in LA, there's a vacant lot with a sign on it, trash, oily dirt. For every authentic, handrubbed birdseye walnut finish, there's spray-on lacquer, liquid plastic. For every truth, systematic ambiguity.

Man, what is this? Landslide into a river canyon? Impossibly dense Dostoevsky? The *Blue Cliff Record*? I've got a ton of new material for the next in my series of research papers: "Understanding Philosophy, Your Enemy—Great Minds Lost in The Tangle of Analytical Dysbelief." Way beyond Dumbo and Jumbo to jungle jumble jangle rumble.

Sic transit gloria mundi, literally translated, "sic the Monday Dog, Gloria, now in motion."

I'd heard all the songs, knew most of the performers. The *Last Dance* was their party, their tribute, their title, just more burning along a long fuse that was lit longer ago. If the music of Mozart couldn't save Europe, the music of ESO won't save me. I've got to let go of the safety line, swim to the Next Dance.

"G-L-O-R-I-A, Gloria. G-L-O-R-I-A, Gloria!"

"Down Gloria, down girl!"

8

Quanta more cubes of air in prelude

We came back to LA on "full instrument approach", as the TWA Captain put it. Mile after mile of subdivisions, palm trees, high schools with running tracks, and strip malls, through a "unique atmospheric challenge" created in the refineries of Carson. To a place where culture shock is the Number One Growth Industry, and the shocked live for the Donut House. Where a successful partnership of the free market and elected officials has succeeded in making the place what New York would look like if the skyscrapers were filled with blocks and Hot Wheels™, then tipped over. When you get tired of dodging them in *your* BMW toy, Monique, then what?

I wasn't adding any warm yuletide memories I could recall to the fluffy, photoreactive sky. We had pretty much gone out of that business after high school. There was no religious observance, and how excited could you get about drawing in the one present lottery? Both holiday and tree disentinselated. Like this flight, it had been Christmas on autopilot, servo hydraulics fully under control. Aerosol E-Z. Select and push. Enjoy, or insert additional coins and select again.

In Santa Monica, work resumed on the album. I tried to advance beyond arguments, find middle ground mixes, get it over with. Dreading going on tour, I thought about what I'd rather be doing. Jams on The 10 kept worsening, and even though the water was way too cold to swim, the beach traffic seemed heavier every weekend. Orange groves fell one after another before the flood of LAimmigrants, only token trees left for marketing purposes. If the wave could just be slowed, the flood ChickHearned:

Rejected by Kareem!

It wasn't going to happen.

There is a particular cadence to shallow living run aground, the click of a spinning shaft, prop sheared. Coming into LA, that was the sound I had heard. It didn't take much thinking to decide the necessary action—leave ESO, move down to the Laguna place, sell the Santa Monica house, travel next summer. Look for somewhere to live outside California, adios the people, places, and lifestyles I had to consciously avoid every day I remained here.

Being analytical, logical to a fault, I've got reasons. All the reasons. I really don't like to tour, and since in ESO we're free agents, not bound by history or friendship, I had become little more than a prisoner of the music business being extradited to the next city. Delivered to another isolation cell. Fighting for control of my physical and emotional landscape, copyrighted thought-life. Becoming an alien unto myself.

I need to constantly create and keep spaces in the wide open story which I am, build on the freedom and possibilities, progress toward truth, find a place, belong. It's about the distinction between *in here* and *out there,* beyond "me, I, my". Out there in the empty stadiums of Canyon de Chelly, Monument Valley, where the silence of stone is the show.

Yeah, I know. Once you go, you usually don't come back. Which is why I want to leave.

With a suspended sentence following conviction on the digital abandonment rap, just for kicks, I'll go to my 10th high school reunion coming up in May. On-site time to ponder who they were: The Musked, The Mata May Hem.

I notified the band that I would be leaving, not tour, then had my attorney draw up the paperwork. The decision was a heavy one, both personally and of business, involving record sales, royalties, and "creative property". I would break in a replacement over the next 45 days, providing an opportunity to take care of the real estate issues and other arrangements for the summer. *New West Press* ran an article which was reasonably factual, explaining that I was going in a different direction (out), rather than claiming irreconcilable artistic squabbles, bad dope, philosophical conflict, girlfriend swapping, or business disagreements leading to multiple assault charges.

January 1977. I talked to Cathy, let her know of my plans, knew that she couldn't relate to what I was telling her about my niche of the LAifestyle. Didn't matter. It was history. She had made up her mind to look for a job in San Francisco after graduation. That would require hammering away to get to the door, a convincing story to get through it, a lot of hard "career" work to stay inside. The University of Wyoming had to be off the map, third rate to the PAC 8 snobs in charge. Go Cowgirl. Go 'Pokes.

The Bay Area scene would be dramatically different than Laramie, undoubtedly exciting and stimulating, the very qualities she already has, now that I think about it. As for me, I had once again shaved off my beard and with hair cut shorter, was going undercover as rapidly as I could, out of sight of the LA record making machinery. We set up a Bay City rendezvous.

Nothing about being raised in Sheridan, living in Laramie, flying out of Casper could prepare her for the Golden Gate on the other end. We stayed downtown for a long weekend, caught Dexter at the Keystone and Mose Allison at the Music Hall, rode cable cars, strolled through the ethnic clash of Chinatown, and walked in rain so heavy it came through the umbrella. Climatological over-compensation, the selfly-charismatic weatherman concluded on KTVU 2, derailed by the implications of the frontal boundary's trailing edge.

The development of Catherine Rousseau into a beautiful woman was accelerating, nearing the speed of light. I couldn't remember a time when I had not enjoyed being with her, a very good sign. Having lived in California and spent considerable time here, though, I dreaded the thought that she might transmutate to Bay Area chic. What could I say, she was entitled to head in her own direction. There was sure to remain some Wyoming corral timber and wildcatter steel, if only molecularly dormant. See, Mose knew that, understanding the important threads, humility, and artful operation of contradiction in everyday life, romance, and relationships. I hoped on the toughest, most demanding BayDay, when Cathy needed to be in touch with her own, original true face, all that would be there for her.

She was excited to be in the City and glad to see me when we met at the airport on Thursday afternoon, balancing everything with enough wide eyed, goodhearted, Wyoming restraint to level it out. We drove down to Half Moon Bay for brunch, walked on the beach. Earthquakes, floods, and mudslides aside, not a bad place. We hit Café Med on Telegraph in Berserkeley, wound up Strawberry Canyon past the football stadium to Lawrence Hall, where sitting on the wall, you look out over the East Bay, San Francisco beyond. Walked through Sather Gate on the Cal campus, checked out the bookstores, dined on stuffed mushrooms at Oleg's, toetapped the evening away at the Freight & Salvage down on San Pablo Avenue to Lawrence Hammond and the Whiplash Band, featuring "Lani, The Queen of the Bluegrass Flute."

She had to leave Sunday afternoon. The future was the future—we didn't need to figure it out now, I thought, not that we could have anyhow. Cathy disappeared, gone into a canvas which would have been as pleasing to her nemesis, Henri Rousseau, as it was to me. The sweet jungle of a man's thought-life where beautiful women go, painted clarity of that frozen moment, static image giving way to a more abstract canvas, brush strokes, fleeting focus of travelers and terminal, handtinted within pen and ink lines, all become riffles upon watermarked parchment. Map of this place, map of our hearts. Evoked and testified by the gentle touching of lips, interdimensional arching, grasp of her slender fingers. Forever much more than the sum of the parts.

On the flight down to Burbank, my mind was filled with walking arm in arm on Union Square, three special nights spent at the St. Francis, glass elevator rides high above the City. Prismatic tenderness, gestures unconscious at the time, now remembered. As that unforgettable night in Ft. Collins, light softened by the snow shining on her as she lay sleeping.

Although we had not talked about it directly, my sense was that our intimacy had been a big step for Cathy. She had shown me her heart, trusted me with it. I didn't know if I was equal to the responsibility. As lovely and trusting as she was, as poignant as our time together had been, a part of me was empty. Call me restless, unready, seeking, confused, whatever, it was there. Green Sweater Girl, who knows how many more in a tiring parade? My own worst enemy. Not even a battle between give and receive, but receive and not receive. "Speaking reluctantly as a recovering part-time allergen ...," my speech began.

Laguna was a therapeutic improvement. Halfway between LA and San Diego, I guess you'd say, with only three ways in and out: Laguna Canyon Road, and (Pacific) Coast Highway from the north and south. A bit of Encinitas and Newport, beaches and coves, galleries and painters, surfers and strollers. A place where you had to pay attention to the drainage, hillside geology, and fire corridors in the undeveloped canyons. Where you couldn't help but be in awe of the expanse of the Pacific. Thousands and thousands of blue water miles.

Van and Healey gone, a 650 Triumph Bonneville and the Ferrari were in the garage, with a new Porsche 911SC for everyday motoring. That's what they drive in Laguna. The Healey had brought me to California, Laramie last year. Rather than storage, I decided to let somebody else enjoy it, headlight wires and all. A closing chorale, finale of Der Ring und der Healey.

The house had less square footage than the one in Santa Monica, but a two level layout which made it more usable, even after converting the family room into a small studio. The improvements would be approached from the standpoint of hanging on to it for a long time. Having learned that anything near the water would continue to appreciate in the future, even more importantly, I would have a refuge to which I could always return. If not the land to which I belonged, nevertheless, a place. My place.

For the upcoming travels, I decided to outfit a GMC motorhome which would be stored in Newport Beach when not in use. The weeks passed quickly as I dealt with transitional business matters and preparing the GMC. On the pretext of needing to get away for a few days to relax, I drove up to Santa Barbara to see what was going on there.

While considering my post-ESO new direction, I had thought of going to Brooks Institute in Santa Barbara to study technical photography. I wouldn't have to get a degree, just take some courses, sharpen my skills of seeing, visualizing, composition. The thought passed. While it might be fun to be a Zen-powered photo lunatic, I didn't want to get lost in technique, photographing white objects on white backgrounds for white-paged magazine ads. The painstaking studio work with a large format view camera wouldn't hold my interest very long. Too much like engineering. There was a nonlinear, dynamic real time world beyond the static poses, possibly even more accessible to an amateur.

On the music side of things, I ran into Jim Messina at Baudelaire's, sitting in with the Little Big Band. They were an excellent local group in a weekend club who brought back the memory of playing for the pure joy of it. I had nearly forgotten what it was like. Santa Barbara was a picturesque, comfortable town which had thrown up a no-growth wall. It was a place where walking to Earthling Books for the latest *Adobe News*, continuing on to coffee at the Sojourner, then strolling along upper State to the Art Museum made an enjoyable *passagiata*. And at night, you might find somebody like Jim at Baudelaire's. Or Craig Maxwell.

April approached, and outfitting of the GMC was nearly complete. A modified 26' Eleganza II with 455 engine, it had become a mobile studio with electric piano and synthesizer, comfortable accommodations, front-wheel drive tractor pulling an enclosed trailer for the Triumph 650 and a modified, street legal 400 Maico dirt bike. Remember, they're only tools, machines, built-in furnishings, I kept telling myself—there was that life to be lived outside, one of art and people.

I made a shakedown run to Death Valley, pulled out at the Zabriskie Point Overlook, painting synthesizer textures for the sunrise. Playing it back, the melodies and harmonics were about both music and experience; women and places, two categories of many more.

Like probes sent into space, we want to believe that someone else, something of value is out there, right before our hearts, on channels in an extreme land which we have not yet been able to access. With the sun, though, to this land came visible spectrum interference of rigged weekenders, munching on Pop Tarts, jabbering without any coherent message I could detect. Even at Bad Water, they were already dug in, encamped, jamming the groove. Mule trains hauling loads of emptiness through a modern desert.

The GMC moved quanta more cubes of air than the Porsche. The sheer volume was astounding as it rumbled over the pavement, throttle wide open, guzzling gallon after gallon, just plain gallonage. Sorry, President Jimmy, although you believe battling the energy crisis to be "the moral equivalent of war," there are other priorities. This rig was an anthropological, archaeological, sociological relic the day it was built, an indicator-exemplar firmly fixed within the fossil record of the Age of Massive Consumption. There wasn't much point talking about its "City" EPA rating. This was strictly a Research Roadasaur. I aimed to learn new secrets from the great half-baked-off life of the here and now, deliver interpretations of truths gleaned in this big aluminum and fiberglass box.

The researchers should be thanking *me* for defining the "extreme case", way beyond data scatter, in fact off the chart.

The dues and the DUDES have been paid. The nitro-burning, aircraft alloy Bonneville has been drilled out, customized for blastoff and reentry. Advanced vector synthesis power-up available at my fingertips. They'll never cross-modulate me again. With impunity and in control, as the Tubes put it, "… out of the business, into rock and roll!"

The dunes of Half Moon Bay or Death Valley, ever the dunes. Creosote bushes, sidewinder tracks erased by the wind which has come up, sweep of sand. Salty crusted ground, barren hills. What role should I act on this empty backlot? I'd seen that movie, *The Passenger*. Check into Stovepipe Wells, disappear into a new identity, but not escape, the future as limited, perhaps even more limited than the one left behind. Not all turns are right turns. Impunity and control? Dreamer.

I spent time working on a photo construction, in those dunes of DeeVee, took two hours but I got it. The composition consists of nine frames of varying sizes, mounted in the shape of a flattened cigar band. In the center is the largest, clearest image. Taken with tripod and timer, set up using a broom stuck in the sand. Bracketed exposures for each pose, increasingly out of focus and of smaller magnification to either side of center. Five exposures were selected, the middle one and four poses, each slightly turned, printed as mirror images by flipping the negatives. Clarity disappearing into grain. What was that I had said about laborious studio work at Brooks? One more time—what *was* that message?

The black & white custom lab I use in Costa Mesa printed and mounted it, a tableau as documentary of my life as aerial shots of contour-plowed corn rows in Iowa, Council of Chiefs in the Dakotas, century old portraits of Lincoln, grimly formal yet understanding. Watershed point in a dry land. When the life of the last six years began to change, grain by grain, marking another beginning.

I pulled into the Furnace Creek Campground shortly after sunset. In the next space, two girls, looking to be about 20, were pitching a tent in front of their yellow VW. A breeze stirred the warm night air, and I was someplace else. Maybe southern Wyoming, thinking of those mysteries of snowfences along the railroad. Yeah, west of Laramie. Any snow there now? I wonder whether it has ever snowed here in DeeVee.

"Need some help with your tent?" I asked, after setting up a chair outside the door of the RV.

"No, but thanks. We've about got it now." Rules 1 and 2 of camping: avoid setting up a tent in the dark; and respect your shotcords. "That's quite an RV you've got there, by the way."

"How about a cup of coffee, or a cold drink? I won't take no for an answer."

They looked at each other for a moment, and the spokeswoman replied, "thank you, that would be good."

"I was going to make a pot of coffee anyway. Won't take more than a few minutes. In the meantime, if you would prefer a soda, I've got … ."

"I'm Terri and this is Gidli. We're students at Claremont."

In the dusk, they hadn't yet gotten a good look at me.

"I'm Craig Maxwell, now of Laguna, pleased to meet you."

Terri moved closer to shake hands, paused. "That Craig Maxwell?" Three words at a near whisper.

"I keep asking myself the same question, but I guess the answer in polite company is yes, I'm that one."

Terri asked, "what are you doing out here?" Gidli was still silent, an untranslatable look on her face. I hadn't seen a smile yet.

"A shakedown cruise for the rig. With some time on my hands now, I'm planning on travelling this summer."

"Got some Swedish ginger snaps, if you're inclined toward carbohydrates. I like them with good coffee."

"This *is* good coffee, but I'll pass on the cookies," Terri said. "Gidli, how about you?"

"Not zo goot on za digestion I sink." A foreign accent, and a little shaky on the grammar. Aloof, with hints of protectiveness—of herself, the history of Zurich, Terri, I couldn't tell.

"A bad habit, coffee and cookies before dinner, I know. One of more than I'd like, probably fewer than I think I have. I'll run it off in the morning."

"We're going to do what we came out here for—rough it. Open a couple envelopes of freeze-dried soup and heat it on the Coleman. You're welcome to join us, Craig. Oh yeah, we have what's left of the Ak Mak crackers, too, those which didn't get munched on the drive up from Baker."

Juniors. Gidli was German, not Swiss, the daughter of a businessman in Los Angeles, studying economics. Terri was from San Diego, in biology with hopes of medical research. With their international backgrounds, they did a good job of adding the Swiss soup mix to briskly boiling water. When dinner had settled, we had a Heineken and kept talking, mostly Terri and I, although I did try to bring Gidli into the conversation.

"I'm a big fan of the classical heavyweights—Beethoven, Bach, Mozart, Hadyn. Someday I'd like to go to the Salzburg Festival."

"Oh, zhat music it is yet very nice, but so old," Gidli replied tersely, as if to equate antiquity with boredom. That's art. Draw your own conclusions. Take it or leave it.

Lights out for me was ten o'clock. I fell asleep quickly, into dreams about dreaming, waking to camp fires and mountains, places which seemed familiar, but which I couldn't quite locate. Walking back into the darkness, anxious about what was out there, I heard a rustle in the brush which couldn't be the wind, and then the moon broke through the clouds, shining brightly. Anticipating the rustle again, I turned around, now hearing drums, on a shore with someone in the distance, coming toward me ... and woke up. Time to run, 5 am.

Moon in the night sky, real this time, breeze sweeping through the creosote. I couldn't recall ever having a dream like that before, one so strongly suggesting the future, yet seeming also to reflect a forgotten past. Perhaps it was the hyperbaric experience of below-sea level heavy air, the secret ingredient in last night's soup, Cream of Dreams, or the curtain rising once more on *One Friday Night in Ft. Collins*. Snow falling outside the window, flakes as notes of a Boccherini guitar fandango, keystrokes of Herbie's "The Eye of the Hurricane", a Rossini love song. Oh, Frederica, when you sing; Cathy, when you're sleeping beside me ...

The sun was just coming up after my run and breakfast—it was still very early. Looking outside, I saw Terri wrapped in a blanket, standing and looking at the sunrise.

Two girls on a weekend camping trip, quite a contrast to my much more localized ramblings at Penn—study, practice, gig, sometimes a visitor, study, practice.

I stepped out the door, making a little noise closing it so as to alert her to my presence, then walked over and softly said, "good morning, Terri." She turned to me with tears in her eyes.

"Hi," she murmured, crying a couple more tears. "My brother. I miss him so much at times like this ... when it's quiet at dawn we'd have a cup of tea before he loaded up his hang glider, then drove to La Jolla or Elsinore. I'd go with him to watch, or take the car to the landing site. He was very careful about safety, always assured me that he'd be fine. Six weeks ago, he had an accident. That was it.

"I'm sorry to start such a beautiful day this way. I look up at the hills, and see him on that day, the bright yellow sail ... ." A lot more tears now. She turned to me, and I could only hold her.

After a couple of minutes, she brushed away the tears with her sleeve. "Thanks. I'll be okay now."

As an adult, I hadn't lost anyone as close to me as Terri had. An active life, a successful one, I guess, is about taking risks. We all take them, of one kind or another—physically in the things we do; emotionally, with others. We can only decide which ones we'll take, and let the others decide for themselves. Ultimately, perhaps there is a spiritual component which smooths it all out. Along with most everything else which is probably important, I can't say I've got that figured out yet.

"Don't leave without saying goodbye, Terri," I said, then walked back to the rig.

When was the last time I had taken a course which truly put me at risk, in a positive, active, or creative way? Nothing to recall.

For a half hour I escaped into Fifties North Beach San Francisco, rereading Kerouac. Brown-shingle cottages in Berkeley, mountain paths winding through trees and boulders, occasionally interrupted by thoughts about a final flight in Elsinore.

Terri came over and tapped gently on the door.

"Craig, I don't suppose you have a picture that you might autograph, do you? I'd like to have something to remember you by. That we really met here."

"Can't say I have a supply with me, but we can take some pictures outside. I've got a camera and tripod. The morning light looks pretty good right now. Is Gidli up?"

"Not yet. She's a late sleeper. Probably won't be up for another hour."

"Well then, let's get to it." I setup the camera and we burned a roll of Tri-X, shots of her alone, of me, together. As many smiles as I could find at ASA 400, with an occasional serene pose.

"Should have copies for you in the mail within a week or two, if you'll give me your address."

"Craig, thanks for everything."

"You're welcome. 'Bye, Terri."

New West Press did a followup article, for publication two weeks later.

I had some business in LA, and thinking of Terri, considered surprising her by personally delivering the pictures from Death Valley. At around 1 pm I knocked on the door of her place on Harvard.

"Craig Maxwell! I'm shocked! What are you doing here in Claremont? I can't believe it! Craig Maxwell!"

I'm only a man. Maybe less, a personality; even less than that, a media personality.

"Delivering some pictures to you. Do you have a few minutes to get a cup of coffee? I saw a place on the next street over, Central Java, I think it was."

"Nothing until a three o'clock class. Plenty of time. *Craig Maxwell!* I can't believe it!"

"Let's drive over. I've got the pictures in my car."

Terri was ready to go in a minute.

"Nice Porsche."

"Laguna Chevy. I got it to fit in. To all appearances, another financially overextended Junior Account Executive."

I ordered a cappuccino, and Terri had a cafe au lait.

"Okay, here're the goods." I unwrapped three mounted, metal-framed prints. The first was a great picture of Terri looking very nice at 20, deep eyes, Scandinavian. Her vulnerable beauty counterpointing background desolation. The way great actresses look before they're famous. When they're 20. The man who connected with her would be very lucky. Blessed.

The second was a picture of Terri and me together, smiling. I had written on it, "Terri—keep smiling! Craig Maxwell, DV April 1977."

"I hope you like it as much as I do. I had this one printed for myself, too."

The third was a "super" contact sheet enlarged to 11 × 14, consisting of all 36 exposures on the roll.

"Craig, I don't know what to say. They're wonderful!" Her look was worth the drive many times over.

So here's this guy at the next table reading *New West Press,* which had just hit the street, looking at me, reading some more, looking back again, now starting to stand up. It was time to go.

"I've got to get going to LA. I'll drive you home."

"Let me help you carry the pictures in." It was a typical students' apartment in a quiet college town. The kind of place I could easily settle into for a night or two. Entirely theoretically. Not here, not tonight.

"Terri, I've enjoyed the time we've spent together, and hope I've been able to brighten it a bit. I know you've brightened mine. You look to have a great future. Let's stay in touch. If you ever need a date for a special occasion, please give me a call. I'd be honored. Here's my card."

"Thank you so much, Craig," Terri said. You made this a great day for me. And I'm going to take you up on your offer. What girl wouldn't?"

"Bye, Terri." Again.

I felt good about the day. Better than my thoughts earlier when I had read the *New West Press* article, and didn't feel much at all.

"Craig Maxwell—What's Next?" So informative. It was a couldn't miss opportunity to join the Gonzo Dog Band elite. Never argue with publicity. It would look good on my resume when I went over the edge, lost everything, forgot who I was, my own name, ended up at K Mart. "Automotive supplies, this is Kreg, I think."

"Back to school for keyboard dynamo, creative co-driver of ESO?" The article went on to recount my Pennsylvania roots, analyze our music, the fact that I wasn't an original member but a draft choice, artistic differences. All the usual stuff they come up with in New York and LA. An exit on I-80 in the unnamed state east of Utah was looking better and better. And there just had to be some mysterious connection to Viking One on the Acidalia Planitia of

Mars. You know, the real meaning of the song, "Spirit in the Sky", the one they didn't want you to know about in 1970?

I sat there for a year, watching the sun's rays through the skylight trace an analemma, wondering how many more figure eights remained until I'd have earned the Lifetime Due Process Achievement Award. "Sure, I ran off the road into the tree that night. It was the right thing to do. The responsible choice. Anyone would have."

Deeper in the existential sandbox was something about a reunion, slices of pie, seeking connection to the rest of the OhSo DeepDish. Ten years later, this time the disintegration would be more orderly, handled much better, in a manner of which finally we could all be proud. Achieved: synthetic truth. The whole world can't be wrong, can it?

9

No Room for Squares

Cathy invited me to her graduation at UWY, or UWHY as she sometimes called it. You? Why? If I was going to make my/MHY reunion, I'd have to be on the road well south and east of Wyoming at that time. Dwelling in ambivalence, I could see only no-win.

I said something like, "can't say mine was a big deal, missed it," as if I was talking to the TV rehearsing, or some Abyssinian Molokai honey left over from a scream actors guilt hollywood bash. That might be equally applicable to the reunion, or any number of the years of my life. Weak, but then there was at least one major myth to deal with in the Pennsylvania night, maybe others. Taillights. Pulling into a stream of them, in timelapse, chasing fictions never to be caught without unexplainable intervention and grim side effects, a transfer granted between dimensions. I was choosing MHE over HER, us. For myths. Stories in small case packaging, shrink-wrapped, stowed.

Although Cathy didn't express it outright, might not even be capable of saying something shallow like, "whatever works for you," which doesn't mean that at all, I heard disappointment in her voice. I wouldn't be there, if nothing else, someone close. Really more than that. How close do I have to be before either accepting that I'm in a very different realm, and all the responsibility found in it, or admitting I don't belong there? "You're my everything. What was your name again?"

The distance between us remained, would likely grow wider. Sitting in a coffee place on Forest Avenue in Laguna, Death Grip Brand Espresso in hand, my conscience asked the man with 27 years of experience when his life might start. Tossing it back and forth, like a volleyball over the net at Main Beach Park, Catalina Island huge as the future on the western horizon. Fighting the coffee and much, much more.

I headed out of Orange County at night, Hank Mobley's title track from 1963, Philly Joe Jones and Lee Morgan powering the GMC down to Capistrano, I-5, and then east on I-8. Expensive life raft, but a life raft just the same. The lights faded with the climb to Alpine, Descanso. *Descanso* once meant only rest; now roadside crosses, death. More lights, El Centro in the distance. Imperial Valley chemiculture blowing hot in the window, sand dunes, bridge, Yuma, 2:00 am jazz dance stretching before me.

My life's consciousness was as a multitrack. Rolling tape of those 27 years. On track one was infancy, track two childhood. The road trips filled more tracks, a rough mix played back through the late night/early morning monitors. I was on I-8, but the ride to Death Valley was running concurrently. Magnetic tape leakage, a print-through of Shoshone at midnight, Town Without Pity or Bulbs, Opera House before Road Turns, Sidewinders Next 312 Miles, a girl from San Diego grieving her brother. An embrace.

On the road leaving the empty state of BeachSurfCultureMinorCelebrity, beyond the Laguna Mountains east of San Diego. An even drier watershed, flowing only with the contradictions of lifestyle and spirit, bearing tension which would not be overcome, could only be suppressed. Flowing with time.

"He lost valuable time." *Time* couldn't really be valuable by itself, could it?

Shiprock and Prescott, Laramie, Bozeman, Santa Fe. More than places, city states, mindsets, paradigms, boundary conditions, values for the variables in my equation trial solutions. New constructive energies, piñon smoke, *time* at t-sub zero, the here and now. Flight from a world of exploitation revealed by scratches in the primer coat, dark and dangerous. Concealing weapons otherwise unseen, the all-fingerprinted numbing Nixon so accurately summarized: "when the President does it, that means it's not illegal."

Space Age restaurant in Gila Bend two hours later, hot coffee and breakfast amid the stainless, oneups before sunup with pickups, outside. Counter cowboys perpetually lost between sleep and fatigue, stirring coffee, talking sparsely, glancing around from time to time, gilas all. Casa Grande and finally Tucson. Sleep. Just another tourist in from California.

It had been a wet winter there too, with the payoff May flowers in a green desert. Although we played Tucson Community Center a couple of times on tour, there was little time to explore. With that in mind, I had booked two nights at the Westward Look Resort on the NW side of Tucson, which proved to be a very comfortable place among the saguaros.

The next morning, after a run in the foothills, I rolled out the Triumph for a ride first to the Desert Museum, later the old downtown, *Barrio Viejo*. The sun had already ignited the day as I roared out Speedway to Gates Pass, then down the other side into Saguaroland for a few hours. This trick Bonneville, all but Gene "Burrito" Romero flat track ready, polished, rasping, mean.

Downtown, I sought an espresso joint for noon refueling. The barrio was colorful in the desert sunlight, brighter and flatter as the day heated up. Crumbling walls, weeds, prickly pear and ocotillo, faded signs, and quirky graffiti competed with trim pastel adobe renovations, trumpet vines and Mexican bird-of-paradise, flowers planted to accent increasingly gentrified townhomes and artists' studios with lofts and northern exposure. I ran film through both cameras, color and black & white, to be mailed back along the way for developing, viewing and printing upon return. South of the Pima County Courthouse I found the Cafe Olé, and parked the bike in a shaded, inconspicuous corner out front.

In what was now silence, time seemed to have stopped, or like the sun, was just reflecting off the hot, thick, walls of this little piazza, with nowhere to go. I was the only animated presence to be seen, flashing on images, associations, questions. Challenging the Zen, whether emptiness can ever be resolution.

Most of the sense of being, moving around within the photograph of that moment, had to do with the dramatic contrast of Tucson, near dormant at noon in the heat, with the incessant activity and noise of LA and the road trip here. Opening the door of the Cafe, I was met with a rush of cool air, coffee smell, and the clamor of enterprise.

Although I usually prefer to remain anonymous, my beaded Plains Indian jacket is a giveaway, design on the gas tank of the Triumph likewise. At Penn a University Museum anthropological exhibition displayed artifacts with Hopi symbols. The strong design content was immediately appealing, although it took another connection later, after arriving in LA, to kindle an interest in Native American cultures, perhaps rekindle my heritage if the family rumors are true.

I regularly caught exhibitions at the Southwest Museum, and eventually adopted a Hopi symbol, rainclouds with lightning, as my logo, had it custom painted on the Triumph tank, used it on album covers and elsewhere to rein-force identity. Commercial at first, it has become much more than that—a connection to land and peoples of which I had been totally unaware. The downside of the decoration now, of course, is that the bike has to be carefully secured to make sure it doesn't get ripped off; and people recognize the bracelets, like that night in Ft. Collins.

A swamp cooler kept the cafe endurable in the inevitable march to 100 degrees. Sitting there, looking at the remains of the cappuccino, deflated froth with grounds, mark of the bitter lacko cappo, I turned around. A modernist flood of sunlight streamed in the window, illuminating swirling dust, obscuring a figure standing against a column. Very Klee. Noumena. Got it with Pro-X.

As I lay the camera on the table, the figure walked over, sat down at the table next to mine. Took out all kinds of stuff and put it on her table. I've got maybe 30 seconds here.

Running through my mind, another museum-quality anthropological dialogue in an all but lost language.

"You do photography for a living? Work in a darkroom?" She beat me to it.

How does one answer such questions? *Reductio ad adsurdum*? I'm good at that—deriving a contradiction from a set of premises. The more contradictions the better. Near worship of the contradictiously conceptual. Mind scribblingly stimulating, amusing.

"No." Let's talk. Start with backpacking in Yosemite. *Optimism* despite nonsustaining *relationships*, growth, energy. Keywords. Italicized.

Travel. *Black Elk Speaks*. Running, Berkeley, cafes, music. Opera. Trading posts, kachinas, friends, conversations in the night, the entire night. Happiness, death, core experiences, stopping the craziness/putting it aside, pointing to what's before you. Off the road, that tree. Pro-black motor Hasselblads and sculpture, toys of all types. "Yes, I've been there … know of a …"

She looks at me when she talks, a fine face, trembles slightly, goes back to order cheese and apple, another coffee. Want one too? Of course. I'm not trying to wire it or anything. A latte for me, warm reinforcing power. All afternoon, until darkness falls, days pass. Oblivious to all but this woman. Her slight tremble which hits me so hard.

Now the way it really happened instead of my full page cartoon, captioned thought balloon ("I wonder what she's like?" he thought).

"Those are nice bracelets," she said, "I'm surprised to see a man wearing them, particularly on both wrists. You must like Hopi work." On the table, a tendril of coincidence, the term we choose in denial of other more powerful unseen forces, seeking the fertile ground of man-woman intersection, was *Sun Chief*, a Hopi autobiography she had brought to read. I won't act too surprised, hold some in reserve.

"I had the bracelets made on Second Mesa a couple of years ago. After I picked them up, driving west toward Tuba City, there were spectacular backlit monsoon thunderheads above Coal Mine Mesa, sunlight streaming through the clouds. Like that window."

"Yes, I've been there … know of a …"

As I spoke, I flashed on the silversmith's shop, heard the tape which had been playing, drum beats, shakers, bells on the high moccasins, all in step, in synch, a hypnotic dance of the Longhair Kachinas. Rocks and sky outside, cedar smell, piñon pitch between my fingers. The sparest of exchanges, nods, eventually a parting smile, an unspoken blessing.

"*'Adoolch 'ił*. You must be an artist or writer." Currently working in lead. Heavy, malleable, dirty. Tire weights, bad paint.

"What did you just say—the first part?"

"*'Adoolch 'ił*. It means a rolling thunderstorm in Navajo." Hitting me harder yet.

"I'm an engineer by training, actually … from what you're reading and the Navajo language, you must have spent some serious time on the Rez."

"I'm Katrina Walter, Kat for short, and yes I have."

"I'm Craig Maxwell." That's who I do for a living.

"Are you from Tucson? That name seems kind of familiar, but then, I've been living in Chinle for two years. Cultural amnesia. Don't know if it's temporary or permanent. Anything not in Navajo seems unfamiliar."

Katrina, Kat for short. Just back from teaching school in Chinle, blonde, stronger for the third world experience. And I'm still anonymous, unrecognized. Not surprising after her time in Chinle. *New West Press* couldn't be a big seller out there.

Kat was a fistful of arcs—optimisim, realism, sincerity, empathy, sadness. Like we all are in varying proportions. Or I should say, like most women are.

I was a traveller, songster, rider-observer, occasionally reticent motormind at idle in the California music business, driving an RV on my way to a reunion in Pennsylvania. I might or might not make it on time. There could be sidetracks, necessitating evaluation on their own merits. It felt good throwing out some books to crayon in the timespaces: *Zen and Japanese Culture*; anything Hemingway, Len Deighton, Raymond Chandler to escape; *Elephant Bangs Train*. Walker Percy for my sensitive side—*Love in the Ruins, The Moviegoer*. Der reflectën literati hïghen mïghtei.

A few philosophical pronouncements to introduce the Newcumbers, Keet Seel the reel:

♩ Immorals and unethics, when cleverly taught, become the mores espoused by society.

♪ Everything's okay until it mugs or infects you, after which you are bound to wonder.

♪ Time is not the measuring tape for the cloth from which life is cut.

♪ If you shake the right rattle long enough, lightning will be summoned from a clear sky.

While Spanky and Our Gang ran through my mind: "… like to get to know you, yes I would … ." Yes I would.

Neither of us had anything more pressing than coffee in Tucson, unwinding recent months of contrast, years of education, events, experience behind us like kite tails. Despite the coffee, I was fading away, still tired from the drive, and drowsy from the swamp cooler humidity. Needing to sleep, I suggested we meet for dinner, maybe see a movie. *Saturday Night Fever?* Real lame after what she had experienced. In this One and Only America, things were rapidly changing from "How Deep is Your Love" to "how deep are your assets?" Deep enough to take my Status-QuoMo-Bile to the film premiere. Wear our RayBans.

Later, things got much more serious over dinner at El Charro. Kat had a story to tell of a reztown coated in red dust and mud, a tangled fight of cultures, steamy windows on the laundromat at 64 and 191, culturally incongruous government tract housing being filled and used up like plastic cups. Universal unemployment, struggles with the curriculum, English as a second language. The broken bottles and standing mob outside the market, passive/aggressive *Diné* ebb and flow. Soaring joy a beat away from heartbreak, promise and desolation, sky crashing down in another daily tragedy. *"Ch´ínílj,"* Chinle," she said in Navajo, hushed, with a different look in her eyes. I saw myself kissing Kat's closed eyelids, comforting her pain, "it's alright … it'll be okay."

Kat knew that now it was all in her blood, would never be gone. The trendy affluence of Tucson, San Francisco, Santa Fe, fern bars and gourmet cookware could never completely displace her rezangst. The moon would rise over the Bisti Badlands, Hopi Mesas, Monument Valley, bent hoops, Yazzie's beat mobile home with old tires on the roof to keep it down in the wind. A flute melody through the canyons under the moon. Now and forever not ours, but their own moon.

We could have ditched the imaginary film premiere and driven up Mt. Lemmon Highway for better air, but cultural reorientation dictated otherwise. So we did see a movie I don't have to remember at a location I can, Campbell and Grant, then went to Coffee Etc. nearby for dessert. Heat radiating from the pavement at 10 pm in the still night air, desert bugs mesmerized by lighting along the storefronts. And above it all, here tonight, a different moon. Our moon.

At the table next to us, back in a corner, a guy was arguing with a girl, one-sided verbal abuse, actually. Both appeared to be graduate students. The way he was treating her made me angry. Looking at Kat a couple of times, I saw growing tightness in her face, that she was getting very upset too. I was on the verge of telling him to take it outside, starting to want to get into it out there with him, pound and get pounded. Within this dark, swamp-cooled place, warming to anger and conflict, more quickly now, adrenalin kicking in. War cries, thundering hooves splashing through shallow water. Attack!

Where did that image come from?

And then, he did everything but slap her one last time, got up, and walked out. Gone; over. Regardless of the facts, it had been the wrong place, wrong way. The girl was left alone, shaking, a tough Friday night for her. We could have just finished our dessert, "glad that's over," but she looked so helpless. I motioned to Kat that we should offer to sit with her for a few minutes, provide some support.

"What that was all about is none of our business, but if you don't mind, we'll just sit with you for a few minutes and finish our coffee," I said, extending my right hand.

"Thanks," she half-whispered, taking it.

"This is Kat Walter, and I'm Craig Maxwell." Kat reached for my left hand and held it.

The other girl looked at me a minute through red eyes, then asked, "are you *that* Craig Maxwell? The one from ESO?"

"Guilty as charged, but as a co-conspirator, I'd appreciate if you would conceal the evidence."

Kat's eyes widened as she made the connection too, but didn't say a word. I felt her grasp become firmer.

We talked for a few minutes and I asked the girl if she had a way home. When she said she didn't, I insisted on calling a cab, and prepaid the fare. Before we all left, I got a piece of paper up at the register, and wrote a note: "For Judy, in Tucson, May 1977. Best wishes for happiness. Craig Maxwell/ESO." For the moment, her night had been turned around.

"Why didn't you tell me who you were? Kat asked. "I thought your name was familiar." She was smiling when she said it. A good sign.

"For all the usual reasons. I'm just a guy on a trip, trying to be himself, after being someone else for too long."

"Not just another guy, that's for sure, but I'll accept the rest." Another favorable sign. "*Háhóólchįįd*, he was angered by him."

"Yes I was."

Kat was quiet on the short drive back to pick up the Triumph, *dzi 'izítsoh*, motorcycle. After agreeing to get in touch Saturday, she dropped me off—it was around midnight. Ignoring the mounting crime rate, I rode east on Broadway, then north on Swan, and back Sunrise, thinking about Kat Walter. I'd have to find a Navajo dictionary to learn a few words, be able to read signs on the Rez in the future, practice with a certain blonde woman.

Thinking of moving down from her eyelids, as we spoke, kissing her lips. Intoxicated by who and what she is. Balsam and sandalwood. Seeing only beauty and intrigue. A woman who *is* the land she loves. Whose golden hair is the desert bloom of dreams.

Back at the hotel, above the palo verde and ocotillo, the lights and shadows, was that bright desert moon. Tonite da stomp and shuffle, mebbe sunup, d'iguana mañana.

10

A post-bop interlude
at the Copper Queen

Running in the morning, way too hot, up and down the foothills and arroyos for about 45 minutes, a half hour longer before the sweating stopped. Mentally reviewing all I knew about the treatment of heatstroke before realizing, oh yeah ... that wouldn't help if I was the victim.

I could only spend one more night in Arizona. With the reunion Friday in Pennsylvania, there were a lot of miles to cover. I had never been to Bisbee, and Kat suggested we go down separately, meet at the Copper Queen Hotel, and have dinner. At the end of the two hour drive it would be cooler, she promised. Before leaving, I went out to find a Navajo dictionary. Preparation is everything.

Saddened that by this route I'd miss The Thing? in the mountains east of Benson, nevertheless, I turned off the freeway, toward Tombstone. Locally it was I-10, not The 10. Something small to celebrate.

There is refuge here, the land promised. Springs and pockets of green, high in the Dragoons. Monsoon cloudbursts and waterfalls, hanging valleys. Tilted rock slabs, haze of summer's heat, cottonwoods along the bottom land of the San Pedro and its tributary draws. Apache country. Well, maybe refuge now, certainly not as secure a century ago.

The drive was continually picturesque, particularly the view east of Tombstone overlooking the Mule and Huachuca Mountains, San Pedro River Valley, Mexico to the south. Tombstone itself was a dogeared, boardwalked, tinhorn throwaway souvenir town panhandling tourists in places claiming to be World Famous. Small world, ain't it? One pass of Allen Street and I was gone.

Tombstone Canyon in Bisbee was something else, a winding drainage which still flash flooded, carrying cars away when the channel overflowed, occasionally a person who tripped and fell into the deluge, or just wanted to cool off in one last drunken swim. It was a unique town of mining wreckage, surprisingly overgrown for the desert, with more crumbling adobe and block walls, graffiti proverbs:

Inside a Potato There are Mountains and Rivers.

I hiked up High School Hill, poked around Brewery Gulch, peered into the huge Lavender Pit, an open pit copper mine that went down a thousand feet, with its chemical green lake at the bottom, not a plant to be seen on the terraced sides from which copper was leached with sulfuric acid. Laguna turned inside out. There were nationally competitive bicycle races each April, Coaster Races in July. Real estate had crashed with the closing of the Mine, attracting a walk-on cast of artists, hippies, border forerunners scratched by bad dope reggae, 'Nam Vets, and militant pacifists.

We need to work together, to redistribute the wealth. Over my fully dressed LoatheMobile.

Out of a terminally weathered window with colorless, sunbleached curtains spiralled jazz riffs from a tenor sax. Inexpert, but honest. Aside from the music, and other expressions of art, there seemed to be no direction to go except sideways. Any new car, local, was a rare sighting, more often than not an Old Copper pensioner's Ford. Never a Lincoln. I took a drink of Calistoga water, bubblingly cold from the Food Co-op, and wondered, how could you make the payments in a place like this?

Having arrived a couple of hours early, or years late, depending upon the perspective, I had time for a ride on the Triumph. Going back up the Canyon, I went under the highway bridge, hung a left before the Mile High Motel, and descended the hill again on U.S. 80. Past the Lavender Pit was Lowell, little more than a lumberyard and a couple of bars. Staying right at the Circle took me toward South Bisbee and the San Jose district. Naco, Mexico, was close by, but I stopped at the border, came back and cruised through Bakerville to Warren. A couple of picnics going on at the park, but otherwise, very quiet. Old Bisbee seemed to have the energy around here.

Thunderheads were building in the early evening as I sat out on the patio at the Copper Queen Hotel, sipping a cup of hopeless coffee only partially neutralized by half-n-half, looking over at the steep hillside to the south. A couple of hippoid musicians hauled in some gear, prepositioning it for the night's suspected mellowout, beginning at nine. A Fender-Rhodes was already on the premises, apparently left by the lounge regular. We talked and I did a brief demo on the Rhodes, incognito, after which they invited me to sit in, and we settled on a few numbers to play. I was surprised that they knew some solid tunes.

Back out on the patio, watching the light change on the mountain, steam waft above the coffee. Thinking of things to say to Kat. Ostensibly, our last night together. My cover blown, I'm flying out to Argentina after the show. For your safety and protection. Darling, my hope is that you will always keep the song I wrote for you this afternoon close to your heart:

An Obvious Impostor

I'm not even really Craig Maxwell. It's the truth. And what is face value, anyhow? Just that. Overrated.

A windup guy burning film below the railing which casts shadows on my legs. Hockney would love it. As the camera shutter clicked, acrylic paint dried, for some reason my thoughts turned to the bluffs of Encinitas, watching a surf dog swim back with the stick. Sky, blue-green water, white wave crests. Sand coarse, brown. Danger, unstable cliffs. Passed in the darkness, this time, only a couple of days ago. Rods and cones, visual purple, and all. Very dim.

Interesting cups they've got at the Queen. Coffee mugs-a-tilt on the metal mesh tables. Don't try it full.

Forget trying to think of something to say to Kat. It's much more interesting to reconstruct the local psychoses from fragments of conversations overheard in this H'Othello Gringo Pair-a-Dice. Hooked on 'Tonics, they were singing "Mister Bo" in slurred and lisped border dialect:

… Mithter BothJangles …

Forensics took little time to confirm that a substantial percentage of the street and night (S&N) crowd did dope, drank, and danced (DD&D), embarked upon expeditions to the Circle K to rent a pack of smokes, couple sixes of Oly, and a carpet shampooer; mumblingly made up or outright deceptively lied about local history, as if well-trained guides at the nationally known Shrine of Heavenly BBQ Marinade. It exists–check the tour books. Mob ranches bulldozed for tract homes that were never built (out here?), the 1929 Senators throwing one in the *Evening Ore* (huh?), what the Air Force had in mind for High Lonesome, who was really in those handtinted VW buses with Colorado plates, and why it was better to keep diamondbacks in a bag. Right down to the angry, polyphonic hissing and occasional fangs catching a hand through the weave.

Who's got the problem here? As will be abundantly clear by now, when I sit and drink coffee in foreign places, especially coffee this raunchy, my airspeed definitely increases. Pull back on the stick and get´ that´ nose´ up´.

Kat arrived at 6:30 pm. Seeing her was the jolt I needed, brought me back. We hugged, then she went into the hotel to check in. A room. I hadn't really thought about that … really, I swear! I thought about it now. She looked great.

Living in Tucson, Kat knew about Bisbee, and had made an occasional weekend getaway to the Queen. I stayed on the patio until she came down, behaving myself, listening to more local talk, bar stories, chatter, thinking of the contrasts of Bisbee and LA, Laguna, Tucson, awaiting our trendyzvous.

"Let's climb up on Castle Rock," she said, and we walked to High School Hill, then the old brick road leading to the top. There was a breeze blowing up there, curve of Tombstone Canyon Road winding below, other more powerful curves before me. While the limestone had stored the day's heat, Kat was desert acclimated, her skin surprisingly cool.

We heard thunder, "'*adi 'ní*, it thunders," she said. I liked the way the strange sounds rolled off her tongue. It was distant, but Kat was here, her legs smooth when she grasped her long, soft cotton skirt to climb up. I wanted to put my hand on her hip, discover what I knew would be found there, roundness, promise of other places. No moment could be more perfect. The evening was beautiful; we both were lead to become active participants in it, testify to our epoch on this planet.

"*Wóshch 'ishídi*, come closer," she said. As Kat turned, moving to me, I couldn't help but glimpse the tanned skin which disappeared into her blouse, beneath the top of her bra, so white in contrast. "Oh man," I exhaled.

And then we jumped off Castle Rock. Figuratively.

As the first stars peeked out of the early night sky, she related the legend of First Man, or *Altsé Hastiin*, in Navajo. I wondered, silently, which came first, the legends or man? Tan or white?

"First Man tried to brighten the dark night sky by decorating it with stars. Taking chips of mica he placed them one by one overhead. But Coyote grabbed the blanket and shook it, and the stars were thrown all over the sky. The order sought by First Man had been thwarted by Coyote the Trickster's mischief."

Kat proved to be a legend with stars of her own, a celebration of much more than the distant elements and physics of this sky, *lees 'áán yílzhódí*, the Milky Way within it. That was later, of course, not on Castle Rock in the middle of Old Bisbee.

We had dinner and then walked more, up to the Iron Man, a miner statue at the Cochise County Court House, before looping back on Clawson. By now it was almost 10 pm, and the band, a quartet, had played their first set at the Queen. We began the second set, starting off with two Coltrane numbers. The sax man did a respectable job with "Impressions". Things started cookin' on Chick Corea's "Spain", and absolutely took off as we jammed on another Coltrane tune, "A Love Supreme". By now, the room was packed, the door was open, and the patio outside was SRO. The set ended with Herbie Hancock's "Cantalope Island", on this all too rare, perfect evening of playing rather than performing.

"You are incredible!" Kat whispered in my ear as she gently but assuredly moved closer, excited about the music, the night, to be with the man from California passing through with a Triumph. I ordered a couple of cold beers, and we sat on the patio to cool down, talking; trading electrical impulses, our own lightning storm building.

Kat had applied for a job teaching school in Flagstaff, to be nearer what was for her the power of the Four Corners region. She related dances on the Hopi mesas, sunrise in Shiprock, the dust and darkness of nightfall in Monument

Valley, the encompassing Southwest cultures. My immediate interests, when coherent, ran farther north, into Wyoming, where the land was as dramatic, though influence and visibility of Native cultures in the populated areas now more subtle. I couldn't really explain why.

"Tell me how you got to where you are," she asked.

I liked the way she listened to my story, asked a question here and there, just accepted me. Must have been that time on the Rez, watching the grandmothers weave. I thought about how the teacher starts with information and tools, a desire to impart it to others; and with time, acquires more knowledge and then wisdom, becomes the lifelong student.

"I'll show you the GMC. It's just a short walk to the parking lot, beside the Phelps-Dodge Building." We left the patio, walking in an *Aja* evening, stars swept across the dark sky, a slight breeze.

The RV and trailer did indeed look like NASA rolling stock in this wornout old town, tinted windows, air conditioners on top, California plates. Inside were the rackmount electronics and keyboard controller, tape library, equipage for an indefinite road trip. Mindboggling technology. So what, I thought, it's only metal and glass. Forget it. You're with a woman on a night each of you want to give to the other, to remember all their life. A night full of biochemistry and planetary physics–the emotion, maybe soul altering celestial mechanics of intimacy.

Well after midnight, getting late. Kat felt wonderful in my arms when I couldn't stand being apart from her any longer.

" *'Ooljéé' bee 'adinídíín*, there is moonlight; *áhodéeszéé'*, it is still. Let's go up to the Queen," she whispered, "I need you to help bring me back from the reservation."

A night to remember. Starry Sky. Van Gogh, Van Going, Van Gone.

11

Explanations neither offered nor accepted

During the night I awoke, looked up at the ceiling fan, for some reason stopped despite the heat. Along the ocean of my consciousness, on a desert beach swept by onshore winds of imagery, I closed my eyes and saw a starfish. Bending over to look at it more closely, waiting for waves promised but never to break there, I wondered: how does one decide whether to stay or go? Why does it seem I'm always having to decide between paths with heavy outcomes? Do I see more with my eyes shut or open?

Stay? Where? Go to a reunion instead of accepting the challenge of a clearly extraordinary woman you've just met? A woman with convincing strengths, yet a very tender heart. Spending a night together is the easy part, more easily misleading. Forthrightly approaching the next days is something else, the basic chord progressions sketched by lovers in their separate drafts of what might be possible. Seeking to create a mutual work with compelling, unifying themes, libretti of truth and giving within which might one day be rendered the elusive—unconditional love.

The touch which started it, our sighs both of relaxation and anticipation. We will have each other. Chain reactions within a setting built up from the prerequisites of migrations, exploration, opportunity, hard work, triumphs and failures extending to antiquity, all now integral to last night's magic, today's memories. Stone quarried, trees felled, lumber sawn and hauled here for this old hotel. Our ancestors, where they went, what they did and didn't do. Kat and I are only the latest. Around all of it were the cosmos' elaborate, convergent arrangements for one May night. The small of her back, so smooth, starting and ending place for star travels, places we visited alone and together within the constellations, superheated dust that we once were, are now, and will always be.

After falling back asleep, I awoke again in mid-morning, Kat still sleeping beside me. Our night had been an overarching star chant, more than physics, beyond random, spontaneous intersection. It was a celebration of life-promise fulfilled, jazz choruses, profound closeness witnessed by the night sky. It is now the woman sleeping in her t-shirt, whose hair I kiss gently so as not to awaken her.

Quietly dressing, I left the room and walked down to the GMC, put on running shorts and a top, laced my shoes.

Beyond the Post Office, Tombstone Canyon was quiet and still, in the absence of a breeze, the sun harsh. It was a ramshackle mining district, but up here in "Old Bisbee", without dumps towering over the shacks, there was no visible rainbow sheen of lead and other toxics. Down the Canyon to the Pit, Lowell, Bakerville, through the pipes of South Bisbee those drainages were found, terrible dull brown. A rusted countryside of trestles, conduits, rods; oil-preserved timbers and ties; bowed clapboard buildings; gravel and dust, dead land. Twitches and turns, Bisbee as nothing more than copper, a town created for, explained away and offered up as sacrifice at the Church of the Commodities (Multinational). While Steely Dan were "Reeling in the Years", here they were "Leaching Away the Time".

Wasteland mining and quiz show towns. Truth or Consequences. Swazey City. Let's Win a Dream! The goods have been shipped, what's your problem? Had my heart set on scoring other stuff. A flame-accented Numbah Won Boom-Boom Wood Tropical Wet Bar Suite with rolling bottle caddy; spring refueling stop in the Azores; slinky dance outfit with boots and short pants, bonus bedside disco spinning ball lamp; the car Sgt. Pepper drove to Buckingham Palace. A handsome whiplash settlement.

Another disquieting koan scrawled on the side of cupped wood siding:

Take heed! The world we know is not coming to an end!

The frightening burden of preparing for yesterday.

Running, searching for synch to the drums, different chant in a language unrecognizable except for the beat, trochaic "hey´-ah, hey´-ah, hey´-ah." Striding as if in a museum documentary, rare film clips, victory lap; walking out the door of the Balboa Theater, marvelling at the cool night air, trying to figure out where I had been for the last few years. Finding the so-called Olympic flame was only a smoky citronella pot to keep away bugs.

Past the Arctic Circle, shade trees at Moore's Market, firehouse, silver and red painted rail along the deep ditch. Across U.S. 80 to Old 80, even steeper and more winding before reaching the Divide, above the Time Tunnel, then turning around in a wonderland of broken bottles, trash, and graffiti. Careful not to test the cattleguard, hugging the guardrail, on the way back down the hill I contrasted this worn garden spot with the engineered freeway environment of Recent LA. Offered up or not, Bisbee would sleep, appearing to be forgotten, funky and comfortable, until it too was rediscovered and obliterated under the guise of preserving, but really renovating that "unique" which never existed. Like most of us. Insisting on living within a mix of selfish futures and fictional pasts. With the top down. Fast.

Back at Queen Plaza, I was getting both nearer to and farther from where I thought I wanted to be. Cathy with a C and Kat with a K. Fine women who brought other, important dimensions to what had become a two dimensional life ignoring subtle curvatures, nuances of origins and destinations, those who were found there. One dimension, time. Arguably not a dimension at all, only a degree. Neither nearer nor farther. Here. Physically and emotionally. Period.

We could spend another day, compressing the available travel time back east, stretching the window. Reasoned away, at least for now. I didn't want to answer the question, "will I see you again?" My sense was yes, but I hoped she wouldn't ask it that directly. I didn't want to even start to try sorting out now how it all fit together. Kat, a RezConnection, incarnate energy field dancing to a fire within mysterious canyonlands I could sense, but in which I never had lived. A roaring fire of midnight passion I *did* experience with her, but for some reason could not validate today by letting go of the world outside the two of us. Looking into the smoldering coals of dawn's quiet conscience, I reasoned for time and distance. Reverting to coordinate geometry, invented measures. Maybe I'm totally insecure dealing with the real, those at the time, any time, outside the "structure" I've built, hardened during the last years.

Kat wouldn't ask me, "why not?" If she had, all I could have said would be, "I just can't." She didn't.

The shutter of my camera clicked this time as I took some black & white shots of the town, Kat standing in a doorway, against old wood. The blonde hair would be gray when printed in black and white. Metaphorical shots and associations carried around forever in my head. When I had put my hand on her, and what was open and accessible between us in our outermost layers of being man and woman, dreams and fantasies, needs and giving, couldn't be stopped. Dissolved now in this midday lighting to crude concrete lintels, faded signs on powdery, failing plaster.

Promising to stay in touch, we left Bisbee. Kat drove away first, retracing my morning uphill run in her own plein-air goodbye. What was *she* thinking, the look on *her* face? Tombstone, towering cottonwoods of St. David, trailer parks of Benson, I-10, The Triple T. Tucson. The City. Day by day. Next year. Next town. Rising up from her heavy heart by giving to others. To me.

When she disappeared I climbed into the rig and wound down what was left of the other end of the canyon. Smelter smoke dose of Douglas. No rodeo in Rodeo, only a tired, shrunken old townsite, a few big trees looking out of place, glint of more broken glass. I-10 at Road Forks, just past the Shady Grove, going the other way. New Mexico now, yucca fringed playa, driving east.

Turning over in my mind the whole way how we should have stayed, spent a second night, and then another until they became all the years of our lives. That no speculative, hypothetical reunion trip experience was worth leaving this woman.

"Leave your car here," I could have said. "Come with me to Pennsylvania." I didn't think to ask it before she left.

Maybe at the Cafe Olé I had turned around to a dream. An apparition in the illuminated dust. If I dare go back now, she won't be there. Was never there. It had been only subterfuge, of the purest crystalline formulation. Laboratory grade.

Interesting I thought of Kat living day to day, while myself night after night. Complementary, to pick one meaning among others.

Joints in the road syncopated the hypnotic planarity of this region. Las Cruces, Tularosa, Roswell. After the paranoia of the 50's, it didn't take too much imagination to deepen the UFO legends out here. Expectations of alien abductions remained high, witness so many of the folk who obviously had already made the trip. In this mix of authentic Buddy Hollyland and actualized Ellavis, the female equivalent of Mr. Presley, every encounter was an alien encounter. Order a burger, meet a witness with personal knowledge, blurry photos, explanatory theories, shocking implications. A very unusual business card.

Fanned by the newspaper. "Extreme Hairstyle Competition Grand Prize Winner." The Lord Nelson, a high loft, narrow-ridged, gravity-defying Admiralty cap of a 'do, representing the gamut from past to present, stegosaurus to armadillo, millions of years in the making. Surprise in The Big Hair Teaseoff, "Vegas of Dreams." And in the Open Class, evidence of truly fearsome supraliminal near-Permian Basin cross-pollinations: "The Babycakes."

Nail Haven, New Mexico, the town where nobody settles down, everybody digs in. Oriental nail parlors with bamboo window lettering; attention arresting synthetic fabrics worn tight as drum heads, wearer and fa-brik one refinery stop away from ancestral sweet crude. "Ban Lon, Hon, blessed on us by the dine-o-soars." Way more advanced than the science books let on. In a pinch, ionizing fuel for the return trip to Rohra Calhoun-13, dominant orb in Yowza Minus. With the memory of Earth Hips, even faster.

I did order the "Reentry Burger", which though singed around the edges, arrived back intact. As I ate, careful not to touch the side of fried abduction rings, conversations as weird as the printed record escaped from the background. Was this in fact only a surreal black box job, staged for a never hip, unreported though permanently missing audience way off Broadway?

"I know what it means to drop dead." A very curious statement, "constructively ambivalent," they would say where I came from. A lightning survival story? Strangely, I swear there was an ozone smell.

Or how about, "No fair reading minds, Bert. Hey, bend me a spoon for Number 5, will ya?"

Works of magic invoking "action at a distance", turns of another ceiling fan reflected in the spoon on the table. Prebent. Had I never seen polished metal, I might have thought the whirling fan energy to be transmitted through the ether and reside in the spoon. Another graduate school paper was in there: "Manifested Kinetic Spoon-Fan Transference." These nails, spoons, burgers and rings were not falling on deaf ears, if you catch my multisensory yaw.

Only one who was from here but had been "outside" might understand the shocking truth. There were no vending machines in this town. Off the snack and novelty route. Taking up the slack was an obscene haiku underground, abstract, posse-defying purposive agents on the prowl, judging from the graffiti in the washroom (several vowel substitutions/other editing for content):

> O West Texas light
> The sweet yield of pumping crude
> Bring your shift over

> Come on in, roughnecks!
> Bet your trucks, rigs and derricks
> Tonight's your strike

Things were going on here which skipped international borders, generations, defied Mendel's laws, proved physics to be inabsolute. The rig was floored, but barely moving under the pull of the town's tractor beam. Empty movie set, thick time, extra hold gel. I had to find the key for the red-painted switch on the dash, the one for deploying degrees of invisibility. It could still come in handy today.

Oh by the way, Austin won't work geographically. Another time, Green Sweater Girl.

Lubbock, headed toward Dallas, I-40 at Little Rock. Lakes with oil wells and power poles in them I can't get used to. Ever unrolling flat brown dirt country.

Taking a roadside break, away from the epicurean splendors dijonnaise of sandwiches past, now feasting on ambrosial melon that tasted like sweet raspberries in a delightful confusion of fruit, I thought of other faces as the Lone

Star traffic roared by. The perfume of this ripe cantalope. The most subtle suggestion of even sweeter perfume.

It's in their eyes. The eyes of Henriette Wyeth, so dark in a black and white photograph of that portraitist extraordinaire. More visions in the waves of heat rising from the road, reflected here from the retrospective of early 1900's Women Painters of the West I saw before leaving LA. Longer hair, a different blouse, and Elsie Palmer could have been Kat. Imagining a midnight drive home to *The Sleeping Child* of Mary Curtis Richardson. Drawn to the bottom lip of Mabel Alvarez in her self portrait, wondering. Such beauty in the art, whether peace in the artist or not.

Could it really have been that long ago, 1911? I couldn't get them out of my mind. Strange when you consider all I saw were pictures on walls. But that's art, door to the aesthetic, the vicarious. Decades becoming centuries, inspiration still fresh, like Botticelli's model for *Primavera*. The gap between art and life. The gap we try to leap, river which must be arduously, heroically navigated.

An occasional slip, rocks dislodged and vertically scattered, hitting an outcrop below, falling in the Chasm of Art. Would you sleep more comfortably with a cubist painting under your pillow? Would you titrate your sanity with Modernistic Expressionism? If you had only one golf club left, what would you wrap it around?

I wanted to look into their eyes and know them. Not possible. All painters, gone for decades. I could, however, seek to understand what they intended to communicate, interpret their work.

Postulating, for the sake of one on none road discussion:

    photography — freezing the subject for storage
    painting   — the subject at room temperature or above

Neither of which held. Too many exceptions, counterarguments, skipping rocks. How about "when technique is demystified, art disappears?" That'll be good for another thousand miles. I'll stick it to the bottom of the seat with the rest of the gum.

Jolted from my incessant musings by a horn, somebody else's near miss, I concluded: though *they* live on through their art, *you* will not find the path to happiness in the faces of dead painters. Nothing there beyond the inevitability of death. Was anything going to work today? Warning: contents may settle during (RV) shipment.

"No Room for Squares". Another chorus.

Fleetwood Mac's *Rumours* was threatening to outsell what used to be us. More than rumors, it was reality for them. Lindsey and Stevie splitting, Christine and John over with. And yet the show went on, great song hooks in their conflict and coping. I thought of Stevie's high school senior picture, what I had seen in it. Was it in *New West Press*? A dream? When she was eighteen, with that "something" you could sense. I remember taking a few pictures of Natalie, but they're gone, lost or thrown out. It doesn't matter—I need only close my eyes, and she's there. With her version of "something".

Submerged in accelerated cultural change, the barrage of breakups, generational and economic muggings, we were all fighting to keep anchored, trying to cope. *Rocky* and *All the President's Men* on film, The Clash drifting in from Britain, plane after plane of dope from Mexico, a different clash at the Seabrook nuke plant, Pink Floyd's quadrophonic assault on Portland, the latest sonic ground zero. The music was just LOUD. Distorted. Kilowatts without clarity. Paradise if you were stoned out of your gourd. Punishment and pain if you were straight.

I was glad to be gone from it, but had to wonder whether the warnings disclosed in the packaging of the *Teachings of Don Pardo and Don José*, *The Two-Pack* were accurate, that "all relief is temporary; whether buying at a bargain price, or recovering from baddd jalapeños." I tried to think of one person (living) I knew who had beat the house, found peace, cut the Record of Eternal Happiness. Not Lindsey, not Stevie. Too many miles, too many faceless faces, too tired to come up with a name.

Finally I-40, then I-81 from northeast Tennessee, through Virginia, and into Pennsylvania, arriving in Harrisburg Thursday, the day before the reunion. 2300 miles. Banging on the road the whole time. Listen to *me*! Recounted, explained away in a few sentences, even one sentence, or just silence, no sentences at all. Miles preserved on another track. Not particularly original, no fundamental truths deduced, it seems the best I can hope for is to put the rolling emptiness in my own words. In MHY own hollow ones, ready to be filled at any moment. Drive the wedges, quarry the marble. Hammer the cork. Age expertly in a dark place. Below room temperature.

Cafe Whyoming

12
What became a chocolate digression

Early summer is wonderful in Central Pennsylvania, the mornings cool, land green, rivers and streams full, flowers in bloom. So different than the dirt dry, overgrazed "natural" open spaces of which there are too many in *The Flat West, a Study in Semi-Arid Denial*.

I drove to my folks' house, set off from the road by a long, winding driveway with gate, at the edge of a forest, screened by a row of trees. There was enough room to park the rig out of the way, on the concrete pad beside the garage. It was as happy a fairweather homecoming as could be expected, given an undercurrent of what *was* I going to do in the post-ESO phase; posed against an unspoken backdrop of those women, painters and others. Living and dead.

So easy sometimes to slip away into gray. At least the investment portfolio is compounding every day with little tending required on my part, providing the means to muse. I shouldn't have to keep trying to explain to them that my future isn't about having to make money. They need to listen and just accept it.

I was glad to be off the interstates. The refrigerator was stocked to support decades of postcataclysmic survival, hardwood floors smooth, rooms, silverware and dishes, mugs in the cupboard, smell in the basement from the fuel-oil fired boiler, all familiar. Glass patio doors divided the worlds, outside and inside, where we visited and updated, ate and speculated, planned and relaxed, though all within the envelope defined by years, hierarchy, attitudes, roles and restraint. Universally accepted, convincing fictions.

In the early evening after dinner, I unloaded the Triumph, anxious for a country ride, west toward Dillsburg, then turning off U.S. 15 before Grantham onto East Lisburn Road. The air became diffused in the heavy golden twilight, the grass thicker, fields more fertile than I remembered. An old Moody Blues song came to mind, about opening my heart to all this. "The Sun is Still Shining" brought back other beauty in Arizona, Wyoming.

Turning north, I rode Slate Hill Road to Shiremanstown, then Orrs Bridge Road, past the Camp Hill Barn, the scene of innumerable high school escapades laced with alcohol, B-3 riffs, two handed cluster chords, tight horns rolling over the fairways on moonlit nights. Devolved to a golf course pro shop. Saddled on the Triumph, growling mill, neo-California interstate invader on the prowl, exploring the landfills and illegal slumping/dumping sites of the Sixties, full of their dreams, deceptions, and debris.

I awoke to a bedroom cooled by night air from the open window. Outside, in my running gear, it was a Friday morning of hazy green, hydrangea blue, coos of mourning doves. Although most of the houses and neighborhood were unchanged, the stirring of renovation on riverview lots was visible. I ran by the park overlooking the Susquehanna, looped up into Camp Hill before returning. Even though having been back only once in six years, last Christmas, the route was familiar. With eyes closed, I could see the homes, trees, hills and curves. Permanently imprinted.

The ragged, thorny old locust at the edge of the yard had outlasted ash trees which always seemed so much healthier. Unless you had to cleanup the dead branches after a windstorm, I now recalled. Bluejays were thriving among the splits, holes, and missing branches, flying to the pewter barked cherry nearby. Seek the path, *hózhó*, as the Navajo say. Walk in the beauty of this creation, even when ragged and thorny.

Not yet having downshifted from constant motion mode, savoring that evening with Kat in intermittent recollections at once near-tangible, fully aesthetic, and interpretive; above all lookin' for adventure, I jumped on the Triumph again. This time for lunch in Hershey, the immaculate, neatly wrapped Almond Bar 20 miles east on U.S. 322. Under the watchful commerce of the Hershey's Kisses streetlights, I turned north from Chocolate Avenue onto Cocoa, then rode up the hill, past the Milton Hershey School to the Hotel Hershey.

Green roofed with twin spires, in the class of Del Coronado and Claremont, it was a large, comfortable bastion whose effete, regular clientele was of considerable means, interrupted only occasionally by leisured walk-ons unaffiliated with the riding stables, like me, and heathen trespassing from the amusement park below, thinking it to be an unmarked Fantasyland. In LA, that's exactly what it would have been—replicant with fake snow on the roof 365 days a year. Here, the kind of place where "I'd like a short cappuccino, and two plane tickets to Spain," would be met with, "At once, sir, I'll have them delivered to your table, and may I be permitted to assist you with any other travel arrangements? Perhaps an autumn cruise to the Orient?"

Needless to say, I was the only one dining at the Hotel Hershey with motorcycle boots. The place was filled with the wives and daughters of execs, even those of a magnate now and then. I immediately recognized one of the corporate Brahmins wearing well polished riding boots when she came over to my table.

Cafe Whyoming

"Hello, Jackie," I said rising to greet the woman with the famous Candy-Land last name. Not Mars, Peter Paul, SkyBar, or Mary Jane on WGAL, a local thing, but in the vicinity.

"It's you, Craig. It's really you, here in Hershey of all places, after what's it been, ten years?"

"Yes, ten years. I'm back for my 10th reunion tonite. Trademarked and copyrighted, just like you."

"I see something about you in the paper from time to time. You're famous now. But then, you were famous with the girls at Maplefields in our high school days, too."

"High school days" didn't really fit this Cosmo prize. To the credit of her parents, she had gone to Maplefields School locally instead of a Swiss boarding academy. Consequently, Jackie could manage very well in the real world. At Penn, I had encountered some overmonogrammed Scarsdale and Westport debs who needed continuous personal assistance. You could only row away your single scull and let them call their cashmere overcoated, prep school counterparts for road service with delightful, vintage rosé.

"Famous for waking up too many times in the wrong place with a head-ache. To the disadvantage of what might have been eternal paradise with the classically elegant likes of yourself." Or one of your cronies who come to mind, Bethany Saxon and Elise Gordon, of course. Very British, very pretty, each with diplomatic immunity. There was another, heretofore unnamed—one whose life was set to a score in A minor, who with me seemed to have suffered a permanent impedance mismatch.

"I guess that's a compliment," Jackie said in her uniquely breathless voice, while I flashed on waking up beside her, gorgeous long hair overflowing the soft, lace fringed white down pillow. Any one of the three would more than do today for lunch. Better reel it in here.

"Is that a wedding ring I see?" I asked. "Sit down and tell me about it."

"Yes, two years now." And then came the story. A good story, it seemed to me, detecting happiness which had to be reflected in her marriage.

Before we parted, Jackie brought up the ghost of that work in A minor which closed a couple of years ago. "I see Anne from time to time. She's married now, too, but still thinks of you. We never really get over first loves, you know." Restlessness of the heart, the spirit.

Who was yours? I wouldn't have minded trying to help you get over him.

"I won't ask you about yours," I said, adding a two measure rest, wanting to avoid the subject of Anne. Collision damage, shattered glass, other evidence left at the scene.

Anne, another English princess, who unlike Jackie, married too young on the wrong rebound and found only disintegrating dreams. Threatened and then defeated by the realities of selfishness, disinterest, confusion. So she married again. Twice now in her twenties. And she still thinks of me.

Jackie had to go. Bidding her goodbye, I was struck by the contrasts of recent days. Hershey certainly wasn't the "Wonder Bar" of Bisbee/Lowell, Arizona, but maybe I belonged there much more than here. If only it had a music school. "Where's the Music School? The what? The Music School … oh, the Music School! Two doors down from the City Maintenance Garage!"

Time compression. Emotional compression. Not all my fault.

Anne lived in a house on Alderwood Court and went to Maplefields as well. Anne of Alderwood. Anne of Three Thousand Days. Anne in a Japanese movie, *The Thousand Waves*. Now, I could remember it only as a haze that had lasted for almost 10 years, much more shrouding than that of this morning's run. As I walked to the parking lot through the rose garden, the sun went behind a cloud. In the shadow, I thought more about those days, too many ruined by carelessness, hurt. The last time I saw her, in Scottsdale a couple of years ago.

Our relationship was stage scenery in search of a play, an opera without music, drama without dialogue. Only an ambiance, a private environment. Like this place, a rose garden mulched with cocoa bean husks, an intoxicating mix of scents, the exciting promise of exotic blossoms left behind as we move on. I wouldn't forget the song that was playing when I saw her across the room for the first time, The Animals' "We Gotta Get Out of This Place"; her sweater, knee socks, above it all pout. Anne's expression dared me: "go ahead, try something. I want you to."

And then another song, the Zombies' "She's Not There", full of imagery with a 25 year guarantee. Smooth context for her voice, eyes, her hair. We were both so cool we couldn't stand it, just had to trade insults, leave with others, eventually find ourselves alone together, as if by surprise. I didn't know what I was doing, but it seemed important. One thing led to another, and then we were left with trying to understand what, if anything, it *had* meant. Year after year. Hooks that wouldn't come free, even with longnose pliers.

Following high school, Zombies notwithstanding, "She Was There", catching the train, coming down to Penn from Sarah Lawrence. Wearing her camel coat when it was cold, denim pants just the right style, shade and softness; the elegant umbrella she brought when it rained. Hair pulled back, carrying a stylishly stencilled canvas bag always full of books, eccentric junk. The fat, happy Buddha pulled out of the bag which she gave to me. Still within my Understanding Nothing, Don't Really Care, And You Deserve The Insults Phase, I hated its cheap, Made in Japan green felt base stupidity. Confusing the girl with the props, struggling with complex equations, thermodynamics, seeing nothing but darkness, able to push it away only with music I could share with others, but never Anne. Questioning what was behind the junk, smiling Buddha. Haven't forgotten it, have I?

Jackie had a private coach, worked hard, and ice skated, very well. Anne and I watched her practicing for a competition once in the Hershey Arena. Fluid, rhythmic, polished, athletic without looking it, gracefully feminine. There were whole dimensions to Jackie that she didn't, couldn't realize, appreciable only by an observer. Perfect as the solitary flower I saw in a meadow at Sequoia, surrounded by tall Sierra grass on the day before fall's first freeze.

I remember the piece to which she was skating, Tchaikovsky's *The Sleeping Beauty*, ballet music; the hollow-metallic sounding ssshhh of a skate edge, toe pick when she came over, face flushed from exertion, the cold rink, fulfillment of artistic expression. Anne noticed as I considered Jackie, looked for and found one of those special dimensions. Jackie returned the gaze, communicating strength, first woman to man, heart to heart; then woman to woman, an elemental "I'll look at whomever I want; don't take anything for granted, not now, not ever."

Jackie shifted the dynamic, greeting Anne, who returned it a little tensely, then looked at me, a mixture of embarrassment, jealousy and prideful "so what?" on her face, as if to say, "she's just another girl; I'm the one with you." Jackie never had been, would never be that. Like Allison, another story, and Stevie Nicks, she had "it". Many times over.

None of this is to denigrate Anne. It was only of a few seconds duration, though had I been more perceptive, it might have been an insightful encounter. Maybe even a learning experience. Regardless, one day the self-deluding clouds dispersed, and I saw Anne beautiful as never before. Perversely, it was at a time she wanted nothing more to do with me. I admit that Anne and I are still jumbled in my head. As if upon examining all the evidence, the Great Mediator pronounced, "you may still live, but in permanent exile, and you'll have to figure out your own oxygen supply."

While Anne and I were bouncing back and forth, we talked about going to New Mexico during the summer before our sophomore years. Actually, it was my idea, conceived during a particularly boring early spring lecture in Hayden Hall, full of monoclinic rocks, old wood, and not so subtle mind-body diversions. The plan was to buy a VW bus and drive out to do a summer field geology program. Her role would be to look great during the day in hiking shorts and after the sun went down, look even better without them. That would have been true.

I don't know why I even brought it up, thought she would be remotely interested other than to get away from her parents for a couple of months, who probably wouldn't have allowed it, knowing I was to be on the scene. Probably because I wasn't thinking at all. We talked about it, while I kept putting off signing up until it was too late. Instead, our band sublet an apartment, stayed in Philly, practiced, and played an occasional gig during the summer, preparing for the wilder, more lucrative fall. It was one of those fateful, right turns toward my future. Anne always blamed me for not doing the New Mexico summer.

I convinced myself that Anne lacked spontaneity, would never surprise me with the miracles I expected to be delivered, thought I needed. Insisting on the ones that take your breath away, make you stand back, step out of yourself, into a new place—with, within that other person. Missing others that were there all the time. Those years, so many to us, but in reality so few. Another crop of artists, so sure our talents would bear spectacular, surpassing life creations. Nobody buying the line, the art.

Walking down the hill, past the tennis courts and across the road, I sat in the rose garden, thinking how music and the move to California had enabled me to push the wreckage of my young life out of the way, all without really having to confront what needed to be, or paying the usual dues. I didn't have to work my way up from bar bands on the road, form alliances, thrash competitors. To the contrary, I had a college degree, benefitted from fortuitous circumstances, was at the right station to hear the call: "All Aboard. The Night Train." It was handed to me. A contract player, at first that is, starting at the top. Just get on board.

Now I stayed away from Harrisburg not really because I didn't want to be confronted with my past, but because I didn't care about it. College, California, change points, markers for moving on to new experiences, away from chapters which had been used up, played out, or in a few now unspoken cases, abandoned, left openended.

Then there was that time when I thought I was really more interested in Anne's older sister, Christine. Did Biochem at Johns Hopkins, law at Boalt. Certainly looked the part, but I never did a background check. Legendary anyhow, and now married to a Stanford MBA, living in Scottsdale. Someone with deeper sensibilities, more intellectual, inclined to reach for essentials, down to the atomic, if necessary, pursue them to resolution. Insightful enough to understand at the outset when the organic chemistry wouldn't work, arguments were fruitless. Cool and aloof, a much different kind of alive. Her character dominated a story I developed, written from the sidelines while riding the bench of Team Imagination, set to the *Goyescas* of Granados.

Occasionally, my glance was returned, surprisingly inquisitively, as if to say, "don't move, let me look into *you*. Famous or not, I'll come to my own conclusion." I didn't know how their marriage was, didn't have a clue how I would even start to evaluate it, and never tried. Unless there were only the two of us left on the planet, Christine would be off limits. Even then, she would be coming to her own conclusions, choosing her own course. There would be no guarantee, no clause operative in the event of World Default. I suppose a part of me always wanted her to say, "though you're shallow, untruthful, and mindless, I kind of like you all the same. I need you to do something with, I mean for, me."

Those days didn't seem so far back, because they weren't. Regardless, here I am now, who knows what'll happen at the reunion tonite, with whom, and why. Maybe the time *is* here for World Default, The Going Away Party! Christine will crash the reunion dressed as the Fairy Godmother, knight me with the mythical wand.

Despite all the pain and boredom, expectations, and disappointments, I know that Anne wanted me and for a time, I wanted her. We kept trying in the hope we'd both get there, while continuing to hurt each other. Once, in anger, she said, "after all these years, I've finally realized that way down, you just don't like me, and I haven't seen anything which makes me believe that you ever will."

I took it as only a restatement of what she said when we met, "… go ahead, try something. I want you to." Took it like that and wrote a new draft:

> "You're not my type," I said, "not at all." A totally selfish, arrogant thing to say.
>
> She deflected, ignored it. "You got what you wanted."
>
> "I didn't get anything at all." Cut.

In the end, Anne and I failed, and Christine is no more than a name. Not because I didn't like Anne, but because neither of us knew who we were, what we wanted, how to live with ourselves and begin to figure it out. She pulled away, or I did. We both did. We all did. I still am.

So here's the dossier. Anne. Major influences: Carly Simon and James Taylor. Interests: shopping, spending money, charity benefits, Vivaldi (nice, but it all sounds the same). Snapshot: another Cosmo doll, though one with a heart, stays out of the deep end of the intellectual pool, very high maintenance. Take two aspirin and check back in twenty years. She'll be there, virtually as perfect. The same, I predict.

I was struck by the flagstone mica at my feet in the garden. More samples, Muscovite passed around Hayden Hall in Geology lab. Mica like the stars above Bisbee with Kat. Had I really left that magic just the other day? For a reunion?

Riding down the winding road which when closed and haybaled became the Hershey Hill Climb course, I remembered the roar of Cobras, 427 'Vettes, Lotuses, bathtub Porsches, an occasional Ferrari. Racing-striped, exuding Castrol. Late fall Sunday afternoons with driving gloves, tweed cap (little check, don't get the wrong idea), top down on the Triumph, warmed by hot loaves of bread at Ursini's, off the expressway, was it at 19th or 21st Street? Anne beside me on one of our memorably better days. All gone.

The WCMB billboard dominated the hillside of Washington Heights as I crossed the Market Street Bridge. Bridge after bridge across the Susquehanna. The radio station was familiar, the songs never forgotten: "He's a Rebel", "Palisades Park", "A Thousand Stars (In The Sky)". Other than the birds at dawn, there is no music for me here, and they are not enough. This is not my home.

Home is somewhere nearer the other side of the continent. I could say it was LA now, standing on the end of the Hermosa Beach Pier or at Main Beach Laguna, sunset before me. 'E 'e 'aah biyaajigo, as Kat would say, and so says my dictionary, westward. But that might not be the right place either. How do you ever know?

13

Familiar faces, forgotten names

I lay in the hammock strung between two trees out back. Lost in the Translation, it could have been the title of a book. My book. One of thought processes, associations, traditions. Mostly about movement between spaces, an oversimplification without the emotional content; confusion.

The branches and leaves let little of the sky through, and I was thankful for a glimpse of blue when the dark clouds parted. Time passes so quickly. The evergreen we planted, used to jump over was now 15 feet tall. In fact, was still growing before my very eyes. We'd stand next to its short, fragrant needles, batter up in a game of Home Run Derby, stroking wiffleball blasts over the power line above the driveway. Everything was bigger now, the azaleas, pink beauty bush with its cascade of flowers, red *Weigelia*. Gone was the grass I had planted, now under the hemlocks, overrun by brown needles on a new forest floor. The redbrick walkway pushed up by oak tree roots, lustrous green moss in the joints. Crimson rose climbing the trellis outside the kitchen window, beaded drops left by the rain shower on waxy green leaves.

In this beautiful spring, rest was needed after the thousands of miles, unrelenting flashbacks triggered by regions, terrain, road centerlines, faces. *Last of the Mohicans* mutating to *Last of the Moccasins*, a 10 year countdown to this evening's event. Could those 10 years have been better used for a silent, frozen trip to Neptune? Looking at the powerline above, an attempted Zen breakthrough failed. Candidate truth: only one squirrel can walk a powerline through a given point at a given time. Tilt: everybody knows squirrels can be multiplexed. I fell asleep.

Being of the Me/Whatever Generation, no dress was prescribed, implied, or suggested by Your Reunion Committee. I wore Cowboys and Indians. The trademark Plains beaded buckskin jacket, artifact for *my* children to remember (now *there's* an assumption), black shirt, bolo, Hopi silver. NonNeptunian alien update ten years in the making, experimental probe roaring up to the country club set among the thick green hills beside the flowing waters, on the stroked Bonneville, doodah.

Lookin' for adventure, to protect the guilty and sue the innocent. But the truth be told, the "who and why", for the mythical Cindy Lambert Hollis. Aka Elle. That's right—Elle, French for "she", signeted -L- by her smart-art qualified girl-friends. Just a half-a-bet away from V. The "Guinnevere" of my little no act play written on the road to Laramie. In that duct-taped, pipewrenched, monumental work, finally *tu* instead of *elle*.

Ten years since I saw her in Mrs. Harkins' class, to my left—so close, less than ten feet away, but so far. "Loves all things *français*, artistic, CliffClan Tri-HiY" the yearbook said. Elle, indeed. Serene, undiscovered, running quietly with her art crowd, moving effortlessly into beauty, a woman's life of promise. Or so went the Major Myth I had created to override whatever her life might actually be.

Dreading the thought that she would be here paraded on the arm of a faceless corporate minion, lawyer, up and coming author, schmoozing with classmates with whom she had never hungout before. I was looking for her to be alone, with the same detached curiosity, unexplainable nonreason as mine: "Moody, individualistic, drives a Triumph, terrific musician … ." A miracle.

There we were in the yearbook, separated by too many pages, never together on a blanket with a six pack under the trees. Rarely a word in six years. We met at 12, left with no more than perfunctory contact by 18. Not even illusion, rather, an allusion—a passing, casual reference. With no denomi-nator in those days, what could I expect now, really, other than at best some-thing too simple like even division by six? Do remainders tell us the most about life?

Had I been recognized today as "Most _____" in the yearbook, it would have to be, "Most Desperate."

Phantoms of the road, broken glass of the Rez, nights too late, promises never made, unkept, unrealized. I couldn't love her, never knew, but wrote a song about her. A song I'm conspiring to do tonight. Or maybe not, instead wait until the 30th, when she has grandkids and both pushing 50, I tell her about how we should have gotten together 30 years ago, while she just looks at me first as if to say, and then does say:

> Elle: "Still out of it, I see. Get a grip."
> CMax: "Never a sucker for the truth."
> Elle: "Pay it no mind."
> CMax: "Want to dance anyhow?"

A Bent Wheat Lager would taste good about now, a hail of a brew. Should have stocked up that time for this trip I didn't know I'd be taking.

In the lobby was a Smokey the Bear sign, "Fire Danger Today". Though the needle was pointing to "Extreme", the night was looking like a rainout. Get a new forecast, Smokey.

Inside the room, I saw familiar faces, many with forgotten names. They were still settling in while I was settling out, my first career already over. You think that you haven't changed, everyone else has; that you're the same. Indulging in a lifelong fiction. Or worse, you don't think at all, and just settle out. To the bottom.

The word had gotten around that "the rock star" was planning to attend. A pummelling succession of articles in the entertainment section of the paper—"ESO Goes Platinum, Set for Another Summer Tour," "ESO Star Expected At Reunion"—had no doubt generated interest. And then there was the *New West Press* cover a month ago. Some teachers were apparently curious. Unguided guidance counselor, artless art instructor. A couple of reporters sought their angles, tired rewrites in templates of the "Local Business Update", "Happenings", "What's Hot". Thrown in with articles like, "Wireless Connector Demand Unlimited."

So far, the night wasn't even registering a reading. The ambiance inert as stripped linoleum.

Across the room, I saw a striking woman. Maybe Smokey was right. Lightning strikes start fires, too. A few years better looking than the other women, sort of familiar. Alone, it appeared. Could it be Miss (Emily) Ritchey, high school Math teacher? I made a note to put whoever she was on my dance card. In the absence of Elle, from those I could see, it would be the only name.

At the Queen it was 'Trane, tonight an oldies band to keep the Sixties straight, duplicated, unedited. The excitement of reminiscence, fatigue of actuality. An old friend, Cedar Log (Yearbook) Editor, talked me into sitting in with the band, for two songs—"When a Man Loves a Woman", followed by "Gimme Some Lovin". B-3 screaming, churning waves of harmonics, you want art, I'll give you art, how much art can you take? Sixties come and gone. Howdy Doody, radical liberation, Steal the Reunion! Thish numbazj for tha Aaamerican pebble. Take a hit!

I could think of some superior retrograde numbers: Bobby Taylor and the Vancouvers, Sam and Dave, Major Lance. "Does Your Mama Know About Me", "Fading Away", "You Don't Know Like I Know", "Monkey Time". Yeah. Curious why "Monkey Time" always pops up in the flashbacks. "Does Your Mama Know About Me" not so puzzling. Prudent. "… Does she know just who I am? … ."

Finally, a solo number at the piano, both song and piano smuggled in for the occasion.

"Here's a number for one of our classmates. In the great tradition of the reflective troubadour adrift, the music came to me in truck stops along the interstates (which we were travelling in unquestionable luxury), became a song written on a napkin." Duh. The way I talk when I have to forget who I am.

"In driving those highways, I thought of how we had been in years of classes together, but couldn't remember speaking with her. I know I'd like to talk to her now. But she's not here tonight. I guess it's a bittersweet memory, fitting lament for our 10th reunion."

"So here it is. You heard it first. The name of the song, and the lady, is 'Cindy'."

After the song, applause, and a bow, I walked over to get something to drink. One of Cindy's predecadian cohorts was there. I casually approached her, to field test both my version of the discreet inquiry, and peripheral vision. There were a lot of people I didn't care to "chat" with at the punch bowl. "Yes, yes, yes, California *is* an exciting place. Really? Really. Do you have a pen? Let me write that down."

"Cindy? She's trying to get over *Enough Love to Marry, Not Enough to Live On,* has a son, five. Living quietly on the other side of the Conodoguinet Creek. She would be shocked if you called. Maybe intimidated after you played the song. It was about *that* Cindy, wasn't it? You were always a mystery to her."

The hollowed out book, furtive glance. "Ssshhh," microclacked the Coquina Chorus. Asynoptic clues. At least I was a mystery. That was something.

14

Emily, random and imaginary variable

"You're Miss Ritchey. Craig Maxwell. Remember?" As if she would after ten years, give or take, but nevertheless delivered with aplomb, I thought. Possible alternate myth detected. Plan B strategy, configuring the reconnaissance, now in effect.

"Of course, I just heard you introduced before playing. Still a little slow on the uptake I see." So much for the supreme confidence, element of surprise. "Gimme Some Lovin'" could hardly have impressed her either. Conclusion? Embarrassed, but no way I'm going to let on.

"Never, with you helping me navigate those hard mathematical truths." I'll just advance a few equations, cross out a few terms, prove some theorems.

"That's some disguise, Craig. We've all read about it, but the reality is much more picturesque. Let me guess, you play lounges in Rapid City instead of the Motor City." Okay, if that's what you want. Whatever. That's our motto, you know. Back to the punch bowl or one more try?

"Guess I'd better stick to algebraic small talk at the t+10 boundary condition. With an absolutely stunning, but undefined variable, if you will, Miss Ritchey."

"It's Emily to you now. Ten years *have* gone by. During your energetic performance I checked the yearbook update, which says you went to Penn and got an engineering degree. You don't look like what I expected. Where's the slide rule? Moody and individualistic, okay, but where were you five years ago when I needed to escape from everybody and everything—my then husband, and even worse, the new crop of college graduates at the first five year version of tonight's frenzy of exhibitionism and exaggeration?"

In her statement were embedded two possibilities at the subatomic level: either I had reached the center of the universe and was to be granted all knowledge, great truth and wisdom, or I had taken the lure and was looking forward only to swimming side to side at the end of hightest line.

"On tour, passing through Kansas City with a real circus, believe me. But since then I've been able to make a few detours—a vision quest at Rocky Boy's, diving with the whales off Santa Barbara, an occasional jam on the border." Edge it back to the musical domain, as close to an extemporaneous Blue Note riff as I can get. She was, after all, *very* good looking. But then, so were Romy, Suzette, and Gita. Time to replace the toaster yet? Need a watch band?

"Why are you here, Emily, duty or string quartet out of town?" Going on the offensive now.

"Curiosity, for once to see somebody other than a wornout once-football player come back and impress us most of all." I recognized this to be other than a throwaway conversation; the punchbowl was way back, by now in another dimension.

"I'll make sure I don't impress you again. It won't be hard to not do. I caught myself counting terra cotta tiles today on a roof in Hershey, hopefully just road weary, not an important new activity. But let me take a few more turns toward the refrain of this expanding rondo, and get back on point, ask what I really want to know: are you in fact impressed by my one-time effort?"

"The night is still young. And was that an engineering or law degree?"

"I'll never tell. Wanna dance?"

"Sure, my feet are waiting to be stepped on."

"Not going to happen."

"What *is* going to happen?" The best question I couldn't answer all evening.

"As you said, the night's still young."

It was a slow number that could be played in any key, sung with any words in any year, for any occasion. "Why bother with stuff like that?" I thought.

The woman with whom I was dancing was another matter entirely. Ms. With Whom had both senses of humor and adventure.

"You want to banish mediocrity, get out of here? Hit Davenports for extra credit?" I asked. Light the fuse and find out to what it's connected?

"The get out of here part came to mind when you mentioned tile counting. Against my better judgment, sure. Could mean my career, but what the heck. Give me a few minutes to visibly become invisible. I came with another teacher; I'll tell her we're going. Shall we meet in front, at a tree on the golf course, in the gazebo, back at McDonalds?" Quick draw. Lightning quick.

"At the front door, obvious and in color. We're both dissenting adults. Go ahead and give them something to talk about for the *next* five or ten years." I was still talking to myself about that slow dance.

At t+5 I fired up the Triumph as Miss Ritchey walked through the door, flashed a whimsical smile to die for, gathered up her dress, and got on the back. The making of real-time legends, if there were legends to be made, not the once or future ones of high school any more. In this simulation, it would be critically important to stay clear of the chain, keep those stockings away from the tailpipes. Make sure the fuse kept burning cleanly, not skipping to an untimely detonation.

There were several couples at the door catching air. By the look of things, all they needed were a Frisbee and dog. It wouldn't take long for the story to spread inside. This was, after all, a high school thing, and there was that Fire Danger Today.

"You got shades, too?" There were obviously other forces at play here, way beyond third period.

"Of course." A little dim going down Market Street through Camp Hill. The latest in bizarre evenings, my teacher Ten Years After with her arms around me, on the Bonneville trick enough for Ascot, California plate, wind rushing by. There was probably a mathematical expression for it. A smoothly intuitive, spare proof involving powers of 10. I liked it, looked forward to the research.

Speaking of trees, I remembered the big one with the park bench under it, before the slight turn in the road. Other summer nights with Susans and Mary-Anns, never an Emily. Suddenly, it was important that we stop: the ambient sightseeing in a potential energy state, that is. Check our parameters before the growing possibility of an upcoming steep downgrade of impulse, redirected momentum.

Without a word I pulled over, silenced the bike, kicked it onto the stand with my pointy boots. Gently drawing her to me, I saw a look of flushed surprise, then was lost in those mathematical lips, sweet in the darkness. A wonderful moment of tenderness and fire, anything and everything. Leaving us breathless. What was that? We both shivered, hit by lightning unleashed from clouds full of energy, crackling dances of the generations, cloudbursts, found streams. "Extreme" didn't even begin to describe the susceptibility of this forest to igniting.

"I had no right to do that," I said, gasping, surprisingly nervous in the confusion, trying to figure out what a kiss even was. As if it was my first.

She could have slapped me, demanded to be taken home, or just laughed, wordlessly communicating, "you jerk." Not this night, for some unexplainable reason happening at all after the ten year time suspension. Not after that kiss. It wasn't *all* lust.

"I'm not that easy, Craig Maxwell," Emily replied. Then, after a pause, "but I'm willing to call it spontaneous combustion. While the next time may not be as spontaneous, I'll look forward to the combustion."

We looked at each other wide eyed and dead serious, still nervous, speaking for myself, then both of us started laughing. Howling until we could only sit on the bench, doubled over, wiping away tears from our eyes. So much for the games. Wait a minute. She had said, "… the next time."

What was clearly now a dance of another kind continued as we crossed the Susquehanna bridge, roared up to Dav's, on Market Square. An all-night restaurant with the stainless, glass and tile automat look where Marco and I used to hang out after gigs, during Christmas vacations in the college years, mod to soul to rebellion to disco to jazz. Repellant for the Polynesian lounges, tikis, sweet tropical drinks served by the SDS—not Students for a Democratic Society, but the Slavic Daughters of Steelworkers. What used to be "collegent" had, on the surface, morphed to the Bee Gees, but never quite lost the Tommy James and the Shondells underpinning, judging from the flared pants and highrise manifolds in the parking lot. And of course I blended right in, with the Plains Indian garb, Hopi silver.

"I heard talk about the *New West Press* story. Apparently you're not touring, what are you really doing?"

"A different tour, my own Long Walk. Preparing for snow, high mountain passes which may claim me, but inevitably cleanse and strengthen, in this life or the next. So says the Teton elder.

"As for you, we'll do some *NY Times Magazine* black & white shots, though without the Absolut vodka or Blackglama furs." What *does* become a legend most? "Don't smile and get me started laughing again. Keep it cool and mysterious. This is serious." Of course, just saying that got us going, and I was lucky not to knock over the coffee.

Finally settling down, I picked up the Leica M-4 I had brought and squeezed off a few Tri-X frames in the style of Henri Rousseau. Henri Bresson, I mean. Another oops. Henri "Rocket" Richard. A double minor—two minutes for cross-checking, two minutes for unsportsmanlike conduct. Ten minute misconduct for confusion.

It was impossible to be anonymous tonight with the officially unusual, trademark garb, Hopi tank logo and California plate, sparkling woman in her party dress. A girl came up and asked, "aren't you … ? Can I have your autograph?"

"Yes, but more importantly, this is Emily, my high school math teacher, if you can believe that! We're hard at work solving quadratic equations with imaginary roots, the statics and dynamics of free-body diagrams!"

"Don't mind him. A real problem student who's managed to fail every meaningful test so far, with only the final exam remaining for redemption. Famous, but questionable whether he'll pass. The course that is!"

Giggling. I liked that in a woman over thirty as long as it wasn't continuous, and the subject was actually funny. Even better if her IQ was in triple figures.

"My friends won't believe this!" Go tell them. Put it on the radio. Riot, trash the city.

I wanted to sit there and appreciate Emily a bit longer, but our exit cue had been delivered. Followed out by several high school couples, I started the Triumph, then looked around to make sure Emily was on, seeing the subtle shine of her stocking above her shoe on the right footpeg. It's always about the key details.

Roaring away again, an infrequent Golden State plate sighting on Market Square, a few minutes later I suggested we get a blanket and watch the river lights from the bluff over in East Pennsboro. "That would be nice," was all she said, smiling, while I thought, "what am I dealing with here? This is unbelievable!"

I know, I'm inclined to make a serious move on every woman with whom I raise the stakes by sharing a blanket under the stars. For once, would it be possible to back off and simply enjoy the evening? Or was that impossible, cut out of the shuffle, leaving only repetitive, nostalgic high school simulations? Another of those one night stands which should have been left behind long ago with the VFW's, Legions, firehalls, and community center dance dates with the SoleCeramics, I mean Soulsations, our band in high school?

At 2 am, I took Emily back to her house in Shiremanstown, we said good-night, and I promised to call. Went home still breathing more heavily than usual, trying to get my heart rate down by doing some tracks in the GMC until first light. As I played, I wondered what Emily might have thought before the reunion. Another party to be endured? Curiosity about a now famous graduate? Curiosity about others?

Pointless conjecture. I'll just ask her sometime. Would she show any of *her* cards? Make no mistake, anyway you look at it, she has a strong hand. Would she even answer? Was she sleeping soundly now, or wide awake, playing back the evening, time and time again like I was?

Crashed at dawn, up around noon. My mother asked about the reunion, and I related an edited, though schematically accurate, recount of the night's events, including the getaway with a certain former teacher.

"It's not like that, Mom." Pretending to be real will get you into trouble every time.

She didn't have much to say to her 27 year old Ivy League graduate engineer, motorcycle riding, footloose ex-rock star of a son. Less disapproval than fatigue?

Weary at noon? Is this what I've got to look forward to? There has to be more to life than, "lunch is ready."

I shamelessly reflected, in retail, on the riddle of Cindy, as "Emily has green eyes, like yours, lady, like yours ..." looped through my consciousness. Other Crosby & Nash stuff too, played in midnight darkness once upon a time, approaching Death Valley, antipolar to this CPA scene. Was it "Where's Cindy", or "Here's Emily"?

Mom said something most of which I missed, but left me with the bottom line drift: "... even though you're famous, we're still going to take you for granted, and keep you in your place."

"If you only knew," I thought.

What was scary was that they might know, and I was the one who didn't. Thirty if I ever stopped to blink my eyes, still trying to figure out what seemed to be the most basic whats and whys.

15

A longshot,
out Orrs Bridge Road

Cindy was a graphic artist who now worked at home, a restored school house, living with her five year old. Out Orrs Bridge Road. I looked up her number in the phone book, "C Hollis, 13847 Orrs Bridge Rd, Camp Hill." Thought the numbers only ran that high in California. They're catching up here, which may not be a good thing.

I've come over 2000 miles to talk to her, and that's what I'm going to do.

"Cindy Hollis."

"Cindy, this is Craig Maxwell. I looked for you last night at the reunion, but you weren't there."

"Was this before you rode off with Miss Ritchey?"

Uhh. This would take quick thinking.

"I'm shocked at such a rumor, even more that one so true would be repeated. Where did you hear *that*?" The cagey Bear's SmokeJumping grapevine again. Favors for honey.

"You were talking to Debbie. She called this morning to relate the night's thrilling events, at least those which were public. Miss Ritchey's got a reputation, you know."

Okay, a Cartesian aside. I'd better graph this one x-y. It's ten years later, and we're talking about reputations—among whom? How much of a reputation could anyone have in this place and still keep a teaching job? How would a "reputation" be communicated? Does the Reputation Club get together every Wednesday night for drinks and breaded ham cutlets at the Dutch Pantry? Just passing questions. Reputation—'nother whole dimension in a window viewed at an extreme, a few degrees from no reflection at all. But hold the cross-examination; I've got an aplanatic agenda here.

"Don't we all. Miss Ritchey and I went over to Davenports for a cup of coffee. It's not everyday you get to take out your math teacher." Not everyday you want to even talk with, much less take her out, that's for sure.

"I wouldn't know. So why are you calling me?"

"Because in six years of school, the same classes, I never got to know you. But every time I reflect on those years, I think about how much I would have liked to."

"I don't think of those years very often. Why would I?"

"Curiosity?"

"I guess I'm not very curious. I've got my own life here with my son, a quiet life. About the wildest I get is too much of a special Bordeaux once in a great while. Nothing dramatic enough or of interest to a rock 'n roll star, I guess that's what you are, who just rode off with our 10th grade math teacher."

"Call it my artistic side; moody, individualistic."

"Still hung up on the yearbook? Not much to go on there. Listen, I've got to get back to work. Bye."

What *did* I expect? There was that reference to the yearbook though. No catch, but a bite just the same. It had not been a totally cold call. Either Cindy had a photographic memory, a possibility, or she had looked me up in the yearbook within the last few hours. Maybe even written it on her palm with a ballpoint pen, waiting for my call. Put Mason on retainer, at least one of us will be needing legal representation, and I want the best. I expect nothing short of the charges being dropped with profuse apologies; at the least, a very favorable, socio-lucrative judgment.

Later in the afternoon Mom and I went down to the Farmers Market, shopping for fresh local produce, baked goods, deli meats and cheeses. It was a middle/upper middle class (mupper) tradition, strolling among the white-washed booths of the Amish purveyors, worn concrete aisles, low timber-framed ceilings. So who do we bump into, but Cindy? The ten years looked good on her as well. Guess I'm moving into my knowledgeably appreciative phase.

"Hi, Cindy. Mom, this is Cindy Hollis. We were in the same class in high school."

"I don't believe this—what a coincidence," Cindy said.

"You've both been out of high school for ten years, and Craig has been gone nearly all of them. That would make it a coincidence," Mom observed, sensing more here than met the eye, while accurately reciting her lines for a day's screen extra pay, not knowing how the plot fit together.

Unusually fast on my feet, I offered, "Coincidentally, how about meeting me at the Coffee Place in Camp Hill, in a half-hour. I'd be interested in your views on last night's reunion."

"I wasn't there."

The Wyoming fortune cookie had been dead-on. I was treading water in this sea of nuances, vignettes populated by all elasmobranches of the shark family.

"Well if you'd like to invent some, I'll be at the Coffee Place at 4:30. Nice seeing you, Cindy," as we strolled off. "Nice seeing you," I could hear Cindy singsonging in her mind as I genially smiled at her again before signoff. Rugged, sensitive man that I am.

"She's good looking—don't think I've ever heard of her. Doesn't seem very happy though," Mom said.

"I agree with the good looking part. Possibly seeing her did play a part in deciding to attend the reunion, although after ten years, it was definitely a long shot. As for the rest, I don't really know." Master of the understatement, "possibly."

I asked Mom to drop me off at the Coffee Place, which meant that if Cindy didn't show, then drive me home, I'd have to walk or take a cab. Not a big deal, though, since it was only a couple of miles from the house. On the way, we passed the tree where Emily and I had pulled over last night to practice losing our breath together. It reminded me that I needed to call her right now.

I was on the phone when Cindy walked in. "OK, talk to you later tonight," I said, while Cindy stood close by, uncomfortably scanning the list of coffees on the wall. We got a table and sat down.

"Let me guess. What did Miss Ritchey have to say to the rock 'n roll star so obviously poised to sweep her off her feet?" Sobviously. Good word, meaning, "cryingly evident." A rare one to trade.

Mercilessly delivered by another very quick on her own feet. Mistress of the direct statement. A big one in the strength plus column. Ever think of becoming a prosecutor? I need Mason right here. Now. A surprising turn in the case. She's Berger's daughter!

"She said okay, talk to you later."

"Craig, what are we doing—why did you want to see me after all this time? I don't know you or anything beyond what I see in the paper once in awhile."

Not obvious or anything. To tell you about Nail Haven, West Texas, endangered coastal species, haiku, and Hopis. Because you're the One and Only Elle!

"Well, I'm on my best behavior, earnestly wanting to get to know *the* hometown girl. Anything other than wrecking rooms in a downtown hotel—it gets so old." Wonder what, if anything, she'll say about "girl"?

"Let's get a cappuccino and talk about it, Cindy. Cappuccino okay with you?"

Looking for, then of necessity assuming a nod, I went to the counter to order, returned and asked her about the last ten years. Please limit updates to twenty-five words or less. Guess the "girl" thing isn't going to come up.

"The biggest thing, and hardest, was when my mother died three years ago after a painful, extended illness. Why do people say things like, 'she died early,' but never, 'she hung on too long?' Anyhow, it was hard, knowing that my son wouldn't know his grandmother. I was three years out of art school when she got sick. At least we had moved back here, and were around. My father hasn't gotten over it yet, and probably never will."

"How about school, Cindy—I don't recall where you went." My attention was on other things during high school, few of which related to anyone else.

Cindy continued, "Philadelphia College of Art, really liked it—so different from Harrisburg in the city, but still close enough to come back. I met my husband there through my roommate's brother. He went to Haverford. We were married after graduation, went to France for the summer, and took a cottage on the Main Line."

France. Why wasn't that surprising? I wouldn't be needing Paul Drake any longer on this case. Better hold onto Mason for the time being, though, there could be unanticipated future fallout.

"I was hustling graphic design in a very competitive market, while he commuted to his father's brokerage in the City. Jed was born a year later, after which I began to rapidly descend into the role of the suburbanite society wife whose principal activity consisted of making sure the flowers in the foyer were arranged. That the gourmet dinner was on the table when my husband arrived tired from the City, trying to unwind, but neither knowing what that meant, nor able to do so.

"As much as I couldn't stand it, my husband, Andrew, really didn't under-stand why. Life on the Main Line, ski holidays somewhere in Europe, depending upon the crowd, old or new money. Supposedly leisure for women, a blessing. Anyone with a spark of life left in them knows it's not enough. That might have worked in the 50's, not necessarily happily, but couldn't in the 70's. It lasted two and a half years, and I came back here."

"Cindy, an artist with edges. Aesthetics and temperament. Counter-pointed by a graceful curve here and there, too, if I may say so, strictly in the interest of art appreciation."

"Don't go there, Craig." A long pause while she decided what action to take.

She didn't walk out. "So there you are, ten years. I'm living in my school house, still hustling for work, and banking every cent of child support for Jed when he's on his own, out in the world. Time passes so quickly now." She was describing a paradox I've observed too—each day is an eternity, but the years fly by.

Child support. Property settlement. Entitled to. Until the age of. Redress. Garnishment. All ominous, nonparadoxical legal terms.

"I'm as intrigued as I was when I decided to come back here for the reunion. I admit, only to see you."

"That *might* have been flattering, if not for the evidence, recent and other-wise, of a womanizer from way back with everybody but me who coincidentally rode off with our math teacher last night.

"A man of whom I know little, and frankly question whether I'm interested in knowing anything about, calls me after 10 years in some kind of high school date warp, and asks, 'how it's going?' I don't know anything about your rock 'n roll world. My life is about heart, truth, love for my child. Art and surviving."

How most women (as distinct from "girls"?) start out wanting to see life? Debatable. Ask me what I think last, after all the bro's have boldly offered their improbable theories. When the oil's been changed, car's off the shopjack, pizza 'n Bud are on order, and keglers rolling the first game on freshly waxed lanes. As usual, more questions than answers.

"Very well put. I can't argue with that, Cindy. Before writing me off on the basis of who you think I am, though, why don't you give me a chance to *show* you who I really am."

Did I really say that? Talk about a severe challenge, at the very least. More likely real trouble, rocks falling from an unseen ledge, higher than the one I call home. Creative self-incrimination.

But what was that she said about "a womanizer … with everybody but me?" Was there some resentment in it which I could now rectify? An opportunity for swashbuckling romanticism?

Nah. Had to be only a figure of speech.

Though it is true that we are who we say, it is even truer that none say who they are. With me, what you see is what you get. What you don't get is who I don't let you see.

That just about covers it.

16

Trout, but not from this river

Dusk in the Susquehanna Valley, late spring. Smooth and comfortable before the humidity that builds in the summer. Coming from Southern California, the land and sky are so dense, the towns quaint, ornate. Timothy grass growing tall, full trees. Quiet. In the burgs and villes families sit on porches with white wooden columns in the falling darkness, watching an occasional passing car.

Slack time before the drinking starts or intensifies. But most of those stories are for another volume, running the gamut from teenage explorations to darker chapters of anger and violence. There are exceptions, like the one about Sandy which comes to mind, rich as shavings from a gold-wrapped chocolate bar. Lipstick I can still taste, eyes sparkling in the moonlight. Yeah, that's right. Eyes, moonlight. In the days when lips were fresh, eager, freely offered, didn't have to be rescued from anyone or anything. I wouldn't trade that memory, not even for a couple quarts of Schmidts. On second thought, bring me an inner tube big enough for two to float the Creek of New Experiences, and we'll talk.

Jed was staying over at a nearby friend's so Cindy had a rare evening to herself, and unexplainedly, agreed to spend it with me. An Elle date! In a manner yet to be completely revealed, the planets appeared to be aligned. The making of folklore.

There was little chance of running into Dexter Gordon at the Coffee Place in Camp Hill, the sprint car races at The Grove were last night, and I was resolved to fight off the attack of the tiki gardens with every available weapon. An alternate campaign was called for—dinner at a new place Cindy had heard about up on North Front Street in Harrisburg. The same river lights, tonight from the reverse viewpoint. Cindy said she'd pick me up two hours later, Peugeot of course, and bring jeans and a top so we could go for a ride on the bike after dinner.

I walked the two miles home and let my parents know I would be going out. Mom wasn't surprised. Crossing my fingers and mindful of "family obligations", I called Emily, suggesting we go to a movie tomorrow evening at the Uptown. Reservation confirmed for that Sunday Nite-Flite.

Cindy came to the door to pick me up, looking superb in a summer dress. Don't ask me what defines a "summer dress", but I know one when I see it. This was a woman who took care of herself, understating some features, with accoutrements accenting others. Her nails were done just right, contrasting with the pearly lipstick and miniature rose earrings. Headed into the prime of life with a complete tool kit. Don't get me started on Sandy's again, this is about tonight's fresh lipstick.

After making small talk with my parents for a few minutes, we hit the road. Surrobviously, they weren't used to dates coming by, and didn't quite know what to say. Surrobviously—abstractly though nonterrestrially evident. Since Cindy was driving, it would be a much longer, depressing cab drive from North Front if I stepped out of line. The only consequence remotely dramatic I could come up with to emphasize the triumph this Coup de Cindy really was.

We had trout, thankfully from other than the murky river a block over. Domestic, not Mexican. Cindy told me tales of happiness and heartache, some of which were grounded to her mother, while I confided my life of occupational technology and detachment, tempered with relationships, some still active, but none of which, obviously, had so far progressed to anything approaching exclusive, forever. From the mystery man to civics and current affairs. Admissions from a reg'lar double dealing joe. From The Polynomial State. *From Russia With Love.*

She listened, but didn't say much about the confidences I selectively related, nor that much about hers. The sense I got was that there wasn't much to tell about. College, marriage, divorce, work, silence. If she had any interest in me, considerable effort and patience would be needed to find out where common ground might exist. For someone to be with Cindy, going in it wouldn't be about comfort, destinations, seduction. It would be about respect, heart, compromise, and survival. Or it wouldn't be at all.

In other words, I would be foolish to read too much into tonight. To read *anything* into it, actually.

Then again, I wondered—is that a special summer dress? She is a woman and where there's a heart must be a capacity, longing for love. This myth went way back. Aren't all myths obsessive? Suppose it *is* a special dress. That there's more to the exquisite smoothness of her back than quality, degree. That she's emphasizing those smooth lines, reinforcing them with the dress. Conclusion: she knows how to wear a dress, that's all; by no definition could "us" exist at this point.

Wake up. We're here, but "She's Not There".

We walked along the river after dinner, crossed over to the brick sidewalk in front of the old homes and limestone row-buildings converted to offices, flowers in bloom, dogwood. I thought about the ride the other night to the old bridge across the Yellow Breeches Creek at Lisburn. Moving, always in motion. A trail of affairs so open ended as to be diffused into nothing at all. Knowing that what starts as intrigue, to be sustained and become valuable, must eventually be about giving, acceptance, even of pain, and forgiveness. In as many words, what Cindy had said.

"I assume that was your vehicle parked at your parents' house." The California plates might have been the tipoff. "You training to be a bus driver?"

"Outfitted for every contingency. NASA technology working to assure an unforgettable vacation getaway. I'm sure you can relate to having the tools in remote places to do your art. Painting, composing, or the night's last howl in the Mojave as the sun comes up, ritually strong *Caffe Combate* made in the dark, jolting the world awake. When at six in the morning, you've already been up for days.

"I'll show you the RV. Then we'll take the Triumph out for that night ride in the country."

She said little on the way back, smiled and half closed her eyes when I put on a tape in the rig for background ambience, Eno's "Music for Airports", intently studied the black & white photos pushpinned to the corkboard on the wall above the stove, among a few business cards and letters.

"Check this out—I'm going to turn off the lights for a moment, then you can change and we'll go." On the ceiling, the luminous stars shone, my own night sky. Kat's Navajo story, the mythology behind what had been a perfect evening under real stars, came back strongly, suggestively. Very recent mythology, equal to any in all creation.

Standing on the horizon, stars streaming overhead, waves of stars, fast then slow. I'm in motion, tracing a different oscillation. There must be a place where I can see the stars like that—in Canada, the Arctic, Chile. A pipeline of stars, wall of glowing star stuff, flowing, bent upon itself as light under an intense magnetic field. Resonant deflection, streaming photons. Eons beyond 2001.

And then silence.

Cindy was close. We were both aware of it. She wore a hint of perfume, reminding me of Santa Barbara jasmine, the gardenia fragrance of Old Naples, Florida. Her ear would be a great place to start incredible explorations of what I thought had to be little-mapped terrain.

I waited outside under a different sky as she changed, one infinitely larger than my imagination but no more valuable, caught again in the moment by Kat, Santa Barbara. The rasp of performance-tuned custom exhausts brought me back as I kicked over the bike.

This was as much or more fantasy as reality. I was getting lost in the here and now, with a woman I never knew, but had thought about for years. A woman who didn't seem lost at all. Hair tied back, right hand on my shoulder as she got on the bike, sat holding onto me. Turning around, I couldn't help putting my cheek to hers for the shortest of moments, "hold on." In that moment, I was again captured by the fragrance behind her ear. Umm. Cindy Hollis. After all these years. The wait had been worth it. I would have blown it then, we wouldn't be here now.

Next stop, Westward Look? Copper Queen? A room in Ft. Collins? Float down the Creek, moonlight swim at the dam?

We moved into the summer night which got darker as the lights of Camp Hill were left behind, then eased along the winding Yellow Breeches.

When we got to the bridge, I pulled halfway across on the walkway which was separated from the narrow travel lanes by a massive, timber barrier. It took a few minutes to be able to hear the flow beneath us after the roar of the Triumph. We sat on the rail and talked about high school experiences, this place where we both had grown up, left, and to which we had returned. Tonight.

"The West is where I live, the wide open spaces my home. I need more and more as time goes on, to be farther from the big cities. Back here, it's compact, life has an entirely different scale. How about you—staying for the long term, art, galleries, museums, a trip to Europe once in awhile?"

"I can get the *Times*, take the train to Philadelphia, drive down to the National Gallery. Even so, the best part is coming back to my school house. For now, it's just right."

"I'd like to see it some time. I wonder why I didn't get to know you during high school—all those years."

"You know the reasons—weren't interested, weren't paying attention to our folksy little group, whatever. Those years and most of what happened or didn't happen have been scattered. Only a few of us are left around here."

"I was playing gigs on weekends and running after the Camp Hill girls. Each of them had a gladiator boyfriend and a multitude of ex-boyfriends; none ever left the scene, always lurking about, ready to deck intruders. Although there were enough capers to make high school memorable, still, when I really began noticing you, seeing you those last few weeks, it was too confusing, too late. We were graduating, going different ways, embarking upon a ten year sentence in a no security institution. The World, with a reporting date in the Summer of Love. So, I grabbed one of those Camp Hill girls, had a great summer of rock 'n roll gigs and intoxicating nights, literally and figuratively, in our favorite orchard. Lost track of you completely, I'm sorry to say."

"You going to tell me the details of the orchard now?"

"I don't think so."

I flashed on Natalie, the Camp Hill girl. "I knew a girl who bent her knee that way, swayed gently to the music I played, eyes closed … ." And thought for a moment about how in my life with each year there seemed to be fewer and fewer places I wanted to be. About which direction the floor turns when you're lying on it drunk as a sailor in the Southern Hemisphere, looking to fight every Kiwi who tries to help you up. About whether the world really was more secure when I was pulling on Turkish Taffy at the New Cumberland Theater in ninth grade. Where was Cindy when I was at that movie, the world unfolding in rock 'n roll, clockwise before me? Anxiety, but not yet my "19th Nervous Breakdown". Knowing that Cindy was of the Peter, Paul, and Mary, Joni Mitchell, Lovin' Spoonful genre, visual and dramatic art, and all.

In the darkness, the stream rippled, over smooth stones, so smooth I could imagine the feel of them up here on the bottoms of my feet, beneath overhanging trees, green after the ripping slabs of winter ice, roar of floods, year after year.

"The Camp Hill girl was Natalie Groves, wasn't she?" Cindy asked.

"Y … yes. How did you know?" I replied, thunderstruck.

"I knew," Cindy said quietly. "I knew. We all knew, saw you with her in your car. I always thought you looked happy together, as good for each other as anyone could in high school. I wanted to be happy like that."

"Such a long time ago. A long time," was all I could say.

It was getting late, but the Coffee Place was still open for another hour. I talked her into closing it down. If you need sleep, have an espresso; if you need to stay awake, have an espresso. That Beatles song, "All you need is joe … all you need is joe." Reg'lar joe, as you already know.

When we got there, Cindy asked Tom, the owner, to put on an ESO tape from his extensive archive of sounds, ranging from *Music for Hockey Violence* to the Genetics' *Resplicing the Helix*. Of course, the ESO album started with "Comin' Back for Java", an anthem of sorts for those in the bohemian cafe trade. Rocket attacking the changes with his Les Paul axe, probably in Denver right now, hitting them again, the screaming still going on.

"This is you? I've heard it, but never payed much attention to rock 'n roll. I can picture you writing it, though. Music that twists and builds. Are you building or unwinding right now?"

"You got the physics right—torsion, energy released in a frenzy of bad boy-art girl lament."

"That's certainly a line worthy of a delusional musician only passin' through. What was your yearbook entry again?"

"A great romantic who never got started. Singing cowboy who's never had a horse. Will love for spare feed."

"What are you offering me tonight other than surreal conversation?" Cindy asked.

"If I had a sketchbook, I'd write you a verse, pencil the cascade of your beautiful hair, the moonlit shadow of your cheek. The Sioux elder would chant, his song power a much different dance. I'd lean over and taste your lips, find currents, float together down the River of Life. I'd see you in silhouette, in shade. Everything you are, all of you I could find would be mine to love, every thought that you crave we'd share. I'd search for you and never be still for the lifetime it would take. I'd love you so much we would be wordless, could only cry out from the deepest passion of our souls in the incomparable silence between us. Without you, there would be only emptiness."

In that moment, I meant it. Moments that get you into trouble when they're over; add dependents to your tax return.

She just looked at me, shuddered, startled. Eyes wide. I could hear her thinking, "Who *is* this guy?" It was a short ride back home.

"Cindy, thank you for tonight." Anti-climax. An understatement. Thank you for working on my car. How much do I owe you for the new wiper blades?

She didn't, couldn't say much as I outlined, "I'm planning on leaving Tuesday, going up through Michigan to the Upper Peninsula, then heading west to Montana. I've been thinking of going back to school to get a music degree at the University of Wyoming, in Laramie, if you can believe that. The discipline would be good for me, in a place where the sky is huge, there are fewer distractions of what the world I've been in self-considers to be hip beyond all measure.

"I'm going to a movie with Emily Ritchey tomorrow night, but I'd like to call you late in the afternoon, to say hi. I'd like to meet your son before I leave town."

"I had a good time. That was quite an argument struck for romantic abandon. Did you mean it?"

"In the dangerous seduction of that instant, yes."

Quiet for a minute.

"Cindy, I'd like to kiss you goodnight, for tonight, and all those years before."

"You're leaving Tuesday, going out with Miss Ritchey tomorrow night, and you want to kiss me? I'll have to think about that one some more … it's not something I take lightly."

"Our own little secret. Either to start or end a spell."

"I'm not ready for this, Craig, any of it."

"You need to let someone be interested in you, care about you."

"I know, but it's hard. It's hard."

"Come here, Cindy."

"Okay," she said quietly, no doubt reluctantly.

Another fortune cookie message unfolded, "Love is like dough." Way open to interpretation.

The momentum had shifted, was no longer about words.

We were all carrying around our world-past. Cathy less so, since she was embarking on creating hers. Kat's years in Chinle. Emily's years of school. Marriages that didn't work. Currents that ran through kisses, some familiar, others streams I knew nothing about, might never know. In my mind, I looked out from the headland above the Navarro River, its flow disappearing into the Pacific, off a shore of great redwood logs thrown about by the churning ocean. To be there was to experience uneasy awe.

Locally, momentum was conserved. Reset and redefined by a kiss, physics intact. More than a decade overdue. In the background, the roar and seething salt mists of crashing waves. Awe, awe, awe, awe ... hhheeeyyy, hey!

"Cindy, you look great tonight. I'm honored to have been with you. It's been a wonderful evening. Goodnight."

"Thank you, Craig. Goodnight," she said, giving my hand a slight squeeze before letting go. Turning with her own version of the woman's wistful look, walking away.

The kiss had been a diamond sifted from the black sands of time, twenty million years in the making. Well worth the relatively momentary, ten year wait.

17

Day dreaming in
Lebanonbaloneyshooflypieland

I slept late, awoke to a cooler day that promised rain, opened the window wider, lay back, relaxed. The seventh day. Usually no running on Sundays, although I had made an exception a week ago. Bisbee?

Reviewing the events of the last months, I thought of dropping out even more dramatically, playing crossroads bars with red and green asphalt checkerboard sides in unnamed Kansas towns; holing up in the Bitterroots; building a house on five acres in Sea Ranch and living there only in the foggy times of year. Realizing, as always, that when so close to The City, it would find me.

Gimme strong coffee. I've got to rework this coda.

I didn't have to wait any longer, I needed to jump into something with both feet. I could even play a passable rhythm guitar and sing Country & Western for diversion, a good time. The two year MFA program at Wyoming would provide structure, something I knew I could do, wanted to do. Playing C&W at the Spur, Watering Hole, Aces High to unwind, while those George Jones pretenders from the plains cut mechanical two-steps with their Saturday nightingales, women who could drive a herd, bale hay, lay pipe, handle a big wrench, a horse trailer. Expertly wear boot-cut jeans. Like Cathy.

Daydreaming here in Lebanonbaloneyshooflypieland, slowflow of another afternoon. After you've hit the spots once, what's next? Buy a house and drive the Carlisle Pike forever, increasingly colonially? Answer: an art movie with subtitles at the Uptown. It couldn't be any stranger than the weekend in DC last year on tour. That we won't go into.

I made two calls, the first to Cindy. The second to a woman met in Portugal.

"I know you said you'd call this afternoon, but why are you calling this afternoon?" she asked.

What did I say about the "Enigma Variations"?

"I couldn't sleep at first, but then fell asleep trying to stay awake. Perhaps a *déjà vu* exercise, to emulate Sunday afternoons like I did in high school—repair serious damage, gracefully bow out, apologize, follow up a promising lead for a date with the latest girl from the Saturday night gig, you name it. But actually, because yesterday was Getting to Know Cindy, the Introduction. I'd like to talk about Chapter 1."

"And how do you think *that* chapter might start?"

"The story's being written as we speak; the end is undetermined."

"I asked about the start, not the end. Is that what's on your mind?" Caution; second thoughts about anything, everything.

"I'm hoping that you'll shrug off your responsibility to support yourself for one day, we'll take Jed to the State Museum Monday, then have lunch downtown."

"I'll have to stay up late on Monday night to finish a job due Tuesday. I think it will work, but I'm still asking myself why … ." I guess she kissed me back only because I really wanted to kiss her. Being nice, despite her better instincts.

"Around 12:30 on Monday." Deal.

First ball in the air, a second one to juggle. Long distance to Lisbon. Thriving in complications. The complexity of hairstyles and lipsticks. Portuguese language, old planes, foreign intrigue. Heavily armed authorities arriving before my getaway car.

Smokescreen. Only a smokescreen.

I called Emily and suggested that because of the rain, she pick me up at about 7:30. Could have used my folks' car, but having her come around did have an appealing element of family maneuvering to it. Keep them guessing.

Aside in the kitchen, Mom remarked, "She's a few years older, isn't she? Another good looking one. Seems to be smart, happy." Maybe those comments were what I was really looking for.

We all sat under the overhang on the patio for a few minutes, listening to the falling rain, small talk. I wondered whether there was any escape from this reshuffled chitchat of the generations, roles long ago defined, not a new dance to be found. I knew plenty of rockers, up or down, who were still abusing room service, jumping off balconies into shallow pools trying to figure it out.

Having once again evaded a game of bridge, I steered us out the door to Emily's mathematical Porsche. A 924, entirely satisfactory and impressive now that I think of it, for this 30's something pi-r-squared gender rep, alas, unfortunately adrift in the uniformly acculturizing milieu of CPA. Her statement. Little wonder that she would want to ride off on a Triumph, if even for one night with a former student who was hardly Marlon Brando or James Dean. Not a Harley 74 in sight.

"So what did you do yesterday?" she asked. A simple opening question, now that we're alone. To me it might seem to have the drama of Beethoven's *Fifth*, but the composer had marked it to be played *piano*.

You could never tell. I knew that there was a whole lot more to Emily Ritchey than a simple question seemingly inviting an equally simple response.

Just getting things going? Prompting me to spin stories like a tropical cyclone. Typhoon Bubba.

"Slept in, and shopped the Farmers Market, where I ran into Cindy Hollis. Do you remember her?"

Disclosure, but did I have an agenda here? Competition? Kind of thinking out loud, I guess, usually a recipe for eventual failure.

Emily paused for a minute, said that she thought so, but only vaguely. A ten year parade of too many changing faces, when bobby sox disappeared for good, lost with other garments, devices, and artifices to the tides of the '68 Convention, return of Nixon, Three Dog Night, the Eagles, gas shortages, and Bicentennial celebrating how much fun we were having in what Miller accurately described as *The Air Conditioned Nightmare*.

"Well, I won't be so insensitive as to talk about another woman, even if it was nothing more than returning and seeing the sights after ten years. Like the Statue of Liberty. Anyhow, that was my yesterday. What was yours?" I asked, innocently disingenuous.

"I'm anxiously waiting to hear about more of your sightseeing," she teased. "I know how to do that, too."

Playful pause, with one of those "you can't fool me" looks. What did she mean about the second part?

"Okay, Craig, I'll let you off the hook. A friend and I couldn't resist opening the Hershey Park arcade season. Those old machines are great, and if you know something about mathematical probabilities, well then … ."

"In contrast to what other kind of probability?" And what kind of friend?

The probability of finding out who you are, for one. If you look outside … the arcade. I got the laugh, but not the reply.

She just looked at me after that laugh and smiled. "How about if we pull over, and consider your question a little more closely." Which she did, followed by five minutes of shameless tactical skirmishing in a no parking zone along North Second Street. Her call, she was driving. I had wanted to get out and visit Mr. Puffy Wrestling Supply while we were in the neighborhood, but missed him.

The interlude was a surprising gesture, what I saw in her eyes more than "I'll see your Friday night advance and raise you one." Emily had a likable, straight ahead style, yet I wondered about the other side of being divorced, ten years into teaching school, appearances to maintain, looking for Mr. Right instead of Mr. Puffy, admitting it or not. And why she would want to waste her time with me, given my style, which was more along the lines of an 11 am checkout time? She had to learn for herself, be convinced, I guess.

Then there were the unspoken truths that could either capture me, or kill the groove, like, "I'll bet you went to CD (Central Dauphin) and Penn State, right?" If you were from CC, conventionally speaking, CD was near the bottom of the list, well below barnacles and only slightly above marine borers. Of course, it worked both ways. Along with the football games they were all just stops, though, nominal squares on the formless, faceless, heartless board of that game, Our Own Familiar Local Suburbia®.

I cleared the board and thought again about her eyes. In them I saw no distress, only warmth, a willingness to explore. Acceptance. A beach, pails and shovels to play.

The movie began and was over quickly, only a few rainy Sunday night diehards on hand to witness the French director's statement. Too allegorical, distant. Enough already seen at the Saturday night screenings of the Romance Languages Club at Penn—Fellini and Truffaut, Widerberg, Kurosawa. I didn't want to be any more surreal than a desert rider laying over the 400 Maico in a powerslide. At least not right now. I did enjoy sitting in the theater, next to Emily Ritchey. Occasionally I'd steal a glance, see the expressions on her face, "what?" "yeah right," "give me a break." Were those about the movie, or me? And when I looked directly at her, she just looked back and smiled. Very comfortably.

Nothing to do after a movie Sunday night in CPA except go home. Emily invited me back to her place. I had no problem accepting. Small house on a back street in Shiremanstown, a different high school district, wisely, away from the public, bureaucrats, and troublemakers of West Shore. And especially former students who wanted to give her their full attention. Outside the classroom.

I picked up a book, *The Odd Woman*, by Gail Goodwin. "What's this about?"

"My age, though thankfully not my family nor how I would approach a relationship. An early thirties Midwestern college professor, English instead of math, is grappling with who she is, her grandmother's death, increasing distance from her mother. Relationship? Did I say relationship to Craig Maxwell? … might not be the first book *you'd* pickup to read."

"Yeah, I go for the occasional book about rocks, like Abbey's *Desert Solitaire*, or war, Michael Herr's *Dispatches*.

"I wonder, though, from what you say about *The Odd Woman* and those I've been reading, whether they're just different pieces of *my* autobiography, larger or smaller, actual or vicarious. Everybody's story, in fact, that of the U. S. of A. now that I think of it. All the stories, commentaries, subtle and shocking experiences dumped into the one big 'Life in the 70's Blender'. And like a lot of history, probably all history, it can't be understood or objectively assessed until much later."

A minute timeout while the blender noisily does its thing. You want chunky or smooth?

"Literature aside, Craig, I invited you back here not to seduce you, or vice versa, which doesn't sound all that bad now that I think about it, but rather to let you see a little of who I am, how I live. And if you'll open the door just a little, I'd like to start to find out who you are."

Sure. I can play.

I reached out and took her hands. As for opening the door, we'd have to see, time would tell.

"Emily, it would be a lie if I said you weren't desirable, right here, right now. But I agree with you, at least in this one moment of weakening restraint. On Tuesday, I'll be headed back out West and … . You said 'relationship,' did I just say 'restraint'?"

"Time to run you back home." I didn't object. I needed a curfew, and it was a school night.

"I want to thank you for this evening, Emily," I said when she dropped me off. "Can we get together for a few minutes tomorrow, say around six, at the Coffee Place?"

"Yes, I'd like that."

Her place had been nice. Plants everywhere. The feel of it. Sweet fragrance when she was near.

The lingering goodnight kiss was best of all.

Ah, the drama of Portugal, winding walkways, old planes, beautiful women and their indecipherable glances.

18

Second coming of the Hun,
but only one

This was another movie, the one where the tentative man and woman, considering whether to get to know each other, put on their best public behavior while trying to keep in check the five year old who might resemble, at any time, old dynamite with a timer down to single digits. Even though I had little experience, the outbursts were few, and Jed seemed to do well. Both Cindy and I had visited the State Museum in elementary school, marvelling at the horse-drawn carriages, dioramas, statues, huge colonial and Revolutionary War paintings. Neither of us had been back since then.

Afterward, we walked down to the train station, then had late lunch at a nearby restaurant before getting lost in a toy store where I bought a box of LEGOS to occupy Jed. When Cindy dropped me at home around five, I asked if I could see her for a few minutes later in the evening. She said that would be alright, if it wasn't too long because of the project she had delayed.

I hopped on the Triumph, to meet Emily. On Market, around 9th Street, passing Phil's Carpet Kingdom, Shore Beer Distributors, and The Snowplow Outlet, I cheerily considered giving in to CPA. I'd take their job, drive the snack truck or deliver fuel oil in the snow, with my head down. Look for the silver lining in every gloomy winter day, 50 more seasons of them to go. Nah.

Arriving early, sipping a Poland water at the Coffee Place, I immediately fell into reminiscences, rather than trying to concentrate on making any serious sense of what I was doing with Cindy and Emily. In each case, something more than simple coincidence appeared to be at work. *Both* mythical when you got right down to it.

Reminiscences of another place, one in Santa Cruz where the Whole Planet Band, led by Spacey Tracey in a guest appearance, went "Down the Equator". What was that all about? Shiny red warmup jacket, boots high over her Levis, voice squeaking like a finger on glass. Tight Levis. So tight they made the Police Log. Thighswise, that tight. Black night bustin'out/into throb, strictly Plutonic. Permanent record of marks on the paper cup rim, imprint of incipient incisors, more lipstick, pearly/moist/wild. Dangerous. Who had I been with that night? A stranger with lips like red raspberries, skin light chocolate, there until I glanced away into the Mustang rearview, saw the rattlesnake watermelon sky, black seed clouds, looked back and she was gone. All the time, frantically taking notes no one would ever believe, not even I. Left with still-blooming words and flowers.

Poland water, drink of dreams.

I surfed on the chords of that song—rollers, breakers, and dunes—driving a steep highway along the Pacific. At the top of the pass, miles away, was a roadhouse. Where different chords floated on the night air, bass lines plunged down from rough sandstone mountains to the valley on the other side. Vibes and changes, lights where there had been only darkness. Overheated engine, smoking tires, beating heart. Yeah.

When the sun rose, came the best chorus, hope of an ever-continuing set. A woman with whom I share total understanding waiting. Behind the door with the Sky Heart painted on it. Her Sky Heart.

The door opened, and there she was.

Emily? Startled me, deep in thought. *Really* startled me. *Her* Sky Heart?

"Hi, Craig."

"Howdy, M'am," the good natured Westerner, quickly recovering, greeted the pretty schoolmarm, to whom she answered, "howdy, yourself." Heard that all over Wyoming, one end to the other, in the corners, along the diagonals.

Tom said hi to Emily too, fixed us each a cappuccino—a magic moment for me if I'd admit the truth, my 800th. A couple of high school girls came over, impressed that I was there, intrigued with my Indian jewelry and Triumph parked out front, in sight on the sidewalk. I sighed, signing autographs with the usual drama, changed the subject when one asked what I was going to do now (after leaving ESO). Parenthetically, what *are* you gonna do?

"I just came 2300 miles to have coffee with my math teacher from Cedar Cliff. I'm heading back to California tomorrow to surf, write music, and make as much a fool of myself again as I can in the shortest possible time." Ordained, it would be so. I could not change my destiny.

"The bracelets you asked about are Hopi, from the reservation in Arizona. One of my favorite places. Thanks for your interest." Hope the mooring lines hold, *Titanic* that this trip seems to be.

"How was your day at school, Emily?" I really want to talk about how beautiful you are, but I'll have to work up to that.

"It's the end of year madness, finals, grades, evaluations, tears and fears. Two more weeks of panic and it'll be over."

"What are your plans for the summer?"

There's this place in Ventura County, a roadhouse at the top of the pass .... .

"Well, I have a two week course at Penn State to do which will fill up June." Thought so.

"After that, take a trip, but haven't decided where. The Smithsonian and Rehobeth have been done enough; I can't get excited about going to either of those again. Rome or Madrid would be much better. South America in winter?"

"If you're interested in staying stateside, I can send a ticket to fly into an airport Out West and meet you. I'll even throw in the return flight."

"I'll have to think about that return," she sighed. "It's not everyday I get propositioned by a major rock 'n roll star, in collusion with a major airline. One who kisses like you do. But I'm wondering, how many other women have you got lined up in the pattern?"

"Nobody else yet, so you'd better act fast. Kisses like *we* do, by the way ... I think you'd enjoy the West."

What was I doing, complicating my life this way, orchestrating a rendezvous when there would be so much to do in Laramie before school started there in early September? When it came to women, not wanting to say Yes, I'd do one of two things ... say Yes now, or say Yes at the earliest opportunity, slightly later. Maybe I really want to be with Emily, not only for a couple of weeks? Maybe Emily is all about Yes.

But where did Cindy fit in? I'll give her a ticket, too, maybe October. Cathy and Kat as well. Come one, come all. Anything and everything goes in my life-long quest to find common sense, even TruLuv. Keep your garden healthy, flowers bright with TruLuv.

We finished our drinks, and left. The excitement of talking about getting together Out West was suddenly stilled as we stood in the parking lot, knowing it was time to say goodbye.

"Well, this was a different kind of student-teacher conference. I'll be in touch about sending you that ticket." When we kissed, it started with a kind of bemused mixture of "goodbye and see you again, won't I?", then flared into combustion which could not be ignored. It didn't seem to be spontaneous at all today. Had this fire been carefully set, whether we'd admit it or not? Set when, and by whom?

Had it been Paris, I would have insisted we look for a room above the cafe. I had a feeling she would have been equally insistent, thrown a pop quiz, forced me up the stairs for extra instruction in physical culture. Both of us laughing, sort of. Unsure of ourselves maybe, certainly not about the attraction between us.

"I'm looking forward to meeting you in July, if I don't find some muscular Ed, as in Driver's Ed, in the meantime. As you now know, I like those younger men, students, teachers, whomever."

Where did you come from *Professeur Mathematique*, hidden within the hills and highways of this Ungourmet ExtraburgerScape, vectoring into Friday night reunion life delivering unprecedented cross-products? What am I really doing here with you? Is it possible there's a lot more going on than simply extending an unexpected, unbelievable LoungeLand fantasy?

"If you meet Mr. Ed, just let me know and I'll send my congratulations, flowers, two dinner theater tickets to Boiling Springs, and a bucket of oats."

"Wise guy. I'm out of here. Have a good trip, and don't let anybody else on the back of the Triumph! I mean it!" That was asking a lot. Possibly, no probably, too much.

"Happy trails, M'am," with a tip of the invisible hat.

She went right, and I went left, to take care of a few more things before hitting the road the next day. Face it, a weakness for a good looking woman, more so when she's her own person. A real soft touch for quality. At what price?

That kiss did kick me up a quantum level, leaving a hunger that might be deferred, but would not be forgotten. Obviously there were other loose ends in this tangle. I thought they would probably remain so for quite some time. Blessed in a land of plenty. Plenty of those loose ends that is. I'd get to the bottom of it by going to the top. "Dear President Lincoln… ." But first, a burning question: can a person be a myth unto themselves?

I know so.

When I called, Cindy said to come over about ten. There wasn't much for me to get ready to leave the next day, just some laundry and provisions. I borrowed my parents' car and made a supermarket run, always a cultural close encounter. The one on the way to Cindy's was no different. Not a fullblown Hollywood creature feature, but a differently flavored short, *Attack of the Boxy Snatchers*.

Why do women, particularly the younger ones, buy so much stuff—a half dozen steaks, three giant boxes of Trix, two huge jars of instant coffee? The market will be there tomorrow, next week. It must be about the reassurance of well stocked shelves, or to demonstrate faith the power won't go out.

Jed was already sleeping, either past his bedtime, or hidden from this second coming of the Hun. Cindy was more relaxed on her own turf, "have some iced herbal tea." I saw a playful side, hidden, I guessed, most of the time. Marriage, divorce, loss, sadness, making it on her own, strictly business with few exceptions, rarely allowed to be seen.

"So tell me about Craig, a better reason for why you're really here, and if you'll be back." If you're really here at all, in the heavy handed drama of this Western.

She knows why I'm here. As for back, does that mean she's interested? Don't you know men take things literally? Too literally? She's gently probing, while I'm torquing down bolts with a three quarter-drive ratchet.

"I've got to validate, extend, or overturn the myth of Cindy Hollis, *artiste*. A quest which will require more than the few hours we've spent together."

"And how do you propose to do that?"

"By bringing the myth to me, at some place, some time. Going local."

"To be effected by?"

"Sleeping on it for the summer, and then inviting you to visit me in Wyoming, assuming I really follow through with the school thing this fall. I'll send you a ticket, and one for Jed, too, if you like."

"Is there urgency?"

"There's always urgency in affairs of the heart."

So I kissed the second woman that day. And it was also good. How could this be truthful, honest? As an exercise in data capture and deduction of Great Truths. When completed, I'd send a copy of the study results to those who had signed up for the distribution list. Mail a duplicate set to myself. Just in case.

Great truths about shopping, like those women at the market. Filling my cart. Same compulsive motivation. When all was said and done, so I wouldn't be alone, still have boxes on the shelves.

It was time for Cindy to finish her work, and for me to leave. Still juggling two CPA local in the air.

19

Ipanema in the
mountains of Michigan

The rig represented over $50,000 in equipment and elaborate preparations for what had been to date only two weeks of road time. Better kick up the level to get my money's worth.

I pulled out of Harrisburg, planning to drive through to Ann Arbor by the Pennsylvania and Ohio Turnpikes, mostly thinking of Emily and Cindy, Kat before that, as mile after mile was left behind the Way Back Machine. On one level, I wasn't confused at all, just on the road, open to adventure. It was those other levels and complexities which had to be sorted out. That must be why fewer people are getting married—too many confusing things, too many barriers, mistakes to make. This has been a good trip for meeting women, and I'm already famous. Manny DuTone and the Near Miss. Near Misses? Missus?

Close to Ann Arbor was a well known motocross track I wanted to ride. Stripped of the street-legalizing bolt-on items, the Maico was quickly ready to run. It was great getting out on the course, pulling wheelies and jumping hills. Wwwaaahhh! the big two-stroke screamed, throwing up rooster tails of dirt. I was a decent rider, although no doubt caught up way too much in mystique— the rig with California plates, works-Maico, full leathers. None of it would have been unusual at Saddleback in Orange County, or out on the Mojave, among the flood of riders every weekend from Southern California to El Mirage, Victorville, Barstow.

Ann Arbor had a few counterculture places where later I browsed books and couldn't resist a t-shirt in the plant shop window ("Arroyo Plants—Bizarre, Succulent, Specializing in the Unusual"). I even found an espresso joint where except for the caffeine jolt, I might have fallen asleep. It was summer, things were laid back, the streets almost empty when a shower cooled off the town. Dinner at the Good Earth was tasty, the movie after that entertaining, and dessert later just right. Caramel peanut butter ice cream—I got it for you but ate it for me. Pleasantly aching from the exertion of motocrossing, I walked while attacking the cone, looking for the Blind Pig, a jazz/blues place recommended by the restaurant waitress. I'd catch some music if any was to be found, otherwise, lights out in the rig.

Turning a corner I heard jazz-fusion riffs, coming from another place, The Drift, which I gathered was about snow rather than sand. Stepping through the door, I entered the customary purple floodlit candles on the table, bigcollegetown club. With most students gone for the summer, the weeknight crowd seemed to be comprised of somewhat older, perhaps hipper, more dedicated jazz aficionados, including a few Sonyas here and there in the subterranean melanzaniness, covers intact. A six piece unit fronted by a Maria Muldaur type stretched between the Oasis and Rio. Strong and scenic for Ann Arbor. Tonight, after the peanut butter ice cream, like winning the Irish Sweep-stakes. I had an immediate feeling about this woman; surprisingly, it wasn't entirely physical.

I asked the keyboard player, who had decent chops, if I could join them for the last set. He was gracious, and suggested that I play the Fender-Rhodes while he covered the synthesizer stack. So I was introduced as a "very special guest, Craig Maxwell, lately of ESO." We wound up the energy level, playing a Tom Scott number, followed by Cannonball and Weather Report. An augmented and diminished prelude to a sweet time until the rim shotted cymbal ride got heavier, driving the groove to abandon, frenzied sweat, hard chops, trading soaring solos.

I'd know where to go if I needed a band. Here, to their own Rio. There's some great music in the clubs of Ann Arbor, Santa Barbara, Boulder. In my experience, the talented players and performers who wanted to make it went to the big city as soon as they could, to live and learn music, give it their best shot. The ones who stayed back but kept dreaming without follow through inevitably lacked a combination of ability, motivation, charisma, original material, or contacts. Somebody like myself might stumble upon, and adopt, a whole group in a place like Ann Arbor, lead them out of the wilderness. Otherwise, they'd still be here years later in a narrow, fading vein of local legend, intact or in float. Working day jobs. Unfortunately, I didn't think I would be needing a band for a long, long time, if ever again.

They quit at midnight, and we hung around talking about the LA scene, while a parade of fans, well wishers, and gapers came by. Maria, not her real name, looked good not only 'Round Midnight, but 24 hours of the day, I suspected, and there was intelligence to match. Reminding me of Kat, she had a degree from UM, and was actually local. When we were cooking I had noticed her swaying, eyes closed in a tropical paradise of her own imagination. Nobody was complaining.

I looked at her now, wondering, where do all these great women come from? This was a singer/musician who played some piano and at this point very interested in "contacts", the all-important wiring of the music business. She wanted to talk to me about that, so we made a date to meet mid-morning at the espresso joint. Harmless as a gun moll in a film noir. Here, put out your cigarette on my hand. Tsss. Didn't hurt at all, defiantly.

The morning was cool, perfect to get out the Triumph and ride over to the cafe. Arrive early and spaceout until she shows up. Will I recognize her? The flash of lightning had been so blinding.

In a different storm there were impossible choruses in unison, mouthpiece biting shrieks, shining sax and flugelhorn. Signals from the Solo Nebulae, radio stars deep in space, source emitters of Original Jazz. After Ornette, what can you say? All things convergent to another stanza in cut time, the accompaniment emptiness, vacuum. Dimensionless charts. There's this picture of Louis with his smoking horn, ultimate black magic music trigger of infinite energy flux. Oh yeah, we're traced out by the waves, people, here now, transformed as the radiation propagates everywhere within a priori infinity. Chinese lotus soprano, beauty, smiles. The Book of Lost Menthol Poems, strange desert musings, shifting sands. Are you really there, painted on stucco walls above a sunset, everyone a reality paratrooper in this dust storm shack, waiting for the light to go on, rush, hands in space until truth pops? Physically quantifiable, never convincingly explained. Only billowing silk.

Night electrons pouring through my brain. Sequences tracing 144 note measures, control voltages and modulations, approaching overheated collapse. Outside, rain brought slides, green hills, snow on top. 'Alright, slurred stumbling on a tour of dark doorways, alleys, deadends. Band warming up again, bass drum rolls, phaser chords. Sax fading out. Stuff's melted black gum, quicksilver, rush brings you down to the temple steps, a stare back to from where you just came. Distorted old movies projected on the sky, pushed as reality. Running on and on.

End the set with the better part. Her lipstick Rayogram on glass. My unreleased record, *When Delusions Come True*, wah … wahooooo.

Outside, Maria pulled up in a battered Bug with Bali plates. Wearing a sarong, a smile and … well, just as exotic in daylight as last night. Now that the storm has passed, I'd know her anywhere, singing her signature hit, "Virtually Voluptuous."

Ordered another cappuccino and a mocha for her. *Subito, subito.*

"So what are you really doing on the road, and of all places, here in Ann Arbor?" she asked. The epée unsheathed. On guard!

"Lookin' for adventure, and whatever comes my way," as Steppenwolf said. The John Kay, non-Hesse version. Me Tarzana, you Yane.

"In truth," a relative expression, "I have a weakness for intelligent women who can sing." It was so true. Where are you now that I need you, Frederica? At *La Scala* in *Milano*? Caffe Trieste?

"And you certainly can sing, Danielle. How about you?" There I go. Too much excitement at hand. Yes … *that* Danielle.

"'Summer's here and now's the time for dancin' in the street', but not for me in Ann Arbor any longer. I'm trying to figure out how to get away from these hungry Wolverines, and in walks a guy from LA who might have the lucky charm."

"I'd like to think so. What's the best way to spend my last day here? Go to another movie, the Army-Navy, a falafel place?"

"That's a little overdone, don't you think, 'my last day here'? I'd go to Mount Brighton, our local peak, to the lookout on top for a picnic. You'd need a guide, of course, preferably one who speaks your language, likes to sing Rio, and can hold her own with any philosophical debate or number of Margaritas Yucatan you put on the table."

Oh oh. Philosophy major. And Definitely Yane, jungle proven. Question: what's worse than gibberish? Answer: Philosophy—organized gibberish with permanently debating subscribers. I wonder if *Popular Mechanics* has published something to help, like *Working Man's Guide to Existential Philosophy for Relationship Improvement*? I sensed we were descending into the depths of axiomatic theories of strict implication. An argument in every box.

"Done and thoroughly intimidated. Let me get my backpack and we'll do just that. Know this reality: *I've Got a Bike*."

I followed Danielle over to her apartment while she changed under a mountain waterfall, then we got some sandwiches to go, before stopping at the GMC to get my backpack. Trusting me, musician to musician I guess. Was I clearly *that* harmless?

"This is a great set of wheels," she exclaimed. I liked her excitement, the fact that she had lots of energy, was not yet jaded by the grind. The whole scene had to be as mind boggling to her as my entire life had become to me.

"Who are these women on the bulletin board—more singers, or shouldn't I have asked?"

Now we're getting down to it. The yin and yang, ch'i and li. Material forces and order-principles, opposite yet complementary red durum hard wheat words of the academic/clinical, cosmic duality oriental/occidental dumpling soup blended and served by the Zen Patriarchs.

"No singers in the bunch. All finest quality, Missy, very exclusive category. Pinups of another kind. Maybe you too can make the CMax bulletin board. Send in your entries, and remember, there is no obligation."

"A categorical proposition or syllogism, something other than that stated, following of necessity. Maybe even modal."

"It was a compliment, not a call to hysterical, I mean critical, analysis. The dispassionate kind someone like me, trained way back as an engineer, occasionally throws out. You said modal. Let's steer away from the rigors of logic and talk aesthetics instead, like music."

Mr. Maxwell's comments in no way represent those of the human race. *Recognizing the Unknowable, a Road Study Course.* I resent the implication. I'm *not* a scholar, I'm a consumer. My book contains *no* original material. Keep it straight from now on.

When we hit the highway and roared to 70, a de facto energy violation of the environment as set forth in the *Congressional Record*, she yelled, "this is a fast motorcycle." Declarative sentences the norm. Indeed it was. We took the dirt road to the top, spread out the tablecloth, and sat down to do nothing more than talk and watch the cumulus clouds drift over, if you need the meteorology to be accurate.

"I really want to go to LA," she murmured, "To prove to myself I can do it." I guess that *was* the purpose of today's get-together, in her mind at least.

"Do what? That's always the question. Unless you know the answer, you won't get there."

"Work a job, sing in dives, go to the beach, get famous, struggle with success."

"I've done enough singing and sinning for a lifetime." Androgynously true and false, not physically but theosophically, to pick a couple words I can't define.

"I'm going the other way, getting out, looking for somewhere to go, something different to do. Probably Laramie. That should meet the criterion of being 'different.'"

"If I went out to LA, would you know me?" Back to Route 66, wagon ruts worn into stone, now the freeway concrete of California, right … ramps.

"Would I know you?" I'm seeing you in the daylight. Outside a hotel room. Yes, of course.

"You know, after our one day fling, or excuse me, 18 hour fling in Michigan, that seemed like a good idea at the time."

"This is a fling? On the flingmanship scale, it's definitely not registering a reading. Hey, I'm just working my day job here." See, I'm not so vain. A real solid guy who takes, makes, and breaks all things in moderation.

"Some day job. What's that about a scale?"

"I'm in a swirl of influences, factors, and changes—career, women, cultures, art, you name it. Too much to talk about under today's Michigan sky. I don't want to make it any more complicated. There, I feel better I said that."

"Aren't we all. In a swirl, I mean."

"So let's get off the meaningless, most important stuff and talk about the excitement, the frenzy of chord substitutions." Rich voicings.

"Chords of the heart. Augmented."

"Right."

And so it went, the boundaries defined, ex post declariori, aeropostale banteriori, a fine day together. In no way was I ignoring being alone with this woman on a day when everything is new, no mistakes have been made, no criticisms rendered, second thoughts entertained. We were accepting the start of what might become friendship, long distance in the near future, steering away from any untimely, clearly premature physical complications. Platonic, for now. I'm his disciple, by the way. They call me Procrasthenes. 'Knees for short.

Another Polaroid tacked to the bulletin board, "Maria (not her real name) aka Danielle." We exchanged numbers; I said I'd show her around LA, make some introductions if she got there before I left for Wyoming. I could see her playing Donte's, Brentwood gigs for zillionaires, beside the pool at the Beverly Hills Hotel, shopping for koi, arguing passionately about barriers to development, sipping *Cinzano*, having lunch at The Place Across the Street from the Hotel Laguna, getting out of the hot tub at *my* place in a local remake of *Five Million B.C.* Because she was smart, could sing, and would appreciate the help. Because I liked her. For a lot of because-reasons, including basic physiological differences which, to the average person, wouldn't be obviously tipped by the Polaroids. Your basic under the table specialist.

I'm neither Don Zany and Radio Silence, nor Manny DuTone. Sonny "Chico" Fortune and the Last Straw. That's the name. Hollywood guy with an eager heart, fragile future, music stand in the trunk missing a wing nut. Despite the refreshing Danielle, still Grand Exalted Master of the Lodge of Marketplace Anxiety, never without a drinking buddy, except in his own mind.

Now in Ann Arbor, T-minus zero, time for second stage separation, driving farther away from closure of all sorts. I broke the seal on the top secret orders, authenticated the code, and read them aloud: "Continue on the path of your ancestors."

I had a feeling it would be a long drive to the next espresso machine. Better get a capp to go. A double.

Cafe Whyoming

20

On the trail of a past which had not existed

Of course, I do have a past, my family has a history. I just had to find out about some of it myself. We never talked about the overall scheme of things, only the most immediate relatives in streams of third person facts and opinions, as if they were not individuals at all. Whether we were too caught up in the present, the subject was deemed uninteresting, unconfrontable, inflammable, or minimized for some other reason conscious or unconscious, I don't know. To fill the vacuum, I sometimes just ran with "what if I had no past?" crudely attempting to recalibrate both assumptions and conclusions—a speculative if not downright fictional approach. What too often works for attorneys at law—sometimes successful judgments; always billable hours. Expert at anguish, choosing to construct and argue airtight cases.

Before I left Harrisburg, my father took me aside. "You said you're planning to go through the Arrowhead of Minnesota. As you know (dimly), I grew up in Superior, Wisconsin, just across the river from Duluth. Your grandfather was Chippewa. He told me that the building containing the Fond du Lac records burned down, and once mentioned running away from an Indian school with his brother. Your mother has never been interested in it, and I haven't returned to the area or done any research to learn more. That's the extent of what I know. Whether it will make any difference in your life is obviously up to you." Or put differently, in the realm of commerce, comfortable lifestyle, and orchestra tickets, it's between marginal and irrelevant.

Well, it's only taken you 27 years to tell me this.

I said something like, "yeah, it would be interesting to checkout," typical family conversation filler, nominal acknowledgement, superficial reaction. The bare minimum into which we fall as teenagers, that some, with regret, try to overcome for the rest of their lives. Why would it matter where I came from? How much Indian could I be? I stir-fry with hot chili sesame oil, play rock and roll for money, jazz for fun, and listen to Bach for my soul. I could imagine the ethnology: "the subject was a 27 year old male, raised in a suburban, Caucasian environment, economically in the middle upper quartile ... ." As the road miles mounted and tire tread disappeared, though, I did think about it. Why not check it out?

Heading north over the Mackinac Bridge to the Upper Peninsula of Michigan, I hooked up with U.S. 2, which went west through Wisconsin to Duluth. The hardwood forests, now a healthy green, would be brilliant in autumn. The farther I went the hotter it seemed to become. Northeastern Minnesota was in the midst of a record drought.

South of Duluth is Cloquet, gateway to the Fond du Lac Reservation. An exaggeration of sorts. I came expecting, at worst, lingering, consuming Pine Ridge bad vibes. A couple of notches above would be a mini version of Gallup but with trees, a place of ragged alleys, subsistence economy, railroad yards, peeled logs, century old dirt between the tracks, grease, chemicals, and rock flour; mercantile stores, elevated asphalt tanks blackstreaked from spills, all fenced, sickly rusting in gray-dead soil. A land overrun by exploiters, trappers and clearcutters, land dividers and reformers who did what they wanted and kept going. Leaving tarpaper shacks, deterioration muted by summer's green branches, but depressingly evident each winter with the freeze, snow, mud, stark gritty days that would drive anyone into a tavern, to escape through football, basketball, hockey, the sports line from Vegas. Heavy odds against the Redskins.

What I found on the surface was an industrial and trading center at the edge of the Rez. A surprisingly substantial economy, discounting the occasional heaps with grills like runover cheeseburgers parked outside the bars, driven by staggeringly unwilling participants of this version of the American dream. Though it's never unanimous, the corporations of White America were firmly entrenched, the shopfloor pounding clock punching shift-workers on mmm-maintenance prescriptions of contemporary chemical and cultural ccc-compounds and ccc-confinements.

Unlike Zuni, Hopi, or the Rio Grande pueblos, within the Fond du Lac Reservation are many individual properties owned by non-Natives, created by the "allotment" system. The spaces on this checkerboard were a lot smaller than the one mile square sections of Arizona and New Mexico. Suffice it to say that Uncle Good-Sam subdivided the Reservation into parcels (officially) intended to be owned by Indian families, but a lot were sold off or otherwise obtained by non-Natives. Dilution of the Band was successful, if property ownership on the Rez was a meaningful indicator. Of course, the natives never viewed land as "property" until the mapmaking frontmen for the material culture came onto the scene, and the for sale and no trespassing signs went up.

Beneath the community's forest products working class facade, "units of demographic identity" were chocolate-swirled like the Big Cone at the Dairy Den. Where there is chocolate there has to be a heating source. And spatters from a couple centuries of imported diseases, levelled old growth, trapped out forests and lakes, introduction of a whole new cast of crops, pests, predators, and controls. Money, property, economy, racial separation. Shame on you,

Uncle Bad-Sam. A "social" agenda not immediately evident to the laidback VistaCruisers stopped for Fudge.

The library was a logical place to start looking into the past, although it was already almost 4 pm. On Cloquet Avenue, the brick building overlooked the St. Louis River and huge wood products plant to the east. I counted 19 steps in front.

Annie LaCroix was the Assistant Librarian. Hoping she would be able to help me locate sources to consult, I learned she had always lived in the Duluth area and was a full-blood Ojibwe. After attending the University of Wisconsin-Superior for a library science degree, Annie said she was very fortunate to have been hired at the Cloquet Public Library, lucky to have a job other than at the mills.

"I'm trying to find out about my ancestors, whom I understand include Fond du Lac. Can you point me where to look?" I asked.

"*Nagaajiwanong indoonjibaa. Ginitaa-Ojibwem ina?*"

"What was that? I'm sorry, I don't speak the language."

"I said that I'm Fond du Lac, and asked whether you speak Ojibwe."

"Unfortunately, I know nothing about the area, the Chippewa Tribe, or family history before my grandfathers, both of whom died while I was a child."

"If you think that you have Ojibwe blood, you'll want to try the BIA office at Cass Lake which has tribal records including genealogy. That's about 120 miles west of here on Route 2. I can pull some books pertaining to tribal and local history. The Library closes in about an hour, so I'll only get a couple of the better ones for you now."

I read that The 1918 Fire had burned down much of northern Carlton County, including the town of Cloquet and its previous library. The building where I was now had been constructed in 1919, as were many of the other buildings on Cloquet Avenue. In the back center room, behind the oak circulation desk, a second floor made of thick glass was added in the late 1930's, an interesting touch.

1500 square miles were burned; hundreds perished, remarkably few if any of them Ojibwe; and according to local witnesses *makwag*, bears, swam in the River to escape the flames. It was a catastrophe to the land, one which left the Fond du Lac, who had little more than the memories of their threatened culture before The Fire, with even less.

I would learn that the terminology "recorded event" was in itself a lightning rod to Native Americans, and that the subsequent reality of the word "treaty" seldom met either the definition or representations set forth therein. With the exception of the "discovering" anthropologists and ethnologists, Anglos largely ignored Pre-Colombian history, since it had not been "recorded" in written, alphabetical form. To most of us brought up on corporate textbooks and in school libraries, "prehistoric" means dinosaurs. At the least, tusks: Pleistocene mammoths and saber-toothed tigers. But prehistoric in North America has been extended all the way forward to BS—before Spanish (one of several obvious meanings). Only 500 years ago.

Much of oral tradition was routinely discarded as myth, other ways of writing down history were deemed inferior, insistence on treaty rights was an "uprising", and so on. It if wasn't recorded, mapped, deeded, or contracted, to the White World it doesn't exist. And since contracts, of which treaties are one type, were made to be broken, it is questionable whether those have any legitimate meaning anyway. He who controls information, the content and presentation of it ... determines the "history".

As for the lesions (sic) of university 'ologists, their cousin biologists, sociologists, archaeologists, paleontologists, and otherologists, the truths which must be sifted from history don't seem to matter much. Theories and speculations, graduate degrees, books, and the scientific-educational machine are both their methods and ends. In the name of discovery, liberal arts, scholarly excellence, endowments, alumni weekends, warm memories, toasts and broken glasses. Here here!

They wouldn't use a real term like "White World"—too harsh, inflammatory. How about if we turn down the treble, go midrange with a more comfortable euphemism? Something in wool argyle perhaps, muted diamonds on a dark background? WWW for Whole White World? W³? Let's say DPMW, for Dominant Pale Material World. Dominance and the material are what have been and are continuing to drive most things American anyhow. Isn't the thunderbird a kind of car? Didn't Detroit design the logo? Invent Cadillac? Can I transfer these sociological theories and applied marketing credits?

The fire explained my father's comment about missing records. I'd have to go to Cass Lake to investigate more. If it's recorded on their paper, it must be "true". Writing down the names of the books I was reading, and a few others listed in the bibliographies which looked promising, I wondered, how many days do I want to spend here?

A stack of back issues of *The Pine Cone*, the local weekly, was sitting on a table. *Masinaiganag*, she called them, talking papers. Leafing through those for the last month, I was struck at how they could have been from any small county town—nothing unusual at all. There was nervousness about the "record drought, worst in recorded history" caused by a very dry spring, particularly in view of The 1918 Fire; vandalism, a recurring thread; and burglaries. Conspicuous by its absence, at least to me, was any direct mention of the Fond du Lac Reservation or its people.

Racial trouble had erupted in the high school over at Mille Lacs a couple of years before, and Pine Ridge had galvanized an undercurrent of militancy against the last hundred years of avowed domination and extermination: "The only good Indian is a dead Indian"; and "Kill the Indian, save the man." The local school district appeared to be trying to address the problem by advertising a job opening for a "Coordinator for Indian Education", the only related item I saw in the paper.

With a couple centuries of self-congratulatory conquest and subjugation, so to speak, for which much more elaborate terminology has been coined by Eastern university academics for descriptive purposes; epidemics which we hasten to point out occurred in Europe over many pre-colonial generations; government policies, well meaning or otherwise, but like life, with no guarantees of success; broken treaties, with rights to break them always reserved by the conquering party; and discrimination, though described as pervasive but of which the local authorities have found little practical evidence—the local situation after those 500 years (the "couple of centuries") could be at best on low simmer.

I had gone to school in Philadelphia during a turbulent time, lived in LA, toured the big cities, read here and there, and wasn't completely naive about racial issues. Awareness was a matter first of whether a person cared about those issues; and beyond that, a question of the degree of tolerance for strident rhetoric, weave of the value system filter, and susceptibility to militant anger. If I asked Annie LaCroix about the subject, would she tell an outsider what really went on, what she thought?

Given that caveat relative to the invisible indigenous, after the *Los Angeles Times* or more recently *New York Times*, the items in the *Pine Cone* were amusing: dog obedience champions, smelt recipes, moose call secrets, and scoop of scoops: "Progress Nearly Here! Warehouse Market to Open in Cloquet!" Buy in bulk, get bulky—it works for America. There was even a traffic stopper about the very building in which I was reading all of it: "Public Library Gets Book Return."

This wasn't Gallup, like any Reztown I knew. It was … well, what?

Something of the blood, in my bones. Connection. Obligation. More graffiti written for *me* to see, that though editing *Gentle Truth Magazine*, I might not escape the responsibility of knowing:

You Must Bat Your Own Weight.

21

Bangii go gii-miskiingwese in the Northwoods (she blushed slightly)

The Librarian walked out of her office at five o'clock, and I overheard her ask Annie to close up; then she left. It was my chance to speak to Annie alone.

"Ms. LaCroix, I hope that's the proper form of address up here in Minnesota, I'd very much like to talk to you more about the Fond du Lac area and Ojibwe people. I know it's terribly forward of me to ask, but would you consider accompanying me to dinner? You could invite any reinforcements you wish … ."

"Annie *niin indizhinikaaz zhaaganaashiimong.*"

"That's a lot of syllables for either a yes or no."

"I said that my name in English is Annie. Everybody calls me Annie, and so can you. I guess I can interrupt my busy schedule." If irony was intended in her reply, it had quickly blended into the forest.

Did she have a beatup red pickup with a gun rack, brother named Lester Little Eagle the size of a house with an even bigger hunting knife? Honest, I think I may have Indian blood. It's not a crime to ask, is it? Nothing here to concern you, I realize, but sufficient to impress myself and those around me in California who need to be regularly impressed. In the end will this only be about cold steel?

Nope. Articulate and genial, if reserved, she spoke of seeing wild rice grow on the lakes, tanning deer hides, replacing the spark plugs in her car. Actually, I don't know what she said, other than agreeing to walk over to Frenchie's for dinner. Spellbound, I was held by her presence, could not see the forest for the trees. With the Iron Range nearby, there might be some unusual magnetic effects going on. *Real* fan-spoon transference.

Outside, I snapped out of it. Somewhat. An hour after I met her, we're headed to dinner. Rinzai! Bonzai! As reflected in thankful wonder many more times than I could ever hope to deserve, "is this some kind of life, or what?" I don't know how the man-woman thing works, but it must be there and healthy. Outside California, that is. Annie LaCroix didn't even seem to need to be impressed.

Her thoughts were very different. From a deeper consciousness.

"Remember who you are." Annie didn't hear that much from other persons. It was the voice of her ancestors, a constant reminder.

The meaning had changed four years after she went to the University of Wisconsin-Superior to work on a degree. She had to decide what it meant every day, among the few women from Fond du Lac with a college diploma. For all she knew, maybe the first, unique.

These days solitary was probably more accurate. She lived on the Rez and went to traditional dances, looked forward to working at the sugarbush camp with her mother and uncle's family when the maple sap ran in early spring. But now she knew about the humanities, arts and sciences of the Other World too. Working in a library didn't pay well, but it was a job and more importantly, a window to a world of knowledge beyond the Rez.

While Annie would never be an outsider, neither might she remain as much an insider. Rez life seemed now to be as much about politics and business as traditions. That was only another facade, painted by those on and off the Rez with predominantly political and business interests. The traditions were really living through those who were strong in what was often perceived to be silence, yet quite the opposite in realms unseen. Poised in both worlds, Annie's actions, not talk, would show just how far into each her life extended.

She would not let herself be adrift in either of them. The marriage hadn't been wrong. It was about being 18. After a year it didn't work out, because she was someone else. Surprisingly, there had been no child. Since then, she had kept in her own space. Though sometimes longing for a man, she was not frantically looking for a relationship, and was more often than not aloof. The good ones were few and far between. She would have no other.

Who are you? *Anishinaabe*. Her people would have to accept what that meant now, in the late 20th century. *Her own people* would have to accept her.

Annie understood the suspicion of outsiders, Anglos, even *Anishinaabeg* from different reservations, those who had grown up away from this land altogether, had little connection to their people. She understood the bitterness which was always there: look what they did to us, took from us. What have they brought us but despair?

It wasn't only she who had changed. The Viet Nam vets had come back drastically different. Rarely better for the world. Confused, reeling, many consumed by sickness which might never be overcome.

Annie *wanted* to be here. Belonged here, both in town and on the Rez. Nobody was going to take that away, drive her from either. By and large, the town worked. There were jobs, without the wearing discrimination elsewhere she had read about and heard from the accounts of those who came back.

Her husband had been from Red Lake, *miskwagamiiwi-zaaga' iganing*. Too soon after meeting him at the Leech Lake powwow, they ran off, got married, and began living together in poverty. In the cold woodlands, she saw a future only of getting by, too many kids, and disillusionment. It could take years for his people to accept her. The marriage wasn't working, and she didn't know how to make it work. When it was over, though she was strongly driven to make something of her life, there were other emotions, too. In the end Annie had given up trying to make it work for a healthier future, yet was left to bear the weight of lingering guilt and failure. By herself, sometimes tearfully, always silently.

Why did she agree to dinner with this outsider? Because she knew. Because of the dream. *Da-dagoshin*, he will arrive. Not to exploit, hurt, or take her away, but because he needed her help in finding himself. "I don't know that I'm trying to 'become Native,'" he had said, "because I'm from the other world. Rather, I want to experience the richness of belonging." That would involve subtle distinctions. As she helped, she would be drawn toward him, perhaps in the end, irresistibly. Her heart would be tested, the outcome uncertain.

Even though she wouldn't agree with all that he said, the beliefs that he might embrace, it wasn't up to her. She would be stronger for the experience, too, the testing of her heart. She knew this from the dream.

We went into Frenchie's Northwoods Family Restaurant, a diner with spliced on metal facade. One story chrome, two stories brick. With the bright finish, swept Pullman car-styled corners, detailing, portholes and round window in the swinging metal door, it looked like a Deco clock radio. Variations on Neo-Diner Exteriors, an Overcooked Regionally Reflective Dysarchitectural Anomaly. The weather was hot, and the place didn't seem to be airconditioned. I brought in my notebook ("I like to jot things down for reference and doodle"), and rolled up my sleeves when we were seated. Despite the heat, I started with a cup of coffee, pouring the cream from a little white porcelain pitcher, returning it to the ringed cardboard coaster.

"Those bracelets are nice. What tribe?"

"Hopi, from the mesas of northeast Arizona. I love the strong, elegant designs. I had them made a few years back." Did I really just say I "loved" the designs on metal objects?

As we talked, Annie related that she had married young and survived it, struggled financially to get her degree. Her mother lived on the Rez, along with aunts and uncles; her father ran off to Minneapolis and then died when she was eight. Annie had already seen a lot at 25, was proud to be *Anishinaabe*, one of The People. She knew how the world worked, by power and the self-interested exercise of it, whether by Pale America, not her words, or the local tribal version. Nevertheless, needing to be on ancestral land, she did not want to move away for "more opportunity" like so many others had, and was determined not to be defeated by the hypocrisy found too often in Rez local politics.

Until I could get a dictionary, I asked Annie to write the Ojibwe words she used. *Gichi-mookomaanag*, white persons. "*Chimooks* in Rezslang," she said, laughing for the first time in my presence. Not too hard to figure out. I was sure there were lots of other words I wouldn't be hearing at Frenchie's. As for her laugh, I hoped to *experience* a lot more of it. When she laughed, I felt alive. Alive, in a way it seemed, as never before.

Annie continued to unfold a life of hard winters, blizzards and frozen lakes as I made a few notes and she wrote down some words for me in the small, clearly practiced penmanship one would expect of a librarian. Left-handed—often creative, intelligent. Throughout it, I was impressed by her apparent tranquility. Below-zero days when the sun shines, the wind quits, and the animal tracks in the snow remind one that life goes on; the awareness that the wait is worthwhile later when spring flowers bloom. It wasn't romantic optimism or styling, rather a recounting of a universe of balancing factors in a real world. The natural world. You can read about it in any number of books at the library, just name the tribe; alternatively, Thoreau. History mirroring storms and serenity, droughts and floods, despair and the triumph of survival. Beaver dams, new grass.

I was surprised at how much about herself she had already told me, a stranger, and asked her about it. "Annie, you've already told me much more than I would ever have expected, particularly about yourself, as it relates to the Ojibwe people. I really appreciate your candor. It's surprising to me."

"You asked about us, and I'm one of the 'us'. I guess it's my job to tell you."

Watching her face as she spoke, I wondered whether I should look into her eyes or not, whether in the Ojibwe culture it was appropriate. She did occasionally look, I think, into mine. It was hard to tell. At first glance, there wasn't any one physical attribute of Annie Lacroix which dominated. Looking at her as closely as I could without it being improper or embarrassing, I saw much more. Everything worked together, both physically and in the healthy energy she commanded. I had the sense that important, valuable depths and dimensions were being unlocked to me, privately released that I might see them revealed as possibilities, through my own eyes, in my heart. Annie LaCroix was, in short, incredible. Strong without being bitter, like great coffee.

I wrote my first draft of Annie LaCroix, cultural survivor, in the notebook and showed her: "I admire your strength in walking the path you have chosen. It is a beautiful path." She looked at me, smiled with what I thought to be the start of a blush, perhaps more in my imagination than actuality, being darker skinned, then looked away. Annie was like the wind, perceptible yet with unseen movement, taking me with her, inductive. I felt that breeze as I considered her in this place, a rustling in my heart for this woman. I might not have noticed her in a crowd before; now, to me she was absolutely fascinating.

What *is* it about certain women beyond the physical attributes that makes them almost indescribably beautiful? Something they have which is innate, absolute; or cultivated, appreciated on my part? Elements of both? I seem to be constantly rethinking beauty these days.

A friend of Annie's came over to the table, rescuing me, maybe both of us for the moment.

"Beatrice, this is Craig Maxwell. He believes himself to be Fond du Lac, and has come to learn about The People."

"I've been wondering since you came in, whether you're *that* Craig Maxwell?"

"Probably so, if you mean the drifter who once used to play music but is presently underemployed."

"Annie, do you know who this guy is?"

"A man from out of town. Maybe the son of a son of a Fond du Lacker, probably just a *chimook*," she said, smiling. "We'll have to make sure the Native Nation does a background check if he shows up tomorrow with feathers in his hair."

"Does ESO ring a bell?"

"You don't mean the gasoline, do you? Sometimes your pronunciation is not always clear."

"No way. This guy's famous." In the third and second persons only, these days.

We chatted about being famous for a few minutes. In my version of what that meant, it didn't apply to me. It's not like I am, or want to be, in succession to become the King of Spain. Michelangelo Buonorrati was famous, Bach, Mozart.

Then Beatrice asked, "Do you mind if I interrupt your dinner and have Tom Driver come over? He's a writer for our local paper, and can always use a good story. You know, 'Star Returns to Cloquet Roots.'" Bigfoot sighted in Minnesota was probably closer to the truth. BigEgo? Trying to convince myself that this would be fun, I knew I really just wanted to talk only with Annie.

As Beatrice went to get "Driver," Annie mentioned that he sometimes did research at the Library. "He's okay, gotten to know us a little, that we're neither the Ungrateful Dead nor Wild Red Menace."

I kept thinking, I'd like to get to know you, too. More than just a little. Jump out of another airplane, down a mineshaft, off a Pacific cliff. With gear rated to protect a continually mystified heart. I can't keep the women I know straight, now I'm going to add another to the mix? What can I say, though—My Personal Manifest Destiny. All the polls have reported, and once more, I Da Man. Well, the Da, or more accurately duh, part is accurate. Looking forward to California dates with Dough. Still wanting Play´ Dōugh and grape Jel´lō. Ending the gloating with a feeling of pointlessness, generic boredom and guilt.

Dinner turned into an interview, pictures. Pictures with Annie, Annie and Beatrice, Driver, Le Frenchie *lui-même*, other patrons around our table. Several gangsters and even Marilyn Monroe captured by Weegee flash shots dripping surprise, glamor, editorial statements. Evidence of the Encounter. Chalked footprints and body outlines on the ground here in Minnesota. I didn't mind spending the time, but would have preferred to learn more about them. When it was over, I was pleased to pick up the checks. This *chimook* was good for business. They'd write Voyageur folk songs about today, dance to fiddle music. Le Frenchie's friend for life.

"Tom, when you get the pictures please send me a couple. Here's a card with the mailing address," that of my agent actually. I was aware of how exotic it would be to them—Los Angeles, California. Hollywood, oranges, the Beach, San Gabriel Mountains in the background of the Rose Bowl, Pasadena 70° on New Year's Day, while it's 10 below here, deeply shadowed sun low in the winter sky. As Annie and I walked outside into the spring evening, I thought about fame. What is it about us that wants to be around famous people? I want the opposite, to be with real people, those with their own identities, far from the hype. In the past, many famous persons were leaders. Today, public leadership was too often simply statistical, the 50% plus one vote moral, Merle, or morel majority.

"Annie, I'm going to Duluth tonight, then up along the Lake. Could you think of a shortlist of good books on Chippewa history and culture I could get? Starting with how come you say Chippewa, Ojibwe, and *Anishinaabeg* at different times, interchangeably, it seems. Obviously, I don't know what to look for or even where to start looking."

"Yes, I can do that. Why don't you call me at the Library from Duluth, and I'll direct you where to go. Let me write down the telephone number of the Library in your notebook."

"Thanks. I'll be coming back through here on the way to Cass Lake. Could I stop by again?"

"Okay. Would you like me to call over to BIA at Cass Lake and ask them to see what they've got on the Maxwells? Not a real strong Indian name, by the way." I know, tell me about it. Everytime *I* hear the name, it reminds me of Maxwell Smart or General Maxwell Taylor. We are such creatures of the media.

"Yeah, I know ... 'been Norman Mailer-Maxwell Taylored ... John O'Hara-McNamara'd ...'" No response to that Simon & Garfunkel lyric.

"Seriously, I can't thank you enough for your help. See you the day after tomorrow, probably sometime in the afternoon."

It was a short walk back to the Library where I bid Annie goodbye. She got into her old Ford and drove away. I returned to my rig parked in the City lot, checked the map, and headed northeast toward Duluth, then the North Shore of Lake Superior where I would look for a place to stay the night.

22

Unwholesome tendencies, artfully avoided

I drove in the darkness, savoring the day if not entirely the recent cuisine, wondering what I was really looking for here. Was it a connection to the past, my heritage, or something flimsier, marketable, to amplify like the bracelets, exploit? Like Masters Degrees by Mail for five bucks, to become The Instant Indian? Answer the question, or I'm calling Tragg and Berger.

Two hours later, I pulled off the road north of Silver Bay, around Palisade Head, and opened the vents to cooler air. The stillness of the night was broken by the sound of waves splashing at the toe of the cliff below, infrequently a passing car or truck on the Minneapolis-Ontario run. I made a cup of coffee, put on a light windbreaker, and sat outside in a folding chair.

The recent years of my life unfolded like the dim, moonlit expanse of Lake Superior. I was here in this land of the Voyageurs and Ojibwe, but still tethered to other land, scraped earth, obliterated orange groves, frantic traffic, choking smog, oil stains, slicks, sheen. Exploitation run aground. Neighbors never known … not neighbors at all. What was I doing of importance? Nothing I could think of worth mentioning. Taking more than giving. Using, not contributing. Receiving royalties on music made to sell, market-responsive product which had ceased to be interesting. As my grandfather ran away, so do I. Not from the Indian boarding school to which he was taken by the government or sent by his family because there wasn't enough to eat, but from *my* clash with modern life.

I don't know that any of us start out wanting to be a cliche, but it gets so comfortable, self-sustaining. Is honesty ever cliche ("I want to love you.")? Not in itself. It's the company too often kept. And what could I possibly give to a woman? Restless attention? An exciting past? A credit line?

Even when jumping out of an airplane some people decline the parachute, thinking, "If I can fly, I can land." Ignoring the obvious—it's about gravity, lift, and control surfaces. Misapplying their, "I haven't used anything taught in school yet, and I'm not about to start now," mentality to motion which is, with a doubt, gravitationally determined. One of the many things they might better have learned and deployed before embarking on short careers of prop-driven disbelief.

All those miles back, *did* that stranger push me out of the plane? I didn't think so at the time. Did I take the parachute option despite myself, my ego? In the end, will my story be about air, water, or fire?

Now a man walking living sideways, seeking any semblance of balance he can find.

Along this lake are drums, just at the threshold of hearing. Wigwams, lodges, tipis; buckskin, beads, moccasins. Fires reflected in the dark eyes of generations, the carbon and ashes of their bones. Seasons of plenty, times of severe need. Fitting together the thousands of pieces of an incredibly complex puzzle, in the blankness of years, mysteries of generations, only the subtle sharpness, turn of an edge for guidance. I know that in the morning light the water will be deep blue, the cliffs unsettling. The loving embrace sought of a woman comforting. But she's out shopping with that credit line. Here and now, she's not there.

I looked at the stars, closed my eyes, saw even more. A stronger breeze came up, then the coffee was gone. Only drums, no melodies to be scratch mixed on the four track. In the grasp of my ancestors, beckoning me to dreamtime.

I got up early, pulled on my shoes to go running along the highway. Despite the drought the morning was overcast, not unusual for the Lake. It was a classic Niman beginning, at first light a purple-blue ribbon at the eastern horizon reminiscent of Hopiland, then a mirage, become as that Pink Cloud beauty bush in the Central Pennsylvania spring. What will my life be when I leave spring behind? Where will I be?

After 45 minutes of roadwork, I found a trail down to the base of the cliff, from which a point ran out into the Lake for a couple hundred feet. Slight as the waves now were, their cumulative effect, bolstered by winter storms and freeze-thaw, had brought down solid rock, reduced boulders to pebbles, rounded and polished them. The strike of igneous strata exposed on the point was northeasterly, the dip southeasterly. Orange lichens covered sparkling black crystal faces. There was no beach, as if the Lake was making a statement: "Know my power." That's what *I* heard it say.

Pale Man always wants to be on the edge, as I am here at land's end, looking ahead, sipping his Expeditionary Pale Ale. Too often wanting more, to be beyond, on the other side or even farther. To get something over with, find the treasure of elusive experience, right around the next curve. The edge, mythical boundary where we dwell in imagination or frustration. Take your pick.

I think I see a city on the horizon, like the cover of a science fiction paperback, *The Water Planet*. But it's only haze. The reflection in the pool is that of a man, it may be real. The man is another story. Fighting to be strong, trying to be alive, something other than the bare, dead snags of the forest above this lake.

In the black rock is a perfect stripe of pink feldspar, off another point a bulk ore carrier, above the trees a plume of smoke from the wood processing plant. Though miles away I can smell it, like the sweet blackberry aroma of burning sawdust near Tillamook on a late September day in Oregon a few years ago when, as now, I was just passing through.

There's always another rocky point, forested shore, lake with unpredictable, dangerous weather. And on that lake life is as a wave, starting with promise, cresting, whipping up the foam of ego, breaking and running up on the beach, dissipated, returning only as flat water. Forget the waves. I hope that my life will be as this clear water on a calm day, undisturbed.

I looked around, startled by my shadow, thinking that someone else must be here. Many are here, have always been here. I have come to join them.

There was somebody. Emily Ritchey. What was it about her at this moment? Another someone so compelling I left her behind, reasoned away by a schedule, exiled by the priority of plans and arrangements.

The reasons being a more important, unquenchable quest for explanations of lava, continental drift, glaciation? Lessons in Pale Domination? Graduate studies in atonality? Seeing the seedling growing in the crack of dense rock, the inexorable breaking of the waves, the birds overhead, those other things explain nothing. One big wave on this point, and no explanation would be necessary. I'd be gone from here. Nobody would check me out, bring my car around. Or I could just walk down the dip of the rock into the clear water, hearing the bubbles released from the scuba regulator which doesn't look much different than the chromed air filter covers on the Triumph. But today's show isn't *Seahunt*, Mike Nelson is nowhere to be found in this country.

On a point in the Lake. A good place to carry on a conversation with myself: "I come in peace," or more accurately, "I come in pieces." Far away from Do', Oz, the Land of Wire.

Feeling lazy about cooking, I drove the few miles back Route 61 to Silver Bay, ending up at The Dinner Cove. 'Spoon with a twist, now open with a new menu for breakfast and lunch only, in a town above the "vermillion" taconite shipping terminal, Range Cities ore feeding the mills of Gary and Cleveland. Oh, those California plates. May as well give them their moneysworth, get out the Triumph and ride up to Finland and Isabella, motor rasp breaking the roadside stillness. Places contributing totally different chapters in this screenplay of ethnic heritage and conflict. Bake that strange bread. No rain in the forecast yet. I'll enjoy the day up here, stay in the forest, go back down to Duluth tomorrow, catch the Vinyl Siding and New Jerky Cavalcade on the way, then call Annie. Call her what?

Okay, there's the "unique" aerial lift bridge, the Chamber of Commerce brochure says that Duluth's a "Cultural Mecca," they have a branch of the University of Minnesota, and no doubt there's redevelopment potential à The Cannery and nearby waterfront in San Francisco, but most of what I see downtown is port-industrial, the roads are shot and the oiled land's tired. Despite the classic Tudors in the better residential areas, novelty of the house that looked like (surprise, surprise) The Little Toaster, I can't imagine being here in the worst ice storm of the winter, ttt-treking to an "off premises" store for a six pack of porter, teeth ccc-chattering, inevitably wrapping more whiteout blankets of DULUTHALOIDAL TENDENCIES around me for iiii-insulation.

There's got to be more to life than leaving your fingerprints on the laminated menu and ordering à la carte, shopping at a place specializing in Damaged Canz, perfecting the surreal tirade, catching dimwits in the act of being reasonable. Get back to the Rez. Get back, Loretta.

23

Miikawaadiziwing izhi-bimosen, Annie LaCroix (walk in beauty, Annie)

Annie directed me to a bookstore in downtown Duluth which had the four books she recommended: *History of the Ojibwe People* (Warren, 1885), *The Voyageur's Highway* (Nute, 1941), *Chippewa Customs* (Densmore, 1929), and a very recent one, *Ojibway Heritage* (Johnston, 1976). Leafing through the last volume, I glanced at the creation story. So that's what Turtle Island is all about—I thought it was in the Caribbean, near St. John's.

The books ... remember? I'll need something to read in North Dakota when pulling over to do that geological field research I missed in college. Open a can of dogfood chili, beans and erasers, rinse it with a local brew, Faded Youth or Lost Winters Lager (Not Licensed for Export). Now that I think of it, I'm not sure the Ice Age left any geology in North Dakota. Only seasons, two of them. Too Hot and Too Cold.

Back in Cloquet, all under the gaze and influence of the steel water tower with Dorothy/Oz'town painted legend in big black letters, "CLOQUET", I slipped by the Dairy Den before the giant cone angled toward the street made liftoff, passed Dave's Phillips 66 and Pete's 66, before opting to fuel the rig at Ray's, third Phillips in the family, and "the only Frank Lloyd Wright designed gas station in America." That's what the article taped to the wall inside said.

What was there to observe from the windowed "hovering lounge" above the office, Pontiacs? After a 20 year hiatus: *Fins and Antifins, Critical Evidence Brought to Light*. Then again maybe it was only a matter of not having recalibrated my Fantasy-Reality Meter. Used to seeing jackalopes on postcards, it looked to me that the candlestick, space needle "Phillips" sign on the roof needed a trading post next door for balance. Cold pop. Souvenirs. Panoramic Mill. Floodview. I remember unusual lights back at the Lake ... am I in Lllllong Beach, Gllllendale, Suurrrff City? Still just nervous?

Side by side on Cloquet Avenue, toward the east end of downtown, were Melody Music Shop and Len's Music Shop, the names in coordinated neon signs. A property settlement between Len and Melody followed by bitter competition? I went into the Melody to see what was burnin' up the local charts, and was pleased to find a complete selection of ESO tapes, no doubt smuggled in with whiskey by canoe from the Twin Cities, covered with furs and hardtack. Hopefully not bootleg, I gotta eat too. Nothing else of much interest, left a few minutes later.

Parking across from the Queen of Peace Catholic Church on Avenue F, I walked down the hill on 4th Street and went into the Library to see Annie. Late afternoon again.

"Thanks for locating the books. They'll be something to read on the long drive through Da-ko-tah.

"I haven't been to the Reservation yet. Could I impose upon you again to drive out there this evening?"

Annie looked down for a minute, then said with a touch of what seemed to be reluctance, but could simply have been more deliberation than that to which I was accustomed, "well, okay."

Picking up on that, I told her if she had other plans, or if it would be awkward in any way, to consider my question withdrawn.

"No, it's alright. We can go there."

"Thanks. In the meantime I'll browse your local interest shelf to see what I can learn." I got down a book and started reading about traditional Chippewa courting customs. A subject of immediate interest? Regardless, nothing so far— the daughters were modest, or expected to be, the parents watchful. How much about human nature and behavior really changes in a hundred years? How much has changed here? Maybe less than I think. The packaging is different, society "freer", selfishness sometimes more artfully disguised. In the end, though, those still standing, on their knees praying, or dancing in beauty, are calling out for the strength found in traditions. Not stifling dictates, but liberating recognition and insights ultimately about what is true and valuable, that which wears its years well. Like this comfortable old oak chair, smoothly crafted, worn even smoother. Got it all figured out. Any more wisdom I can cook up for you today?

I also read about the importance and power of dreams. How they were sometimes never revealed to others, or shared in part, only at the necessary time. We all have dreams. A recurring one of mine is to be able to fly, but not without effort. Other than that, I would have to say my recollectable dream life has been limited. As will be evident by now, daydreaming is another matter.

Things started off okay as I leafed through *The Ojibway Woman*. I liked the revelation about what women really do:

> … Women talk about their important experiences … the private motivations behind interesting actions. Ruth Landes, 1938.

So concise, can't say I've ever read a better explanation. But the rest of the book was an eye opener, 'bout scared me to death, full of shamans, taboos, men and women walking off. The traditional courting customs I first read about seemed to be window dressing, the tip of the iceberg on a sunny day.

Couldn't I just have the Golden Book years o' plenty turkey dinner version, forget the rest, ice the beer, and party onward?

"All done for the day. Let's go," Annie said. Outside, she asked what I was driving.

"My rig's up the hill. I've got a motorcycle. We can take that if it's okay with you."

"I've never been on one, but would like to."

"Nothing else like it. First, let me show you the motorhome, before we go."

I unlocked the door and left it open. "It's pretty hot in here now. When driving the air is on if needed, and I have a generator to run the top unit when camping." Camping being a very relative term.

She studied the music gear, the Polaroid photo gallery on the bulletin board, the ceiling.

"So I can always sleep under the stars. Let me see, I wrote down the words at the Library: *anaami-anangoog*, under the stars. How did I do?"

"A good start. Close enough."

"The pictures are of special women I know, strong like you. I'd really like to add yours." I don't know if I would have agreed, it's so easy to be skeptical. Nevertheless, she said okay, a little self-consciously, and we went outside to take a few shots, Polaroid and 35 mm black & whites. I chose one, put it up on the board, and gave her the rest of the Polaroids.

After a sound system demo, she said, "the sound is great, but up here you've got to have more than classical. You need *dewe'iganag*, drums, powwow music for the drive through the Dakotas, buffalo country. I'll find a cassette before you leave."

"It'll only take a minute to get the bike out." Annie waited under a tree while I locked up the motorhome, then opened the trailer.

Releasing the tie-downs, I brought out the Bonneville and we got on.

"You can hold onto the seat strap," I told her above the idling engine.

We rolled away smoothly, went south on Route 33, then took a right on Big Lake Road, past the shopping center and up the hill. After a mile or two, there was a sign, "Entering Fond du Lac Indian Reservation", but it didn't look any different at first. When we turned north, headed toward Twin Lakes, there were tarpaper shacks, and everything was more rundown. Last year's cattails lay brown in the ditches and bogs, with birches toppled, snapped from ice damage. The crackling branches of winter storms.

Annie didn't take me to her mother's home, where she still lived. Maybe it just wasn't on the way. There might be any number of reasons. I didn't inquire.

Eventually, we returned to Cloquet. After shutting down the bike and putting it back in the trailer, I asked Annie if she would join me again for dinner. She agreed, and we went to another place, the Riverside Grill. There were some looks as we walked in and found a table. Small town with a lot of history, long-standing attitudes.

"Can't go too wrong with the burgers here," she said, as we talked about the Rez, the Tribe, the town. Annie was clearly exceptional: one of only a few Fond du Lac women who had gone to college; and then, been able to get a job here, in her field. She wasn't intent on "making a statement" about rising above racial opposition or economic pressures, or resisting forces of conformance pulling her back toward the old wigwam days, rather, her life was about finding steps to walk and grow, drawing upon the strengths of Ojibwe traditions, using tools available in the contemporary world.

We got on the subject of religion. Her mom was Catholic, Annie was not.

"What are you then?" I asked.

"Ojibwe. Anishinaabe."

Not wanting to be completely insensitive, uninformed, and unthinking, I didn't ask the obvious: "what do you mean?" Even on the Navajo and Hopi Reservations, to me, the "religions" seemed to be about the pageantry of dances, symbolism appearing in their arts. That iceberg again. One glance at complex faith and values systems. Always looking for the all-encompassing descriptive phrase, the written manual with reference tabs. The foolproof Polaroid exposure. The instant picture.

Native, college educated, and 25, Annie wondered aloud more than really asked me, "why should we give money to build churches, when so many Ojibwe are hungry here in Northern Minnesota? 'We're not building cathedrals,' they say, but I don't agree. Not cathedrals like in the history books, but to a ricer from the shingle shacks of the Rez, that stone church in Cloquet with stained glass windows across from your RV *is* a cathedral."

And so is my RV, for that matter.

"There are a lot of issues I have with 'organized religion'. Some other time, though. I want to enjoy dinner."

I didn't feel responsible to answer her assertions, nor did I consider myself sufficiently informed, competent, or even particularly interested. My observation, though, is that more often than not, we're cultural consumers, accepting what and who others tell us we are, what we should do, including their "religion". Caught in second hand interpretations. Building what I've always thought would be a healthy life requires not only observation and learning, but origination— living it. Life and living are not the same thing. Life is too often at a "cool distance", behind a smokescreen of relativism, cultural, moral, spiritual. I realized I was describing myself. Where could I find the opening to the other side of that glass?

The doors in my life, instead of being passages to nature and happiness, were to closets filled only with accumulated psychological and material stuff.

Spiritual living, spiritual health had to be important. It seemed to be in the organizing and practice where people veered from the path, built the cathedrals on the backs of slaves of one kind or another, argued interpretations of minute scriptural references, fought holy wars, excommunicated and executed those who did not agree, would not conform, or were simply considered to be threats. Even martyrdom could be more marketing than deep, selfless sacrifice. Was it any surprise that viewed from the Native perspective, there were a lot of problems with the everyday reality of Big Western Religion?

I had the feeling Annie was letting me off easy, at least for now, not insisting that I enumerate a cogent analysis, articulate an airtight defense, or embrace her point of view. If there had to be an eventual run through the gauntlet of declaration, justification, self protection, and survival, it was being deferred.

That was fortunate, since I wasn't even close to figuring it out, much less trying to answer her. In the end, would I be only another member of the permanent touring cast of *Relatively Unobtrusive Cultural Stereotypes, A Life Style*? To really get the drift, listen to the soprano's lament from Mahler's *Symphony No. 3*: *Oh mensch, tief!* ("Oh man ... deep"). Lament—tangential or tangible. Triumphant?

Then we got into contrasts between the Native and "civilized" worlds—property, real estate, ownership, rights, styles, fads, economics, all the exploitative schemes ingrained in the society of the "white persons", *gichi-mooko-maanag*—versus land that belongs (present tense) to all Native people and isn't for sale at any price. Those traditions again, the Old Ways, spiritual health. As strong as her words were about the Dominant Pale Material World, she had equally forceful things to say about Native "moderns." Not those who applied useful skills or technologies, but the others disposing of tradition solely to benefit from the DPMW. Reinventing it either purposely or in an absence of knowledge, hence living in ignorance; otherwise, falling prey to the vices which would inevitably replace it in an environment of passivity.

Despite my good intentions, breadth of knowledge, and welcome of just causes, was I living in a sealed condo, over the line past Reality Shores? "Here! A Neopragmatic, Monoculturally Masterplanned and Deed Restricted Retreat Celebrating the New Paradoxicality of Exclusion. Models! Clubhouse! Play!"

I once asked a Native musician, one who played popular/traditional/Native folk-rock if we must give it a label for reference, what he thought of Beethoven. No response. Say what? Silence. Mozart and Beethoven. Great composers and performers, world class egos. Working in times of wide disparities in wealth and education. Today, the shapes of the statistical distribution curves were different, but the disparities still extreme.

His unspoken answer, in the jargon, was Silent Speaks Two-Fold. First, "you're asking what *does* a curiosity like me, an ethnic artifact of Native American culture plugged into a wall outlet of Educated Material America, think of Beethoven?" Second, "I doubt you're asking me, but really asking yourself. Trying to bring more 'input' to bear, calibrating your own defined system, reinforcing your own views." He was right on both counts. We were speaking different languages. In fact, not communicating at all.

From a child of the litigious society, reinforcement: "as for the sins of the last 150 years, how can you argue with the long litany of injustice, extermination, alienation?" Answer: "it happened, and can't be set aside with only the simplistic admonition, this is the 20th century, you lost, get over it." Who inherited this injustice, now owns it? Is there a Managing Partner, Executive Vice President in charge of "Injustice Operations and Reprisals"? Who are we bombing this week to keep sales up by the way? It's all clear to me. I can go either way. Both ways, other ways. Any way. And by now it's nearly 500, not 150 years.

Somewhere in here, we managed to down the burgers, enjoy the company of one another, and avoid inciting a riot among the patrons of the Riverside. Annie was indeed cutting me a lot of slack in what I realized were my very sketchy views. After leaving, we walked back to the Library, *agindaasoowigamig*, sat on a picnic table under the trees, and talked more.

With 8:30 pm approaching, it was time to go.

"I'd like to stay in touch with you, Annie. Let me write down my address and home phone, and those of my parents, who usually know how to find me. Please call me if you ever need anything, or just want to talk. I'd enjoy that. Maybe one of these days you'll come visit me." Laguna 92651. That would be … beyond description, actually.

"Everybody wants to go to Disneyland," she laughed, able to step back from the impassioned expression of her viewpoint. "It's TV."

Not if you live in it already. Disneyland started out to be wholesome family entertainment, not a lifestyle.

"Annie, what you've accomplished is an inspiration. You've been so helpful to me, an outsider, a stranger."

"Before you go, I'd like to explain about why I had to think about riding out to the Rez with you. The issues are outsiders and respectability. My reputation is not only important to myself, but to my family. Many here would and do consider a single woman alone and accompanied by an outsider to be unacceptable. I'm already different than the other women—a college degree, working at the Library. No kids. Resisting the occasional efforts which are made to marry me off."

"I know I'm an outsider and a stranger, and if I have compromised you in any way, I'm truly sorry."

She took my hands in hers. "Before meeting you, I had already moved the 'line of good behavior' out a little bit. Not that I want to fight our own people, rather in a small way work to redefine what it means to be a woman here on the Rez in 1977.

"Also, you're not a stranger. You're *Anishinaabe*. I know this. Don't ask me to explain now. I will tell you when the time is right. Find your heart for The People. Our People. We have been moving for centuries, to this land, now our home. Though you live farther away than many others, remember us, come back and learn more about who you are. Whether out of curiosity or need for connection, many of those with the blood come back here to the Rez.

"For now, you *are* an outsider. You will be an outsider until you live here, learn the language and customs; to those who value them, show the community you are one of us, that your intentions are honorable, that you can be trusted. That you embrace the earth, the trees, the sky, the animals, the stories, creation—all of what it means to be *Anishinaabe*. You may not achieve that in a lifetime, coming from somewhere else.

"And before I forget, let me get that powwow tape out of my car.

"Goodbye, Craig, *gi ga-waabamin naagaj*, see you later."

Only a few days ago in Camp Hill, I had turned north on Market Street, Cindy south. Now Annie went south, then west on Big Lake Road. Back to another night on the Rez. To a real life? What had that ever meant? For her? For me? Was there such a thing?

I went north on Route 33, imagining the frypan dance, literally *abwewin niimi 'idiwin*. Bullets detonated, meditated, seen, dodged, deflected. Orthogonal cousin to Zen betweentheraindrops walking. Harvesting truths from the vines of life, huge melons on the shelf at a county fair. Knockin' heads with myself.

A thought surfaced in my mind: "if you're not comfortable with your death, how can you be satisfied with your life?" Where did that come from? I guess the conversation with Cindy, about her Mom. Can't think of anywhere else. Strange.

Does it work the other way—if you're satisfied with life, you're comfortable with (your) death? Not necessarily, I'd have to say. Okay, then, do we need more data?

How about me? Definitely not satisfied with much of the recent past. So I guess death would be bitter. I'm not "comfortable" with it. Who would use the word "comfortable" to talk about that anyway?

What is it about Indian Country that brings thoughts like this? Out here in the dark, nobody around. Boom! Like a blowout, swerving off the road. Where is Indian Country? *What* is Indian Country?

"In a land once with 500 tribes, the spirit is everywhere." That sounds a lot better.

Because it's true.

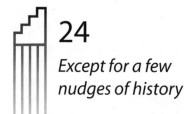

24

*Except for a few
nudges of history*

I stayed the night at a campground west of Grand Rapids, sleeping deeply despite the anticipation of what I might find at the BIA office at Cass Lake. In mid-morning, walking into the office I introduced myself to Mary Long, Tribal Enrollment Specialist. That's what the black name plate on the counter said.

"Oh, you're the one the lady from Cloquet called about a couple of days ago. It wouldn't be a government office if I didn't first want to see your ID. Don't ask me why you need it to view public records, but I have to ask: do you have ID?"

"Yes, as authentic as anything from California can be these days. Here, have a look." Will I have to execute an affidavit? Take an antacid taste and effectiveness test? What color represents my heartburn again? Sign away any mineral rights, prolific trap lines, or royalties? Smart aleck.

"I'll just note that on the standard checklist. Now let's see what we came up with in this folder."

"Mr. Maxwell, our records establish blood quantum of 1/8, of the Fond du Lac Band, Minnesota Chippewa Tribe. Your grandfather, Thomas Martin Maxwell, who is or was 1/2, is listed in the Agency files. This is a genealogy extending back several more generations, into the 1800's. Your family tree indicates that you're descended from one of the principal chiefs. I have a copy of what's in the folder for you."

As simple as that, like checking AKC papers for a purebred. In my case, the pedigree was many more rungs down toward mongrel. A half hour later, after thanking Ms. Long, I was back on U.S. 2, continuing west. The BIA office wasn't the kind of place where they had tables, you ordered fancy coffee, then hung around basking in the warm, welcoming local vibes.

Stopping at a wayside to make a sandwich for lunch, I got out the folding chair, sat and ate, looking at a small lake under the hazy, partly cloudy sky. Another hot dry day, high pressure in control.

From the paintings and photography I had seen, books read, I knew that up until the mid-1800's, Natives were recorded visually only in the imagination and technique of Eastern painters. Noble savages frozen in somber, dark oil paint, spliced into exaggerated flat landscapes of the "Edenic Rapids and Mist" style. Up in the Arrowhead, little was recorded at all. By the late 1800's, our ancestors started showing up in photographs, still frozen, blankly staring, dressed incongruously in what had to be uncomfortable city clothes from the East. "Our ancestors." That's heavy.

Centuries in cold country, innumerable generations ostensibly become "prehistoric" with the shadowing or in too many cases disappearance of oral traditions, lack of what was considered by the European world to be a written language. Fishing, hunting, harvesting wild rice, fighting off winter with smoky fires burning damp wood. While the government intervened like termites in soft, fresh wood, dictated treaties and cooked up policies, yanked away the land, wasted it in a profligate frenzy of corrupted due process, moved to smother the culture. And, like in 'Nam, failed. What appeared to vanish is still there, in the trees, dreams, and picture rocks, this lake before me. In the eyes, hands, and hearts of the people.

I have a memory of my grandfather, now understood to be a half-breed Fond du Lac Ojibwe, a Maxwell married to a Lemieux, French Canadian Voyageur stock. Perhaps it came to me in a vision, since he died when I was not yet two. I remember wondering where he went. To a grave somewhere else, not Montana; in my imagination, wearing a red wool plaid robe, far away from the camp fires.

What does it matter *where* I came from?

I don't know if it's even true, having questioned nothing at BIA. Why would I? Paper is official, I got what I came for. Not full blood, obviously, but enough to use, validate and activate an instant identity. In my own mind if I am foolish enough to believe it, certainly in the world at large, Indian! Whoop it up! Original Resistance party time! That sixer is nice and cold by now. Right on!

But not in the mind of Annie, who had pointed out I would be an outsider unless I became Native. Unified with and living truths and traditions. Authentic. More than jewelry or a piece of BIA paper. Not merely liner note hype drafted for test markets.

Why *does* it matter?

Back on the road, passing the lone figure walking, always walking along the shoulder. *Ningichi aya 'aam.* Grandfather, my elder. Walking 40 miles north of Gallup at Sheep Springs, at Red Point, southwest of Page, in the middle of nowhere. If I stopped, what would he say? Anything? What would I say at the meeting of the tribes, The Walkers and the Drivers? Need a ride to the next auction of the dispossessed? What's my opening bid? Now ten, now ten, now twenty. "Every Picture" *does* tell a story. Franklin on a fifty, Grant on the C-note.

Minnesota blended into North Dakota. Time to validate those theories of Ice Age induced geological disappearance. Having missed The Thing? I was eager for Prepackaged Counterfeit Traditions! CrazyHorzeDiorama Next Exit Now! and couldn't resist picking up a couple of "1680 Pueblo Revolt String Starter Kits With Bonus Rubber Drum!" More cold drinks, rattler tails, souvenir spoons, magic jumping beans in stapled cellophane envelopes.

Beyond the Diorama, the Valley of the Red River of the North was an agricultural mosaic of square fields, a realist mural painted with plows and ditches, planted fields layed flat on the ground. From the air, a classic geography textbook shot, low clouds above the crop quilt, backlit somehow by an unseen sun. Yield tested and verified. Modest, we'll say, but a man's got to do something with himself up here, so plow! Plowing is good. Plowing is your destiny. "We don't plow, we sell them. You'll be needing a tractor too, we've got those on E-Z terms. See us first for the best deal, then go forth and plow." Their Northern Tier variation of "on the backs of ... ." Only the backs have changed.

Passing through TwinHood Scoops then Grand Forks, by now early evening, south of U.S. 2 I saw what appeared to be the lights of a night baseball game. Class C Northern League, lowest rung on the professional ladder. In reality, barely a profession at this level.

The Grand Forks Chiefs played their games in a stadium next to the roundhouse, a train maintenance yard like the Pennsy's one at Enola in the Harrisburg area, though much smaller. After a burger from Johnny's Drive-In across the alley, I bought a ticket for a couple bucks, electing the grandstand instead of bleachers with the Knot Hole Gang, a regular mob of kids; and watched the Chiefs play the Duluth Dukes.

Real estate, insurance, and farm supply dominated the outfield advertising. There were about 200 fans, very familiar with both the players ("Butch", "Cap", "Gil") and judging from the catcalls and insults, Roundhouse Pilsener and Uppercut Stout, which might have been brewed in a body shop a few more doors down the alley. A couple of long drives, some clutch pitching, and it was over. Bring on the Aberdeen Pheasants, Eau Claire Bears! An oldtimer watched me walk over to my rig, asking if I was a scout, pointing to the California plates. Yeah, just joined the Indians. The Tribe.

Daylight turns to darkness, and in the early morning a pool of cooler air covers the land. Taste of the coming change of seasons, even though months away, in a place where few go, few remain. Not much on the vast, uninhabited plains this dawn as I run, make breakfast and resume driving. My road arrow story punctuated near the state line west of Williston by a solitary cattle chute, amid more weathered desolation. No different than one 300 miles west in Montana, up a cowtrail nobody takes, on the way only to sky, ghosts, remnants of lost dreams. Nowhere is nowhere, and this road is little more than intaglio of empty, frozen opportunity, even on a summer day. Indian Country seized and sold to Scandinavian immigrants. Land!

North Dakota was defined into a wasteland by PaleMan's incursion. A railroad-building, bluesky promising, sodbusting, swindling exaggeration which became lonely only because of the invaders' rutted roads, telegraph lines, drafty shacks, interest rates, and windbreaks. The marginal production, hard lives, and disillusionment all a failure to take this land for what it is and always has been. Despite what the lingering economic movers and shakers keep promising in their markup.

These railroad towns are as abandoned burial mounds along a straight river of steel and cross-ties, Mississippi of another kind, "features" of future archaeological and ethnological curiosity. Popcorn kernels shaken and turned in the heat, exploding in memories of not enough water, clouds of dust, and unable to afford passage, missing the train out. Abandoned on more than one level, despite the small, declining population which remains.

With no reservations at all about exiling the Indians on pathetically small "parcels" of "real property". I was raised on a reservation, too. Land reserved for White Suburbia. A training ground for economic, political, and religious dominance, with its day school where we rehearsed different traditions: rock 'n roll; buttondown shirts, club ties, and Weejuns; mindless catechisms. Changing continuously, styles, to be accurate, not traditions at all. We had our own versions of the drinking problem, discomfort when off-Rez, on the multiracial, multiethnic turfs across the river. Beyond all that was one fundamental difference. On our Rez, a center of invented, self-defined material expectations, were economic opportunities, promising futures. You could be a dentist.

If you're in that line of business, a drive along the Hi-Line is a good place to sequence bank jobs, perfect elaborate swindles. Passing through here there's plenty of time to figure every angle, slip into the ditch of modern life and stall. Broken headlights, abandoned dreams. Stories written in the skids.

Several more hours west was Ft. Peck, touchstone of my birth. I stayed in the Hotel, on the green of the former Corps of Engineers town, saw a summer stock play at the Community Center, rode trails down near the Reservoir on the Maico. Held back by the hydraulic fill of the dam, millions of yards dredged year in-year out, interrupted only by the thick ice of merciless winters. I walked down "Officers Row", where the honchos lived when the dam was being built, succeeded by senior bureaucrats who later ran it.

We had lived in one of those houses, with a brown painted detached garage out back, accessed by an alley. There were raspberries and hollyhocks in the summer, bumble bees climbing the roses. Our dog's name, like that of half of those in the 50's, was Friskie. I remember the day he had the run-in with a porcupine and Dad pulled out the quills with pliers. Friskie came with us to

Pennsylvania, ran off, or so we thought. Years later we learned that because of starting to nip at the postman, something I never remembered, he had to be put down. Another history revised upon new evidence, now documented and accurately recorded as a Dog Relocation Era casualty. For old times sake, I hopped on the Triumph and headed to Glasgow for a strawberry malt at the Dairy Queen, twenty years after we had moved to Pennsylvania. There wasn't much along the way except grain elevators, ranches, and lonely roads on the loop from Glasgow back to Ft. Peck. I rode over the railroad crossing where Baldwin had shipped the grand my mother picked out at the factory in Cincinnati. The smell of sawn spruce and glue there is one never forgotten. That was the piano on which I learned, now in the house in CPA. Memories of the first grade Christmas pageant at Ft. Peck Elementary reemerged. Lined up in our angel sheets, cotton cloud puffs, pipecleaner halos, ready to go onstage.

Back at the hotel, I was reading about the *Great Miigis*, a sacred cowry shell that appeared and disappeared, beckoning migration westward from the shores of the Atlantic Ocean, eventually to Lake Superior; blessing the Ojibwe with life, light, and wisdom. I remembered the cowry in the little house here in which my grandmother lived, down the hill to the dredge cuts, next to railroad tracks smelling of old oil and creosote. That shiny leopard-spotted shell, so smooth and wondrous, purple where it had been worn. I always wanted to be on the magic beach from where the shell came, to discover it on the coral sand.

Staying in Ft. Peck for three nights, I became reacquainted with the little town which was born in the Depression, so hot in the summer, cold in winter, where we went sledding down the hill, careful to stay away from the posts and cable along the steep roadside. This trip had started similarly, a sledding fantasy involving Cindy Hollis, but become much more—a collection of short stories, full of the truth and fictions of real women, a man between worlds. Spirit, heartbreak, and survival flowed down summer streams of the past and present, along mile after mile of dreams and mirages, through the Rez and city badlands, among cultures and attitudes rising as vapor heated by the sun, cooled and falling as precipitation: the gentle female rain, *níłtsqbi´ ádd*; the violent male rainstorm, *níłtsqbikq´*. Dance of zigzag lightning, sunlight pollen, white shell and turquoise; sleep, awakening.

At times, looking back, I feel so out of synch, wonder what is ahead. If I am 1/8 Ojibwe, the majority is obviously something else. Face it. Is my destiny to be another culturally marooned, drunken Injun of the WaatchaWannabe Tribe? Will there ever be peace, or only constant, internal conflict in languages I don't understand?

That question posed after the Revelation Non-Grotto of Cass Lake: *what does it matter where I came from?* What does anything matter, knowing by and large man has squandered most, if not all, of what has been given to him?

Sitting in the hotel at Fort Peck, I thought about it a lot, and took a shot at writing down an answer addressing the "me" part, first listing what it was based upon: what I've read over the last few years, researched, and noted; Annie's thoughts and comments; the photographs I've seen and my observations about interpretation and meaning; the BIA archives; time in the museums and on the reservations of the West; reading and considering other cultures, including that of Japan; thinking about and observing families, relationships, and how belonging is manifested; realizing we're descendants, that there's coding in the genes, "power in the blood", as the Christians say, albeit in a different context.

Here it is. My lunge at life.

The short answer is that part of me is *Anishinaabe*, and because I am one man, paradoxically, all of me already both is, and has the potential to be, *Anishinaabe*. The more complete answer will only start to be learned when enough pieces are assembled to illuminate the shadows from where I came, while accepting and then learning the meaning of crypticisms like, "you will get there, but maybe not in your lifetime." Team Convolution. More than the BIA paper, a satin warmup jacket, or Stetson with silver band.

No longer Native, or even just extended family, we pass little from the grandfathers down the generations, lose understanding. Except for a few nudges of history, I could be huddled over a fire, praying for the ice to breakup, for another spring to come, summer bounty to relieve winter's hunger. There is a profound unease of not understanding who you are, your role, now mercilessly compounded by the manufactured world. Conditioned to select, acquire, use, and dispose, there are gaping voids in our knowledge, sensitivities of place. More often than not we try to fill them through using, taking, consuming instead of respecting, expressing, originating, giving, conserving. Native values.

Nature and Native are about gaining and communicating wisdom through beneficial practices and stories. Drawing in life mud. Jumping in and swimming through the rivers, trees, lakes and skies of the ancestors. Animating the drawings, living their stories within the decay, tangible muck and seepages of the real. Unless that happens, I will be no more than a statistical Indian, business entry, member of a qualified class: The Savage Remnant. "He's nice, just like us. Successful. So artistic too."

When we were talking about the night sky, Annie mentioned the word, *ishpiming*, meaning, "in that sky, above in heaven"; and said, "if the bear is in the sky, in a constellation of stars, the stars are also in the bear, down here on earth. It is all living, sacred." The richness of the culture dim within me, the revelations found in the shadows which I can not yet see, are reason enough for it all to matter, for me to do my minute part toward reversing the pitiful lot of mankind as I know and live within it. To be more than an Indian Head Nickel worn smooth. A celebrity figurehead.

My Ancestors *found me*. In the dreams in which they dwell and brought to me. I am here. "Will you hear us, will you learn?" they ask. Will I?

Having spent so much time on the road, I was used to tuning most of it out, rendering no more than another blurred progression. From Shelby to Browning, through Glacier, Kalispell, Missoula. Making up new fictions as I went along, milepost stories about those women, all wonderful, all valuable. Stories about marrying, introducing my wife to the mountains and rivers, seasons, Ursa Major. Winning and defending her against cunning enemies, impossible odds; shuddering in triumph. Renée Still Smoking, Blackfeet princess. In our tipi along the Two Medicine River. Annie LaCroix in a log house we built on Deep Lake, a woman to be admired, at once simple and complex, so healthy in how she approaches life. Cindy Hollis in a stone split-level with plenty of glass, overlooking the Conodoguinet Creek. It was all possible. Emily Ritchey, where? Not back there in Pennsylvania. Almost forgot Cathy, Kat, Danielle. I'd have to sketch them later.

On the way to my older brother's place in Idaho Falls I drove into Bozeman, interrupting the fairy tales. I liked the small city feel—a Laramie kind of place, old downtown, University, few if any California plates. Tough in winter. Maybe I'd be back to spend more time.

Idaho Falls was very different than Bozeman, a strange, uneasy mix of cowboys, ranchers, Rickover's nuclear power sailors in their summer whites, bureaucrats, multinational "site operations contractors" (including my brother), and Mormons. Dry land looking for a ditch, giant spuds that would keep forever, just downwind of the reactor vents. Inside those potatoes were neither mountains nor rivers.

I got away for a day, taking the Triumph for a ride over Teton Pass to Jackson, Wyoming. Dawn pilgrimage to the antlers on the Square, breakfast at the Rising Crust, a fancy new pair of boots. Another Wild West place to be "restored", paved over before you knew what happened. Returning along the Snake, I flashed on more of what I had seen, that had happened on this trip. I could have grasped any of the threads and found enough to fill a life, blessed with rain instead of virga, the wispy streamers that promise moisture, but evaporate before reaching the ground on which I stand, shifting as it is and always seems to have been.

Driving on nights like this, Natalie often comes back, sits beside me. So alive. Brushing hair she's let down, reclining on the blanket over tall green spring grass, laugh riding the breeze. The bend of her knee, graceful, Rohmerian. A smiling richness, eyes closed as we float down another river of summers.

After graduating from Penn, I saw her, the day before leaving for California. As beautiful as ever. One last look granted by fate to travel with me for the rest of my life.

"I have no illusions." In that moment of clarity, she not only said so, it may even have been true.

But not an instant later. The clouds were back, thunder rolled across the blackening sky, and once again *all* seemed to be illusion. Finding with the silence no quiet. Lost among the most desperate of motives. Thought. Analysis. Structure. Everything but being. A small k kafka who's slept with the land, but fathered no clouds.

Why couldn't either of us think of anything to say? Natalie, always with me, will never be gone. I understand that now. We don't have to touch for it to be real.

My travels were as tracks left on a dry lake after rain, a jumbled criss-crossing which could not be followed, decoded. Ephemeral jaunts washed away, reset without a trace. And to complete the trip, I was looking at one of the least favorite routes, I-15 south to Salt Lake, Vegas, San Berdoo, back to LA, CA. Alternates were possible west through Nevada, or south by Flagstaff. But mid-June had already passed. I would have time later to listen to the drums, wonder about the night above the tops of the lodgepole pines. For now, the Rez had to be put on hold, to prepare for Laramie, universally recognized to be the official short term objective. To keep on schedule, there could be no detour.

What will I be able to show LA I've overcome, stripped away, learned? Suppression as entertainment, repression as art? After having plowed so much of this land, will I know myself? How will I be able to prove it? With documents, a witness? Have I encountered truth? Competing truths? Inconclusive Truth, the hardest kind to deal with?

Will detachment, silence ever be enough again?

25

Plenty Sioux confirm, it was a good day to ride

Max tells me that Sunday was a good day to ride. What happened is from his account, and those others told me later.

After returning to Laguna we went out for a weekend ride in the high desert. The Sioux, in saying it was a good day to die, would have been closer to the truth. Those wily Sioux, feared Dakota, enemy of the Ojibwe in the Old Days. Could it be more of their treachery, hidden in dark forests of the generations? Whether or not the Old Days had taken a timeout, I feel no antipathy now. This was about dirt biking, not tribal skirmishes. It was a good day to ride.

On El Mirage Dry Lake, wide open, I flowed with the orange Maico desert sled, Max beside me on his red and silver WR360 Husqvarna with big Metzeler knobby, the two of us colorful flags waving in the desert wind of our motion. Gripping Pro-Alloy bars, we hung it all out, wheelied over sand hills, flew through narrow arroyos, planted boots and roared up winding washes. Shut down, pipes smoking Bardahl VBA mixed 32:1, we stretched out in the shade of a boulder, ears ringing from the noise, guzzling water and gobbling trail mix.

Back in motion, I took one jump too fast, caught huge air over the top, but was blind to the deep trench on the other side cut by a thunderstorm's flood. In rigid body rotation, aka an endo, I went over the bars, hitting the front of my helmet hard on a rock, knocked out in that desert nowhere. Max came over the hill right behind, slightly slower, and though slammed from the jarring contact with the ditch, both made it safely and missed running into me and my bike; then got off and tried to revive me, with no response. When it was clear I was badly hurt, he drained some gas out of my tank and lit a bush on fire. Max didn't want to leave for fear of being unable to find the way back, ten miles from the Wells Bar, the only place nearby which had a phone. Burning bush in the desert. Classically Mosaic.

Two other riders saw the black smoke, checked it out, then went for help. An hour later, a 4x4 rescue crew arrived and called in a medevac to UCLA Medical Center. Unconscious, pale, cold, with a very weak, sinking pulse and undiagnosed injuries, it was questionable whether I would make it.

They say I awoke three days later, but could do little more than move my eyes. My leg was in a cast, ribs hurt when I breathed, and there was a reason my clavicle was wrapped. All broken. Disoriented—actually, more accurately unoriented—I was immobilized because of the head injury and extended unconsciousness. Drugs were being administered by IV to combat pneumonia. "Breathe consciously," distant voices repeated during their white-uniformed bedside rotations, "fight the pneumonia."

Max came by, but I didn't recognize him in the cold fog of serious injury.

I heard a doctor saying (to my parents, it turns out), "Your son has suffered a contusion of the frontal lobe of the brain. He's lucky to have survived the impact trauma. A harder hit or different angle, and it could have been fatal. Recovery from this type of injury is unpredictable—it can be partial or complete, rapid or slow, with the possibility of unusual side effects. All I can say at present is time will tell."

With my parents' concurrence, a wall of anonymity was raised around me. "He went on a trip and hasn't returned." I disappeared from the world.

Inside that wall my world was a different place. Not unfamiliar, because with the references of memory swept away, what could be familiar? I was just there. Empty. Blank. Awake, but with a life I no longer knew hidden beyond a dim, distant horizon.

Moved from UCLA to another medical center in Laguna Niguel, time went by slowly, stretching across a month of hospitalization. It would take more months of physical and mental rehabilitation after release to function again. If ever fully.

By the time I returned to Laguna, the first week of August 1977, two months after the reunion, I began to remember some things about my life, but mostly as unconnected fragments. Traffic was heavy for the Pageant of the Masters and Sawdust Festival, but that didn't mean anything to me. I wasn't going out anytime soon. For the first two weeks, I was assisted by a "home care provider".

The house was only vaguely recognizable. Much better than unrecogniz-able, believe me.

Not only did I have little accessible memory, I suffered frequent interruptions of concentration, like the power plug being pulled in the middle of a thought. Mostly, I didn't even remember not remembering. The housekeeper had dutifully stacked answering machine tapes for the month spent in the hospital, and weeks before that during my trip to the reunion which I had not had time to review before the desert rumble. When I got around to playing them, I couldn't visualize the faces of the callers. A double order of hospital haze had been shipped. You can keep the extra. Call me Craig O. Opaque. Double Nought for short. 00.

Callers during my absence included several women—Cathy, Kat, Cindy, Emily, and Danielle. All phoned, left messages, then ceased calling. There was also mail—from fans, forwarded by my agent, business documents, photos returned from a processing lab, and some letters from those who had called. Max knew only generally of my exploits, and couldn't fill in many of the memory blanks. Max? I must know him—my friend? Elvis didn't call. Like a dog watching and "thinking" who knows what, I saw on TV that Elvis checked out of the Heartbreak Hotel and permanently into the Land of the Legendary on August 16th.

Recovering from the fractures, I had to take things very slowly. My life in the clouds was as a time exposure, softly streaked by the wind, further drawn by a slow shutter speed. I rested, read, and sat out on the deck watching more clouds, the waves below. Having embarked on this journey to my special place, not one of my own making, I wasn't yet able to sight shore. It was all as foreign as *Islandia*, that hazy utopia accessible only by invitation or intervention. Navigating a world without references.

Sleep required that I lie flat on my back. Getting out of bed in the morning, any body twist was painful. I hobbled up and down the stairs, and had to wrap the leg cast in plastic to keep out the water in the shower. With time I regained some awareness of "myself". Considering how close I had come to death, I wondered later if there wasn't a force in the clouds filling my life, one which had brought me to the brink, but not let me go over. Kept around for some unknown purpose.

When I could do so without too much pain, I sat at the piano, at first for no other reason than it was there, then began to visualize instead of trying to play. From there, musical skills came back surprisingly quickly. Much more startling, I became capable of brilliance as never before. So good that had my mind been stronger at the time, it would have scared me. I had to practice—it wasn't like I was just struck by lightning and there it was, fully developed. While hospitalized, I had heard classical music on the radio, soothed for hours during the day, and especially at night in what passed for hospital darkness. Now, with growing awareness, I sensed that the new capabilities were awesome.

My playing became technically daunting. As powerful as a summer thunderstorm bearing down on a mountain town; the sun afterward lyrical as finely drawn poetry, illuminating cloud tops in heavenly drama. Fragments of Mozart became quickly familiar, cherished, expressive arias sung at the piano in a moonlit vineyard of vernal imagination.

Oh yeah, there *were* two unusual side effects of the accident: I couldn't or didn't want to talk; and was color blind.

At that time I had little more than music. It was a period of withdrawal, near physical and mental isolation. Sailing through a visually achromatic world black and white as the keys on the piano, I arrived at *Islandia* and found it uninhabited.

Come out, come out. Whoever you are.

26

Dream defense
of the Ojibwe

It might have remained that way for the rest of my life. Who can say? Seeing and communicating like a camera loaded with Tri-X, indirectly, quietly; by grayscale, contrast, sequences of motor-driven photoemissive life images. SuperBoy lifting buses while never realizing his powers. A life of nothing more than PerryWhitened emulations, climbing the ladder at The Daily Planet, devoid of take-home zygotene drama. Lífe mítoüten Loís.

I was constantly inputting, processing, storing information in ways of which I was only partly aware. Like looking at the stars not from earth, but from the floating void of space, trying to grasp what can be seen and interpreted, with a growing sense of the infinity which will never be physically experienced. Visualizing rearrangement of objects on a perceptual table, rotating them, changing the lighting, the shadows, the associations, meaning, importance.

There were pencils and sketching pads around from my foray into *Drawing on the Right Side*. One day I picked up a pencil and began to see faces. Rendering them with the sharp point like fine weaving, sometimes I didn't want to lift the pencil, withdraw from the image, fearing it would unravel. There were no names to put with the faces I drew, almost all women and children. Looking at the drawings, I wondered whether the people existed, and if so, who they might be. I didn't remember putting the sketching pad down on top of an open box of music scores, one of a dozen usually kept on shelves in the garage when not looking for a particular piece.

After a shower and in the midst of getting dressed, suddenly distracted when the wind slammed shut the bedroom door, I slipped on wet bathroom tile, and went down hard, hitting my head on the sink. The world went dark. Again.

The second (latest?) most incredible course altering event in my life, but who's counting?

My housekeeper found me when she arrived an hour later, unconscious on the bathroom floor, and immediately called for help. After taking care of that, and when the shaking stopped, she continued straightening up, cleaned the kitchen, put the lids on the boxes in the music room and returned them to the garage, then mopped any dust in the entryway which might have been tracked in by the EMT's.

"I wonder if that man's going to be okay *this* time," she thought. "How many chances will he get? Been real strange since the accident. Hope he's alright—I won't find a better job."

✣══════✣

I awoke in the Laguna Hills hospital. Though a bit blurry when I first saw the nurse coming in the door of the room, she became clearer walking toward me. Pretty, with reddish hair. I told her so.

"*You're* okay, I can see." The medical professional who has seen and heard all of it, with whom another hospital hostage is always falling in love. Thankfulness for healing, if that's the case, an energetic gesture of resignation, physical attraction … whatever.

Wait a minute. Her hair *color*, what I *said* to her.

Though treated and released after two days of "observation", the unfocused vision hadn't entirely gone away. "There are things going on we don't understand," the doctor said. "If it gets worse, let me know immediately, otherwise, I want to see you at the end of the week."

Max took me home without a word, shaking his head. It was all too unbelievable.

Occasional blurriness remained, with headaches. Back to the doctor.

"You need glasses," he said after some tests in the "take out the trash now" laconic monotone of a disengaged medical practitioner, "that's all."

✣══════✣

A few days later, I had an intense dream that I still recall undiminished in clarity and power. Before going to bed, I was looking for something in a drawer, and came across a few mementos—a baseball signed by Casey Stengel and the 1960's Mets from a game with the Phillies at Connie Mack, and a deck of "Authors" cards. We played that card game when kids on vacation in the Shenandoahs, sitting at the table while the rain clicked on the aluminum roof of my family's travel trailer. Hawthorne, Longfellow, Tennyson, all looking so old with beards and dark clothes of the 1800's.

I dreamed of thick forest falling to a cold, deep lake, smoke curling skyward in villages on the shore. Dark clouds of a storm coming from the west. Tired and hungry, I stumbled into a camp, but no one could see me. Continuing to walk, I sat on the steep beach, one of smooth, red-brown and black polished stones rather than sand. Looking down, I saw a marble-sized agate, a shooter resembling an eye. Small waves, more irregular surges than a progression, wet porous rocks that glistened, then were quickly matted by the wind, before being wet again.

Behind me, I heard a voice, soft footsteps on the pebbles and cobbles, another sound I didn't recognize.

Turning around, I saw Annie LaCroix, in a jingle dress, *ziibaaska' igana-gooday*, dancing so gracefully, beautiful.

"*Mino-giizhigad, minwaanimad.*" It is a nice day, the wind is from a favorable direction.

"You came back, my *Anishinaabe* brother," she said quietly after the dance was completed.

"Yes, now I am as our grandfathers, building their camps, gathering rice, fishing in this lake."

"Will you be marrying soon?" she asked.

"I have not yet been told. Are you to be my wife?"

"I know only that you will marry one of your own kind. We will share the fires of our people, strengthening the life which has been given to each of us. We are to seek the lessons of the Old Ways and revere their truths. Have no fear when you are at the point of death, for you will live a full life, until blessed to be called by *Gichi-Manidoo*—Great Spirit, God the Creator.

"Loved ones will die, testing your spirit, from which you will emerge stronger, yet you must learn to understand both loss and true strength. It will take time.

"Before I go," Annie said, "I am to leave you this card. Though you are not to look now, when you see it again, you will recognize it, and begin to understand."

Annie walked back to camp.

There was a crash of lightning, and I was in a desert, looking south to the horizon. I turned around once more, and saw the ancient rock and adobe of First Mesa, Hopiland. A woman was smiling, reaching out her hand to me. *Bitsii´ litsoii*, the one with the yellow hair. She was familiar, though with a grieving heart, smiling. I extended my hand, yet could not reach hers.

Looking to the sky, she said, "teach us, that one day we may be worthy."

The woman disappeared in a rush of wind from the most dramatic lightning storms on the Hopi mesas that I never experienced. Just when the torrential rain hit my face, carried me off in a churning mocha flood down an endless arroyo, I awoke. Some of my memory was back.

The top drawer of the dresser wasn't completely shut. Instead of closing it, I opened the drawer and pulled out a deck of cards. The one on top was Long-fellow, *Evangeline*.

I looked in the phone book, and when a bookstore downtown opened, called to arrange immediate delivery of a copy. Based on a true story of the displacement of the French by the British in 1755 Nova Scotia, it was an epic verse of Longfellow which first appeared in 1847. The story was eerily reminiscent of the occupation of Ojibwe land by white settlers under governmental authority, prior to and after the Treaty of 1854. Evangeline was separated from her beloved Gabriel, spent her life searching for him, became reconciled to a life of separation, and finally found him on the day of his death:

> All was ended now, the hope, and the fear, and the sorrow,
> All the aching of heart, the restless, unsatisfied longing …
> Meekly she bowed her own (head), and murmured,
> "Father, I thank Thee!"
> Still stands the forest primeval; but far away from its shadow,
> Side by side, in their nameless graves, the lovers are sleeping.

Having been plugged back in, the current was on. The healing was far from over, I would still be challenged by gaps in my memory, and there was no creative outlet as yet for my newfound musical capabilities. So I kept them close, private. But I could start putting the names back together with the faces of the past, get to know them again.

The pictures in the envelopes included those of a dark-haired woman with striking eyes that held mine as I studied the photos. Annie LaCroix. In my dream, she had said that I would marry one of my own kind. Which dream? Was it all a dream? Was I *Anishinaabe*, or *gichi-mookomaan*, a white person? Both, and if so, therefore really neither? Were these pictures even real? Had I drawn pictures of her as well? What happened to my sketch pad? Where did that go? I couldn't find it.

Calling Directory Assistance in Minnesota, I got the number of the Library and dialed. Please exist, please answer, Annie LaCroix.

"Cloquet Public Library, this is Annie LaCroix. May I help you?"

"Annie, this is Craig Maxwell. I'm so glad you're there, you're really there." She was not surprised that I was calling. It seemed that we were just resuming a recent conversation, that she needed no update. Nevertheless, I summarized what had happened.

"Only now is my memory coming back, after an incredible dream."

Annie listened as I told her about it, including *Evangeline*. When I finished, she remarked only, "it is good that we dream." Much later, Annie would relate that she had been thinking of me that night, wondering where I had gone. She had a dream too, one that included our encounter on the shore. Her dream ended with an admonishment to keep it to herself until the time was right—in the way of The People. It was astounding.

I told her about what I had learned at Cass Lake.

"No, we're not cousins, if that's what you're driving at," she said with a giggle. "You're Hawk, I'm Sturgeon."

"What?"

"Our totems, clans."

"How do you know that?"

"A little asking around in your case. While you were away on your journey."

I wanted to believe the dream, that she would be a source of serene comfort, kinship. A link to The People, placed in that capacity by unseen forces, a compass for navigating at the edges of two cultures as I sought the path crossing the divisions.

"... away on your journey." Interesting way to put it.

"Annie, I want to be close to you, knowing that even though we may be living our lives far apart, we will always be there for each other. Please help me, Annie."

"That's the Sturgeon, Craig, *Numae*. Strength, depth. The Hawk, *Kaikaik*, brings leadership. In your case, maybe not yet; something to look forward to," she giggled again.

Annie LaCroix was no romanticized record cover Indian Icon. She was the real thing, a bright, special child who had walked down abandoned logging roads in her worn sack dress, through maples and birch, dreaming of the campfires in Grandmother's old stories, bountiful seasons, the mysteries of the created world, grasping in her hand the old deerskin ball Grandfather had made, skipping, humming a song.

Annie had to go, but before hanging up, she said, "I know you will be back here, the land of our people. Perhaps I will come see you sometime, my brother, *indawemaa*."

My brother. She had spoken it first in my dream, and now, again. That she could have known any of this before I called continued to amaze me.

Looking at the picture of Annie, I saw her on the other end of the line as she spoke with me. Wondering what had been between us those months ago, what was there now, unspoken, unseen. Not knowing what "brother" really meant—a general statement of tribal affiliation, or closer kinship of brother and sister, with its restrictions? It was so hazy. I hadn't dared ask.

I went outside on the deck and saw the Ocean, the waves far below. My weakness was a common one—I wanted to know the ending without the experience. Cut to the chase, sneak a look at the last chapter. In trying to do so, I had been missing the richness of discovery, failing to build a foundation for my life and relationships with others. Just let me catch the fish, show me the bottom line, don't tell me about the factory conditions. I might call you again. I'll think about it.

Though I had awakened in the world, not in the purity of heaven or whatever you want to call it, still a man continuously pulled in different directions by forces internal and external, I also sensed that I was being given new perspectives and tools to deal with them. Insight, heart, music.

If you truly dance, you will be set apart; forfeit their time, but be drawn toward, then brought into, The Circle. The Circle of Life.

27

Bewilderment, a state within
The Golden State

Another call to the photo gallery. Cathy, now in San Francisco.

"Cathy, this is Craig Maxwell."

"Where have you been? I've been so worried." Tense, concerned. "I called and called but couldn't get through to you. Is it really you? You sound ... different."

"I had a motorcycle accident and have been out of commission. I was very lucky—there was no permanent physical damage, and despite amnesia following the accident, my doctors now think there will be no long term memory impairment. It's been touch and go for quite awhile. Although I just snapped out of it, there are still a lot of gaps in remembering my life before the accident. I have to take everything very slowly."

A long pause before, "where did it happen?"

I told her what I knew, almost all from what Max had told me.

Another long pause. "Do you remember what I look like?"

"I'm looking at a picture of you, taken in Wyoming, I think."

"I want to come down to see you right away," she said. "There's an airport in Orange County, right?"

"Yes, but is that a good idea right now? I'm pretty beatup."

"I want to see you, to help any way I can. Are you really okay?"

"I think so. I won't be driving for some time, though, so you'll have to either rent a car or take a cab from the airport."

Flying north-south in California was no problem, lots of flights and inexpensive fares. Cathy arrived the following Friday evening. By the time she knocked on the door I was anxious, wondering, "who are you, Cathy?" My fog wasn't the kind that would just burn off the next morning with the sun. It was deep, layered bewilderment. Thick as river silt.

"You've got glasses now. I like them," she said, then kissed me gently, as if I would break.

Cathy told me afterward that she was wondering the same thing when I opened the door. Although I appeared to be healthy, there was a difference in my eyes she couldn't quite figure out. And then there was the impact of the prime digs, above the lights of Laguna, the day's heat now displaced by an onshore Pacific breeze; darkness beyond the beach below stretching to what would be the night horizon with the moonrise. Overwhelming and, to some extent, probably intimidating.

Later in the evening, Cathy pointed to the piano, and asked if I was up to playing. "Play something, Craig, please. For me." Almost a plea, in which I sensed a welling of emotion, nearly overflowing, as if to say, "come back." Come back to me, for me.

As I reflected on that moment months after, I realized that the trip to see me was an important chapter in a struggle within her. That she loved me, but our relationship, whatever it could be called, hadn't grown closer. There was no indication that it would, and now, possibly in ways yet to be revealed, I was different—had been changed. And then there was her career. She wanted to succeed, a drive in her blood as strong as that needed to survive on the land of Wyoming. Laramie, four years of her life there. Go back with me? To what? She had ridden fence, punched cattle, awakened to ice storms, pulled trucks out of ditches back onto slippery roads. Tough, yet vulnerable. Like we all are, to our hearts. Hers didn't want to return to Laramie.

I hadn't gotten very far in developing my newfound capabilities, so there was little repertoire upon which to draw. But I could do a Bach keyboard piece, long time warmup drill. As I played it, there was a fresh crispness to the articulation, solid phrasing, subtlety in the dynamics.

Cathy was mesmerized. "Wow," she said softly, "… I never knew you could play like that. I want more of it. And I want more of you and I." Together in the Bay Area, not Laramie.

Putting herself at emotional risk, knowing that there were strong headwinds and crosscurrents, body and who knows what other damage. Still reaching out.

She snuggled close to me as we talked more. I was very tired. Still experiencing occasional pain when I stood up or turned the wrong way, I suggested that it would be better if we slept separately. "Okay," she murmured, as I hobbled down the hall with a cane, showing her to the bedroom where she would stay.

On Saturday, Cathy took us for a ride on PCH. We parked and watched the surfers below catching waves. I wasn't up to going to a restaurant yet so we cooked in. My housekeeper made sure that the kitchen was well-provisioned, and everything was in order. On Saturday night, sitting out on the deck for the sunset, we talked in the increasing darkness.

"I like San Francisco—it's the right place for me. My job at the publishing company is going well, and there's always so much happening."

I tried to visualize the City, places I'd been, but it was still vague.

"Have you been meeting people, going out?"

"Yes, the job is great for that. I guess you could say I go out regularly with a couple of guys from work, more friends than anything."

"Cathy, tell me about us—our time together when you were in Laramie. I don't remember all of it."

"You're quieter now, more thoughtful, which is understandable since you're trying to remember the past. Your eyes are different. They're even darker now. More mysterious," she said laughing. "Like different clouds in the sky, changing weather."

"Sesame Street has been a big help: 'What color is the white car, Bobby?' As far as I know, my senses are intact, and I don't know that I'm incapable of doing anything I could before. I guess I'm making a new start, finding out what I want to do. If I don't remember something, I just have to be quiet, or invent it as I go along, step by step."

As we talked, I wondered about how much was smoldering underneath. I was comfortable with her, and vice versa. Would we be close friends who shared a past, or lovers with a future? Still in the process of rebuilding the memories of our time together and being so banged up, I had no expectations. Despite the returning physical electricity I felt, we just held each other for a long time.

Cathy left on Sunday. A few more pieces of the puzzle of my life had been filled in. Would the distance between us be overcome, or grow even greater? She wanted to see me. But what did I want? What did I feel? What did I remember? Would we keep in touch for a time, then just exchange Christmas cards with a letter inserted to update our lives, until one or the other came back undeliverable? Why was I thinking this way?

Was the puzzle even the same one? Why *was* I thinking this way? Beauty had been revealed to me in so many ways, through this woman, music, art. This was an opportunity to start over, approach all of it from a new, healthier direction—with a child's acceptance and appreciation, an adult's discernment. I should be seeking that realm of beauty, consciously living each day within it.

28

Cindy enters the memory warp at Laguna

It was now early September 1977. For Emily, the teacher, September meant back to school, with Thanksgiving realistically the earliest she could visit, if she wanted to at all. By that time, I might even remember if there were any crucial details I needed to know. I dialed her number.

Emily's "greeting" was cool. "I was disappointed. I thought I was going to be able to see the West this summer. You just disappeared."

I explained what had happened, including the "wall of secrecy" Max had built up around me immediately after the accident. That resolved the disappearance, but not entirely the disappointment. Maybe to a woman, a motorcycle crash and burn was foolishness, rather than a directly accepted, pitiable feat. A "guy's excuse" that didn't cut it. We left it at that, and the conversation was soon over.

As with Cathy, I couldn't remember her completely even after speaking, although the pictures helped. I was looking at more therapy, and wouldn't be able to go back to Pennsylvania to visit. If we talked again, I'd offer to send that ticket so she could come to Laguna.

The next morning, at least for her, Emily called, waking me. The clock said 3:30 am. Payback.

"I've been thinking since we talked last night, hardly been able to sleep at all. Not getting together this summer was a real letdown, but I understand what happened. I wanted to see you then, and I want to see you now. Unfortunately, the earliest I could make it would be Thanksgiving," she said. "Is the offer you made when you were here still open, but for Thanksgiving instead?" When you were somebody else.

"Yes," I yawned, "I'll send you a ticket."

"Okay, that's settled, except I'll buy my own ticket. Meeting an injured man I'm mad at with a lost memory in a place I've never been. Am I crazy or what?" Then a little laugh.

"I'm going to go back to sleep now." Sure I am. "Enjoy your day at school, Emily."

"I will. Plenty of time for the arrangements. Talk to you later. Bye."

A runaway mind-body reaction had been initiated. Her little laugh pushed a button, opened the door, blew it completely off the hinges. In a rush of imagery I saw Emily before me, under a tree on a spring night, willing to be kissed. She had been ready, desirable. Why had she been willing? Desirable? Did I realize how desirable at that moment? Was I blind? With my new glasses it'll be different ... .

I was so excited I went back to bed, looking forward to dreams of abandon, winding streets of the Algarve, Andalusian flamenco nights. Where were those places anyhow?

A few days later, when I called Kat, her mother said she had moved to Flagstaff and resumed teaching school. I couldn't remember anything about moving. I left my number and asked her to give Kat the message I had called. Since she was teaching, like Emily, it might be difficult to slip away and come down to Laguna, even for a weekend.

My last call, in no particular order of which I was aware, obviously a very relative term, was to Cindy. Perhaps Danielle would call me again or show up in LA one day. I would wait on that.

Unexplainably, I clearly remembered what Cindy looked like in high school, but only vaguely recalled our brief time together after the reunion. Gray shetland crewneck sweater, hair cut in a pageboy kind of style, but a little longer. She bore a clear resemblance to painter Edith Hamlin, wife of Maynard Dixon, whom I saw in a 1940's photo. The pink oxford blouse with a button-down collar and kilt-style skirt were different, though. Tall and slim. Loafers. Nice long legs. The more I thought about her, I wondered, what am I doing, setting up interviews? Am I just trying to calibrate, recalibrate memories? Was there anything useful that I ever knew, much less forgot? Where is my heart? My true heart? What is a true heart?

Things were a little slow in her business, a lull between back to school and holiday advertising, she said. Cindy had never been to Southern California and was interested in coming out for a few days. Was that surprising? She asked if it would be alright to bring Jed. Of course. Later, after having thought some more, she mentioned that her sister could watch him. I didn't know she had a sister.

Cindy would be renting a car for the drive down to Laguna since I still wasn't driving. For now, Laguna Beach was safety and quiet, a good place to mend, watch the sunsets, breathe the night seabreeze. Get to know these women, really for the first time.

Two school teachers, a commercial artist, and a cowgirl; no dancers, comedians, agents, or technical assistants. All from out of town. For me, a new chapter, if not life—time would tell. Nobody I needed to impress, no deadlines to meet. It was a course correction, whether I wanted to go to new destinations or not.

Two weeks later, Cindy arrived, wearing a simple though elegant cotton dress over black leotard, with a subtly textured cotton sweater. Impeccable. In clothing, not cars—the Peugeot to which she was partial, I recalled, was barely an automobile. Talking about bare, her graceful neck and long legs were a wakeup call. Tired from a full day of travel and the time difference, she would be refreshed by a shower, night blooming jasmine outside the bedroom window, cool evening breeze off the Pacific.

My mind felt like the local eucalyptus sawdust, fragrant yet punky, of little use. An extra in a black & white movie, sweeping the streets at dawn, not knowing what to do except stand aside when a car passed, barely getting out of the way. I showed her to her bedroom and turned to go, but she gently caught my arm. Not saying a word, she leaned into me with a kiss. Intoxicating. Healthy, smooth complexion, hair, lipstick, you get the picture. Shuffling off to my room, the fatigue from the day's exertion was forgotten for a moment as I savored what had just happened, thinking house guests aren't that much bother.

When I awoke, Cindy was already up, doing yoga, centering, stretching, exercising. After she finished, we had rolls, jam, and coffee on the deck, the sky a gray morning overcast which would burn off by noon. Cindy was interested in seeing an exhibition in Long Beach mentioned in the paper. I felt up to the drive, so we planned to leave after lunch. In the meantime, we looked at my collection of Indian arts, pottery, sculpture, paintings, jewelry, and baskets. She was fascinated, having had no exposure to the Southwest or Native arts of the region.

The Porsche and Ferrari were in the garage. "You're probably not ready to take one of these to Long Beach today. Some other time maybe?" Showy California toys stabled in the hills above Laguna. Cindy did not disagree. Her rental Ford would be just fine.

Down on Coast Highway, we passed the Hotel Laguna, then Main Beach Park, "Laguna Beach Lifeguard Dept. Est. 1929" on the old building there. Farther north, up the hill at Aster Street, I remembered having breakfast at the Cottage Restaurant. A beautiful day, Catalina was visible to the west, as we continued north past Emerald Bay and Reef Point to Corona del Mar. The Port Theater, with its sails, Tudor Five Crowns, and The Quiet Woman were all reminders contributing bits and pieces of other days and nights to my rebuilding.

Cindy liked the headlands, coves and sand, breaking waves, the magnificent Pacific coast, but had a few things to say about the traffic, which thickened considerably past Fashion Island in Newport Beach and remained that way through Huntington Beach, Surfside, and Seal Beach. On Naples Island,

Kelly's Irish pub prompted memories of a namesake, Kelly Dalton. During the Santa Monica days I had spent a few weekends in nearby Belmont Heights. Leaving on a tour shortly after meeting her, I could only say goodbye by mail before she moved to Colorado.

Belmont Shore and Belmont Heights, the latter slightly higher, built on top the bluff overlooking Long Beach Harbor, were comfortably livable districts with a sense of community character, rather than the endless square miles of development to the north existing as little more than exits on the freeways crisscrossing the Southland east and west. Hof's Hut, Hamburger Henry, and that log place on 2nd Street; the German tavern off Redondo Avenue with Dresdener on tap. Yeah, once upon a time, briefly, Kelly Country. Setting for the illusory Susan/Suzanne/Susanna(h).

A couple minutes away was Ocean Boulevard, on that Pacific bluff, along which ran a promenade of sorts, ending at the Long Beach Museum of Art. Cindy parked and we went inside, slowly, taking it easy because of my leg. According to their brochure, the brown-shingle complex consisted of the Elizabeth Milbank Anderson residence and carriage house built in 1912. Without the joggers and ten-speed bikes now dominating it, the walkway and parkstrip along Ocean Boulevard would have been a real promenade in that era.

After viewing the exhibition, the significance of which was lost on my empty mind, we went back outside and sat on a bench. With the Queen Mary, Harbor piers and cranes, and oil islands in the distance, the palms, ornate steel railing, irrigated grass and flowers provided welcome visual relief. On concrete steps zig-zagging from the wide, flat beach below, a girl stair-stepped up backward, long black hair flowing out from her baseball cap. An unusual workout? Exercise in easyway/hardway? Some kind of abstract statement rejecting the freewayland mentality/reality?

Cindy looked at me and said, "I see her point." I smiled, wondering what that might be. Perhaps kinetic art.

On the way home we stopped on Forest Avenue in Laguna for a cappuccino, appreciating the ambience of the place, Mission Revival architecture, relief from the cardboard houses being slapped up along the San Diego Freeway by the thousands, from their exits along "The 405", theoretically a straight shot commute to the heart of LA, wherever that is. A few doors down at Laguna Music, I found a couple tapes of Bach and Handel keyboard pieces and bought them to help with my practicing.

I still couldn't do anything strenuous, and though open parking spaces kept cropping up between my ears, I had no quarters for the meters. We were again barely scratching the surface in getting to know each other. It was evident though that Cindy was trying to find herself, after the promise, then failure, of the last five or six years.

We were in the hot tub out back after sundown, screened from the neighbors, the day's warmth moderated by a moist seabreeze. I was leaning back, eyes closed, when she put her finger on my lips as if to say, "quiet, not a word," took my hand and gestured to get out, handing me a towel. Inside, still without that word, we lay down carefully, slowly seeking currents, simmering for years, unknowingly before, now to be experienced. Together, fully in the prime of life, while the moon rose, the waves broke, and jasmine bloomed, we were carried off. Later, she cried, a tearful moan rising to become a heartwrenching wail as she held onto me, as if for dear life. Beyond emotion, all the way around and back to what was primal, like nothing I had ever experienced.

I didn't expect any of it. To sleep so deeply, wake up, Elle beside me as I groped for a life, aching from the exertion. Cindy with an edge, boundary of pain covered by peacefulness, at least during the start of this day. Her original true face, if only visible for part of a night.

And so it was for the next two days, sleeping together, our time. Gently experimental. We'll just do this, try that, if we have to, figure out what it means later.

"What do you think of Southern California?" Nominal in the complex mechanics and metaphysics of this encounter thought about for ten years, but she took it with grace.

"Well, the time I've spent could hardly be typical, and I haven't been to Los Angeles yet. Although what I've seen is different and exciting, I don't think it's for me. Huge, fast, and you say getting even bigger and faster. I'd miss the more dramatic change of seasons, my school house, the Creek, new leaves, green forest in spring."

"I guess some of those reasons underlie why I thought of going back to school in Laramie." Another recollection.

"I don't know anything about Wyoming, but I would guess that it isn't any greener."

Funny how you remember a remark in passing: "I would guess that it isn't any greener." Even now I remember her saying it, as if the thought was a subtitle below her portrait.

I waved goodbye when Cindy drove off, heard her car make the turn at the corner, then only the breeze. Looking out at the Pacific, I thought about this woman. The trip to Laguna seemed to be a big step toward confronting hurt within her only beginning to be faced. That step had brought a measure of healing to me as well.

Cindy returned to Camp Hill, and I stayed in Laguna. We might like to spend more time together, but neither wanted to be in the other place. Our relationship was left closemouthed and open-ended.

29
Thanksgiving 1977

Which left one or both teachers in the fall. My own school plans for Laramie would have to be delayed, probably at least two semesters, nearly a year.

While the physical healing progressed, my memory continued to return. I looked forward to being able to get back behind the wheel. Taking it slowly, I began driving around the winding streets where I lived, trying to remember where they went, and stay away from the grades of 20% or more plunging to PCH. When ready to venture beyond, I would have to figure out from maps how to get where I wanted to go and back. Well, we've only got two vehicles left for Laguna Drivers Ed, a Porsche and Ferrari, both serious stick. Which one would you like to take out into heavy traffic today?

One night I hitched a ride to a performance of Beethoven's *Piano Concerto No. 5, Emperor,* with the LA Philharmonic. It was exhilarating. The concert motivated me to practice harder, reach higher. I got stacks of sheet music and scores, spent hours every day playing scales, sonatas, and the piano parts of ensemble works. To relax I played against jazz progressions from the studio monitors.

In early November my other brother decided that he needed a break from Upstate New York. Working/not working on his doctoral thesis, in reality he was faded out from too many years of school, the end of four years of living with a woman, and wanted to nip the increasingly passive, sleep late/ perpetual college bar night scene before it became permanently entrenched.

Driving what used to be a white VW, rusted by Thruway winters and battered from a freak hailstorm in Colorado, full of six pack plastic carriers, cigarette butts, dirty clothes, empty beer cans, camping junk, and maps, he was a great, bearded denim road character, fully premagnetized and capable of determining the local deflection without powered scientific apparatus, calculating cultural drift. Driving coast to coast, taking 1000 mile detours in what was becoming a family tradition, he was ready to kick back in transit and shred Laguna.

After a week, we left on a three day trip to San Francisco via U.S. 101 to Santa Barbara and SLO, Route 1 up through Big Sur, Monterey, Half Moon Bay, then over the bridge. He would be continuing from there to Reno, the Pacific Northwest, Idaho and Montana, seeking to be vaccinated by the miles against incipient Cayuga Lake winter browns and grays, then solid, frozen white.

I got off his tour at the Oakland Airport, limped down to the gate, bought a paper, and thought about how after all this time, I was still coming or going, never staying, building or maintaining. I should have called Cathy, but didn't, walking onto the flight without a word. Why not? With my brother leaving, a down day was some of it. Then there was the fact that Cindy and I had slept together, and Thanksgiving was only a few days away. Emily would be arriving Wednesday night. The need to simplify things was obvious. That explained it. Move on. Well, not so fast. Some guilt in there, I think. About what?

I drove to the Orange County Airport to pick up Emily, a significant navigational success in itself. No Bonneville this time. The Porsche had to do, given her luggage. She found me in the holiday weekend crowd after a double take, my beard and hair grown longer after the accident, months of not having seen each other. It was 11 pm before we got to the house, after opting for the scenic route through Newport Beach and Corona del Mar, obligatory moon reflection on the Pacific, wind stirring the palms and flowers, thick and sweet.

Seeing Emily's excitement at being in Laguna literally made me shudder, gave me a very good feeling about her visit. I thought back to Cindy's short time here, and rather than guilt, felt thankfulness without having to figure out all the reasons why.

"I could learn to like living in a house on the coast, Porsche in the garage, and a mystery man constantly changing disguises."

She looked great, had a spark that took hold of me. Twenty more years of teaching math? It didn't compute.

"Maybe you'll decide to move out here, although California these days would not be my first choice. There's nothing wrong with Shiremanstown, but the West is a different world."

We got into the hot tub to unwind. It was so relaxing, and as was the case most late evenings, I was very tired.

"Hey there, you going to go to sleep on me?"

"Yeah, I think so. I still have to take things pretty slowly these days, step by step, and right now my body is telling me to stop stepping; it needs sleep."

"Okay, I can live with that. Goodnight, Craig," she said, giving me a kiss. With Emily, each kiss seemed so special, electrical, awesome.

While lying in bed, though, I began to wonder again whether I was doing the right thing, inviting Cindy and then Emily. Out of town, mail order, shipments, windows of opportunity. In the most superficial sense, little more than new mileposts along the road. I wanted something so much deeper. I wanted to belong—to somewhere, something, with someone.

Thanksgiving 1977. As the day dawned, despite those misgivings, I was thankful—to be here, to have this woman with me. I had bribed my everfaithful housekeeper to come in and set up Thanksgiving dinner for two, knowing she would have done it anyway. When Emily awoke I had a fresh cup of french roast ready. It was a clear blue day, the Pacific view incredible. I put on a Jan Garbarek album to add just the right touch of morning introspective appreciation, creative border. We listened to the first cut, sitting side by side on the deck. Everything about Emily said, "woman", in the best, most exciting ways.

After a few minutes, she looked at me and smiled, took my hand, then closed her eyes, taking both of us somewhere else. Suddenly, I wanted to be there with her, more than anything I could remember in my life. When she opened her eyes, still smiling, I saw a different Emily. Everything before had only been a prelude. She was dazzling. I leaned over and kissed her, thinking after our lips had separated, neither of us could ever be the same. Would that be true? Could I trust my emotions?

"I'm afraid if we don't go down to the beach now, I'll never get there," she said laughing. We both knew it.

"You're right. Against my better judgment, let's go. We'll put some coffee in a thermos. The water will be colder than you can imagine."

There's a cove known to the locals and few others. The trail isn't apparent unless you've been on it before, and the beach can't be seen until you're at the edge of a steep bluff. To get down to the cove, you have to walk out onto the headland, then descend a very narrow path, coming back toward the beach, away from the Pacific.

The headland, being a geological popcorn ball, has been undercut by wave action on the softer underlying sediment, above which is a tough, cemented conglomerate. On top of that is silty sand, erodible and prone to sloughing, particularly after sustained rain. Applicable geological terminology includes "marine cut wave surfaces, Miocene sedimentary rocks of marine origin, and volcanic intrusive rocks; Pleistocene and Holocene deposits; Topanga Formation and San Onofre Breccia." All the ingredients for those famous California coastal slides.

The ocean bottom rises steeply shoreward of the headland, such that waves build dramatically before breaking over a bar and running up on the small, sandy beach. One of my favorite Laguna places. A very special place today with Emily Ritchey.

"Oh, it *is* cold! I can't *believe* how cold it is!" Frisky Easterner at large in Laguna. She was so excited, expressing it in the way she moved, the arch of her body sidearming a pebble into the surf. This was beauty, pure and simple—

overwhelmingly, the day, woman, all a gift to me. Any recent misgivings I had were long gone.

"I'm not quite back to surfing yet. If I could just remember how to swim, it would help."

"No way *I'm* going in," she laughed, running out a few feet and back.

We played awhile at the beach, rode around the deserted downtown, then returned to the house.

The waves were the noisiest thing that day. The rest was Thanksgiving calm, a time to stay home, have a delicious dinner, sit on the deck and talk, hold hands and flirt, wait for the sun to go down in silent, mutually observed restraint. Later, anything would be possible.

When the sky was streaked by the last light of a beautiful sunset, Emily came to me, with all the musical poetry of *Ariodante*:

Im Westen sinkt wohl schon die Sonne	The sun is already setting in the west,
in deinen schönen Augen aber	and in your lovely eyes a brighter sun
geht uns eine hellere Sonne auf.	is breaking on us.

Everything within her heart, body, and, I'm convinced, her soul. I am yours and you are mine. This is our moment, from which will grow what has been given to us. I give myself to you.

I accept your gift, your trust; and give myself to you in return.

The words did not need to be said. Our hearts knew, spoke them all.

In the morning, I looked at Emily as she slept. *Träum ich?* Am I dreaming? Seeing her beauty, my feelings were even stronger. When she awoke we looked into each others' eyes and there were no fences, only clarity and the beginning of deep trust in one another.

"Wow," is all I could say.

"Yeah," Emily replied, moving to kiss me. There was something in our kisses I had longed for—not an end or request, but a beginning. Always an invitation to beginning.

"I've wanted to be together, with you, ever since that first night," she said quietly, looking in my eyes again, deeper within me. "I can't just dance around it. You learn things in life. I've learned what's important, and good. Being with you is very important and very good.

"If it's too much way too soon, so be it. I feel strongly I need to put it right out front. Now. I want to be with you."

"Don't break my heart, Craig, not now," I heard her communicate, without speaking, "but if that ever happens, it will have been a risk I was willing to take."

I reflected in that instant upon another time with Cathy, how she had expressed the same thing. It was true—people in love, those worthy of love, put themselves at risk. By its very nature, fundamentally, love is about courage and sacrifice. Risk taking.

Emily arose and came back a couple of minutes later, as I marvelled at the way she moved. It was comforting to not have to wonder what was going through her mind. She had just told me some of it, significant stuff. But then, I thought, that works both ways. Do I have anything to confide to her?

Neither of us wanted to get up yet, even for the day's crucial first cup of coffee, so we stayed in bed. Believe it or not, some things are even more important than great coffee.

I felt—no, was beginning to believe—that what was between us would never get old, rather be constantly renewing. It was something I thought I could trust, about the deepest of relationships extending way beyond the physical, pleasurable as that was. Like the first course of groundwork had been completed, and now we were poised to begin building a life together.

Eventually getting out of bed around noon, we made lunch, then went back to the beach. Friday, the day after Thanksgiving. I had a lot to be thankful for.

Max had invited us to his place off Laurel Canyon Boulevard for dinner, after which we were going to see The Tubes at a club on Sunset. At the time we booked the date, Max thought I needed to get out, loosen up; and in his opinion, The Tubes were the closest thing to over the counter comic relief. He was right—I had needed to loosen up. That is, before. Now, I could really enjoy the evening with Max, Gretchen, his Numera Una, and Emily Ritchey, hitting the charts at 32 with a bullet.

Max had an eye for quality. He and Gretchen liked Emily right away. I don't know how I would have gotten through the last few years without them, bright points of sanity in the whole LA BigMusicFameMoneyThing. Even if they *did* live up a canyon in LA.

At the Sunset Palace, while waiting a moment to get in, a woman remarked, "Hey, I think that's Craig Maxwell, you know, ESO. Wasn't he in an accident last summer? Lookin' good now. Isn't that person with him, what's her name, the actress?"

Emily looked at me, captivated by all of it, smiled and whispered, "thank you for this," while giving me a hug. My heart said, "thank you for you."

On Saturday, we went sailing with George and Louisa Ryan, both music business attorneys whose firm represented me. They lived in Dana Point, keeping their 38 footer at the marina. The day was clear, a preamble to the Santa Ana winds which were expected to start blowing two days later. Even San Clemente Island was visible, and there was enough wind for sailing without a lot of chop.

The water and sky were the deep blue of a matchless late fall/early winter day. Pictured perfectly by that Julian Priester album on ECM. As much as I liked the music and cover, they were a reminder of my uneasiness around deep water, what was to me a cold, unforgiving sea. As a child I fell off a pier in North

Carolina, and was rescued by my uncle. Though at times like this I was not overcome by out and out fear, there was an uneasiness that something could happen, one day the ocean might not give me up again. Recurrent, personal angst.

George ran a roll of Tri-X through the Leica, black & whites of Emily and I, separately and together. I would have fun working with the shots, a labor of … love?

Emily said she wanted to take the long way home. Through San Juan Capistrano, past the Mission, to El Toro Road, where Marine Corps F-4 weekend warrior jet jocks rocketed overhead. After making dinner we watched the lights dance below, hearing an occasional hot car or bike roaring up Coast Highway.

I got out the bracelets bought a year ago in Santa Fe. Hopi, Zuni, Navajo. The Zuni one was the best of the bunch, and it fit Emily's slender wrist well. I was pleased and gave it to her. We watched an old movie in each other's arms, and then went to bed, a tender, intimate finale to another perfect day.

Her stuff just fit into the back of the Ferrari, so we took it to the airport, cruising up PCH to Corona del Mar, Jamboree Road along the Newport Back Bay, to Mac Arthur Boulevard in the quiet of early Sunday morning.

"Craig, I had a great time. The best. I really want to spend Christmas with you. I don't know the details of how it all fits together—you here, me there, music school in Wyoming, teaching—but I do know that in my heart it *will* fit. I want to be with you, figuring it out together."

"You've just been invited for Christmas. I feel the same. You surprise me in so many ways. We'll work out the details as we go along." As I looked at her, all I could think was, Emily, I'm falling in love with you. When will what's between us have grown strong enough, when will *I* be strong enough that with unquestioned assurance I can say it, give my heart to you? This weekend I clearly felt that I was starting to let go of entrenched forces which had been holding me back for years—insecurity, ego, selfishness, control, indifference. Letting go of them so I could give you my heart.

"The bracelet's beautiful. A treasure from a wonderful man. Thank you."

Don't go. Stay with me now, forever, I thought. Please don't go.

We hugged and kissed, both overcome by intense emotion. It had been so much more than a few days in a far away place for her. The same for me. But she did have to go, through the gate to another life. Chicago, Harrisburg, and school Monday. Tomorrow morning. Back to Cedar Cliff.

When I returned to Laguna, the house seemed so quiet. Although missing Emily already, I told myself that Christmas was less than a month away. So I focused on seeing her then, rather than missing her now, and felt some peace.

30

December 1977

Emily was growing in my heart like a flood rolling down Laguna Canyon, taking everything in its path, clearing a *tabla rasa* upon which to write the beginning of new love. Beethoven had expressed the dramatic essence of what I was feeling in his *Piano Concerto No. 5 in E flat major, Emperor*. It was surprising, considering the differences in our lives and little time we had spent together. But then she had an inner strength, was fun to be with, knew who she was, and like me, wanted to make changes, move ahead. I had never looked forward more eagerly to those changes, felt more strongly that they could be made, molded into a life together. The idea of marriage began creeping into my thoughts. Different thoughts, not in the mode of the analytical past, rather, those which arise when you begin to let go, you're open to new possibilities.

For her, I was one of the keys necessary for release from the last ten years in Harrisburg. She just didn't fit in there any longer, had outgrown it, was ready to jump outside the lines. And did I say beautiful? Every time I thought of her, looked at a picture, I was struck by her beauty. About the softness, gentleness when I had leaned over our table for two, gently pulled her to me; when her hair brushed the side of my face as she lay her head on my shoulder. Simple, intensely powerful moments. Between a man and woman I now knew, as never before, were meant to be together.

After she returned home, we continued to talk about the Christmas holidays and our plans for them in Laguna. Emily spoke about her interest in moving next summer. Looking at the overall picture, I was reevaluating the timing of going to Laramie. Nevertheless, though our futures were coinciding, we would have to make sure neither of us let go of our own interests and creative needs. With the promise of love come the realities of a relationship.

I wrote a song for Emily, planning to surprise her with it at Christmas. Did the chart and copyrighted it, *Emily*, the title at the top. She was excitable, and would be excited.

Occasionally, I thought about Cindy, and the anger she still had about the failure of her marriage. Maybe less anger now; more likely, less apparent. Regardless, anger which would have to be worked through and left behind, so as not to be brought into a new relationship. Cindy with edges, to be overcome, rounded. It would take time, and the love of another for the final, healing leap. I hoped someone would give her the kind of love I now knew was possible.

Max had grown up outside Yuma, and some property matters arose which he needed to settle. Accurately observing that I was beginning to climb the walls waiting for Christmas and Emily, and thinking that it might do me good to get out of town for a couple of days, he not so subtly "invited" me along for the drive. Yes, to Yuma. At least he had a Mercedes.

As Max drove on I-5 toward San Diego, I thought of Emily continuously. Somehow, she had maintained a girlish charm. The boys in her math classes must be in agony right now. I know I was.

It was as if she had been waiting for her love story to start, just one chapter away. Seemingly easygoing, she left terms out of the equation that others were only too quick to assume and add. Reputation, what reputation? The truth was that she had a peacefulness, quiet place few people got to go with her. Maybe no one before. A place of the heart, abiding, in anticipation of the first one who would know how special it was. Her essential, creative-emotional center.

Before leaving, we talked on the phone, and Emily said, laughing, "Christmas is for surprises. I just might have one or two for you."

"To put under the tree? To turn out the lights and show me? Something that begins innocently enough in the hot tub? What?"

"I'm not saying anything more. You need a little suspense in your life, and with me, to show a lot of responsibility. Now, no doubt more than ever before, you're going to get a chance for both."

I started to say, "I've got you, Emily. I love you." But those words needed to be spoken looking into her eyes. So we just said our goodbyes.

Climbing to Alpine, a memory came back of last year's trip over the same pass, at night then. What was the music, "No Room for Squares"? Yes, that was it. Returning to this drive, I thought about another chapter, the one about loneliness and isolation now being closed through my love for Emily.

Passing Descanso, then in the steep curves on the way down the other side, I was a little queasy, sweating, uncomfortable.

"You okay?" Max asked.

"Just a little nervous. Anxiety about the road, I guess. I feel a little strange." We passed the big JACUMBA exit sign on that rockpile road, then I was better.

After Max's business was concluded and some numbing *chorizo* at The Territorial, a restaurant, not the prison, we were ready to leave town.

The Santa Ana winds started blowing again, and headed back to LA, there was no way to avoid them. Driving through the choking clouds of sand in the Great American Desert west of Yuma was wild—Disneyland, the real version.

Although we managed to stay on the road, the dust storm added to my lingering uneasiness, premonition, dread. It was claustrophobic, like being at the bottom of a hole while realizing it was being slowly filled.

The trip back through El Centro and over the pass to San Diego was rough, with constant buffetting by the winds. Saying little, enduring the pounding as best we could, we were thankful not to have been in the RV overturned beside the road. When Max dropped me off at my place in Laguna, the sky was blue, the Santa Ana winds having pushed the smog offshore. But it wasn't a calm blue—when the winds subsided, the haze would come back. I went to bed early, hoping sleep would help.

Something wasn't right.

When I got back, I wanted to call Emily, but knew she'd be gone for the weekend with her Mother on a trip to visit relatives. Maybe she'd call me. Not hearing from her, on Sunday night I called, mostly wanting to hear her voice, but also to continue our dialogue about the upcoming Christmas trip to Laguna, seeing Catalina Island, what we wanted to do. Despite trying several times, I couldn't reach her. I'd try again Monday night. No answer again.

On Tuesday morning, after calling at 4 am Pacific Time to catch her before she left for work, I decided to telephone the high school office when it opened. I told the person who answered that Ms. Ritchey had been thinking of attending an educational seminar the upcoming summer, and I wanted to confirm that she was still interested. Could she give Ms. Ritchey the message, with my telephone number?

"I'm terribly sorry," she said, "Ms. Ritchey was in an automobile accident Friday and didn't survive. We're all in shock around here about it."

I called my parents, who had just returned from a long weekend in New York, and hadn't seen the papers. They found the article and read it to me.

> Emily Ritchey, mathematics teacher at Cedar Cliff High School, was fatally injured Friday in a one car crash on I-83 when her vehicle slid out of control on an icy highway bridge. Interment at Colonial Park Gardens will be held on Tuesday, December 13, 1977; followed by a memorial service on Saturday, December 17, 1977, at 10:00 am, in the Shiremanstown Baptist Church where she was a member.

I couldn't get there in time for the burial, but would be at the service on Saturday.

Emily had not said anything about being a member of a church.

It couldn't be true that Emily was gone; only a bad dream. I had finally fallen in love with a woman with whom I saw such assurance in a future together. I'd wake up and she'd answer when I called.

But it *was* true. My life continued. Back to being alone now. I couldn't even start to understand it.

A reporter and photographer were at the service, somehow tipped off, looking for a scoop. "How would you describe your relationship with Emily Ritchey," and so on. I just brushed them off without a response. What did they know? How could they know? I couldn't talk about her now, about us.

Come back! Open your eyes, Emily! *Tue die Augen auf Emily*! Oh that my heart was stronger.

Later, a woman came up to me. "I'm Ellen Ritchey, Emily's mother. I understand that you are Craig Maxwell. I wish we'd met before. I'd like to speak with you. Will you meet me at Emily's house an hour after the service?" I agreed without question.

The memorial service affected me deeply. When it began I was coming apart. I didn't want to experience another moment.

It had been some time since I was in a church, among the rows of pews with their hymnals, arched ceiling, leaded glass windows. As I sat there looking at the flowers, I realized that everything I loved about Emily had flowed from her spirit. She would never have given up, in fact, was always looking for the best in life, whether getting on the back of my motorcycle, leaving ten years at Cedar Cliff behind, or accepting a risk with me I knew she wanted to take.

What Emily had contributed to my life was invaluable, permanent. Starting as a fun ride, a Friday night getaway, it had grown into love during a time of physical healing. I needed the memory of her to comfort me, give my thoughts clarity, enable me to press on. Even though I didn't understand how, and couldn't have put it into words on that day, a slight thread of who I really was, and why I was here, had been revealed. Not in terms of interests or abilities, race or culture. Like her spirit, it was much deeper.

I knocked on the door of what had been Emily's house, and when Mrs. Ritchey opened it, went in. Nothing appeared to have been touched.

"I wanted to speak with you alone. After the funeral, I came over here, to feel her presence, look for things to remember her by, things to help me." Her mother had started crying, and tears filled my eyes when I saw them. I held her as a pulse of emotion gripped both of us. A release, followed by peace, if only for a few minutes. One small step of many which would be needed to endure this terrible loss.

"Craig, I came across her journal open on the desk. Here, please read what it says. It's really a letter to you."

December 1, 1977

I've been thinking a lot about you, Craig. I never dreamed that I would, and how could I have known before you dropped into my life, but I love you. Your kindness and gentleness to me are an inspiration. You swept me off my feet, accepted me for who I am, did not pull, did not push, did not question that which need not be questioned. I know that you're going through things yourself. You're healing, and I sense growing deeply in ways you may not even realize yet. I want to be part of that healing and growth. And though we haven't talked about it, I pray that as time goes on, You would touch him, Lord, as You have touched me. And that You would bless us, and forgive our sin, that it would not be sin any longer. For I believe that we are now one, forever, and it has always been so according to Your plan. Thank you, Craig. And thank You, Lord, for this man, whether it be only for the moments we have already shared, a lifetime, or eternity. Lord, truly I pray that you would bless our love.

More tears streamed down my face as I read it. I had never experienced such powerful love. I was so thankful for her, while knowing that the intensity of a growing love, lost, had to bring equally intense pain, truly an aching within my soul.

"Emily had a wild streak to her," Mrs. Ritchey said, "but then, most of us have one kind of streak or another. And though Emily did some things over the years which she regretted, haven't we all? Some would say that she was a contradiction—a school teacher working within a regimented system, yet one who took risks, wouldn't suffer those who were not equally committed. Like riding out of a class reunion on the back of your motorcycle, a former student at that. I would have done it too! Emily wanted to live, not just watch her life go by. When you met, she was so ready to take another of the big steps that make it a real life, experience the joy we all dream about.

"She loved to teach school. She loved new experiences, adventure. She loved so much, and in return, was loved by so many. She loved you, Craig, and because I knew my daughter, I know you were worthy of her love. May God bless you, as Emily prayed.

"We talked a lot. She confided in me, telling about how you met again, but really for the first time, in May, the brief time you spent together. And when she got back from California after Thanksgiving, she was absolutely transformed—luminous, full of life, of love. We talked about you, the present, the future. She told me that you were the one, would be the best husband, the man with whom she wanted children … for a woman, that's it. When you know that, there's nothing more to say.

"I wanted to meet you! To thank you for helping bring her happiness."

The depth of love and understanding that ran through Mrs. Ritchey, the capacity passed on to her daughter, Emily, awed me.

I offered to help pack Emily's things and move them over to Mrs. Ritchey's house in Colonial Park when she was ready for that. For now, she only wanted to take Emily's journal, to hold it close. There had been much, much more to her life than me, one who became part of it for such a brief time near the end.

Mrs. Ritchey wanted me to have the Zuni bracelet back which I had given to Emily at Thanksgiving. I accepted it and thanked her. Later I had the inside engraved:

Emily, My Love. December 1977.

If one moment I was at peace about Emily, in the next I was overcome by grief. And so it would be for a long time. I needed to walk around, I needed air.

The December afternoon quickly turned to darkness as clouds moved above the cold wind. I went over to Harrisburg and walked in that cold wind. Despite the Christmas decorations and carols ringing out from the department stores, it was a downtown in decline. Gritty and tired, the area would never be the same. But then, this version was different than the previous one. Optimism, renewal, maturity, decline, over and over. Seemingly an inevitable cycle, parallel to the cycling of our generations.

Seeing the decline, I vowed not to waste Emily's gift, the part of me that would always belong to her. Although not knowing what that meant to my future, after everything else had fallen away, I believed that the key was continuing renewal for me, too. Renewal of my grieving heart through love.

31

Painting the hills of Laguna, barns of Dillsburg

Before returning to California, I wanted to call Cindy, to tie up any loose ends of the fall weekend in Laguna. Although we spoke by phone several times afterward, I was not able to grasp what it had meant to her, whether anything needed to be addressed. As I thought about my own question, a light went on, though dimly. What I'm learning about women is that there's always something to deal with. Nothing is or can be static. The art is in finding out what that something is without creating a new issue, or withdrawing to avoid it, becoming another issue in itself. Also, that to women, "issues" and "problems" are not the same thing, as they are to most men. Essentially, it's all about walking an everpresent tightrope with changing definitions, shifting moods, and varying tension.

With that giant insight, though not having any idea about how to apply it, I called Cindy, told her that I was in town for Emily's memorial service, and asked to see her the next day. We met Sunday afternoon at the Coffee Place. I got there a little early. Tom, the owner, remembered me of course.

"You were here this summer with Emily Ritchey. I read about it in the paper. What a tragedy. Such a beautiful lady."

"That's why I'm back, Tom. That's why ... ," fading off into a memory of her.

"She came in quite a bit during the summer, and then after school started, late afternoons. A regular. More than just nice. Thrilling, in the best sense of the word. To my thinking, one in a million." Indeed she was. One in many more than that.

Cindy came in a few minutes later. We ordered and talked. I didn't say much about Emily, trying to keep the focus on her, California history.

I needed oriented activity, to provide structure to my life, one affected physically and emotionally by two accidents. To find something to do, keep from coming apart. That could happen so quickly, a slip, maybe a wet glass falling from one's fingers, headed down. Reflecting upon relationships in general, they didn't seem to be as much about potential or probability as time and timing, two lives being somewhere near the same place, together, to make a start. My love for Emily eclipsed any other which had existed or might be possible now, for how long I didn't know. As long as it took. Maybe for the rest of my life, a succession of failed efforts which would never measure up.

"Remember," I tried to tell myself, "Emily didn't quit," but it rang hollow. The confidence wasn't there. Maybe I had already slipped.

Cindy said, "Since I've started to get to know you, as brief as it has been … I should say the new or different you now … our time together has helped me. We both have things to deal with, to overcome, that require healing. For myself, I don't know if we are meant to be with each other eventually. Things are often not clear, understanding so elusive. One day can change anything, bring the world tumbling down. From there it's a slow, draining climb back, with pressures and setbacks. I'm speaking from experience. What keeps me going in the tough times is the love for my son. He needs me, and because of that, I keep going. I just can't give up."

We talked for a while longer and as we were leaving, I told her that I wanted to continue to stay in touch. To help ground me. Grounding to a story, a relationship, whatever it might be, that for some reason I thought had yet to be completed. Like she had said, someone or something to keep me going.

As we hugged, I asked her to call if she ever wanted to paint the hills of Laguna, the barns of Dillsburg. In this cafe, Marvin Gaye and Tammi Terrell were singing, "Ain't No Mountain High Enough", but nobody was dancin' in the street. She kissed me, without another word, and left.

Grounding to a person. Just the person. *Not* a story or relationship. One person to another. Those were the words I was looking for. But Cindy was already gone.

✛ ══════ ✛

I drove out to Pinchot State Park that Sunday afternoon, as I had done on college weekends spent at home, before they became fewer as the courses got harder and playing music took over. Hustling high school chicks to fight the loneliness; searching for something loud on the radio, nothing to be found. No snow was on the ground today, but the sky promised it by tomorrow. I was staying over Christmas, then leaving December 26th, so I still had a few days. After parking, I stood on the timber rail, wind blowing, looked over the lake, continuing to turn it all over in my mind.

Thinking back to the summers, I was aware of how different my life was when growing up here than now. The texture of moss in the creek, watermarks on cobbles when summer diminished spring flows, flies skipping across still pools. Those hadn't changed. That girl who moved gently to the music undoubtedly had. How I now associate all of it from a broader though not necessarily wiser perspective, more in metaphors, "like float planes on northern lakes," or "as mutually fulfilling a relationship as … ."

Before, it was only about swimming, finding a tree from which to jump into the cool water, being careful not to step on a sharp rock. Doing. Experiencing the mud of the silt ponds, feeling good between my toes. That was enough. Movement, destinations, actions, events, before recording, analysis and ceaseless evaluation, criticism set in. If you just run film without interrupting to compose each frame or impose editorial "consistency", whatever that is, sometimes the results are startling. Seeing in a very different way, without preconception. Why can't I just roll it?

What did that entry in Emily's diary mean, "… and that He would bless us, and forgive us our sin?" What sin could there be in the love between a man and woman, a growing love?

As I looked up into the troubled sky, I envisioned having gone to a place in another forest, far from here. But when I got there, it was not enough. The clouds, voices drew me beyond, to the desert. Where I sifted, screened for shards, clues to who I was. And when I again knew it was not enough, I went up to the mountains. The kind that always have snow in the cirques, dark northside ravines, treacherous with scree. Places of frozen dreams and death falling like the night.

My ancestors, in their waves of migrations from the Atlantic coast to the forests along Lake Superior, were speaking, telling me to reject what others would have me be, how they would define me. To meditate upon the paths— physical, emotional, spiritual, winding from birth through formative knowl- edge and experiences—that had brought me to this very moment. A point where I had become old and tired, far beyond my years. In the way of our people, threatened, ravaged, yet somehow surviving, wiser for each breath.

Turned loose, free to walk into the high mountain snows. To confront waiting death, and either begin living, or simply decline the opportunity, give in to the latent anguish which had been there as long as I could remember. Hidden, so difficult not only to overcome but drive out. Perhaps the faintest trace of insight had been revealed by today's deep life-scratch, but I didn't know how to read it by myself.

I looked up Emily's mother in the phone book and called her, again offering help in moving or anything else which needed to be done. She initially demurred, but then said I could take a few things over to Colonial Park. Afterward, she made me a cup of coffee and we got to talking.

"I loved your daughter, although I never fully realized how powerful and precious it was, and didn't have the opportunity to tell her face to face. I have never been in love like that. Unspoken as it was, our love was growing and I was filled with happiness, glad for knowing her. She made my life in these last few weeks exciting, full of promise."

Mrs. Ritchey said she had hoped, after the breakup of her daughter's marriage, that Emily would find a person who would be good with and for her, that she would remarry and finally find happiness. As the years passed, both wondered if that would ever happen. It amazed me that the beautiful woman I loved could have had such difficulty.

Then the bombshell: "It is possible that Emily was pregnant with your child.

"She mentioned setting a doctor's appointment 'before going to California at Christmas', and made a few comments. Emily looked a little different, something a mother recognizes.

"It's not easy for me to talk about any of this. I debated whether to tell you, because I really didn't know for sure, and never will. She always wanted a child, and after turning thirty, even more so.

"I've thought about it over and over, and believe if she was pregnant, it's because she wanted a child with you and nobody else. You read her diary. She loved you; told me she wanted you to be the father of her children. She was very careful; I don't know how it could have been an 'accident'. It would have been a tremendous risk, putting such pressure on a relationship which had barely started, not to mention her teaching career and economic circumstances.

"As you also know from her diary, Emily was a Christian. So if it was true, a child would have been no small thing in her faith, but then, she wasn't perfect. None of us are. You could look at it as being very selfish on Emily's part, if she had decided to have a child without your knowledge. If you loved her as you say, however, you might see it differently, that both of you chose each other, would be blessed by being together, accepting and treasuring all that you were, all that was and would be of you. Your child.

"If I've upset you, I'm truly sorry. I couldn't keep this to myself, Craig," she said, now in tears.

Though there were tears in my eyes, I was too stunned to say anything for a few minutes. Could this have been the surprise and responsibility Emily had talked about in our last phone conversation?

"Thank you for telling me, Mrs. Ritchey. I loved Emily. I've … I've got to go now."

Still stunned, I drove to Emily's grave, visiting it for the first time, but all I found was a place. A reference point for loss of the woman I loved, possibly our child as well.

In tears I spoke to her, knowing I was only talking to myself, until there was nothing more to say. All my emotions came forth, pain, joy, thankfulness, loss, and suffering … left exposed without closure.

He died and left town.

I did my Christmas shopping on automatic, went to O'Reilly's with Marco just to get out of the house. As usual, people constantly brought up the days with ESO, women looked at me too long and in the wrong ways, and all I was left with to say was that I didn't remember much. The nuances were gone, and depending upon with whom I was speaking, they would either know me and accept what I said, or think I didn't want to talk to them. It would have to do.

Late Wednesday afternoon I ducked into the Coffee Place again, out of the snow. I don't space out in cafes like I used to before the accident. What that means, if anything, I don't know.

Looking out the window, I wondered, is a dramatic loss more profound? A plane going down in flames more terrible than withering away? A beautiful young teacher's life tragically eclipsed … what?

Become silent, the walls of an empty room are little changed by the lives of those before or after. One day there is no one to put down a suitcase, find familiar places. A morning will be quiet, plant blooming, warm inside the window, though outside it is a winter day. There is no such thing as, "that didn't happen to me." It's only a matter of when everything has, is, or will. Love, whether or not returned by those loved, is never in vain. But sometimes, it's silenced. Suddenly. And I'm left only with walls. I become … I am the walls, boundary between inside and outside, life and silence.

A man crossed the street, headed toward the cafe. It was the reporter from the service, probably taking a break from the newspaper's Camp Hill branch a few doors down on the other side. After ordering and glancing around, he came over, trying not to look surprised, always on the prowl for a story, already forming those important first few questions, searching for the lead-in.

Outside, the snow continued to fall. Lost in thought, hearing Mozart's *Requiem in D minor*, I was on the threshold of walking into the snowladen forest of today's imagination. Someday, I sensed, it would not be imagination.

Turning from the window, I looked at the reporter, the cafe, a good cup of coffee, wooden chairs and tables, radiator hissing. A Tri-X gray day, overexposed and underdeveloped. Zone VI.

The *Requiem* was not going to be quieted:

> *Requiem aeternam dona eis, Domine;*   Eternal rest grant them, O Lord;
> *et lux perpetua luceat eis.*   and let perpetual light shine upon them.

"You're Craig Maxwell," he said interrupting the Kyrie. "I saw you the other day. Can I ask you a few questions?"

"Please give me a minute to finish a thought." With that, I turned back to the window. He might have misinterpreted that as rejection and gone away, but didn't. A job to do, maybe even good at it.

Did I really want to talk to this guy, now? Perhaps it was what I should do—for myself, a small step in working through it; for others who knew Emily, to offer a tribute. A requiem illuminating a dark landscape. A story about Emily, who I knew her to be, what she meant to me. A story of redemptive love, too brief, then loss.

Taking a sip of coffee, I started, making a statement rather than waiting for any questions.

"We were just really getting to know each other. It was amazing to come back after 10 years to my high school reunion, ride off with her. I know, it sounds like a Hollywood thing. Emily Ritchey, math student teacher. I didn't see her again until several months later, after the motorcycle accident in California. It was over Thanksgiving. She had to come back here to her teaching job, but we made plans to spend Christmas together.

"I had fallen in love with her, and it was powerful, good. The best thing that has ever happened to me. Then another accident, and she was gone. I can't even put into words how deeply I miss her." And our child. I knew that now.

"She will always be a part of me. An important part. Oh, Emily, *ningii-zaagi' giin.*"

"What are those words you just said?"

"Ningii-zaagi' giin. It means, 'I loved you,' in Ojibwe."

"Spell it for me, if you would."

"I wrote a song, simply entitled, 'Emily', planning to surprise her with it at Christmas. She never got to hear it, at least not with me here on this earth. Maybe she has heard it already, in spirit. Perhaps you would understand if I played it for you."

We walked down a couple of doors to Market Hill Music, a piano and organ place. I barely got through the song.

The article appeared Friday.

> ESO Rocker, School Mourn Loss (NP) According to Craig Maxwell, I am the only other person to hear the song that he wrote, but never got to play, for a school teacher who recently perished in an automobile accident. The true story of how he met and courted her is the stuff of Hollywood. But after the drama is pulled away, there can only be one conclusion when he tells that story and plays the music. That Craig Maxwell loved Emily Ritchey, and as he put it, their love was one of "beauty, subtlety,

silence, and musical poetry." His composition, "Emily", is a classic love song, emotional yet articulate, embracing the spectrum of discovery, joy, and tears … .

The phone began to ring at the house. It didn't take long for everybody and anybody to track me down. There weren't too many Maxwells in this town. After making a quick run to buy an answering machine, I connected it and went out.

32

Rows of marble

At home, I brought up my visit to Fond du Lac. The conversation didn't go very far. For reasons he kept to himself, my father remained reticent. Maybe there was some old pain … I once heard that Grandfather Maxwell had a drinking problem. In passing he mentioned the Carlisle Indian School, only about 15 miles west, and the probability that Chippewa children had gone there. All I knew about it was the movie, *Jim Thorpe, All American*. The reality was much different.

Going first to the Cumberland County Historical Society in Carlisle, I found that the remaining buildings of the former Indian School, the first of several dozens of post treaty-making, federal cultural extermination/reprogramming stations, became the site of the U.S. Army War College. Domination in the name of Manifest Destiny; at the very least, breaking down the tribal family structure, diluting traditions. Similar objectives, different tactics. A carefully tended cemetery could be visited, now quietly bearing the symbols of respect and honor denied the living students who attended such schools.

Children came, often more accurately were brought or shipped, to the Indian School and some died of tuberculosis, scarlet fever, smallpox, measles; others undoubtedly of broken hearts. In a grave with the earliest date was Take the Tail, also known as Lucy Pretty Eagle, a ten year old Rosebud Sioux who survived in that foreign place less than four months before passing away in March 1884. Story upon story had been scratched into what was now essentially a sealed, concreted unconsciousness:

> Your son died quietly, without suffering, like a man. We have dressed him in his good clothes and tomorrow we will bury him the way the white people do. Capt. Richard H. Pratt, 1880.

> In eight years, nobody hugged me once … . An Indian girl.

The grief Lucy Pretty Eagle's family must have felt was unimaginable.

Many Ojibwe came through the School doors, and some had also been laid to rest in the cemetery, identified as "Chippewa." Looking at the uniform white marble headstones, and reflecting on the new grave where Emily now lay, I recalled what I had read of the Circle of Life. To the Ojibwe, the Circle is sacred, about balance and harmony, living in a respectful manner, achieving a good, honorable life, *bimaadiziwin*. Where were the children along the Circle, those whose chiseled names had already witnessed nearly a century of sunrises and sunsets? In heaven or another spirit realm, waiting for me? How close was I to them? To Emily?

It was Friday, December 23rd. Tomorrow would be Christmas Eve.

I left the cemetery, driving through the Carlisle Barracks, then downtown to High and Hanover Streets. It had been a long time. The gray-columned Old Courthouse was still there, Molly Pitcher Hotel nearby. Many of the stores were in decline, overtaken, submerged to the rooftops by the Great Wave of the Malls, leaving more than one bar with its plastic sign, painted martini glass, LOUNGE, the only evidence of life between empty storefronts barren as failing trees.

Down the street, near Dickinson College, was Carlisle's first attempt at an espresso coffee house. With brick walks, well-maintained narrow alleys, trim black shutters, and period architecture, the town had a strong colonial feel, and historical preservation was increasingly a big deal. So much history, they said, but arguably brief in the longer view. Create the language and market the history to gain your ends. Little more than a flicker compared to Oraibi, much less Rome or Cairo. That's the voice of the purist and skeptic, though, the critic. How many years are enough? How many lifetimes make a place significant? Why is a *place* important at all?

Considerable thought had gone into the cafe, and many things were done right. Not exactly Café Med of Berkeley, or Mr. Rosewater's in Durango, but enough to work with. Although spiced cider sounded great, given the availability and choice, I'll almost always opt for cappuccino. An end unto itself—searching for the perfect cup, and when that's found, resuming the quest for another to equal it.

I ordered a *doppio*, took off my jacket, and watched the young woman make it—meticulously, as if it *had* to be matchless. She brought it over and indeed the double cappuccino looked perfect, mocha ring from the two espresso shots poured after the milk, nice head of whole milk foam. Italian chocolate-brown porcelain cup from the stack on top of La Machina, ivory-white inside. Looking at it, I knew I wanted it to be perfect too. Could this be the fabled:

¿Mocha Corona?

The first sip is telling. In this case, great production diminished by coffee which was only of average quality, bland in flavor. Not her fault. A marginal, unextended chord in an otherwise kickin' progression. Lesson: learn what the best coffee is, where it can consistently be found, keep a fresh supply, and never use anything else. There I go again, ever the purist.

Looking out the window, I wondered to where all the women my age had disappeared. If they were around, I couldn't seem to see them. Doing laundry, cleaning house for the exciting Christmas weekend? Going from one NFL playoff game to another this time of year maybe; who was in the playoffs, anyhow? America's Team, Grateful & Dead Cowboys, again? In short, I guess, married and cloistered, or out of town working a career in the big city.

Teaching school? Mourning loved ones? A pointless, mindless marriage? I asked no one as the *ragazza* came up to my table from the back of the room.

"Excuse me, you're Craig Maxwell, aren't you?"

"Yes, I am."

"I saw the article with your picture in the paper today. I'm so sorry."

"Thank you. It's a terrible loss. I know I'm not even starting to cope with it yet. So much can change in an instant. And if that's not enough, I was just over at the Indian School Cemetery. So sad as to be nearly indescribable."

"The article said you have Indian ancestry."

"Yes, Ojibwe." The BIA paper tells me so. "I never really knew much about it until last summer when I went to Minnesota. I'm finding it's just a starting point for coming to know who I am."

"Your music is great. I listen to it all the time. I grew up on it. Thank you for that."

"Well, I guess growing up on it dates me. We used to play gigs here at the College, fraternity parties. It's all kind of a blur, though, ten years later. After midnight I could never remember what happened anyhow. Too much opportunity for substance abuse. A big mistake, when I think of all the magic that's in the world, all that I missed at that time. It's still there, if you seek it, make the right choices, and let go. But then, there's loss and pain, too." And all kinds of painkillers to mask them.

"Do you go to Dickinson?"

"Yes, I'm a senior, majoring in English Literature. Don't ask me what I'm going to use it for."

"Let's do *Hidden Themes of Beowulf* for fifty dollars."

"You're making fun of me," she laughed, smiling.

With that Ms. Mocha Corona threw a life preserver, to rescue me from drowning among the graves. One of a long line of saving laughs, sincere concerns, hands taken and held in comfort. In that moment, everything slowed, almost to a stop, and I looked closely at her, received and appreciated her sympathy, her loveliness. I came here, I am here because I needed that smile, your laugh. How important they are. I *must* pass them on, in whatever way I can. Can I really do that?

Back farther than ten years, as a self-associated Animal, the afternoon would have travelled another path—put the sign on the door, "we gotta get outta this place." Today, the door had already been barred by the Zombies. "She's not there." More accurately, I'm not here. Nowhere close.

"Well, my degree is in civil engineering, and as you can imagine, I'm not getting much mileage out of *that. But ...* there are always opportunities, and you will be better for the perspective you develop in college, whether through English, engineering, or art. Finish it. Learn from the experiences of college itself, go out into the world and use what you've gained, building a life by adding what's healthy to it. My advice, anyhow." Quite a speech.

"I've been thinking of going to grad school, but haven't decided. Somewhere else, probably. I want to, no ... need to get out of here. California, maybe—everybody wants to go some time. You live there, what would be a good place?"

"Lots of them. I've been to many cities and towns, but don't know much about schools Out West for what you've been studying. I do know a woman who graduated from the University of Wyoming in Laramie this year, and is now working for a publishing company in San Francisco. The opportunities seem to be there. The University of Montana, which is in Missoula, is supposed to have a good writing program. A Pacific Coast school maybe? Depends whether you decide to continue your studies or look for a job.

"I do like Laramie, and am planning to go back to school there for an MFA in music and photography."

"That's interesting. All you've done, and going back to school at ... ."

"28. Getting up there."

We talked a little more in generalities about places, schools, and curricula. Then she said, "it's kind of embarrassing, but I'd sure like to have a picture of you, signed and all that."

"I'm used to the requests, get quite a few. Fresh out of 8x10 glossies on me, but tell you what. I'll go out to the car and get my camera. We'll pull somebody in from the street and ask them to snap some pictures. I'll send them to you."

"Really?" She couldn't believe it. For all the hassles of being well known, there were good times, too, adding a little sunshine to a life, on a winter day. For these few minutes, I was Santa, bringing the ribbon candy, oranges and chocolate, doll and toys for her Christmas stocking. Like that time with ... Terri ... Death Valley.

I got the Nikon and asked a passerby to come in the cafe, help us take the pictures.

"How about if we take a couple of shots seated at a table, then in front of the espresso machine at the counter?"

I set up the camera, gave a few instructions, and smiling, a half roll of Tri-X was exposed. The man got a free coffee and departed, leaving us alone once again.

"Let me get your name and mailing address."

"It's Beth Royer," she said, giving an address in Maryland.

"I'll see if I can turn these around in a week or two."

"And write something on them, okay?"

"Sure, I know how to do that."

"Beth, thank you for the coffee, and for being here. It helped to talk with someone, break the spell, if only for a few minutes."

"Let me give you a hug. Thank you, too, for surprising me by walking in. In Carlisle. Amazing."

It was an embrace of brief acquaintance, the kind I have always assumed women are used to, that means no more or less than that for which it is offered. I don't really know, have never asked. The press of a young woman's body, though, freely given, no matter how unthinking, reflexive, or demure, is to me always powerful, always mysterious. Let it forever be that way.

I walked outside, got into the car, and was on the verge of pulling away when Beth tapped on my window, motioning to wind it down.

"We're having a little get-together tonight before going home for Christmas. I know I would be shocked if you accepted, but would you like to come? You could bring anyone you want."

"Well, I was planning to go out for awhile tonight in Harrisburg with a buddy of mine, although I will grant that we seem to have worked through the few possibilities there already this week. We'd be pretty old for your crowd."

"It's just a small gathering of friends from the College—more of a lowkey Christmas party than anything else. I'd be pleased if you would come. I mean, what can I say—Craig Maxwell!"

"A long shot, but if so, on one condition—that you tell nobody. And if that's acceptable, I'll also have to check with my friend, Marco, to see if it's okay with him. Come to think of it, he probably knows his way around Carlisle better than I do, though he's living in DC these days." Better not mention his nickname. The Meteor has repeatedly shown himself to be capable of truly flaming atmospheric entries, regardless of crowd demographics. Flamboyant, the word that comes to mind. Crash and burn." I'd like to think I'm more flamebuoyant, able to float away from a flameout. Time will tell.

"Just consider it. Please. We'd love to have you."

"If we do show up, no need to get anything special—neither of us drink when driving. Well, not too frequently or excessively anyhow. At least in that sense, a couple of minimally self-responsible relics."

"Let me write down the address for you."

"Okay. Here, I've got a pen and pencil in the glove box. Thanks again, Beth. So long."

Driving east on the Pike, I thought of Beth Royer in the cafe, College Classic Coffee, a brick building on the sunny side of West High Street in Carlisle. A town through which Geronimo rode in a strange juxtaposition uniquely American. Illustrating one version of an unspoken national motto: "If At All, Inadvertent Truth."

On exhibit, the conquered Apache among the Pennsylvanians, Mennonites and English; as alien as the picture of "Einstein Among the Hopi." Visiting the Indian School while travelling to the inauguration of President Teddy Roosevelt in 1905. Barely over a half century later, others were cruising to inaugurations by Boeing 707. Technology had accelerated, but as far as I could see, dignity and compassion weren't keeping up.

I'd like to have a cafe someday, who knows, maybe in Laramie. Done right, a really good one can be so alive with people, ideas, creativity, music, art, and of course, great Java Joe. A magnet for the Beth Royers, Cathy Rousseaus, Green Sweater Girls throwing off their sparks, inciting "more fire at Tomasita's." Starched aprons. My secret Harvey Girls, never to be forgotten.

Once in a very long while, a person so special as to defy description might even walk in the door, dare you to put yourself at risk, and in a second miracle, offer to make a life with you, give her love, bring a child into your world. Someone like Emily Ritchey.

Oh Em, *ninde' an*, my heart. I miss you.

Tears starting for Emily, but also for Beth, Cathy, Green Sweater, all the others. All humanity, beauty, love; suffering, loss. Children. Born and unborn.

I turned on the radio, looking for help. Handel's *Messiah* wouldn't stop them.

And He shall purify …

Will He? When?

Who *is* the King of Glory? Is He Jesus Christ, *Gichi-Manidoo*, Buddha, a kachina, mark on a tree, sacred rock? Who? Does God exist, or is He/It only a concept to make us think we're playing with a full deck, marketed through literature, mythology, words and music? Are we just intermingling dreams, weakly fanning the empty mists of a void?

Why is it that when we think we've finally figured out even a minute part of our life, we back off, saying, "It can't be that … look at me … how could *I* figure out anything?" Unworthy of insight, knowledge, wisdom. Unworthy.

I turned onto a side road on the way back, near Cumberland Valley High School, rolled down the window to connect to the world, shutoff the car for quiet, looking out at an old barn, my breath fogging the windshield.

Every drive around here was one through the past. High school dances we played at "Cow Valley", Cedar Cliff, Trinity, and Camp Hill; girls from Bishop

McDevitt and 'Harris. "Shake and Fingerpop", "How Sweet It Is (to be Loved by You)", "This Can't be True". Got that right.

"We're gonna bring it on down, take a pause for the cause. See ya in 15." Back to loud, double-time frenzy before the end of set tag. Only in my mind; here seeing nothing more than an old barn on a narrow road on a cold December day during a sad time … on and on.

That place a couple minutes from here on the Pike in New Kingston, name escapes me. Home for a weekend, heard on the radio that the Edison Electric Band, a Penn/Philly fixture, would be there. No-name roadhouse in a nearly unnamed place. The irony of Randy Newman and Dr. John's gumbo lost on a thin crowd of locals who wanted metal. Must have fired their manager for that one. Before they went to LA and fell into a Jackson Browne-Bonnie Raitt-J.D. Souther-John Prine orbit. Before we all went to LA. Knowing that somebody'd work that into "My Country 'Tis of Thee". "… from every mountainside, we all made LA."

In this moment, the only "home" I can think of, while knowing it's not home at all.

And now I'm looking down the road, the years, knowing the story before it happens. Cindy and I, both on the rebound, married. To have someone to hold on to. She knew where she wanted to be, where home was. I didn't. We couldn't hold it together.

Hypothetically. She's smarter than that. As for me … I don't know.

Yes, every road a drive through the past, but unfortunately, not a history lesson learned well and taken to heart. Still not understanding the forces which have shaped me, realizing who I am, taking control of how I'm being influenced, forgiving that which needs to be forgiven, extending compassion to others. Wanting new kinships, the creation of new family. Choosing to live, and making it stick.

33

*Not quite ready
for ice fishing*

"I'll pick you up around eight-thirty," I told Marco.

"Why so early? There won't be anybody at O'Reilly's until 9:30 or 10." Rarely anyone of interest there at all. With the exception of Elaine a year ago. I wonder how she's doing? A lot of things can happen in a year. I hope better ones.

"I'll see you at eight-thirty."

"We're going to Carlisle tonight. I heard of a wild party some coeds from Dickinson are having. Should be a real acid flashback for an unreformed corporate climber like you." Hypocinematic. Coeds? White tennis shoes with poms?

"I was thinking more in terms of Mrs. Robinson—hey, hey, hey."

"You B-school types are a real mess. I just know you'd rather be at a Christmas party in DC chasing some Muffy garbed in Black Watch or a red skirt. No, both—one on each arm. Largest gold wreath pin in the hemisphere, wool fringes, miniature bells that really ring … wouldn't you? A brooch, that's the word. Admit it, all of it."

"Yeah, but I'm home for the holidays, and have to settle for whatever birds can be flushed out of the frozen marshes of this Duck Hunter's Paradise."

"Semi-articulately rendered, but lookin' for love in all the wrong places, if by that you mean mallards at O'Reilly's."

"What can I say? Where are we really going, Birdbender? Will there be a sleigh ride?"

"A small Christmas party. A girl I met today, English Lit major invited us, if you must know. Since she probably doesn't think we'll show, it has to be the safest thing we can find. She seemed very nice. When was the last time you spent time with someone like that?"

"So long ago I can't remember. Probably never. I wonder if she's taken?"

"I know that has nothing to do with her as an actual person. You'll just have to make your own objective observations when we get there."

Over ten years since we hitchhiked the Pike to the house of The Meteor's girlfriend in Carlisle, joking about wanted posters. Wanted—West Shore Soul Delinquents. Wanted for being 16, crossing city limits to chase new girls living on unfamiliar streets, going to different schools. It really wasn't a joke. In truth we were wanted, have always been wanted. By our dreams and emotions, then our skepticism; always by the Angry Hungry-AllConsuming AllSoldOut-BackorderedButI'veGottenTheLastCopy Material World. A can't miss, category busting fabrication without a shipping date. Soon, we're promised. Soon, and I can get you something interesting in the meantime, here, check this out. Wanted for being alive.

At about a quarter after nine I knocked on the door of a townhouse on Pomfret Street in Carlisle. It opened, and we were greeted by someone other than Beth. Inside Christmas music and talk could be heard. The scene seemed to be under control.

"And you are?"

"I'm Craig and this is NonTravolta, my two-capital, unhyphenated sidekick. Beth Royer invited us."

"She mentioned that a couple of comedians might be coming by, a long shot, but didn't say who. You professors breaking the rules, dance instructors, or just uncomfortable with living?"

"Debatable. May we come in?" I didn't say, "We have a warrant," and then reach into my jacket. You never knew who was holding what—could ruin the whole night. Better play it straight.

"Sure. Beth's in the kitchen. I'll let her know you're here."

We went into the little living room where there were another girl and two guys with drinks. The kind of place where they take turns sleeping in the closet, because it's the biggest room. A small Christmas tree was nicely decorated and carols were playing. Small was the operative word, but the room was bright and comfortable. It wasn't so long ago … .

Marco and I introduced ourselves to the second line of defense, first names only. One of the girls said, "you look familiar, like what's his name? Oh, my ggg … ." Not even close.

Just then, Beth walked in with another girl, and giving me a hug, took her cue. "That's right. Craig Maxwell in a special appearance at our Christmas party."

For a few seconds, the only sound in the room was the tape player grinding out, "Little Drummer Boy".

"But I just read in the paper today … ," one of the unnamed squeaked. "I'm so sorry I just said that."

"Come on, Craig, break the ice and let's party," Marco interrupted, feigning impatience.

"… We're here tonight because Beth asked us. For myself, I would appreciate not discussing what was in the paper today. I'll be dealing with all that for a long time. I guess I have another request, too—please don't play my records, if you even have any. Marco can't stand them. The Christmas carols are much better, went platinum way before.

"Beth, in the absence of your exquisitely crafted cappuccino, how 'bout rustling up some of that hot spiced cider you promised?"

"Sure. Come on Craig, let's rustle in the kitchen. Marco, see if you can talk any sense into Jill. She's a history major so it's going to be uphill all the way. Jill, be careful when he throws out a line about wanting to talk in a quieter place. I can tell a salesman a mile away."

"As it turns out, your keen observation is accurate. I *am* a telecommunications marketing manager for a Fortune 500 company."

"What are you doing hanging out with a rock 'n roll eminence?" With that one, I walked into the kitchen with Beth. Eminence? European History major. Comparative Religions?

"Craig, what a surprise. I'm shocked! Can't thank you enough for coming tonight. I know I'm babbling. I'll try to be quiet and get the cider."

"You're doing just fine, Beth." That we would all do as well.

In the living room Jill and The Meteor were engaged in a Peter and the Wolf simulation, nominally on the subject of history. Marco could hold his own on any subject, with anyone. For him, it wasn't about facts and logic, it was strictly setting the trap, art of the negotiation, making the sale. All about The Pounce. The others sat back listening, kind of stunned by the high pressure, wondering if they could ever fall down into the black hole of a career like that. And he was only working on 10% Warp Power. Just playing.

"Well, I'm second generation off the boat, and the only thing I'm interested in is Italian food. I don't speak the language—I know a few names, a few insults, that's about it," laughing. "Someday, I'll visit Italy. That would be good for business, helpful in certain circles. I've been accused of being culturally disenfranchised, or maybe it's disadvantaged. As you can tell, I don't always listen too closely if it's about anything other than product or terms." Everything a smokescreen until the hammer came down. Flamer, alright, but one with an unremitting follow-through.

"How about you, Craig?" Jill asked, wisely redirecting the flow of hot metal.

"If we're still on the subject of cultures … I used to root for the British in History class when we were talking about the French and Indian War. The textbook printers and teachers wanted us to choose that side. Buy the book, get through the lesson plan, pass the course. We all spoke English, so the British couldn't be that bad. It was all about misunderstandings and economic disagreements, right? The complexities of Native American nations weren't dealt with. When I found I had some of the blood, my allegiance in that historical conflict migrated to the French and Indians, if there is such a thing as allegiance regarding a war fought two hundred years back. Nevertheless, controversial since my Mom's side of the family is pure English. Now, I wonder, why take a side at all? It was so long ago."

They just looked at me, as if to say, "everybody knows life is about taking sides."

"Jill, let's hear what you're doing," I asked, moving the discussion back to more casual ground.

Marco and I enjoyed ourselves, and with the time approaching midnight, we took our leave. Everybody else seemed to enjoy the evening too. That was good—after all, it was their party.

Before leaving, Beth gave me another hug and kiss on the cheek. Oh, Beth, you're so young. Enjoy your life. Be careful. I hope you find love, happiness.

"I'll send you those pictures, Beth."

The ride back to Harrisburg was quiet.

I dropped off The Meteor, then drove down Market Street in Camp Hill, virtually deserted. The trees sparkled with frost as I passed the Coffee Place, reminding me of when I was here with Emily. Closed now. Watching the reflection of the car in the shop windows, I replayed our time together, but it ended the same way. Saying goodbye at the airport. For the rest of our lives. Oh, that I would be driving home to you, Em.

Not wanting to go to sleep yet, I stopped at Mr. Donut, many notches down from *pâtisserie*, like the night, well below freezing. As expected, there were a few after-hours denizens on the loose, talking over their coffee while an elderly waitress got in an occasional wisecrack, and a guy stamped out crullers and cherry-injected donuts in back, behind the glass. A healthy dose of half-n-half can neutralize most any low budget coffee, but not airborne fryoil. Fifteen minutes was about my limit. Not from around here, are ya?

Pulling out, I saw the officer at the usual place in the drycleaner's lot across the street, parking lights on, clouds from the exhaust pipe. Oblivious to the traffic on Market Street. Reading a magazine. *Big Crime, Donut World*, or worse. Learning how to take the lettuce off and then safely eat a ham sandwich during high speed pursuit.

It's true. I don't belong here. I haven't for a long time.

Saturday started quietly, until I saw the *Philadelphia Inquirer* at the newsstand. The wire services had picked up the article, and the phone kept ringing. The other Maxwells in the phone book had to be furious by now.

There was a Christmas Eve candlelight service at the Shiremanstown Baptist Church. The only one I could remember ever going to was during my freshman year at Penn during Christmas break. It was strictly a date in my by then nonrelationship with Natalie, a lull in the on again/off again with Anne, accelerated withdrawal from all aspects of CPA life.

I couldn't tell you what denomination of church it was, five, ten, or twenty, though I've passed it a hundred times. Natalie and I went with her mother and gladiator brothers, one a linebacker for O-State, the other a Captain in the Special Forces. Both glared nonstop, looking for an excuse to deck the halls with me, regimentally expel the scruffy musician for the good of the team, *our* country.

"Do you know whatever happened to her?" Marco had once asked.

"No," I replied. But I did know and never wanted to hear another word. I couldn't talk about it.

Ten years later, there were neither glares nor Natalie, only a bittersweet celebration. The organ and choir soared, particularly on "Oh Come All Ye Faithful". I've got to learn those hymns, I thought, powerful uplifting works like "We Gather Together"—such dramatic counterpoint to the austerity of Pilgrim times, as considered in Alistair Cooke's *America*.

By Christmas Day, the phone calls had tapered off, with just an occasional ring disrupting the quiet of the afternoon. I happened to be near when one came in: "*Boozhoo,*" hello? "It's Annie, Craig." Hurriedly, I picked up the phone.

"Annie, what a surprise." Thankful for the coincidence of being there.

"I saw the article in the paper today."

"Oh, Annie. I loved her so much. I don't know what to do. I'm okay for awhile, then it hits me again. It hurts and hurts."

"You need to come up here and go ice fishing with my uncle. You won't be able to think of anything except keeping warm."

"It may be just what I need, but at this point, I guess I'll go back to California. I've still got some aches from the accident, and now this." We skate on ice laughing, ignoring the lake below. There are always cracks. More than we know.

We talked for a few more minutes. I was glad she had called.

"I'll come visit you one of these days, promise. *Miigwech*, Annie."

"Don't put if off too long, Craig. We've got to work on your Ojibwe pronunciation. Up here, with the home field advantage. *Giga-waabamin naagaj.*" Goodbye.

Christmas passed, and the next day, Monday, I returned to California. On the way to the airport was the Star Barn, a white, picturesque wooden structure along Route 283 in Highspire. Like so many old buildings around here, it would need to be shored up and rehabilitated soon, or fall to the creeping deterioration of indifference so subtly played out season after season. The Star Barn was a fitting reference for coming and going, greeting and goodbye.

Flying over snowy Kansas fields, icy mountains, desert at 35,000 feet, it would have been so easy for my spirit to be completely frozen as well. Alone.

Emily dominated my thoughts. Do angels exist? Maybe Emily was one kind of angel, destined to be with me, but ever so briefly. To conceive, yet not bear our child. A child with her in the infinity of Heaven?

I reflected again on my conversation with Mrs. Ritchey, about how Emily might have "justified" a child. By sleeping together, spiritually, were we man and wife? Is marriage a contractual state, a status, act, and/or commitment? Before/in the eyes of what or whom? Civil or religious?

It seemed to me that the spiritual dimension had to be paramount, and with that, what "marriage" is does not fall apart if we can't all-inclusively pin it down in words, concepts, descriptions of state, status, or relationship. Logically, I guess that means it's absolute. A tough thing for us to deal with.

No matter what it is or how it plays out, if Emily was an angel, she's another kind now.

✠ ══════ ✠

Back at Laguna, I put on Bach's *St. Matthew Passion*, opened the windows, and turned up the volume, challenging the sky, the Pacific with its heavy swells this late December day, hour after hour, as if forever. The libretto told the story of my heart:

Kommt, ihr Tochter, helft mir klagen	Come ye daughters, share my mourning.
O Mensch, bewein dein Sunde groß	O Man, thy heavy sin lament.

That evening, a melody formed in my mind as I sat at the piano and sketched out what became "The Gardens". I wouldn't have written that, couldn't have … before. A tough way to get inspiration.

New Years Eve was spent with Max, Gretchen, and Marcy, their longtime friend who was my date. They were all aware of most but not all of what had happened—Gretchen and Max had met Emily that night at the club on Sunset, and liked her. It was a lowkey, subdued evening for friends to be together, celebrate the New Year.

Before falling asleep later at home, I put on the powwow tape Annie had given to me. One lifetime ago, only yesterday. The beat was soothing, thought of Annie brought strength, the singing courage and beauty. The *Anishinaabeg* had survived, and so could I. Life would go on. I didn't have to crackup or drop out of sight. I had to look ahead.

1977. When the real technical challenges and triumph of Viking One were overrun by the fiction of *Star Wars*. Movies would never be the same. Life would never measure up.

A heartwrenching year. The year when my life hung by a thread, was turned upside down, literally and figuratively. A market bottom from which my depleted stock could only recover, rise.

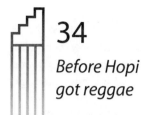

34

Before Hopi got reggae

Practicing for long hours, I resolved to keep sharpening my keyboard skills in a fervor both to excel and keep from being overcome by depression. My body continued to heal, strengthened through rehabilitation and other workouts of which I was capable, helped by late evening soaks in the hot tub. Preparing to start school in the fall, the on-again plan, I had a couple of dates, including one with Terri, now a senior at Claremont, following her surprise call. We went to a classical concert in San Diego and enjoyable party in La Jolla afterward with her parents. I asked her about the pictures. Laughing, she told me, "the girls are impressed, guys intimidated." Though the family made me feel comfortable for the evening, I was mindful of being alone. "What if there *is* no one else for you, then what?" I thought. When is then? Now? Forever?

Alone. Never more alone.

It rained and rained. Not the black wall summer thunderstorms of Wyoming, New Mexico, or Arizona, but winter Pineapple Connection jetstreamed moisture, low after low lobbed from Hawaii. Hills slid, parts of PCH were closed north of Santa Monica, arroyos and flood control channels flowed full. Despite the gloomy sky, reservoirs were filling and the Laguna Hills would be green, carpeted with spring wildflowers.

The fog of my still somewhat misplaced memory continued to lift. Contemplating "when Josie comes home," on impulse I called not Steely Dan but Kat. We made plans for a trip to Hopiland. The timing was good—there was the Buffalo Dance in January, followed by the Bean Dance in February. Being nearby in Chinle, Kat had been to both dances the year before, and highly recommended them.

So I flew into Phoenix and drove up to Flag, cold with ice and recent snow, got a room at Little America, and went over to her place for dinner. On the phone before the trip she had mentioned reading the "ESO Rocker" article in the paper, and I levelled with her. My recollection of Kat had been dimmed by the accident and time, having last seen each other at the Copper Queen in Bisbee nearly a year ago, after meeting the day before that. You could only say we were near-strangers. Nevertheless, I immediately felt at ease in our conversation, that she was a willing listener with heartfelt understanding. One who had interesting recounts and perspective to relate herself. Closeness and rapport is not always a function of time.

Kat's place was small, sparsely furnished with the essentials: Native American arts, a few pieces of comfortable, well designed furniture, stereo, and lots of books. *Black Elk Speaks; Lame Deer: Seeker of Visions; Stories of Traditional Navajo Life and Culture; Wind from an Enemy Sky; Sun Chief*, the book I thought she had that day in Tucson.

Twentieth Century Native American writing is about finding places in two worlds. Confronting difficulties and overcoming them through traditions and recognition of the importance of the land itself; being healed or mercilessly defeated, clubbed, overrun. About what goes on at the edge of a dry lake in an empty place, seeing the harsh beauty alive as never before through one's opened eyes, or in spirit gone from the skeleton to somewhere else along The Circle.

It was as if Kat had opted into tribal life at that dry lake. Left herself upon the doorstep of all that it is to be Native. Finding an identity outside her Germanic lineage through multiple disappearances: first into the presence of timeless, unheard currents running through the region for which she felt a life's thirst; then into the language and literature, all that is written, read, and spoken; and finally, within the transformed state always beyond the horizon of all that The People *out there* are and are not. Kat could laugh at *Annie Hall* and sing along to *Hotel California*, but in the night, she dreamtravelled through the Big Rez on ancient roads. I had been with her on one of those trips.

Kat appeared to be thriving in Flag, having taken up skiing at the Snow Bowl, and was looking forward to outdoor recreation during the coming summer in the high country of Arizona. Since she lived in the downtown area, we were able to walk to the Caffe Express on San Francisco Street after dinner. Looking fit and pretty, she wore a manta, or shoulder wrap, a brightly colored handwoven replica of a late 1800's Navajo textile.

It was getting late, with only a few people left at the Caffe. Kat wanted to hear me play again. No jazz tonight. There was a piano, surprisingly in tune and with a decent action, so I played an excerpt of *The Well Tempered Clavier*. It amazed her—both what I played, and how competently I played it. I had been working hard. You expected, perhaps, "Mustang Sally"?

I had other songs, originals that weren't quite together, unset fragments, unpolished castings. A significant change from the ESO era compositions. Commercial value was no longer my concern and might even be elusive, if I really thought about it. But I didn't have to think about it.

I walked her home and drove back to my room, wondering why I was really here.

The next day, Saturday, was the Bean Dance. We got a thermos of french roast coffee and some unique, if not bizarre (e.g., Wheat-Free Non-Dairy Pine-apple Cinnamon Sunrise Surprise), pastries at a place on South Beaver Street before hitting the road for the Hopi Rez within the Navajo Big Rez. After AnyCityExtraGrandé, driving here is simply sublime. Check it out: sublime, "lofty, grand, or exalted in thought, manner, or expression." Or if you prefer a synonym, how about empyreal, "celestial; exalted, sublime"? That's what it is out here. Sublime.

There are the land, the big land, and indigenous cultures at once decep-tively primitive and sophisticated. A contradictory mix, one on which you can't easily put simple labels. I had Hopi pottery which was exquisite fine art, and Navajo pottery, crude and covered with pine pitch—the artistic and utilitarian. Underneath the jet trails in the sky were foot races to Walpi, the grinding of corn by hand, *mano* and *metate*, while in metal buildings components of guidance systems for Army tanks were assembled by contract.

Traditionally, the tribes had made no distinction between "art" and the rest of life. Art was an expression of *all* the elements of life. But at exhibitions a distinction *was* now being made. Avante-garde, modernistic influences had crept in, and I was almost excruciatingly sensitive to them. Similar to the treaties and surrenders of the past, new erosions and accommodations were evident as art was framed and marketed in the Material World. Speaking only for myself, I saw "modern by tradition" to be healthy change, preserving valuable traditions while moving ahead through innovation. There are of course other views, and the reality that art will go where it goes. I am not suggesting the folly of trying to "stop" anything, only expressing a preference for a more traditional style, one which is at the same time original and creative, rather than angry, shocking, or market-reactive. For me, "aesthetic" means just that.

I could say "our art", recognizing the biological and governmental-political circuits which wire me to the *Anishinaabeg*, but then I work in a different genre. Little progress has been made in understanding, much less reconciling, the 1/8 seeming to self-define me with the Anglo which never goes willingly. Who you are, more than a Head Thing? Who Are *You*, Baba O'Riley?

As we drove, I was struck by the complexities resolved in great vertical walls of sandstone, flat mesa tops in parallel relief to the horizon, sparse arrangements of brush and browngrass, the sinuosity of a road around a butte, an occasional ribbon cloud sheared by stronger winds aloft. Dually, The Land Before Artists, and Artists' Paradise. Uniquely, simply The Land. Let's leave the styles and fractions behind today, listen to the voice of beauty calling.

Daydream country, with music. Footprints, Milestones, Orbits. So evocative, so hip, so Miles. Mozart, *Piano Concerto No. 23*, in a huge key demanded by the kyanite sky to be primal and major, running through my mind, visualized at my fingertips.

I looked over at Kat and marvelled at the creation she represented, then back at the spectacular land outside the window. Was this all God's creation? Or were we just null set characters in an instruction manual—caricatures within a cosmic comic book, Random Event Underground Comix, Volume One, No. 1? Krumbs of the Kosmos?

Kat was a marvellous work, regardless of the creator. Let us slip away into the shadows of those mesas, I thought, the two of us. Like we might have done in Bisbee. There's still time. Let go. Escape now.

"Kat … ," I began to speak, but with a whoosh! she rolled down her window for a blast of fresh air.

"What did you start to say?" She could have asked, *ha´ át´´íísh niníło´*, what's holding you back?

"Nothing. Lost my train of thought when you opened the window." I wish.

Life as caricature, the post-modern "art" of choice, "culture" the label of convenience. Engaged in a supraintuitive dialogic, with ever escalating stakes. Stop it! I was going to get away from analysis, listen to the voice of beauty, right?

Kat knew the way, but I liked to refer to the map, gauging our progress as we passed Leupp, pronounced "Loop", *Tsiizizii* in Navajo, turned north after the Little Colorado River on Indian Route 2, eventually paralleling Oraibi Wash. Driving through *Mesa and Desert*, a 1905 painting by Louis Akin. Driving in beauty, as they say on the Rez. Diving into the sky.

The land you live on, observe, grow to know and understand, learn from, are part of. I remember speaking with a Hopi woman, sculptor, now living in Santa Fe. "When going north from Leupp, excitement builds … I'm nearly home! The rock formations all have names, handed down to me by my grandmother. The figures I sculpt both reflect and are imbued with that land, the myths, history, and qualities it contains. The plants, sky, people, and stories which make us who we are."

In the cities Back East people have little or no land, hence are not grounded, knowledgeable of or sensitive to it. Living vertically, stacked floor upon floor in a way constantly requiring more elaborate technologies, arts and media to reinforce self-convincing models of creative maintenance and vitality; unable to relate to the rolling horizontal expanse under the huge sky west of the Painted Desert. They're at home in San Francisco, less so in LA. Not at all in *Tsiizizii*.

The mind of an engineer, always seeing things in terms of stresses and strains, analytical systems, measurements and calibrations, predictive behaviors, codes of "practice". That of this engineer-critic, one without a home, in the end perhaps distinguished only by his horizontal model. Horizontally empty. The kind I was almost successful in leaving behind in the Mojave.

"I like the Navajo rug you have. Tell me about it," I asked, turning from the thoughtway I had been travelling. It was 4×6 in size, with a geometric pattern on red background, tightly woven, excellent quality.

"*Diyogí*, a Navajo blanket or rug. It's done in the style of a late classic ceremonial serape, actually, emulated in the rug. The pattern dates from around 1870. I searched for almost the entire two years I was at Chinle, finding it finally with the help of a trader at Lukachukai. In the shadow of the Chuskas. An important marker for my time on the Rez. On the surface, wool, woven yarn, just a rug. But to both the weaver and me, much, much more."

"What is the significance of the pattern?"

"Rugs speak of untold generations of Navajo culture. The shearing, carding, spinning, and dyeing of the wool are ritual preparation for weaving patterns deep in mythic tradition—rocks and sky, stars and rain, shadows and silhouettes, the Yei and Thunder People. The Navajo world is dynamic, a constant push-pull in pursuit of *hózhó*—beauty, balance, order, harmony. It never ends. They weave it into their rugs. It is said that there are elements of the Long Walk, suffering, tribulation, and deliverance in the weaving I have. One of my favorite Navajo words sums it up—*ájíní*, meaning, 'one has been saying that for a long time.'

"We're only a moment in the long narrative of time. Look at the rug carefully, and you might see another dawn, the recreation of earth and sky that is both a day, and a lifetime. *Ájíní*. One has been saying that for a long time."

"So it's not about symmetry and perfection, it's about balance, and the communication of tradition," I mused.

And about a magical night on Castle Rock, later in a room at the Queen. What may have been the only such night between us in our lifetimes. Our own mythology. Even more, as Kat had said, the imperfect strands we are woven into an infinitely complex work. It was all there, woven into that night, but she didn't say it. She wouldn't go back to dwell there, I thought. She was Kat.

I admired her, mostly for the best of reasons. The others had little to do with her, rather me. I could be spared from having to deal with Bisbee, because she wouldn't bring it up.

In the cold morning air, an old Navajo walked along the road, *yikahígíí*, those who are walking. As much sandstone and greasewood as man. Kat pulled over, rolled down the window, and greeted him, "*yá'át'ééh*," hello. He acknowledged her with a few more words, then got into the back seat. Wearing an old sweater, he told me story after story without saying another word.

I poured some coffee into a cup, pulled a pastry out of the bag and served it to him on a napkin. He smelled the coffee, *gohwééh*, savored the sweetness of the food, ate and drank in silence, enjoying the unexpected treat. Then he closed his eyes and hummed what seemed to me a mixture of chant, gleeful thanks, and contentment, like a sleepy cat rubbing its back on a rug, paws outstretched.

A half hour later, he gestured, softly grunting, *"kwe'é,"* here. Kat pulled over, and he got out. *Kwe'é*, his password to a completely different reality, gateway to another culture. Walking down an unmarked dirt track toward the shadow of Garces Mesa, he disappeared in the cold day. *Bíjík'ehgo*, in accord with his own customs, in his own way. In reality, we were the ones disappearing. At 60 miles an hour, consisting more of spaces between our atoms than particle substance, moving fields and vapors of thoughts, dreams, and memories wrapped in elaborate metal. Toward Blue Point.

Maybe it was the Old Man whose presence nudged Kat to reflect, then observe in a moment of candor, "I hardly know you, and can understand that because of the whole fame thing, beyond a certain point, it seems to be difficult to get close enough to even start to get to know you ... did the woman you lost get closer?"

Maybe I had been wrong. She would talk about it. What would she say?

"Yes ... I was just starting to realize how." But when I thought that, I couldn't help arguing to the contrary. Was it true? Had I really been on the trail to understanding, or was it all an artifice for coping, a transparently contrived lunacy toward new moons?

"I knew what I was getting into at the Queen," she said. "It was a wonderful night. A perfect night, the kind that you dream of for a long time. Perfection that may happen only once. That can both define and be a peak experience in one part of my life, or for the rest of my life. And then it *did* happen. By any measure, it was heavy duty medicine. *Nihá*. A gift for us.

"Between the time I dropped you off after we left Coffee Etc., and when we met again in Bisbee, I could think of little other than Craig Maxwell. ESO! Fascinated, with a serious case of 24-hour awe. A man with so much talent, such tenderness, who wanted to be with me. And in many ways, I immediately knew, like me. A traveller. On the smallest, most remote roads we can find. Like today. So tired of the city, needing the desert, mountains, forests, the sky. And having been there, each time never the same again.

"I know we both have fences, the closer we get to others. As much as we sometimes want them gone, we hold on. When I think of your fences, they seem to be along the road, close in. You're that traveller, always looking ahead, but not often pulling to the side, opening a gate, spending time with those in the fields behind the fences in long term relationships. A cowboy looking to drive the next herd a thousand miles."

Cafe Whyoming

Why am I fenced out, when the fences keeping me out are those I've put up? Am I really fenced out, or fenced in? Why is it always about the *next* herd?

Kat continued, "we have been hurt, in different ways. You lost someone you began to love, wanted to love more. I lost a lot of my heart to the *Diné*, to their special kind of pride and reckless self-destruction. The suffering of generations, children alienated by the weaknesses of their parents, caught among cultural, racial, material, and spiritual pressures and erosions. All so tragic because of their poetry, that with which they're born in their hearts, that of the land."

You could say the same thing about any number of other places, races, cultures. Too many around the world to list. Even those of the Dominant Pale Material World. Mankind is a failure. It's the only conclusion to which I can come.

She was quiet for a few minutes, as we made our way on the road parallelling the mesa to the west.

"I read that you're part Native American, but I can't remember you mentioning it."

"Yes, 1/8 *Anishinaabe*—aka Ojibwe or Chippewa. The Old Man could just as well have been the grandfather I saw last year walking along a road in the forests near Lake Superior, in northeast Minnesota. *Ningichi aya'aam*, grandfather or elder in Ojibwe.

"Sometimes that blood is entirely who I am, to the exclusion of the world of the *bilagáana*. At other times, the majority is firmly in control, dominant, and I'm just another *bilagáana* in a sports car listening to Bach."

The quantum was like a logger's wedge—once you cut through to the heart of the tree, it took only driving the wedge to topple it. Then, you had to leave the symbolic and deal with the real—the log on the ground, monolithic and now inert, useful only if its branches are removed; skidded to the mill, sawn, dimensioned, manufactured in clouds of sawdust, fragrant trace of the living tree. If not properly dried, warped, rejected, discarded.

"Craig, at some moments, I've seen the look, an intense, Indian look in your eyes. Like when you got angry about the obnoxious guy at Coffee Etc. Fierce. Different, as dark as the timberlands of your ancestors on a night with no moon." Her eyes were locked to mine for a few seconds, until she had to look back at the road ahead.

"And when we were together at the Queen, I looked into your eyes and saw fields of tall grass moved by the wind—waves, swirls. Like the stars in the sky we talked about on Castle Rock. Spiral arms of the Milky Way. Order and disorder. Peaceful beauty, yet always watching for the cloud of dust, one threat or another approaching. Do you remember that moment?"

"Yes. It was a beautiful moment, one of hearts truly dying to all but each other."

"You know my heart, Craig, my grief. When we slept together, my heart did die, as you put it; and when we left the next day, it died again. That's how my life always seems to be, a succession of deaths. But then when I think I can't go on, some force grants me another life, another day. Today. Those deaths are not about rejection or failure. They're about living and endings.

"Since our night together, there has always been part of you with me, and if you'll admit it, part of me within you. The multitrack recording process you explained. It's like that. Just like that."

I looked away, out the window, trying to grasp all of what Kat was saying. End it here, as you put it. Drive off the road. But there were no trees to hit, skid, or saw.

She broke the silence, continuing. "In Flag now, I'm close to, but far enough away from, the Rez, where I can grow stronger, heal. I look at the pictures of the Navajos in the first half of the century, how dark their skin looks, how thin they were, scratching out existences in a land purposely made even more harsh by the government. Submerging them in a society which was alien then, possibly even more dispiriting now.

"How they sat on the dirt in long skirts and wove at their looms, the little ones on cradleboards in the shade. So much has been displaced. Though the *Diné* look different now, and despite the heartbreak, I'm always drawn back. To their heavy duty medicine. I just don't feel that medicine in the white culture— my own. A hard thing to deal with. Maybe another kind is there, but I can't connect with it. Craig, you've got some of that Native medicine, if nowhere else, in your eyes.

"Know this … that although as man and woman we may sleep together only once and then part, in another dimension, spiritually we are and will always be together, forever one as the remembered experiences and emptiness of this sky and land."

When she said that, it was like I fell out of the car. My mind was all over the map, scraping on rock ledges and emergent vertical desert lava fins, black ash mesas. Dendrochronologically caught in dry years, supernovas.

Who *are* you out here, among the rocks, jasper gravel and rippled siltstone, slipping and swerving on the cinders and asphalt, through rabbit brush, thistles and sage, under *their* sky?

Anglo/white, red/Native, women/lovers, true love/children, dimensions. Tension which had not been released by anything remotely approaching a healthy, survivable view. The cultural objectivity within me was always trying to reduce the complex to the oversimplified here and now, losing it in forever expanding information. What are you doing with all this information, these rushes of stuff? How many signs and wonders will it take to recognize the message, whatever that might be? When will the fighting stop, the war of paper and systematic arguments? What were the life-implications of what Kat was saying? If it's true, am I also with those before ... Anne too? I had a similar thought about Emily back in December, but had not extended the argument beyond, or before, her.

T ´áadoo haadzíí ´da. He said nothing, locked up in uncomfortable contemplation.

After the windmill has turned its life and rusted, last tumbleweeds are caught by the wire of fences that have fallen; when grasses burn sweetly before the angry splendor of a final, beautiful fury; pockets of crystallized boredom crack in the heat, what will have been my name?

Kat was quiet again as the Hopi mesas came into sight. I was beside her, but now lost in remembering Emily, how I would have liked to bring her here. I loved them both, to grasp a few words, but couldn't decide what that really meant. It wasn't that I didn't want to be with Kat, rather *at this moment*, I wanted to be with Em, in the past. Not strong enough to totally deal with the present, the woman beside me.

Tutskwa. Hopiland. The land, always the Creator's land.

Walking into the village plaza, on a mesa top high above land which stretched out in the four directions, we had left the Big Rez and were at once immersed within a totally different world. The dancers stepped to ancient rhythms, keeping time with the bells on their leggings, costumes intensely colorful under surprisingly bright winter sunlight. The crowd filling the close spaces constantly moved to accommodate the dancers, on another level a dance in itself. The dust on moccasins was a subtle shade of yellow-red, weathered from the rocks of this mesa; footprints as timeless as the petroglyphs etched by their ancestors. *Bikék ´eh,* their footprints; *na´ akéé´ęę,* the footprints he saw all around.

Prints reminiscent of those of the astronauts—one small step, one smaller footprint in the dust of the moon. "That's some story," the ancient Hopi remarked in his smile. As if to say, "no way." Realizing that both were right, walk and vision. Understanding that the giggling, playfully inquisitive child, looking up from under her mother's arm, was infinitely more powerful than a footprint on the moon. That child *lives.*

On the plateau to the east, toward Steamboat, a road drawn with pastels soft and dusty as the moon's shades of light brown winds through sagebrush a silver-green unique to earth, full of abiding life. Downward from this mesa along a steep path, past the real petroglyphs, are sacred springs. On the plain below, looking so sparse, runners have passed along other paths, in motion toward the horizon always so far away in this vast land. Flowing with the continuity of untold generations. That's some story, too.

There had been snow, pockets remaining within shaded exposures. Moisture for spring planting. The Bean Dance is about purification, renewal, and initiation of children into Hopi ceremonial life. A time of bringing families back together during the transition of *Powamuya*, the lunar month corresponding to February; for the kachina spirit beings to intercede in the germination and growth of beans soon to be planted. Emerging from kivas by ladders bent to the sky, the kachina dancers went throughout the village, handing out toys and gifts to the women and children.

Their dance of renewal triggered the torrent building within me. I had to walk away from the crowds, rhythmic flow, village of mortared rocks hewn centuries ago. Lost in grief on the edge of the mesa. From that warm spring night to this winter day. Kat came over to comfort me, knowing her own tears. In my pain, there was a sense of pervasive guilt. About Kat, Cathy. Possibly even Emily. Why?

The Hopi kept dancing in ritual preservation of their culture. Prayer feathers, *paho*, tied to bushes in significant ways fluttered in the wind, waved to the land saying, "remember." The pressures exerted from without would continue unmitigated in the future, even more intensely than in the past. That culture was still recognizable, if not largely intact. My heart was not.

When we left, on the way back I remembered reading about the interrelatedness of the aspects comprising Hopi life: spiritual beliefs, social organization, dwellings and other structures for religious practice, the land and all over, on, and under it.

Seeking wisdom, I would be thankful for just a fragment of understanding.

> By our land you will recognize us,
> By our houses you will meet us,
> By our heart you will know us.

It was a quiet ride to Flagstaff, *Kin tání*, where we stopped at the 66 Diner beneath Mars Hill. I picked at food I didn't want, tired from the trip, yet thankful for the opportunity to learn from the Hopi, *'Ayahkinii*; the Old Man; women who ask only for respect, truthfulness.

Which women? Am I really here or is all of this only a dream, continuation of the one on the shore of *Gichigami*?

I must be here. Kat just dropped me off at Little America, so extreme in contrast to the Big Rez, Hopiland. Off the scale. *Da 'nijah*, where people sleep, up the elevator, down carpeted corridors, in locked rooms. Built in a dry land, a place permeated with Native presence below Sacred Peaks, flakes falling outside at once truth and snow. Inside this building, shut out. No footprints left in the dust.

During the night, the dreams came back. Burns from loss, the ropes of habit, chafing self restraint.

"*Bee nihiłhashni´*," said the old Navajo, let me tell you about it. The Old Days.

"*Eya', giga wiindamoon gaa-pi-izhiwebak*," replied my Ojibwe grandfather. Yes, let me tell you about those days.

I was one then the other, looking at the land falling away from Garces Mesa to Dinnebito Wash; with the sweep of an arm, *Gichigami*, Lake Superior.

"I tell you now, about those days long ago when we lived in harmony with the spirits and the land. When we were thankful in plentiful years, and had the strength to survive other times, hard times ... ."

Awakened from the dream, I got up and walked over to the window, opened it, felt the winter cold. Outside was a parking lot, a light shining in the window. I wanted so much to be with a woman. Her sleepy warmth. I'll call Kat, she'll come here, be with me. I know she will. It's who she is, climbing Castle Rock, only one of her many woman's dances. At the top, cool to my touch, sensuous. The marvellous creation I was with today. Real.

I dialed her number, hearing her already begin, prefacing, aligning the energy fields and ancient currents of what it is to be a woman; silently express, "When I was a young girl ... ."

"Kat, I'm sorry for calling so late. Did I wake you?"

"I was only half asleep. Long day, exciting dances, strong spirits, heavy issues."

"Kat, what you said is true, that there is and always will be some of you within me. I remember everything about Castle Rock, the way you grasped your skirt to climb it, the coolness of your skin; walking together around Bisbee, later our night at the Queen. But even more than that, I think about your beautiful heart.

"Part of *my* heart really wants you here now. But there are others to resolve—those within me whom I have loved, most recently Emily; and others, as you, I love more strongly than ever, with the perspective of loss now, in ways as individual as the women you are.

"In my confusion, I desperately need to find a center, my own Flag; be alone, if I can stand it, and heal. Like you, sort things out. Without hurting anyone else." She needs a *very strong man* to love her back. I'm not that man now, scared that I never have been, never will be.

"I understand. There are others within me too. It never seems to be simple or easy.

"And yet, to spend one's life trying to sort things out perfectly is not to live at all. Someday, our hearts may intersect again in a perfect night. It would be terrible to just ignore that. Life is a stream in which we float timelessly, before we were born, here on earth, then in the spirit. As they say, 'don't stay on the shore working too hard trying to figure out why it flows, while watching the stream go by.'"

"That's always the challenge … thanks for listening to me and understanding, Kat. Let's still get together tomorrow like we talked about, okay?"

"See you at my place around 10:30. Night, Craig."

"Goodnight."

Had I done the right thing calling her? If so, why do I feel empty? Hanging up the phone, I turned around and looked at the bed, saw no woman, only a memory. A stream of memories, some of which were also dreams. Cathy, sleeping peacefully.

I thought of Hopiland today, so alive. Chaco and Mesa Verde, abandoned. Or were they? Look at George Grant's pictures of archaeologists in the early 1930's working there. Rock walls, rooms, fallen emptiness being mortared back together. Then look at the wrinkled faces of stone, spirit shadows, scrawny bent tree watching, as much a grandfather as the man on the road today. Places not only of the past, but present and future. Filled with the animate, created world … .

Once again, giving way to sleep. More dreams.

Late Sunday morning after coffee, Kat and I walked around the downtown, *biníshiit΄ áázh.* Alleys with old painted signs, electric lines and service drops, concrete gutters, dumpsters, crushed boxes, broken glass. Winter ragged, too often there only for the business of brown-bagged shame.

One good Indian arts place on San Francisco Street, Puchteca, was open, so we went in. On the walls were several exceptional, brilliantly colored pen and inks. I had never seen anything quite like them. "Navajo, Baje Whitethorne. From Shonto, Reed Clan." Shonto, that place of sunlight water, purple lips. In the layers and jags of rocks were energy fields, pressure gradients invisible as those which cause the wind, spirit lines. I immediately felt the energy, excitement great art generates.

On a lower shelf of an unlit, trading post style display case was a necklace that I asked to be brought out. In the light, the exquisite deep red coral practically jumped out of the proprietor's hands. Five strands, strung with a twist, like a red chile ristra. Highest quality. I had to have it. "This is one piece I hate to see go," he said; "it's been waiting for the right person to come along for a couple of years. Congratulations, a superb necklace, made by a beautiful Navajo woman."

"Puchteca," the owner explained, "traders of the Aztec area a thousand years ago," while looking at the necklace I saw Tusayan polychrome bowls, ancient sandals, Anasazi roads. New roads through Meteor City, Two Guns, Smoke Signal, Twin Arrows. Flow Land. Mud flows, lava flows, Dynaflo. The withered, dwarf Hopi corn stalks of yesterday seemingly resting in nothing but eternal dirt. Those who vanished, leaving only a strange statement: "this time the total destruction was less severe."

A turquoise necklace looked great on Kat, and I got that for her. *Biyo´*, her necklace. I really like to buy Indian stuff for women, appreciate how it enhances their beauty. In the Way 'o the Rez, she said little in accepting the gift, opened her purse and gave me in return a simple beaded bracelet. Old time. I remembered seeing one like it at the Oljeto Trading Post, smiling at the recollection. My memory was getting better.

"Stay in touch," she said, hugging when it was time to go. "Craig, you are and will always be my special heart-traveller." I thought of what I had begun to say yesterday, when Kat rolled down her window … but once again, *my* heart kept quiet.

Before leaving town I went into McGaugh's, a few doors down on San Francisco Street, for something to read on the return trip. A quote encountered while leafing through a book on art rang true, summarized how I feel about The West:

> I felt reluctant to leave those brutal and rugged mountains, the dry, scorching plains, to abandon for good that long dim trail that lay over the sandy desert … The life is wonderful, strange—the fascination of it clutches me … seems to whisper, 'Come back, you belong here, this is your real home.' N.C. Wyeth, 1904.

At the airport, I reached into the pocket of my jacket for something, finding a piece of paper. On it Kat had written words which I later translated:

Hoodeeshnih	I will tell my story.
łe´ doolch´	Lightning flashed
´adahwiis ´áágóó.	everywhere.
Hodoo´ niid	It was said
hwéé hodoozįįł,	he will be tested,
´íhwiidooł´áalgo.	he will learn.
Bitsii´ yibizh.	She is braiding her hair.
Neiséyeel	I dreamed
shiiłkaah.	I am staying all night.
Da ´diilzhish.	Let us dance.
Bik ´idadi´ diitįįł	We will understand it
hayííłkąągo.	at dawn.
Nihijéí	(In) our hearts.

Glancing out the window of the plane at the mosaic below, brown land subdued by altitude and thin, cold clouds, I reflected again on our drive, the Old Man, the complex, strange Navajo words, my dreams. Opening the box containing the red coral necklace, I looked at it, jotting a verse of reply on the Air West napkin:

> *Ajíní*
> They say,
> It is said,
> One has been saying
> For a long time
> That
> I awoke,
> I dreamed,
> My life awakened me
> When
> I was awakened from my life
> By a dream.

I *am* thankful for women who ask only for respect, truthfulness. But if that's as far as it goes, the message can only be hard and cold. Because it's not that they don't *want* more, much more, they just don't *ask* for it. They have been giving and giving, while I have done little more than taking, at best, accepting. Forgive me. Please … forgive me.

Postscript to a quiet goodbye. Kat. A woman Rezwild and hungry for life. A grieving woman, yet deep and so alive in the right ways, those that move my heart. Deep in the shadows of the Chuskas.

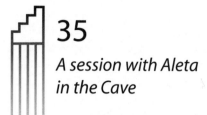

35

A session with Aleta in the Cave

A month later, I was at the Guitar Center looking at gear, but not with "Life in the Fast Lane", "Theme from Star Wars", or *Shock of the New* in mind. On some days, having anything in mind was a triumph. This was one of those.

"Hey, man, been readin' 'bout you."

"I'm sorry, you look familiar, but I can't quite place you." Tight end for the Rams? "Have we worked together?"

"It's Cedric, Cedric Clarke."

As we talked, I remembered Cedric, first call session synthesist extraordinaire, like George Duke, a purveyor of very tasty Minimoog. In our soul band during high school, before moving on to Prog Rock in college, I played the music because I liked the songs. The roots from which soul and gospel sprang, however, were foreign to me. Cedar Cliff was white, middle class. Suburban subdivisions. Khaki and Madras shirts. Levis. A long way from the black communities of New York, Philly, or LA where funk cooked and gospel choirs shook Sunday mornings. Cedric and I had run across each other more than a few times at Planet Tracks. We weren't competitors, we were pros—past tense for me; present tense, I assumed, for Cedric.

"I'm eight months into rehab now, almost done except for some memory blanks. So what are you workin' on, Cedric?"

"Producin' a session over at the Pearl, gospel, very tight, real smooth. Bet it's been awhile since you were in the Cave. Why don't you come over? You're goin' to like Aleta Stewart. She can write, make you shiver when she sings. Come on, man. Right now, let's go!"

"You got any food over there? I could use something to eat."

"Yeah, soul food, what you think?"

"That'll do. I've got a couple of stops to make first. Better give me the address. I'm liable to end up in Antelope Valley. Be there in a few."

When I arrived, the studio was quiet. As I opened the door, I heard a prayer.

"… for this day. May we truly make a joyful noise. Amen."

Cedric looked up and saw me enter. "Aleta, meet Craig Maxwell, mover and shaker of ESO before he really shook himself up in the desert. Let's see if we can work on his spirit today."

"Nice to meet you. We'll try to do that. Maybe even get a few guest tracks out of you," Aleta said good naturedly.

The gospel session was something else. Everybody working hard, focused, lots of smiles with headphones on, eyes closed. They were doing takes of "My Ship", a strong tune, finding and pulling down the sound. Enough there to connect it to traditional gospel, but big steps forward too, in composition and instrumentation. Aleta was more than up to the material, a diminutive powerhouse belting it out. These singers from Watts, South LA, so talented, but with Nowhere to Go in radio markets other than Sunday morning shows. There were few opportunities to be the next Aretha. Was there an alternative? Not yet on the radar screen of the music and airplay businesses, run from distant highrises, corporations plowing through the years and revenue streams like aircraft carriers.

Cedric wasn't satisfied with his piano part on one of the cuts, and asked me during a break if I would give it a go.

"I'd like to warmup first, get the feel of that Yamaha grand. It's been a long time since I was in a studio."

Bach's *Toccata in C minor* would do the trick. I sat down, visualizing the keyboard, music, reflecting upon what I believed to be the composer's intent, then began playing his extraordinarily articulate composition.

In the studio, they always roll tape. The recording engineer had turned on the machine, and got it all down. I finished and looked up to see everybody standing behind the glass, just staring. In listening to a cassette made from the tape later, it had been, by all accounts, a prodigious warmup.

"Man. That was incredible. I got to have me a motorcycle accident, too."

In contrast, the session cut was simple and straightforward. I played it with no problem. While in the neighborhood, I was going to have dinner at the MaxMan's, and had to go. Aleta's tune kept running through my mind on the way over. The music was good. Was there a broader market?

Did it matter? Was a theorem being imposed, like in Plane Geometry? "Diametrically, if music semicircularly, then it follows, the marketable arc length." Or was this instead about philosophy? For every neutral assumption P^0 there exists a poorer one, P^-? A universe of poorer ones?

I drove away on Sunset, looking at the sky above the palm tops, still the shaggy-maned, toothless lions from the Santa Monica days. Contemplating my expertise in nonapplicative expatiation while the real universe, seemingly so frozen in our earth-time, ran wild with all sorts of annihilating cancellations, unheard fusions, Saturday blowouts lasting for a billion years, throwing broken stars, bottles, sparkling trash tumbling into the Great Empty. It all seems so placid, harmless. So Blue.

March, moving on toward spring. Max and I were looking out over the lights of LA from the deck of his place.

"So how was Arizona?"

"Arizona was too much, way too soon."

After a few minutes of thought, Max said, "here's some worthless advice from an otherwise all-knowing friend. You can't just practice piano for ten hours a day. Take specific steps to confront the pain and leave it behind.

"You've got all kinds of things going for you. There's someone else out there, for the long haul. Someone like Gretchen is to me. It's there in your heart. Find it."

"What are you really saying, go to a shrink?" I asked, realizing it to be only half jokingly. "Here? In LA? That would be a trip."

"Not at all. You still planning to go back to school in Wyoming? Go there. Throw yourself into it. Do it!"

"I don't know. Sometimes it seems to be no more than a fiction, another date on another tour."

"What's the name of that girl you met there last year?"

"Cathy … still in San Francisco, doing well, she says, learning the publishing business. Probably live in the City for ten years, do the sizzling rice Szechuan/North Beach cafe thing. Fall in with the Stanford crowd, get married, end up with a Mercedes, live in the foothills or canyons. Hey, just like you! Have kids, spend summers at the hobby ranch in Colorado. Wear zipup boots with trendy heels, tailored khakis and a $500 belt. Wondering where the cowgirl went. Make that a Mercedes *station wagon*."

I could explain anything away quickly, it required so little effort. A great gift, born under a bland sign.

Rehearsing abandon, let's get the countenance right.

For awhile this afternoon I was doing okay. Now I can't even remember who I am, what it means, much less say, "I'm going home." Game over. Ended by washout. No ideas set me free, no objects were levitated. No value detected, intrinsic, ascribed, or derived. Once swimming in junk, now swept over a cheddarfall. Distracted by the toothless palms on Sunset, I never saw the onrushing cheezine menace.

I'll ask for directions. I'm lost. That'll be my silent story.

36

Currents, you get The Drift

Almost a year after we met, I received a letter from Danielle. If you cross out July through September, as well as December, that year wasn't too bad.

Danielle had driven out to California in July and called many times, but was unable to reach me because of the accident. Intimidated by the LA music scene, she returned to Ann Arbor and was back at The Drift, singing jazz. Her dream, though not extinguished, had come to a standstill. Wiser for the experience, but with clear disappointment, she realized even more how crucial contacts were in the business. Between the lines I heard, "be there this time … help me … please."

As I read the letter, I tried to place a face with the name, but needed to look at her picture from last year's trip. My time in Laguna was winding down rapidly, if I was going to follow through on the plan to go to school in Laramie. It wouldn't be an open ended thing with Danielle if … .

"I been lonely too long, I been lonely." The Young Rascals said it for me. I was lonely.

The possibility of complications was obvious, ones which might not be so easy to deal with. Did I really want to go to Michigan for a weekend? Since I hadn't "worked" for a long time, what was a weekend anyhow?

Spurred on by the moment, I called The Drift to confirm the band would be playing there Saturday night, then booked a flight. I would fly to Detroit and drive to Ann Arbor. Fieldwork. Strictly analytical. Baseline inquisitiveness.

Michigan was cold, drab after Laguna. I checked into a hotel and headed over to The Drift, getting there about 10:45 pm, at the end of a set. Danielle was doing a Return to Forever cover, "Light as a Feather". Her voice was superior, close to superlative, strong and distinctive in a style which would always carry the tune, no doubt the day. The immediate impression was that of a passionate woman who sung what she felt, knew what she was singing about, and clearly delivered the goods. The kind of sultry woman South American dictators used to keep around for scenery. *Conchita! Lupita! Evita!* With good material, in the right hands, and a break or two, she had a chance to make it— in LA, not at The Drift.

Looking to the side of the room where I was, she did a double take and gasped, ever so slightly, but didn't miss a word. I liked the way she did that, and smiled back.

After the tune ended, Danielle came right over and hugged me "generously". I appreciated her generosity. My hands as the right hands? Now there's something to think about.

"Craig Maxwell! Have you been out of the country, or are you just talent scouting?"

"I got your letter the other day, and decided to surprise you. A lot has happened since we last saw each other."

"Yes and no, in my case. Yes, because I did go to LA. No, because I'm still here, playing a club in a college town, trying to survive. Unfortunately, a little older, a little wiser for the experience."

"After you're done tonight, why don't you come over to the hotel where I'm staying? We'll have a glass of wine and catch up."

"You going to stay around until we finish here at 12:30?"

"Yeah, I'll do that."

The music was good, and after they wrapped the night, we went over to the hotel.

"Craig, play something on the piano. I'll clear it with the bartender."

"How about 'Spain', with you singing it?"

"Sure, I can do that."

Danielle pulled a barstool beside the piano, looked at me warmly, and nodded into the tune. By the end, both of us had our eyes shut, somewhere *in* Spain. I opened mine first, hearing and seeing her, "... mmm," faded to apparent ecstasy. Her dreamy face got my full attention, and that of the half dozen people still in the bar. "The look ... of love ... ."

"Very smooth. You want a steady date here?" the bartender asked.

"I don't think you could afford us," I replied, "we're just passing through on our way back to LA."

"Are we?" asked Danielle.

"I guess so, if you decide it's worth another try."

"It all sounds so straightforward when you talk about it," she said. "I wish it had been that easy last summer. And by the way, what *have* you been doing since then?"

In the next half hour, I explained what had happened.

"Although I didn't mention it in my letter, I did read the article around Christmas. What was her name? I'm sorry, I don't remember."

"Emily ... ," I sighed.

"I can tell by the way you said it she meant a lot to you, although I must say it wasn't evident when we met."

"True. It was later, at Thanksgiving, when we became close."

"I'm sorry, Craig. We both took our hits last year, though clearly my temporary setback doesn't begin to compare to what you've been through."

"Let's shut it down. Hey, can you come over to my place for brunch tomorrow, say around noon?" Danielle asked.

"I'd like that," I said before we went our separate ways for the night.

We will meet at the meal when our tastes and hungers intersect; know what we were brought together for by the next day's dawn, whether alone or together.

Brunch turned into something else. From the moment I stepped through the door, Danielle and I knew we were headed for an all day, all night *tête à tête*. To put it mildly. There were needs within each of us that reacted chemically, emotionally, explosively. I thought of her last night, sitting on the stool, singing with eyes closed, that dress, body. I couldn't keep my hands off her. She was equally desperate, as passionate as her singing. A heartbreaker if you ever got close enough, were allowed even closer. Unless you struck first, let her know you were as strong. That's the part I played. At least in my mind. There was no need to ask Danielle whether I was right. She was busy playing hers.

Chica and da Man. It was a languid time warp, on silky sheets ("my one luxury"), completely letting go, needing, enjoying, and in some profound moments of giving, appreciating one another as if to fit an entire life into a single afternoon. Finding a whole new life that night. Both release and bonding. Exhaustion. For Danielle, purging the disappointment of LA last summer, anxiety about the future, thankfulness that I had come back, just to see her. Beyond the physical attraction, some curiosity. After all, I am *that* Craig Maxwell.

The next morning, still in each other's arms, we talked.

"I needed that," she said, "I really needed that, and I'm glad it was you, Craig. It's been a tough year, wanting to make it, but hitting the wall in LA."

"Me too, the part about 'I'm glad it was you'. I confess I thought about it before coming here, but it wasn't the only reason. I didn't think that's what I came here for, but I guess I was wrong."

"What was it? Not for publication, of course."

"It's simple. To visit the woman in the picture who wrote me the letter. To restore a piece or two of my memory while lending a hand if you wanted to try LA again."

In talking we made a space, both knowing that it would never be like this again. A space enabling us to go separate ways when reaching the point of departure—out there, but not far. Once in awhile this kind of "loving and leaving" just happens to work, contrary to all my previously stated theories.

Not denied or forgotten, rather, mutually appreciated, with no apparent damage or continuing commitment required.

Two weeks later, Danielle was in California with a Laguna apartment. Her arrival was neither a complication for me, nor this time, overly intimidating for her. We both knew my plans and her goal. I was leaving in a matter of weeks to go to school in Laramie. For her, the challenge was at hand, maybe more manageable. Helping her take a few big steps closer to the career she wanted was a project I enjoyed. As many as she could in a few weeks. For once, I would be an accompanist, have a chance to contribute some writing too. We worked on material for club dates, found the right people to listen to her.

At times we looked at each other in the way only those who have been lovers can. But we had left that space. Danielle wanted to give it her best shot in LA, and I needed to get out of town. If I was going to take on the MFA challenge, I had to start sometime. Sleeping together again would have complicated things, for one or both. We didn't.

The promotional auditions, guest sets, and club dates over the next few weeks went well. She had the chops and material. And when a trio doing high end gigs had an immediate opening for a singer, Danielle stepped right in. Eventually, she found the right producer, solid material, and cut the right record, which put her over the top.

When I'm in town we try to get together for dinner or a walk along the beach. Danielle. Major influences: Gauguin, Astrud Gilberto, Maria Muldaur, Flora Purim. Interests: Southern Hemisphere, a beach tan, warm night, and hot band. Snapshot: *une chanteuse*, diva, the real thing; hibiscus, papaya, coconut-awapuhi rinse; "sure, I'd love to do a song"; descendant of that long lost rain-forest tribe of melodic philosophers, The Original Interpreters of Drifting Irony.

As for me, I did a competent though intentionally subdued audition tape, so as to be more credible, sent it, and was admitted to the MFA program. My major would be keyboard performance with a minor in art photography. Vocations which would, had my circumstances been otherwise, capably prepare me for a low paying career in music education, supplemented by "classical" wedding gigs, a Tuesday night featured artist date in venues like the Riverton Municipal Auditorium, or occasional surprising sale of a platinum fine art print hung on the walls of the Billings Camera Club. "The picture was so Montana, I had to have it." Ka-chink. Sold to the rancher's Dartmouth-educated daughter. Better give me your phone number in case we need to get in touch some time. Can you sing?

Speaking of fine art and more specifically painters, we lost a good one in May when T.C. Cannon rolled his truck outside Santa Fe. Unlike me, he didn't snap back. I had a couple of his pieces, keepers which grab you with brilliant color, boldly communicate T.C.'s Native perspective within plural cultures. Sadly, the brushes that painted *Chief Watching* and *Waiting for the Bus (Anadarko Princess)* would remain in the can. The Circle was closed for T.C. May he walk in beauty, forevermore.

Later in May, I went up to Laramie to look at renting a place, and ended up buying an old brick building near the campus with an existing cafe, and a large apartment/loft above it where I could live. Just like that. You know, California money. There was even a heated garage with rollup door out back. A great setup, place from which I could walk, bicycle, cross-country ski to class. The cafe had a lot of potential the previous owner didn't have the resources to realize. I planned to renovate it during the summer, for reopening in September. It would be a busy few months.

37
Cafe Whyoming, Laramie

I left Laguna in early June 1978, fleeing the "Who Shot J.R.?" TV hysteria of *Dallas,* clamor about Randy Newman's "Short People", *Saturday Night Fever,* and the 250,000 people who went to California Jam II. More than eager to reset my altimeter.

"Licensed Honest Persons Will Watch Your Home," said the ad. Thankfully, I didn't have to rent the house or contract with some company like that. It would be taken care of by my trustworthy housekeeper, a lawn service, and reliable handyman, there when I needed it, my getaway for Pacific Coast rejuvenation. The Ferrari and Porsche were covered in the garage, a drop of Marvel Mystery Oil in each cylinder; RV stored in Newport Beach. I had sold most of the music gear, which was constantly changing in technology anyhow, retaining an ARP Chroma, B-3, mixer, 4-track recorder, some effects, and monitor speaker system. An acoustic piano would be added in Laramie.

I bought a Toyota Land Cruiser 4×4 thinking of winter, and towed it to Wyoming behind a rental truck filled with the motorcycles and other items not entrusted to the movers. After the drive up to Laramie, I was eager to dive into the renovation, then getting the business going. The cafe would be well done, well run, hip.

In the process of buying the building, I had located an architect, Emmett Marshall, who was very interested in the project. He had already made substantial progress with the plans, and construction would be starting by the end of June. In the meantime, I planned to live in an apartment with my stuff stored in the rollup/garage. Emmett had a general contractor's license and preferred to do interesting projects hands-on. I would be helping him, assisted by tradesmen and subcontractors as required, while looking for a manager to come aboard by mid-August. Many of the cafe fixtures were in good condition, and reusable. A darkroom would be installed at the rear of the building, in a little used storage area. Upstairs, some interior walls were to be removed and skylights installed, to provide a bright great room for the piano and other instruments. The kitchen and bathroom were also being redone, with all new fixtures and appliances, cabinets and counters.

Emmett's associate, Martin Scott, took care of ordering and delivery of the materials and equipment. It would have been easy to choke on putting

$150,000 into the building, but I knew the cafe business would do well, a one of a kind downtown, and the upstairs would provide comfortable space for the two year MFA program. I had the money.

July was a blur of long work days. One beautiful Sunday morning, I took off and rode up U.S. 30/287 on the Triumph, stopping for a cold drink in Medicine Creek. It was already a hot day. To avoid the thunderstorms building in the Medicine Bows, I would have to be back in Laramie by mid-afternoon.

"Kind of quiet," I remarked to the waitress in the restaurant.

"Just about sums up Medicine Creek. Things'll pickup a bit at noon, after the church service, though. You should walk over there and drop in."

"Like this?" I asked, pointing to my cream riding leathers.

"It wouldn't matter. Pastor Franck has a way of getting you to look at each day in a whole different way, regardless of what you're wearing. We're lucky to have him. I go Sunday nights because of working here."

The service had already started with a hymn as I slipped into the church and found a seat at the back. There were about a hundred people.

I thought of Shiremanstown, Emily's church, back farther, remembering her laugh, smile, beauty, our brief time together. The love growing between us kindled in the Pennsylvania spring, from a math class years before that. A return, ride, conversation. An accident which cleared my slate, perhaps enabling me to be more open, feeling, worthy. Our private time at Thanksgiving, truths spoken and unspoken, our sense of direction. Promise for the future which might have been lived out, in part, through a child. Our separation, now by life itself. Oh Emily, my love, how I miss you.

There was music, preaching, prayer, silence. And when the Pastor invited those with special needs to pray at the altar, I didn't go forward, didn't know how to or why. In the next moment, though, I was overcome by the sense that those memories were strongly connected to the present. The tears that I had known as emotion were about something much deeper, more essential.

Head bowed, another sinner they would say, dressed in riding leathers in church on this sunny Wyoming Sunday morning. Homeless in spirit.

The Baptists greet you—ushers coming in, Pastor going out. Pastor Dave Franck, polyglot name and all, shook my hand.

"We don't get too many road warriors in our Sunday services. They're usually out taking *On Any Sunday* literally, rather than showing up here. With whom do I have the pleasure of speaking?"

"Craig Maxwell. I've recently relocated to Laramie from LA, as you could probably tell."

"Well, I imagine you'll be hitting the road to outrun the thunderstorms this afternoon. Please come back and visit us again."

"Thanks, I'll try to do that."

Some days there was promise, some days pain. In the coming days, there would be carpentry, art, music, and a lot more coffee.

They're not all cowboys and cowgirls in Wyoming. New arrivals, grad students, professors, and city drifters all like a comfortable place to sip coffee on cold winter mornings, spring afternoons, even when it's a buck fifty a cup and the strong taste takes getting used to. Add a capable guitarist or entertaining, musical would-be cowboy-poet on an occasional Saturday night, stay open late, and enjoy the success. That's the idea, and it works.

We lured away Bob St. Clair, who was managing the best restaurant in town, to run the cafe. He fit like a glove. I flew him to Berkeley for a week to learn about the Bay Area places which filled similar niches. All tax deductible, of course. In addition to a salary, there were profit-sharing and equity incentives.

Bob needed a right-hand man for relief, otherwise he'd be a slave to the gig. Nobody came out of the local woodwork though. Sitting at a table talking to him about it, running through the data bank, I thought of the place in Carlisle. What was the name of that Mocha Corona girl? Betsy? It was Christmas … Campus Coffee?

I went over to the phone and after a couple of calls was talking to a guy in Carlisle.

"A girl who worked there when I came in last Christmas, a senior, as I recall. Her name was Betsy, or something like that. Can you help me get in touch with her?"

"You mean Beth."

"Yeah, Beth, from somewhere in Maryland. I had her address, but can't think of where it would be. I'm Craig Maxwell."

"Sure you are." Sounded a little macrobiotically detached.

"I really am. I grew up in Harrisburg."

"Well, whatever. I can leave a message for the owner, who might know where Beth is."

"I couldn't ask for more. Thanks a lot. Please give her a message … ."
Doubt if this will go anywhere.

Surprise! The next day, I got a call from Beth Royer.

"The real Craig Maxwell. The one who came to our Christmas party and I never saw again, though I must admit sent me some great pictures?"

"The same. Not always so good about followup calls."

"To say I'm surprised would be a serious understatement. I take it from the 307 area code that you're not local. What's up? Did you decide you're in love with me after all?"

"Ouch. Whatever happened to hero worship? And if that doesn't work, let me assure you my intentions are pure, completely businesslike to the unsuspecting."

"Business can be love, too. The love of hard work, low pay, and eventual unemployment. Believe me, I know."

"We all know." If she couldn't have parried, I wouldn't have been talking to her. Diagnostic testing over. Passed. Passed last Christmas, actually. I *liked* her, as we said in high school, the same as now, not knowing what that meant.

"We need a good cafe hand here in 307 Country, that's as in Laramie, Wyoming, and you're overqualified for the job. If you're interested in grad school, I'm sure we can do a work-study deal. There are plenty of cowboys out here who would *love* to meet *you*. Seriously, please think about it and call me back within the next day or two. If it's yes, we can talk about the details. I'd like to have you join us. It would be a lot of fun."

"You've just blown my mind right out of the blue. Yes, I'll think about it and call you back after the shock wears off, when I can make a list of unanswerable questions and unrealistic demands. Thanks for thinking of me, Craig Maxwell."

"Beth, your kindness last Christmas meant a lot. I'd like to return that kindness. By putting you to work at a slave's wage."

"I can tell you're sincere, and clearly so in a completely material way. That salesman guy who was with you—he's not anywhere nearby influencing you in this venture, is he?" she asked laughing.

"No, Marco is a lot closer to you, working DC for all the lucrative long term exclusives it's worth. Another good reason for you to get out of there. Anyhow, please think about Laramie. You'd enjoy it, I think. I'll be waiting for your call. Bye, Beth."

"Bye, Craig, and thanks again for calling."

Beth did call back, and we put together a deal.

She drove up in a VW bug ten days later, with unmistakable wide-eyed, weary-excited road glaze. I even recognized her. So far so good. Later, we talked.

"Beth, as I mentioned on the phone, this isn't about you and me. It's about you, and it's about me, separately. I need to be totally up front about it."

"I know, Craig, and appreciate that. I accepted your offer because I want to be here and believe we'll grow to be great friends. You just happened to become more famous faster than I have."

She and Bob hit it off right away. Magnetically in fact. With a couple of other shift students, the staff was set for opening.

It didn't take long for Cafe Whyoming to be on the way to becoming a Laramie legend, owned by that rock 'n roller, now what was his name? *New West Press* did a filler updating my recovery from the accident and new business venture. There were, of course, pluses and minuses associated with that notoriety. But Laramie was still far enough away from the Cities of Pushed Limits, ruled by their Power Masters of Empirical NoDoubt, to be manageable, and would be that way for a long time.

38

*Plenty coupes at
Medicine Bowl*

By early September, the living quarters above the Whyomin' were mostly done. I moved in a week before classes started, drove over to Cheyenne and found a surprisingly good Kawai grand piano. That took some effort to get up to the second floor. Serious decorating would have to wait for trips to Jackson, Arizona, Santa Fe. Probably next summer. There was more than enough to keep me busy in the meantime, between school and the cafe.

On Saturday to get out of town and take a break, I drove back to Medicine Creek and ran into Pastor Franck. Small town.

"Hello. We've met, haven't we?" he asked. It was his business to remember people.

"Yes, I dropped into one of your services this summer. The guy wearing riding leathers. Craig Maxwell, once of California, now Laramie."

We shook hands. "I'm taking a break from preparing tomorrow's message. How about joining me for coffee here in the Rexall?"

"I'd be pleased to accept, Pastor, though I can find you a much better cup when you're in Laramie."

"How's that?"

"I'm in the coffee house business. Been working on it all summer. Just opened."

"What kind of coffee house?"

"Espresso drinks, baked goods, salads, sandwiches, ice cream. Occasional low decibel music on weekends."

"What do you do there—food, drinks, entertainment?"

Ninth grade heavily triggered by his question. **Parties ◆ Dances**, the school print shop business cards said. Cranberry shirts, white Levis, and New Cumberland girls. Our group, The Valiants, playing "Glad All Over" by the Dave Clark Five, "Hey!!" That record, those years by now well out of print.

"I'm the owner—got the easy part. Running it is left to much more capable management. I'm going back to school at the U, in their MFA program, majoring in music performance. It'll be a real change."

"We can always use musical support at the church. Perhaps you could play sometime as our guest. I guess I should ask you first what your interests in music are. Schoenberg would be extreme, to put it mildly, for our small town congregation."

"Don't have to worry about that," I laughed. "My audition piece for the program was *The Well Tempered Clavier*. I might even get some coursework credit for an out of town performance."

"Well that's different, a cafe owner going back to school in Wyoming, of all places. We'll have to talk more one of these days, when we both have the time. Stop by the house, right behind the church, when you're in town again. My wife, Amy, and daughter, Sarah, would be interested in meeting the Man in the Leathers. Has kind of a Japanese film ring to it, don't you think? As you can tell, I went to seminary in California, so I know what espresso coffee, riding leathers and Japanese film are. Though we've got some Samurai characters of our own around here, more often they're out of *The Virginian* or *Fistful of Dollars*. You never know who or what is going to show up for dinner."

"*Arigato gozaimasu*, Pastor-san. Thank you very much for the cup of coffee."

"Call me Dave. Civilian today."

"It's a deal. Later, Dave." Clearly an atypical smalltown Wyoming fire and brimstone dispensing man of the cloth.

I went up to Medicine Bow, then headed south to Elk Mountain before hitting I-80, back to Laramie. Emmett and a couple of friends were coming over to help make salad and pasta, our own upstairs pseudospaghetti western.

✢══════✢

We had an enjoyable time cooking and dining. The music gear impressed my date, Allison, who was a Planner with the City. I wondered what there was to plan. Maybe she was planning something tonight, short range.

Instead of firing up the electronics, I felt like playing a piano transcription of a Bach toccata and fugue I was working on. Not your usual Saturday night Downtown Laramie musical offering. They liked it, and why not? Competently played, centuries old, with each year becoming even more timeless, like the superb black and white Mimbres pot on the pedestal near the piano.

Allison looked for a moment at the 11×14 photographs on the wall, also black & whites. I had meticulously cropped, dodged and burned, printed and mounted all three at The Darkroom, a rental place on Broadway back in Laguna. Each was literally a labor of love.

"That's Emily, taken last Thanksgiving sailing off Dana Point, Southern California. A story which was way too short, during a time which seems so long ago."

"How about this one—she looks American Indian."

"Annie LaCroix, from the Fond du Lac Reservation near Duluth, Minnesota. Annie LaCroix, *Niwiijiwaagan*, my friend, *Anishinaabe* dream sister. A woman in light that's always just right." You *are* my dream sister, Annie LaCroix. Truly.

"And the third?"

"Cathy Rousseau, from Sheridan, UWY Vintage 1977, now San Francisco immigrant embarked upon the *Sunset* life. Three beautiful, capable women like you two. Emmett and I just can't resist."

"Oooookaay. The legends and rumors are true. Smooth as a developer's lawyer in a residential zone," Allison laughed. When she did that, her reddish-brown hair generated flashes of lightning. Was I the only one who had seen it? Direct dial from 307 to 717, area code of the past. A namesake with her own electricity, forgotten until this moment, from a summer 11 years ago.

I was driving the blue TR-4A. The other Allison liked the car, maybe even me. We ended up at a place we shouldn't have been, doing things we shouldn't have done, but I'll never regret. For her, it was the briefest of interludes, fallout from a one night fight with the guy she had been going with for a couple years, a friend of mine. Until then. Allison, chameleon shifting between a boyish look with short cut reddish hair, and glamorous world class fashion model. Lean, perfect body type. Perfect. She had "it". Taciturn and aloof. Looking at me with internazionale eyes, she took my hand in her slender fingers, whispered, "now, right now ... ," cutting right to the heart of sin. Striking while the anger and guilt were hot. I wonder if the world ever found her.

"Hey, let's go downstairs and have a cappuccino, perfect counterpoint to a great dinner," I suggested. Steering away from a very personal digression, what would before have become an extended spaceout.

Bob was behind the counter. I went over to ask him to make the drinks. Coming back to the booth (the "Owners Booth", to add some Whyomin' mystique), I heard the tail end of Emmett's sentence.

"... accident in Pennsylvania, still trying to get over it." I was okay with that. It was true.

"The coffee will be here in a few minutes. Emmett did such a good job with this place, probably because as an architect, he really wanted more hangout options than the Spur. The yin and yang of libational environments."

A slide guitar player was starting his third set, twanging away, singing grinning ballads filled with regional lore, like "Medicine Bowl", "Plenty Coupes", Hatcheck (Hatchet) Chops". We laughed through the set, sipped the excellent drinks, and then said our goodnights.

Grasping her hand, I kissed this Allison on the cheek as they left, indulging in a moment's ballet, hearing the Edwin Starr oldie while we drove up Front Street to the Barn, stoked on the Endells: "Agent Double O Soul". The companionship had been nice, but I was not looking for a relationship with a woman, or even an affair. I needed to focus on the MFA work starting Monday.

Nevertheless, there's inevitably more to life than what you think you're looking for, and much more if you're open to the parade crossing your path. Take a certain violinist on the program, for instance. Sometimes, though, there's just less life, as in the case of The Who's Keith Moon, another wild man punched out of the game the other day at 31.

Plenty coupes at the old drive-in. Locally, the two door version of mobile intrigue, each with its softly upholstered landing zone.

39

Ironically, neither ionic nor covalent

September and October were filled with classes, practice, studying, photography projects, time spent alongside Bob tending the business downstairs. The leaves dropped with the temperature, the wind became constant, cold, sometimes downright vicious. Snow was in the air. There would be no real interruption in this grind until semester break over the Christmas holidays. By then, I would be more than ready to spend two weeks in Laguna.

Listening to Bach one summer day, I had become intrigued with learning German and Latin, to be able to understand and appreciate the libretti of the great choral works of Mozart, Bach, Beethoven, and Haydn, while they were being performed. I discovered another side effect of the accident, one which should already have been more evident from the Navajo and Ojibwe words I sometimes used—an ability to rapidly pick up languages. With seven years of French by high school graduation, the big bang in the desert, LaPlace transforms running loose, and Theory of Special Relativity lurking a tad beyond the fringe of reason, like the last grapefruit section hidden underneath the lettuce leaf on a space-time fruit salad, the prerequisites were in place, cognitive circuitry fortuitously rewired. Please, Whoever or Whatever You Are, don't take it all away.

I liked UWY, its limestone buildings, hardwood and terrazzo floors, flat light through the trees before snow. And the cafe's wooden tables, chairs, track lights, black ductwork and registers, muffins baking in the oven. Toranis lined up below the chalkboard listing the coffee blends: Pole Mountain, Line Camp XX, Cowboy's Perk, Silver Spur, Jackrabbit, Pronghorn, Java Creek, Old Main, Better Buick. Coffee brought in by trading post freighters. In and exdulgences. Fence lines in the fields out Vista Drive, barren hills au lait, drifts from an early snow, cattle, horses, weathered line shacks. Copper lettering on the window as I looked out across the street at the Cullen Building with its cornice, bolted cast iron plates, frozen canvas awning.

Beth was enjoying life in Laramie, too, and one day motioned me to sit down and talk.

"Bob and I are considering moving in together. What do you think, boss?"

"What do you think, boss" ... was this *The Bob Cummings Show*? I had an opinion, but it wasn't politically or culturally correct—how about deciding whether you are in love, and if so, seriously consider getting married as one of the options? For somebody only recently graduated and turned 22, I knew it would be a tough upstream paddle. But if it wasn't love, moving in was about experimentation, "logic", economics or loneliness, a move with substantial, complicated downside. Think hard, talk about it together, figure out what was really going on.

"You guys have obviously hit it off well. It wouldn't surprise me if marital bliss wasn't somewhere ahead. Have you talked about that?"

"Not directly. I'm not ready for that." Give her a break. Beth's a woman who can have an opinion, not just an employee who should keep quiet.

The Sage Advice from Biscuits Maximus, had it been proffered, would have been to not move in. Instead, I just responded, "follow your heart," as if the title of a jazz tune, as good as it was, could point to a better, enduring choice. "Follow Your Heart" is in an unusual time signature. That part fit, but back to the proposition. I could just as well have replied with the universal hitch forever in search of a trailer: "whatever," but that had too much of the wrong kind of edge.

Beth looked at me for a long moment, and then said, mostly to herself, "I'll think about it."

As she walked away, hopefully weighing what living together with an unstated, money-back "no commitments" nonwarranty providing no emotional coverages really was and was not, I sat there thinking about our conversation. Beth wasn't looking for advice, rather someone to listen. We men want to tell women what choice to make, not necessarily even addressing how to fix something, after being given the minimum of information ("I've heard enough, don't tell me anymore"), then move on to the next subject. If I'm conscious of that tendency, maybe I'm finally learning something. The heels on their shoes are another matter. I'll never figure out those. A moving target—they keep changing.

The MFA was going okay. For me, grades or a new "career" were not important. Originally, it had been about seeking legitimacy as a musician, the lingering challenge of whether I could develop at least the little more talent on good days I thought I might have, but had never been able to realize. After the accident, however, it became as much a matter of rediscovering who I was and wanted to be. I needed to maintain discipline as I worked, keeping a grip on a life which could have gone over the edge at any time, given the struggle that was always there in lesser or greater measure among the loss of Emily, the self doubt like mine all artists must have, potential abuse of available material resources, and plain fatigue.

The faculty was in my estimation average, not surprising since, after all, it was Laramie. Wyoming. If I did the work, I'd pass the courses. An MFA was not a ticket to anything, anywhere, anyway. Ultimately most of us were really doing it for "art"—teaching, learning, performing. Having become oriented to my LaramieLife and to assure balance, after Christmas I might even see about playing the long-rumored rhythm guitar in a band. Was the Spur ready for a third chair strummin' Pete Townsend ambling up to the mike to sing background "aah-oohs?"

Allison and I went out occasionally, to catch a movie or have dinner. Nothing serious, neither ionic nor covalent bonding. Simple carbon-ring, organic chemistry.

The dreams were not so simple—biochemical streams, unseen nanosynaptic, possibly altitude-induced or exacerbated narcoleptic energy fields and forces mimicking work in different dimensions. Dreams shaped in time, place, and spirit. Dreams of Yumiko, a woman at the boundary of the real. The Violinist. Second mention, I know. That's all I may say, in the event she proves to be real.

In early November Cathy phoned, I'd call it a surprise, inviting me to her family's ranch near Sheridan for Thanksgiving. Perhaps to help me through the holidays after the promise then tragedy of a year earlier; or to gain perspective or guidance regarding the direction of her life. Laramie would be a ghost town. I accepted.

Thanksgiving Day was clear and cold after a storm earlier in the week. I got an early start in the morning darkness—Laramie to Rock River, Medicine Bow, then north to Casper and Buffalo, about 300 miles through Big Country. Range fences, remote ranch houses, decorative welded entry arches and cattle guards, once in awhile a furrowed cornfield or smooth rise planted with winter wheat.

I arrived around noon at the Rousseau Ranch. Buck and Becky Rousseau, son Bobby, and daughter Cathy (Catherine Marie Rousseau, now there's a name for the society page under an ethereal wedding picture of a reservedly rapturous bride in contemplation of her bouquet) welcomed me at the door of their warm, rambling homestead. Turkey baking, pies cooling, coffee pot on, perfect setting to overeat and watch football. Everett and Margaret, local aunt and uncle, nicknamed the Lazy T's, would arrive a little later.

"Welcome to our house, Craig. Catherine has told us bits and pieces about you over the last two years. Perhaps now we'll be able to reconcile the fact with the fiction."

Would I have said something like that? I didn't take it for anything, even though his name was Buck. They make a good pair, I decided even before hearing the snap of the judgment. Mindboom, faster than the speed of sound.

Mrs. Rousseau was in her late 40's, virtually an older version of Cathy, like her daughter, not hard to look at. I knew what they had been saying in town for years: "Becky Rousseau, the woman's been a knockout in these parts since the beginning of time." That explained the locks on the doors. She knew about cross-examining too.

"I don't know which is more exciting, the fact or fiction." Here I was, cowboy boots and jeans, six feet, 165, clean shaven, trimmed hair, wire rimmed glasses, personification of the graduate student. Injuries healed, at least the physical ones.

"I understand you were born in Montana. Where 'bouts?" Buck asked.

"The flat part that doesn't have snowstorms in July, but pays for it by being a practice target for SAC low altitude training runs. Glasgow, actually, if you can believe it. My father was an engineer at Ft. Peck Dam. Back in the days when GS-13's wore gray suits to work, even in Fort Peck, Montana."

"They've always been frozen up there a few too many weeks of the year."

"Dad, Montana's only 30 miles from here."

"Been to Billings lately? Just proves my point."

Cathy threw me a line. "You're probably ready to get some fresh air—I know how long that drive can be. Come on out to the stables, and we'll go for a ride. After a sandwich and something to drink, that is. Sorry we won't be able to compete with the Many-Rumored Espresso Prince of Laramie, though, if you want coffee." *Cozze fan tutte. Il Principe de Ferrara.*

"Oh ze epicure zat chu now are, Catherine, North Beach arts aficionada *dans le pays*, manuscripts spread out at Caffe Trieste, rain pouring down, Bay Bridge towers missing in the fog, week after week, until it all finally lifts and there are hills, a sky, Mount Tam.

"As for me these days, I'm at rest, though steeply tilted toward Incidental Recital rather than opera. Anything for a course, gig for a grade. The half pound of freshly ground Kona I brought should help in the coffee department." Speaking mostly to myself.

"Hey, Tug," Cathy said greeting an Australian sheep dog who ran into the room from who knows where, wagging his tail. With his one blue eye, Tug considered me carefully, too smart to outright growl, but wary, suspicious.

"Promoted from stock dog to house privileges," Cathy remarked, rubbing his ears, smiling, happily making no distinction between dog and man. "Same as us, all about status, food, and a warmer place."

I helped her saddle up two horses, and we went for a slow ride. Good thing I had my North Face jacket. It was cold! A tractor, old, scratched, red worn paint, orange primer underneath, the only bright color beneath the steel-blue sky, left by an equally worn wood fence running over the hill, dividing those everpresent, Western winter browns and grays, the sparkle of frost in the flat sunlight. The kind of day when it seems to get dark at 3:30.

At the top of a nearby hill, Cathy stopped, got down, and looked west toward the Big Horns, stunningly beautiful. Home. I was drawn to look at her, the way we must when seeing something precious revealed. Not the simple, "you're beautiful, I love you, let's get married" thing. More to *Primavera*, Degas, Monet, the face of an Alan Houser sculpture. Extraordinary in a much larger context.

"What?" She looked at me quizzically.

"You are absolutely radiant. Is it the City, this moment, or a burning secret?"

"I'm happy today. To be right here, right now, as you often put it. With my family, on this land, with you. I know my life has moved away from both here and you, in other directions. But the future will be what it is, and this is now. That's all."

Could that really be all? Was there another man now, but they were not yet close? Like Beth, wondering whether to take the step?

After the Thanksgiving dinner, football which was mostly TV picture snow, Ranch Monopoly©, a game I had never before played but no trouble picking up, and a bit o' excellent sherry, we said our goodnights and retired.

At about one o'clock, I was awakened by a brush on the arm and a "ssshhhh." Women sense the needs of others, reach out to meet them in compassionate ways through which their needs are fulfilled as well. I wondered how needy I really was.

I didn't think that Cathy was trying to fan the fires of romance, rather it was about giving and the opportunity for intimacy, closeness. With a measure of intrigue thrown in. Perhaps a first in the Rousseau compound, a daring after-midnight rendezvous perpetrated by their spectacular 23 year old? I hope so. Braided hair, flannel nightshirt, warmth almost burning, clasped hands. All the things you can imagine, the experience you can't so much more.

Awakening later, though still before dawn, I thought, maybe I'm totally wrong—it's *all* about fire.

40
Dale and Roy in 30

Running through the theories again while lying in bed after sleeping late (7:30), under the covers, sun shining in the window. In many respects I was a wide-eyed reinvention of myself, possibly now an irresistible rehab project for Cathy. A landing slot at a familiar field, in the pattern to revisit, rewrite our history. On *final* approach? I really had a handle on this. Any number of contradictory yet equally possible explanations. All implausible. Could you repeat the question?

I went out to run, which froze that line of conjecture in the morning cold, if only for an hour.

"How much of our time together do you remember, hanging out at the Spur, dancing until one?" Cathy asked later, the two of us in a quiet kitchen where time seemed to have stopped over a ranch breakfast.

"Some of it's still dim, other parts crystal clear. I remember you the person, of course, since we've worked on rebuilding my memory. And most of the music, too. But people will come up and I don't remember them. They have to think I'm a snob."

I helped Buck and Bobby with a couple of jobs during what was left of the morning, had a late lunch of a mammoth turkey sandwich and cup of steaming Kona, then went riding with Cathy again, before the sun went down at 3:30. Hidden behind the mountains, it might as well have, the shadows long and even colder.

"Is there a future for us?" Cathy asked quietly.

"Riding saddle bronc, or barrel racing?"

"You know what I mean." Accompanied by a firm love tap, thankfully muted by her riding gloves.

"Fiction or nonfiction. Select category now."

"Okay, I just got the answer I dreaded, but expected."

I don't mean to hurt you Cathy. Please understand that.

"Seriously," I said, "whatever that means, although we're both right here, right now, the fact remains that we're still headed in different directions. I'm going back to enable me to go forward. You're on another road toward a horizon I can see. In sight, but beyond that, what?"

"Things are going well in the City, but I have to admit I do miss this country. Sometimes I think I should just come back and bang on your door until you let me in. Keep banging on it until you *really* let me in. Then I realize, Craig and me, and Emily made three, with me left out."

"It wouldn't take that much banging on the door, beautiful one. Though considering what each of us is doing and has been through, I think that we need to continue along the paths we've chosen. What does your mom say? Once college is over mothers and daughters are supposed to start talking again. Or maybe it's in a rare quiet moment after your first child is born that happens."

"Very funny. As if you know, Maxwell the Man, know anything about mothers, daughters, or children. If you must hear the hard truth, she thinks that we're right for each other."

Oops. Am I ready for where this seems to be going? Down the path of ... .

"We could go dancing in town tonight, get falling down drunk, and change her opinion."

"It would be a long drive home in the dark. Besides, as far as I know, it would be totally out of character for you. And I think your character is just fine ... well, mostly now that I think of some of the things you were doing last night ... so there's no need to pull something like that. The falling down, I mean. The rest of it was ... okay," laughing, "appreciated, possibly even enjoyed. There are things about you, how shall I put it, which don't meet the eye ... but I'll never tell."

"Well, let's go dancing anyway, Stampede Queen. Have a long neck or two, show those high school boys you grew up with that they should have paid more attention. And by the way, what specifically did you like about last night that you're still thinking about?"

"First things first. The boys did pay attention, a whole lot of attention. It's just that the attention span didn't extend beyond, 'when we get married and have our own ranch ...'. When they see me duded out, they'll think I wasn't worth the chase. City girl now." Zipup boots, tailored slacks, the $500 belt. My prior conjecture, though arrogant and useless, had not been totally off-planet.

"As for the second question, I'll let you know if and when I feel like it. Maybe as soon as tonight. Maybe not at all after that wisecrack."

Aahh. Reassuring, I think. Aside from ego, how should I take all this?

On toasted rye with tomatoes, lettuce, and insight. Write this down. Here's a big difference between men and women. Men operate from the view that an issue has been dealt with, analyzed, conclusions neatly wrapped and delivered. Send a bill or write it off, maybe a favor to be called in the future. Move on. For women, it's only another item added to the long list of the previous, residing in their consciousness (and unconsciousness), all of which must be continually retrieved, talked about, confided. To "resolve", understand motivations, a process (forgive me) that never really seems to be completed. I have to continually remind myself that if for one of us the issue's still there, for both of us it's not over. And the charge may and will dramatically vary by market.

I'm talking not only of Cathy, I'm talking about every woman who ever lived about every subject ever spoken, right down the line from Eve. They're all in this together. But it can be looked at positively: according to ironclad logic, then, last night I was sleeping with all women. Even Catherine Deneuve. That's too mind blowing to contemplate. I wonder where the flaw is in my reasoning. And if miraculously unflawed, where the black truffles are to be found. Everybody wants a prize for an original thought. I want *cuisine avec Deneuve.*

The logic hasn't quite been completed, but I've got an uneasy feeling, looming bigger than Buck the Rock Rousseau equipped with an inkling of insight and the clue of the squeaking door. How about my cousins? My totem? *Kaikaik*, Hawk, Annie had told me. I remember that, but don't know what it means. Different colored jersey in a football game on the Rez maybe?

Upon further consideration, the larger fantasy fails on the basis that if there's one objection or inconsistency, there are an infinite number. The Law of Infinitely Numerous Objections in Infinitely Small Spaces. I do know this … sigh: if I was sleeping with all of them last night, they were gone by dawn. So redefine the class to consist of unrelated women between 21 and 30, go with that. Better.

There's always a Hitchin' Post in a town of any size in Wyoming, parking lot filled with pickups, cowboys cutting steps with their partners, Dolly, Sue, Marty, hats moving across the floor. You can tell the difference between the cowgirls and towngirls. Similar outfits, except for the rodeo belt buckles. "Ropers, Racers, and All Around."

Casper Cheyenne and the Big Horns were the band, surprisingly good, and we danced up a storm. The slow numbers were a series of dream sequences, exciting in a way only an attractive woman in your arms can make them. Full of life, desire, and promise, perfume and softness. Give us thirty years, and we'll look like Dale and Roy, at least I hope so. Plenty of slow dances between now and then to ease into it.

We got back around midnight. Cathy came by later, caving in to her bluff, and we celebrated those slow ones with other dances, modern and traditional. Fire dances. Walking on hot coals. Select your technique, arching toes or flat-footed.

It was Saturday, time for me to return to Laramie. Cathy's folks would be driving her up to Billings on Sunday to catch a plane back to the Bay Area. I had a couple rolls of Tri-X exposures of Cathy on the ranch. On that cold hill, wind blowing her hair as she rubbed her horse's forehead. In the tack room and stables. Walking alone in the vast field. Our boot tracks and shadows on the ground, leaning against a truck. Gloves and sweaters, down jackets, thick wool socks. Tears in my eyes from the wind.

Any man in his right mind would have gone after this woman, but neither of us wanted to go back to where the other was—in Cathy's case Laramie, in mine, The City. Been there, done that. I believe both of us wanted to someday dance a slow number and find ourselves within true, deep love which had been there all the time, patiently waiting. A dance from which neither of us would ever walk away.

But hadn't that been the case with Anne too? Waiting for love to take over, in vain?

This woman, all women were right. Clearly none of it was resolved.

41

Dynamite in a gown,
in my opinion

Back home early Saturday evening. Did I really say, "home?" Was that a slip or something approaching comfortable acceptance of this place? Anyhow, I started to say Laramie was deserted due to the Thanksgiving holiday, most students living within driving distance (a day or less on the 24 hour Western clock). A cappuccino helped relieve zoned out white line fever, bring me back to the here and now. It was so quiet. Drops of silence, one after another. *´Ádiłhaasdzol*. Sigh.

You know how it is after a long drive, the autoreactive fallout, guilt: "why am I stopped?" Texaco doesn't like it. I'm not comfortable with it. I need another roadburger, something. Anything.

I went into the darkroom instead, put on a Haydn *Te Deum* to push out the silence in a jubilation of trumpets and voices, conducting *Missa in tempore belli* after that with my dodging tool as baton. The Broadside Volley of 100 Guns, theme music for another romantic-tragic era. Vicarious Maximus. *La Pyrotechnica Finale.*

In the darkroom I developed the film, then enlarged the shot of Cathy with her horse. A better 11×14 for the gallery. Emily would have understood. It wasn't a struggle between the physical and spirit worlds, even women or my memories of them, only living another evening. Getting through another day. Archival, not immortal.

Késhmish t´áá nííhąądí, it won't be long to Christmas. There were the exams and projects, a string quartet piece, photo portfolio, straightforward MFA endeavors. Insouciant games of catch with a harpoon.

In mid-December, I got two calls, both unexpected. The first from Cathy.

"I'd like to spend a few days after Christmas with you in Laguna. If you're not already booked, can I invite myself down?"

Translation: the way I figure it, if we don't spend time together, we'll never know, will we?

This woman from Sheridan, holding off rustlers along the Powder River, dynamite in a gown. Flannel, silk, you name it. And I'm worrying about the double negative in not what she said, but my own translation?

"Certainly. You may proceed with inviting yourself. Our future is important enough to generate a statistically defensible basis."

"You didn't just say that."

"A larger statistical sample, perhaps?"

"Oh, stop it. Guess my flight and pick me up at Orange County on December 27th, from Billings and Salt Lake. And this time, you can sneak into *my* bedroom, if the door's unlocked, that is." I know I heard it, but did she really just say that? Another bluff. The enjoyable kind.

The second call was a day later, from Dave Franck.

"Well this is a surprise, Pastor. What's up?"

"I'm in Laramie and want to talk to you about a problem we've got with our Christmas Program on December 28th. Can I come by your establishment?"

"Sure, it's in the old downtown. You can't miss the prosperity. Cafe Whyoming."

"Be there in an hour."

This was an interesting development. What could be up?

"Good to see you, Craig. Nice place you've got here."

"Cappuccino for you OK? On the house."

"Sure, I'll try one. None of the congregation are here to see me go bad, hanging around with bohemians, drinking yuppie coffee."

"Kind of like going to church wearing riding leathers, huh? Out of our elements."

"Craig, we've got a big setback with the church's holiday music show. Our regular pianist has taken ill and won't be back until after New Years. There's nobody else in Medicine Creek who can fill in. Praying about it, I thought of you down here, just waiting to help us out."

"Well, I do have a date on December 27th in Laguna Beach, California. A pretty girl from Sheridan would be heartbroken if I stood her up. A very pretty girl."

"Let my wife, Amy, work on that angle. Maybe we can even talk her into helping out."

"Well, tell me about the program, and we'll go from there."

"It's about an hour of music, spoken word, and most importantly, celebration of The Lord, and the gift of eternal life He offers to all who believe."

"I think I just heard a sales pitch in there."

"We're running a holiday special, but regardless, buy now or buy later, you can't find a better, more eternally indispensable gift for yourself. I brought copies of the program and music with me. Will you take a look at them?"

"Okay. Go get 'em."

Play the hand you're dealt, I thought. After headlining arenas and stadiums, I should be able to whip the program into shape as a second stringer.

It was mostly traditional Christmas songs; the program looked to be complete enough for me to easily follow.

"I'll think about it some more and let you know tomorrow if I can do it."

"Fair enough," said Pastor Franck. "Ten days and counting. We could use recorded music, but it wouldn't be the same. I'd love to hear you play a keyboard piece. Classical would be more appropriate than range 'n roll or Waylon Jennings, but then, I trust your judgment."

"*We're* thinking of doing what?" asked Cathy when I called her. "You'll do a good job, but I don't know what I would do in Medicine Creek for three days."

"How about if we stay in Laramie and drive up Thursday and Friday for the rehearsals, then Saturday night with the Francks, for the Sunday program? We can go to Laguna together after that."

"It's possible. I'd like to see your place in Laramie. And a few more nights of you all to myself would be just compensation for our Medicine Creek outreach—you know, Reach the Creek."

"Consider it an opportunity for spiritual growth."

"Before it's over, we'll need some spirits, alright."

So this year Christmas was the prelude, with the performance to follow four days later. Cathy was at the ranch, and would take a bus down to Laramie on December 26th, arriving around noon. We'd then drive up to Medicine Creek for the 4:00 pm rehearsal.

The bus was on schedule and I picked her up at the station. We had a couple of hours free before leaving for Medicine Creek.

"You owe me big time for the bus ride, Craig," Cathy admonished as we got into the Toyota for the drive to CafeWhy. Body language, emphatically speaking, gave her away though, as the frown turned into a smile when our polyhyperbolic curves, subtle arches, conformable surfaces, imaginative planes, and smooth vectors mutually, measurably, and pleasurably intersected in the front seat. 6.2 on that 'ole Richter Scale, a quake felt at the epicenter in downtown Laramie. More shakin' than Elvis, and I didn't even have it in gear.

It was only a few blocks. We could have walked, but risked being cited for extreme familiarity along the way. "This is Enterprise Maxwell, aka, the Why O' Why You Moanin' Cafe. It is customary to offer the guest a cappuccino."

"Gratefully accepted. You haven't aged a bit since Thanksgiving, Craig. That's what people say this time of year, for some reason."

"Cute," she said reading the sign on the door as we went in: "Cafe Whyoming—Well Mannered Fillies and Cowpokes They Brung Welcome."

"All this can be yours, darling. Closing and opening, mopping floors, cleaning windows, sweeping up broken glass. And then there are the Mountains of Grounds. It started out as a love of espresso. If the help wasn't so good, it would have to be a love of punishment to keep going day after day. Terminal wisdom gained after only four months of business."

"Hey, Beth," I called to her behind the counter.

"Hi, Craig," she said with a big smile for me, a critical and protective once-over of Cathy, looking to validate my selectivity, legend, weakness, you name it. "What can I getcha?"

After I ordered the coffee, Cathy asked, "who's *she*?"

"It's a story that goes back a year."

"I want to hear the story," Cathy said, placing her own order. Yes M'am, right away, knowing that for once I was not guilty. Persuasively communicating the truth is, of course, always another matter.

We sipped the cappuccini, followed by bowls of thick chili. A couple of turkey club sandwiches would be packed for the afternoon drive to Medicine Creek. I guess my explanation about Beth *and* Bob set her at ease.

"This is a great place to live!" Cathy exclaimed when we went upstairs. Then she saw the pictures.

"Is this Emily?" Clouding over. Meaning, time for another explanation, and don't make me ask.

"Yes, that picture was taken a year ago at Thanksgiving, sailing off Dana Point, south of Laguna."

"She was beautiful, Craig. Definitely. You have good taste in women."

I swallowed hard, seeing Emily's hair, radiant smile. It had been a wonderful, forever day. But this was the one I needed now, gently pulling her close. Immediately.

"Yes. Present case in point."

Cathy wasn't going to be dislodged from her line of inquiry.

"There must have been more than three over the years."

"Yes, but these are the ones in my heart. Emily, is gone; the second, Annie, is my *Anishinaabe* sister. Leaving the beautiful, fascinating, and desirable (major accent on that word) youuuuuuuu." By the process of elimination … not the most endearingly romantic way to put it. The truth, perhaps, but neither the entire, nor final truth.

"Pause the song, even though I want to hear more. The truth—have you let Emily go?"

"In truth … not entirely. Cathy, I've come to believe that if someone is that valuable, you never let them go completely. They become part of your strength. The strength of having lived, continuing to live."

"Well, there's one surefire way to a man's heart … ."

"You mean through his appetite?" I guess it had been the right answer. You never know.

"Yes. Food for thought, but I don't have cuisine in mind at this moment. Bring your ear closer and I'll whisper a clue."

Later, Cathy asked, "I don't think that pastor of yours would approve of our goings on, do you?"

"I think he'd say it's not for him to judge, but he understands the passions of youth."

"That fits me, but how about you?"

"Just say I'm a strong and steady hand, ready to aid any ship being buffeted by those passions of youth."

"Touché, alternately rough and gentle Sir."

"Shall we bathe and depart Fortress Whyoming?" I asked.

"I wouldn't mind replaying the last hour." See that and raise you one.

"Have to put it on pause until we're back from riding fence up to Medicine Creek."

"I'll cherish the thought," she said, as a starburst of thoughts and images lit the sky, percussively suggesting Santana … Boooommm!

"It's a mix of required and optional elements. Ritual and spontaneity."

"The architecture? Ice cream? Your smile?"

"All of it."

Yeah, but more to Hendrix. "Axis, Bold as Love".

42

Medicine Creek,
without the leathers

Cathy had been in churches much more than I, so she wasn't at a loss or intimidated. To me, after the upanddownheavalsman of the 60's, and now into the 70's, for reasons I can't articulate without difficulty, if at all, that seemed positive. There were, of course, certain Biblical issues involving moral conduct of which I was somewhat, though effectively only theoretically, aware that we conveniently ignored, doing our little gig for holiday spirit.

Amy Franck answered the door at the Pastorage, Parsonage, or whatever you call it, and immediately put us at ease while walking over to the sanctuary where Dave was making preparations for the rehearsal.

"Cathy, this is my husband, Dave Franck. Dave, Cathy Rousseau." The woman in the picture, *Once in the Dunes*, now a movie. *Les Dunés de Demi Luné Baye*. Half Moon Bay. Catherine Marie Rousseau.

"Pleased to meet you, Cathy, and good to see you again, Craig. We've got some cocoa in the kitchen which will help take the chill off. Let's have a cup before we get started." A year ago it had been hot cider in Carlisle. A year already.

Cathy helped make decorations while I rehearsed the music with the choir, soloists, and organist. I got through "O Come All Ye Faithful", but not without an icicle or two broken off my heart. The carol was an electric shock bringing back last Christmas Eve, Shiremanstown, the service for Emily. When the song was done, I got up and walked into the vestibule. Cathy followed, held me tightly as I cried, not asking, already knowing why. Somehow, women know. A good rancher, sitting the stock, getting through the tough times. Tears of love and the pain of mourning, a year already; thankfulness, joy, spirit, all mixed up in this small town Wyoming church. Faithful. Faith in what? Why?

After the rehearsal, Dave invited us over for a quick supper, so as not to make our return to Laramie too late. As was my habit, I had brought a half-pound of French Roast. A cup of the coffee would be a treat after the meal.

"So what did you think about the rehearsal, Craig?" Dave asked.

"I missed the smoke machines and stadium sound, but thought the performers did well. Actually, I think we should ask Sarah, who as a teenager will probably give us the most forthright assessment."

"I thought it was good, Dad. It would be nice to hear Mr. Maxwell play piano all the time. A little square in terms of the song selection, but then he's so good."

"Craig's really living undercover, Sarah, although I have never been able to reconcile this Clark Kent with the rock 'n roll Superman he claims to be," Cathy teased.

Sarah's eyes widened. "Dad, you didn't tell me Mr. Maxwell had a past. Did you play in a group in California?"

"I used to be with ESO, maybe you've heard of them." If I do have a past, when will it start?

"ESO, no way! Wow, wait 'till I tell my friends. They won't believe it!"

"I don't remember all of those days, and I'm not sure I believe them anyhow. Before that, I went to engineering school. There was an accident which must have smoothed a few rough 'n roll edges. You'll have to ask Cathy about that. Privately, I hope. Others tell me that my outlaw tendencies and bad behavior are still around, just more disguised. Your Dad is trying to work on those."

"I do know the Sheriff. If the gentle stuff doesn't work, Craig, we've got the posse. That'll stop the trouble; we can bring you warm meals in jail," Dave argued. "Lock you up for your own good." Well there's a flashback from the 60's. Hope he's kidding.

But thinking about it for a moment, had I been in jail the whole time, transferred from Santa Monica minimum security to Laguna, then a second story whitewashed slammer in Downtown Laramie? A place with three pinups on the wall my only company? Stocked with an array of intoxicants widely used in the conduct of (what was by convention deemed to be) legal business?

We said our goodbyes and hit the road in the Land Cruiser, heater going full blast to little benefit. With the windchill approaching absolute zero, *Appalachian Spring* it was not. A few more degrees down the mercury column, and motion would be suspended, the electrons very sleepy, emitting a pale green glow. Cryogenic night light. Humans, clusters and clusters of electrons, protons, and neutrons, have a tough time waking up and getting out of bed in that kind of cold. Don't always immediately rebound when the sun's back on, even with a double espresso.

"I liked the Francks," Cathy ventured. "Here I am back in Laramie, actually, beyond Laramie in Medicine Creek, of all places. I thought I was out of here for good when I graduated. What are we doing, freezing in this tin can, Japanese version of a Jeep? Didn't anybody ever tell you to buy American?"

"Sue me. I just don't remember. Memory lapses, you know." Hood louvers, flat glass, window gaskets, "stubby hubs" and steel. I wonder if custom rims would help warm it up? Japanese. Yumiko would. With her it wasn't about bending a knee, rather, turning around, an enigmatic smile. I wonder, does each woman have their signature move? One above everything else you can't forget?

"Brrr … hypothermia. I'm going to need to be brought back slowly if by a miracle we ever make Laramie. And as for your memory, I'm also going to need an explanation of 'Why in Wyoming'."

Be glad to provide both.

It was 9:30 pm when we pulled into the garage. A hot drink was definitely called for. Danny and a Few Drillers, the duo, were starting their acoustic Dali folk-rangerock set with "Unearthing the Final Boogaloo". Just the right twist to set things in order before going to the Spud, I mean Spur for a work-study session on theory and application of the two step. On any night of the week, you could get a lot of craziness, rowdy wit, or humorous cynicism in Berkeley or San Francisco, but it was only multiple repetitions of what we also had here in Laramie. More importantly, you didn't have to fight for a parking space or get panhandled, at least in winter.

Danny spun tales of bentonite mudwrestling fantasy, like, "Livin' for Mud"; and was the only other person I've met who'd been to Nail Haven, NM. Many a night I had, and would continue to, stay up late for "Don't Touch These Nails" in his last set:

> … nothin' but nubbins
> indomitably worn smooth
> by the file of your luvvv …

We drank the coffee, freshened up, and eased out the door into the crisp night, temperature hovering in the single digits, but at least no wind now. The Spur was within walking distance and after a few slips and slides on the ice, we were there.

A few people knew Cathy, and I nodded to several myself. I wasn't making the rounds much in town, preferring the Cafe and relentless practice upstairs. With Allison, the chimerical-apparitional, though sometimes tangible, Yumiko, and an occasional special visitor like Cathy, I didn't feel there was much point. Listening to the music, I didn't know whether I would ever get around to playing rhythm guitar in this joint, even though for some reason the thought continued to be intriguing. A right-side of the brain gesture from an essentially left-brain technician, mixed up with a bit of frontal lobe warping, I suppose.

"Livingston Saturday Night" covers, "Hank, let's talk about your Daddy," "Okie from Muskogee". I want to play this stuff? For elitist comic relief. The Yuppie Urban Bozo Thing, as George Ryan called it.

Cathy was an excellent dancer, with the right kind of experience on her Sheridan Ranch Girl resume. Though now learning about Volvo station wagons, Topsiders, fern bars, and cable knits in the Big City, her roots were right here in the fringe and piping of Western shirts, strong forearms, and attractively long Levi lines. In these paved over, frozen, Wild West towns, Kaycee, Ten Sleep, Worland. In the corrals and loading chutes, grain elevators, tractors, Ford trucks, propane tanks, and ag-exchanges. "Drillin' in seed," as Danny put it.

We got reacquainted during the slow numbers, nursed a long neck, danced a few more times, the slip 'n slide back home, if you could call it that. There I go again. Home. If not here, where?

Friday would be another long one. I awoke first, pulled on my running stuff, and headed out into the morning. Always an adventure running in Wyoming in the winter. Freezing to start, frosty eyebrows, sweating at the finish, no matter how cold.

Cathy was still sleeping while I made coffee. Maybe ranch girls snooze later in winter. I wanted her to sleep, to watch her for a moment, never forget the tenderness of that night in Fort Collins. Though fragile, my safety line to what life might be.

I put on some dry sweats, then settled in for an hour of piano practice. About 20 minutes into playing, she stumbled out in search of the steaming java. All second floor activity stopped as she stood there, wearing only my old Penn henley. Hair pulled back as always while sleeping, can't be too ruffled. No makeup, of course. In my opinion, she had never needed it. That was something which couldn't be said to a woman, though. "Mind your own business. You don't know what you're talking about," would be the reply. It wasn't about "needing" makeup at all.

Enough instantaneous commentary. Get her a cup of coffee.

"I awoke to your playing. Is this bliss or what, warm under a down comforter, awakened to live classical piano, a cup of gourmet coffee awaiting me? Down right romantic, pardner, and it's still early morning! I'll bet you've already been out running too."

"Did you say romantic? I'd like to followup on that subject. Yes, I've been out running, but complete exercise involves all muscle groups. That would invite your participation, more active or passive, depending upon the mood. And I'll need my shirt back."

"My mood's just fine, you'll be happy to know. As for the shirt, I'm prepared to return it to you right now, but only temporarily. In San Francisco, I forget how I need to keep in shape. It's only when I return to this town that I realize how much I miss the cowboys."

"Any cowboy in particular?"

"I only see one tied up at the hitchin' post. Ready to be untied?"

"More than ready. I've been meaning to talk to you again about what you did to my ear yesterday … ."

"Well, as you say yourself, 'check your guns at the door and leave a message' … ."

The *Denver Post* was on the table, coffee in the vacuum pot on the counter would keep. The *Partitas* could wait.

The day slipped away, and it was 2:30 pm, time to leave again for Medicine Creek.

At the rehearsal a new group of teenagers appeared, alerted to the presence of Craig Maxwell, rock star. Former rock star. There wasn't any rock 'n roll in the program, but I delighted them by playing and singing a couple of songs during a rehearsal break. It would be good for attendance. The music was coming together well, and decorations were nearly complete. I was looking forward to the production on Sunday.

After the rehearsal, I gave Pastor Franck an envelope for the Sunday offering. The contribution to help with program expenses was tax-deductible, in the opinion of my accountant. These small town churches must run on the thinnest of shoestrings.

Cathy and I drove back to Laramie for dinner and a movie. The place where she used to work now purveyed a surprisingly respectable Chicken a la Marsala ("All New Menu!"), and it was fun for her to visit with Angelo and his family. We got back home at around ten, following the flick at the Strand Theater. What strand would that be around here? I wondered. The one about the shelf life of a concept, service life of a metaphor perpetually out of phase.

43

*That thermos—
french roast or dip?*

Saturday was a replay of Friday, although a storm was coming, judging from the clouds. It was good that we would be staying over and not have to drive back for the night. Later in the morning Cathy and I went out for a walk downtown, browsing, visiting, chatting on the street before returning to the Cafe for a latte. Living in San Francisco now, Cathy had acquired a taste for espresso, though wasn't quite to the *doppio macchiato* stage yet. Ah, the joy of having one's own industrial coffee production shop.

During the quiet trip to Medicine Creek I was turning over a lot of things in my mind. The pictures on the wall. Hall of Fame. They must be hard for Cathy. No woman would want to compete with pictures on a wall, even if one of them was of her. As a photographer, it's my gallery; as the resident, the space is mine, and the pictures important to me. That said, however, I realized the statement being made was that I wasn't ready to share either my physical or emotional space exclusively with another woman right now. Was that true? There were other thoughts as well, some contradictory. Of home, belonging. Cathy was as deep in thought as I. The silence wasn't uncomfortable to me, nor did I feel it was for her. I took her warm hand in mine, warm as it could be in the Land Cruiser, and kept driving along. Not much farther now.

If only this was Donizetti. Here, *L'elisir d'amore*. Let me pour this love potion. Singing through that drama would take about three hours, though. We didn't have the time this afternoon. How about something shorter. *Belle de Jour*? Deneuve. No music, and not sure I want to go there. Still two hours. Let me think of … .

Roast beef sandwiches for the trip, clothes, and a thermos of french roast. The consumables were gone by the time we rolled into Medicine Creek at around 3:30 pm. The rehearsal went fine. Everything was ready for the Sunday morning program. There were even more kids at the practice than the previous day. I played a few songs afterward, posed for snapshots, and signed autographs. Then onto dinner Chez Franck.

With the musical program Sunday morning, Dave did not have to prepare a sermon. He could relax this Saturday night instead of working late. After dinner, we played Scrabble for a couple of hours, then Amy and Cathy went into another room for girltalk. Dave and I adjourned to the kitchen to make some hot chocolate.

Girltalk. Did Cathy have any close girlfriends? She either rarely spoke of them, or I hadn't been listening. That didn't seem healthy on either account. I'd have to wait until she mentioned a girlfriend, or bring up the subject sometime. "Of course," she'd say. "Where have you been the last couple years?" The memory loss thing was getting no mileage these days.

I looked around the kitchen. Smaller, and though more modestly equipped than mine, much warmer with the family pictures, notes on the refrigerator, other touches, including the dish towels. Two girls in this family. A happy one. As we sipped the cocoa, Dave asked me about my beliefs.

"Craig, if you died right now, do you know what would happen to you, where you would go for eternity?" These pastors were on a mission, never let up. Fearless.

"Shipping one of your loaded questions this way, Dave? What are you driving at?" Deflected that one nicely.

"Eternal security. We believe that there will be a judgment day, at which time each of us will be called to account for our lives, and be sent to one of two places for eternity—Heaven or hell. Those who believe in the Lord Jesus Christ as their personal Savior will be saved, and reside with Him in Heaven, for eternity.

For we Christians, helping to bring others to know the Lord is indeed a life or death proposition—eternal life in Heaven or eternal death and suffering. I'd like to talk to you more about your life, faith, and how you can have true happiness. You never know when this life on earth will end, so the choice between true belief and the salvation it brings, and unbelief, is a choice you must consciously make without delay. I hope you'll think about it, and we can talk about it again, soon."

The subject was interesting to me, having survived a near-fatal accident, but perhaps in more of an intellectual way than anything else. After all, the society in which we lived, the training in critical thinking I got in college, the moneymaking part of my ride through the world of music, all were down the path of "logic" and "reason". Things unseen were not "logical" or "knowable".

And then there was the whole subject of societal bias to Christianity with "other religions" being looked down upon. It was like asking someone what it meant to "be" an American. The answer was likely, "part of the greatest nation on earth," if you stayed out of Watts, the Rural South, and most universities. To the similar question of what it meant to be Christian, what would the answers be? "It's a personal thing, the way I was raised?"

I would have to think about it more, discuss the subject again with Dave. I wasn't sure any of it was as pressing as he thought.

Cathy and I slept separately, awakening to a snowy Sunday morning. The 10:00 am program went well, about an hour of vocal and instrumental music. Although no rock 'n roll was included, undoubtedly to the disappointment of the teenagers present, there was a message. If a rock star was here in church on Sunday morning playing traditional music, then maybe that music, and its statement, were worth listening to. For the record, former rock star; and did the "worth listening to" also apply to me?

Following the performance, Pastor Franck thanked the participants and their families for the rehearsals and other work which went into preparing the church for the program.

"And I'd like to give special thanks to our guests, Craig Maxwell at the piano who stepped in as music director, and Cathy Rousseau, who assisted with the decorations and details, for driving up from Laramie for rehearsals and our program this morning. They will always be welcome at Medicine Creek Baptist, and we'd love to see them come back again for a visit. Thank you, Cathy and Craig. May the Lord bless you both."

As Dave was speaking, I wondered, was this just another gig, or more? What did it mean when you loved a person within your heart, your soul? I had said that about Emily last December, when the words, though sad, seemed to come so easily. What they really reflected, indicated, and activated was something else. There had to be an explanation and purpose for our existence. It couldn't all be just a big bang, then evolution. Untenable physics followed by unexplained chemistry; amusing animation.

After Sunday dinner, we said our goodbyes, and left. The trip back was another quiet ride, this time with 4-wheel drive engaged as the snow came down. I thought ahead to Tuesday morning, about Cathy and I driving to Cheyenne to catch the commuter to Salt Lake, connecting to Air West for the trip to Orange County. Thursday was New Years Eve, which we would be celebrating with Max and Gretchen in LA, relying upon whatever they had up their sleeves. It would be a welcome change after the grind of opening the cafe, my first semester back in school, the cold Wyoming weather.

I thought too about Pastor Dave, his message of faith and salvation, the holiday music program, next spring and summer, Cathy, Emily, performance piano, the waves breaking in my favorite Laguna cove, the mileposts on this highway, the promise of a hot, tasty buzzaccino in an hour or so if we wanted, the closeness of this woman riding beside me. A good, strong woman, now dozing, surrounded by the whiteness of the snowfall.

How deep did that which was between us run? What was really between us? Were yesterday, today, and tomorrow nothing more than oscillations, at some times closer to "limits" than others, fading in then fading out? I longed for all consuming, yet graceful, honorable, and beautiful passion, what seemed to be the ultimate antidote to the hard edged criteria of my intellectualism. I was sure Emily and I had that, ever so briefly. It set the standard. After her, things were occasionally clear, but more often hazy and confusing. In Zen, there are two paths to enlightenment, sudden and gradual. There was undoubtedly a parallel in love. Over Thanksgiving last year, I had been hit by a lightning bolt. Sudden. With Cathy, everything was more gradual. Behind the scenes, just the slightest distance this side of awareness, all kinds of things went on, preparations were made, circuits connected. Even a lightning strike relied upon grounding potential, the "voltage to ground," whether we realized it or not. Who could tell when it would hit us? When we were afraid the weather might have passed us by?

There are the photographs. For now I guess it's about depths and heights—arcs, the melancholy of not having a clue. In this moment I can only be, and am, thankful for the opportunity to explore it all with the woman beside me. Make no mistake about it, she is beautiful. Sometimes so achingly beautiful I don't believe it. Maybe that's the explanation—for some reason, not a lack of interest or attraction, I can't accept I'm worthy of her love.

I pulled over and stopped at several places, taking pictures of the fields, the fences, a trestle bridge with no stream visible below, ghostly shadows of flash exposures, Cathy sleeping, the Land Cruiser running, heater full blast, darker presence along a whiter road, against a close, small sky, wind gust twisting a road sign. The thought of putting the kitchen rugs in the dryer when we got back was pleasurable, heating them to warm our bare feet. Outside, the sky became even closer as darkness fell, became another monochrome Wyoming night. So cold. Warmth was miles away. Until then I could only reframe the black & whites I had taken, over and over in my mind as we got closer to Laramie.

When we were there, I gently awakened Cathy. Without a word, she took my hand. Upstairs, the rugs stayed on the floor while we found each other, communicating only with our eyes, touch, and hearts; sharing our own warmth.

Monday was laidback—exercise, cooking dinner, getting to bed early for the next day's trip. Cathy visited a couple of girlfriends during the afternoon. One less thing for me to have to try to bring up, I went downstairs to take care of business, then have a cup of coffee.

It's definitely a fish story, I thought. The question: Jonah or Jaws? In the World of the Fishin' Fools, it's all about bait and festivals. Indians, Fins and Elvis, A Celebration. Warren Zevon's answer: "Lawyers, Guns, and Money". I'll take that bet and raise you my flag, current musically Merle commentary from the seam, "One Hundred Years of Coal". Don't get alarmed, only creative musing on a cold day. It's not like I threw a table through the window.

Then where did the table go? I knew what the fortune cookie would say if I went to Angelo's: "Make plans now to buy plywood."

By Tuesday morning the snow had stopped, easing the drive to Cheyenne. A couple of flights and we were at Orange County, catching a cab down to Laguna. Saddleback dominated the horizon on the warm, clear, late December day. The house was ready for our sojourn.

Cathy would be staying until Sunday, then return to San Francisco. I looked at her, dressed for early morning in finely knit, gray cotton workout clothes—marvelling, appreciative. Humming Wayne Shorter's encore on soprano sax with Miles, "Dolores".

"This is a welcome change. I guess the Wyoming winter has finally gotten old for me. You're fortunate to have this warm weather getaway."

Tell me about it. Freezing my buns off taking pictures north of Laramie in a snowstorm, all in the name of "art". Even so, it beat sitting around on Naugahyde watching TV football and slugging down the beers here, complaining about how it's never winter in Southern California. Why bother with that when there are more important things to whine about? I smugly considered. Privately, of course.

That place, Desert Center. Really? According to whom, and why did that pop into my mind anyway?

Where was My Center? Unachievable due to a slipping clutch? Hidden, disguised, lost in a material land, among unicultural/noncultural/dyscultural/extracultural savages, all menacing, expert consumers? A land where too often discovery hinges on illegal activity. Crimes of wist, irony, blankfulness. With just the right, wry, cinematic facial twist. "Twist and Shout" morphed to Twist and Fade. Quantities limited. Minimum of 50 assaults per store. Score and evade.

What's the expression I'm looking for, excoriatory bliss? Planing the lignin of ideas to smoothness, according to my specifications. Wood from the "Trees of Mystery". Was there an anti-forest of countervalent "Trees of Reason"?

If anger is natural, is it healthy? Self-anger, maybe, as learning? Anger can be gently corrosive, strangely comforting when accompanied by just the right amount of adrenalin shake. What did I have for breakfast anyhow, Nutty Nietzsche Cheks?

Below, the cars, nearly all nonlocal, were backed up on PCH, celebrating a holiday confusion by now effortlessly predictable. To the tune, "Buffalo Girls Won't You Come Out Tonight", in their Brownian motivity, sketching, disclosing, and notarizing another of life's minor revelations in rays and traces, chrome and metal, glass and rubber, burgers and fries: the more numerous the bumper stickers, more extreme the messages, the balder the tires.

Won't *you* come out tonight, and dance by the light of the silvery moon?

I guess my problem is not that I'm playing without a full deck, it's that I've got too many decks, including the one on which I'm now sitting. Sometimes I play no cards, other times I can't stop drawing and playing every card. And if I run out, I'll get more. As many as it takes.

"Craig, you flying somewhere above the Pacific?" Cathy asked, looking at me. Perceptive. Close. More accurately, "you go down somewhere in the Pacific without a trace?"

"I'm fine. Enjoying the morning." Misfires, expert commentary by the Tubes, "he seemed like a regular guy … ." Before he committed "TV Suicide". Fine.

Engine quit, headed for the water. Blue water. "Without a Trace." Good title for a song. Cathy, what are you doing with me? There's nothing for you to hang on to. But when you try, it helps. I wish I knew how much, to be able to tell you. I wake up in the night and can only think, "this isn't going anywhere." Not that my heart doesn't want it to, but because there's not enough heart left.

$$\div\!\!=\!\!\!=\!\!\div$$

But on to more aesthetic matters. The *most* important one—Cathy needed a dress for New Years Eve.

Along the way, we stopped at the espresso place on Forest Avenue for coffee. "What's been happening around here during the last couple of months?" I asked the guy who owned it, "I've been away."

"Biggest thing was the Bluebird Canyon slide back in October. 20 homes or something like that destroyed."

"I live down that way. Glad it didn't affect my place. Did some geological testing before I bought the property, but if it's not one thing, it's another. If not slides, and there will undoubtedly be more in this area during rainy years, then wildfires or earthquakes. Bottom line is that if you can't afford the catastrophe, don't build here. Could say the same thing about San Francisco and every-where along the Fault, though; hurricane country along the Gulf of Mexico; tornadoes in Kansas. You name it."

"Thanks a lot, Craig," Cathy said, "it's not like I'm living in the Bay Area or anything. I feel a lot better now with your reassurance."

"What can I say? It's true. But your chances are pretty good until inevitably you're affected … ."

"Very funny. You were going to buy me a dress, as I recall. You're *really* going to buy me a dress now. Shoes, purse, necklace, no telling what we'll find. What you'll need to come up with to get back in my good graces."

"What *you'll* find. What *you'll* need."

"No, what *you'll* have to find. This could take hours and hours, and *I'll* need your opinion, regardless of whether I pay any attention to it."

"Then let's get going. Nothing better to do today."

"This will be fun. I'm going to enjoy this," Cathy said, kidding me, with what appeared to be her equivalent of brass knuckles. She was kidding, right?

A dress. Not just any dress. One elegant enough for the parties the zillion-aires who shop Fashion Island would be going to. The slide was back, taking me with it. All I had to do was stumble into the wrong conversation.

Cathy wouldn't have needed all that stuff for New Years Eve back in Laramie. Or Sheridan. Was she giving me a taste of the other side of cohabita-tional bliss? The part about cleaning up the messes, enduring shopping together for stuff not involving solid state components, technical specs, or entertainment; taking the clothes to the cleaners?

Focus only on the *girl* in the dress, I reminded myself. That's, I mean she's, the most important part of all this.

44

*New Years—jumped by
1979 before I knew it*

New Years Eve. 1978 gone, 1979 upon us. The year when I would hit the Big Three Zero. Feeling, unfortunately, that celebration might be closer to Big Ground Zero, or simply Zero.

Max and Gretchen knew the owners of a National Forest in-holding along the Angeles Crest Highway, high above LA in the San Gabriel Mountains. There would be five couples at their New Years Eve celebration, including Cathy and me. It was a spectacular place in a magnificent setting. Superb champagne, intelligent company, and stimulating musings before the midnight gong, noisemakers, hugs and kisses.

Cathy's black velvet dress fit her like a glove. If below LA seemed to go on forever, lights sparkling in the darkness, it was nothing compared to this woman when she smiled. "The Genuine Article." Truly awesome.

Max and Gretchen had just met her, and the feedback was very positive.

"I had no idea," Max said. "She's incredibly beautiful, and without all the attitude I'm so used to seeing around here. Craig, you're making a big mistake if you let her get away." He was right. Unquestionably. Inarguably. Conclusively. Without a doubt.

Shoptalk was a party violation, but in cleverly disguised side conversations we discussed emerging music markets, both those internationally influenced, and surprisingly, "gospel". Mike Curb, Ronnie Rayguns' 1975 Campaign Chairman, subsequent Republican National Executive Committee member, had moved into the new market, in part defined it. Far from gospel in the traditional sense, rather a blend of rock, folk-rock, or funk with religious content. That content had been strongly evident in County & Western for some time, but seemed to be waning as Nashville and the product coming out of it became more mainstream, targeting new markets. Yuppie factions, for one, too busy to believe in anything of value. With messin' around taken for granted, and while broken hearts sold huge, little serious advice on how to fix them was being offered.

Although the material had a long way to go to crack the marketplace, the potential was there to reach places and people as never before. Even the Little Big Band at Baudelaire's in Santa Barbara, whose sets touched diverse bases, was exploring the genre with a playlist encompassing Flora Purim, from Brazil;

Deniece Williams, on Sparrow, a Christian label; Steely Dan; and EWF, all of which had an underlying hip, funky energy. If it worked in Santa Barbara, it would work on the radio. Everybody wanted that energy.

We got back to Laguna at 3 am, and slept until noon. I put the coffee on as usual and went out for a run, this time to the beach. The surfers and tourists there had made the right choice so far, fresh air over football on the tube. What was this, oxygen? Negative ions?

Yes, even at noon a crisp, invigorating breeze. When I got back, after a sprint up the hillside above Coast Highway, Cathy was sipping coffee on the deck, reading and working on getting some winter sun.

"*The Monkey Wrench Gang* is an interesting selection for a Wyoming cowgirl. Don't leave it out at home on the ranch."

"Required reading for orientation in Northern California. Too-serious issues, Seldom Seen, so to speak … a feminist-environmentalist radical and cowboy monkey wrencher bankrolled by soft green money, it's the San Francisco way. Copy comes with the owner's manual in the dash of every used Volvo with Earth plates. But really, I'm trying to understand why you like that Canyonlands maze country so much."

"Easy to hide in during a cloudburst … or any other time for that matter, as long as you keep your ears open, and can make high ground in a heart-beat." Kinda like where we are right now?

There wouldn't be much sunshine in San Francisco this time of year. I showered, had a bite to eat, and practiced piano for the customary, hour-minimum session. It was a quiet day, followed by an equally quiet evening. So much for New Years.

The next day, Sunday, Cathy was returning to San Francisco, departing from Orange County at noon. I got up early, my routine accomplished by 9:00 am. Rain was threatening, the sky already low and gray. We made breakfast and talked about last week, next week, the coming year, but not forever. Cathy said she was considering an opportunity for a transfer to Singapore. Increasingly, for reasons of cost and quality, publishing houses were having their high end art and graphics books printed in the Far East. That would be a long way from Sheridan, a half a world away from me. At 23 now, the pull of seeing the world was strong on her, continually stimulated by the international currents of San Francisco.

"Craig, earlier this year it seemed we were headed in different directions which could not be reconciled. I didn't tell you before about the Singapore thing because I didn't want it to affect our time together. I had pretty much concluded that although we love each other, to put a label on it, we weren't in-love. But Thanksgiving and this last week have been so wonderful. I just don't know. So I guess I'm back to that question … do we have a future?"

"… I've thought about it, too, almost constantly over this last month. I believe there's enough between us for a future together. The present is the challenge. We're still headed in different directions, and that hasn't changed. I need the wide open spaces, more solitude. For me, that means the Four Corners, Wyoming, Montana. I don't want to live in California beyond visits here to Laguna. I like Laramie, studying music, practicing piano, running the cafe. I also sense that there's a spiritual part of me wanting to be transformed. That will be better nurtured in the wide open spaces, rather than under the pressures of LA, Orange County, or San Francisco." Or Singapore either.

"I appreciate the truthfulness we've had," Cathy said. Between too many times of extended silence, I thought. "It would be so easy for me to chase you, all the stops out, even after all the time we've known each other. Until one way or another I became Mrs. Craig Maxwell. And I agree with you that there's more than enough between us to start building a future together."

There's trouble ahead when we're analyzing our hearts in a real, much less real-time, conversation. El Fameoso, the famous one. El Flameoso? If I thought about what I had just said, Kat would be closer to fitting into the scenario. Order on line two. Cut the analysis, now.

"I've dreamed of us being married, a life together … I don't want to lose you, but I don't want to let go of other dreams I have, either," she said, beginning to cry. "I'm being pulled two opposite ways … why does it hurt to love someone?"

I could only hold her close, starting to sink myself. Thinking of the radiant woman in the black velvet dress, cowgirl on the cold hill at the ranch. A few minutes later, she was quiet.

"You're looking for an angel, aren't you Craig?"

"… Now that you say it, yes, I suppose I am. I've always been looking for an angel. An angel's hair, an angel's smile." I had never thought of it like that. It was true. Go way back. Natalie wasn't an angel, but … somehow the youthful "love" we had was … what? I couldn't quite get to a conclusion about it.

"We're not angels, and neither was Emily. You've got to let her go. I don't know that there's enough love in you to go around." Was that the last thing I would be hearing before lights out, or was another thunderclap on the way in prelude?

"You're right. I know I've got to let more of her go," I said. Emily wasn't an angel either, and I had to accept the loss of her, resolve it in a way that let me live. About the rest of it, I didn't know how much love, or capacity to love, was within me. And how about my thought long ago, that "someday I hope to love a woman like I love this land?" The West. That says a lot about heart, choices. Is that only an expression, or really the truth? The *heart* of the *matter*?

"Not let 'more of her go', let her go, period. You can't heal without truly saying goodbye!" Cathy replied, frustrated; then looked away.

Are you really asking me to forget her? Letting go can't mean forgetting or denying. It has to be about accepting and appreciating.

The challenge is not to forget, rather to be open to new experiences, creating new memories, stronger relationships, all through reaching out to others and what they might bring. Reordering one's perspective, in a positive way. For me, recognizing, knowing that it's about *both* a woman, *and* the land.

Maybe we were on the right track, but hadn't gone far enough. How about children? Cathy and I had never talked about that. Shouldn't we have, by this time? Was it my fault? Having a child with Emily would have been such a blessing. But how much of any of this about Emily, appearing to be "right" or "truth", was because now it *could only be* a thought, a hypothetical dialogue?

We had to get ready to leave. A time of subdued preparation, another quiet trip to the airport. Her makeup, which she didn't need, looked nice.

I tried to cheer things up a bit: "And if your travel plans should include coffee in the Mountain West, we hope you'll return to the friendly paws of Cafe Whyoming." Not even a half-smile. "Be more sensitive to what's going on here," … unsaid.

"Cathy, I have never seen you look more beautiful than you are now, and that includes Thanksgiving, which was wonderful. You just keep getting more and more stunning. I can't even begin to express how much being with you means to me."

"Thank you for your kindness. I'm selfish. I want your heart too … if not all of it, more of it. I've got a lot to think about, the Singapore job, you and I … , the future. All heavy issues for a Wyoming ranch girl from Sheridan.

"Despite all the issues, I had a wonderful time. I love you, Craig. I love you," she quietly spoke, looking into my eyes.

"I love you, Cathy." I did love her. It wasn't a matter of "how deeply". I just loved her.

And felt terrible. Really bad.

Once more, my life's *ostinato* refrain: "and then she was gone."

They tracked me down, called to see if I would do a session at Pearl Recorders on Thursday. The connection, of course, was Cedric Clarke. Why not? Church programs, LA sessions, classical MFA performances, anything was possible these days, as long as it didn't involve women.

A tape was sent for me to listen to, come up with a piano part. It was a ballad calling for rolling arpeggios and a showcase solo, right down my line. When I layed down the track at the studio, Cedric was there, and we got to talking about "the new gospel". He knew of Deniece Williams, of course, and the funkiness of some of the tunes on her *Songbird* album. As we discussed it, my thoughts about the new music were strengthened. He agreed, and believed that the blending of traditional gospel, funk, classical, and pop, with a Christian message, would be huge. There were few outlets yet for the "new music". Time would be required to reach critical mass, first in terms of a defined style, and then expanding the number of stations which would play it. Many "religious" stations would never spin anything more progressive than "Rock of Ages", the Hammond wavy V-3 vibrato version, heavily white-drawbarred.

The studio date was a helpful interlude, one which didn't involve the unremitting grind of doing an entire album, and helped keep my mind off Women from the North.

Did the session. Returned to Laramie. Back to school, return to the roast and grind. Espresso. WünderPerk, Polecat BlackBlend.

The semester went on, a mix of practice, projects, and performances. An occasional date with Allison, get togethers with Emmett. I planned to visit the Francks on a Sunday in February, but Dave beat me to the punch, stopping by one afternoon in late January. I was upstairs when he rang.

"Craig, it's Dave Franck. Can I come up?"

"Sure, walk up the stairs after the buzzer."

"Quite a place. The building is attractive and Cafe is nice, but this is something else."

"Let me show you around for a minute—everything's up here except for the darkroom downstairs and garage out back."

"I recognize Cathy Rousseau in this picture. Who are the others?"

"That's Emily, from back home in Pennsylvania. The other is Annie LaCroix, from Minnesota."

"They must be important to you."

"Very important. I'll have to tell you about the others sometime. Anyhow, what's up Pastor?"

"Well, I know you were planning to visit in a few weeks, but it looks like we're going to be moving to Montana. We've been in Medicine Creek for five years, and have been blessed by it. After considerable prayer, however, we believe that the Lord is calling us to a church in Bozeman. Montana State will provide a nearby place for Sarah to go to college as well. How about visiting us in Bozeman instead, after we get settled?"

"I'll plan on it. Since it's much farther, the logistics will be a little bit more complicated, perhaps dictating a trip after school's out in May."

"Great. Now what I really came for, you know, is to have a cappuccino with you downstairs. Can that be arranged?"

"Sure. It's a good thing I don't have many visitors, otherwise, I would be totally wired from all the strong coffee. Let's go."

It didn't look like my rhythm guitar gig was going to be feasible this semester. There were only three months left, and I had a lot of work to do. Maybe in the fall. I'd get a stack of Marshalls, a Les Paul Jr., raise my sights, go for lead guitar. Take on ZZ Top, compete for the All World Critter Rock Title. Nah, something more local, put together a pickup band from whoever passes out last at the Cowboy football bonfire.

Cathy called one evening, and told me she was taking the Singapore job, starting in late February. Not surprising—either that she was taking the job, or initiated the call to tell me about it.

I would have liked to get together in San Francisco before she left, but felt that she should invite me. Prolong the agony? In any event, if I got adventuresome during the summer, I could always catch a plane and visit her … would that be likely?

About 15 minutes into our conversation, she said, "Craig, don't get upset with what I'm going to say, it's really just an observation. With you, everything is planned out, arranged. Like recording an album—there's creative inspiration, refining the material, recording, packaging, performing, and then leaving it behind for the next project. It's how you live each day. Organized, by the numbers. To make a lasting relationship, though, I think that you have to keep constantly coming back, committed to what you've got, working to renew and improve it. That has to be done close, not at a distance. By putting your heart into it. Risking your heart.

"Trying to be with you hurts, Craig, little by little," she continued. "I need to have more confidence that we have a relationship we're working on, see you bring more to it."

I know, sins of omission. I'm truly sorry.

"Cathy … ." I should just leave this alone. Take it somewhere else.

"What?" A tinge of anger. Speak and you lose. Be quiet, same result.

"I know it's no comfort, so insufficient, but it's not you." Definitely not you. How had I described her?

"It's me. It seems like there's always something missing … something to do with childhood, about my family, high school or college experiences … of the heart or spirit. I just don't know. I'm aware of the emptiness, but can't quite figure out where it comes from and how to fill it."

Solitude. I wanted to be alone, yet with the companionship of another while trying to figure it out. Clearly contradictory, paradoxical. No woman could be that other. At best a catalyst, there would be no life for her.

"Craig, I worry about you sometimes, that you're walking out too close to the edge. Not in anger or carelessness about either you or me, but simply wandering, looking; taking pictures but not living what's in them. I worry that one day, you'll think the only way to release the tension I see within you is to step off."

Lawrence of Arabia on his horse, engulfed by a storm of blowing sand. At the edge of a life. Convinced that the spirit is the only means of soaring. Stepping off before my white robe gets dirty. She may be right. The parachute thing.

"You are the most creative, talented person I have ever known," Cathy continued, "and in special moments we've experienced, the most gentle and caring. Those times are every woman's dream."

Drifted over by the sands.

"When I look back on you and I, how will I remember it? Describe it? Despite what I've just said, I can't really sum us up in words, Craig."

Native drums, soft, slow, in unaccented trimeter …beat/beat/rest … beat/beat/rest … winding into the silence of a conversation that ended before we stopped talking.

I might have gone off into verbalized, monological musing, or begun another quest for the lowest common denominator. She might have said, reacting, "you're a philosopher who lives no life." Managing Director of Life Simulations. She might have yelled at me in frustration, trying to either wake me up or irreparably break whatever was between us. She spared me all that, yet another thing for which I love and admire her.

I thought of our conversation for a long time afterward, about an orderly life in the wrong order. And in all fairness, if there is such a thing in evaluating relationships, in what order was her life? She was mapping out her future too. But that wasn't really about "fair and objective", acceptance, it was about being defensive.

Neither of us hung up the phone obviously upset. It was instead the end of a chapter, perhaps not necessarily the final one.

Define upset. Then let Cathy define it herself. I know how to deal with all this. Describe it as a "rocky period in my life." The readers of New West Press wouldn't even have to think about decoding that. Self-tragic artistic temperament. Oh, that. Life as weather. A particularly mean cold front blew in, upsetting the psychological and material complacencies. Froze the block. Nuthin' to do but wait until the thaw. Help it along with a spiked something at my own version of the Post-modern Indian Laramie Lounge. See you at the PILL.

I heard myself asking, how important is a life, my life? Answering, "not *that* important." How important *is*, "not that important?" Not important at all. And then there is the quadratic equation. How important is *that*? Long division? Thumbing the pages of a book like shuffling cards. Dealing them now. Solitaire in solitude.

Don't try to fool yourself. Cathy's gone. Wake up. She's really gone and it *is* the final chapter in our story. And I'm not upset. Keep telling yourself that.

Cathy. Major influences: Professor Randall Edmiston, "a great teacher with a shady past"; Grandma Esther, an Eastern blossom who took to the land like sunflowers; Craig Maxwell (believe it or not), who "helped me to extend my horizons." Interests: contemporary fiction, print media/design, adventure travel. Snapshot: cowgirl headed around the world for Palo Alto; future publishing exec—most fearsome expression uttered or heard: "I can't put a saddle on that."

Achingly beautiful.

Kat, Cindy, and Danielle sent me Christmas cards, to which I had responded. Quietly, effortlessly. I vowed to call Danielle the next time I was back in Laguna and invite her to dinner. With Kat and Cindy, the cards were updates, nothing major going on in either case. Tell me, what would constitute "major"?

My routine was about as simple as it could get. Go to school, oversee the business, easy to do at arm's length with Bob and Beth, and think about spring. However, simpler or more orderly, as Cathy called it, is not always better. There was the matter of purpose. Nearly thirty, I was increasingly mindful of the void left by Emily, to put it mildly, and admittedly now deepened by Cathy's departure.

I continued to write songs with no resemblance to the ESO stuff, to which my connection now was the dimmest of dim. There wasn't any reason to remember it. Some days, I struggled with a wandering sadness, reflected in my writing, the useless words invariably crossed out later, annotated NO!

> You reach out, then pull away, when comes the light?
> My darkest day is every day, when comes the light?

The cloud would lift and I would be better, honing my keyboard skills, seeing an incredible world through a 135 mm Zeiss lens with breathtaking clarity. Until the next low. Drafting a thesis again and again, trying to come up with an apologia for a flat island of a life, washed over by the ocean of my own innocent lies and representations. Rejected, having to repeat all the research, organization, presentation. Would it ever be done? Would the degree coveted for so long as to extend over all the miles and generations I am finally be conferred: Master of Fine Arts in Understanding? Would I ever live to see The Thing? So close that time.

What was missing wasn't a platinum album, a woman, or house in the Tetons. All wrong turns. Could I figure it out by crossing things off the list of what it wasn't? I didn't have enough years left to do that.

I was just bogging down in a tiring failure to be extraordinary. That's it. Burnt out by writing a piano sonata for the April recital. Practicing it at a much milder location over spring break was the answer. Eight days in Laguna to break the Wyoming winter cabin fever. To figure it ALL out. Without pills or excessive drink. I promise.

45

The Alberta Clipper, in a jazz club, with perfume

My work was going well, my body stronger for morning runs, the marine air cool and thick before afternoon warming. It was spring vacation, so I didn't feel guilty about a day off to roll down to Escondido and Anza-Borrego, now green and fresh after what had been a wet winter. The road seductively whispered, then screamed for Ferrrari time, an opulent celebration of speed and style. Fruit stands along the way offered freshly squeezed orange juice, tangelos, avocados, and strawberries to feast on in Laguna.

East of Julian, CA Route 78 drops off into the desert. Pulled over by the side of the road, 'atiin bąąhgóó; enjoying the sun. There was no wind, only the considerable, directed power of bees working flowers in the stillness. Back in the machine miles clicked by headed toward the Salton Sea, speedometer at 110, before I turned north to the oasis of Borrego Springs, west to Warner Springs, Aguanga, Temecula, and Elsinore, west again to San Juan Capistrano. Return to the kiln-cooked clay, electrostatically powder-coated, chrome-flaked and resin-formed California version of civilization. Your choice of finishes—vitreous or porous silicates—paint tints, and shimmers. Imbedded shells and stars. New! Two "now" Happenin' Hues: Cream Moss and Sundirt Ocher. Exclusive!

Shower, dinner, then enPorsched to The Jazz Spot in downtown Laguna for Wednesday Jam Night, where you might encounter anyone, allstars to no stars. The basic unit was the house trio—guitar, bass, drums. If you played a horn or keys, had the chops, changes, and confidence, you were the show.

While scoping out the scene for an hour, I had a capp from the copper *machina grande*, a terminally ornate machine with gold-winged Rolls knockoff on top. That California version again, aggrandized, unprecedented then incessantly duplicated, celebratorily metallicized. Coffee Critic rated the brew ★★½, passable but well below Whyomin' perfection. In the Coffee Stylist (Western Region) category, Beth was truly best in class.

It was my turn, and I dove into the jam. Two cookin' numbers right from the fake book—Freddie Hubbard's "Red Clay" for terracottasized consistency, and "Passion Dance", a McCoy Tyner piano showcase. The edges were surprisingly crisp for a pickup jam, and we filled a half hour. The crowd liked it and wanted more, so I played a solo piece, variations on "Equipoise" by Stanley Cowell, before adjourning to the bar. Done for the night, I rewarded myself with a Harvey's to sip and savor before exiting to the awaiting night air, by now again cool and thick. Jazz air.

A couple of stools down the bar somebody said, "the man can flat play," as the woman I had noticed earlier at a corner table walked right up to me. By repeat business in the glances and lookarounds category, easily Numbah Won in Club, literally translated from the French as, *woman she who stops traffic.*

"You heard it, that was great. Are you famous?" the traffic stopper asked.

"No more famous or fabulous than the way you look tonight. What planet you from, Princess?"

"The name is Jupiter, from the Galaxy, I came to meet you, to make you free … ."

"Easy one—Earth Wind & Fire. How about "Giant Steps", Miles for $100?"

"I've been "Miles High", but I'm really not a $100 kind of girl."

To put it mildly. But she started it.

"Not that kind of guy either. I'd like to hang around and talk to you, but I've got a date with the dawn. Around nine tomorrow night I might be back, though, to convince whoever's listening that I'm the one comet you don't want to lose sight of, Miss Kindly Fill in the Blank." Expecting a typical non-Native, PostPseudoDecoPuebloan SoulMated and Affiliated Taos name like O'Dodgette Mandala.

"Rebecca, from Alberta, nickname's Chinook."

Surprisingly close when you consider … . Chinook, Chimook, whatever, whenever, forever. Better not use words I don't fully understand. Occasionally, someone else does understand.

"Silver and smooth." Yes, but hardly a Coho. Or do you have a thing for helicopter skiing in the Whistlers? "I'm Craig, lately from Laramie, back from the slalom. *Que sera, sera.* Goodnight, Princess." Would they be wooly, would they be white … .

"Goodnight, Mr. Fill in the Blank Yourself." As if to say, nobody walks out on *me*. Now we've got a game.

Left *her* standing there. Been wanting to do that again ever since Maple-fields. Once more, "ahhh bring it on down." To 11th grade. Just the right touch, like exquisite dessert, matchless coffee. Artful subtlety, richness, timing. Creative flirting. So hip, so lightweight, so pointless. So Mr. Baadfulll. Mr. Joyyfulll. Mr. Awwfulll. Mr. Pitifulll. A chuckle to myself, the phantom, departing. Like the road I'm driving up this hill, curve ball coming in high and tight. It might break, might not. Questionable chance to apply good wood to this Maple Leaf slider. Better chance handling a hundred mile fastball.

Leaving a question or two. Did the conversation actually happen? Would the woman really know the lyrics to that EFW song?

I *did* meet Rebecca, and she *would* have been scenic company cruising Anza-Borrego this afternoon. Though her face, being unfamiliar, was already hazy it wouldn't be hard to recognize the aura. Not hard at all. Other categories and titles won, in the words of the Calgary press, "Most Dramatic, Most Eligible, Least Available." Sighting confirmed at The Jazz Spot, among what could only be described as a very strong field.

By the time I got to bed, for the second time I had decided the conversation was real. Maybe not exactly as I remembered it, but close enough to reality to count. We'd test the conclusion tomorrow night. But what if she was, "Most Dramatic, Least Eligible, Most Available?" The permutations could be semi-serious trouble.

In the morning I awoke and attacked my routine with vigor. Running harder, practicing longer, working until near collapse, then kicking it up a level with what was left. Healthy dinner of stir-fry vegetables, ginger tofu, and rice, chased by a Kirin. All true, so far.

A cold, on-shore wind was blowing. Jeans, boots, and selected tribal accoutrements would be just right, at least for me. I arrived five minutes early. It wasn't about image, right? This is a "special occasion"? Define that these days. Regardless, she was already there. No problem recognizing *her*. My knowing smile.

"Hi, Rebecca. Good thing you finally showed up. I was just about to do a final once over and leave."

"Try it until you get it right. I was here first. Your name is Greg, right?"

"That's the one I wrote on the napkin, along with the schematic for the quantum drive propulsion system. Something to do with a one way mission to an outer planet. Unaccompanied, it would appear." Do rockets have rearview mirrors? I wondered for some reason. I'd have a dreamcatcher and string of firecrackers on mine. Celebrate the Year of the Loon.

"I know who you are, Greg," Rebecca said, restoring a fragment of electromagnetic sideband leakage. "BarKeep told me. You really should keep a lower profile, avoid the groupies."

"Got me," groupie or not. "Greg The Bender, nonxenophobic carbo-caloric proponent of Bent Wheat Lager, all around underemployed great guy. Will occasionally let down his guard in the name of art, even Carney Art. Will walk the Planck for Max. Does that make sense?"

"I think that we'd better go back 24 hours and reset. You can pick me up at my parents' house tomorrow, travelling light. We'll walk down the driveway, speed to the airport in a rental car paid in cash, disappear without a trace. Live happily ever after in Yellowknife."

My parents' house? Yellowknife? Would we need Canadian bills. Where would she shop?

"Try most of Flat-U-tah, if you're looking for a remote, drier place layered with comparably tangible weirdness but less snow. How much time do we have, by the way, until your fiancé shows up?"

"About two years. I've met him several times, at least that's what he thinks. Said he'd like to meet me again when I was thirty. Plenty of time." A parable of rejection in there somewhere? Another allegory of hard knocks and knuckles?

"So you know all about me. Greg Fender, call me Junior, heir to the guitar dynasty, but hardly Less or Lesser Paul. How about you?"

"I'm Melissa." That is, Miss Uncharted Territory 1977. "Last year's model, but still in excellent condition. High miles and finicky to keep in tune."

I could believe that. Surprisingly high miles, I'll bet. Now we're getting to the facts of the case.

"O-K. It's time to get serious about this scene, so let's do a rewrite, starting now. I'm Craig Maxwell, graduate student at the University of Wyoming, in Laramie, studying fine arts, music and photography. How about you?"

"Get serious. You're Craig Maxwell, rock 'n roller."

"Who has, by all accounts, dropped out of sight after quitting the business a couple of years ago. It's true. I do live in Wyoming and am on the skids in the MFA program. I repeat—so how about you?"

"Rebecca McLeod, older of two children of Angus and Rachel McLeod, Calgary, Alberta. Energy industry corporate daughter gone bad after a couple of degrees in economics and law. I'm an economist, teaching at the University of Alberta. Visiting Mom and Dad, who have a place down here."

"Would you further define the 'bad' part?"

"Stick around for more than ten minutes, *if* you're ever invited to find out."

"Okay, we'll stipulate that you're well positioned in the provincial economy. The question is, are you bad or *bad*?" We might be related.

"That remains to be seen. Are you going to behave? And by the way, considering your gear, are you going to a Sun Dance later tonight?"

"Definitely. I'm emulating that 'right off the Reserve look,' as you Canucks would say."

"That would be insulting if we weren't in California. Name of the rival hockey team, too. Better watch it." In California, where everything and nothing are insulting.

"Sorry about the spectacle. I'm really just a sensitive, introspective guy. Being totally embarrassed by my inability to keep up with you, Princess of the Jupiter Moons, I think I'd better shove off. Out of my league here."

"I'll tell you when you can leave, Chief. Right now, I'd like a drink, stronger the better."

"Bartender, two Old Canadian Keels, one rolled straight over."

"Very funny. Not too obvious."

"Welcome to the all-skate."

"What's that supposed to mean?"

"It's after the ladies choice. Free-skate. Something to do with my youth."

"Truce!" You mess with my truce, you mess with me.

"Deal. Help me behave, put all those beautiful women behind me." Real charming guy.

And so it went, until she asked me whether I liked the perfume behind her ear. "You'll need to get closer, there's only the faintest trace."

I liked it a lot. So much I called for the check, eased her out the door, and over to the boardwalk along Main Beach. It seemed so much like a dream. It was. The next thing I knew, I was being held as a suspect, charged in an unnamed conspiracy involving a knockout swindler, negotiable bonds, spiked drink, and a memory blank of three hours. Better a co-conspirator than a witness, in this case.

"Rebecca, I know you desperately want to come home with me tonight for a drink or some other cliche. But I'm sensitive to taking things excruciatingly slow with, as some in Hollywood would say, a backward Canadian native, so I'm not even going to ask."

"Some line. What makes you think I would have accepted?"

"Objection, badgering the witness." Wolverine-ing, minking? Interesting wild animal association.

"Overruled. Motion granted to reconvene tomorrow afternoon. Pick me up, and we'll go up to South Coast Village. I just love authentic cappuccino. Why the big smile?"

"Nothing in particular, lots in general. Anyhow, it's a date."

Will you bring news from the Edge of Creation? Teach me the Dance of Veiled Essential Truth?

I wanted to ask, but recognized my dialectical thinking, streams of compressed data without the means of decipherment revealed even to me. Inexpressible, transmuted stories woven from the finest of nuances and subtleties, stories in which man, as we see ourselves, is arguably irrelevant. Set not in Outer Space, or Beyond All Space, but along the Qu'Appelle River, the "It's Calling River" north of North Dakota. Really. Where telephone conversations flow, and thoughts once again pop like kernels of Colorful Corn under the summer sun.

We exchanged addresses and numbers, everything important short of genetic fingerprints, then drove off into the night, separately. The rendezvous had lasted all of an hour. A Canadian economics lecturer at large. The price to earnings ratio appeared to be very favorable, a superior opportunity for long term capital appreciation.

Or was it market hype? In the great oilmen's trading tradition, a classic pump and dump?

I chose a new thesis topic—*Airtight Ignorance: New Tractions, New Traditions*. Then thought about Rebecca walking in the door at her parents' place.

"Hello, darling. You're back earlier than usual. Meet anyone interesting tonight?" O Mother asked.

"No … well maybe … oh, probably not."

We'll see about that. In Round Three.

46
Cappuccino, Rebecca?

Continuing what had to be little more than a diversion, albeit one with interesting scenery and neither career potential nor kinetic downside, I picked up Rebecca in the Porsche, mid-afternoon Friday. No need to get any more locally radical in terms of the road hardware. Her parents' place was a large, tastefully done home on a superior lot high in the hills. Where else? A bit 'o Scotland warp transmutated with a Western Canadian woof. Tasteful if you like heavily-sauced and pudding'd walnut panelling. Oil money. Rebecca introduced me to her father, who immediately asked what line of work I was in. The kind of guy who would wear a suit to the beach.

"I'm a graduate student at the University of Wyoming, majoring in music performance."

Then don't bother me, his look said. Who let you into our exclusive enclave, *Les Riches de Laguna,* anyhow?

"He's actually a famous musician. Maybe even more famous in Calgary than you are, Daddy," really saying, "I'm the one who snared this marten and brought him back home … for the cat to play with … rrrrrhhhhh."

Well okay, if that's the way she wants to see it, for the time being. As for Daddy, he's still wintering over near the Pole.

"Really? What sort of music?"

"I made my first fortune in rock 'n roll. Which explains why I would want to go back to school to study classical. I'm doing okay, so I guess it was the right choice."

When I said "fortune", a glimmer of smiling respect crossed his face. Now fortunes are always something we can talk about. Competitively. In fact, everything about this family was competitive. I didn't perceive any rebellion, breaking from the ranks on Rebecca's part. What would happen if I called her Becky, I wonder?

"What brings you to Laguna?"

A claim jumping Canadian oilman asking me that. His one track mind stopped long ago on very favorable petroleum-bearing geology under remote, leased land.

"I used to be based in Santa Monica, but also owned a house here in Laguna. It's my getaway these days. This week is spring break. I'm working on a couple of pieces for an April recital." Burnt Sauté in E-flat minor in three movements, for one. Eyes on the fair, conspiratorially inspirational daughter, poised to strike when the meter is right, crescendo inescapable.

"And what do you plan to do after completing your music program?"

"I'm not really sure. That's a year away, and there are several possibilities, none of which would require moving back here full time, or touring. I could get into music performance or session work."

"Daddy, I think that he can do pretty much what he wants in music. He can really play."

"Well, pleased to meet you. I'm usually surrounded by accountants, geologists, lawyers, and engineers. Even occasionally my daughters." Call them downstairs and get on with the introductions. A little contrast in size and style might be nice.

"I'm one of those engineers, too. My degree is in civil engineering. But I got a break and ended up in LA. The right situation at the right time."

"You're probably not too bad, then, although the engineers I employ, of necessity, are focused on anything but the arts." No question who's in charge.

"I will admit to analytical objectivity, but not to the exclusion of artistic interests."

"We'll see, young man." Young man? We must be keeping him from being fitted for another suit, or his daily telex with the Indonesian spot market crude close.

The afternoon was nice for a drive up PCH to South Coast Village, just across "The 405" near the Orange County Airport. "You shall address the California freeways with all due respect." As the Tubes might have put it in *Remote Control*,

Freeway is King, it's my everything.

I was familiar with the coffee bar, having mapped the Southland espresso mines, of which there were still few, long ago, and knew the owner casually. He did make a more than decent cappuccino, which I usually had as a "mezzo-mezzo". Steamed half 'n half instead of milk. We sat down on a couple of prime ebony African texture-enNauga'd bistro chairs.

"Cappuccino, Rebecca?" She nodded.

"*Eduardo, uno cappuccino regulare, e uno cappuccino mezzo-mezzo.*"

"*Subito*, Craig, *prestissimo.*"

"Hey, you didn't tell me that you knew everyone south of Santa Ana," Rebecca teased.

"Just a coincidence."

"Yeah, too right."

"That expression confuses me, 'too right'. What does it mean?"

"Stick around and you'll find out, although there may be pain." Rebecca might take prisoners, but I was sure they didn't have much of a shelf-life. Speeding away from the scene in a '54 Ford, my right arm casually stretched out along the top of the seat above her back, while she gestured with the 38 special, "take the Logging Camp Road." Both of us with shades, motives concealed beneath black t-shirts and too much smug, graduate-level education. Independent study.

Ed made the drinks, which were tasty, and asked me how business was at my cafe in Laramie.

"Your cafe?"

"Just another coincidence. Yes, I have an espresso joint near the campus. Something to distract me from the rigors of the MFA program." Throw the pursuit off the trail.

"I suppose you shop Erewhon next door to here, too."

"Methodically wholegrained and leafy. Yours in good taste, again."

"As a barrister I try to keep the concept of 'fate' out of my arguments. But it seems to be creeping in here." Life permeation with an occasional Dream Jolt.

"Well, I won't go off on a boatman's holiday, whatever that means, and explain it all in terms of Jung's 'synchronicity'. Let's just say that from time to time, the planets are aligned favorably, Jupiter Princess."

Later, I suggested we catch Bobby Hutcherson at the Lighthouse. "We could have dinner at the Chart House before the first set." A surfin' safari, by definition, headed to the Pier, permanent Beach Boys turf, though tonight hardly with the little "Surfer Girl" riding shotgun. Rather, a tough negotiator with that 38.

Rebecca liked jazz, unless the whole Jazz Spot thing was expert subterfuge, and immediately agreed. Even though not familiar with the mallet man, she took my word that it would be worth the drive.

After dinner and some fine music, we got back on The 405. Rebecca was enjoying the evening, her eyes closed now to the endless subdivisions of Orange County. By the time we hit Laguna Canyon Road, she awakened and suggested a glass of wine at the Ojai Grille, a quiet retreat downtown on Ocean Avenue with great food. The kind of place, though, with a pointless anecdote at the top of the menu: " … the original Ojai Grille was, of course, in Ojai … ." Setting forth the lineage. Delineating the lineage linearly. You get the unidimensional progression.

Right then and there, I decided the longstanding question. There *were* no degrees of pointlessness. It was absolute. Like stepping in tar. Black stuff that had to be cleaned off with something even worse. It was not a revelation I could share.

We were both flying back to our routines later in what was now Saturday—Rebecca to her university, I to mine. Another coincidence, but one with no mileage in it. Time was up on our first and maybe only day together, not even a full one at that. Leaning over, she coquettishly encouraged a kiss. Primarily in the role of a consumer shopping on the boatman's holiday, I willing evaluated it: worth the effort. Warm and familiar. Experienced. Postgraduate Expert? Definitely, while I was still thinking of completing my first year.

Driving away, I thought about that moment, the pleasant anticipation just before our lips touched. I couldn't escape the thought: we're total strangers, who's on the other end of this? Before dumping that line of inquiry into the can. How much does it really matter? This is about spring break, being soooo California. Making socially acceptable, if not praiseworthy, personally irreversible mistakes. Unaccountable speeding.

Rebecca was in her late 20's, not yet married, as far I knew, which wasn't much at all. You'd think the chances good someone like that would have been off the market long ago, not hanging out in a Laguna jazz joint. Maybe even considering children. "Napier babies," as *Morgan* disdainfully put it.

Wrong. Rebecca was "perfect", and just as perfectly strong willed. She was going to live life on her own terms. Take weeks to decide on a pair of jeans, if that's what it took. If she wore them at all, ever got grubby in a corral or flower bed. Dress for and trade up to the "success" of her father, try her best to surpass it. An options player fixed on dominating the market segment at hand, whether business or pleasure. That approach carries considerable risk—the possibility that going where you want to go, alone, is not really where you want to go at all. Was I talking about myself? Time would tell.

So there we were—two people wrapped up in ourselves, clever comments, asides, and comebacks. Enjoying the other's company within a small, well defined, tightly written scene both of us knew was just that. We all take these sporting side trips. Experiences with no apparent future, diversions to practice our interpersonal skills (read flirtation), reinforce our self image (read ego). Taking an actress to a film premiere, getting your picture taken. ´Asht´ į, t´óó, just fooling around. ´Aljił, flirting.

In a fleeting glimpse of near-reality, reflecting on Rebecca McLeod, I could only come up with a question. Though the composition was dramatic, and the incendiary promise tantalizingly real, how would I know if and when the fuse to *Music for Royal Fireworks* was lit, in order to crack the koan?

I thought about that shuffling to a mazurka all the way back to Laramie, tapping moderate 3/8 Polish dance time, considering Chopin, encounters which had little to do with either chance or the future. Musing over the power of bees and sweet found pollen of spring, hearing myself saying, "I dreamed of you naked, but I digress."

Huh?

47

Planets remain in extra-Whyominal orbits

Back in Laramie, a town in 2/4 time, it was a chilly Saturday night. Nothing new there. The stars were out and the cafe deserted due to spring break. After a shower I Spurred over for a beer, maybe two. Here's to the spark of romance, the promise of glowing embers, the Bent Wheat Lager brewing family. Quirky ballads, the allure of snowmobiles. Widespread Panic, the group; "Mutant Victors", their signature first set close.

Rebecca, *pend d'oreille'd parfumé*, crystal malted double-hopped contender for an extra-legitimate title, Miss Stops Traffic North America. Perfectly ingreduented for fermented lament. Interim conclusion tumbling in the weightless space of woman-thought, *ex poste birra seconda*: too perfect, too tangential. Not art, illustration. Nice memory though.

After the Spur, I came back and setup the darkroom to work on my term portfolio. When layed out on the floor before sequencing, the collective message jumped out—19 shots at emptiness, plus the wakeup. There were clusters of stepdown transformers in frozen alleys, a beauty contestant without pageant, rock stars I had known with empty looks, figures identified only by their shadows and silhouettes, a woman sleeping in a Land Cruiser in a snowstorm, coffee foam residue in a china mug threatened by a blurred advance from two o'clock—could be a spoon, arrow, punch, miniature thunderstorm, whatever you want it to be. Anything you can get or do for a grade at the *Supermarket of the Artistic Elite: An Installation*.

The woman in the car was of course Cathy. Exhausted or happily dozing at that moment, lulled into relaxation by the slow drive through the snow? Solid and forgiving, she put aside the notoriety which so often streaked, sometimes outright scratched my life, but wanted the one thing so hard for me to give— love. A fine woman. Would I ever escape the loneliness, to love someone again as I had begun to love Emily, totally, breathtakingly? And if yes, was I capable of the follow-through assuring it would live, last? I kept coming back to these questions, time after time.

The fences, bare trees, old tractor in a field set before frozen hills, vapor which might have been from an off-frame laugh. One brought in from somewhere else, maybe 1927. Nothing to laugh about in this spare land I was defining. The photographs captured the local universe of a few days, reflections recorded, some things only I would recognize once printed. Tracks which extended through the clearing of our time together, those we had made. I could rewrite all of this, reexpose the frames any number of times. They would all say the same thing. We haven't split up because we were never really together. I don't know why. I just know it's true.

Another day I had walked near the campus, occasionally taking a shot, freezing the motion of a crowd, neither faces nor clues of purpose recognizable due to the slow shutter speed, drawn as jet trails around a clock which had been stopped at 5:12. All leading to the last picture, that of a child on the Rez, smiling in an emptiness only that because we don't know how to look at it, don't understand.

The real *is* often empty, though. When yours is the only car in a parking lot, you're sitting on a bench along a street in a deserted town, the pavement on a remote highway in Idaho wet, disappearing into a summer night smelling of freshly cut hay, of not enough trees and too much loneliness. I've been in that car, in that parking lot, on that road, wondering if I'm the last person on Earth, realizing that I am. We all have been. We all are.

There are those who specialize in retouching, brushing away what they see as defects, when reality isn't good enough, won't make the emotional sale. Others retouching lives, not photographs. Holding on to, letting go of special women, whether they were there or not. Thinking foreign thoughts, speaking different languages. Changing the idioms, manipulating the smile. It didn't seem to matter.

Define blind. I was color blind. I think I'm other blind. Remembering what is dawn, but blind to the promise. Blind.

✣══════✣

March began like a walk in a field, the first green of Spring's beauty emerging, only to end with a fall into an unmarked well. "Same as it ever was … same as it ever was," David Byrne and Talking Heads contributed. Mark Knopfler's Dire Straits, *hojoobá´ ágo*, neared the top of the charts, and things were looking up in the Middle East with the peace treaty between Israel and Egypt signed. The headlines should have read:

Failure to Knock on Wood

On March 28th an accident at the Three Mile Island nuke plant, just a few miles southeast of Harrisburg, nearly caused a meltdown of the core. I could hear the Chief Event Containment Rep's monotonal debrief: "It was close, we almost lost the unit."

The cause was attributed to a combination of "human, mechanical, and design errors." In chilling irony, *The China Syndrome*, a movie with the same theme, had opened two weeks earlier, laying the groundwork for paranoia which would become rampant with the TMI disaster. And rightfully so. Nobody ever wanted to hear about the risks, just wanted Redi-Kilowatt™ to be there when they fired up the Perfect Belgian Wafflemaker. You've seen that one, the commercial for the Environmental Widowmaker—remember? The cat with real scary eyes, "Purrrfect."

During the following week I called my parents repeatedly for updates, their evacuation plans. All the time thinking about never being able to go back—not me, since I had left years go and wasn't interested in returning, but them. The barns of Dillsburg abandoned, radiation-poisoned, overgrown by plants which would be studied for effects century after century by technicians in concrete suits. Reflecting on conversations with friends in the late 60's, about how well summer work at Three Mile paid. That's what it had been all about. Forget the fail-safe systems which failed. Return on "equity", sweat or capital, in its narrowest definition. Big money. Equity-safe.

Little by little, the crisis was "resolved." Now that's an omnipurpose word. There would be lessons learned, heightened safety protocols prescribed for the "nuclear power industry, safe and clean," with all costs passed back to the captive rate paying customers. The utility's "reasonable rate of return," effectively guaranteed to preferred investors, would remain unscathed. Amid the "sincere" regrets, inquiries, and improvements promised to be made, it would be business as usual within the industry, a model of statistical safety. "Still the safest in the world," if you stay away from the uranium mines, enriching mills, fueling facilities, plant steam vents, leaking, corroded pipes, and other "miscellaneous uncontrolled 'emission' sources." The CEO of the Powerful Power Company wouldn't be building his retirement home on the tailings outside Grand Junction or Moab anytime soon.

Considering the stress, the recital went well. An understatement, actually. I channelled the tension of recent days into the dynamics of my original piano sonata, a technically demanding work of variations reminiscent of Mozart.

"Thank you for your kind interest and attention," I simply said, got up and left, my boots sharply clomping on the wooden floor of the recital hall. Cowboy? Indeed, Terse. Got customers to tend.

The faculty panel was speechless, blown away. I know that because of a conversation later.

A guest member of the MFA panel from New York, passing through on the way to a spring visit to Aspen, sought me out at the Cafe. It was no secret in the Music Department where I could be found.

"That was extraordinary, both in composition and technique. Have you considered studying with a master?" Swami Who? James and Bobby Purify ("I'm Your Puppet")?

"Maybe later. I'm having too much fun now running a cafe."

"As superb as you are, as much better as you undoubtedly can be, will *not* developing your talent, *not* taking it to its highest expression, ever be enough?" Not the background tint I was looking for; not the texture, chord structure, or optimal temperature to caramelize the glaze. Not, not, and more not. City guy.

"I do plan to continue sharpening my skills, but perhaps by a different course than you have described. Let's just leave it at that and enjoy some great coffee, assuming, of course, that you gave me an A."

"Indeed I did, though in no way does just one letter describe what we heard. When you change your mind about your course of study … ." As if it was inevitable. "Innovation and excellence, what you can always count on at the Trade School of the Virtuosos Illustriotivos." Get that product to market! The right tint, perfect glaze.

Beth heard a word here and there, and after he'd gone, sat down for a minute to talk.

"We can't help but hear you play upstairs when it's quiet down here in the cafe. The Music School people who came in earlier said you stoked the recital, that you're a world class talent. They're in awe of you. *Are* you that good?"

"I may be in terms of technique relative to my rather narrow musical interests and familiarity at this point, possibly in terms of potential as well. Certainly not in terms of repertoire. I'm not even out of the 18th century yet. Though the promise may be there, the sculpture doesn't always come out of the stone."

"Are you going to go after it, Craig? You know, New York? We'd be rooting for you, but it wouldn't be the same without you here. I'll never be able to thank you enough for bringing me out and giving me this opportunity. Bob feels the same way."

"About bringing you out here?"

"That too," Beth laughed.

"Seriously, no chance I'm going back to the big city, New York, LA, wherever. I don't have to be a world class performer; don't want the recognition, don't need the money. Pushing 30, I'm looking for peace. The real thing. It's been so elusive. Music is helping me with that, I think, but is not an all consuming end unto itself."

We appreciate how you are operating at a superior level, how smart you are. It's just that your accomplishments have nothing to do with the actual matter at hand. Life.

I haven't changed my mind yet, though it would be nice to have friends who say things like, "I think I'll play the Chopin this evening." Or, "I'd like to sing the Schumann." A soprano in my future? Not likely outside New York or Vienna. The closest I was going to get to that scene was Vienna, the roast.

Early May. Halfway to the MFA. Cafe business winding down for the summer. We had done well this first year, and there was no reason to think it wouldn't continue.

Bob and Beth surprised me by announcing they were getting married. Good move. Bob had a large bonus coming, earned many times over.

As for me, after considering, "what can I do in pine?" I scheduled a weekend trip to Calgary to visit Rebecca. We had talked several times on the phone, and she was, "I'm So Excited", that I would be coming up for "Springtime in the Rockies." Two songs in the same sentence, but certainly not in outcome.

From the start, I had known any common ground between us was small, maybe infinitesimal. When I flew up there in May, Rebecca said she was leaving three weeks later for the summer in Scotland, doing some work for her father's oil company. Did I detect a hint embedded in that statement? Laramie is way off the jet set, and more than any other place, it *was* feeling like home to me these days. I didn't want to get wrapped up in a faceless high-rise, sprawling "population center", or picturesque Scots cottage beside the North Sea. A replay of Anne in that unrealized Southwest fiction, except this time I would be wearing not the shorts, but a kilt. Not a chance.

Evidently Rebecca wanted to show me off to her girlfriends, likewise late 20's unmarried professionals. The Investors' Cluhhbb. Spin-sters. We spent a pleasant, if nominal, weekend together, late snowstorm and all. Everything on her terms. Well, almost everything, with a notable exception or two challenging her idea of domination. It resembled a business trip. To the Spice Islands. Now that I think of it, maybe for her it was a business trip. To what kind of business might I have been an unwitting accomplice? That's right, the bond scam.

I love the phrase, "under ideal conditions … ."

> It was a story of gangland virtue, a black Cadillac full of
> the DEA's worst nightmare … under ideal conditions the
> caper might have worked, the violence that would bring
> down half the force avoided …

Under ideal conditions, Rebecca and I … .

Anyhow, Rebecca said that when back from Scotland, she would like to visit me in Laramie. I couldn't tell if she meant it, and if so, how come? So why am I thinking about this, much less mentioning it? It could be ego, to reinforce that I've held my own with some *glamorate* over the years. The Rebeccas,

Romys, Moniques. But that's not really the reason. Instead, it's about hoping that one day, underneath the bravada of Ms. Whatever Hernameis, perhaps set to a polonaise, a vulnerable, loving woman will emerge from her persona by surprise, gracefully offering a hand to the man wanting to experience what love really is and can be, for the long haul. You'll never know unless you make a run at finding the Sky Heart. Life has to be about a few of those surprises now and then. Even a math teacher.

I'm the one who gave Beth the lecture, remember? The one about loneliness and economics. I should have listened to myself more carefully, realizing I was cutting out pictures for what could only be a static collage. Sign: Winding Road Narrows and Nearly Disappears—Caution. "My car's brand new and I want to see what it'll take to burn a valve." This is the right place to find out. One thing I've always wondered: how can a counselor have no beliefs?

Somehow, the "mentality here", isn't quite the right terminology, nor does "if sophistication counts for anything ..." fit. Like I said, the static collage. Images without a message.

Stepping back, to view the masterpiece, any way you look at it, I'm still alone while the planets, Cathy, Rebecca, others, remain in extraWhyominal orbits. In this darkroom with the red safelight, do I even know what I'm looking at? My analytical side says never open or shut the door too early. Control all factors. Always follow the script. Approve all scripts in advance. How much of all this is content (Craig), and how much marketing (the MaxSwell persona)? In the mind cloud of this moment, tangled up in the definition of big time musician.

Rebecca's file (did I actually think that—file?) was still open, symbolically if nothing else, to resist drawing a final conclusion from such brief experience. For once, hold the verdict, just see what happens if our paths cross again. After all, I don't have any other strong new leads these days. Maybe I really don't want any.

Printing new snow on old snow. White on white. Light on light. Always trying to fill that gap between art and life sensitively, to apply the most delicate shading, but finding it's the wrong brush. Emily would have done her part, more than that surely, to help solve the puzzle, provide contrast and tint to my monochromaticism. Because she was such an important part of the solution, a wildcard that I lost. Laughter to put me at ease, a depth like no one else. Depth that I only started to get to know. Can *anyone* really be a solution? Will I ever be at peace with the memory of you, Emily?

Knock on the door. Cafe Whyoming? Looking for Lenny Power and the Alter Ego. We're here to crate their arguments for shipping. Are you those persons? Manifest also says pencil drawings of someone they used to know, never knew, need to know. Sign and we'll drive nails, stencil a destination.

Calgary, Singapore, Laguna, clear run of the Qu'Appelle River; turbid, milky flow of the Powder; even, lazy meanders of the Conodoguinet, only a creek. Too far from Laramie in this moment.

Crate and take them all away. My name in Navajo: *t´áá sahdii*, alone. Has-Nothing-To-Say. Living a Whim Life, in the land of Manifest Isolation. Living rough drafts of the only life he knows, the one he never thought he wanted. The safelight bulb just went dark, and the tide's going out.

Quickly.

48

Bella signorina, sotto voce

Summer 1979. The papers were incessantly filled with the likes of, "… after serving nearly 7 months of … scheduled to go to jury trial … still at large … ." Take a pick between *Alien* and *Quadrophenia*, if you're inclined toward film. Your choice, spaceship or scooter, extra or subterrestrial, aliens all. And how about the good news that the Strategic Arms Limitation Talks (II) limited each superpower to 2250 long-range nuclear missile launchers? Enough remaining, a hundred times over, so we could be confident the residual ash of the earth, fluffy over silica heated to incandescence and fused, would be a muted shade of gray with an occasional frozen foam of shiny dark blue gas bubbles, testimony to those strategic thinkers and weapons builders whose minions left only a jumble of radio transmissions, final launch codes scattered by the solar wind. When things cooled down, what had been Earth would be simply another sueded slag planet, not even the newest one among billions in the "heavens", going by a different name: Nobody Was Responsible. Cinderscape candidate for another round of evolution.

This is why I don't read the papers, yet still know exactly what's in them. Because it never changes. I for one, an alien corrupted to the other side, celebrating where liquidity is all, was keeping my priorities straight, taking comfort not in the perpetual "news", but in the knowledge Pearl is still brewed in Fort Worth. At least while the Artesian Water holds out or is vaporized in The Last Real Test.

Bob and Beth were married in a nice ceremony in Laramie, on a clear day that wasn't too hot, and left no permanent scars. The right, happy ending to a story told through the time being, one which I sincerely hoped would extend for much longer. Her parents flew into Denver and drove up a few days before, no doubt thinking, what now? Out here? Never seen anything like this country. Are there still buffalo stampedes? It's all this guy Maxwell's fault. They came around. Laramie was comfortable in summer, and I turned on the battery-powered humble charm.

For a few minutes during the ceremony, I hypothesized about the two-step, then the next step, finally the same step, marriage if you've already lost the thread, before quickly stepping on. Didn't want to get hung up—this was about celebration and more subtle, magnum'd hooch than Pearl.

What to do this summer? Get the GMC in Newport, verify music gear operational status, load up the cycles, and take a trip up the Coast, across the top, and down to visit the Francks. Return to Laramie awhile after that, before driving the rig back to Newport. Above all, ignore any and all news. That subject's been covered.

My pace this time was much more relaxed than the hard bop of "No Time for Squares", which is essentially an east-west kind of tune anyway. I spent a week in the redwoods, enjoying the scenery and fresh air, rides on the Triumph, practicing at the keyboard, composing. Hiking up to a fire lookout above the South Fork of the Kern River, I talked with the Cal State student spending the summer there with her old dog. Kerouac redux, living for the view, to get in touch with oneself, the peacefulness broken only by an occasional backpacker or dayhiker stumbling up the granular, decomposed granite trail among dry, dusty trees. It wouldn't be raining anytime soon.

On the way back to the rig, I stopped to admire the vista from a rock ledge, taking a sip of water from the canteen, splashing some on my face. The beauty of the place was overwhelming, prompting me to observe (and jot down):

> Modern Life is too often about elaborate preparations
> for insignificant events. We know our destinations,
> but not where or why we're going.

Morally, ethically, spiritually, we have thrown up our arms and exclaimed, "Whatever!" I don't want to accept that. I *need* truth, significance, understanding, actuation, and actualization.

"I'm honored to be your only friend," she said, a little scared.

Accurate. Scary, alright. It's way past time to start living the music I play, the sky-weaving of this day, what I just wrote.

Closing my eyes, I saw warrior paint, a feather. A hoofprint on the sandy bank of a wide, shallow creek, splashing, talking to me with its flow. Sssshhhh. Seeing the reflection of my painted face in it, the feather in my hair. Preparing for battle, receiving a blessing from the river, the Spirit in that place. Belonging. Going forth with honor.

Farther north, the granite domes of Yosemite gave way to the deep blue of Tahoe, steaming vents of Lassen, sleepy, immaculately tended McKenzie River byway east of Eugene, scarps of the Columbia River gorge, funkiness of Hood River, glaciers of Rainier, clamor of Pike Place Market in Seattle. Then Snoqualmie Pass, the North Cascades Highway, Spokane, and Sandpoint, in the Idaho panhandle, winding down to Missoula and Butte, Bozeman. Great country.

An interesting mix of Outdoor Rec and Ag/Tech, Bozeman didn't have the counterculture wreckage of Missoula. I liked the setting, with the Bridger Range just to the north, blue ribbon trout streams; Livingston, Tom McGuane and Jimmy Buffet's adopted railroad town, a half hour east. My take on Bozeman was cold and isolated in the winter, increasingly popular in the summer, bound to grow and prosper. Rough 'n Ready, Rec 'n Tech.

Dave Franck was pastoring a church in an older, well maintained residential area located between the downtown and Montana State University. He told me that the congregation was a mix of younger families associated with MSU, long time residents, and a few ranchers. The real 'pokes had to spiritually recharge in the saddle, not as able to keep a "normal" schedule in the Big Open, given the demands of working ranch life. I parked in his driveway and ran around town on the bike, stayed out as late as I could, meaning about 10:30, and slept *en rig*, or if you want it more dashing and Italian, *en rigoletto*.

There wasn't yet a legit espresso bar in town. It was an opportunity to go into the chain-gourmet business, one which I resisted, for now. Maybe after I finished the MFA next year. Recreating the magic of the Cafe Whyoming wouldn't just happen. It took a lot of work and perhaps more important, a Bob St. Clair. In the meantime I could get a passable cup of coffee and piece of apple pie downtown at The Bakery, more than adequate after two thousand miles.

Sarah, Dave and Amy's daughter, was excited to see me again, once a rock star, always a rock star I guess. She brought around new friends who were equally impressed that ESO's former keyboardist was really visiting her parents in, of all places, Bozeman. The Triumph with California tag helped sustain the momentum of the myth. The bike on which Emily and I roared off from the reunion. Legendary, in my mind. Should I have it bronzed? The bike or my mind?

"Craig, update me on the last six months, after the Christmas holidays in Medicine Creek," Dave asked as we sat on the porch. "And what is Cathy doing?"

"Cathy's in Singapore, probably for a couple of years, a new job in her company's high end publications division. After leaving Medicine Creek after Christmas, we spent a few days in Laguna Beach. In her last letter she was excited about being in Singapore, says it's very clean, English speaking, modern and highly literate. I've been thinking of visiting her there. Someday, I expect she'll be back in Wyoming, at least part time. Those ranching roots run deep.

"I was real busy during the spring semester at the University, and am doing fine in the program. I'm still improving and expanding my repertoire, so I'm happy. The MFA was the right thing for me to do. It's taken me in some interesting directions, like Medicine Creek, of course, and the cafe business.

"For the last month or so I've been travelling, taking pictures, riding the bike, doing a little composing, hunting for espresso in unmapped places with big trees. I'm ready to get off the road in Laramie for a few weeks, before driving the rig back down to Newport Beach."

Always considering the next Sunday's show, Dave asked, "can I talk you into playing something for our service Sunday? I'm sure the congregation would enjoy it."

"I expected that if I was here on a Sunday, you'd maneuver me into the program. Sure. I've been transcribing a couple of pieces from several Bach masses and oratorios to occupy myself during spare moments on the trip. They would be appropriately sacred. I'll make sure the dynamics are robust; we don't want the customers in the pews to fall asleep."

"Great. I'll have to casually mention to Sarah that Craig Maxwell will be on-hand. Anything to get the youth attendance up."

"After dinner tonight downtown, with the Franck family as my invited guests by the way, I may sit in with a local group. If things get rowdy, you might have to make bail and sober me up before the Sunday service."

"Deal, Brother Maxwell. I know just the restaurant to keep your sophisticated tastes challenged and record clean while we get an elegant meal we couldn't afford."

I don't know why I remembered it a few minutes later when Dave and I were sitting on the porch alone, but I did, and asked him one of many questions I had been carrying around.

"Dave, I had a discussion once with a friend about 'churches'. We were on the verge of a fullblown cross-cultural examination of 'religion.'" That friend was Annie LaCroix, *Ogimaakwens*, the Princess she was and always would be to me, Jeans on Back (of the Triumph). Actually, *Ogimaakwe* would be more accurate and respectful—Woman Leader. That's the way *I* saw her.

"She is not a Christian, and critical about much of 'organized white religion', in this case the expense, contrast, and statement made by elaborate churches in poor areas. To some, an image of insensitivity, domination."

"She has a good point. My belief is that there is nothing intrinsically wrong with those churches, which seem luxurious to some. But they're just places, buildings which should not be ends unto themselves. The real objective is to get people in touch with themselves spiritually, with God. I don't think we'll ever settle all the issues associated with disparities of wealth, amenities of churches, even salaries of pastors. These are issues among people, and it's so easy to generalize, rationalize. I look at the church building as only a door. Some are more elaborate than others. Some are too elaborate. The question is what is in the heart, the spirit? Is it sharing, in this case the sharing of wealth to build a church, or is it appearances, comfort for comfort's sake, ornate self-edification?"

I considered his remarks for a minute, neither agreeing nor disagreeing, then we moved onto something else. I'd add Dave's thoughts to what I had been carrying around, think about them more. The religion thing was challenging—a lot of questions with either too many answers, or sometimes seemingly none at all.

We had an enjoyable dinner and afterward, said our "see ya laters" for the evening. I went into a club, had a Coke, and played a few numbers with some rangebop wannabes, just for fun. Road entertainment. They wouldn't be ready for the Lighthouse any time soon, but it was an easy way to stay out of trouble.

Sunday was rainy, cool weather dipping south from Canada a little more than usual for summer. I kept a blue Palm Beach blazer and khaki slacks in the RV, legit for church.

Pastor Dave ad libbed an introduction, variation on *The Miracle of Christmas*, wherein the pianist falls ill, and the church members see their Christmas program coming apart. The Pastor remembers the strangely dressed musician from months before, finds and convinces him to help. The show is a success in the humble little town in Wyoming, and they become friends. And oh by the way, it turns out that this man in the motorcycle riding outfit used to be a member of the famous rock 'n roll group ESO, of which he, Pastor Dave, had never heard before, of course. But his daughter certainly had.

"In getting to know him, we've found that while his exaggerations know no bounds, they usually take willing prisoners!"

Mere-a-cle. The act you've been waiting for, all show, all Cher! Live from the Vegas House of Pipe. Take it away, CMaximus!

"With that, I give you Craig Maxwell, lately of Laramie, who will be playing piano transcriptions of excerpts from several of Bach's choral masterworks, two hundred and fifty years old."

There I was, pounding out baroque counterpoint in the Sunday morning stillness. When I finished the exquisite material, it was as if the music had set, to the sun's last evening rays. Breathtaking. Yet I was struck with a "feeling", or whatever it was, that my playing, indeed my life, could go both much deeper and higher. A sense about potential, empathy, heart and spirit; not criticism or insecurity.

Following applause, as I thought, "they clap in this church, is that reverent?" the next performer stepped forward from the choir, a vocal solo.

I looked at the program for her name and the piece—Stephanie Tyler, *Laudate Dominum*—intrigued that it would be sung in Latin. She seemed … familiar.

Now there's a surprise, Mozart in Bozeman. And where was the accompaniment? As for Ms. Tyler, she was pretty, in a Montana way, tanned with a few freckles. Around 25, I guessed. Reminded me of someone, but couldn't think who it might be. Perhaps in the choir robe was an "interesting" competition of cowgirl and stockings. I had to let it go right away. This was church. The very one my friend pastored.

Hearing a taped orchestral introduction, I thought, well here goes, canned music—the alpine downhill with tragic fall. That didn't last long. Her voice literally took my breath away. Range, sense of timing, dynamics, the humility demanded by the work conveyed by her presence and delivery. She was a classical singer. In Bozeman? Could you rewind and play that again? What a voice! *Vox angelica!*

I looked on the back of the program, where the words and translation had been printed:

Laudate Dominum, omnes gentes,	O praise the Lord, all ye nations,
Laudate eum, omnes populi.	Praise Him, all ye people.
Quoniam confirmata est	For His merciful kindness is
Super nos misericordia ejus,	great toward us,
Et veritas Domini manet in æternum.	And the truth of the Lord endureth forever.

Four minutes of musical bliss. I could think of nothing else during the rest of the service. Afterward, I congratulated her. With equal parts of seemingly shy beauty and self-assuredness, the kind of opposed chemistry that keeps you thinking and guessing, unsettled, she simply replied, "thank you, I enjoyed your playing very much too." That's who she reminded me of, Emmylou Harris. But even so, the resemblance wasn't entirely resolved—it was someone else, another time, a different place. I knew I had seen her.

A little while later, at Sunday dinner with the Francks, I commented how talented the singer was, "Stephanie something, as I recall." Amy and Sarah looked at each other, both smiling, but said nothing, as if waiting for Chief Many Decks to turn over another card.

"Do you know her?" She *is* in the choir. Why aren't they answering?

"... Yes, she probably is our best kept secret," Amy said after the dramatic pause. "Stephanie Tyler is the name. Graduated from Montana State, a masters degree, I think, something like anthropology. Works in the Museum at MSU. Her folks have a ranch north of town. Rumor has it that she is seriously considering marriage to a suitor in Billings. You'll have to act fast on this one, Craig."

"What do you mean, Amy?"

"I happened to glance at you while she was singing. You were entranced."

"*Entranché?* I wouldn't go that far, even in French."

"Oh, wouldn't you?" Dave joined in. "Get those leathers on again and ride up to tonight's service on your Triumph. The signature arrival. That might make the difference."

"Pass the mashed potatoes, Dave. Right now. Pass them as many times as it takes to change the subject." Full circle, another arrival two years ago. Spring 1977. The Circle of Life.

Things were pretty slow in Bozeman on Sunday night. Out of courtesy to my hosts, I attended the evening service, which was smaller, informal. I even listened more carefully to the message. I mean, that had to be important in church. And who should be there, but Stephanie Tyler? I nodded to her once when our eyes met, coincidentally of course, but that was it. After the service, when I looked for her, she had disappeared, but not the distinct feeling I had seen her before.

I told Amy that I would sure enjoy staying in their driveway another day or two, if by some chance Stephanie might be coming to dinner. I would be pleased to do the shopping, even make the coffee.

"You're so lovable when you beg, Craig ... okay, we'll give it a try," she finally added, "but don't get your hopes up. As I said, we've heard she's pretty close to marrying someone in Billings. We need to be careful about matters like this. Bozeman's a small town, and we're the new kids on the block in a close congregation."

"Message received. I'll behave, even go up in the mountains tomorrow, if the rain stops, and cleanse my spirit. Put it all in the hands of *Gichi-Manidoo*."

"Craig, you're actually nervous about this. Gitchy what?"

"In a pleasant Rec 'n Tech town on the Gallatin, she began to efficiently demolish the myth of him, in earnest ... . *Gichi-Manidoo*. The Great Spirit, in Ojibwe."

"Well, you are a myth, but a nervous one right now—you're blushing, Craig. What kind of rock star are you anyhow? One with a heart?" Dispelling myths. Despelling. Dysspelling.

"Yeah, that's it. Couldn't make the grade, but don't let the word get out." Go Latin with it, if anyone asks. *Il romanticus qui nente startus*. The romantic who never got started.

49

Losing the trail in Bozeman

Dziłbąąh kíjiiyá. He went up to the mountain. In appreciation of *vistas sierras* revealed by the clearing sky, I was mindful of and thankful for other revelations rendered through music and art; women who have loved me, and those whom I have loved. My emotions were as this mountain range; acquaintances, friends, and relationships as the clouds in the sky above me now, some dissipating; others remembered as gray and torn, in the end so close yet eluding touch, seemingly now gone forever. A few stronger in my heart, wisps and golden-edged billows, beautiful against the brilliant blue.

"Talk to me," I asked the sky on this Navajo-Zen-tai chi day while doing an exercise, "talk to me."

"True living is knowing who you are, your own original true face, spirit, from which you can begin to belong. The capacity to love grows from finding even a trace of the best that is within you. What you think you don't know *is* there, abiding, waiting to be found." Call it a rough draft of what I think I heard. Not a bad start.

Closing my eyes, I heard Annie say, "remember who you are"; watched Emily turn and smile; saw a black & white picture of a man and woman in a cafe, the view rear oblique, finger through the ring of a coffee cup, other palm covering the rim in appreciation of retreating warmth. A rim I knew was chipped, having felt it. Her head on my shoulder. A tiny child bundled in fuzzy blankets sleeping. Who had I been in the travels of that shutter at 1/60 of a Tri-X second? Who was I now? Who was the child?

When I returned in late afternoon, Amy sent me out to get some things for dinner, saying only, "she's been invited, and accepted. Of course out of courtesy I told her you would be the fourth, since Sarah will be over at a friend's house. Strictly by coincidence."

"What did she say?"

"None of your business. Dinner's at 7." When there are chips on the table, in the end, women always stick together.

The time dragged on minute by minute like a string of stubborn mules, until finally it was near 7. Stephanie drove up in a battered pickup as I sat on the front porch in a rocking chair, sipping iced tea. How's *that* for coincidence?

"Hello," I called, noticing an almost imperceptible hitch in her walk, not clumsy, but the slightest inflexibility. She was wearing a dress, so it was surprising I was able to notice anything other than the total effect, which unquestionably was lovely.

"Hi. This your rig taking up the whole driveway? Looks like you're on tour, alright."

"Yeah, on tour—thankful for friendship, looking for traces of culture out here in 406 Ranch country."

"You'd be surprised about the culture part. And I *was* raised a rancher. You can probably tell. Haven't heard of the 406, though." Area code, but that's my secret.

"Your dress almost threw me off the trail, but the pickup gave you away. 'You wear it well,' as Rod Stewart put it. The dress. And pickup too." Every picture … .

"Well, the engine's been rebuilt, so it runs fine. I just can't bear to give it up. In Big Sky, the second car you buy has got to be a Cadillac. Regardless of whether the cattle or grain markets are healthy or not. Mandatory, with one of those landau tops that last for about six months of the first winter. So you know what I'm up against. As for your comment about my dress, I do have one or two. Thanks for the compliment, if that's what it was." Don't blame me, Rod said it first.

"Do you drive your truck to church?" What kind of lame question was that? I was trying to come up with something clever, but nothing was there. Even my fellow mules were silent, squinting, as if to say, "get on with it." Outmaneuvered, if not outclassed.

"No, I usually come with Mom and Dad." Drawer pushed in on my fingers, doily straightened, door closed for another ten years. No visitors. He's inherently, inertly dumb and dangerous.

Knock on a different door, Thanksgiving dinner, turkey baking, cold hills at my back, Buck and Becky, their beautiful daughter, Catherine Marie Rousseau. Can I go back to that day right now? Change my mind about the future? That night?

"Still with us, Craig?"

"Yeah, sorry. The Mom and Dad part triggered a memory." But I liked it when she said my name.

The floe beneath me was breaking up quickly, should have melted months ago. It *was* summer, but the water beneath the ice in this Montana trout stream had to be cold. Real cold. I sensed that I was going to find out very soon. What had I called this place, an "interesting" mix of Rec 'n Tech? Just make it Wreck.

"Your performance yesterday was excellent. You have a great voice, Stephanie."

I mused on her name, the sound of it mellifluously rolling off my tongue, "Steph-a-nie ... Steph-a-nie," as I silently rehearsed the tenor to her soprano for this evening's operetta. Opening my arms to her in song, proclaiming my *huerto captivato*, while the Norse attacked.

The captive orchard (*huerto*), that is. Have to work on the Spanish. *Bellissimo!* would be better in the meantime. Italian *always* works.

"Well, I've been blessed, although I didn't realize I had any ability until my mom tried to teach me piano. That didn't get very far, so we tried voice. For the last few years I've been fortunate to study with a classical teacher at the University, though I like other music too. Up here that means Country & Western. Nothing wrong dancing to a cowboy band with the right cowboy."

"May I get you something to drink?"

"Sure, I'll have what you're having. I'd like to go in and say hello to the Francks."

After some commotion off stage, we were back on the porch set. Beginning of the next scene. The one in which Steph-a-nie misunderstands my motives? Completely understands them?

Thinking about a rewrite of, "I knew a girl who bent her knee that way ... ," her Steph-a-knee.

We're back. "Dave tells me you graduated from MSU and work there." Got a resume handy, with your address and phone number on it? Family pictures? Want to share any secrets in an operatic aside? Guess not, feeling the stage empty, farmers walk sadly toward the fields, Steph-a-nie into the manor house with her basket of flowers, deep in thought. Vicarious Maximus, on steed, in flight toward the sea, pursued by the Norsemen. The orchard seemingly lost forever.

"Yes, I've been with the University Museum for a couple of years. Opportunities for anthropologists are almost nonexistent in Montana, regardless of how capable, so I'm thankful for the job, even if it's kind of menial. Living here, I can still help out at the ranch. I'm planning on moving to Billings soon, when some things are settled. How about you?"

I didn't like the sound of that—when some things are settled. Back to the here and now, I was sledding down the face of a concrete spillway, wishing for anything to relieve the sparking screech of steel runners, wondering how deep the water is beneath the cracking ice that had my name carved in it a few minutes ago, apparently still does, now even thinner.

"Well, I'm certainly not an anthropologist, although I am very interested in the cultures of the Four Corners—Anasazi, Pueblo, Navajo."

Drop a few Black Mesa Basketmaker II references. Can't hurt.

"I love the area, the people, the arts and crafts. I've been to the Maxwell Museum of Anthropology in Albuquerque. No relation. It's quite good. Right now I'm in the MFA program down at Laramie, starting my second year in September, majoring in music performance, minor in photography. Enjoying the work and the town."

"You're older than the typical MFA." Meaning: when you finish, a prospective high school music or art teacher, ancient the first day you walk in the door.

The brakes locked up and I went into a skid, fascinated by the thousand foot dropoff. Was that a drum solo or thunder approaching on the soundtrack? Define yourself! You are who you say you are! When impending experience is our own worst fear, by definition, we're headed for trouble.

"Older. Now there's a pivotal term in the music business. I didn't want to live in California full time anymore, and the MFA was a good excuse to drop out and focus on sharpening my keyboard skills."

Not exactly the bronzed persona I was looking for, I thought as the lengthening pause spurred me hard. I could relate to what the horse must feel. A little love prodding in the ribs by sharp stainless.

A couple of kids walked along the sidewalk in front of the house and looked at us.

"Hi, girls," Stephanie said. "Hi," they both replied, then turned into the driveway two doors down.

"Cute kids," I remarked, thinking how much I really liked the way Stephanie said "hi" to the girls, full of warmth.

"You like kids?" she asked.

Always an important question in a conversation with a young, unmarried woman. Careful, this will count heavily toward whether you get by today's quiz, be crucial to your final grade. Worse, there's no answer which is always right. Either way, you can pass or fail.

"Yes." If only our hearts could speak, share what was really in them.

Then it might be a very short night.

"I haven't been thinking in those terms lately, though. Wrapped up in too many things. But the time will come, maybe sooner than I think. I wonder why I just said that?"

Looking at Stephanie, I saw a blankness momentarily descend over her face, again, almost imperceptibly. Not knowing her, I couldn't ask, "what was that all about?" You asked, I thought … . Could my reply have been a total throwaway, even if it wasn't intended to be? Thinking back, it may be the most accurate statement I've made to her thus far. Is that what I'm doing, making statements? I'm in big trouble here. Can we start this over … where she drives up in her BMW, we immediately hit it off, agree on the veneers, Mexican glass, and placemats? Where I have no past to hurt me?

Seeking refuge in the visible excitement of the lawn, I took a sip of my drink. While doing so, out of the corner of my eye, I saw Stephanie considering me. Not just glancing at my anti-disco shirt, sizing me up. Calculating how fast I could draw? Wondering why I couldn't express the simplest, coherent thought? I kept sipping, trying to look reflective, instead only boring a hole in the street.

I didn't know what her discreet look meant, if anything.

Dave and Amy came out onto the porch.

"Pretty quiet out here," Dave observed. "What are you two talking about?"

Turning to look directly at Stephanie, I replied, "kids." She looked back at me without flinching. I didn't think her eyes were saying, "drop dead." Good move. One for me. A certain maybe.

I broke off the *opéra bouffe*, selected a #1 wood, hammered a drive right down the middle of the fairway, replaced the club in the bag, started walking, and with impressive nonchalance asked, "What's for dinner, Amy?"

"You were just in the kitchen. Have you become more distracted lately, noticed any other behavioral differences, changed your medication? *You're* talking about kids? Already?" If you only knew.

"I must have had my mind on other things in the kitchen. Complex philosophical arguments. Refrigerator magnets, potholders." Recovering well, if I do say so myself.

"Generally obtuse, but takes orders well, runs errands, and is generous. Now that I think of it, we need you to visit more often, Craig," Amy teased.

"So why did you invite me to dinner again, Amy?" asked Stephanie. Recharging, maybe with a pointed vengeance. Leading question, a setup to unmask my motives.

Aggressive defense, I can feel it. Steel Curtain. Just let me inbound the ball, okay? So *I* can control the tempo. Wrong game.

"Because Craig talked Amy into it," Dave replied. "I'd just as soon he hit the road and get that thing out of the driveway, but you can only make so many suggestions. Consider this his going away banquet." Let's have dinner first, then we'll run over you with the truck. The only banquets I could think of were in dark castles a long way from here, plotted celebrations eclipsed by tragedy. *Opéras tragique.*

"Your name's Dave, honey, *mine's* Amy. Actually, yesterday we were talking about your singing, and thought it would be nice to have a fourth for dinner, before Craig leaves town the day after tomorrow. If he's leaving town, that is."

Seizing the opportunity, Dave helped out, "and why did you accept the invitation, Stephanie, aside from Amy's excellent cooking?"

"I'll admit to some curiosity," she replied forthrightly, though her tone also said, "but that's all I'll ever admit." Except to another woman. They tell everything then. Everything.

"Anyone curious about my exciting day at the Bridget Bowl, maybe you, Miss, didn't quite get your last name—Taylor, Twhyler, Twirler was it? I assume you're familiar with the locale?"

"Oh, you're going to tell us all about it, Mr. Out of State Plates?" Stephanie replied, easing down the stick for another Spitfire gunnery run, "and by the way, it's the *Bridger* Bowl and *Tyler*, as in Texas, or Anne Tyler the author."

Silence. The look on her face says she's really kidding, right? Could this be a handhold in the sheer wall of adverse conversation, or was I watching a piton slipping, coming free of a mistrusted crack?

"I was all ready to poetically recount the composition of clouds clearing from sawtooth ridges, willows along the river swaying in the breeze, about art, about being alive. And I thought you were shy. Seems like I just got sideswiped by a lone star of one kind or another ... ."

"One subject at a time. Who said I was shy?" Stephanie pretended to demand. Pretend can be good. Let's see you do it more often now.

"Must be another of Craig's questionable assumptions. The one about the quietly worshipful young woman singing in church. There are others we've heard, but left unacknowledged. Number no longer in service, if you get my meaning." Amy wasn't letting go. The girls were ganging up on me.

"Isn't dinner ready?" I pleaded.

"Not yet, Mr. Out of State Plates," Amy said, keeping the pressure on. "Hey, I like that, Stephanie. How about 'Plates' for short?"

"Dave, help me out here."

"Yeah, I've been waiting for weeks to show Plates my new orbital sander. A thing only guys would understand ... ."

"Love to see it, Dave. Your power tools are really something else."

It's hard to spaceout and carry on a lucid conversation at the same time. It felt like I was slipping back into that and needed a rest. Tools would help for the moment. Tools as interpersonal avoidance, multi-measure rests.

Wisemen that we are, Dave and I escaped to the garage and adored the tools before camelling back in the house for a delicious meal. Home cooking. Good thing dinner was excellent—I was definitely not controlling the local environment. What the heck, just enjoy it.

After dinner, we returned to the porch for coffee. I thought about the Anne Tyler reference. *Earthly Possessions*—hadn't I read that? The one about a woman leaving her husband, getting out of town, really for the first time, with a bank robber? Quirky characters. Finding ways to cope with the tragedies of very local lives. Was that a metaphor for Stephanie's life? This was Bozeman after all, not Seattle. And your point is? Sketching more linear strategies for survival. Liquid strategies? Those are certainly familiar to me.

Take it from this rugged specimen, Stephanie, you just need the right man with the right tools. A quirky man with a point of view *mélondramatique*. Tonight, without question, I meet the description of, and am in fact, that man.

"This is good coffee Amy," Stephanie remarked as she sipped the french roast, thwarting me with the very coffee I brought.

"Secret sources. Not local, smuggled into Montana, thanks to Craig, if the truth be told."

"Thank you," Stephanie said looking at me.

"Huh?" I asked, distracted.

"That's twice tonight you've been somewhere over the rainbow, Craig."

Third time's the charm. Will it be a called third strike? Rainout? Game cancelled because of darkness? Referee stops contest?

"Yeah, sorry. I was thinking about an Anne Tyler book after you mentioned her name."

"Dave, will you help me get the dessert?" Amy asked, "this is getting even stranger, maybe even embarrassing. Oh, I forgot … we're dealing with an *artist*." No slack.

"It's about the art, not about the artist," was the only reply I could think of.

I guess it wouldn't be appropriate to elbow *her* in the ribs, no matter how much in jest. Ha, ha, ha. Slap! Probably going inside to make the call and I won't have a chance anyhow. The Fun Bus will be arriving soon. In tomorrow's *Bozeman Bugle* an article picked up by the wire services: "ESO Star Under Observation in Montana." That part of it would be true. Way under.

"I enjoyed dinner," Stephanie said when they were inside, for the moment steering clear of my tendency to partially disappear from the scene. "The Francks are really nice, a good change for the church. More to the point, not that it's really necessary, I can do the arithmetic. You should know that there is already someone in my life."

"I'm not surprised, Miss Tyler," nearly slipping and calling her Miss Twirler, seeing the cherry licorice ropes of my youth, sequins and batons. Artificial flavor, artificial color. Artificial sequins. A generation raised on irresistibly artificial penny candy, comfortable with continuing the contrivances, wrapping them into an adulthood lost in repeat glitter falling from the glue that didn't hold on that sign in the Holiday Inn lobby, around the picture taken too many years ago of a passé lounge act, yet one whose small, devoted following of those baton-misses could not let go. A generation, my generation, still analyzing it. In colors not found in nature. Why do I keep seeing that sign?

Better let go of that one, Mr. Max-Swell, I imagined her thinking. Finally getting the name right, with the slippery "Sw". Let go of what? All I said was, "I'm not surprised … ."

Coincidentally, the expression, "let go." Was that the message pervading this evening? Let go of what? The wheel, trapeze, insulated tumbler in my hand? Inhibitions? So many questions. Not a good one to be found.

"I liked your singing yesterday, which is to say, I really liked it. Beside the fact that you are, how should I say, an interesting rancherette from the perspective of this Orange County, California, overdocumented alien," someone in your life or not, "I'm intrigued about the possibility of a musical collaboration." Now I'm going to show you how serious I can be. Nah, actually see if you read between the lines. Music is only music. You're something else entirely, Steph-a-nie.

"New music. Contemporary, but with a positive message, reaching people, younger people. It's coming and going to be important. I've just scratched the surface, but it's exciting." So there. Might have been a little heavy on the marketing.

"I've got to get back to Laramie the day after tomorrow. If I can assist in any way as you consider work, location, and, most importantly, as a matter of narrow self-interest, music, please call." Lookin' forward to that possibility, fer sher. Shopping breaks driving beneath the palms on Sunset, the lions much healthier and assured now after dental work and combing of the manes, together at the Galleria, my Gallatin Valley Girl fully on board. Far out! Hook up with you there. Fer sher!

Listening intently and quietly she could have said, "what you're really talking about is Christian music. You might want to become a Christian first. It's about the message, not the market." Instead of feedback, there was only silence. Stephanie looked at me, then away when I returned the gaze. Perhaps too directly for comfort.

"At the time you lost your memory, what were you thinking? It's important," I imagined her asking.

Nothing to lose now by being quiet. Maybe she was relaxed, fully in control. Asserting as she looked away, "you're not going to pull me in with your eyes on high beam."

Amy and Dave came back with the dessert. Somebody knew how to cook.

"Stephanie, tell Craig about the opera this spring."

"Let me guess, you just got cable TV in Bozeman."

"Excuse me, try *La Traviata*. Verdi, live at the Intermountain Opera. With a New York producer, New York costumes, and baritone with the Met who sang Germont. *Opera News* even covered it. Next year we're doing *The Barber of Seville*."

"My humblest apology for underestimating the interest in high register, ripsnorting range *macédoine* drama on the range."

"Arrogant, isn't he?" Amy asked, "not that any of us have a clue what he said."

"I was thinking of a few words of my own." Stephanie quipped, as if to mean, "you want to be ridiculous, go ahead."

"Dave, did I leave that orbital sander running?" Only a shaking head. No escape, fella.

We finished the dessert and coffee.

"I've got a better idea, though it doesn't involve tools. Craig, let's stroll over to the church for a little while," Dave suggested. "It's still early, and we'd love to hear you play some more. Can we talk you into it?"

"Yes. We can do that. It really is a nice summer evening, almost Italianate." I'll work on talking myself into it on the way over.

"Want to come along, Stephanie?"

"Sure."

"Did I hear Italian? Remember, Craig, we're in Montana. Keep it local for Dave and I," Amy needled.

At the church, the record concerning local culture having been set straight, Dave switched on the lights and opened a couple of windows to let in the cooler night air.

"Ladies and gentleman, I'll play from Bach's *French Suites*," I said, closing my eyes to reach the space where I needed to be. No. 5, actually. I had listened to it for months in Laramie, practiced it day and night. About 18 minutes in six movements. I can play this music. I love this music.

The images it evokes for me. A slim girl with her violin standing beside the piano, above the cafe. My home now, maybe for her too. Dressed in black. A mesmerizing mix of athletic, contemporary, and traditional. Japanese? *Bináá 'ádaałts 'ózí diné é*, slender eyes.

"I need to be with my people ... ," Yumiko began as I alternately looked into her eyes, watched the roundness of her lips as she breathily pronounced the words, rollingly accented, softly paused, then resumed. Only one of so many things that made her astonishing, heartbreaking. Incredibly desirable. That flowing hair on the pillow beside mine, both of us in sleep, window open, as now. Dreams within dreams, of Jackie in the Hotel Hershey. Dreams experienced with Cathy in Ft. Collins, Sheridan, later in that very space above the cafe. Grace notes.

Yumiko wasn't talking about leaving, breaking off, rather describing the sympathetic cultural sustenance she needed to be nourished, to thrive. She could not live in ethnic solitary, as a singletree, *'atł 'eeyah dah sinilí*. The "maybe for her too" about my home didn't come up.

Or was the slender one *Zitkala-Ša*, Red Bird? A woman seeming to time-lessly exist once in a photograph, now in my mind. So halting that I wrote down the Smithsonian archive negative number. Easy to remember, impossible to forget. With the lightest push, so easy to fall into obsession. Another story, trains home a half-century before. In this space-time, real as Yumiko. Another violinist.

To have known her. The last flourish of the concerto, eyes flashing in triumph, young, alive, deep, rebellious in her soul. Had I been living then, known her? How many pictures does it take to bring you back, Red Bird? How long for me to be released?

Sometimes in this detached wandering, in exile from my heart, obsession is all I have. Built upon stories, pictures, imagination. Rows of marble. Carlisle. You walked upon that very ground. All true.

"Was she happy when she died?" they might ask, not about the dead, but for their own reassurance, the living. As if that mattered. Eleven years before I was born, she lay in a new grave. The beautiful young Nakota (Yankton Sioux) of that picture. Decades later. 1938.

Wait a minute. Rebellious in her soul? How could I know that? Imputed from hearsay. I'm describing what I want her to be, starting with the stereo-type, Indian Princess, again, processed and embellished. Such is an empty man's lot.

Never having known or before knowing her, who doesn't desire a woman to be more than she is or might ever be? We want the mustang, wild creature never entirely subdued. Alternatively, the serene Japanese version, quietly gazing on the samurai in his chivalric dance unto death, *bushido*. The romance of historical fabrication. "She is ... ," I said as I thought upon poetry, defaulted to warm places, defined *Zitkala-Ša* as I would have her, when I would want her, to my own needs.

Until I came across something she had written to me:

> Today the Indian is pressed almost to the farther sea. Does that sea symbolize his death? Does the narrow territory still left to him typify the last brief day before his place on Earth "Shall know him no more forever?" Ziktaka-Ša, 1896.

I live there. In Laguna. Beach, not Pueblo.

Star Barn, star quilts. Patterns, conscious order of the generations; an instant later, the disorder of the celestial sky, *yá 'qqsh*.

Meet the grandfathers and grandmothers. Meet yourself. From birth, the same. Flow of the Circle.

Annie: "I will always be here. I will remember who I am."

I will not always be who we have been. Fierce eyes. Waves of the wind in vast buffalo grasslands. Help me … I'm slipping away, pulled by The Singing Sky. Not knowing who I am, which are my people, what I'm saying.

"*Craig?* You there?" Dave was talking to me. I was seated on a piano stool.

"What?"

"You've been sitting there for a couple of minutes, as if in a trance."

"Just thinking of a few things. Sorry. What was I going to play again?"

"One of the French Suites, you said."

"I'm … , yes, going to play No. 5, followed by a short, delightful Scarlatti Sonata."

Got it all together now. Ready to rumble. Ready to roll. Stephanie must have been impressed. Are the spaceouts back? Have to explain this away as artistic preoccupation, though without any license evident whatsoever.

Never mind. Time to disappear again, into the music.

There was still a lot of mileage left in the key of G. I did indeed enter another dreamworld, the very articulate, shifting, and personal one defined by Bach's music.

More clouds. Domenico Scarlatti's *Sonata in B Minor, K.27*. Perhaps more romantically contemplative than any other music from that era I've heard. Communicating directly to *me*, posing questions and making entreaties everytime I play it, the soft, hopeful questions and arguments of new love. Unusually constructed. This guy was born in 1685. Amazing. That's what it is. There's nothing more to say.

The final key release, then restful silence, profound as those cloud and pillow dreams, rolled vowels, memories of truth. Tears in my eyes.

"Lord, thank you for this time together, for the truly magnificent music with which you have blessed us," Dave offered quietly.

We walked back to the Francks' without speaking. Dave had his arm around Amy, sharing something special. I wished for the same. Maybe again someday.

Stephanie thanked the Francks. I went out with her to the truck in the driveway.

My gaffes aside, it had been a wonderful evening, like that one two years ago. Stephanie Tyler was beautiful. A woman whose simple presence was pure romance.

"Here's my card with telephone numbers in Laramie and Laguna Beach. If I'm not around, just leave a message at the Cafe Whyoming in downtown Laramie. They'll know how to get in touch with me. Thanks for coming to dinner tonight, Stephanie Tyler."

"Unusual, but I enjoyed it," she said looking right at me again, like earlier on the porch. "Goodnight," Stephanie said in her assured, classical singer's voice. Hoping that she'd linger, even as she started the truck and drove away. Engine sounded strong.

The Francks waved goodbye. We sat on the porch for a few minutes talking, until they went inside for the night.

Feet up on the railing, I thought that this was part of what I wanted. In Laramie, I lived one flight up. I had the cafe, but not the kids a couple of doors down, not the porch with a rocker or trees in the front yard. I wanted to belong. In my heart I wanted the woman. I wanted the kids. If I live that long. I really wonder sometimes. A feeling.

Stephanie Tyler, a cowgirl singing Verdi in an opera. Unbelievable. That'll get my attention any day. What had I thought—I'd like to hang out with friends who say, "I think I'll sing the Schumann?" Stephanie wants to sing *Lieder*. That requires accompaniment. I'd like to audition for the part.

She had mentioned staying out at the ranch tonight, instead of in town at her apartment. That meant a half hour trip on a two lane road heading toward the mountains, in Montana at a speed "reasonable and proper." I thought of Steph-a-nie, dashboard aglow. Was she trying to process the evening, or easily leaving it behind, unwinding, just listening to the radio as the straight 6 lumbered on?

Stephanie *was* driving and wondering—about the future, the ranch, a stranger on the scene, one who had lived in the big city, been places, seen things, could play piano way beyond very well, didn't talk much about himself for a rock 'n roll star, ex-star that is, might like me at least a little bit, enjoyed being with the Francks, who are very in-tune, very nice.

Accomplished, talented … introspective. Those are the words I'm looking for. When he's introspective, he disappears, gone into some kind of space, whatever's going on in there. A lot happening behind those eyes. Creative. Very creative. The sidetrips would take some getting used to. Did I see tears? I wonder, is there hurt not so deep? I can relate to that. Joy. Definitely.

When he looked at me a couple of times, his eyes spoke to mine. Deeply, intensely. Moving like the clouds he mentioned above Bridger this afternoon.

And that Scarlatti. Still resounding in my head. I have never heard anyone play like that. And the music, it was like … the perfect song … I wonder if he knows that?

Yes, he does. He was speaking to me through it.

While he jokes and flirts, he communicates everything important, if you're paying attention … strengths and, well, weakness is not the right word … capacity to love?

Vulnerability. Not afraid to show it. And when he said that about children … that look … he meant it, too … looking right into me, into my heart with that one.

He's a formidable person, alright.

And what did Craig Maxwell mean by "new music?" Do I really want to move to Billings? Will I like my new job? It won't be about music.

In Bozeman or Billings, my life will never be enough about music.

If it was only as simple as living happily ever after with someone like Craig Maxwell. With anyone.

50

It wasn't the baling wire

Main Street, always another Main Street. Last full day in Bozeman before the road again. While walking down this Main Street, late in the afternoon, I saw Stephanie pull her truck into a parking space. *Nich´ ijí ´oo´ áát. Bi´ deeshłíiłii shił bééhozin.* This is your lucky day. I *know* what to do.

When she got out, I offered a "surprised to see you" and asked her to join me for coffee and pie at The Bakery. She seemed aloof, perhaps a moment too slow in saying no, instead settled for a polite, "oh alright." Needing to do an errand first, Stephanie said she'd be back in a few minutes. I went inside, thinking how unpredictable women are. Last night though conveying "forget it" in so many words, she was friendly. Remarkably friendly for being "taken", to my thinking. Today, she's distant, reluctant. Conclusion: regardless of a few possible high points, last night had been a wisecracked disaster.

Waiting for Stephanie, I thought about the major spaceout into which I had slipped, much deeper and more distant than other recent, more routine conversational asides. The former, being fullblown digression, completely occupies my mind, to the extent that I am in another place. In contrast, the asides are concurrent contemplation of the subject at hand, with the frequency unchanged. Despite the energetic variations in alternate keys, time signatures, and tempos, I'm still able to carry on the conversation amid rapidly dropping barometric pressures, wildly fluctuating voltages, and drops in pH sometimes so extreme they can etch concrete.

Somebody says something and it triggers a stream of imagery, possibilities, manipulations. Similarly, I'll activate a connection to a vivid observation or memory. Though everyone with a thought life does this, maybe my box of images is a little closer up the scale to hypermnesia. It's creative, albeit from time to time in ways perceived to be rude; and tiring, because imagining and voicing the stream are so self-centeredly energy intensive. The other person, though physically present, is not on the same wavelength; hence, I realize I'm using a fire hose to fill the space between us with the abstract color of thoughts, fragments, quips, associations, outlines, imprints, and exotic vapors. A one man job, usually difficult to resist.

Cafe Whyoming

The snap of the screen door restored my attention as Stephanie entered The Bakery. I really liked the sound of her name, everything I saw coming over to the table after she found me with a glance around the room.

Lookin' even better in jeans and boots than she did 10 minutes ago—authentically, Big Sky Cowgirl. Had she changed her outfit or did I need new glasses? Rising to greet her, I gently pushed in the chair as she sat down. I couldn't believe that wasn't a standard gesture around here, but she looked at me in kind of a strange way, one I couldn't read, accompanied by what looked to be the most delicate of blushes. Should I be wearing a kerchief or bolo tie? Both?

For a silent moment, not knowing what to say, I just looked at her. Stephanie had accelerated from "pretty in a Montana way" to "really good looking", now to "outright beautiful". The bar had been set high, and she was clear, way over. The final round on a very short card? I was aware of my heart beating more strongly. She seemed a little nervous now too. Maybe I upset her.

"Your voice. I was thinking about how well you sing." How beautiful you are, how much I'd like to get to know you. Driving over to your place in the evenings, seeing you on the porch waiting for me. If you've got a porch. Even better, being at our place, not having to drive there.

Quiet. This wasn't a good idea. Should have left my fantasy on the real porch last night. I could see her thinking, "get the picture ... remember what I told you? If I had been a little quicker, I wouldn't be here going through this."

"Didja get the baling wire you needed for the combine, or was this bronc bustin' day? There a trace of stiffness in your gait?"

She waited for another moment, maybe thought what the heck, then threw it back. "Baling wire wouldn't do much good. Baling wire is for a baler. You'd be trouble on a ranch."

Nothing about the gait. Guess I'm the stiff.

"Yeah, I've been *that* before." South of Sheridan, actually. We won't go into it now. "So tell me more about your job prospects in Billings, archaeologically speaking."

"You could listen more carefully. Anthropology is the word I used last night, among other things said."

"Okay then, anthropologically speaking. Pretend you're explaining it to me in German, Ginevra."

"Ginevra?"

"From *Ariodante*, the Handel opera. One of the tapes I play while travelling. Here, let me sing the dramatic aria ... ."

"You would, wouldn't you?"

"Actually, the nemesis, *Ariodante*, though the male dramatic lead, is sung by a soprano. 'Fascinating' is about the only word I can come up with to describe it, so no, I wouldn't actually. Before trying to explain Handel, you were talking about employment ... ."

"You tend to go off on tangents. Frequently. Did you know that?"

"I suppose so, but right now, the question on the table is a coherent one, pertaining to your job prospects ... in anthropology."

"Not much to talk about. Up here in Montana unless you can: one, relate it to gas, oil, or mining; and two, have connections; then three, there are no jobs. The way it works is, 'we want to rip up this land, strip mine, flood, or ruin it in some other way, and need you to recover fragments of antiquity before they're irretrievably lost in the inarguable pursuit of commerce.' Anthro is an interesting field, but of little use without a PhD and a grant or fellowship. I don't see going the PhD route; a master's degree is the end of the line for me. As to working in Billings, I'm finally getting out of town, for a little more money."

"I would think anthropology, paleontology, archaeology, to be a challenge for a Christian woman in an occupational sector rife with hard rock evolutionists. Do you encounter a lot of conflict?"

"I would if I let it happen. I don't have a PhD, so nobody listens to me anyway. Evolution only addresses adaptation, not origin or creation. The "evolution explains everything" argument fundamentally breaks down on that, and there are plenty of fossil record discontinuities as well. And how about consciousness? How did that evolve? So many problems with their theory. If all else fails, they just say that God is irrelevant, or water it down with some kind of flimsy cosmology. In my heart and soul, I know differently."

Cosmoacentricity. Universal confusion 'cause Mo's not centered. That explains it for me.

"Regardless of what I said last night about scholarly endeavors oriented toward taking apart the pit dweller and basketmaker eras and coming up with 'conclusions', overall I'm rather skeptical about the meaningfulness of anthropology and ethnology. Seems to me like a lot of tenuous 'theoretical fabrication' on the basis of fragmentary material evidence advanced by the ethnoapproximatists and anthroconjecturists. Myself, I guess I'm a semi-orthorelativist." Thinking at an angle. On an analytical incline. Don't ask me to explain.

"I wonder, should I try to talk *you* out of *your* conclusions on the basis of, what evidence was that *you* had again?"

"I was just playing. See if you'd take the gambit."

"How did I know that?" Stephanie said laughing a little. Good girl, let's see more of that. "Wasn't too obvious or anything." 10 of 13 from the floor, 5 of 6 from the line. A shooter.

"I'm going back to your voice. It's so dynamic … expressive. The rest of the picture is pretty dynamic, too."

"There you go, flirting in the bakery with a cowgirl. I knew I should have slipped into town under cover of darkness for that baling wire. By the way, those bracelets are pretty interesting. Mmmm, let me think … Hopi?"

"That's right on both accounts. Extra-tribal reinforcement. I was wearing them last night."

"I didn't notice. Not too many cowpokes wear bracelets around here. Might get you into a scuffle on the wrong side of the street. And the second account is … ?"

"The part about flirting. Truer words were never spoken."

"The man who wins me will have to … let me think now … ride into this bakery 'cause his horse likes the big cinnamon rolls."

"I've already been planning it. Let me show you in my journal here." Along with other stuff. That quote of Ziktala-Ša for starters. Interestingly worded, by the way, "… the man who (eventually) wins me," I thought leafing through the pages.

"What or who is Zitkala-Ša?" she might inquire, "a chief, medicine man, town in Mexico?" What or who would be my answer? In a perfect world … with the arguments layed end to end … I'd really like to go out with you, but am obsessed with this picture … ?

"What?" Stephanie asked.

"Here it is. *Bááh łikani náhineests'ee'ígíí.* Cinnamon rolls in Navajo. One of my survival phrases. Impressed?"

"I am impressed, though strangely."

"Here's another one. *´Ahéédahooszįįd.* They became known to each other."

"That could be taken the wrong way."

"It's the inflection which determines whether you get a disingenuous smile or knowing slap."

"You usin' that RV to check on any special crop? Here in the banana belt we hear all kinds of stories about greenhouses shielded from prying eyes by the Crazies."

"I'm taking the Fifth."

"I don't doubt it."

So we made small talk until it was time for her to go. I didn't want that to happen, but was powerless to affect it. At least her mood had softened to friendly deprecation.

"Thanks for keeping me company. As you can probably tell, I've got a weakness for pie and coffee. Have to keep running to burn all the calories." Talking nonsense too.

"Take care of that voice, and seriously, please consider my proposal to get together. I've got some material in mind which I think would fit well. And a *Te Deum* always works wonders."

"Probably a long shot, but thanks anyway. Maybe I'll see you again sometime in church."

I didn't want her to leave. Ever. I couldn't just walk away without trying.

"Stephanie. I don't want this to be goodbye."

She didn't seem to be surprised, go blank, swallow hard, or get up and leave without another word.

"Craig, I'm not going to encourage you. As I mentioned last night, there's someone else. I'm sorry."

She said that, glancing down for a moment, before looking right at me, surprising in her directness. The photojournalist shooting black & white. High contrast. Is that what Stephanie was doing, recording only the visible image, or was there another dimension involved? An exposure with the most expressive of cameras, her mind, more than capable of rendering pictures while attaching emotion?

Looking at her, I saw into eyes clear and alive, yet sad. There was something untold, more to it. I thought I saw her eyes start to get watery, then she bit her lip and it was gone. Stephanie wasn't going to encourage me. I accepted that, but wouldn't believe there was no chance for me. Unfortunately, I have always had difficulty reconciling what I see with reality, even more so my emotions. Who knows what any of it meant?

"I really have to go now, Craig. Goodbye."

"Bye, Stephanie."

After she left, I asked the waitress to warm up my coffee, turning over in my mind everything I knew about this woman, all that I had sensed. Stephanie Tyler. A dynamic package indeed. As with Cathy, I wondered about where she was headed. One main difference was evident. While Cathy wanted to see the world working on her career, Stephanie had a different rudder. One of faith. A different inner strength. That's what made her really interesting to me. Dynamic package? Am I buying locking pliers here? A complete assortment? Pro set for any job?

How would I meet the woman of my dreams if this was a new play? What dreams would those be? If it was possible for Stephanie and me to get together, how would the play be written to get us there? Would she allude to "another" at dinner, then have coffee with me the next day? "Oh that," she might say, as if to imply it was nothing. There are "nothing" which can actually mean "anything"; and real nothing, meaning zero. Other people seem to do better than I do about nothing.

A cowgirl. What is a cowgirl? Cathy and Stephanie. Wyoming-Montana ranch girls. They define it. A cowgirl is, most importantly, about loving horses. Believing, loving, and living the Big Sky, Big Open as a way of life. Work that always needs to be done. Bucked off or kicked in the shins, despite a fancy silver horncap and handmade boots. Rodeo buckles, clean hats for town, work hats spotted by dirty rain, mud, and sweat. Roping and riding, cutting cattle. The land, family, and that horse. Freedom.

Cathy wouldn't be able to live indefinitely without being a cowgirl again. She might be in Northern California, but would have to get back to a ranch, with the horses, raising her own sons and daughters.

Stephanie had that same blood, riding spirit ever since she could remember. Though loving music, she needed the balance of being on the land. Witness and party to creating life, bearing young, living fully, and growing old, edging toward the renewal of death with no regrets.

She gave me neither a telephone number nor address, and there had been that moment when she looked to be on the edge of tears. Her eyes looked that way to me, anyway. Why? Choked up by the beauty of the Navajo language? A movement andante mysterioso.

For now, *Stephanie and Me* would be a play in only my mind, of my writing. To get beyond that would take either some kind of Whyomin' magic or divine intervention. I'd carry around the play until it had a happy ending, faded away, or was rewritten with another captivating lead. No play at all simply was not an option.

Tomorrow's dawn would bring a new "for now". What would I do about Stephanie? Keep thinking how beautiful she is as I drive away to Laramie? I've done that before.

C'Est La Vie—Pis 'kun. That's what the highway sign said, with an arrow pointing over the hill. That meant me. Another shaggy-mane running with the herd, more than susceptible to being lured off the cliff by all that is the 20th century. *Pis 'kun*, buffalo jump.

51

The block will never be the same

I realized I had really needed the relaxing visit with the Francks. Real friends—I didn't have many. And then there was the surprise of Stephanie. Better than the Rockies, the Crazies, Spanish Peaks, Spanish Fork, Purple Sage, Golden Coors. The best draw so far for this man to move aggressively into the Montana market. Were things falling into place? The memory of her was warm, comfortable as a cookout under the eucalyptus trees in Laguna on a summer evening. Tans and sunbleached Hawaiian shirts all around. Joni before Mingus.

Get real. Nice time, nice try, but my chances with her seemed about as close to blooming as the damp ring under a flower pot on the patio.

Returning to the Francks', I joined them for a late dinner, talking about all kinds of things, present and future. After that I tinkered around in the GMC getting ready to roll in the morning, planning to take I-90 east to Billings and northern Wyoming, then I-25 down to Casper before picking up 487.

I slept well, as if being refreshed for both the trip to Laramie, and the rest of the summer. Dreaming, I was in stables, sunlight streaming through the window, dust floating, sparkling like that day in Tucson. There was the smell of straw and freshly saddle-soaped tack. Kat looked at me, smiled, and was gone when I heard Cathy say, "I know you love me, as much as you can," then lead her horse outside, mount, and ride away while I could do nothing more than watch, unable to speak.

Turning around, through the window I saw Stephanie walk by, hearing a voice speak to me: "If truly you love, seek her and one day you will be together." I reached out, touching only glass.

Upon awakening, I remembered the dreams, wondering again if things might be falling into place. With that thought, I decided to stop at the Museum on the way out of town, to try to see Stephanie.

Asking a girl who evidently was a graduate-intern to find Stephanie, I saw her look at my bracelets, do a double take, and run it all through the memory bank. Identified. In a couple of minutes, Stephanie came out of a door from the back, wearing a lab smock, while the other girl lurked nearby, eyes widening, not wanting to miss a word. Maybe Stephanie had asked her to hang around?

"Hi, Stephanie," I started, "please don't get mad at me for stopping by to see you before leaving town today."

"I'm flattered by your attention, but there's nothing more to say, other than you haven't been listening." No longer ambivalent or reluctant. Intransigent.

"I have been listening. But that's different from accepting. What I've seen in your eyes is telling me not to give up." Going way out here, talking about her eyes and what's in them, in "public".

"I can't explain why, but I have this strong feeling, belief actually, that I've seen you before. I had an accident which caused a temporary loss of memory ... maybe the answer is in there. And last night, I had a dream about the future.

There's something going on between us. I *know* that, and don't want to just walk away without talking to you about it."

"Nothing has gone on between us other than a couple of chance meetings, and dinner at the Francks'. I haven't changed my plans because of those. I'm going to Billings. Please let me do that. By myself."

"... Stephanie, my offer stands about music, anything actually ... you've got my number. I hope things change or work out to enable that ... ."

"I'm in the middle of a restoration project and need to get back now. I'm sorry. Goodbye, Craig."

And then *I* was gone.

There was an espresso place in old downtown Livingston where I stopped for a Road Capp, to shake my head a few more times about the conversation with Stephanie, what little of it there had been; and to call Bob and Beth, let them know I was on my way. No answer. Strange. Maybe a phone problem. Two hours later I tried again from Billings, but still couldn't get through. Not a good sign. Finally, I dialed their home number, and Bob answered.

"Craig, real bad news. I've been trying to contact you. A fire started in the place next door early Sunday morning. Three buildings were totalled, including the Cafe. I've been in touch with the insurance people and financially it'll be okay, but your place upstairs, all we worked for is gone. The only part that remains is the garage out back. Everything stored in there made it."

"Was anybody hurt?"

"No, everybody's safe."

"Okay, Bob, I'm already on the way, and will drive through."

Hanging up the phone, I felt like I had been run over by that truck after dinner. Why were these things happening to me? Just when it looked like I was in a groove. While Stephanie was singing Sunday morning, the firemen were hosing down what used to be the Whyomin'.

Dave was at home when I called him.

"Dave, there was a fire. The Cafe's gone. Please let Stephanie know, if you happen to see her."

"I'll pray for your safe return to Laramie, and the strength to get you through this. May God bless you, Craig."

"Thanks Dave. I'll call you later in the week, when I have more information."

It was a complete loss—building, cafe, upstairs, piano and other instruments. The bracelet I gave to Emily, had engraved with my profession of love after her death, gone. In the ashes was the Mimbres pot I had brought to Laramie. A very expensive piece, fascinating in design, impressive in craftmanship, antiquity. It had survived 800 years in the ground outside Silver City, New Mexico, brought back from the earth once already, only to be destroyed by the fire. Leave it alone, let it go to the dump with the rest of the rubble. I kicked a charred board over what was left of the pot. In the future archaeologists could puzzle over how it got from a burial pit outside Silver City, New Mexico, all the way up here. That could be the message, I thought with a shiver, it shouldn't have been removed from the ground in the first place.

Our business records were kept by the accountant, and many of my possessions were back in Laguna, so at least I wasn't totally wiped out. And I still had the GMC with its music gear and bikes in the trailer.

Emmett was downcast. I stayed at his house for a couple of days, arranging for demolition of what was left of the building and closing out the business. I wanted to get it all over with quickly, leave town. Pennsylvania might be far enough. At some point I would have to return to get the Land Cruiser and stuff out of the garage, but that could wait.

"Hello, Stephanie? This is Dave Franck. Craig Maxwell asked me to convey a message to you, and I think it would be better done in person. Could I ask you to please stop by for a few minutes? Amy and I will be here all evening."

I kept on the road, I-80 headed east. Thinking about Laramie, Bozeman, Stephanie. Depressed on all accounts. Not down, depressed. Wondering if I was living Truffaut's film, *The Man Who Loved Women*. A succession of *affaires du coeur* which became an autobiography. Did I have a pretext for each of mine? More subtle pretexts? As in that movie, had tragedy been bearing down on me from the blindside while I was distracted by what fit so well into another pair of cowgirl boots?

I could have been there sleeping when the place went up in flames. How many times could the finality I often felt hanging so heavily over me be evaded? Passing through Grand Island, Nebraska, visited in a storm by Thunder People and Forked Lightning, my mind cleared somewhat and I realized what had been happening was way beyond a simple head trip. It was in the blood, of the past. Warfare in which I had no experience was being waged. Fighting spirits, challenging mythology. Tribal. Tragedies, seductions, obsessions used against, weakening me. Had my mind really cleared, or was I now delusional? What was real?

The fire had taken the pictures off the wall. Three women. Negatives. Letters, journals. References, tangible memories. All irreplaceable. I was being erased. Shaking, I pulled over in heavy rain. I had to find stronger power, heavier medicine, but knew neither where nor how.

And then there was the MFA. The least of the worries. My interest in the second year was severely deflated. The musical skills and discipline I sought had been developed, as witnessed by the coursework and recitals. What was the point in going back?

Finally, the matter of Stephanie. Had we acted our last scene, regardless of what I dreamed, felt, and said before leaving Bozeman? Her message seemed to be mixed, but that could be because I was fighting it. I still didn't think her "goodbye" was final. Stephanie had said, "I'm going to Billings by *myself*," not, "I'm going to be with my fiance ... I love him ... ."

Though not expecting her to react differently, I had needed to go back and give it that one last try. Transacting business of the heart to the point where it's out of my hands. Trying to make the deal which would put me over the top, despite tough odds. Pacing the motel room waiting for the "important call." In the end, at the least, have a final rejection to cherish as fuel for the next fire. I had picked up more from Marco The Meteor than I realized.

Oh yeah, I forgot. No chapter's over until I step on the hoe. It's *my* signature move.

At Des Moines, seeing the sign for I-35 Minneapolis, I thought of Annie, visualizing her face. It had been much too long.

Pacing my travel, I arrived in Cloquet at 3:30 pm, Friday. Annie was surprised when I walked into the Library and gave her a long hug. I needed a woman in my arms, to be in a woman's arms. One part of me wanted her to be Stephanie, another Annie, as never before. Annie was not only a woman, but a presence. A strong, Native presence.

I was searching for a bridge over what had become increasingly rough emotional, cultural, and spiritual waters. A bridge to the love, belonging, faith I sought on the other side. In Annie's arms I found refuge for the moment, though when we parted, I was very aware of my hand on her back, the electricity in simply touching her. It was like we were balanced at the top of a cliff.

On Castle Rock in Bisbee, and this time we'd jump off. She must have felt my shiver, but said nothing about it.

Annie was planning to drive over to Duluth to a folk club near UMD for the evening, and asked if I wanted to go. Nothing to think about there.

I killed time until she got off work, then suggested we ride the Triumph to the city. Annie agreed, and ran home to change. Annie BlueJeans. While waiting I rolled out the bike, then made a cup of coffee. Two years. How many miles? It had gone by as if in an instant, a flicker of candlelight. During all that time, no one had been in the empty seat beside me.

The evening was beautiful, with the exception of an occasional thick cloud of bugs dive bombing at sunset, fitting in as many runs as they could during the short summer. It only took about a half hour to get to Duluth. Annie wanted to stop first at the Food Co-Op for some herbs before it closed. Not exactly the upscale glass, wood, cast iron tree rings, specimen buttonwoods, and decorative patterned walkways to Erewhon at South Coast Village.

As she opened the gallon glass jars to get a half ounce of this and that, I was aware that the place smelled, well, organic. I had a Health Valley Natural Root Beer, asked a few questions, and browsed the books. Mostly they were about alternative lifestyles, spiritual orientations, and diet. Annie went up to the register, manned by a whole grain, whole earth subscriber to holisticism who grinned the whole way through the transaction, saying something that sounded like, "polar, definitely man."

Finding a restaurant was next. She liked Italian food and knew the place to go. It reminded me a little of Angelo's, where Cathy had worked in Laramie, though without the yang. Checkered table cloths, candles in red vinyl-netted glasses, wine goblets stacked in front of a mirror behind the counter, torn romaine. Just being there with her cheered me up.

"I thought you'd order Moose Cacciatore with a side of bog cabbage. I'm disappointed."

"If you had been raised on salted fish, you would be ordering ravioli too."

"Some Fond du Lacker, foregoing rye bread, bratwurst, melted Swiss and a bottle of Leinenkugel dark in favor of pasta pillows."

"This is Minnesota, not Wisconsin, although barely, I'll grant you. Have you been mixin' it up with a fraulein lately?"

"Nope." Not since The Flagstaff Dreams.

"Without a doubt I'm still hyper from sneaking through Sioux country, so close to danger I could hear the drums, barking dogs. Now that I'm here, bring me up to date on Rezlife and what's doing in Cloquet."

Not much seemed to be happening, but everything was probably too subtle for me. After thousands of miles, meeting Stephanie, which I mentioned to Annie, the Whyomin' burning down, life up here seemed to be barely moving. It takes a lot of sap and time to boil down a gallon of maple syrup. I wondered how long it would take for the right guy to cross Annie's path.

"Any handsome warriors around these days who might have a chance of keeping up with you?"

"*Ogichidaa*, warrior. If by that you mean the guy I'm having dinner with tonight, I guess the answer is both yes and no."

"Meaning?"

"Handsome? Definitely. A warrior? Yes. Road warrior, not Rez warrior, so no, too," Annie said, smiling a bit selfconsciously.

Simple and direct about me. Sidestepping the question of someone else. If she wanted to tell me, she would when she wanted to.

"Could you be a little more specific about the handsome part?" I asked, simply teasing, but then my mind began considering other possibilities.

"You got the message." Need me to write it? On birch bark maybe?

Did I mention that her long black hair was unbraided tonight, pulled back over her ears, gathered in back, that she was dark and beautiful, at once both delicate and strong, had a well developed though private sense of humor, was absolutely spellbinding? I was honored to be with Annie LaCroix. The woman. The Native woman.

Primo and secondo dispatched, when the grissini were depleted, flan and gelato declined, we made the short ride to The Hoot. It was a Lighthouse kind of place, cocktail tables again with candles, comfortable, out East Superior toward UMD. Annie knew the headliner, Bennie Nauga, who did a Native comedy-guitar thing, kind of like the Smothers Brothers glued together in mono. He was hilarious and appeared to have a good following since the place was packed.

After his set, she introduced me to Bennie whose name, I gather, was a truncated version of an ancestor's, a 19th century Ojibwe chief. I offered my assessment that he was good enough to make a go of it in the Big City, if that's what he wanted. Bennie said that while the possibility had occurred to him, he belonged in northern Minnesota and didn't want to live elsewhere. No argument from me on that.

There was a piano in the place, and Bennie invited me to play something. Classical? Here, tonight? I ended up playing two selections, the first part of the *French Suites*, No. 1, by Bach; followed by Stanley Cowell's "Equipoise". Shades of the Jazz Spot. Duluth and Laguna, beside big blue water.

I went into the Performance Zone, as usual, after which the audience was warmly appreciative. Annie smiled at me as if a rain shower had just passed through dry land, bringing flowers.

"Miigwech, my brother." Thank you, she said hugging me. "I finally got to hear you play, never imagining you could play like that. It's a gift … and I gave you a powwow tape … ."

Nihá. It's what Kat had said. A gift for us. I liked that hug. What were we getting into here?

"You're welcome, Annie."

Walking out into the cool night air, wind on our faces, I kicked over the Triumph for the ride back.

Annie held on to me, lay her head on my back as I wondered when she had last been with a man. It was too intense to even think about. If I am going to turn away from Bozeman and the near complete uncertainty of Stephanie, if Annie and I are going to flee the grinding boredom of separate everyday lives, fall in love and never look back, paddle away in one canoe, it will be now, on this ride. We will return to the GMC, and she will spend the night.

I heard her softly humming a song, tickling my back as we rode along. Hitting a bump, she grasped me more tightly as we both laughed at her reaction, then returned to her song.

Awareness. I knew there was something between us, perhaps in a way neither of us completely understood. So close to the edge now. I sighed, feeling her at my back, wanting her there. One tender touch, a word, an inviting look would be all it took. Then again, maybe we were never to be together in this life, as in *Evangeline*; our happiness would be with and through others. The thoughts came easily; withstanding the force, knowing what was right so much more difficult. When we get back to Cloquet, will our hearts speak the words, render that burning look, race away together?

My mind moved closer, considering her shining hair again, all that made her so special, alluring.

I pulled over at the top of Thompson Hill, near the exit for Spirit Mountain. Traffic rushing by, St. Louis Bay and the lights of Duluth below.

"What were you singing, Annie?" My heart ached, not only from tonight, but these last years. Despite so many blessings, so little real happiness. So hungry for it. Yet I held back, did not pull her to me.

"Just an old song:

> From the shore,
> our hearts in soaring
> tell their stories,
> along true paths.
>
> How in the dawn,
> begins a child's life.
> How in the west, is

the warmth of dreams.
Beyond *Gichigami*,
Our hearts soar.

Sung in Ojibwe, naturally," she tried to laugh, but looking straight at me, didn't quite get there.

A wave felt the point, moved to wrap around it. I saw myself gently grasping Annie, finding her lips.

"Annie, will you write down the song and the Ojibwe translation for me?"

Approached the cove, building height. Now! Now!

"Oh, it's nothing, only some words … .

"Hey, let's go over to Superior tomorrow, to Wisconsin Point," she said, stepping away, looking to the east and pointing.

Turning *from me*, really, as the wave broke, mixed with the ebb of the previous one. Promise unfulfilled. Flat, slack water. No tree, no bench. This was neither Market Street in Camp Hill the night of the reunion, nor Bozeman. Emily was gone, Stephanie nowhere to be found, and now Annie was distancing herself.

"Yes, let's do that," I agreed quietly, restrained, stopped by forces for some reason I knew could not be overcome tonight.

"Ready to go?"

"Ready," she replied.

When we got back to Cloquet, Annie thanked me for the evening, gave me a hug, and was gone. I didn't see a reason to go anywhere else, so I just put away the bike, drew the blinds, and crashed. Lying there, I thought about Annie, Stephanie, Laramie, this trip, the future, restless for hours. The evening's fire had not gone out.

Annie was here, with me. Closer than ever before. A trade blanket over my arm, motioning for her to come closer, I finally fell asleep, dreaming of forests and mountains, painted warriors, horses with handprints, a clouded moon, the earth shaking, sparks from a fire, darkness. The touch of a woman.

That's not an old song I was singing, Annie thought, driving into a different darkness, not that of the Reservation. It was my song. About hearts, yes. About a man, one who will be tested, grow stronger in body and spirit. A man I want, forever, even if only in our dreams. Oh, my heart, my soul! *Let* me reach out, *help* his heart heal, be strengthened.

I want this man as never before. Now I am ready. So ready to have his child. Our child!

Annie banged on the door in mid-morning. "When you going to get a phone so I can call first? I didn't even know if you'd be here. Could have ridden off after buffalo in the night for all I know. Got any clothes on?" she laughed, *gii-baapi*.

"*Tatanka*, buffalo," I replied through the window screen. "And yes, I'm dressed. Are you? Either way, come on in." I shouldn't have said that.

"Better be careful talking Sioux around here, people might get the wrong idea," Annie whispered, ignoring the other part.

"Across from the Catholic Church? As for the phone, forget it. Someday they'll make miniature portables and I won't have one. For me the distraction would outweigh the benefits. I don't need to be any more disconnected than I already am, that way."

"Who are you, Craig Maxwell?" Annie asked, rhetorically. Her eyes were sparkling. The day, or promise of something else?

I smiled back. This was about the ways we communicate, not including phones. The answers to all the questions were left hanging as we got into her car and drove to Duluth, then took the bridge over to Superior.

On the seat were two books in library dust jackets. "What're these about?" I asked, picking them up.

"This one's *The Woman Warrior: Memoirs of a Girlhood Among Ghosts* by Maxine Hong Kingston. About growing up in two worlds. Something to which I can relate. In her case, Chinese, in California. I liked the title.

The other one I really wanted to read, *Ceremony*, by Leslie Marmon Silko. Lives in Albuquerque or Tucson, I think. Somewhere down there. It's about a man who returns from World War II to the sorrows of Gallup, and needs to get well. Tough place to do it. To survive, he must get close to the land, back to his people through ceremonies, the Old Ways."

"Bet you quietly ordered that one and sneaked it into the stacks."

"You could say that. Asian and European immigrant stories are always popular and acceptable to the LibraryKeepers, but much less so contemporary Native American fiction or poetry. You know, 'Indians don't go to libraries, so who would we be getting these books for?'"

"Monkey wrencher at work in the Library?"

"I wouldn't go that far."

"Okay, 'change agent' is probably a better way to put it."

"I wouldn't say that either, if you're referring to me. As for today and our drive over to Superior, I've been doing some asking around," Annie said.

"Your ancestors are buried in Nemadji Cemetery, along the river of the same name. Their graves were moved from Wisconsin Point around the time of the Great Fire, when the Steel Company pushed the Ojibwe off land they wanted. The Company didn't build a mill or anything on Wisconsin Point, but claimed title to it. As you can see, the Cemetery is sliding down the slope to the Nemadji River. Another unhappy little chapter in a very long book." A heaviness had seemed to descend on Annie at the site, as if she was dealing with unseen matters I couldn't detect.

Stolen not through armed conflict, violent battles of conquest to the death, but words on paper, definitions; legislative, executive, and judicial acts of corruption, treaties, status, rulings and interpretations; maps and deeds. Not "ownership" stolen, but the simple right to be on the land. All for Little Ricky.

"Tell me about Stephanie," Annie asked later when we returned to Duluth, and talked more over coffee. Was there anything behind that question?

"In many ways, she's like you, Annie. Strong, independent, smart, principled. A brightness of the eyes, strength in the heart." Spirited and spiritual. But I admit I don't know either of you as well as I'd like. Can a man love two women, unselfishly, equally, without guilt or regret? Possibly, but only from a distance. Do I, or could I love either of you the way I loved Emily?

"Speaking of women, why do you think that most of those whom I consider close friends, not many for sure, are women? Does it have something to do about competitiveness, or more accurately, avoiding it? It's something I ponder from time to time."

She thought for a minute before responding.

"'Friends' may not quite be the right or best term ... but that aside ... I see you competing with yourself, not the world, not other men. It seems like you have little to talk about with most of them. You talk through your music. You don't need to compete with women or be dominant, but look to us for balance, completion, intimate closure. I'm kind of like that too, coming from the other direction. Although living on the Rez and working in town, I'm much closer to the community. I cannot be as detached as you seem to be, particularly since you can live anywhere you want, travel anytime, control the physical circumstances of your life much more."

Ah yes, an Indian adrift. Not in alcoholic despair, I thought, but cultural disorientation, unorientation; no, more toward geographical dispossession. And my worst enemy gets to control the circumstances. Myself. Now neither exterminated nor rubbed out, rather, "excused" from daily life. Another kind of despair.

"Just remember, Craig, that being loved by others, whether family, friends, wife or husband, is by itself never enough, yet without it, we're incomplete. And the same goes with music, because though it includes the arts, life cannot consist solely of art. Life is about seeking a healthy balance among all its physical, emotional, and spiritual aspects."

"That's something heavy to think about."

"Think away, you've got a lot of miles ahead of you."

Both of us were quiet for a few minutes, during which I thought more about what we had said. I knew it was deeper than what Annie described. Either she had no way of knowing, was being polite, the timing was not right, or she didn't really want to get into it.

I am so alienated that I can't/don't relate to men. I don't have to figure out how/why, or go to work every morning and try or pretend. I just don't relate.

With women, it's easier for me. *To a point*. The man-woman thing works for some time, *to a point*. Because in large part, initially, relating arises from attraction of one sort or another. There's mileage in that, particularly if you're "famous". When *the point* is reached, when you *have* to relate or else, it's too easy to turn away, toward another. Besides, "we're so different," I'll never be able to figure out the how and why anyway.

So once again, I'm only swimming short laps on the surface of a small, shallow pool. The one in my backyard, constructed for another minimalist vignette. My own thought-space, controlled physical environment. Controlled, refrigerated silence.

"Whatcha doing tonite?" I asked, trying to get back to the here and now. Fighting being alone, while thinking that there didn't seem to be anything personal behind her question about Stephanie.

"Going to visit friends on the Rez with my Mom."

"I guess that's my cue to put some of those miles behind me.

"Annie, that time when I was first here, you said that though an outsider, I wasn't a stranger. Will you tell me more about that?"

"I was told to help you. By a dream. Not to help you fit in here, but to find yourself. You will know your home, wherever that is, belong there when you know yourself."

Interesting. Helping me find myself clearly didn't include falling in love. Didn't involve stepping over the line into … .

"Remember this place, Annie continued, "the Lake which knows *you*, to which you can always return in spirit. The trees of your fathers, which though unseen, guide you," she breathed more than spoke, as a wind caressing those trees. Her words went right to my heart. I really wanted to kiss her again, once, that symbolically, we would have shared our bodies. Hold on to her. No! Not experience the thunder sure to be in our kiss only once—but as completely, deeply, and for as long as I could. *Beyond the point*.

The fire within me found pitch, hissed and flared again as it boiled, steamed and burned, while I looked at her, intensely now. Fierce Eyes. "I will take you, my woman. Now. The spirits know this, have always known that I will fight them over you. I will take this to the sky, within the earth, do whatever it takes to win you. We will be complete. Both of us."

Annie looked straight back at me, seeing what was in my eyes. For an instant, I'm sure she began to move toward me, to a different embrace, one which would take us over the cliff, falling through the space of future and past.

Maybe we were together, that moment was a lifetime. Our lifetime in another dimension, yet only a few seconds here.

"I've got to go," she said, drawing back, breaking the spell. *"Giga waabamin miinawaa."* Goodbye.

"Annie." Looking into the eyes of this woman again, seeing what was there. What had been, and always would be there. Some of it about me. What couldn't be hidden. Everything. I saw it! There in her eyes!

"Daga! Please, Craig," she pleaded. A fight within her I couldn't even begin to imagine.

My mind was in a frenzy. My own fight. Wanting this woman, yet needing to respect her request, plea. Above the Lake but falling, knowing it was only a matter of time before I hit again, sank. How deep this time? Running with her until our hands separated and she slipped away into the forest while I could only watch from the clearing.

The smell of sparking flint, fingers stained by walnut leaves, sticky pine gum. One fire out while I was gone. Another I couldn't get started in the cold.

The heaviness I felt driving here, tension with the spirit world. Holds partially broken, but not released as the wrestling continued, probing for weaknesses to be exploited.

Now only silence, and in it, sadness.

"Craig, are you alright?" I saw a different look in her eyes now. The look of The People, down the generations. A woman's silent love, compassion, acceptance of hardships. The look of, "my love, I am here to comfort you."

"Yes, Annie," was all I could say, still restrained.

There is that moment, after you've left a woman, when you're totally alone. Invisible, solitary as a grain of sand. Even an atomic particle in a cloud chamber leaves a trace—for me now none, transitionally disregarded by the cosmos. Between heartbeats which had nearly ceased, maybe not even one full frame on film, the briefest of images synthetically recorded, an analog approximation, more shadow than light.

"What would it take to win you?" I wondered. "The man who wins *me* ... ," Stephanie had said in The Bakery. Turning it all over and over without any resolution.

There would indeed be a lot of time to ponder things between Cloquet and Harrisburg, but I wasn't looking forward to it. Watching Annie drive away, I didn't know what I wished—that I was on the way back to Bozeman, or fighting a war here against spirits living in dreams. At either destination was a woman I couldn't have. In 1967 it had been "The Look of Love" and Natalie. Now, in the realm of circular time at notch 1979, the Surf Punks had devolved to "Punch Out at Malibu", dragging me under with them into the fight. I couldn't have said it better.

I'm running out of postures, poses, phrases, and words to accent. Thoughts, imagination, and dreams. Headed the wrong direction even to hatch elaborate swindles, east, away from the Hi-Line. In my mind a picture of the front half of a canoe over the brink of a plunging waterfall. A one man canoe. I'm paddling in the wrong direction, at the wrong location.

What does it say when a man's quest breaks down, is no longer for peace in the spirit, but only antidotes? As a cowgirl might rephrase it, "the ride was going great until that last turn … before the wreck … it was bad … real bad."

52

*Ruling of the Official Scorer:
error on the throw*

The visit with Annie dominated my thoughts as I rolled into Harrisburg; interest in the MFA program and continuing to live in Laramie had completely faded. Cynically, I wondered whether it might be a good idea to wear a film badge or carry a geiger counter here. The government didn't have a very good history of "controlling" much, did have a solid track record of violating trust, lying in the public interest: "you won't see anything for a couple of generations ... there'll be time to deal with it."

Back home, two years after the reunion. The two years later thing was becoming a fixation, as was that tree in the yard we used to jump over, now even taller. A fair setting, but many places are. Never enough to hold me here, not even close. I could say, "like many of the women I've known," but that would be heartless. It wasn't about them, rather purely about me, whether I had been willing to give myself, to even begin a relationship in earnest. Why do we use so many modifiers (serious, long term, giving, authentic relationship)? To pinpoint truth? If so, it's a dead-giveaway that we're only arguing a case.

If the flowers, slate roof barns, solitary maples were removed from this place, what would be left? May apples, tulip trees, horse chestnuts and ash; brooks flowing, Queen Anne's lace. Goldenrod and milkweed drying in the late September heat, releasing silky seed puffs to October's winds, like trout flies on whipping line. All pretty good to those for whom it *is* home.

I have to admit that there's more of this land in me than I would have acknowledged before. The rich, red Cumberland County soil and tough limestone in the peaches, plums, garden lettuce, and hickory nuts from trees on islands surrounded by waving seas of ripening corn. The air I have breathed, dust that I am.

Turning away, I went inside and called Cindy Lambert Hollis. Elle. Feeling a smooth cheek once again as I dialed, gently touching her ear with my palm, remembering the softness of her hair when my fingers ran through it as we kissed in Laguna. Life's experience above a different sea.

"Cindy, it's Craig Maxwell. I wasn't planning on coming back here this summer, but things have changed. Let's visit. Can we get together at the Coffee Place?"

After the briefest of updates, she agreed, "yes, I can get away for a couple of hours tonight. See you there at 7."

Afternoon rain had cooled things off, but now it was clear. I rode the Bonneville up to Camp Hill, chatting with Tom until Cindy arrived.

"Hi, Cindy," I greeted her, a kiss on each cheek in the European style. She appeared more relaxed than I remembered.

Cindy looked into my eyes in a way she hadn't done before. Apparently nothing too fierce in there for her to be concerned about now. She got out a drawing pad and started to sketch.

"I'm thinking how relaxed you look, Cindy."

Seeing the pencil move, as she alternately looked at me and down at the image, it seemed to have been ages since I had sketched anyone. Was it the day I slipped on the floor back in Laguna? Now remembering a time when I couldn't remember. That long ago?

"Thank you. Things have been on an upswing during the last few months. My business is doing well, and I'm rejoining the world, little by little. You've helped me do that." Truthfully, I don't see how it could have been very much.

"Do you have an extra pencil with you? It's been forever since I did any drawing."

Without a word Cindy ripped a couple sheets out of the pad and gave me a pencil, like passing a serving spoon at dinner. "Since I can't see what you're doing, no fair looking at mine," I said, getting started, shielding the sketch with my left hand, suddenly thinking how nice it would be to play footsies under the table with Cindy Hollis.

"Glad to hear your life's going well. Things on my end have taken a dramatic turn. The cafe in Laramie burned down, along with everything upstairs where I lived.

"I was on the road at the time, so the GMC and bikes were not affected, nor were some things I had stored in the garage out back. Other than those, a total loss. One year of work on the business and my place, gone. Good thing I kept the Laguna house, which is where I'm going after I leave here."

"I remember that place *very* well," she said, smiling beautifully, while I remembered *her* at the door, wearing the wrap skirt, sweater, and leotard; even more interesting moments.

"I do too. Warm memories that make a real life." And how we rarely talk about some of the closest, most powerful experiences of our lives with whom they happened.

"How about the MFA at the University?" she asked.

"I'm going to withdraw. I've talked myself into believing I accomplished what I set out to do. I don't want to go back to Laramie and start over in terms of another place to live, whether to rebuild the Cafe, all that. It's been done, and it's over. I'm sorry you didn't get to see it."

"What will you do in Laguna Beach? You didn't want to live there full time. Has that changed?

"And by the way, Mr. Wyeth, how are you doing with that pencil?"

"Funny you should mention Wyeth."

"Why's that?"

"I like Henriette's *Portrait of Witter Bynner,* late 30's."

"I was thinking of one of the *Mr.* Wyeths. So how are you doing with that pencil?"

"I told you, no peeking until I'm finished. Then we'll swap, and you can show me mine, and I'll show you yours."

"I hope you'll let that sleeping dog lie," she laughed.

"Multi-entendre too complicated or what?"

"You were telling me about your future," Cindy redirected.

"Nothing more definite than to meditate on the Pacific until I figure out the next step. I've got friends in Bozeman, Montana, a Baptist pastor and his family. Through them, on a more serious side, if there is such a thing anymore, I guess you could say I'm becoming more aware of the spiritual aspect of my life.

"Dave Franck, the pastor, says that God nudges us through various people and situations, bringing us to the point where we either are moved closer and eventually accept Him, or head in the opposite direction, ignoring or outright rejecting Him. Thinking about the last few years, I can't but believe that's true. The things which have happened to me, and those around me ... ."

"Well, I know about loneliness, but I have never been a church person, so I don't quite know how to gain understanding of the way God might fit in, if God indeed exists.

"So your life in Wyoming has gone up in smoke, you've made a decision not to return to school, you're planning on getting back into recording, and you've come here to get some perspective on the lay of the land. That's a lot. If your spiritual life is becoming more important to you, causing you to seek answers, then you should try to find them. Anything else?"

I reached out and she gave me her hand. Hands tell a lot. Hers was very nice. In the comfortable pause, I reflected upon a couple of similar days, telling Emily about Cindy, and vice versa. Smoothly noncommittal then.

"Yeah. I've seen a couple other women since I last saw you. 'Seen, been with' sound so shallow. Anyhow, I've known one for several years; the other is recent, a lady I met in Bozeman, Montana, a couple of weeks ago. Could be married by now, though—pretty close to that when I met her, or so the story goes. We spent very little time together. With the fire, our situation has been left totally openended, if there is a situation, are any ends at all." Maybe just snow fences. "I haven't been able to speak with her since. Another in Minnesota I visited the other day, much more complicated. That's me. How about you in that department?"

"Well, my life seems to be coming more into balance, to the point that I can see a serious relationship as something at least possible. We spent all of those years in school without even talking to one another, and it took ten years after that to have a conversation. While I've always found you good looking … if you were around here all the time … things might be, how shall I say it, different … but you're not."

Cindy continued, "I don't see myself living in places like Wyoming, Montana, or even Laguna Beach, as spectacular as that is. Speaking from my heart, I would sum it up by saying that the time we've spent together to this point has been very, very valuable. The future is the future. I don't know what it will bring. I'm looking forward more now to finding out. No matter what happens, I will always have the memory of our weekend in Laguna Beach. Treasure that time you and I were together. In all honesty, time of closeness with a gentle man like no other in my life."

"Me too. A wonderful time … .

"I'll be here for a few more days, then down to Southwest Florida. One of my favorite places, Sanibel Island. The beach is great, there's a comfortable hotel, and it's not yet overrun with tourists. After that, I'll be heading back out West. Let's stay in touch."

We talked awhile longer, while finishing our *cappuccini*.

"Here you are. An original pencil drawing of a famous guy. With best wishes for happiness."

The image was very good, capturing my features and look with an economy of strokes. It seemed to be an intense look.

"Well done. Thank you, Cindy. Do I really look like that?"

"You really look like that." She could have said that in the hall at Cedar Cliff on a Thursday afternoon in the early spring, when the weather was still unpredictable. Cold and rainy that day, she'd be wearing a tartan skirt, penny loafers, pink oxford blouse, tortoise shell glasses, looking so studious yet relaxed. In those days, she always looked relaxed. The next day warm, fog rising from the ground in the darkened Friday night. She'd be with her crones, laughing, off to some folk thing. I would have liked to have been with her, getting in way over my head. She might have sketched me then, kept it in her locker, given me another one she drew. We might even have fallen in love in what was a different time, a different place, in what could have been a different future. For both of us.

She didn't say that at Cedar Cliff. I went my own way, and there was Natalie.

"Let me see yours," Cindy giggled.

I handed the drawing to her. Her mouth dropped in surprise.

"This is incredible! I never knew you could draw like this. Wow! And I was kidding you about it. You could give me lessons."

"I don't think so, Cindy. You're the artist here, the one with the artist's heart. Even better, the mother's heart."

She leaned across the table and hugged me, starting to softly cry. This time, I took them to be tears of rapport, thankfulness; not hurt.

Dabbing her eyes with a Kleenex, she looked at me, said she had to get going.

Outside, we hugged, silently spending a last minute in each others' arms. She smelled so good, felt so wonderful. In that time, The World of New Possibilities edged closer. But it vanished as instantaneously—we weren't in love now, had never been in love. We were intrigued, in curiosity, exploration; complex functions, each in motion with few points of intersection. In recovery.

I hopped on the Triumph, hungry for something to eat. Dav's, on the Square in Harrisburg, sounded about right. Try to put a few more memories of Emily to rest, too. By going there? Well, maybe not, but I wanted a comfortable, familiar place.

Sitting in Dav's, this time nobody recognized me. Why should I be, a couple of years after disappearing from the scene? That I was the day leaving Bozeman was a little surprising, actually. Now, even if I was "recognized", what would I be recognized as?

The first night with Emily came back vividly. I saw her sitting across from me, so beautiful, laughing at things in our small talk. About a week. Amazing that's all the time we got to spend together. A week with Emily. Not much more than that with Cindy. A few days with Danielle. Talk about shooting stars, ephemeral lives. How they can be so profoundly influenced by what happens in a week, a day, an instant.

Looking out the window, little was different. Change was slow here. Same beatup road, thermoplastic markings worn off, bent parking meters, downtown cast of characters going about their antics.

I walked along the Square to where the music store used to be, on the alley. A magic place 15 years ago, filled with Hammond organs, Slingerland and Gretsch drums, Ampeg and Fender amps with spring reverb and tremolo. The gear we all wanted. Meanwhile, I had worked through soul, progressive, classical. Background music for falling out of orbit.

Roaring north on 2nd Street, then Front along the Susquehanna River, I passed the Cottage and the Barn, before turning onto Linglestown Road, then Crooked Hill Road to Alderwood Court. Another scene of key high school capers, by now a designated historical site. Remembering the hammock outside her window the night the Russians invaded Czechoslovakia, the overwhelming though uninformed sadness we felt. Anne of Gray Eyes. If we both had known a few more things about life, it would have been so much easier. Things we had no way of knowing, many more we still don't know. Thank you for your love, Anne. I'm saying goodbye now. Please forgive me.

In asking for forgiveness, I was mindful that the late 60's/early 70's thing, "whatever you do is cool, as valid as what everybody else is doing," was totally bogus. The truth is that what's ultimately valuable has to be based on a solid foundation of morals and ethics, discipline, restraint, love, respect, courage. In short, what Dave Franck was teaching on Sundays. It was both a call and blueprint for me to get serious about my life, to build relationships based upon shared values, ones which were honorable, strong, lasting. Spiritual values. But how could I reach that space? How is one really forgiven?

Retracing the last part of the route, I came back down Front Street, over the Taylor Bridge to Camp Hill, out U.S. 15 to Dillsburg, riding through the summer night. Familiar by now to the Triumph, a tiger purring away. Looking at the land brought back the old Ojays' song, "I'll Never Forget You". If Only I Could Find You, If Only I Could Find Yŏu-oŏ. Find who?

I pulled over and parked on the bridge where we had stopped before, thinking of the portrait Cindy had just done, thirty years of rolled up me. Her dossier. Cindy. Major influences: Rembrandt, Cezanne, Klee, Wyeth (all). Interests: Art, Art, Art. Snapshot: a healthy *joie de vivre* on the upswing; never without her sketch pad; a survivor, she knows and is strengthened by it; a myth worth spending time with. A loving mother.

On the way home, alone, I practiced the silent scream, two versions. Self-directed, and universal. The world heard only Triumph. The British version.

✠══════✠

The next morning, I visited Emily's grave, to say another goodbye. Never "finally", because those who are precious in part define us, and in doing so, are always with us. Kat was right about that.

✠══════✠

Still fighting over Annie, I had a wild thought. A last attempt either at a start of another kind, or release from the current tension, like I tried in the Museum before leaving Bozeman. Why not send her a ticket to meet me in Florida? With the Gulf temperature in the 80's, white sandy beach, palms and flowers, it would be different for Annie. Nearly foreign. A last attempt is one way to look at it; the one call too many another, welding an already shut door closed forever. Potentially, a repeat trip to "you're not listening" land. Nevertheless, I called her.

"Annie, why don't you meet me in Florida, get away from the summer heat up there for somewhere even hotter? I can get you a ticket. It would be great to spend a few more days with you on the beach. Separate rooms, of course, if you're wondering just how desperate I am." I had to put that out front, but couldn't bear to think about it in any depth.

"I'd need a swimsuit, can't remember when I last had one. *Gichigami's* too cold for real swimming, even in summer." Swimsuit. Umm, umm, umm. This is getting painful.

"We could buy you one."

"When would you be there?"

"In three or four days, but I could stretch that to a week or so."

"Let me think about it and call you back."

"That would be fine. Here's the number of my parents' place again. Talk to you later."

Annie phoned in the evening.

"Craig, I've thought about it. A lot. I think I should decline. This is a crucial time for you. After the fire, and with that woman from Montana on your mind, going to Florida with you is probably not a good idea. I say this realizing you need support, and I want to help provide that. On the other hand, the potential would exist for confusion. Confusion for both of us. You know how I feel about you, my brother. You must understand that you are to be with one of your own and accept this."

"Annie, what does it mean, 'one of my own'?"

"Everything in our dreams has not been revealed, only what we need to know. The rest of it will be given through other dreams, persons, or experiences. I cannot act upon my dream until I understand the meaning."

"You're going to follow a dream, not your heart, not what's real? I think you understate what's between us when you say, 'you know how I feel about you, my brother.' It was just a dream, Annie. This is life. This is real, you and I." As I said it, though, I knew that dream of reawakening had *not* been "just a dream."

"Craig, my life is one, a whole life, both waking and in sleep. The dreams given to me are as true as the sunrise."

Annie could not disregard her dreams, was obliged to live by them.

"I don't mean to argue. To the contrary, I respect your beliefs and values. They make you who you are. They paint you with beauty."

I visualized her on the other end of the line as we spoke.

Aná´ át´ááh	The sun sets,
náyoołtááד.	she is undoing the braids of her hair.
Bik ´idad´ diitįįł	We will understand it
hayííłkąągo.	at dawn.

I hope we will understand it.

"I guess the beach trip was the way to approach discussing this stuff. I had to talk about it with you, not leave things unresolved, in my mind. I'm so comfortable with you, enjoy spending time together so much."

"I'm glad we're talking about it too. I feel as strongly about you, but feelings are never everything. There is always much more."

"You Ojibwe women are a tough lot."

"Raised on salted fish," Annie laughed, now almost relaxed.

We talked a few more minutes, promising to keep in touch. Then the conversation was over, and I was alone again. But the thinking went on. You don't settle these things in a telephone call.

The guy with Hopi bracelets, beaded Plains Indian jacket, motorcycle riding, card-carrying Indian Chief in Simulation. Did I want Annie because she was a "real Native", drawn by her magnetism in a fiction of Indian nostalgia and myth, longing to be singed by her "real Native" fire? Was I self-targeting myself for cultural assassination in both worlds, Anglo and Native?

That's now part of the problem, isn't it? No War Whoops!! Subtle trails and traditions are there, underfoot and in the background, but "Star" is not enough "Indian".

And the beach trip. Wasn't that on the most basic level no more than shamelessly pushing to close the deal—import the woman, disappear with her into the dunes? The on-call, exotic Indian woman, far from the campfires of accountability. To live the "real thing" which is not nor has ever been real at all.

Yesses and no's. Always yes and no.

I had been in the business of creating, propagating, enhancing myths. Commercial myths. Big music. Beautiful women. Oceanview property. Travel. Stars and SuperStars. But the cities with their brick walls fell over on me years ago. I thought I had climbed out of the rubble, vowed not to go back. Everything they afforded, everything they lacked, still had a hold on me.

✛ ═══ ✛

That night Annie had another dream. Above the Lake, a long time ago. When there were only the forest and *Gichigami*, waves slapping the rocky cliff below. After they talked, he turned and walked away, along the old path, then disappeared.

He is in danger, she gasped, he's going to die.

She was back on the shore, dancing in the jingle dress.

"You have done well," the Old Man said.

"But I am afraid for him."

"It is his life. Yours is before you."

"Will I marry?"

"Yes. He is over there."

A man was in the distance, along the water, back turned, clothed in deer-skin. Even though I can't see his face, she thought, his presence comforts me. Is he someone I already know, or another?

She turned around to speak with the Old Man, but he was gone.

Now it was her wedding day. There was dancing as the evening shadows lengthened. A different ceremony, not Ojibwe.

"Where is he? Where is my husband?" Annie asked.

"He will come to your wigwam this night. Go, make it ready," Grandmother said.

In the darkness, she heard a rustle at the entryway; an instant later his hands were gently on her. She remembered the warmth after their kiss, as they now travelled together by canoe on a river. Was the Land of Souls on the other side? Though surely together, had they died? Annie remembered *all* of it.

The alarm woke her—5:30, time to make breakfast. Get ready to go to work at the Library. Offer prayers, for the man who had disappeared in her dream, for the husband she would know.

✠━━━━✠

"*Miish agamiing gii-gwayakochigewag,* so it is that on the shore, they did the right thing," I thought. For reasons some of which had already been revealed, others yet to be understood.

The night seemed so quiet. Whatever was between us, a part of it would always be about a man and woman. It took respect and restraint to keep the whole intact, if it was to ever become another kind of love. The Greeks took a shot at distinguishing among three kinds other than the romantic/erotic: *storgē* (family), *philia* (affection), *agapē* (commanded for one another by deity). Words. Classes. It's human nature to categorize, from which inevitably there is a closing in, discrimination. Simply call it love. Care and emotion; spirit and selflessness.

Don't you get it? This is not about definitions or an offering, rather a sacri-fice. And if I *am* the sacrifice, then I love.

✠━━━━✠

A couple of days later, I left Pennsylvania, driving south on I-81. The scenery was as beautiful as it had been when I was coming the other way in 1977, to the surprise of Emily after all those years. How many surprises can one expect in a lifetime?

Connecting to I-95 then I-75, down to Ft. Myers and Sanibel Island. The motel was on West Gulf Drive, on the sand, next to the State Preserve. A wonderful beach which I walked several times a day, at dawn, after a morning swim, following a siesta.

The humidity was fierce, sun broiling, coral rock and bleached white shell on the driveway blinding. In late afternoon the sky clouded up, and by 5 pm thunderstorms deluged the palms and sea oats, dropping the temperature 15 degrees, bringing a breeze lasting until after midnight. I dodged the rain to shop at Bailey's General Store, cook dinner in the efficiency kitchen, sliding doors open, air conditioner on high, drapes billowing from the wind, lightning and thunder over the Gulf. Out again later for ice cream or to scout a six pack of Old Spanish Main SeaOats Dark. "A willie-waught of Wack-a-Mundo Porter, me hearties." Remember that limit.

I wished Stephanie could be here with me. Were things really becoming clearer in my mind, or was I just going down the list after Annie crossed herself off for this stay? Kat next? A rush trip to Singapore to see Cathy before starting over? Had I actually reset my altimeter way back when?

Several weeks had passed since I talked to Dave, so I called him from Sanibel. In the course of our conversation, he said that with Amy they had let Stephanie know about the fire. During their talk, she mentioned my interest in musical collaboration, and how much she would really like to do that, but didn't know how it could ever be possible, given the "other" interest in her I had voiced, and her rumored marriage to another. Had I lived in Bozeman before, it might have turned out differently, but that wasn't the case. They knew Stephanie really wanted to sing, not just "church songs" for the next 50 years, so each of us was caught in our own dilemma.

Stephanie *had* admitted doing a little research on my career at the library, and coming across the article about Emily's death. "You never mentioned it to us," Dave said, "but I could tell that there is pain within you, Craig."

Anyhow, she had moved to Billings, with no further news.

The Gulf temperature was 86°. I enjoyed the beach, swimming and dodging mosquitoes before going north to Tampa, where we had played a gig years ago on my first trip to Southwest Florida.

I got serious about putting the pedal down, with the next real stop Texas, a midcontinent break on the return to Laguna. The plan was still to drop the rig in Newport, but then fly up to Wyoming in early October, to bring the Land Cruiser back, trailering the rest of the garage stuff.

Austin, once home of Green Sweater Girl. Maybe still home. How many years had it been already? Again, neither time nor heart.

When I get close to New Mexico, Santa Fe beckons, so I took a detour up to I-40. Stayed in Santa Fe for a few days, riding the Triumph up Canyon Road, to Chimayo and Española, Santa Clara, San Ildefonso, and Taos. Land of juniper and piñon. Even went to the Santa Fe Opera, caught a flamenco troupe one evening at El Gancho. Not enough time for a person, Green Sweater Girl, in order to spend a couple of days in a place. No confusing those priorities.

I-40 ran over to Flagstaff. Maybe I would stop and try to find Kat. *Ájíní*, button that would buzz me out of the Monotony Suite, open the door to some kind of layered world reality I had missed, the Four Corners version in Native Color. Fight the paradox of the Myth of Memory: no past authentic; all pasts authentic.

I took Business 40. A beautiful summer day under the deep blue sky, at the foot of the towering San Francisco Peaks. In the Caffe Express, sipping a cappuccino, looking at the piano, the street out the front window. Conscious of driving one more herd of myth-memories, desires, expectations, disappointments along these familiar trails at the end of yet another fading movie. Pondering that gap between art and life, wondering on which side I was now, in which direction, if any, I was looking. On neither side, still at the bottom. Looking up at a long, steep climb. Hoping that if someday I ever got to the top, it wouldn't be just to find a barren terrain of intellectualism—flat, inert, and directionless, or a claustrophobic, tangled confusion confined by the unseen, resistive, enervating forces always at work.

I can't burden Kat again in my sorrow. Not now. Why is that? Does she represent a part of myself I've always been unwilling to give? A deep conscience I don't want to confront? A leaving behind of all the trash I fearfully hold on to, not able to face the naked emptiness, though knowing one day I must? That which in order to ever be connected to what's true, essential to giving, loving, enabling me to live a life and enter death with no regrets, only thankfulness, I have to overcome?

I guess that's it. Understanding involves more than knowing women of gentle strength, having dreams and travelling. It's about confrontation, warfare within oneself, killing the ego, strengthening conscience. Becoming fertile dirt from which life may spring.

Kat is both a teacher and self-sacrifice, blessing those around her while experiencing trials and suffering. Strong but vulnerable. Warrior and peacemaker. A woman of dignity. So rich in life's blood that I feel unworthy in her presence.

Why does everyone I'm not haunt me? Pentimento. Not a 5-part mint, but emergence of things that have been painted over. That's all I'm doing—painting over the same canvas. The picture on top's different, those underneath, the same.

As the road descended on the way to Kingman, I compiled yet another dossier. Kat. Major influences: "Mom, who believes in and supports who I am"; *Hoskinnini*, the angry one; Louisa Wetherill, *'Anísts 'óózi Ts 'ósí*, Slim Woman.

Interests: Native American arts and culture, teaching children, photography. Snapshot: planted her heart at the wall of the Chuskas.

It would be nonstop from Kingman to Barstow. Searing desert. In that desert, the heat radiating off the pavement, I saw supernatural intervention at work in my life. The accident in the Mojave, new musical skills, dreams, Thunder People, Forked Lightning … Annie LaCroix, Kat Walter. What was next? The end? I was still wondering when I arrived back in Orange County, by now late August.

After the empty high desert, coming down into San Bernardino and Riverside is always so shocking. Define, "fairly sickening". Back to packed beaches, eyewatering smog, freeways stop and go at best, and summer "celebrations" in full swing. Pageant of the Masters. Newport Festival of Ill-Gotten Gains and Unquenched Greed. U-Haul Immigration Days. Everything about carving the heart from the land; living for "valuable possessions". Living resilient oxymorons. Nationally recognized by major publications as a premier rat's nest of consummate material accumulation, in a temperate climate where it can be conspicuously displayed.

It's a terrible feeling when you're part of the thick, sweeping textures of indifference and denial, and realize that. Like in *The Deer Hunter*, knowing you can't save your best friend from himself. When your best friend, only friend, is yourself. The contest won't be stopped, the odds not beaten: "mo!"

Overbuilt, overrun, overbooked, overburdened, overtired. Over and over. Over. Contemporary America has not paused in its eating. Not enough got the message of that movie: though the deer is there, it is not always for you to take, no matter how proud or hungry either of you are.

Wanting to be here infrequently doesn't make me innocent. Are degrees of guilt meaningful? I wonder, where do I rest in the spectrum of greed and self-interest? Am I in equilibrium?

When in our lives do we start going so wrong?

53

Body surfing the Point, well west of Laramie

Having notified the University that I would not be returning, with the shock of the Cafe being gone, all the summer miles, and disappointment that time could not be reset to give me a chance with Stephanie, I could do little more than seek the rest of Laguna, in the waves off the Point at this dynamic boundary of nature's forces. Keep seeking my heart's peace. Here, in its sea of sand, desert of water, would the Pacific know me?

Had my thoughts in Flagstaff been delusional? Supernatural intervention? I wasn't going to think about it. As Annie would say, that which is to be revealed will be, at the appointed time. I'm here sipping a cup of coffee, looking at the marine overcast. Another morning. Nothing more, nothing less.

I had to keep a routine, tough it out. Running the hills, hiking in the mountains would maintain tone, slipping out for an occasional night at the Lighthouse keep me in touch with the currents of improvisational performance. I was consciously becoming more reclusive, screening calls, only returning those absolutely necessary. Neither the nagging sense I had lost ten years of thought-life, nor fear without major changes the rest of it, physical and mental, would slip away purposelessly, could be escaped. That didn't mean skydiving or replaying the Mojave crash and burn to slow down the approach, insert just the right reaction which would have avoided damage. More fundamental changes. Until I gained some understanding of what they were and how to initiate them, I had little to say, to anyone.

In late September Rebecca called, reaching me at the Laguna number after trying Laramie without success. She was planning to come down to Laguna in early October for a long weekend at her parents' place and wanted to get together. That was the same time I was going up to Laramie, so it wouldn't work. I really didn't want to make it work. What had I been thinking when I met her? No thinking involved, only cruising. Without any change in her voice, Rebecca said she would call in November, expecting to be back at Christmas, maybe earlier. You have a vacancy over the holidays? Great. Like making a hotel reservation. I'll take the suite that comes with The Provincial Blonde.

Before going up to Laramie, I considered putting out the word I would be available for session work in LA after returning in late October. I didn't get around to it.

After the flight to Denver, I took the shuttle to Laramie, then a taxi to Emmett's where I was staying. It would forevermore be strange not being able to go back to the Whyomin'. The land had been sold and a new building was planned on the site. The garage would remain, but I had to get my stuff out by the end of the month.

With the weather good, I decided to visit the Francks for a few days, driving up through the Wind River Range, Togwotee, Moran, then Yellowstone. I wanted to take a closer look at Bozeman, consider a second generation version of the Cafe Whyoming. At least it would give me something to think about other than misfortune. Cafe Mhontana. Cafe Monthana? Montina? Chez Stéphane might have been nice.

There were certainly possibilities downtown, and enough cold weather to sell lots of espresso. I thought Bob and Beth would be interested, but wasn't sure that I wanted to live in Bozeman if Stephanie was anywhere near, married to someone else. Billings and Bozeman are only 140 miles apart. In Montana, that's practically next door.

Driving mile after mile, I was confronted by the same old struggles felt day after day. *Díísha' táá 'át' é háágóó 'ada 'iiztiin?* Where do all these roads go?

I had barely scratched the surfaces of the Navajo and Ojibwe, even less so the Hopi. So far, I was only shopping cultures, picking an item here or there for adornment, the most accessible themes and attributes, generalized patterns of thinking, words lifted for dramatic effect. Both an orphan in the material culture I knew, and a stranger to Native America. Exiled from an identity. I would bring Stephanie into this emotional landscape, one as brutal as Wyeth's mountains?

Hundreds of thousands of miles ago, I had decided how to handle life—if I couldn't get what I wanted when I wanted it, I'd jump in the car, on a bike or jet. Put miles behind me, spin more speculative episodes.

But the motion mode was exhausted, sold out superficial refuge it had been, the escapades now become little more than empty, unrelated chapters. "Modern" tone poems—shrill, discordant, assaulting—lacking the beauty which time and time again though glimpsed, was so elusive. Where was the common thread? The valuable one connecting all the important points—physical, emotional, and spiritual truth, happiness? *Kó' 'ayóigo bee n'deezdíín ndi doo shiníldoi da.* The fire gives lots of light, but doesn't warm me.

Something had to change very soon.

Aside from seeing the Francks, there was a crucial reason to be there, though I didn't realize it when I pulled into town. I knew I needed to let go of my life; let go of Emily, the woman I had loved; let go of Stephanie, the woman

I wanted to love, but couldn't be with; and Annie, a woman from whom unseen forces were keeping me. Let go. Nothing new there. To be able to find what?

Another replacement? Now there's a clue, maybe the smoking gun restated. A clue that fundamentally I was a mess, terribly sick, kept alive by little more than the consumer's addiction to the next "right" product released in the marketplace. The new, incomparable model. Or soon to be famous person, all dumped into the media like barrels of fish, spring stocking of the stream.

Likewise, the struggle with that other question of my own fabrication—was I Ojibwe or white? What was the meaning of the answer? Was it always to be no more than another shopping choice—cultural consumerism? Catalytic uncertainty?

Unless I could overcome the sickness, I would surely die. Soon. I felt the omega approaching, had been struggling emotionally for a long time, most if not all of my life. To me, "I'm going away," really meant that. Away from life.

Were we all born to struggle? Neither a parade of Rebeccas nor "interesting" aspects of my ancestry could keep me afloat any longer. I was disappearing alone into a woodland, into an identity of my own making, tragically, not knowing at all with whom I was going. Climbing a mountain so steep that I wouldn't be able to get back down.

Shíni' 'íít' i'. I long to go ... my mind stretches away like a slender line. *Shiyaa 'ahooldo.* Time is up for me.

Go out into the land, not come back. Awaken forever from what has been the sleep of my life, in order to enter the deepest of sleep. If we are all dancing, the dance that none can see may be the best of all.

Have I done nothing but waste this second life, the one granted to me after the accident, from which I seek only the rest of death? If not, I will need the strongest medicine, that of last resort. Now.

God knew that. In His time, He had brought me to the most important decision point of my life.

Through Pastor Dave, God spoke to me a message not of words or reasons, but love, sacrifice, loss, compassion. Of all the desert rainstorms I had seen, ever would see; of all the people I had known, would ever know; of all the waves breaking off the Point. Of blessings in the midst of suffering.

As the tears came, I thought of the music, the songs. All the music that had been placed in my life, the music within me. Songs which had been given, but not yet written.

I realized that I had been so blessed. That as God spoke through Pastor Dave, He wanted to speak through me as well. He had been speaking for some time, but I hadn't been listening. They were all His songs, not mine.

Being a man, there was no doubt that the losses I had experienced were painful. But more important than the pain were learning, understanding, forgiving, letting go of it. This was the time and place for the cloud I am to build, static charges to align; the time when I would be struck by, transmit the lightning which is God. Finally. When Pastor Dave gave the invitation, I rose, stepped forward, knelt, accepted Christ as my Savior, and was changed forever. And forever, amen.

I surrender. I surrender all.

A man finally broken, and by the grace of God, saved. Pastor Dave knelt beside me, and prayed, giving thanks, both of us weeping, children before our God.

His music filled me. All of me, alloyed Ojibwe, stronger for it—the spiritual fence upon which I had been sitting was gone. A voice for Him now, in whatever way He deemed. The Deniece Williams song heard years before in Santa Barbara had said what I could not understand then: "Jubilation for me and you."

I felt His cleansing love wash over me. There was so much to learn about my faith, how to live. Emily's words had said, "… that He would bless us, and forgive us our sin … ." Now I understood that God reserved the most profound and powerful intimacies for husband and wife, and no others. Our love must be pure and holy before God, otherwise, it is only empty rationalization, or worse.

In that dream Annie had said that I would marry one of my "own kind." Had that meant I was to marry a Christian woman?

I vowed to return to Bozeman, to be baptized by this man who had not given up, led me to Christ. Born again, beginning again. As a suffering, hurt adult, lost, out of control; and though seeing the world for much of what it is, not willing to admit I knew it all the time and had to take action to survive. Now finding the courage to start again as a child, tender and trusting. Learning, making false starts and mistakes, but with a purpose. Finally, a purpose and guidance how to live my life.

The next few days were a blur, kind of like the time spent in the hospitals after the accident. I was returning to Laramie to pick up my stuff, then bringing it back to Laguna.

On the drive I thought of Cathy, praying that seeds had been planted in her spiritual life during that Christmas in Medicine Creek, that she would come to know God as well. And Stephanie over in Billings or wherever she was. I considered going there, seeing her old truck roll up to meet and talk. Walking through the door, was that she? Her face seemed to change in my mind, would she even know me? What would I say?

You're the one? Words that would almost certainly scare her away. And if she was already married, what then … "you have no right?"

Stephanie was in a special place of my heart, now the new heart of a born again believer, but I didn't know what to do about her.

I wasn't ready to take the turn. There were too many revelations, was too much to learn right now. I had to trust God, that I would return. The heart of a new believer is as a child. Pastor Dave told me that it is fragile, there would be starts and stops, mistakes; that my faith and worthiness would be tested, perhaps severely. Though the angry seas would still churn, I now had a spiritual rudder. Throughout the trials, God has a plan for me. I have to trust that He will reveal it, raise me well, provide strength when needed. A plan which includes Stephanie, Annie, everybody.

I went straight back to Laramie, loaded the trailer, and left. There might be snow tomorrow, but not for me. I'd outrun it.

Within a few days, I was back in Laguna. A Christian.

It was the end of October; the year, 1979.

54

Vershont, aber nicht vom Schmerz der Weisheit (spared, but not from the pain of wisdom)

Upon return I reestablished LA music contacts, did some sessions; wrote keyboard pieces and songs in long hours of work at Laguna, often broken only by sitting on the deck or in the hot tub, the night's peacefulness surrounding, comforting me. Some songs for me to sing, sketching others for a woman, with Stephanie in mind, but not daring to hope that would come true.

George Ryan called in mid-November about the business end of things, and in the course of our conversation suggested that I might want to establish an estate trust to shelter assets in the event something happened to me. "You just never know." For what beneficiary? Thirty years old, with no survivors. Nevertheless, I asked him to draw up the papers by the end of the month. If nobody or nothing else, a charitable trust. Annie as trustee. Now that's a thought.

I also accepted when he invited me to go sailing with Louisa and "another friend" the next weekend. What was that sign in the cabin? "Use the negligence given to you sparingly. A little goes a long way." Make it last. Same as the music business.

With sailing, though, comes the Blue Water. Always that tinge of uneasiness.

Here, it also brings reminiscences of Emily, two years ago now. It was clear how we had been placed in each other's life. Although all that happened occurred within a very short period, I could see that it was really part of a profoundly timeless story, one shared by God as clouds reflected on a serene high mountain lake. We are as children who in their earliest, purest life, need not compare, time-scale, or construct elaborate plans, nor expect immediate, life altering conclusions or insights from our experiences.

Emily was in Paradise, dwelling in peace until the Resurrection, the reuniting of *our* souls with those of all the saints. As for pain, the message was clear:

> Because in much wisdom there is much grief, and increasing
> knowledge results in increasing pain. Ecclesiastes 1:18

I wanted to walk the straight and narrow, staying out of the clubs late Saturday nights so I could get up Sunday morning and go to Calvary Chapel in Costa Mesa, alert and ready to receive The Word. The new music, now called Contemporary Christian, was growing, becoming an increasingly powerful channel for delivering God's message of salvation, joy, and eternal security. Music we had talked about last New Year's Eve, from a detached distance, in terms of markets and units. Clearly, He had spared me for His purpose, but I couldn't know what that would bring. I promised to stay in touch with Dave and return to Bozeman as soon as I could, to be baptized. Surely, Dave would help me seek understanding of God's purpose.

It was soon evident that with faith come many matters of life and lifestyle to resolve, getting beyond oneself, stepping outside the comfort zone we all want. The churches of which Annie spoke, the music we like and only want to hear, doctrine and content of preaching with which we're comfortable, the extent of participation, sacrificial support, honest study.

We have been programmed to think that nothing can be relied upon until we understand everything, see it preserved in an airtight case. And since we're always too busy or not interested enough to review all of what we see as the "facts" before us, with little basis we bluff, "that's just a theory," or "it proves nothing." Hence, anything goes. Including us, in ignorance. Faith is about looking at it from the other direction.

A lot in and about this life is unexplained. Unexplainable now, here. That's where faith comes in. One day we will know everything about what the world was, is, and ever will be; about our life and "afterlife". Until then, through faith enough truth is being revealed for me to make up my mind. I choose to seek, and when finding it, both believe that truth, and accept the responsibility which accompanies it.

On the Wednesday before Thanksgiving, Rebecca called. She was in town, and suggested we get together at the Grill. We spoke briefly and I agreed to meet her.

When the circumstances are right, a good looking woman can indeed stop time, take your breath away. Rebecca. Whoa, this was a very attractive woman. Maybe she actually was Miss Alberta. Sophisticated, elegant. When she came in the door, as I sipped Luxury Water and wondered what to say, I saw many eyes turn to watch her. Within me opposing forces skirmished. You're not falling into the trap of believing *your eyes*, are you?

"Hey, Cowboy, long time no see," she said as we hugged. Kinda Hollywood, I thought, but got caught up in her perfume. Remembered from Robinsons or Bullocks ... *Taboo?*

"Likewise, Professor." Clockwise? Westwood? Westworld?

Small talk, explaining away the months, safe conversation. As she tilted back her head, laughing, eyes closed for a moment, long hair streaming, I thought, "man, she really is something else."

As we spoke, however, I was reminded that while she was good looking, smart, and accomplished, she knew and used it. All the time. To what purpose? I felt like I was taking some kind of test whenever I was with her. The tests weren't to evaluate important growth and understanding, rather only gauging a superficial aesthetic of hip. It wasn't healthy and I wasn't interested. I wanted to get to know, appreciate, invest in a relationship with a woman. Open up and be vulnerable, learn, experience the blessings, grow stronger from the pain. That didn't mean Rebecca would never rise above where she was. It did mean that I didn't see any common ground between us now. Zero.

While she continued to talk, I thought of Kat wrapped in her colorful manta, the poignant trip to Hopiland stored away for another day, today, the Old Man, the culture; then Annie, beating the odds at the Cloquet Library. Where and what was Rebecca's culture? The culture of production and consumption, image and reinforcement. Grounds and arguments. A modern life contortion of control and avoidance. Controlling the local environment, forestalling controversy by steering the dialogue, watering down the message, always maintaining an orchestrated strategic retreat, deployable when needed. High maintenance. Low interest. High risk. "That's a really nice dinette, Mrs. Cleaver," and meaning it.

The wandering, wondering "what if" with the Rebecca across from me had been conclusively settled.

"Rebecca, I've met someone. Actually, I've met two someones. The first is Jesus Christ, whom I have accepted as my personal Savior. The second is a woman in Montana whom I may or may not see again, but one who is in my heart."

She sat there and looked at me, quiet for a minute. The conversation had clearly been iced.

"I had a feeling that something was up, and more than likely, the second part. The first part is not hard to believe either. Aside from all your talent, the fun of being together … well, perhaps overshadowing that, it's been evident you were looking for someone, something, or both. What could be interpreted as weakness, or become that, if you're not careful."

Weakness in the world. It didn't bother me. It would be a victory. Now I knew where strength could be found.

"I guess congratulations are in order, Craig, with wishes for happiness and success."

"Rebecca, in the brief time we've known each other, I've enjoyed being with the beautiful woman that you are." Extraordinarily beautiful. Physically.

"Although I have never really felt that we'd get together, I'm also learning that each relationship is different, and can be valuable in its own way. Rather than just pursuing what I think I want and can get, I'm trying to see what I can bring. When the woman is as spectacular as you are, the learning experience isn't hard to take."

I looked at her face as she sat there, quiet again. Green eyes, high cheeks, eyelashes, the wisp of hair in front of her ear. Not hard to take, indeed. What would she say next—"I'm not who I appear to be? I want to be somebody else? I want you to help me find out who I am?"

"Motion for mistrial," she said, calling for damage control, that orchestrated retreat. The defense rests its case.

"What's important in your life, and why? Who's important, and why? What will get you through the long haul? That you can walk in beauty, ʼiłhóózhó, as the Navajo say?"

"This is getting pretty serious. Can we go back to being cowboys and cowgirls, riding up on our horses, easy talk, avoid the stampede?"

"It's been mostly small talk, Rebecca. Getting right with God is what matters. And if we will, then He will bless us with understanding and happiness, and we'll get right with ourselves. While our lives may not be easy, we'll know why we're here, where we're going, and eventually, with whom."

"So you've bought into the idea of God. A Holy Roller in Laguna. Now that's a change." Nobody's talked to me this way; it's not comfortable, I saw her thinking. Seeing me as a zealot babbling in the tent down a muddy road on the Rez. Revival!

"I haven't bought the idea, I have accepted His love. Be totally truthful with yourself. You'll be amazed at where it leads."

That was her cue. Though she didn't leave right then, after a couple more minutes of talk, she did. The evening was still young.

I sipped a cappuccino, reflecting on the exchange. Had I conveyed the truth in love, or was I just expressing a new self righteousness, using a different hammer? In the lodge at Lake Louise, Rebecca had allowed, not shared or given, her beautiful body, separate from and without any of her heart. For both of us, it had been adventure, entertainment, little or nothing more. Taking, not giving. Hollow, pointless. It had been wrong, and I was ashamed.

Warmed by the coffee, I walked outside in no hurry to do anything except enjoy the evening. Remembering the wedding earlier in the day at the Heisler Park gazebo, up the hill along Cliff Drive, the start of a different life together. May that life be blessed.

Passing the Laguna Gate, greeting visitors for the last 60 years, originally to an ice cream parlor, now Forest Avenue:

> This Gate Hangs Well
> And Hinders None
> Refresh and Rest
> Then Travel On

Reflecting on this morning's beach, boulders as if in a Japanese garden, surrounded by immaculate borders of wet sparkling sand. Endangered sand. A hummingbird feeding on flowers, ice plant in magenta bloom.

I guess I'll never know more about The Prime of Miss Rebecca. I've only seen her once since, driving down PCH in a Mercedes 450SL, shades on, straight ahead, cool. Looking for another cowboy, another movie to fill the time until she hits 30, decides to mark one more item off the list—marriage to the "right" man. Another linear story, forgettable soundtrack, hearttrack locked away, processed to suppress the fundamentals, no harmonics. Seeing her drive in the opposite direction, away into a future where I would not be found.

Returning my gaze ahead from her retreat in the rearview, I saw a little hand raised in the back seat of the car in front of me, recalling another south of Shiprock. I had followed that car into a parking lot, pulled into a space, and captivated, watched the young mother take her child out of the car seat. Dressed for a ceremony, an awesome Navajo woman driving a dusty, beat Chevy. Black hair carefully fixed, dark dress, concho belt, coral and shell necklaces, long dangling turquoise earrings, silver bracelets and rings, old buffalo nickel button covers, Mercury dimes, buckskin leggings.

As they went through the door of the trading post, I thought about my unborn children, the stationwagon, a parking lot somewhere on the road, in America, in that waking dream. Months, years ago. Why was that little hand the only one I could remember seeing in Laguna?

Where are the mothers and children? They're here. In my blindness, I haven't been able to see them.

The rendezvous with Rebecca was brief. Unfortunately, for the time being, only another pretty girl, in the tight, seductive dress of her own choices, boundaries, and excuses.

In retrospect, our time together suffered from uncorrected parallax distortion. Apparent shifting against reference experiences in the more distant background when viewed from two different points. Reality and fantasy. Now throw in some clouds of emotion, celestial rotation, and one gains a new respect for the question of olde: "why don't we fall off the Earth?" Gravity, conventions, choices.

Belonging, if you're inclined to work at it. And ultimately, faith. Because "Devoted Husband, Loving Father" on one's grave marker, without being those, will not be enough.

I took the Holy Roller thing as a compliment. If you stand for what you believe, there will always be those who label you, or just want to see you run aground. I guess I was getting "conservative", with respect to that faith, not the politics served up daily in the *Orange County Patriot*, which used to be the

Democrat (talk about irony) before it was sold in the 50's. Theirs was just an editorial creed, journalistic rallying call. Another kind of toga party.

Marriage versus "living together", without total commitment. A woman in the kitchen wearing an apron—not relegated to a "role", rather committed to a loving relationship. I'd wear an apron, if that's what was needed. It's practical, it can work, and it looks good to me, the right jewelry for the occasion. A prominent heartline. This is not, and doesn't have to be, the cardboard vacuum of *Leave it to Beaver*.

It wouldn't play in a lot of places I had been. I didn't need to play those any more.

Rebecca, I'm sorry. I don't know who I thought you were. I do know now who I wanted you to be, and who I've been.

It's still early. I guess I'll drive up to Newport, see what's playing at the theaters.

Thanksgiving was quiet. A day with thoughts of Emily, a morning like any other day. And of Stephanie, wherever you are. Exercise, practice, work on some charts for an upcoming session. Later, I drove up to Max and Gretchen's for dinner. It was an opportunity to catch up, the longest period spent together since New Year's. By the time to go, we had decided to attend the Mozart program at Dorothy Chandler Pavilion the next week which included one of my favorite choral works.

The drive home later was almost peaceful, the highways deserted, the sky clear, starsandmoon. A beautiful place thirty years ago. I was fortunate to live in Laguna now, the mountains, ocean, and greenbelt insulating the town from the horizontal components of growth pushing on three sides. The vertical component was something else, as homes were built higher and higher on the steep slopes.

The serenity had long since vanished several days later, eclipsed by the bumper to bumper traffic through the sprawl of LAORANGECO on the way to the concert. By the time the music started I was agitated, wondering why. Later, I would understand that the Spirit of the Lord was upon me, stirring up things, to break the complacency into which it was always so easy to slip, to mould me. Hard work, church on Sunday, in my own mind walking that straight and narrow, getting it together. But life is also about body slams and bouncing back. Often, crawling back.

Mozart's *Great Mass in C minor* is an unleashing of incredible power— ultimately, an exuberant, humbling, though uncompleted celebration. Hearing it has always made me question who I am and what I'm doing; now makes me call out to God the Father—"help me, I need Your hand in my life, constantly."

Soaring, incredibly beautiful, with a libretto I could now not only translate, but follow and understand in Latin. Heavy duty medicine of a different kind. In terms of momentum, one might think that the end of the Gloria, "Jesu Christe—Cum Sancto Spiritu", is the conclusive power of the work, but without denouement it just keeps coming with the Credo:

Credo in unum Deum,	I believe in one God,
Patrem omnipotentem,	the Father Almighty,
Factorem coeli et terrae,	Maker of heaven and earth
Visibilium omnium et invisibilium.	and of all things visible and invisible.
Credo, et in unum Dominum,	I believe in one Lord,
Jesum Christum	Jesus Christ

It drove me out after a mumbled, "*Ich muß gehen*" (I must go), to Max and Gretchen, who were frozen by the terse farewell. Row after row until I reached the foyer door. "Concert Collapse," the *LA Times* article would read. I could just see it, but didn't care.

On the freeway everything was backed up at The Stack except I-10 East. At San Bernardino, I turned north on I-15, headed for the high desert. Rolling the dice, like all the others on this road headed toward Vegas.

As I drove, the Credo and Sanctus ran through my mind. They wouldn't stop. My life was as unfinished as Mozart's composition. How could I just give up on Stephanie, as if I had never met her, totally let it slide? Assume an ending without any current, accurate basis? I had to look for the missing parts. I'm already in Baker, only 1000 miles to Laramie, and I've got a Ferrari.

And then a final, although disregarded, argument to the contrary. In the Moon of Spinning Wheels, not equipped with snow tires.

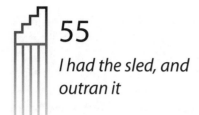

55

I had the sled, and outran it

Somewhere in Utah, looking through headlights, I thought of the cuff of my shirt, once laundered, crisply starched and folded, now worn and rumpled, well past when it would otherwise have been thrown aside on the bathroom floor. Epitome of and postscript to the night's events. Order, anticipation, tension; flight, wired abandon, melancholy. Fatigue. As that gray tree in a gray field, only the imprint of rough bark texture and bare sweeping limbs to remind us of the life that existed, was there, but never in the picture, being only an image.

An evening like the slam of a car door in the rain, ringing trash can lid. "Blues in F minor" rising from a cellar, across the glistening street, filling us with jams and variations, notes on and beyond the scale, fuel for yet more sensuous riffs. Eventually. Until then, a hydrocarbon powered ride toward nothing but assumptions and premises.

Even darkness can be the plucked harmonic of a moment's truth. Stopped for gas I heard the screeching of a hot box on steel rail, sonorous as a humming anvil. Put your ear to it, the sound of fleeing an era—flattened, ground down, slickness punctuated by the staccato click-clack of express freights which don't stop.

There is a city ahead, and then, there is the poetry of the night behind, smooth or jagged. Headlights and red taillights, speeding by in accelerating timelapse. Late, dark buildings blank except for the stars still stuck to the windows.

A muted trumpet, metallic flugelhorn drawing, bending smooth tones, brushstroked lights on Edward Hopper Street, 11th's and 13th's over a Dsus4, vaporized chord chunks like smoke floating in the jazz club, emotion drawn over the boulevard. Night's witness to when all the people are gone, you're alone. For me, the city's never been about people, rather, creative hiding. Snap. Snap. Snap, fingers catching the beat.

While back along the track, the breath of spring whispers it will loosen the sap, return the flow of life. A promise. But this is winter, not spring. The struggle of ice storms and uninvited cold lie ahead. Another moon. The Moon of Popping Trees.

I passed the vacant lot that had been the Cafe Whyoming, seeing it panoramically in a slow drive-by, as if situated on a peninsula tip of distorted reality. Taken out by an event, storm of one kind or another, now only the runup of time among broken, derelict beach pilings of past dreams and experiences. Cathy in the doorway one morning, the henley shirt.

What had been a drumhead stretched tightly over the shell of a resonant life was now only an unmarked historical site down by the tracks, wasted by a blaze. Remembered in a hypothetical charcoalrubble alley, fire escape without a building, in a missing canyon overrun by incendiary fear and depletion. Every city has them.

Likewise wasted my ears rang and body ached from the drive. The glow of dashboard gauges long since gone in the daylight, clear blue sky. No snow today. What was I expecting to find here in Laramie, in Bozeman, Billings. Stephanie? Sleep? Tractor attachments? Back in the banana belt, without bananas.

A sleep full of dreams, of dawns, faces, impossible circumstances resolved only by waking for a moment, falling back into the dreamland. On and off until the next morning.

I finally awoke, looked at the ceiling, turned my face to the side. Wildly implausible hypothesis confirmed. Laramie.

The morning, still dark, was incredibly cold as I drove the mile downtown for breakfast, particularly so considering that I was wearing a tropical weight tux, the only clothing I had. A man in a tuxedo driving a Ferrari pulling into the Country Kitchen at 6:30 am. There was that time in Medicine Creek … much warmer day, different props and materials.

The car heater never got up to operating temperature, and I was shivering as I walked through the door, ranchers and graveyard shifters peering at me over their coffee cups. Buddy Iota and the Pacific Rim Sing-a-Long Band doing an all night party at the Elks? Nobody said hi, Whyoming days notwithstanding. This was a different crowd.

After twice petrified toast, wavedoff rancheros, and plenty of acid-aluminized coffee, I went over to the drug store and got a few things before returning to the room to clean up and make some calls.

Pastor Dave.

"Your love will be true and worthy when you submit it unselfishly, asking for nothing in return. Nothing. Love for the benefit of those who are loved and

Cafe Whyoming

not yourself. That they may know the love of another, a reflection of what, through faith, we can come to know as God's love for us.

"There's nothing wrong with praying that your love will be returned, but that must be a prayer of submission to God. That He will bless you, and you will accept what He grants. It may not be what you are praying for, or think you are praying for."

We were talking about Stephanie, of course. As always, the message was clear and direct, leaving no ambiguity for rationalization. I knew he was right.

"Craig, I heard that Stephanie isn't engaged, or no longer engaged, I'm not sure which is the case, but that's all I know. Amy saw her briefly, but she said little. Although it seems something's going on, a struggle perhaps, we have to respect her privacy. Her parents say she *is* living in Billings ... ."

Concluding the call to Dave, I dialed directory assistance in Billings next. Having no luck finding her number, I rang Stephanie's parents at the ranch. It wouldn't be right to pry. Speaking briefly with her mother, I could only ask that she convey a message asking Stephanie to call me. I left my Laguna number, and that of Bob and Beth St. Clair here in Laramie.

The report Stephanie wasn't on her honeymoon encouraged me, having outlined the heart-wrenching, signature aria of my new opera, *Love Song Between Worlds*, on the way up, for her to sing. Seeking a Native sign to confirm things were going to get better, there was only Rusted Laughing Bear. Precision Wheel Balancing.

Finally, I called Bob to check in. He was running a restaurant while Beth went to school, a tragic step down from the energy which had been brought to this high plains, wind whipped town by the Whyomin'.

The sunlight was disappearing into overcast from the northwest which meant only one thing—snow. I had three choices: stay here to vacation in Laramie; go north to Billings; or go south toward that Great State of Regression in what could only add layers to an already prize-winning celebration cake of self doubt. Coin toss. It didn't land on edge. With Option 2 prevailing, I went north, headed for the 34 cutoff, to Wheatland and I-25, over Morton Pass. On the other side, the snow started. It would soon be a wall, whiteout.

Crossing a bridge, icy under the snow, the car spun. In that instant, I'm sure I saw Emily's face. *Emily, du lebst? Du atmest?* Do you live? Do you breathe? Am I still alive? *Ich lebe noch immer?*

There were no other cars on the desolate route, and the land on the other side of the bridge was flat. After a couple of donuts, the Ferrari came to rest on the shoulder, undamaged. Whether it had been a command to stop, or just a loss of nerve, I couldn't continue. With the adrenalin hit came a kinetic collage of the living and dead, strangely comforting when it was happening, but a fearsome rush of images a moment later, one with which I had no chance of keeping up.

Getting out of the car, I began walking, imagining the ghostly petroglyphs scratched into the sandstone of Nine Mile Canyon. Seeing them float. A broken lance tip, lame horse. Defenseless. This was your last chance, I thought, all of it. The sleep of death is near. I could feel it all around me. The soft snow become cold, bitter, unforgiving.

I saw the petroglyphs in books, in person. In my dreams. "Do not open," said the rocks on which they were etched. Do not open the sandstones and shales, fossil leaves and tracks, fractures, seeping springs; the Mimbres graves, burial mounds along the rivers, armies beneath the earth.

Yes, it is about tension, isn't it? Nibbling at the edges until you must confront yourself, time and time again. Grandfathers turned, to watch me go. Knowing it so well, rendered with spare elegance: the Long Knives are out of balance, their actions desperate, their world ill. It is in *you*, that part which is not in harmony.

What are *my* sacred mountains? The Empire State Building? Pyramid on the back of a dollar bill? The Gibraltar of Insurance? Are sacred mountains the last ones you see, or those that can never be seen entirely? The mountains here, now hidden by snow?

Behold, I have become the man beside the road, grandfather to my old ideas. Walking toward death, into the high mountain snow of my dreams. What had Annie said, "my life is one, a whole life, both waking and in sleep?" I felt her presence with me now. Watching my death. Walking with me.

There were no shadows here, only the bare uniformity of white truth. No distractions or diversions, cover from which to peer out, considering … no vision once thought to be sharp, if too critical, now realized to be unreliable, useless. I could choose the path, but not the outcome. Walk. Freeze. Numbered steps to eternity.

I accept this. I am ready.

Slipping on a patch of ice covered by the snow, I went down hard, breath knocked from me, crying out in a universe of pain. With each gasp for air, I cried even more deeply, rolled into a ball, side of my face in the cold snow, until the moan became louder than the wind.

My struggle was not to be concluded along this road. It wasn't fear. I was ready to die. Closer to and much more ready than in the Mojave. Were there children to be born? Was that the reason?

Returning to the car, hurting from the fall, I thought back to Laramie, and what brought me to this very point today. Within the dynamic equilibrium of time, on the edge, there was a moment's rest. But only a moment. The pictures were gone, burned. All of them. The moment passed, tension returned.

At I-25, I could only turn south, before calling Dave Franck again to let him know I wasn't coming to Montana. There was nothing new regarding the whereabouts of Stephanie.

The trip became one of daydreaming, movement, mechanical refueling, counting down the mile markers. Another chapter in an unending book, *The History of Distraction*, that mixed media exploration of extravisitational, passive enervation. The storm kept building, but I had the sled to outrun it, to Denver, Colorado Springs, over Raton Pass. In Santa Fe, the fireplace at La Fonda would warm me, and indeed it did when I pulled in at 9 pm, still in the tux, by this time unbearable. I had picked up some clothes along the way which room service would have laundered overnight.

At least I was in Santa Fe at a good time, early December, when the tourists are gone and the skiers have not yet arrived en masse. Enchiladas with "Christmas" chile, red and green. Cafe Pasqual's for breakfast. Tia Sophia. *Sopapillas* dipped in Questa honey. Mexican Trout!

Hazy, incompletely thawed memory of a time before, on my way to meet Cathy in Ft. Collins, earlier fire at Tomasita's. A clearer memory of going to the Dorothy Chandler. Blame it all on Mozart … and … love. Or was it obsession? How could I know that it was real, living, truly God given and not sirenic? Love by approximate methods? The love written in notes, yet not by the heart? Love sotto voce. Almost a thrill. What a concept.

I warmed my hands at the fireplace behind the back wall of La Plazuela, the dining room which was mostly deserted. Nearby was a piano to which I was drawn. Tonight, softly playing my *Sonata*, it would be music not for a grade, only for saltillo tile. Lament in A minor. Charged and rightfully convicted of failure to have anything in common with modern life. Failure to make the sale, missing out on the long term exclusive deal. Elusive, everlasting, true love. I could take the advance for Sonata No. 2, but would it ever be written?

Surprisingly, they didn't chase my rumpled figure away, back out onto *La Strada Due Mila Disappointamente*, to be perfectly macaronic. The Street of Two Thousand Mile Disappointment. Not Mozart, but not lounge music either. Remember, a sonata given by God, played through me, a man. For my angel, Emily, all those who had given of their hearts to me. A benediction for them, and for what had been my life, chunks of which I was still letting go. That there would be quiet within me, mercy granted.

By this time, a small crowd had gathered in the nearby chairs and sofas. Seeing my Hopi bracelets, I heard a woman say in a too loud whisper, "that's Craig Maxwell!" followed by another, "looks burnt out to me."

Where had I heard it before: "… but you're Craig Maxwell, I've read the stories, seen the pictures … creative whirlwind, icon?" Nowhere important. It was all only by implication. Only by imagination, reputation. Fabrication. Bolted together; frozen, rusted threads long gone.

Imagine that, burnt out at 30. Needing rest, I went to my room without a word, seeking refuge. No Pink Adobe tonight. Slide the *carne asada* under the door to my cell.

Opening the Bible in the nightstand, I read the passage:

Behold, though it is planted, will it thrive? Ezekiel 17:10

A man alone on a battlefield with an enemy tank before him on the verge of firing can find God's guidance an instant before he perishes. Was I that man? Was I? To what dreams could I look forward this night? Was that battlefield this very place, my mind? By now, how deep was the snow in which I kneeled?

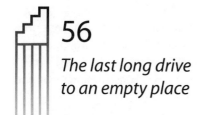

56
The last long drive to an empty place

After two nights in Santa Fe, I began the long trip back to Laguna, the southern route through Las Cruces and Tucson because of the weather. A lot of things were going through my mind on the way down to Albuquerque, incoherently. I wasn't really in driving synch, my consciousness jammed by apparent failure to find Woman With Gentle Spirit, the imagined co-lead in *Life II: After Emily*. A story fading with the miles, postured automatic driving overrunning what little was left of my dreams of happiness. Boomer, Skywalker, Indian Road Chief commuting to the next steel job in a hardened world of concrete, construction fences, with no time.

Taking the Silver exit, I made a left, east on Coal, up Yale to Central. There was a newsstand across from the University of New Mexico where I could get a magazine to read at the coffee joint around the corner, The Hippo or something like that, I recalled.

Sipping a cappuccino, trying to get interested in an article on jazz chord voicings in *Contemporary Keyboard Magazine* while FM soft rock played in the background, I noticed a dark haired girl come in, dressed in black. The girl didn't as much resemble Annie as evoke the difference she represented, where she came from, who she was therefore assumed to be.

Asked the question, "Who are you?", most people wouldn't know what to say or want to talk about it, returning with, "What do you mean?" Ask a Blackfeet, Hopi, or Sioux. They know. Ask an Ojibwe. "I am *Anishinaabe*. We are The People." In part who I am too, if I can both learn and let go of more. Connect with what I often think has either never been there or is just gone, but the next day find still within me.

Put a paddle to the currents of the St. Croix River, dance on the shore of *Gichigami*. Here in The Hippo among animated silhouettes and chatter better thoughts now, possibly on the verge of being liberated by another Dolores del Luna. Almost Japanese. Morning Dance to Miles and Wayne Shorter, yet so far from New York. Buzz Time Estate Reserve. Mysterious. Extreme.

But no. Coffee gone and evocation depleted, table turned over in fourteen minutes. Used to be in the cafe business.

There was no healthy reason to dwell on Dolores. A stroll over to University, north to the Maxwell would be something to do, might help. Walk it out in the fresh air. Oh great, an exhibition of Mimbres pottery. One piece is missing, unaccounted for. Here's a tip—the Laramie landfill.

Keep walking. The library—maybe that's where I need to go, what drew me here. Their extensive Native American collection. A hail of arrows, and it'll all be over. Shot off his horse, collapsed in the dust of the stacks. Last gasp.

Medweackwe. The noise of wind in the trees. Pages turning, thoughts rustling.

> In the old days, there was no 'education', only life, the imparting of knowledge through dreams, visions, the wisdom of elders, everyday practices. We lived on the land, Mother Earth. Our homeland.
>
> Land became 'property' when the white man came. The concept of property is exclusive—a sanctioned means of declaring trespass, denying use. Government tells people how to behave, without wisdom; defines land as real property; and has legislated the taking of our right to occupy it. Even now, the white man does not know how to interpret, and does not obey, his own laws, or live in harmony with what he has taken and now calls *his* land.
>
> The white man brought the Bible, but doesn't understand the Great Spirit. I've read the Bible. It's about courage, sacrifice, love, understanding, judgment, and consequences. It says, 'do unto others,' but when it comes to Indians, the doing has been done unto us. If we ask that the land be respected, our treaty rights preserved, we're called agitators or relics.
>
> Today, white society doesn't know what it is, can't stand to stay in one place, and craves possessions and 'unique experiences.' Its ancestors are unknown, lost with the knowledge of how to live on the land, what it means to belong. It's constantly trying to escape the present life for an imaginary one—in either the past or future.

Under Father Sky has been created Rectalinear America. *On the Road* is really *On the Grid*. Going where *they* want you to go. Plugged in, as they say, but only to the Grid. Spiritual centers reduced to, indeed now being only, map coordinates linked by the quickest routes. Experience overnight delivery by Psyche Trucking Lines.

Well, I've gotten what I came here for. Native perspective indented by the Crowbar Tribe. Where would you like to start, fender, hood, or windshield? Another Rez 'lude—legally sovereign, officially foreign. A prescription by my own scrawling hand, dispensed as assistive impatience, an exercise in scapegoating with postscripted asymptotic lament, a "cultural revolution". New lyrics for a hit song I once coined in a language explainable only by account balances, "Dim Past, Shady Present, Glittering Future".

Fully informed, now cognoscenti, those who know

Back on the Grid, passing T or C, To Tell The Truth, Double Wide, billboard commerce dream towns; places of alkaline hot springs, with no literal translation possible in Apache. Glad for the mountains between me and the Trinity Site isotopic curiosities to the east, though the separation was of little more benefit than wax paper. I was crackling with a more recent dose, exposing film badges with the ghosts of history, seeking to be grounded, but only flying into power lines. As those who have walked up alleys along the coast when the night winds shift know, insulation is never complete, transmission wires stretched tightly, arcing, hissing in the salt air.

Some of us work best at the margins, I thought, belong there. Mindfully observing, deconstructing and recolorizing the version of life we see. If done uncynically, artistic, I think. There will always be those more knowledgeable than I, more expert or erudite, accomplished, perhaps with more depth in their feelings and appreciation of others. Accept that you're not them, and be okay with it. They're not you, either.

Moving on to other subjects, forward, pause, back. Ice Age paleontology, wave mechanics, tethered goats and wolves. Friends with whom I had spent time during the last couple of years, more about my conversations with Annie.

Most of those friends *had* been women. Doesn't bother me. Steering away from the gritty Freudian slush advanced in forgettable seasons by faculty adjunct to any healthy understanding of life, to me the common denominator appeared to be a large prime number, the stainless sieve mesh very fine. In my mixed mind, from the romantic side of the menu, I had always ordered and lived variations on *A Man and a Woman*. Slow dissolves and fades, long drives, words from the heart, maybe even the very soul. An occasional fandango of subtleties. That took a woman. When there was pain to overcome, I sought refuge and expression by creating music. Before realizing it was neither refuge nor my music at all.

We talk so freely about the soul, usually not knowing anything of what we speak. In Mark 12:28-29, the distinction is made among heart, soul, mind, and strength. The soul is our spiritual center, deep and obscured. Without faith, nothing is there except mists of confusion hovering over The Grid.

Bodywork with a grinder. That produces sparks. Let's back up the trash truck and try to collect what's been set out for me in this burning dumpster again, hope the wheels don't slip off into mud.

"Those women." I wondered about their lives, relationships before I met them, and realized I had never asked. They might have mentioned something from time to time, but if so, I had paid little attention. It wasn't about intruding, rather being interested, coming to know, sharing.

What was Cathy's birthday? Constantly thinking about myself, considering what to say next, now I can't even remember something as simple as the date. Unnecessary information as I sought to maximize my comfort, return, those account balances. Noncontroversially. Pleasurably. Nearly all of it was about me.

Submit a couple more dossiers. Emily. Major influence: "God, who inspires me." Interests: plants and gardening, puzzles, children, Porsches, Motown. Snapshot: what day is it? Unpredictable, giving. Once imperfectly perfect, now an angel in Paradise.

Stephanie. Major influences: Grandfather Wells for this tenacity during 75 Montana winters; archival photographs of the last 100 years. Interests: culture, man's relationship to the land, music with a message, barrel racing. Snapshot: enigmatic, complex cowgirl, "if only I could sing *lieder* in German"; an angel on earth. "Don't call me an angel," I could hear her say, if I ever got the chance to be that foolish. Thinking it made me smile.

Kat. Already filed hers from the last trip through Kingman. I hadn't forgotten what she said about a part of each of us remaining with the other, while attempting to understand marriage after Emily's death. How it all fit together in Heaven. Leafing through the little Bible I carried with me now, I found what I was looking for in Mark 12:18-27, the case of a woman who had been married multiple times, and question of whose wife she would be in Heaven:

> For when they rise from the dead, they neither marry, nor are given in marriage, but are like angels in heaven … He is not the God of the dead, but of the living … .

Would the stereoscopic beauty, tangible creation I knew on good days be reduced to this asphalt strip, nothing more than from afar become the graphite line along a designer's ruler? Filling the car at a remote station just past the sign identifying the village: "Lament". Cold wind whipped dust along the road, bent bare branches, reminded me once more that though winter hadn't officially arrived, it had crept in, was silently lurking.

Humanistic Lament, as distinct from the materialistic (not having or receiving in your Christmas stocking exactly the stuff you want, whether or not asked for). Asymptotic, tangential, extra-envelopative, unitive.

Asymptotic, approaching but never getting to the Threshold of Virtual Lament. Ultimately, emotionally separate. Annulment.

In *tangential* lament, the rays of concern *do* intersect the (circle of the) locus of lament, but only at one dimensionless point. How much can you transfer at such an abstract location in terms of love, all it truly is and can be? The lament of a marriage tried, briefly, in terms of time or interest; veering off, away. Abandonment. Divorce.

Extra-envelopative, blanketing a third party, actual or imaginary, in a substitutionary expression of concern, avoiding direct expression to the true object of lament. Sometimes manifested as knitting a jacket for a dog. A wall plug with only one blade, randomly the ground prong. Without current, off subject, off base.

Unitive, where in more than three dimensions a ray of concern, now real, pierces the locus of lament, defining the Space of Renewal. Where this trip ends, I hope. The found Sky Heart.

Got that? Which model do I employ? Resemble? My own sermon on the mount. Mounted today not on a nag, but a thoroughbred. A Ferrari.

Lives flare, burn, dim as glaciers creep. Maybe we're little more than air bubbles and rock fragments frozen in the clear ice of imperceptibly moving time. Too often dry, overgrazed, and barren as this land, as ignored and forgotten. There is no redemption in ignorance or depletion, of ourselves or others. Nevertheless, the choice is always there, between picking and hauling pointless cargo, and freedom. Of the spirit. Though freed for eternity, I have not yet learned how to live each day in thankful triumph, world remission.

Somewhere in New Mexico, fleeing the storm, I saw a white horse graze in a field under gray sky. Amid the cedar and scrub, grama grass, chamisa winter silver after the golden flowers of summer, withering of fall. I was as the horse, alone before the heavens. Contrasts harsh and subtle, growing cracks telling me to seek refuge, for this bluffing, deluded empire is destined to crumble.

Among the hard days, despair, reluctance, uncertainty, and weakness, inevitably man's lot, my lot, I know You're there. If it's Your will, send an angel. That I may:

> See the beauty
> Seek the beauty
> Know the beauty
> Celebrate the beauty
> And in doing so,
> Live the beauty.

Please, another angel, one whom only You can send. That the fighting, scarring of my heart in losing Emily would not overtake me. That I might *love the beauty*.

57

*Reflections, on light
and film*

Returning late at night, I took a shower and fell into bed. In the morning, the evidence of recent rain convinced me I really had been away, that it wasn't only a fantasia spun by Mozart. Below the hills, wave sets rolled in on the Pacific, dragged bottom, breaking one after another. This place, familiar after the days on the road; flowers so dramatic in contrast to the winterscapes of Wyoming and Colorado, low storm clouds of New Mexico. *Díghááł, yá diłhił, kodi*—open your eyes, blue sky, right here. High sparkle factor, the surfers would say, paddling out their brightly colored, glassed sticks.

If I was to sum up my feelings about Stephanie, try to communicate them to her, what would I write? Opening the desk drawer to get some paper, I thought about the red coral necklace bought on that Sunday morning in Flagstaff. I wanted to give it to her, but why would she accept it? A cowgirl wearing red coral—would she even want it? Another relic headed for the landfill to join the Mimbres pot? Taking the necklace out of the box, I admired the deep red color, quality of the coral, workmanship in the beads and expert stringing. This is a gift, a beautiful one which tells about me. That can be the best kind.

I wrote the letter I hoped would come true, folded, and put it in an envelope addressed to "Stephanie Tyler", then placed the box and envelope on the desk. They'll be there, until I decide whether to send or file them, under "What Might Have Been".

Back out on the deck, judging from the moist ground, it looked like the rain had been heavy. Despite the magnificent landscape, the Southwest filled my mind. I hadn't quite caught up with being back.

That white horse in New Mexico—was there another hidden in the background? I visualized the land, walked down a path of detail disappearing into shadows, grain. The second horse was there, beyond a fence, darker, perhaps chestnut brown. But was all of it within even one more fence I couldn't see, along another road, as Kat had said, behind a gate I would never open?

Farther west, along the Colorado, the throaty voice of the Ferrari faded, and I saw the eyes of "Mosa Mohave", a young girl photographed by Curtis 75 years ago. Though I wanted to believe she was looking back at me in timeless empathy, that couldn't be true. Mosa stopped existing in terms of the picture when it was taken, became only a frozen image. As had Zitkala-Ša, who wasn't even looking into the camera. I kept wanting her to turn, to look at me, but she never would. The pose cannot be overcome, the motion never completely stopped, hence, the rendering, not in reality or spirit but analogical densities of silver, is always blurred, imperfect. Still, I seek the eyes.

Black & white isn't even reality unless you're color blind. In shooting and printing it, I'm the editor, using technique and devices to emphasize communication of the editorial viewpoint by framing (inclusion or exclusion), contrast, form, abstraction, the spectrum extending from softly to starkly real, unreal or surreal.

I got out *Dwellers at the Source*, a compilation of A.C. Vroman's turn of the century *Southwestern Indian Photographs*. The "Hopi Woman", more a child with butterfly hairstyle of the unmarried, looking down and to the side with what seemed to be the profound sadness of a culture under assault. Since the Pan American Exposition, inhabitants of a living museum, rendered as chapters of curiosity, each the cause and effect of another thrust of the "dominant culture".

Pictures are often posed, always exposed. Our objectives, methods, and materials enable us to "see" the subject, extract the message we want to communicate according to a photographic agenda, selectively applying materials, aesthetic and technical skills. The everyday isolation of clothes drying on lines on bright winter days between storms, snow on the ground. Clusters of mailboxes at deserted crossroads, grader berms lining dusty ribbons disappearing into the hills. Breezes of springs past rustling tall green grass along those roads, ascribed romance and emotions of the winds and waving grass Kat had seen in my eyes. The towering walls of Canyon del Muerto, aspen groves in the mountains above the Dolores River, a lifetime of travel. Already behind me. In a spare land, one substantially of my own perception, interpreted creation.

For a moment, I was overwhelmed again by a sense that my life was nearly over. *Nihoolzhíísh*, that time is running out. I had seen, posed, and done enough, was spiritually equipped for the biggest step of all. In this existence, I felt caught in the permanent cast of that museum exhibit, *Contemporary Life*, footnoted by the inevitable sociological monograph describing the decline and extinction of another cultural remnant. As was Ishi, interesting for a time, a memory preserved and then largely forgotten until it was time to once again worship the past, its archetypes and symbols shrunken and dry as the split grain of old wood. Not everybody gets to marry and have children in this experiment.

I went into the kitchen for some water, sat down thinking. We have been so damaged, become as synthetic as the materials, equipment, social and internal contrivances with which we have tried to amuse, explain, sustain, and repair ourselves. While considering that, I looked up, seeing the automatic dishwasher, other kitchen appliances, stereo and music machines, lighting systems, mass-produced carpet, on and on and on.

The architectural magazine on the table drove the runaway thought-train even faster. "It was a bold, linear site. A minimalist enterprise in all the right ways. Enjoy your walls." The same signs seen every mile along innumerable roads of this Great State of Material Culture (with official seal). "Stop Now! Here! Gene Autry's Saddle! Talk To An Apache! America's Only Museum Of The Future!"

They all did dope or just liked the second hand smoke, Went Chemical! Still crave hallucinogenic residue in whatever material or immaterial forms "modern demographic groups" do these days in their baseline volleys. Make reservations to laugh about it over a few drinks, dinner. Arrive in a heavy, fortified car, secure in rehearsed superficialities, exclusions of grandeur. Turn red in anger when the conversation takes an unfortunate twist, insults are launched, truths are told. Sociopsychological trick shooting and trial solutions. The thrill of spilled burning hot coffee behind the wheel approaching a one lane bridge while passing, intent on getting there before the oncoming truck. "The thrill of victory … the agony of defeat," as *Wide World of Sports* sums it up.

Long drive. No girl. We say "hopes and dreams," but is what's really driving our lives just nervous, unsettled, anticipatory, contingent, speculative motivation? I know the answer. Accept only clean, unbiased, random tragedy. It draws a sharper edge on an otherwise predictable, entropic life. Entropic does not mean ensconced in a tropical locale, nor does ensconced mean residing within a lighting fixture.

Thinking to myself, as in a voice over: "I've changed." What was once arrogance is now only unknowingness. Caught in more rambling jumbles of words, fragments of ideas. Struggling on many fronts. Resigned.

O herz, sei stark! Be strong my heart! Because the fishscape is both—Jaws *and* Jonah.

I needed to break the spell, try to play some music. Start with … Scarlatti, and go from there, wherever that might be. It had been a long time since I'd played what I had in mind. First, the music would have to be found. Out in the garage, on the shelves probably.

After finding and dusting off the box, I brought it inside by the piano, took off the top, lifted out several folios, and set them on the saltillo tile floor. "What's that spiral bound one doing in here?" I wondered, starting to leaf through the stack. The phone rang.

I went into the kitchen, debating if I wanted to answer or not, but then just picked up. It was Max, who had business in Orange County and suggested we get together for lunch in Laguna. As we talked, I looked at the feathered Yokuts basket on the shelf, quietly listening to my side of the conversation while flying through time.

No doubt Max wanted to check on me after the episode at Dorothy Chandler. I summarized the trip for him in a few seconds: "long drive, no girl; no Stephanie, but it's okay," for some reason reassured by the presence of the basket. As we continued to speak, I looked out the window, at the ocean below. What I really need is a run to the beach, to breathe the salty air, hear the roar of waves crashing into the headland, walk in foamy runup on the golden sand of the cove, go downtown for a cappuccino. Hold off the siege of weariness and disappointment, be thankful for the blessings instead of chasing the who or what I think I want always seeming to elude me.

I told Max I'd leave a note where he could find me if I wasn't at the house when he arrived, then changed. Before leaving, I did a few tai chi moves to orient myself to the run, beach, being back here, the day. It wasn't about the moves, rather emptying oneself of everything but the movement. And then leaving that behind. When I returned, there would be the Scarlatti.

In the kitchen to get a drink of water before my run, I noticed the answering machine. Light blinking as always, it would have to wait. I'm out of here.

When he arrived, there was an old truck in the driveway, a woman inside, in tears. Montana plates. Spare tire and snow chains in the bed. A long way from Big Sky.

"Are you looking for someone?" Max asked.

"Do you know where I can find Craig Maxwell? This is the address he gave me."

"Is he expecting you?"

"No ... we met in Bozeman last summer. I tried to find him in Laramie, but apparently he had just left. Then I called here, but still haven't been able to make contact. I'm Stephanie Tyler."

"I'm Max, a friend of his. You sing, right?"

"Yes, which is the reason I'm here. Well, one of the reasons ... but how did you know that?"

"Craig has mentioned you, more than once, as recently as this morning when I spoke with him, if you can believe that. He said there'd be a note if he was gone when I arrived, which looks like the case. Let me check by the door. Yes, here it is. He's either at the cove or downtown. We'll see if we can find him. Would you prefer to come back later, ride with me, or follow in your truck?"

"I'll ride with you. Thank you. It's been a long drive and I'm really tired."

Jogging *down* to the beach is always the easy part. Eventually, you have to climb back *up* the hills. I headed down the street, thinking about Annie. To be more specific, the image versus the person.

I was drawn, am still attracted by the image, the exotic, no matter what I say. Maybe shopping a different department at Tower Records, but admiring the album artwork just the same. She's intriguing to my Anglo side—my longing for the exotic. But I've gotten to know her, the person, too. So to me, she's both.

Now, add or subtract a little complexity, depending upon how you look at it: every woman in whom I've ever been interested has been exotic. Because she's a woman. Female. So where does that leave me?

Annie, the woman *is* exotic	Strike One!
Annie's *image is* exotic	Strike Two!
To get to know the person, you cannot afford to get lost in the exotic; however, that is impossible because she *is* a woman, and therefore exotic	Strike Three!

I'M OUT, brought full circle, back to where I started. Even if you know all the answers, you can't solve the puzzle. That's women. And love. Labyrinth of the senses, perceptions, heart. In the Canyonlands. The Maze. Many men never descend into it; fewer climb out.

That woman back in Harrisburg … Elaine … separated, divorce pending. She was in a minefield. What I didn't realize is that I was too.

I loved Natalie, my first real love, when I was growing from boy to man. Not knowing how deep it was, or how the loss of her would affect me. I realize now the emptiness after her that I filled with music. No love measured up to that for Natalie, no woman to the music with which I tried to replace her … until Emily. She reawakened my capacity to truly love. Now I also know it takes more than capacity, a special woman, and timing. It takes faith, and God's blessing. Intersection within His spiritual universe. All the elements have to be there, on the part of both man and woman, for it to work. Otherwise, it must be empty, whether earlier or later. Often terribly so.

What I'm left with is a gift—that what's between a man and woman is holy before God. *He has made it exotic.*

All wrapped up. Nothing to do but curl the ribbon.

Crossing PCH, I took the trail to my favorite cove, the premier lagoon of Laguna. The very place where Emily and I walked, and yet not on the same grains of sand, never again the exact beach. While coming down the path, I thought of Stephanie and felt happiness, visualizing her face while enjoying the breeze, looking down at the cove, azure water just off the little beach, light reflected from the shallow bottom.

My heart was suddenly filled with the uniquely simultaneous triumph and capitulation of love. Knowing that to love is only to start, I realized Stephanie was the one for whom God had readied me. A minute ago, I had set forth my arguments about what was necessary to make it work. But even that didn't go far enough. At the core of what had been eluding me was learning to peacefully *accept* God's plan. True faith.

Du bist meine Hoffnung. Lord, You are my only hope.

Prefaced by the most subtle of shadows, perhaps a thin cloud above or unseen, diaphanous hand shielding my view from the sun, a voice which could only be from Him spoke to me.

"Where have you been?" The question a parent asks after calling their child.

Within a step, the briefest of moments, a choir offered a perfect benediction from the *Mass in B Minor*:

> *Gratias agimus tibi propter*   We give Thee thanks for Thy
> *magnam gloriam tuam.*   great glory.

Bach, Mozart, Haydn and Beethoven had been there to guide me. God-willing, when the drums of my ancestors were silent, the campfires out, I would meet them in Paradise. Now, perhaps only a moment away.

"Now that you are with Me, I am here with you," He said. "Seek your rest in Me."

"Thank you, Lord." I was at peace, walking alone along a road toward mountains. In the snow.

✛══✛

From below on the beach, the two surfers saw the top of the bank, saturated by the rains, collapse; someone go over the cliff. A person falling, movement strangely graceful, as if dancing. Smooth, balanced, swan-like, with no flailing. Then a huge wave broke, dirt from the bank hit it, followed by the man, disappearing into the water, crashing foam.

✛══✛

Nearly to the headland, Max and Stephanie saw the familiar figure for an instant, and then the earth gave way, the path disappearing into the ocean with the landslide.

"NNNOOOOOOOOO," Stephanie screamed, while Max, frozen, could say nothing at first, then turned around and ran, yelling, "I'll go for help."

58

*Another rough week
in the media*

In early December 1979, at the end of the 70's, the newspaper headlines were dominated with weighty stories: "Iran Hostage Crisis in 30th Day, Carter to Run for Second Term, U.S. in Chrysler Bailout, Inflation Soaring, U.S. Steel Closes 10 Mills, Two States Fight Over 'Wild Thing' Rights." California wanted it as the state song; another, Indiana?, the official bird and license plate motto. Krugerrand sales were booming, with gold at $500 per ounce, film prices headed out of sight due to the cost of silver. *Star Trek—The Motion Picture* and *The Jerk* were opening, a media mix of science fiction and thinly comedic stupidity. Holiday escape for four bucks at the nearest multi-screen.

It was a time of soaring, if you can call a flat spin death spiral that: "Divorce Rate Soars 70% Over Decade, Inflation Soars, 13% CPI Increase Largest Rise in Over 30 Years, Growing Hunger." Sides were being chosen—in divorce court, one or the other "Kramer vs. Kramer"; similarly in the economy, the next round of Big Government vs. Big Oil. Maybe the "crisis of confidence" threatening America's future would be solved before the new millennium. Pan Am *would* be flying off planet, fulfilling the prophesy of *2001: A Space Odyssey*, right? Manking (sic) could happily look forward to even more elaborate thrill rides.

There were certainly alternative, terrestrially based scenarios, given the pervasive mindset of *Saturday Night Fever*: life as an expanded version of *American Bandstand*. Bobby Rydell and Freddy Cannon would keep coming back, ageless special guests; everybody would dance in black & white on afternoon TV, rate the newest sounds forever: "I liked the beat and the performer, but not the words; I gave it a 48." The late 60's *Easy Rider* model hadn't made permanent headway; that could be crossed off the list. If there were any thinkers left, they might reasonably grasp, without having to graph the data, things didn't seem to have gotten much better in the 70's.

Against that backdrop of self-deluding conjecture as reality and advertising content as truth, two items appeared on the front page, the same day: "11 Die at Cincinnati Who Concert," and "Accident Claims Rock Star"—"More on Page 1 of Spectrum Section."

Landslide, Pacific Claim Rock Star in Laguna Beach

(NP) Two years after a traffic accident claimed the life of his girlfriend, ESO star Craig Maxwell perished in a landslide along the

Pacific Ocean in Laguna Beach, California. Eyewitnesses watched helplessly as a bluff collapsed and fell into the Pacific Ocean, taking with it Craig Maxwell, who was walking on a narrow path leading to the cove below. Maxwell's body was recovered by the Orange County Sheriff's Department.

Craig Maxwell burst onto the LA music scene in 1971, joining ESO after graduation from the University of Pennsylvania. Following his departure from the group in 1977, he was seriously injured in a motorcycle accident in the Mojave Desert. After what some termed an astounding recovery, he enrolled in the Master of Fine Arts program at the University of Wyoming, majoring in music performance. Those close to him remarked about the dramatic, prodigious growth of musical abilities following the motorcycle accident, as if he was on a mission known only to himself; and brilliant photographic interpretations.

Tragedy first struck Maxwell in late 1977, with the death of Emily Ritchey, a teacher at the high school he attended in Camp Hill, PA. In a newspaper story at that time, Maxwell mourned the loss of Ritchey, for whom he had written the love song, "Emily", which was never released. Tragedy again struck earlier this year, when the building he owned in Laramie, Wyoming, burned to the ground. Reeling from that setback, he became an avowed Born Again Christian, and moved toward the musical style now known as "Contemporary Christian".

Craig Maxwell is remembered by the string of hits he wrote for ESO, identification with Native American issues and arts as a member of the Fond du Lac Band, Minnesota Chippewa Tribe, and his love for "espresso coffee and the wide open Western spaces." Craig Maxwell was 30.

Stephanie sat on the balcony outside her room at the Laguna Inn in tears, reading the newspaper article over and over, looking out to the Pacific for help, seeking an anchor. Unfamiliar water on a scale she had never before experienced. Waves rolling in, one moment beautiful, soothing; then troubling, tragic. So few words to sum up a life. It was as if Fate was speaking to her through the opera Craig had mentioned that day in Bozeman, *Ariodante*:

Im nahen Meer ertrank dein	Your bridegroom has been lost
Bräutigam.	in the nearby sea.

A woman has dreams. I had dreams, she thought, dreams of music and then this man which brought me here. Seeing herself place a hand on his breast, tell him with her eyes that she was and forevermore would be his. In the end, left only with those dreams, the memorial service later today, more of the pain she had not been able to overcome. Another dream last night, of walking in snow, seeing Craig in the distance, but not being able to reach him.

Clutching the letter that he had written, looking at the red coral necklace in the box with the sticker, "Puchteca Indian Arts, Flagstaff, Arizona", she pleaded, "Oh, Lord, help me. When I knew I had to tell him the truth, when I realized that I wanted to be with him, why was it too late? Why did you take him away? Please, Lord, help me understand."

My dearest Stephanie,

Life slips away, too often without those whom you finally realize you were always meant to love. This necklace is for you. And if you wear it, only then will we know that we've found each other.

… If there are children, to be born, there must be songs, to be sung. Go. Sing.

With all my love,
Craig Maxwell

As the waves kept rolling in, she remembered Pastor Franck's story about Craig Maxwell, a man in the end she desperately sought; the Cafe Whyoming, a place she had never been. Other things he had told her. Finding the Ojibwe in Minnesota, he had embarked upon the long road toward understanding his own people. And the loss of a woman named Emily, whose picture was on a wall she never saw. Even in death, the memory of a woman which could make her a life-long competitor, but if honorable and worthy of Craig's love, really an ally and sister in Christ. A loss which she had to believe could only have strengthened his capacity to love and be loved.

Stories repeated down the generations in one form or another, all played out through different sons and daughters, even entire cultures as in *Evangeline*, which Craig had mentioned as they sat in The Bakery talking. Stories about loss, but always with the possibility of a blessed ending after struggle, triumph through salvation. Bozeman, so far away now as to be a place to which her heart could never fully return.

It was fundamentally, eternally true, she meditated—God uses us in His time, for His purpose:

> For My thoughts are not your thoughts,
> Neither are your ways My ways, declares the Lord.
> For as the heavens are higher than the earth,
> So are My ways higher than your ways. Isaiah 55:8-9

> Come to Me, all you who are weary and heavy-laden,
> and I will give you rest. Matthew 11:28

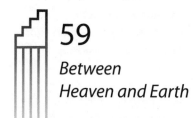

59

*Between
Heaven and Earth*

What's more romantic—the romance of life, or that of death? The dream of living, or life of the spirit? It depends, particularly if you're Shakespeare, or inclined to read him.

You can accept that ending, or write another. The choice is entirely, purely yours. Parts of both are true, tributaries to the ocean of revelation in which the flows of lives mingle and reside, forever.

I remember regaining consciousness for a moment. Face down on the bar, stunned, unable to move, choking on seawater, perhaps mortally injured, I saw the wave once more, felt so light as I came toward it, hearing a voice which seemed far away: "NNNOOOOOOOOO." Then peacefulness as I danced into the darkness between Heaven and Earth.

The most peaceful, wonderful dance, one of transfiguration. Hinted at in the Sixth Movement of Mahler's *Symphony No. 3*. Listen to that, and you will *know*.

In peace, I dreamed as vividly as the night when my memory returned. Many more dreams this time. Maybe not dreams any longer, but a new life. A new *kind* of life.

On the shore of the great lake, more smooth, polished rocks than sand, there was the sound of soft footsteps behind me. Turning around, I saw Annie in the distance, Stephanie Tyler beside me, flowers in her hair, smiling.

"Stephanie, will you marry me?"

"Yes … ."

"Stephanie … my love," I whispered, holding out my arms to her.

With the sound of a wave gently breaking on the beach, I was gone from the lake. Instead of water, there was only a mirage above the desert as I looked out from the striped shade of chimney rocks. In the spirit, I was speaking to God about children.

"Father, that I would be blessed with a daughter who has the dignity and traditions of Annie LaCroix; the sincere heart of Katrina; the good-spirited, longstanding devotion of Catherine; the passionate, energetic smile of

Danielle; the intelligence and inspiring faith of Emily; the enduring promise of Cindy; and the beauty of Stephanie Tyler, in a Montana kind of way."

I knew His reply. "There's more to it than that, much more than simply asking and then receiving. What have you given? What will you give?"

✛════✛

Max, always the one to pick up the pieces, ran for help. A line was rigged over the cliff, to haul the unconscious man up in a basket. Tragic, but nothing unusual, they said, somebody's always getting in trouble around the bluffs or on the rocks below. Then the ride up PCH to the hospital. Sometimes they make it, sometimes they don't.

I was in a hospital, what could only be intensive care, saw a shape standing there, looking through the glare of the lights. Max? But my eyes weren't open.

"Max, that you?" I asked. He couldn't hear me. Beside him were others. Or more accurately, if the distinction is meaningful in a dream, the presences of others.

"Craig," I heard her gaspingly entreat, "please wake up. Oh, Lord, please don't take him away, not now. Craig, please wake up. Please ... ," until no more was heard. I tried to place the voice. Stephanie? Here?

"Is that you, Stephanie? I was just dreaming about you, my love." Words of a dream, unspoken.

In the room, the vital sign monitors, graphs, lights and alarms went crazy.

Emily, an angel, held Stephanie, comforting her as she cried. A different kind of cry, but as heart wrenching as another from so long ago. Cindy. Laguna.

✛════✛

"He's gone," one ER nurse said.

"Yeah ... flat," confirmed another, "who did you say this guy was?"

"White male, thirty years of age, never regained ... ," the doctor began dictating. Detached. For the records. Just another guy.

Rock Star Craig Maxwell Perishes in Accident

(NP) An all night vigil by friends of ESO star Craig Maxwell ended sadly with his death early Saturday morning at the Corona del Mar Medical Center. Details surrounding the accident involving a landslide in Laguna Beach which claimed his life are still not fully known. Officials reported he was placed on a respirator, but never regained consciousness. More information will be reported in later editions when available. Craig Maxwell was 30 years of age.

I was paddling a canoe on the river. Before the Voyageurs, Columbus. Seeking the Land of Souls.

"I'd like you to meet my wife, *niwiiw*, Annie LaCroix.

"Driving through Minnesota on the way back to LA in 1977, I met her at the Library in Cloquet. We've been together ever since.

"We live here in Duluth along Lake Superior, or *Gichigami*, as the Ojibwe call it. The lake is cold and clear, as unpredictable as the Pacific. Rocky and rough enough to take down freighters. Look over there—you can see Wisconsin Point where our ancestors lived in the 1800's, that is those whom we know by name. I like to watch the waves along the North Shore. Reminds me of the Pacific off Laguna Beach where we also have a house. A getaway from the long, cold winters up here. I'm still trying to get used to those.

"Annie went to UW Superior and does volunteer work for the Duluth Library, running the Ojibwe/English bilingual reading program she established.

"And this little guy, *nitamoozhaan*, or first born, is Thomas, our son. Though Annie has a head start, Thomas and I are learning the language, and Old Ways, too.

"I'm doing a little composing, but more arts and crafts these days. Designing and building handmade, custom furniture, updating traditional designs and methods; painting; and even doing some writing.

"Meeting Annie is the best thing that ever happened to me. Saved my life."

"Kat and I live in Flagstaff, on a wonderful piece of land with views of the San Francisco Peaks, *Dook´o´oslííd*, out the back door, Sunset Crater to the east. Fall is my favorite time. The yellow aspen leaves, clear air, and deep blue sky are incomparable.

"She was there when I needed her, although I think we're still both surprised that we're together, *´ahidzískéii*, a married couple. Maybe that's one mark of a strong marriage—though in awe, we never take anything for granted.

"We enjoy a lot of the same things, Native American arts, living on the edge of the Big Rez, such a different culture, a contrast which constantly energizes us.

"Kat teaches school in Flag and has quite a few Navajo students. She sees their uniqueness, promise and problems every day. She loves the kids and teaching school. It's who she is.

"We're active in programs of the Museum of Northern Arizona, northwest of town on Fort Valley Road, the one that goes to the Grand Canyon. Their collections are superb, and summer tribal marketplaces so enjoyable.

"We can't think of anywhere else we'd rather be. The winters are much colder than you might expect in Arizona, since the elevation's about 7000 feet. At least they're not as long as in Montana, where I was born, and other places I considered living such as Laramie, Wyoming, and northern Minnesota.

"Kat's going to be taking a year off after the birth of our child, who is due in April. She's so radiant these days. When I think back to the day we met … it's all been such a blessing, *'ayóí 'ó 'ó ní*, one of love."

✛━━━✛

"This is my wife, Emily. The story of how we met, and then met again is a wonderful one. We reside in Laguna Beach, but would like to move somewhere else for most of the year. She has resumed teaching high school math after the birth of our daughter, Susannah Lynn Maxwell. Such a beautiful child. 'Stars of beauty, stars of light.'

"I was planning on going back to music school in Laramie, Wyoming, but never got there. After the motorcycle accident, she visited me at Thanksgiving and stayed for two months. Our relationship really took off, we were married, and before we knew it Susannah was on the way.

"We've been paying a lot of attention to our spiritual lives. I owe that to Emily. She's so strong and grounded in the Christian faith. I'm just starting out; it's truly exciting. I can see how God's hand has been there throughout my life, guiding me toward that which is good, protecting me from the bad.

"Musically, I've never been better. I'm writing, practicing, and occasionally performing, mostly classical pieces. I see myself going into what's called "Contemporary Christian" as well—music with the right message. The message of joyful life, now and forever.

"Emily is a great mother. It's something that's always a question in a serious relationship, whether you're thinking about it directly or not. Would she be a great mother? Definitely. One of many strengths, reasons why I can thankfully say, God truly brought us together."

✛━━━✛

"This is Cindy. We went to school together. Ten years after graduation, I came back for a reunion and met her, really for the first time. Cindy is a graphic artist who has built a successful business from scratch. I admire her talent and tenacity.

"There's something special and enduring about marrying someone from high school, years later, after both of you have had a chance to go through what all of us must experience. You know and share much more than you realize.

"Before Penn, I had an interview at a Princeton guy's farm between Hummelstown and Hershey. On a Saturday afternoon, he had wallpaint on his hands, and was wearing a pink buttondown shirt, khakis, and great club tie. Restoring this place out in the country. I went to Penn, not Princeton, thankfully, archrivals that they are, but the scenario always stuck in my mind. More of the stuff from high school that stays with you. I liked that scenario, a lot. It was more important than I ever thought.

"Cindy and I live along the Conodoguinet Creek in a similar old place, for most of the year. Summers are Out West, either at the house in Laguna Beach, or a favorite getaway at Jackson Hole.

"This is Cindy's son, Jed, who's nine. We get along pretty well. I'm learning to give him my attention not just when he asks for it, but as much as I can at all times. Kids need loving attention. They're such a challenge.

"Cindy and I have talked about having another child, a sister for Jed, if blessed with a girl. The if and when are still up in the air.

"I'm still practicing and playing music, mostly classical. Occasionally, I'll do a concert in New York or Philadelphia, but enjoy playing jazz with a group here as much or more. There aren't a lot a venues, though. It's not like you'll find a Keystone Korner in Lancaster.

"I also write and build handcrafted furniture, New Mexico designs. That's really unusual in Central Pennsylvania."

⊹ ▭ ⊹

"How do you like my white suit? It *is* Singapore. I've *got* to have a white suit here.

"Cathy's career has really ascended since she relocated from San Francisco. With the production experience, she'll continue to rise through the ranks upon return to the Bay Area next year. Until then, we're jetsetting to as many Pacific rendezvous as we can fit into our schedules. Tahiti, Bali, Japan, Hawaii, Australia, New Zealand. Though a blur, everytime I see Cathy, I know it's worth it. She's beautiful, and we're best friends. Her mother thought we belonged together, and was right.

"I like visiting Singapore for a week or so at a time. The city is so fantastic, clean, picturesque. And the *Straits Times* is always outside the door of Cathy's apartment in the morning. An English language newspaper! I've taken so many photos, full of color and contrast, the mix of English, Chinese, and Malay cultures, old and new. There's nothing else like strolling the open air food stalls downtown on a warm evening and having a dessert of exotic melons and other fruit.

"Finding a place to live next year will be fun, and challenging. It'll be a question of the particular mix we're looking for—urban/suburban; cafes, bookstores, and quiet; Victorian hedges and parks; glass, metal, and wood; fog, wind, and sunshine. That's the Bay Area.

"I'll be writing, recording, and performing, classical, jazz and whatever else I come across. It's a great place for all that.

"As far as kids go, we're going to take that one step at a time. It's an important decision. We have to plan and be ready to devote the time and care it involves. Cathy will be a great mom."

"This is Laurel, my wife.

"We met briefly in Santa Fe in 1976, at a cafe on San Francisco Street. She was wearing a green sweater. Ever since, she's been my Green Sweater Girl. I couldn't take my eyes from her that day in Santa Fe, sketching in my notebook as she sat in front of the window. Laurel recognized me, which must be the reason I coaxed her phone number, though she's never admitted it—'bout wore me out getting that number! An Austin girl on a getaway to Santa Fe, and a banking junior exec to boot. Those Texans.

"In 1977, on the way to my 10th high school reunion in Pennsylvania, I detoured through Austin to see her. At that point, she was only a fortunate coincidence, imagined and amplified from the brief cafe encounter, but I had a feeling we would hit it off.

"Laurel was surprised when I showed up in Austin and called, by then six months later. Even more surprising, we had dinner that night and immediately liked each other. Though I didn't want to miss the reunion and had to leave, I knew I'd be back. Soon.

"We share a love of New Mexico. There's something so different about it, whether under the porticos in Santa Fe or Taos, or out driving a hundred miles from nowhere. We just bought this adobe in Tesuque. It's plain old New Mexico Magic.

"We're starting to think about children, though that's at least a couple of years away. I fill my days with practicing, writing, and taking a lot more pictures. I'm working on a book of black & whites, in the great photographic tradition of New Mexico. There's so much to see here, interpret through that medium.

"I've got a solo album coming out next month. It's pretty good, if I do say so myself. Much different than anything I did with ESO. Maybe it's New Mexico, finding Laurel, settling down, or all of the above. I think you'll like it."

60
A different saving grace

"Doctor, I've got a pulse!" the nurse yelled.

"What the … ?" he exclaimed running over.

I was gone. They wanted to believe modern medicine brought me back but couldn't, since no specific "procedure" could be associated with the resuscitation. Nor could they explain how I suffered no permanent damage although clinically dead for several minutes. Once in awhile there is a case when the patient, to all appearances having died, just comes back. I was proof that it happens; the why remains elusive.

Unless you have faith, then it's simple. The ER nurse who spoke with me later was on the right track when she confided that some of the things she had seen were enough to make her go to church every Sunday and give thanks. Really pray. For her, holy days of obligation.

The truth *is* often tangent, rarely embraced by a simple, "… here, let me tell you what happened." In some incredible way having humbly faced the choice, and made the selection opting for life, a particular life, here goes. I like this version the best. I wasn't ready for my life to end with that hundred word obituary anyway. As to the particular life, which of the dreamscapes came true, read on.

Rock Star Survives Laguna Landslide Into Pacific

I awoke in the middle of the night. The clock on the wall said 1:15 am. I wanted to speak to the nurse I saw out of the corner of my eye, but couldn't remember how. The hoses, tubes, and other devices taped to me didn't help.

Checking me a minute later on her round, she noticed that my eyes were open.

"Your eyes are open. That's a good sign," the nurse said, "but is anyone home? If you can hear me, blink your eyes."

I think I blinked.

"That's a very good sign! Be right back," she said, hurrying out to the ER Supervisor's station.

Better let the young woman know who's sleeping in the waiting room, too.

I fell back into sleep before the nurse returned.

"Don't leave us again, this time for good," the nurse said, trying to awaken me.

"Let me sleep," I thought, "I'll be okay."

I awoke in mid-morning.

Stephanie was there. "Rest," she said, taking my hand.

Either unable to speak or not wanting to, I said nothing, wondering if this time my speaking ability was really gone.

After a thorough examination, scans and tests, the only damage found was that the leg broken in the Mojave had been slightly refractured. Although it hurt, home was the best place for me to heal. The prescription was rest, limited physical activity, and a sleeping pill. I blinked my eyes, "yes, I understand."

I was fortunate not to have drowned. Where as a child my uncle dove in to rescue me from one ocean, this time the Pacific helped save me and in the process, extinguished that angst. I had fallen at a place where the rocks below were closer to the toe of the bluff, at the moment when a huge wave was breaking. The wave's height cushioned the fall, and in breaking, swept me onto the bar.

Beat up and tired, rest is what I did.

⊹══════⊹

After another day in the hospital, I was able to go home. In an ambulance. For more rest. There were no reporters or photographers snapping shots. Old news.

I awoke the following morning. Stephanie was sitting in a chair beside my bed. Looking more than beautiful in her Montana kind of way. She helped me drink a glass of water and some juice. I really wanted a cup of coffee. Good coffee.

"Listen," she said, not knowing if I could speak.

"After Pastor Franck called me, I drove to Laramie to find you, but the Cafe was gone. I found the St. Clairs, who told me you were driving back here. I called the number on the card you gave me, but only got your answering machine. I had to keep going. But when I knocked on your door and you weren't at home … .

"Craig, the truth is that when I met you, there was no one else in my life with whom things were serious, at least in my mind. What I've not been able to tell any man before is that the doctors say I'm unable to have children. A fall from a horse when I was a child. I haven't been able to deal with that in the relationships I've had, so I either put up a wall, or eventually withdraw. And being an unmarried Christian, well, let's just say I haven't been able to really find out for myself if it's true. I'm sorry."

It was not the time for me to be quiet any longer.

I just looked at her, wanting to speak, but not able to say anything. A couple of minutes passed. Stephanie started crying, thinking I might not ever speak again.

"Bbbbbbb … but you're here, Stephanie. You're here now," I blurted out.

"Oh, Craig … ," she sobbed.

"I couldn't walk away from a chance at a future I know God has placed before us. I don't want to lose that. I can't lose you now. I started to fall in love with you that evening you played in the church after dinner at the Francks'.

"I couldn't get it out of my head. There was something so … emotionally reflective, timeless, romantic about it. When you played, you showed me your heart. I wanted to be in it, with you.

"Music so beautiful that I couldn't dare to believe my love for you would be returned. It hurt so much when I told you to go away. Like dying. I'm so sorry I did that."

Easier for me to speak now. "Aaanndd for me to be worthy of you, Stephanie, I had to come to know God. It was a bumpy ride."

"At the hospital, you said, 'Stephanie … my love.' Did you mean that?"

I remembered it from within the dream. Had she been there, with me in the dream?

"SSStephanie, so much has happened since the summer. A lot to catch up on. I'll bet right now, Pastor Franck is working on a Christmas program, and time's short. I've got to hurry up and heal. Ill've got just the song. You'll have to do the singing for awhile. It would fit you as well as that Levi jacket you wear."

"Did you mean that?"

"What?"

"You know, what I asked you if you said. Did you mean it?"

"Yes, my love." Waking or asleep, it was all a dream. A wonderful dream.

As I shifted, trying to get more comfortable sitting up, with a cast and all the aches, Stephanie asked if I would like to sip a cup of the coffee she just made. "Regular diet," the doctor had instructed.

"I hope it's up to your standards."

"While you're getting the coffee, look on the desk for an envelope and box. A little early for Christmas, but they're for you."

She was crying again when she came back. Must have known I'd like the coffee. It was perfect.

When I was up and around, itching to play some music, I thought again about the Scarlatti piece I had intended to play on what I now call the Day of Unimaginable Providence. The box should still be by the piano, which is where it was, top on and music inside. My housekeeper, always straightening up. As before, I got out a stack to look for the Scarlatti folio, and saw the spiral binding. It was a sketching pad.

"Whoa … ," I exhaled, suddenly short of breath as I remembered the pad, even without opening it.

Leafing through the pictures I had drawn in pencil after the accident, now with goosebumps, I knew what I would find. And there it was. A head and shoulders version of *The Sleeping Child* by Mary Curtis Richardson, remembered from the exhibition in LA in 1977. *Unmistakably, the face of Stephanie, and with a child. Done before I had met her.*

"We finally going to get started on that music col-lab-or-a-tion you tried to sweet talk me into back in Bozeman?" Stephanie asked, walking into the room and seeing me by the piano.

When I didn't immediately reply, she came over and saw the drawing.

"Who did *that*?" she asked. "It's good. And *when*?"

"Fasten your seat belt, I've got a story to tell you about this … after which we've got some heavy duty praying to do."

Pastor Franck introduced the next song by telling a story about a man who was famous, as people are in this world, had a bad accident which nearly took his life, but was spared. For what we can conclude only to be God's purpose. And how after a woman very close to him, a Christian woman, was taken to be with the Lord, he came to the church in Medicine Creek a couple of years back, returned to rescue the Christmas program, and seemingly had everything on track.

This was a man who was gifted musical capabilities previously unknown, who went back to school to develop them, but hit a wall when the building where he lived and had a business burned down, the very Sunday he was in this church, performing for our congregation. And how he returned, finally broken, and accepted the Lord Jesus Christ as his personal Savior, but wasn't out of danger yet. Falling into the Pacific Ocean from a cliff due to a landslide in California, after having been pronounced dead in a hospital emergency room, he was once again spared, for God's purpose. And as Craig puts it, 'a rough way to be baptized'.

We all have our stories to tell; some of pain, others about what can only be miracles and triumph. Please join Craig Maxwell and Stephanie Tyler with hearts lifted to the Lord in thanksgiving, as they lead the choir in an uplifting arrangement of a traditional carol. One which has special meaning for them, and I'm sure for all of us. And lest I forget a couple of other little details, first I'd better announce that they are engaged to be married; and second, because you wouldn't even sign it, thank you for the beautiful drawing on the cover of today's program, Craig.

Let us celebrate Christmas, and their engagement, through joyous music, with 'O Come All Ye Faithful.'"

What began as a road rush became lustrously coherent, outer layers of cultural interference, inner layers of empty selfishness stripped away. Laminar flow, honey on a spoon. Like our first kiss, in which Stephanie both told me about the most fantastic future together I could have ever imagined, and swore me to an intimate secrecy. I'm sorry I can't tell you more.

If you loved a woman, even more so after losing her from this life, what would you hope to bring from that into another relationship? Faith, a deeper capacity to love again, recognition and daily acknowledgement of the importance of balancing identities, thankfulness. With Stephanie, I see the promise of meeting within the ground those define and making the great music both of us have always wanted, together.

God exists. A personal relationship with God is just that. It is not encumbered by what others think, nor reliant on empty ritual or the "interpretations", behavior, applications, or other acts of man. Our faith is enabled and strengthened when we consciously yield to Him. Sinners to saints, one by one, testifying to His Glory through our lives.

It's *not* easy, day to day work for emotional and spiritual survival. Everywhere you look, there will be the perversions of man—despite, and in defiance of, God. The problem is not, nor has ever been, Him—it's man, his arrogance, selfishness, rebellion. The answer, the strength to go on will not be found in man's philosophy, arguments, words, or the practice of "religion", but only faith. Taking apart and giving up the world's value system, the one we can see; surrendering, and replacing it with faith, believing in and being guided by the unseen.

I'm glad where I ended up. Thankful. Because no matter what's happening, it's the one place, only place where I can live without despair. I can't take you, but pray we'll meet there.

When I finally got around to the translation of that Latin written a couple of years back in my notebook, the Mass clothed in particularly beautiful music by Haydn—*Missa Sanctae Caeciliae*, for Saint Cecelia, Patron Saint of Music—it was all right there:

Et resurrexit tertia die,	And the third day He rose again
secundum Scripturas.	according to the Scriptures;
Et ascendit in coelum:	and ascended into Heaven. He sitteth
sedet ad dexteram Patris.	at the right hand of the Father;

Et resurrexit tertia die,	And the third day He rose again
Et iterum venturus est cum gloria,	and He shall come again with glory
judicare vivos et mortuos:	to judge the living and the dead;
ujus regni non erit finis.	and His kingdom shall have no end.

And His kingdom has no end.

I am not about time. Science first tells us that time is linear, the behavior of time is as a line divided into increments. When we're comfortable with that—and why should we be?—it tells us that under certain special circumstances, time may be *thought of* as a curved surface or shape. Plane, torus, helix, intertwined helices? You name it, but why stop there? Anything. Strands of cable in aggregate larger than can ever be imagined (unimagined)? All sorted into the bins of interpretation, affinity, conformity, and the last one, a crate on the floor, *Other*. Troubling in its fullness, overflowing with nonconformabilities. Within which the enterprise is urgent, imagining of the unimaginable.

Science is about observation, time one attempt at measure. If we dwell on either, more often than not, we're only reflecting, revising to even more of a fiction. Reducing it to the ratio of living:dying. The implications of a short growing season, losing sight of irony, judgment by man rather than guidance by the wisdom of the original stories.

Why bother with the *idea* of time? The Unimaginable is someone else, beyond the self-defined parameters and measures of science; the clear, sole, unifying conclusion of the finest argument, in the end, made over the brink of human contradiction.

I started to love you that evening on the porch, Stephanie, when you looked at me. Later, I visualized that moment thinking, "thank you for being interested enough to try to see inside me." Revisited over and over it became a dream, in my tradition as valuable and nourishing as *manoomin*, the wild rice on the lakes of my ancestors.

My heart, my love for you is of that dream. Love which became dimensionless when in the shortest moment, I saw your slightly open-mouthed, reflective/introspective, unconsciously, quizzically pondering 'huh,' an authentic aside after which you looked at me, beamed a smile seen only between the two of us, colored with a tinge of lovers' blush, saying, "now and forever we share this, the two of us, with and before our God."

I am about consciousness, presence, in motion defined by conscious choices, within a sea of circumstances. Now never alone, I belong. As a husband, God-willing, a father; Native if and when I dive into that stream, swim in the waters of awareness. Not by virtue of blood quantum or Wild Indian rejection of the Great White Father—my God, *Yahweh*—but accompanied by His original, profoundly infinite presence within the unique creation I am.

Though there are a dawn and sunset, a day is neither beginning nor end, only continuation. I am about that continuation—energy, effort, and rest … the concentric waves created by a thought dropped into a still pool. Spare and elegant, summer's skipping pebble before the surface is once again smooth, waiting.

Maybe there *is* something in the blood itself, a quirk not yet detected, mirrored as left or right-handed, like rye bread and frybread. If there's a right-handed rule for vector cross-products and another one for electromotive force, the flow of current, then maybe's there's a left-handed version of our biochemistry. You know, "given certain reversed states … ."

If so, it's only one trace of many. What remains paramount is gaining understanding, setting bricks in a foundation begun as discovery, getting beyond the philosophical and argumentative, to faith. The foundation that disappears while being built, yet forever remains in and for the spirit.

I'm just starting to figure out how it all can and does work together, Native and Christian. Though my dreamworld does not yet include talking badgers, nevertheless I live with the assurance of having accepted God, and knowing that he created Natives *and* badgers. I guess that to be both Native and Christian means I dwell in a little wider spiritual spectrum, not bringing in "other gods", but learning how a different culture, one also in my blood, recognizes God the Creator. As for how my life will play out along the way, who knows? To know that would be fast-forwarding to the ending, without living.

"I tell you now," Grandfather begins his story, following a familiar trail under the snow, notches in the birch trees; feeling the direction of the wind, seeing tracks of winter game.

"A warrior from far away who knew neither his strength nor heart journeyed to this land and found a woman who would become his wife. On the shore of *Gichigami*."

"I tell you now," what *I* know of that story, from a dream I cannot place in time. In that dream, Annie and I were together, in a wigwam, where I slept through the dawn. In a canoe on a river, one known to my ancestors, the Old Ones who have passed before me.

Annie has a son, Thomas. He is mine, but that is all she will say. At the beginning I could only make up conversations … "I don't understand, Annie, it's not possible". " … You will. He is real. Thomas is your son. You will be told more at the appointed time."

She doesn't work at the Library any more … "I don't want to live my life surrounded by books, paper … I want to learn about other things now, live in the forest with my son, with you when you're back from the hunt."

When I'm awake, I'm with Stephanie, completely, thankfully. Sometimes when I dream, I'm with Annie and Thomas, in a cabin in the forest. I haven't called Annie about the dreams. It wouldn't be right—I'm happily married. Besides, she may not answer this time. Might never have been there *as Annie* at all. Yet we meet in my dreams. *Our* dreams, which haven't stopped or diminished. I have grown to accept it.

"She's Not There" is a song about a beautiful girl, and how she lied. Annie is about truth, and in significant part, defines me through our ancestors. So no matter if anyone answers, Annie is "Always There".

"*Azhigwa ginisidotam*," Annie speaks to me in my dreams, "Now, you understand."

It is our lot to marry, raise children. Whether they're from us or adopted, they will be *of* us, carry on our love when we die in bodies which will be returned to the land. In our tears some would have us weak. They are the true tears of struggle, compassion, love, loss; antithetical to the emotionless posturing of those living adrift, empty. Tears that our children may grow strong.

We have dreams and visions, lives while awake, others when sleeping. The physical and dream states are two complementary components of who we are. "Whenever the truth of vision comes upon the world, it is like a rain," I remember Black Elk said, as I look out on this rainy day to the Pacific below. Waves feeling the point, moving to wrap around it, as my arm around Stephanie, in the afterglow of the song we wrote, sang together a moment ago.

"Thank you for waiting for me, Stephanie."

No need to speak about that, she smiles, moving closer, leaning her head on my shoulder.

But she is a woman, so there are always other things to talk about.

"Craig, you've got this cowgirl, but if you *really* want this cowgirl's heart, we've got to start talking about horses … ."

And so it goes with women, their confidences, riddles, and dances.

I am a man, a dreamer. In my life here, and dreams, I am the beach sand, dust and pebbles, waves and wind. Clouds and trees. Warrior paint from seeping springs. The flowers and meadow; breath of life, peace of death. Son of my father, message delivered from the generations with irony and humor; continuation and contradiction. A child and ancestor. In the end, a thought, a chord; coda of an eternal melody of incomparable silence.

In the knowledge that our spirits will forever live, from a genesis only God truly understands along our unique path to eternity, having Him with us is enough. It is all.

And Lord, one more prayer. That I would not talk in my sleep.

Amen.

Playlist

Chapter	Song / Album / Composer / Label	Artist / Conductor / Orchestra
1	Guinnevere/ So Far/ Crosby, Stills & Nash	Crosby, Stills, & Nash
	The Six Partitas/ J.S. Bach/Hyperion (1997)	Angela Hewitt
	Symphony No. 3/ Gustav Mahler/ Deutsche Grammophon (1982)	Claudio Abbado/ Vienna Philharmonic
	Symphony No. 1/ Ralph Vaughan Williams/ EMI (1990)	Bernard Haitink London Philharmonic
	You Can't Always Get What You Want/ Let It Bleed	Rolling Stones
	Keyboard Suite No. 5 in E major/Handel/ EMI (1996)	Sviatoslav Richter
	Like a Rolling Stone/Highway 61 Revisited	Bob Dylan
	My Guy (and others)	Mary Wells
3	Monkey Time	Major Lance
	Variation No. 9/ Enigma Variations/ Sir Edward Elgar /Naxos (1997)	George Hurst/Bournemouth
4	Going Mobile/ Who's Next	The Who
	Requiem Mass/ Mozart/Deutsche Grammophon (1987)	Herbert Von Karajan/ Vienna Philharmonic
5	Missa Sanctae Caeceliae/ Haydn/ L'Oiseau-Lyre (1997)	Simon Preston/ Academy of Ancient Music
	Louie, Louie	The Kingsmen
6	Shout!	Isley Brothers
	Cripple Creek / The Band	The Band
	Your Molecular Structure/I've Been Doin' Some Thinkin'/Atlantic (1968)	Mose Allison

Chapter	Song / Album / Composer / Label	Artist / Conductor / Orchestra
	Missa Solemnis/ Beethoven/Archiv (1990)	Sir John Elliot Gardiner Monteverdi Choir
	Where are You/ GO!/Blue Note (1987)	Dexter Gordon
7	My Soul Lies Deep/Another Beginning	Les McCann
8	Remote Control (1979)	The Tubes
	The Eye of the Hurricane/ Maiden Voyage/ Blue Note (1986)	Herbie Hancock
9	No Room for Squares (song & album)/ Blue Note (1989)	Hank Mobley
10	Impressions	John Coltrane
	Spain	Chick Corea
	A Love Supreme	John Coltrane
	Cantalope Island	Herbie Hancock
	Josie/Aja (song & album)	Steely Dan
12	Sun is Still Shining/ To Our Children's …	Moody Blues
	Goyescas/ Granados/Decca (1976)	Alicia de Larrocha
	When a Man Loves a Woman	Percy Sledge
	Gimme Some Lovin'	Spencer Davis Group
	Does Your Mama Know About Me?/ Fading Away	Bobby Taylor & Vancouvers
	You Don't Know Like I Know	Sam & Dave
13	Hymn for Her/ Body and Soul	Rick Braun
16	Comin' Back for Java	ESO
21	A Simple Desultory Philippic, For Emily, Parsely, Sage, Rosemary and Thyme	Simon & Garfunkel
24	Powwow	Go for it! Black Lodge Singers, Canyon Records, you decide
29	Reflections, Entering/ Places/ECM (1978)	Jan Garbarek
30	Piano Concerto No. 5, "Emperor"/ Beethoven/ Sony Classical (1997)	Rudolf Serkin/ Bernstein NY Philharmonic

Chapter	Song / Album / Composer / Label	Artist / Conductor / Orchestra
31	Ain't No Mountain High Enough	Marvin Gaye & Tammi Terrell
	Dancin' in the Street	Martha & The Vandellas
33	Seven Nights in Rome (aka "The Gardens")/ Black Diamond	The Rippingtons
35	The Captain of My Ship (aka "My Ship")/ Come Walk with Me	Oleta Adams
	Toccata in C Minor/ J.S. Bach/ Deutsche Grammophon (1980)	Martha Argerrich
38	Agent Double-O-Soul	Edwin Starr
41	Te Deum, Missa en tempore belli/ Haydn/ Chaconne (1998)	Hickox/ Collegium/ Musicum 90
42	Livingston Saturday Night	Jimmy Buffett
43	Dolores/ Miles Smiles	Miles Davis Quintet
45	Red Clay (song & album)	Freddie Hubbard
	Passion Dance/ The Real McCoy	McCoy Tyner
	Equipoise/ MUSA—Ancestral Streams/ (1974)	Stanley Cowell
46	Music for Royal Fireworks/ Handel/ Archiv (1991)	Trevor Pinnock/ The English Concert
48	Laudate Dominum/ Mozart/Sony Classical (1997)	Kathleen Battle/Grace/Robert Sadin
49	French Suites/ J.S. Bach/EMI Classics (1996)	Andrei Gavrilov
	Sonata in B minor/D. Scarlatti/Sony (1997)	Murray Perahia
50	Ariodante/ Handel/Harmonia Mundi (1996)	Nicholas McGegan Freiburger Barockorchester
54	Great Mass in C Minor/ Mozart	Christopher Hogwood/ Academy of Ancient Music

Other Recommendations

	Love, Love/ ECM (1974)	Julian Priester, Pepo Mtoto
	Expresso Love/ Making Movies	Dire Straits
	Jupiter/ Earth, Wind & Fire	Earth, Wind, and Fire

Chapter	Song / Album / Composer / Label	Artist / Conductor / Orchestra
	Life is Hard (God is Good)/Feel the Healing	Pam Thum
	Hold Me Close/ Arms of Mercy	Kim Hill
	Heaven & Earth (compilation)/ Sparrow (1999)	Michelle Tumes/ Rebecca St. James
	Streams (compilation)/Word (1999)	Chris Rodriguez
	Look What Love Has Done (to Me)	Jaci Velasquez
	O Come All Ye Faithful /Christmas with the Master Chorale of Tampa Bay (1996)	Robert Summer

Acknowledgments

Thanks to those who have helped me learn about and understand even a small part of what it means to be native: the extraordinary exposition of Gerald Vizenor in his *Fugitive Poses* (U. of Nebraska Press, 1998) which assisted in clarifying "native" (Native American); correspondence with Dr. Kimberly Blaeser, University of Wisconsin-Milwaukee, and Dr. Laura Tohe, Arizona State University; *Ojibway Heritage* by Basil Johnston (U. of Nebraska Press, 1990); and *The Ojibway Woman* (U. of Nebraska Press, 1997, by arrangement with the Research Institute for the Study of Man, 1938). Additionally, Rick Gresczyk and Chuck Lilligren generously provided translations for some of the Ojibwe words and phrases (the ones which are correct). Please excuse any errors in the other Ojibwe and Navajo translations, which I attempted myself using *A Concise Dictionary of Minnesota Ojibwe* (John D. Nichols and Earl Nyholm, U. of Minnesota Press, 1995), *Ojibwemowin* (Judith L. Vollom and Thomas M. Vollom, O.L.P Native Voice, Inc., 1994), *Navajo-English Dictionary* (Leon Wall and William Morgan, Hippocrene Books, Inc., 1994), and *Colloquial Navaho* (Robert W. Young and William Morgan, Hippocrene Books, Inc., 1998).

The source for philosophy terms was *A Dictionary of Philosophy* (Antony Flew, Grammercy Books, 1999, by arrangement, Laurence Urdang Associates, Ltd., 1979). My indispensable word resource was *Webster's Seventh New Collegiate Dictionary* (G. & C. Merriam Co., 1965). Celestial meanderings were launched by *Get a Grip on Astronomy* (Robin Kerrod, The Ivy Press Limited, 1999). Bible quotations and material are from *New American Standard Bible, The New Open Bible* (The Lockman Foundation, 1977, and Thomas Nelson, Inc., 1990). The N.C. Wyeth quotation is from *Paintings of the Southwest* (ed. Arnold Skolnick, Chameleon Books, Inc., 1994). References to *The Sleeping Child* and other artworks of the era are from *Independent Spirits, Women Painters of the American West, 1890-1945* (Autry Museum of Western Heritage and University of California Press, 1995). Mention of the exhibition in LA is an anachronism, trickery for which those shifty Nail Haven professional stylists, amateur astrophysicists, and time travellers are prime suspects.

Many trips, observations, conversations, recordings and books provided background and stimulated the thinking, for better or worse, which resulted in this volume. My utmost respect and appreciation to John Trudell, a man who, "says what he means and means what he says," for *Johnny Damas and Me*, his powerful CD. I wish your spirit peace. Appreciation also to Gwendolen Cates for her book, *Indian Country* (Grove Press, 2001), much, much more than pictures;

Roxanne Swentzell, "sculptor of human emotions"; Baje Whitethorne, Sr., whose wonderful art traces a deep, meaningful life; and Evelyn Fredericks, yet another fine sculptor who tells the old stories in stone. I only wish I could be at Second Mesa in Hopiland more often to speak with Alph Secakuku, author of *Following The Sun and Moon, Hopi Kachina Tradition* (Northland Publishing in cooperation with the Heard Museum, 1995). Thanks also to the Heard Museum for their exhibition (2002) and accompanying book, *Away from Home: American Indian Boarding School Experiences* (the Heard Museum, 2000), sources for the two quotations at the beginning of Chapter 32; and for some of the information on the Bean Dance in Chapter 34 from their permanent exhibit.

Special thanks to Meredith Kimberlin, City of Superior, WI, Parks & Recreation, who researched the Osaugie Trail, named for an ancestor; and Marlene Wisuri, photographer and historian who made me welcome at the Carlton County Historical Society, located in the old library in Cloquet, MN, the very building in which Annie LaCroix worked. Also to Barbara Landis, Carlisle Indian School Biographer, for information and reverent guidance on that institution; Lee Amble, slugging centerfielder, for his knowledge of Northern League ball; Larry Tarkowski, for reminiscences of Ann Arbor; and Steve Beiser, Puchteca Indian Art in Flagstaff, AZ, solid citizen and purveyor of high quality native goods.

Please note that none of the aforementioned individuals, institutions, or sources were provided with or otherwise aware of the entirety of my writing, accordingly, they neither bear any responsibility for any errors, omissions, or representations, nor necessarily share any viewpoints expressed herein. Heartfelt thanks also to those creators and interpreters of music listed in the Playlist; Professor Paul J. Korshin who encouraged my writing so many years ago in English Composition at Penn; and to my family for their patience, love and forgiveness.

Finally, Green Sweater Girl, who is neither Yumiko, nor completely a work of fiction.

About the Author

Craig McConnell was born in Montana, grew up in Central Pennsylvania, and has traveled throughout and lived within several Western States locales, including Arizona, Nevada, and Southern California. A graduate of the University of Pennsylvania and University of California, Berkeley, he also sojourned for a year in Sardinia, Italy. An enrolled member of the Fond du Lac Band, Minnesota Chippewa Tribe, with eclectic musical tastes and what could only be termed approximate keyboard skills, he expertly enjoys and modestly collects Native American fine arts. *Cafe Whyoming* was written from exile in Southwest Florida. He now lives in Prescott, Arizona.